Pamela Belle lives in Wiltshire with her partner Steve and baby son Hugh, and is the author of five previous novels including *The Lodestar* and *Wintercombe*. *Herald of Joy* is the second book in the Wintercombe series.

PAMELA BELLE

HERALD
❧ of ❧
JOY

PAN BOOKS
in association with The Bodley Head

For Kathryn and Matthew,
who are not really like
William and Deb!

First published 1989 by The Bodley Head Ltd
This edition published 1990 by Pan Books Ltd,
Cavaye Place, London SW10 9PG
9 8 7 6 5 4 3 2 1
© Pamela Belle 1989
ISBN 0 330 31242 1
Printed in England by Clays Ltd, St Ives plc

'Silence is the perfectest herald of joy'
(*Much Ado About Nothing*)

HISTORICAL NOTE

As with my previous novel about Wintercombe, *Herald of Joy* is firmly rooted in fact. Although the St. Barbe family are my own invention, their beloved home is largely based on the National Trust manor of Great Chalfield, in Wiltshire, and most of their servants are drawn from the contemporary population of Norton St. Philip. The events surrounding the Battle of Worcester took place much as depicted. Unlikely as it may seem, Mervyn Touchet, later to become Earl of Castlehaven, did exist, and took part in the battle, although his subsequent adventures are not on record, and I may well have done his character, and his appearance, some injustice. The diary of John Harington of Kelston, however, reveals a man very much as I have portrayed him, although his son John is a more shadowy figure.

I would like to pay tribute to all those who have helped me with the research for this book. Once more, Mrs. Pat Lawless, of Norton St. Philip, and Dave Ryan, of Caliver Books, provided valuable assistance. I would also like to thank Mr. and Mrs. Robert Floyd, of Great Chalfield, for their kindness in letting me take liberties with their lovely home, and the various local history experts, particularly those in the Somerset Record Office and the Bath City Archives, who have answered all sorts of obscure queries at various times.

Finally, as ever, I am indebted to my mother, who has done her best to eliminate my more major errors of spelling, grammar and continuity, and offered numerous useful suggestions; to the rest of my family, and my friends, who have never been less than enthusiastic and encouraging; and, last but not least, to Steve, without whom the writing of this story would have taken much longer, and been much more difficult, and a great deal less fun!

P.D.A.B.
JANUARY, 1989

PART
❦ I ❦

THE SORROWING WIDOW

(May – August, 1651)

❦ CHAPTER ONE ❦

'The contract of her marriage'
(*As You Like It*)

It was the middle of May, in the year 1651, and Sir George St. Barbe was dying.

They all kept up a cheerful appearance, of course, but he knew better. That doctor, one of the many leeches who fed on the fashionably sick of Bath, might put on his false smile and assure him that he would be up and riding his estate before midsummer, but his patient, listening sourly from his bed, did not believe a word of it. The pain in his chest, his laboured, wheezing breath, told him another tale, and in truth, he would not be sorry to leave this world of disappointment, disillusion and grievous error.

Where was that smooth young attorney, Harley? He did not care for the fellow, never had, too self-assured and urbane for his taste, but there was no denying that he was a competent man of law. Sir George had recalled, in the pain-racked and sleepless watches of the previous night, that his will, made many years previously, took no account of subsequent changes in his family's circumstances. Before the creeping weakness conquered him, he must have it altered: and at dawn, one of the grooms had gone galloping off to Bath to fetch Master Harley.

'Rachael!' said Sir George, on a difficult, rasping breath.

His eldest daughter stopped reading. All morning, his thoughts had been accompanied by her rather loud, monotonous voice plodding through Holy Writ. Today it was the Psalms, but it had been some time since he had given the words his full attention. He peered at the thin, serious girl sitting beside the bed and added, 'What time is it?'

'It wants an hour to dinner, Father,' said Rachael. The sun, and the growls of her hungry belly, confirmed it.

'Then where's that lawyer? He should be here by now.'

'Perhaps he had other business,' Rachael suggested.

Sir George uttered a wheeze of derision. 'He knows mine can't wait. I suppose he thinks it's not important – just a dying man's whim.'

As if triggered by clockwork, his daughter said at once, with the same spurious cheer as the doctor, 'Oh, no, Father, don't speak like that – you're not dying.'

Sir George, who was not a sensitive person, failed to discern that she was endeavouring to convince herself of this delusion. He grunted, and waved a feeble hand. 'Continue – go on, girl. From where you left off.'

There was a brief pause. Rachael, her blue eyes distended, stared at him for a moment. Then she swallowed, and bent her head obediently to the book. Her voice came surprisingly faint and faltering at first, and then, entering into the rhythm of the Psalms, grew stronger.

'"Blessed is the nation whose God is the Lord; and the people whom he hath chosen for his own inheritance."'

Sir George, his thoughts drifting away once more, bitterly considered the irony of those words. He had fought against the misguided King and his evil Councillors for four years of civil war, and suffered greatly for his beliefs. His other manor at Chard had succumbed to Royalist pillagers, this house, Wintercombe, had been occupied, though not greatly damaged, and, worst of all, he had lost his beloved eldest son Samuel, dead after the second battle of Newbury. He, and all his comrades, had fought for the rule of law, for the rights of an elected Parliament, and against Popery. The hand of the Lord had given them victory: the King had been defeated, his supporters humiliated and scattered, and the Parliament's army was left supreme in the land. Sir George had looked forward to a return to normal life: himself in his manor; the King in his palace, though with his power drastically circumscribed; Parliament in session, ruling sensibly and moderately with due respect to property and the Presbyterian mode of worship, and the army disbanded.

But it had all turned out quite different. The army had refused to be so summarily dismissed, and the defender of the rights of Parliament seemed suddenly to have changed into a menacing monster, with many and dreadful aspects: radical and lunatic religious sects; illiterate labourers demanding a share of property; a most dangerous tolerance of anarchy and a contempt for all the tenets of order and degree which Sir George, and thousands like him, held so dear. In the space of two brief years, the world had indeed been turned upside-down. Honest Presbyterians were expelled from the Commons by insolent soldiers; the Scots, once allies, were reduced to bargaining with the King and invading the country in his support; and, worst of all, King Charles had been put on trial for his life, and executed.

It was not the victory for which Sir George had fought so fervently. He was old, approaching sixty. Disheartened, his health failing, he had finally left the army and returned to the lovely house of Wintercombe, his inheritance, where he had left his young second wife and his children, to live out the war under the sheltered wing of his father and mother.

And that, too, had been a profound disappointment. His father, Sir Samuel St. Barbe, had died in his absence: since he was well over seventy, this had not been a surprise, nor a cause for too much grief, as Sir George had never accorded well with his sire. He suffered the loss of his mother, Dame Ursula, much more keenly. She had doted on him, her only son, nourished his religion and his self-esteem, filled him with a sense of his own grace and the certainty that he would find his allotted place in Heaven, one of the Lord's Elect. To discover that she had died, only a few weeks before his regiment recaptured Wintercombe from the Royalist garrison, was a bitter blow indeed, and one which he still felt most grievously.

Nor was his wife a help and comfort in his time of trial. True, she had managed the house for a year while it was under occupation by the enemy soldiers, a thankless task at best, and, to do her justice, she seemed to have coped remarkably well. But the meek little mouse he had left at Wintercombe had been transformed under pressure, like base metal in an alchemist's laboratory, into something much less malleable, and he disliked the change intensely. It was not that she was insolent or openly ungovernable: far from it. Nevertheless, it was evident that she enjoyed the tacit support of all the servants, who had likewise endured the unhappy rule of the brutal Royalist soldiers. He discovered on many, many occasions that his wishes were thwarted, manipulated, disobeyed or ignored, so quietly and subtly that it was some time before he became aware of it.

To outward eyes, Silence was still the perfect wife. She had, after all, given him another child with gratifying speed, barely nine months after his return. However, he had left precise instructions as to its naming – Samuel if a boy, Ursula for a girl – before going back to his regiment, and had not been best pleased to find that his youngest daughter had instead been called Katherine.

It was yet another symptom of his wife's changed attitude. It seemed as if the baby's name, as well as her sex, were an affront to him, done from spite. Nor had there been any more pregnancies, and when children died so readily, to have just two sons remaining, and one a weakling, was perilous for a man's posterity. But despite himself, he had grown fond of little Kate, though she did not in the least resemble him, being a small brown oddity with no flesh on her bones. And now, nearly five years after her birth, this youngest daughter was dearer to him than all his other living children, save one: the girl who read to him every day, and tried to force him back into health with the fierce strength of her will and her prayers.

Rachael had reached the thirty-seventh Psalm, with its comforting words. "'I have seen the wicked in great power, and spreading himself like a green bay tree.'

"'Yet he passed away, and, lo, he was not: yea, I sought him, but he could not be found.'"

So, alas, had His Majesty perished, although even now Sir George could not be persuaded that his monarch had been wicked rather than misguided. And so, he hoped, would that overmighty and despicable hypocrite, the Lord General Oliver Cromwell, be cast down by the wrath of God. The only reason that Sir George might have to regret his own impending demise was that he would not live to see the General's inevitable downfall.

His mind wandered from the lamentable state of the realm — or the Commonwealth, as it now was, lacking a king save the one in exile — to contemplation of his eldest surviving child. On the whole, he was pleased with her transformation. Once she had been a sullen, gawky, unattractive little girl, prey to moods and terrifying rages. But she was twenty-one now, adult, and her raw fierce unfeminine nature had been well tempered by maturity. Her voice could still grate, her step still tread too heavy, but she had made sincere efforts to moderate her behaviour, and had succeeded. Moreover, she showed a most encouraging godliness, and a sense of filial duty and obedience that was conspicuous by its absence in his other children. Only Rachael came every day to read to him on his sick bed; only Rachael listened to him with such attentiveness, and thereby calmed his nagging sense of disappointment, the uneasy feeling of being superfluous in his own house.

It was time she took a husband: she was ready for it. He could fault his wife Silence on many things, but this at least he must grudgingly allow her, that she had taught Rachael the duties of a housewife exceeding thoroughly. She would be well dowered, and as such would make a good match for any country gentleman's son.

He had often pondered the problem this last year, mentally reviewing a procession of eligible young men, who had only their godliness and sobriety in common. He had come to his final decision some months previously, in the certain knowledge that the boy's father would be in complete agreement: indeed, they had already discussed the matter informally. That was another matter which Master Harley – if he ever arrived – would be instructed to set in hand, but the time had come to tell Rachael of his plans for her future.

She was stumbling over the words of the thirty-eighth Psalm, which were hideously appropriate. '"I am feeble and sore broken: I have roared by reason of the disquietness of my heart."' She was glad when her father spoke to her again, in that dreadful voice which wheezed and spluttered, and she could lay down the Bible. She knew that he was dying: everyone did, despite their brave faces, but she fought against her knowledge, as if by doing so she could turn the grim hour aside. 'Yes, Father?' she said quietly.

'I have been giving some thought to your future,' said that labouring voice, more clearly and distinctly than for some days. 'As I trust that you have also been doing, Daughter.'

Rachael's mind had not yet travelled beyond the imminent day of her father's death. It was strange that this should have affected her so greatly: as a child, she had always feared his distant, authoritarian figure. And yet, the ogre of her earlier years had returned to Wintercombe diminished by war, shrunken in girth as well as influence. She had found herself feeling sorry for him, making a special effort to please him, and had made the gratifying discovery that her endeavours were rewarded by his favour. Since her father was not an emotional nor a demonstrative man, this meant no more than companionable discussions of religious topics, and even, rarely, a word or two of limited and reluctant praise. But to Rachael, always parched and thirsty for any drop of love, however small and unsatisfactory, this scanty evidence of paternal feeling was as manna from Heaven.

From habit, she gave the answer which would satisfy him, rather than the truth. 'Yes, Father.'

'You are a woman grown – time you took a husband,' said Sir

George. In happier, healthier times he would have used many more words to express the same idea, but speaking cost him so much painful effort that he was always, now, uncharacteristically brief.

Rachael could not hide her astonishment. She gaped at him, and her voice came so loud that her father winced. 'Me? A *husband*?'

'Of course — you are of age, I would like to see you betrothed before I die.'

So surprised was Rachael by this novel suggestion that she omitted to protest at the mention of his imminent demise. Then slowly, the implications of what he had said began to dawn on her.

A betrothal. A husband. Someone who would promise to love — *love* — and honour her. Her own place in the world, her own household to run, instead of acting as her stepmother's deputy. She had no particular young man in mind to fulfil the role, despite the numerous suitable sons of local gentry whom she had known from childhood. One disastrous experience of calf-love, nearly six years ago, had, she thought, cured her of such things. She had not really cared whom she might marry, so long as one day there would be someone willing to do it.

And now, it seemed, there was. She closed her mouth, somewhat tardily, and said, 'I would . . . I would like that very much indeed, Father.' She paused, and then, belatedly curious, added, 'Who? Who are you thinking of? Has he asked for me? Has he said anything about me?'

'Patience, Daughter . . . have patience. Nothing is settled yet, but I do have a young man in mind, yes. His father is one of my oldest friends, and we have often talked of this . . . I would like you to marry Jack Harington, John Harington's son.'

Rachael stared at him. The Haringtons lived at Kelston, some eight or nine miles away on the western side of Bath. The elder was a wealthy landowner, very much respected in Somerset, a lawyer, a justice and a Member for the Shire in Parliament. He was of her father's age, and shared the same political and religious beliefs. A few months ago, all the St. Barbes had gone to Kelston for the wedding of his daughter Moll, who was a year or so older than Rachael. She remembered, with sudden clarity, the tall, rather plump figure of Jack, asking her earnestly how she had liked the marriage sermon.

And that young man, with his round flushed serious face and untidy-looking brown hair, might soon be her husband, in her bed and at her board, and her home would be the beautiful Italianate house overlooking the River Avon, or the lesser Harington manor of Corston on the opposite bank. Beside the gracious mansion of Kelston, lovely Wintercombe seemed little better than a farmhouse. A small glow of delight and excitement settled somewhere in Rachael's stomach.

'Well, what do you think, child?' Sir George said, struggling up against the piled pillows. Quickly, Rachael leaned over to help him. He sat still for a moment, sweat breaking out on his haggard grey face, his eyes closed. Her heart pounding with mingled anticipation and anxiety, Rachael wiped his brow with a cool damp cloth kept in a bowl on the bedside table, along with ranks of physic in glass vials, cups and jugs of water, and a bottle of her stepmother's violet and hyssop water, an excellent remedy for sickness in the lungs. After a moment or two, her father had recovered: his eyes, the same blue as her own but less vivid by far, opened again, and he repeated, 'What do you think . . . of Jack Harington?'

'I . . . oh, yes, I like him,' said Rachael. In truth, she hardly knew him, and it would be more accurate to say that she did not dislike him, but so wonderful was the prospect of being a wife at last, of having some standing in the world, that any doubts in her mind, or in her father's, must be laid to rest at once. 'Does . . . does he like me?'

'He did not seem averse to the marriage . . . when I spoke with him and his father . . . in January,' said Sir George laboriously. 'All was settled then . . . a thousand pounds for your portion . . . needs only to send word to Harington . . . he's in London at present, alas . . . and that man Harley . . . if he can bestir himself . . . can draw up the contract today.' He paused for a series of difficult, wheezing breaths, and added in a gasping whisper, 'Does . . . does it please you, Daughter?'

'Of course it does,' said Rachael, and with a return of the impetuous affection which she had put away with other, childish things, she bent and kissed his clammy brow. 'It's wonderful news, Father – thank you, thank you so much!'

There was a knock on the door. Suddenly self-conscious, Rachael hastily settled back on her chair. The sick man spluttered a command to enter, and his manservant, Giles Stone, came in. 'Master Harley be here, Sir George.'

'At last.' Her father heaved himself further upright against the

pillows and glared expectantly at the door. 'About time too —
we'll hardly be done now before dark.'

'My most profound apologies, Sir George,' said the attorney,
bowing at the entrance. He was a long, lean greyhound of a man in
his late thirties, fair-haired, with a sharp, intelligent face, dominated by brilliant green eyes. 'Your servant, Mistress St. Barbe.'

Rachael made her curtsey. Jonathan Harley had always given her
a sense of unease: those extraordinary eyes saw altogether too far
and too deep and too much, as if her head were made of glass and
all her thoughts visible. She avoided his gaze and spoke to Sir
George. 'Shall I leave you now, Father? Is there any errand you
wish me to run?'

'My wife . . . should be told too, I suppose,' he said. 'Go fetch
her, Daughter.'

'Of course,' said Rachael, poised for flight. She added, buoyed
up by her happiness, 'Father — can I tell her? Can I tell her about
. . . about Jack?'

'Yes, you may . . . it will do no harm,' Sir George told her, and,
his face unusually soft, watched her precipitate exit from his
chamber.

Rachael knew where her stepmother could be found: on a sunny
day in May, it was unlikely that she would be anywhere else. She
leapt like a hoyden down the stone stairs, almost knocked one of
the maids flying at the bottom, and remembered belatedly that she
was shortly to become a respectable married woman. Her back
straight, her eyes modestly downcast and her walk slow and
graceful, she stepped out on to the first of the three sunny, fragrant
terraces that formed the chief part of Wintercombe's gardens.

*

Silence, Lady St. Barbe, was sitting in a niche set into the lowest
wall of the three terraces. Before her lay the orchard, at this season
a mass of blossom, pink and white. Quinces, apples, pears, mul-
berries and plums all grew there, and the warm air was thickly
scented and dangerous with bees. She had come here, as she did
whenever she could, to escape for a brief while the bustle and noise
and suffocating closeness of the house behind her, the trivial
complaints of her children, the endless domestic round, and the
inevitably gloomy atmosphere of approaching death. Today,
especially, she needed peace to think.

A letter had been brought to her yesterday. It lay now in her hands and she stared down at it as if she had never seen it before, although she knew its contents by heart. Usually, news from her brother Joseph was passed around the family, to be read again and again, and then kept safe in the box in her chamber with all the rest.

This one, she should have burned already.

She had not felt so frightened for years, not since the war ended, and the Royalist soldiers marched out of Wintercombe and out of her life. She had emerged from that nightmare a different woman, stronger, feeling that if she had survived that terrible year of death and danger, she could survive anything else that grim Fortune might place in her way. George had not understood: he saw only the surface of things, and had been disturbed, bewildered and ultimately defeated by her transformation. But she knew, far better than he, that she could never return to the obedient, uncomplaining, dutiful wife that she had been before war violated her life. And not only war: but that was a secret known to only three other people at Wintercombe.

It was all six years in the past, however, and she had more immediate concerns. There was her husband and his slow, painful and inevitable progress towards death, which had now dragged on agonisingly for some weeks and looked certain to continue for several more. She pushed that unpleasant fact to the back of her mind with the rest of her troubles, and concentrated her thoughts on the letter on her lap.

Her brother Joseph Woods lived in London, a flourishing draper like his father before him. He was some four years younger than Silence and had always tended to defer to his eldest sister, asking her advice on all kinds of matters concerning both business and family. Every fortnight or so, one of his haphazardly written letters would be delivered to Wintercombe by the Post, with the usual chaotic mixture of complaints about rising prices and the difficulty of attracting customers, the doings of all her nephews and nieces, his own two and sister Prue's four, scraps of news gathered from all corners of the country, Scots battles and two-headed calves treated with equal importance. And, in every letter, like a tale of doom, recounted with a mixture of horror and relish, the latest transgressions of their sister Patience.

Silence had left London to come as a bride of nineteen to Somerset. Busy with her life at Wintercombe, and separated by war and distance, she had not seen her youngest sister for nearly sixteen years. It was difficult to reconcile the lively, pretty, wilful child whom she remembered with the young Jezebel of Joseph's letters, and Silence, adept at reading between her brother's lines, had never taken his tales of Patience's misdemeanours very seriously. What if she did spend money on fripperies, refuse to work all hours in the shop, give pert answers to Joseph's wife and reject all suitable offers for her hand? Silence, well aware of the essential failure of her own marriage — although to most onlookers it seemed placid enough — could not but sympathise with her little sister's obstinate dismissal of all those boring and sober young men who would meet with the unimaginative Joseph's approval.

But this was no trivial transgression. Incredibly, this was treason.

Wondering for the twentieth time if there could possibly be some mistake, she read the letter again. Joseph's hand had always been somewhat erratic and here, under pressure of panic and fury, it had all but disintegrated into illegibility. Even she, who knew his writing like her own, was hard put to make out more than a quarter of it without difficulty. She wished that she had paid more attention to the seal when she opened it: now, it was impossible to tell if it had been tampered with. In view of the contents, however unreadable, she prayed most earnestly that it had not.

And yet, could this rambling, almost incoherent letter possibly be telling the truth about her little sister Patience?

'We would have known nothing,' Joseph wrote, the words almost flat in his haste,

if my dear wife had not come by chance upon a piece of paper in her chamber, which her eye fell upon, she would have looked no further had she not seen that the words seemed to be in some sort of cipher. She being somewhat alarmed, by reason of the plots lately discovered in this city, showed the paper to me, and I judged it fit to tax our sister with it. She, however, proved most obdurate, and would speak not one word to us concerning the paper, save that she accused my dear wife most intemperately of spying upon her, and hot words followed hard upon, from both sides. Considering her obstinacy to be in itself an admission of her guilt, and in great fear both for her and for ourselves, should her part in any conspiracy be discovered, my dear wife and I have decided that it were best to carry her out of the city for a space, until the Council of State and its officers have completed all investigation into the late plots. To this end, my dear sister, we would all be exceeding grateful if you would give shelter to Patience, for since Somerset is so far from London, she should be safe from chance discovery, and she will moreover have no further opportunity to continue her wicked plotting.

There was more, heavily blotched and splattered with ink. Silence wondered wryly how many quills Joseph had ruined in the writing of it. But it did seem to be true, most dreadfully so: and she still did not understand why, why her little sister, her favourite, whom she had last seen a mischievous eight-year-old child, who should by now be betrothed or wed, had somehow become involved in a plot against the government.

She pushed her hands against her hot forehead, trying to think clearly. It must be true: there was the letter in cipher, and if there was an innocent explanation, why not give it?

She could sympathise with Joseph, who was happiest when dealing with absolutes and certainties, the quality of a bolt of cloth or the amount needed for a gown. She loved him, but she knew his limitations. It occurred to her, not for the first time, that she herself, and not her brother, was better equipped, both by nature and by circumstance, to deal with the headstrong Patience, and that sending her to Wintercombe was long overdue.

And yet, with George so ill, her arrival could not have come at a worse time. He had never admitted it, but her husband undoubtedly looked down upon his second wife's family. His grandfather had travelled Europe on diplomatic missions, a favourite of Queen Elizabeth, and his wife had been the daughter of an earl. Silence's grandmother had sold fish in Billingsgate at the age of fourteen, and she had always suspected that for George thoughts of her family came trailing the odour of herring. True, he had respected her father, a most godly man and assuredly one of the Elect, and enjoyed cordial relations with Joseph, who was admittedly devout and well-meaning, but if the Patience described in the letters bore the remotest resemblance to the reality, she would soon set Sir George, and Wintercombe, by the ears.

However, George was dying, confined to his bed. He would barely notice his sister-in-law's presence, having, not unnaturally, other concerns on his mind. Silence, wondering what Patience had become, found herself suddenly wishing for her company. True, she had the children, and now that Rachael and her twin Nat were adult, she could be their friend, rather than their stepmother. Nevertheless, Rachael had never been easy to know, or even to like, and Nat had been much absent, completing his education. The thought of her sister, a friend, companion, ally, and comfort in the bleak and difficult days that lay ahead, was suddenly very tempting.

She looked down at Joseph's last paragraph. He would waste no time waiting for her answer, the case was too urgent: he would set out the very next day to bring his wayward sister safe to Wintercombe, out of harm's way.

The letter was dated the previous Tuesday, the thirteenth of May. It was now Friday. Joseph had sent one of his own servants, riding Post, to deliver it to her, and that at least showed some sense, for it was unlikely to have been opened and read by unfriendly eyes, unless the man was lying, or careless, or disloyal. She wondered how long it would take for her brother and sister to ride from London: three or four days at the least, for it was a hundred miles, and neither of them, city bred, was accomplished on horseback. Joseph, who followed, with indifferent success, the strict morality of his father, would not want to travel on the Sabbath, and so she might expect them tomorrow, or on the Monday.

She would have to tell George, of course, but the reason for Patience's arrival at Wintercombe must be kept a secret. A convincing explanation would not be difficult to find. If nothing better, she could always say that her sister had come to offer comfort in her time of affliction.

She must destroy the letter, and at once: she had been foolish not to do so immediately. Silence thought, however, smiling with rueful affection at Joseph's scrawl, that any government agent casting curious eyes over it would be hard-pressed to decipher a single word of it, let alone discern treasonous intent.

She screwed up the paper in her hands and got to her feet. At once her little white greyhound, Lily, jumped up and looked at her expectantly. Then the dog turned her narrow, sharp-nosed head to the steps, and pricked her ears.

It was her stepdaughter. Silence, watching her descend with studied care, thought with a pang of the old impetuous Rachael, rushing, shouting, never pausing to think. This stilted behaviour did not represent the girl's true character, which had been sternly repressed over the past few years, leaving only the dutiful daughter that Sir George wanted. Of his six remaining children, only Rachael had been so hungry for love and approval that she had sacrificed her self on the altar of filial duty and obedience, and Silence, knowing that the reason for it would vanish with Sir George's death, could see no good in this transformation.

But there was something left of that fierce and vigorous child: as she saw her stepmother, she ran down the remaining steps and came to a breathless halt in front of Silence, her eyes wide and shining with excitement. 'Oh, Mother, the most wonderful news – I'm going to be married!'

It was utterly unexpected. Silence stared at the girl, whose face was transfigured into beauty by her happiness, and knew that this must be entirely George's doing: Rachael, sheltered and dutiful, had neither the opportunity nor the inclination to seek out her own husband. She said, trying to disguise her astonishment and sudden anger, 'Married? Who? Who is he?'

Rachael did not seem to think it strange that her stepmother should not have been consulted on such an important matter: after all, she herself had not been informed either. She said, 'Father's arranged it all, and Master Harley's here to draw up the contract, I'm going to marry Jack Harington!'

There was no denying, it was a most suitable, not to say excellent match. The two fathers were alike in age, wealth, and religious beliefs, although Harington was a great deal more intellectual than Sir George: Silence could not imagine her husband reading books in Arabic or Hebrew, as was the worthy Esquire's habit. She thought of Jack Harington, whom she hardly knew, but who did not seem the sort of young man who would suit Rachael's tempestuous nature. On her limited acquaintance, she had thought him vain, thoughtless, and rather shallow and, unlike his father, he made a great parade of his zealous godliness, as if a man's worth could be judged by the hours he spent on his knees. How would he deal with Rachael, who above all needed sensitivity, understanding, and love – real love, not careless, dutiful affection? With clear eyes, Silence knew that he would not make her happy for a week.

However, she could not say that to the pretty, glowing girl before her, transported with delight. She must speak with her husband, try to tell him that Jack Harington would not do for Rachael, that someone else must be found. She knew her stepdaughter well enough to guess that it was the idea of marriage in general which excited her, not marriage to Jack Harington in particular. If only she could persuade Sir George that there were other young men in Somerset or Wiltshire, and that Rachael's husband need not necessarily be the priggish son of one of his oldest friends.

'Do you know when it will be?' she asked Rachael, letting none of her doubts show in her face or voice. From long, long habit her dissembling was perfect, and the girl was in any case too caught up in her intoxicating future to notice anything untoward.

Rachael launched at full spate into everything that her father had told her, while Silence kept her own growing anger in check. So this had been arranged four months ago, and not a word breathed till now! It was typical of George that he should not deign to consult her: he had always thought his wife to be apart from such things and had treated her with an insulting lack of consideration that, once, she had accepted. Now, she would not, but she had too active a conscience, still, to harangue him on his death-bed. Unless a miracle happened, it would not be very long before she was a widow and George would never know, till his dying day, of his wife's true feelings towards him.

Yes, she was a hypocrite: she was always honest with herself, if with few others. But her strict, harsh, dreary Puritan childhood had taught her to say what would be pleasing when her heart and thought ran quite opposite, and she could see so clearly the similar pattern in Rachael.

They walked back together up through the sunny gardens. Sir George's cosmopolitan grandfather had laid them out in the Italian manner, with terraces and balustrades, but somehow in the building they had been transmuted into something much less formal and typically English. The knots and the arbour of cherry trees, the sweet wallflowers, the clipped box and lavender and the flowers that shouted of spring, in voices made of scent and colour, were her solace and her delight. Other, more godly wives sought comfort for their trials and afflictions in prayer and fasting: Silence, Lady St. Barbe, found true peace only in her garden.

'Mother,' said Rachael hesitantly, on the top terrace by the south door. She stopped and turned to face Silence, the excitement suddenly drained from her pale, intense face, the lines of wilfulness and hard-held temper already traced around her long, slender nose and between the narrow brows. 'Mother . . . what did you feel, when you heard that you were going to be married to Father?'

It was an unexpected question from Rachael, who so rarely

opened her heart, but Silence thought that she could see the reason for it. She considered, and then said carefully, 'A great many things, all quite different. I was younger than you are, of course, and marriage hadn't entered my head. I think I was surprised, and flattered too, to be asked by an important and well-respected man like your father. Even though he was so much older, and had already been married, and had three children — I felt sorry for you, and Nat, and Sam, when he described how unhappy you all were without a mother to look after you. He made me feel that I would be needed and I liked that. And . . . well, as you know, I was not very happy at that time, my father was very stern, and I think I wanted to escape. To live so far away, with a house to manage and a husband and children to look after . . . it was exciting, but, I must admit, rather frightening too.'

'I feel like that,' Rachael confessed. 'Even though Jack is only a little older than I am, and there are no children, and he lives less than two hours' ride away. I do want to be married,' she added. 'And Jack is very godly, and he wants to marry me. But . . . I can't help feeling a little frightened all the same. Kelston is so big, so grand, it's not like Wintercombe.'

'You wouldn't live at Kelston, not while his father is still alive — I expect you'd be at the other manor, Corston, and that's a much more friendly place,' Silence said. She was touched by the secretive Rachael's untypical admission, but it was very difficult to calm the girl's fears without seeming to approve of the match, and that she most assuredly did not. She added quietly, 'Rachael — I know that you are very pleased and excited, and that's only natural, but do, I beg you, do think very carefully about this betrothal. I know you're of age to be wed, but are you quite sure that it's Jack Harington you want to marry? You hardly know him, after all. And you don't have to snatch at the first person who offers — there are plenty of other young men in Somerset: Horners, Ashes, many who'd suit you just as well, if not better.'

As she had feared, the shutters closed down over Rachael's face. 'Plenty of young men? I suppose there are, but they've all known me for years and not one of them has ever made an offer for me, until now, and if I refuse Jack, I don't suppose any of them ever will! I *want* to marry him, and Father wants it, and Jack and his father, and that's all there is to it.' And, with her mind once more firmly bolted and barred against inconvenient truths, she turned and marched indignantly into the house.

Oh, dear, thought Silence unhappily: when will I ever learn to read her right? Rachael, though she had acquired some maturity, some skill at hiding her feelings as well as her thoughts, was still unpredictable, still essentially at the mercy of her vacillating moods and emotions. She could not really be blamed for leaping at the chance of marriage to Jack Harington, apparently so suitable. One of Rachael's closest friends, Eleanor Flower, who was the same age, had been wed for two years and had a little son. No wonder the girl was frightened that no one else would offer. Perhaps she had secretly entertained hopes of Eleanor's brother Tom, whose own wedding had recently taken place: but the Flowers were only minor gentry, who leased, and did not own, the Manor Farm half a mile away in Philip's Norton. Rachael, a baronet's daughter, could surely not have expected to marry into such a family.

All the same, Silence thought, I was far beneath George when I married him. My large dowry obviously influenced his choice, but in the main he was seeking a godly girl of good Puritan stock. Certainly considerations of that sort should outweigh any mercenary motives – but whoever marries Rachael should be marrying *her*, not her family or her dowry. And that, I am sure, Jack Harington will not be doing.

Love, which Rachael needed so much, did not enter the bargain either. Once, long ago, Silence had not thought it so important. She had never loved George, and early affection had grown only because, like a puppy in its new home, she had no one else on whom to fix her feelings. The children which she bore to him had amply supplanted him in her heart, and for all of them, her predecessor's as well as her own, she felt a deep and fierce love. She had remained a good and dutiful wife until the Royalist soldiers invaded Wintercombe, shattering her sheltered contentment, bringing destruction and danger. Six years ago, she had discovered what love for a man could mean: and even now, the memory, sudden, piercingly and agonisingly sweet, had the power to melt her bones with hopeless longing.

He had gone with the rest of the enemy soldiers, her autumn-coloured man, and she had never seen him again. He could be anywhere in the world: he could be dead. She would probably never know what had become of him, but he had left her two gifts beyond all price: he had taught her the meaning of love, and given her the strength to endure the empty days without him, for she knew now what it was to be beloved. And he had given her Kate.

George did not know, would, she prayed, never know that he had been cuckolded by an enemy captain, and that the little girl on whom he doted was not in fact his own but another man's sowing. Only her maid, Mally, and the twins Nat and Rachael knew the truth. Nat, her friend always, despised by his father for a feeble weakling, would never betray her, but Rachael, torn by hectic moods, driven by whim and impulse, was a different matter. She had never spoken to her stepmother about her adultery, and it was as if it had never happened. Silence had often wondered if the girl had been drawn to her father out of pity, because she wanted somehow to atone for his wife's sin, and for her own guilty complicity.

It was a bad time to think of the past, when the future was so uncertain and so difficult. Silence walked up the stone stairs to her husband's sickroom, her heart cold with guilt and compassion. She had married him in innocence, for better, for worse, and in all the vows of her wedding day, she had betrayed him. Small point in complaining that he had treated her as a child, disregarded her views, taken her for granted, continually criticised her, and shown a lack of sensitivity to her feelings that would have given many men pause if he had done the same to his horse. He was still her husband: she had promised. Women up and down the country, in their thousands, were used as thoughtlessly and did not cuckold their husbands. Her wickedness was very great, and yet she could not regret what she had done.

She knocked on the door and entered. The chamber in which Sir George lay dying faced north and was a beautiful room, with a splendid oriel window, a high, beamed ceiling and a stone mantel richly carved, with the St. Barbe arms proudly displayed in the centre. However, for Silence this place was forever associated with her husband's fearsome mother, Dame Ursula, who had occupied it until her death six years previously. There was still a close, frowsty smell in the chamber, a lack of fresh air and the heavy presence of remedies and potions, and she longed to open a window.

Master Harley rose and bowed. She inclined her head graciously, seeing with a sinking heart the parchment, ink and quills on the table beside him. George beckoned her closer to the bed. 'There you are, Wife. Has Rachael found you?'

'She has indeed,' said Silence, ignoring the impatient tone in his voice. She found that she wanted to shake the sick and shrunken man lying against the pillows, to shout at him, to ask how he dared arrange his daughter's future without a word to either of them, but because of the brief days left to him, she would not. She added, 'She tells me that you have arranged for her to marry Jack Harington.'

'I have,' said her husband. 'Talked it over with his father . . . in January, at Moll's wedding. Master Harley here will see to the contract — she's to have a dowry of a thousand pounds and the lands at Bruton and Shepton for her jointure.'

He did not ask if she approved, but that came as no surprise, for he never sought her opinion. She had intended to remain silent, but the anger within her was growing too great to be denied. She said, 'Have you consulted Rachael on this? Have you given her any choice?'

George looked at her in genuine bewilderment. He said eventually, 'She needs none. She is quite happy with the arrangement — she is a good and dutiful daughter.'

'Could you not have discovered her thoughts before you spoke with John Harington?' Silence asked. Her voice was quiet, but there was a sharpness in her tone which made Master Harley, politely contemplating his fingernails, look at her keenly. He had long ago ascertained that this ill-matched couple, outwardly quite conventional, were more fundamentally at odds than any other husband and wife of his wide acquaintance. It was fortunate that the doctors were so positive as to the nature of their patient's ailment, or he would have entertained dire suspicions about Lady St. Barbe and her vast store of remedies and potions.

'What need? She is gracious and obedient — marriage to Jack Harington pleases her mightily, she told me so herself,' said Sir George impatiently, and began to cough. Silence dutifully tended him with a kerchief and a cup of water, trying to fight down her indignation. This was no trivial matter, this concerned Rachael's future, her happiness, and yet George saw nothing wrong in presenting it to her as a foregone conclusion, relying on his daughter's convenient sense of duty and her desire for her own place in the world to overcome any doubts. She knew that her objections were futile, but she could not surrender so tamely. She said, 'Have you not considered that she would agree to whatever you suggest, even if she did not want it? Can you not see that you might be exploiting her sense of duty?'

'She is happy with the match,' Sir George repeated, his voice cracking with annoyance. 'She has no reason to be otherwise.' He succumbed to another fit of coughing, muffled by the kerchief, which was crumpled and stained. Silence, ready with more water, glanced at the lawyer and found him looking at her with a curious mixture of speculation and sympathy on his lean, unemotional face. If it had been Nat standing there, she would have given him the benefit of a smile. Feeling strangely encouraged, as if she had received a tacit message of support, she turned back to her husband. He was dying: she could at least give him peace in his last days on this earth, and make a show of acquiescence. With a hypocrisy that saddened her, she said quietly, 'If that is indeed so, then I will say no more. My only concern is for Rachael's happiness.'

George stared at her suspiciously. He had learned, these last few years, to look beyond the surface value of her words, and to wonder, with increasingly frustrated bewilderment, what she really meant. Her eyes, a clear and lovely hazel, met his without guile, and he leaned back on the pillows, too sick and weary to delve for any deeper significance. 'As it is mine, Wife,' he said, and waved a feeble hand. 'Leave us now – go to your duties. Master Harley is drawing up the contract and my will. We have much to discuss.'

And so she was dismissed. The lawyer bowed her out, and again she saw the sympathy in those unusual eyes and was a little heartened by it. She said softly, 'I thank you for your help, sir. I am sure it is a great comfort to my husband to have such an honest and trustworthy man at his service.' She paused and on impulse added, 'Will you speak with me before you leave Wintercombe, Master Harley? There are some matters which I wish to raise with you on my own account.'

He smiled, a movement that involved only his thin lips, and said that it would be a pleasure. Silence descended the twisting stairs, wondering if she had been wise to presume too much upon his compassion. Covert sympathy with the downtrodden wife was one matter, but interfering on her behalf in her husband's business was quite another. Yet, she must find out what George intended in the marriage contract and in his will. She did not trust him to be fair: and she was not thinking of her own situation, but of the children.

*

Master Jonathan Harley was ushered into her chamber much later that afternoon. Silence had occupied this room since coming to Wintercombe at the outbreak of civil war, nearly nine years previously, and had gradually made it her own. The books that George despised, poetry, histories and travellers' tales, the works of Sir Francis Bacon and William Shakespeare, lined the deep windowsills, and bowls of tulips and hazy blue forget-me-nots and heavy-scented wallflowers decorated the hearth and the two walnut tables. It was larger than her husband's chamber, and constructed in similar fashion, but the atmosphere was quite different. The windows were open, sunlight streamed across the polished boards, and in the yellow warmth a pretty grey and white cat lay contentedly dozing on the bed. Master Harley, who appreciated neatness and order, looked about him approvingly, noting with surprise the abundant evidence that Lady St. Barbe was made of a very different metal to her husband. The virginals, on which a stack of music sheets had been placed; the flowers, the books, the fragrance and the animals — a little white dog was curled amongst the cushions on the sunniest windowsill — all spoke of a delight in her surroundings which he suspected Sir George entirely lacked. He himself also liked beautiful things, and he could not help but take pleasure in this lovely room.

Lady St. Barbe greeted him with a smile, and sent down her little red-haired maid for cider and pasties. He knew that she must be almost as old as himself, but it barely showed on that serene, oval face, lacking beauty yet nevertheless very pleasant to behold. He remarked, indicating the virginals, that he had not known that she played any instrument, and she gave him a smile that suddenly lit up her eyes. 'I am afraid that I do not, Master Harley. I have only to look at them for the strings to fall out of tune. It's my daughter Tabitha who plays them, and though I should not boast of her accomplishment, she performs most beautifully. Have you any music skills, sir?'

He confessed that he had learned to play the viol in his youth, though not so well as he would have liked. They passed some time in such idle conversation, until the maid returned with a tray, two pewter mugs of cool yellow cider, and a plate of warm spiced pasties. When she had curtseyed and left, her mistress fixed the lawyer with that direct gaze and said without preamble, 'Have you finished your business with my husband, Master Harley?'

'I have, my lady. The will and the contract are alike drawn up, and want only the necessary seals and signatures. Sir George is resting at present, but wants to sign both documents before I leave today. Then I am to take the contract to Master Harington, who is at present at Lincoln's Inn, for his approval and signature.'

'And – forgive me, I know that you are bound by your duty to my husband to keep his business private, but I feel I should know – what provisions has Sir George made for his children in his will?'

Harley stared at her in some surprise. He had assumed that his client had at least discussed such things with his wife, even if the final decision had been his alone. He said at last, 'Has he not spoken to you at all?'

Her wry expression was answer enough. 'No,' she said. 'I am afraid that it has probably never entered his head to do so. Let me make it clear, Master Harley, I am not anxious for myself, I have my jointure at least, as agreed in my marriage contract, and I will not starve. It is the children who concern me, and I would like to know what plans Sir George has made for them.'

He had never had such a request in all his years of practice in Bath: in his experience, every husband at least paid lip service to the courtesy of consulting his wife on such matters. Moreover, any gentleman could be trusted to make good provision for his family, especially when they were as young as Sir George's off-spring. But as he had drawn up the will to the sick man's dictation, he had begun to realise that his client, although seemingly bene-volent, was determined to influence his children, and his wife, from beyond the grave. How Lady St. Barbe had managed to guess this, he did not know, but she had every right to be anxious.

He debated with his professional scruples, weighing the rules of confidence against the sympathy he felt for her. She was watching him closely, and he realised she must know that there was some-thing amiss. He came to a decision, put down the mug of cider, and leaned forward in his chair. 'Very well, Lady St. Barbe – I know it is not the acceptable practice, but I will give you some indication of what your husband has ordained. The contents of his will are quite straightforward. Wintercombe itself, of course, and the bulk of his estate, is left to his eldest son Nathaniel, with a small competence for William. Sir George expresses the hope that he will enter some worthy occupation and make his own way in the world. Each of his daughters – Rachael, Tabitha, Deborah and Katherine – is to receive the sum of one thousand pounds as their dowry, upon their marriage. However, if Rachael should not wish to marry Master Harington, as set out in the marriage contract, then her dowry is withdrawn, and divided between the other daughters.'

Silence stared at him in dismay. This provision was aimed at her, she knew it: by this means, George had ensured that Rachael would marry the man of his choice, or nobody. Without a doubt, her attempts to persuade him to think again about Jack Harington had led to this, and it was her fault. She should have known that her husband, who could be so stubborn and unreasonable, might well stoop to this. And there was nothing she could do.

'Poor Rachael,' she said sadly, thinking of her stepdaughter's transparent joy that morning. How long would it be before merciless reality shattered her illusions?

'You may be wrong,' Harley pointed out. 'Surely there is every chance that she will be perfectly happy? Certainly, she is very pleased at the prospect, and that is an excellent beginning.'

'Perhaps,' Silence said, though she had no great hopes of it. She would, for Rachael's sake, have to swallow all her doubts and fears, and lend her support to a marriage of which she had such profound misgivings, and she was not sure whether, once George had gone, she could continue to be such a hypocrite.

She must. She took a deep breath, and said, 'What other provisions has my husband made?'

'It seems that Sir George is most concerned for his son's poor health.'

'Not so concerned, that he could not send Nat away to study at Oxford for three years,' said Silence with some asperity.

'Sir George fears that his son will die untimely, leaving no heir save his brother, William, who is yet a child. That is one reason why he has left so little to his younger son. Therefore, he has stipulated that, if this should happen, you are to be William's guardian and manage Wintercombe until the boy comes of age. However, he did not at first see fit to make any other provision for you, and could not see the necessity of giving you the right of residence here, in your widowhood, unless Nathaniel were to die. I pointed out that you must have somewhere to live, and also asked him what he felt should happen, should you at any time wish to marry again. He seemed most surprised by the idea, but decided that if you did you would naturally want to live at your new husband's house. I said that I felt that you should have some independence, or you would be forced to rely on your stepson's charity. I eventually managed to persuade him to leave you the Chard property, to be yours absolutely for your life, and after your death to your heirs.'

Silence closed her eyes. The room seemed suddenly, suffocatingly hot. She tried desperately to order her thoughts through a fog of anger and achieved some little success. She said, looking straight at Master Harley, 'Let me confirm this. I have no right of residence at Wintercombe, but I inherit the house at Chard. However, if Nat dies, and William inherits while still a minor, then I can stay here – with my new husband if I choose to marry again. Do I have the right of it?'

'You do,' said the lawyer. He added, 'My lady – I can see that this information has been something of a surprise for you. Believe me, I understand your feelings. I have spent most of this afternoon attempting to persuade your husband to show a little more concern for your welfare. It has been something of a struggle, but I think I have succeeded in convincing him that he must make more efforts on your behalf.'

'I thank you,' Silence said. She wanted suddenly to be alone, to think over George's will, and all the problems and tensions and difficulties it would undoubtedly create. It seemed almost as if he had wanted to humiliate her and to drive a wedge between Nat and herself – and yet, she had not thought him capable of foreseeing the inevitable dissensions that would result, nor indeed of such spite.

At best, he was thoughtless and naïve. At worst, he wished to disrupt her happy relations with all the children. His mother, Dame Ursula, would have been delighted to do such a thing, but surely George had more regard for his family than this?

She would have no right to stay at Wintercombe, which she loved so much, save by Nat's permission. True, he would grant it gladly, as a matter of course, but the very fact that she would be here as his guest might put a subtle strain on their friendship – of which George had always been rather suspicious. True, he would leave her the Chard house, but that was more in the nature of a millstone than a blessing: he knew full well how she had disliked the place, and after the ravages of the war it was little better than a ruin. This did not really matter: she and Nat could overcome such difficulties, for their relationship was strong enough. What really enraged her was his forcing of Rachael into a marriage which she might come to regret.

There was nothing she could do, no words she could use to persuade George to change this part of his will. Harley would not intervene, and he would certainly pay no attention whatsoever to his wife. In the long and subtle battle that had been their marriage, he had inflicted this final, and somehow most crushing, defeat.

She thanked Master Harley again, with genuine gratitude for his efforts on her behalf, and he left her, the sympathy even more marked in his lean, fine-featured face. She knew that, if she wanted it, he would be an ally, albeit one almost as powerless against her husband as herself. Then she sat down in the warm sunshine, hugging Lily to her, appalled by the thoughts within her, unleashed by her husband's injustice.

His death, so imminent and inevitable, no longer seemed to be an occasion for mourning and regret, however muted. Now she could no longer deny it, evil though her feelings were.

She would be so very glad, to be at last a widow.

❧ CHAPTER TWO ❧

'Patience herself'
(*As You Like It*)

In the third-best parlour of the White Hart in Stall Street, Bath, the two occupants were locked in an argument that they had, in essence, carried with them all the way from London, to the profit of neither and the annoyance of both.

'I'm not going to stay here for a whole day, just because you don't want to travel on the Sabbath,' said Patience Woods. She fixed her brother with a cold brown gaze and folded her arms. 'Tell me, Joseph — why can we not go on to Wintercombe now? It's a fine sunny afternoon, and there are only a few more miles. Otherwise, we won't be there until Monday.'

Joseph in self-defence took too large a gulp of the frothy warm beer, and all but choked on it. He swallowed it with difficulty, growing very red in the face, while his younger sister watched him without sympathy. 'Saddle-sore?' she suggested, with callous perspicacity.

'No, no, of course not,' said Joseph, with unconvincing haste. 'My concern is entirely for you, dear Sister. We have ridden many miles today and you must be weary.'

'Not so tired that I can't ride a few more,' said Patience. She walked over to the table and picked up her own tankard, wrinkling her nose at its bitter, heavy aroma, quite unlike the smoother brew favoured in London. 'And if you don't want to, Joseph, I swear I'll go alone.'

Joseph Woods, draper, of Paternoster Row in the City of London, was a man of middle height, just over thirty years old, with a rather straggling head of brown hair already going bald at the crown, and an expression of extreme harassment. He had known that this journey would be difficult, but if he had been able to foresee just how awkward and uncomfortable the exclusive companionship of his sister Patience could be, he would never have left London with her, treason or no treason. And he knew that when she uttered a threat such as this, she was perfectly capable of carrying it out.

Besides, he thought, putting a brave face on it, saddle-sore or no, he did not relish the thought of staying for two nights at this inn, with Patience in such close proximity. Better to reach Winter-combe this evening, at whatever cost to his painful fundament, and return to London, home and family on the Monday, rested and refreshed and blessedly alone.

'Very well,' he said, unaware of the petulant note in his voice. 'When we have finished, we will continue our journey. It is not so far, after all.'

Patience gave him the brilliant smile that had enchanted many stronger men than Joseph. 'Good,' she said, swallowing her beer with unladylike fervour. 'I knew you'd see sense. You've been here before, after all – but I haven't seen Silence for sixteen years, and I can't wait to see her again.'

'I have only visited Wintercombe once, and that was four years ago,' Joseph pointed out. He consulted his watch, a rather futile exercise since the jolting of the journey had set its already erratic timing completely adrift. 'Well, if you would make yourself ready, Patience, we should be gone, or we shall not arrive before dark.'

'I *am* ready,' said his sister. 'And we won't need to waste time hiring a guide, will we? You know the way, after all.'

Joseph, with a memory of bleak bare downs and waterlogged valleys, hoped devoutly that he would remember it. He considered that Patience would be entirely to blame if they lost their way and were benighted on some lonely hill. With a sigh of longing for his own comfortable London bed, and his busy, brisk, efficient wife Grace, he ushered his impetuous sister from the parlour.

They rode out of Bath through the Southgate, over the bridge across the River Avon, quiet and midge-infested in the westering sunlight, and began the climb up through the downs towards Philip's Norton, and Wintercombe. Joseph, weary and irritated by Patience's cheerfully insensitive conversation, soon stopped talking, his attention occupied by the tickling nose and streaming eyes that always afflicted him at this time of the year, whenever he rode in the country.

After a while, she decided to ignore his martyred snufflings and sneezings. Really, he was such a prosy prig! On the whole, she was glad to be leaving London, glad of the prospect of something new and different in her life, instead of the unending tedium of her days at Paternoster Row, enduring the insinuating remarks of her nosy sister-in-law, resenting the hours spent over her needle or serving customers in the dark little shop, living only for the brief snatches of freedom that had, quite by chance, led her into intoxicating danger.

She had met John Jackel at the church that the Woods family attended every Sunday. He was quite young, and evidently attracted to her, for he soon found an excuse to speak with her. Patience was used to young men seeking her acquaintance, but not so much accustomed to the attentions of one so handsome and amusing. She flirted with him outrageously, enjoying the game, and very well aware of the dubious glances of Joseph and Grace. But when Master Jackel presented himself at the shop, it did not take her brother long to decide that he liked the fellow — as if, Patience had thought with annoyance, his was the only opinion that mattered. There had been no formal arrangement, but Jackel was given to understand that Joseph would allow him to pay court to Patience.

That last winter had been a brief, almost magical time. Patience, bored with her restricted life, had welcomed the attentions of this well-informed and erudite man, a few years older than herself. Like the Woods family, and many others in London, he was a Presbyterian, and Joseph happily allowed him to escort his sister to sermons and prayer meetings. Once, Patience would have laughed to imagine herself grown so godly, but, under Jackel's influence and in his company, the most tedious gathering became an event to be savoured both in anticipation and in memory.

She could not now remember when she had first begun to suspect that the meetings at Minister Love's house were not as innocent as she had thought, but she could vividly recall the moment when she had discovered the truth about John Jackel. He had been perusing a letter, thinking her out of the room. Playfully, she had crept up behind him and snatched it away.

He had not laughed: he had been alarmed and angry. Indignantly, Patience had whisked it further out of his reach, the better to discover what it contained.

It was in cipher. As she stared at it, trying to work out the sense, he tore it from her hands. Angry in her turn, she had accused him of plotting with the King of Scots.

Aghast, he stared at her. 'How do you know?'

'It says so, in your letter,' Patience told him. 'Cipher? That wouldn't deceive the Council of State for five minutes!'

He could not understand how she knew so much of what had

been written. Patience eventually took pity on him and explained. Her father had been a man of unusual severity, ruling his children with a rod of iron, which they could evade only with secrecy and deception. Together, Joseph and his three sisters – she seemed to remember that Silence had been the chief instigator – had devised a series of codes, used to communicate with each other when speech or contact were forbidden. Patience had learned the various devices early and never forgotten them: indeed, she had poured out her adolescent heart in a succession of journals, all written in ciphers of increasing complexity to thwart Grace's prying eyes.

'You can write in code?' John had said at the end of her explanation, rather as if she had boasted of her prowess in Arabic or Hebrew. 'Then – will you help us in this enterprise?'

And Patience, welcoming the excitement and the danger, had thus been willingly drawn into conspiracy and treason.

The plotters, however, had been careless, and a Royalist agent, taken into custody on another matter, had confessed to everything he knew. In April, the arrests had started, and a fine mixed haul of Presbyterian ministers, Royalists, old army officers and small merchants and shopkeepers, were committed to the Tower. John Jackel had simply vanished – presumably into hiding – and Patience, for the first time really frightened, made no attempt to seek him out. There was no knowing, now, who her friends might be and, without John, she had no idea whom to trust. She told Joseph, casually convincing, that he had been called into the country to visit a sick relative, and prayed that no emissary of the Council of State would come knocking at her brother's door to drag his foolish little sister off to the Tower with the rest of the traitors.

Nothing happened. The peril receded and it had all begun to seem like a game again, even with all those men in the Tower and John gone from her life. For amusement, she had written a letter in her latest cipher, one that she had devised over the weeks of suspense, assuring the King of Scots in extravagant language of the undying devotion of his loyal City of London. It was this that Grace had discovered where Patience had thought it well hidden, secreted in her clothes-press, and it had brought her here, to the high hills of Somerset, to the sister she had not seen for sixteen years and the family who were strangers to her.

Joseph, sneezing just behind her, was riding as if his fundament pained him. Patience, grinning to herself, thought that it served him right if it did. There had been no need for this drastic remedy, no reason to whisk her out of London as if the headsman were after her, but Joseph had always made soaring peaks out of very small molehills. And she welcomed the change in her life. She had never been so far out of London before, and the greenness, the quiet, the open spaces and distant views delighted her. She looked around, breathing the deep clean air, tossing her hair free, and almost lost her hat in a sudden warm breeze. This was Silence's country, and this road along the ridges, clear of the wet soggy valleys, one which she must know well. And the next village, already visible as a smudge of tile and stone and thatch, was Philip's Norton.

Her body was tired, but not her mind. She straightened her aching shoulders, surreptitiously flexed a stiff knee, and adjusted her ample skirts. She had bought this riding-habit from a neighbour's wife especially for the journey, notice being too short to have one made for her in time. The rich russet suited her colouring, and she knew she looked well in it. She glanced back at Joseph, glumly riding some twenty paces behind, and wished that she were a better horsewoman. She would love to set heels to her weary hired horse and gallop dashingly up to Wintercombe in a cloud of dust, to the admiration of all. But she knew that her experience was too limited, and it would be extremely embarrassing were she to fall off a somnolent old nag like this one. She concentrated instead on achieving the upright but relaxed posture that was held to mark the proficient rider.

The village was large and prosperous-looking, with a fine market place and a cross, rather battered, and two inns on opposite sides of the street. One was much larger than the other, a handsome building with a half-timbered upper storey oversailing a base of stone. A sign swung above the door and she identified it without difficulty. Any depiction of a man in armour spearing a monster, however crudely drawn, must indicate the George.

There were people about, at a smithy, leading horses or driving cattle, fetching water or gossiping in doorways. She looked at the broad brown country faces, so different from the pale-skinned Londoners. She must take care to keep her own complexion smooth and white, and sheltered from sun and wind. But at least these vigorous people did not seem to suffer so much from the smallpox and other disfigurements.

Her belief that rural air was cleaner and healthier than that of the city, however, was dissolved by the noisome midden that spilt on to the street, and made even her sleepy old horse snort and sidestep. She glanced at Joseph and saw him press a kerchief to his mouth. A child, filthy and barefoot, called out something completely unintelligible. Patience gave it her most brilliant smile and let her brother lead the way through the village streets.

They passed a mill, its wide pond dangerously close to flooding, and the lane became increasingly wet and muddy: the last few days here had obviously seen a great deal of rain. The hedges were high, and new-sprouting with leaf, so that it was hard to look over. As the way turned slightly to the left, she saw a little group ahead.

The sun was in her eyes, and she pulled her hat-brim down. There was a pony, busily cropping the new grass at the hedge foot, and a gate, with three children sitting on it.

She glanced round. Joseph had dropped behind again, succumbing to one of the sneezing fits that had plagued him all the way from Bath. He was bent over his kerchief, while his horse snatched something tasty amongst the fresh green hawthorns. She drew rein and smiled at the children.

They stared unwinkingly back. There was a girl, perhaps eleven or twelve years old, stoutly built, with curling fair hair and a rosy, sunflushed complexion. The boy, a couple of years younger, was more slender, with paler hair, but evidently her brother. Between them was a little mite of five or so, with straight brown elf-locks and a pointed, mischievous face, at present wearing a most solemn expression. They were all dressed plainly but cleanly in mulberry-coloured wool that had probably come from the same bolt of cloth, and were obviously of good family.

Patience decided to pretend that she did not know who they might be. She addressed them cheerfully. 'Can you tell me the way to Wintercombe? Sir George St. Barbe's house?'

The older two exchanged glances and covert grins. Then the girl said, in a heavy but passable imitation of the local dialect, 'Ooh, aargh, oi doan't roightly know that, ma'am.' The effect was somewhat spoiled when she burst into hilarious giggles, and the boy joined her.

The smallest child, however, was unimpressed. She cast them both a scornful glance and then jumped down from the gate, which was nearly her height, in a flurry of skirts. 'I know who you are,' she said in triumph, coming fearlessly up to the horse. 'You're our Aunt Imp!'

That confirmed the identification. It had been many years since

Patience had heard her nickname, bestowed on her in childhood by her eldest sister. It had been a joke amongst the three girls, that Silence could not refrain from talking, that Prudence was so careless, and Patience so eager to snatch at whatever life had to offer. And so Impatience she had become, an Imp of mischief. Prue, now a respectable married woman, had not called her younger sister thus for years, and humourless Joseph never had, but to hear her old name bestowed on her by these children heartened Patience immensely. She gave the little girl her sunniest smile, and said, 'Indeed I am – and you must be Kate.'

'Yes, I'm Kate,' said the child, her expression still serious. 'And that's William, and that's Deb, only they're too rude to climb off the gate.' And her small face suddenly split into a huge, infectious, three-cornered grin.

'Hallo, Deb, hallo, William,' said Patience to the older children, who hastily scrambled down from their perch and made rather belated courtesies. 'Your Uncle Joseph is just behind,' she added. 'Do not forget him.'

This was somewhat difficult, since he was still sneezing explosively. Summer sunlight, flowers and grass always seemed to bring on these fits, and Patience had seen it too often to be sympathetic. She watched with amusement as he blew his nose, wiped his streaming eyes and endeavoured to be pleasant to his nieces and nephew. Then, with Deb and Kate perched on the fat brown pony, and William trotting by his aunt's side, they turned left up the low hill towards Wintercombe.

Patience had not known what to expect: something more grand, perhaps, or a shabby old place little better than a farmhouse. What she had not thought to see was this, a long lovely building around two sides of a courtyard, constructed in the grey-gold local stone, with gables and statues and three tall windows in the centre, and a beautiful rounded oriel on either side. It was not large, nor imposing, but it was perfect.

'Where are the rest of you?' she asked William, loping like a tireless small dog beside her.

He grinned, pushing his heavy yellow hair out of his eyes, which were brown. 'Tabby's playing the virginals – Nat's with the bailiff – Rachael will be reading to Father – he's very ill, you know.'

'I am sorry to hear that,' said Patience, though she had decided long ago, from sundry brief encounters with Sir George on his visits to London, not to mention Silence's letters, that she did not care for her sister's husband. 'But your mother was always so good with simples and remedies – I'm sure he will soon recover.'

'I heard Eliza saying that the doctors have given him over,' said Kate, twisting round on the pony's broad back to stare anxiously at her aunt. 'Does that mean he's going to die?'

'Of course not,' said Deb stoutly. She hauled the pony's head round to lead them under the arch of the gateway and into the gravelled courtyard in front of the house. 'You don't want to believe what the doctors tell you, that's what Mama always says.'

She sounded defensive, and rather frightened, and Patience felt sorry for her nieces and nephew. She reined in her weary horse, and looked up at the weathered stones of the house that would be her home for some time to come, liking what she saw. Wintercombe had survived siege and storm in the civil wars, as it had successfully endured all the ravages of the past two hundred years or so, and looked as if it would stand for ever. She wondered where lay the gardens that were her sister's pride and joy. Patience loved the colour and scent of flowers, but they grew too slow for her liking: she had never understood why Silence should be so happy among things that took so long to come to maturity.

William had called for grooms, and a stable-lad came running to take the horses. Patience gave him a smile and a groat – he was a handsome boy – and dismounted, so stiff and sore that it was a real effort to disguise how she felt. Joseph, less concerned for his dignity, groaned in agony and hobbled across the gravel to the door.

'I'll go and find Mama,' said Deb, and vanished past her uncle into the house, the gravel spraying from her stout wooden heels.

William, very conscious of his temporary role as master of the house, grinned up at Patience. She had little memory of her sister's appearance, but thought that she recognised his level brows, wide mouth, and the dark eyes. Certain mannerisms seemed somehow familiar, the turn of his head, the movement of his hands. 'Mother didn't think you'd be here so soon,' he explained. 'She thought you wouldn't arrive till Monday.'

'We nearly didn't,' Patience told him. 'But your Uncle Joseph doesn't like to travel on the Sabbath unless he has to, and we thought that we had time to reach Wintercombe before dark.'

'And you did!' said William. 'It won't be dark for another hour yet. How far have you travelled today? Which way did you come? Did you come by way of Bath, or The Devizes?'

Laughing, Patience allowed herself to be escorted into Winter-combe. This pattern of house, with its high central hall and screened passage at one end, was lamentably old-fashioned now, and she had never been inside such a place before. She looked around her with interest, while Joseph sat wincing on a chair. William pointed out the portraits of his parents, and the three spyholes looking down from upstairs chambers, each disguised by a carved stone mask. 'So you must always be very careful what you say and do, down here in the hall — you never know who might be watching or listening!'

'No indeed,' said a woman's voice, and Patience, turning, beheld her eldest sister for the first time in sixteen years.

She had remembered, vaguely, a plain tall girl, quiet and shy in adult company, bright and sparkling with inventive mischief amongst her younger sisters and brother. The woman standing by the screens, dressed in a plain gown of deep blue, a narrow edging of lace bordering cap and collar, cuffs and apron, was the Silence she remembered in their father's presence, shrunken and diminished by fear. For a moment, Patience felt appalling apprehension, worse by far than the weeks when she had waited for discovery by the Council of State. Her sister had turned out just like Grace, and she wished she had not come.

Silence, for her part, was also startled. Logically, she had known, of course, that the sister whom she could only remember as a child had now grown up, and was a young woman of twenty-four. But somehow, she had still expected a little girl, all smiles and curls and repressed giggles, in an apron that was never quite clean, and collars that were always creased, and caps that refused to stay on her head.

Was this really Patience? With a sinking heart, she saw the slender, graceful young woman, the windswept brown ringlets, the handsome riding habit that set off her figure and enhanced her beauty without offending Joseph's Puritan principles, the flushed, vivid face, red lips and bright brown eyes, the lovely skin only slightly marred, on one otherwise flawless cheek, by a dark mole that Silence prayed earnestly was not a patch. Her little Imp had turned into a swan, an alien and treasonous swan, and whatever was she to do with such a creature, immured deep in Somerset?

And then the spell of awkwardness was broken, as Kate

appeared at her aunt's side, took her hand, and led her forward, laughing. 'Look, Mama – here's Aunt Imp!'

Patience, her apprehension suddenly evaporating, gave her sister the benefit of her dazzling smile. 'What stories have you been telling them? I haven't been called Imp for years!'

They embraced, both laughing and emotional, while Kate watched with bright-eyed glee, and Silence encountered for the first time the warm rose and orris fragrance and vibrant life of her little sister. Then they stood and looked at each other, seeing differences and similarities, the tricks that memory had played. Patience, no longer a child, realised that she was now taller, by a finger's width, than her big sister, and that the calm, serene face which had soothed her infant tantrums and rebellions bore, at close quarters, the indelible marks of strain and sorrow, and inexorably advancing maturity. Patience, who had given no thought at all to the inevitable decline of her own beauty, which Silence had never possessed, remembered with a shock that she herself was only eleven years the younger.

'It's strange,' Silence said, smiling. 'Before I saw you, I could only imagine our little Imp. And now you're here, you're not her at all!'

'Oh, but I am,' said Patience. She spun round gracefully, the shining hair and russet skirts flying, and indicated poor Joseph, still slumped in the leather chair under the south windows. 'You tell her, Joseph – aren't I the same Patience I've always been?'

Her brother's reply was more groan than word. Kate, her mischievous little face all concern, approached him and laid a small paw on his sleeve. 'Please don't worry, Uncle, Mama has lots of very good ointment, and you'll be better in no time.'

Silence caught her sister's eye, and Patience put her hand over her mouth, vainly attempting to smother her rather snuffling laugh. It was a sound, and a gesture, that Silence remembered with sudden, vivid clarity from her life in London. Just so had the child Patience giggled irrepressibly, even when faced with the full fire of their father's wrath. Yes, this lovely, charming, rather frighteningly self-assured young woman was still the little Imp at heart: and Silence, remembering just how much trouble her youngest sister had been capable of instigating, thought that she would do well to bear that fact in mind.

The chief maid, Eliza Davison, appeared, decorous and sour, to do her bidding. Once, Silence had felt intimidated by this gloomy

Puritan, and had been in severe danger of allowing herself to be browbeaten by her own servant. Early antagonism and resentment had slowly changed to a grudging respect, and certainly there was no doubt about Eliza's competence, nor her ability to rule the younger maids with a scathing tongue and curdling eye. She was in her thirties, a year or two younger than her mistress, and thus late in life was being courted by a farmer from Wellow, who coveted her housekeeping skills, if not her tongue. Silence, who had never felt wholly at ease in her company, had found herself, to her surprise, contemplating a Wintercombe bereft of Eliza's services with something approaching alarm.

The maid surveyed Patience, travel-stained and yet somehow exotic, and Silence saw her thin mouth turn down with covert disapproval. There was no denying it — even clad in respectable, orderly garments, an aura of worldliness and frivolity clung to her sister like a cloud. Eliza, now, would never dream of airing her opinions to anyone concerning something so personal to her mistress, but her thoughts were as obvious as if she had spoken them aloud. Silence, with an inward smile, asked her to escort the visitors to the quarters prepared for them, and added that supper was to be served in her own chamber in half an hour.

'And you must off to bed, Binnick,' she said to Kate, who hovered still: Deb and William had already gone, with some reluctance, to make themselves tidy for the meal.

The little girl twirled merrily in the centre of the hall, her mulberry skirts flying out around her, in exuberant imitation of her Aunt Imp. 'Oh, Mama, please — can't I stay up? Please? Just this once?'

Silence knew full well that if she gave in to her youngest child on this matter, she would be laying up trouble for herself in the future. Kate was already too much indulged, too reliant for her own good on her bright-eyed charm to get her way. And yet Silence, every time she looked at the child, saw, standing like a ghost behind her, the wild, reckless, laughing man who was Kate's true father, and her heart melted. It was not that she resembled the Cavalier captain so closely: her small pointed face, her huge smile, her quick grace were hers alone, and only in the warm chestnut eyes could any definite likeness be discerned. Certainly, no one at Wintercombe who was not already party to the secret had ever suspected the truth of Kate's parentage, even though most of them had known Captain Hellier well. It was fortunate for Kate, and for

Silence herself, that no suspicion of her wickedness had ever crossed anyone's mind.

'Please?' Kate said beseechingly, gazing up at her mother, the autumn-brown eyes wide and imploring. Oh, Nick, Silence thought, with a stab of anguish she had not felt for a long time: where are you now?

Anywhere in this world, or the next: and he had a wife and children of his own. She must forget him for ever and hold fast to this most precious child, her only memento of a joy altogether too brief.

She bent down and picked up the little girl, feeling her fragile bones, so different from the sturdy, well-covered bodies of William or Deb. Binnick, Tabby had called her smallest sister: it meant minnow, in the Somerset dialect, and suited Kate's swift, darting movements to perfection. Tabby had always had a facility for words and had named all the animals. She also shared Kate's slender build and fine features, so that the child's difference was not so obvious, to eyes that did not know the truth.

Kate's arms wound round her neck. 'Please,' she said again.

'No, Binnick,' Silence told her firmly. 'You saw how tired your Uncle Joseph was, and your aunt was too, only she didn't show it so much. They want a peaceful quiet supper without being bothered by your chatter, and an early night in nice soft beds. You'll have chance enough tomorrow to quiz them all you want, if they'll put up with you. Now come up with me and say goodnight to your father.'

It was the ritual end to the day, since the onset of George's illness. All the children gathered in his chamber before supper for prayers and quiet talk. To Silence, it was unpleasantly reminiscent of the bad old days, when her husband's crippled mother had attempted to rule her daughter-in-law and grandchildren from that same room, and all the household had gone in fear of her. But George, weak and gasping, had now little authority over any of his offspring, and his inevitable disapproval of their manner and their doings no longer held much sting. His wife insisted on this meeting, however, morning and evening, haunted by his approaching death and by her duty, even her wish, to keep up the pretence that his word still mattered. Even her illicit knowledge of the provisions of his will would not alter her outward show of wifely duty. If he had been in good health, she knew that she would have fought him openly, for the sake of her own future and her children's: but his imminent death had forced her to be kind.

Kate accepted her mother's decision calmly. She was not yet so spoilt that she grew cross or whining when her wishes were thwarted, though Silence knew there was some risk of it. Besides, she looked forward eagerly to her brief moments with the sick man she called Father, enjoying his attention and his obvious pleasure in her company. Silence, standing quietly by the bed as Kate babbled on about the excitements of the day, saw the softening of her husband's face and felt the usual pangs of conscience and disquiet. Guiltily, she realised she was glad that George would not have the chance to distort this child's life with his love, as he had already distorted Rachael's.

He was appreciably weaker than in the morning, and the end would not be long now. The doctor had bled him again today, but it had done him no good at all. He could hardly speak, and it was plain that Kate's vigorous chatter exhausted him. Silence made them all kneel for a few prayers and then ushered her brood from the chamber, leaving the manservant with instructions to administer a soothing draught to aid peaceful sleep.

Nat had been conspicuous by his absence, and she knew that George had noticed it. She was hardly surprised, though, for whenever his son and heir appeared at his bedside, her husband invariably took the opportunity to issue a stream of criticism, advice and complaint that ran off Nat like rainwater from a duck's feathers. She loved her stepson dearly, and he had been a bulwark of sense, reason and affection during the dreadful year of occupation by the Royalist soldiers, but she saw, with deep unease, the growing hardness in him engendered by his father's dislike.

He came in as she was crossing the hall with the older children: Kate, still protesting her case, had been firmly sent off to bed in the charge of her nurse. As a child, Nat had been undersized and frail, coming much later to maturity than his twin sister Rachael, as if she had stolen most of his health and growth to fuel her own. Only in the past few years had his fragile body caught up at last with his entirely adult mind. At twenty-one, he was not tall, only an inch or so higher than Silence, and still slender and delicate-looking, with a thin, pale, sharp face and watchful, observant blue eyes. It was not very long since she had stopped worrying about him at the start of each winter, in case he failed to survive it.

'Hallo,' he said to her, with cheerful resignation. 'I hear they've arrived – Nan Russell told me. What have you done with them?'

'Your aunt and uncle are at present making themselves ready for supper,' Silence told him, feeling that a proper respect ought to be shown, even though Joseph would be gone on Monday and Patience was hardly likely to stand on ceremony.

Nat glanced down at his filthy, workaday clothes – he had spent the day with Jesse Russell, the new young bailiff, and looked as though he had assisted at a calving. 'Is that a hint, dear Silence? I'd best go and change at once. And they're not really my aunt and uncle, are they? In fact, they're no relation to me at all.'

'And I hope you don't make them feel glad of it,' said his stepmother, with some asperity. Nat laughed and vanished upstairs.

*

Patience had been shown to a lovely, sunny chamber overlooking the garden. She thanked Eliza, to whom she had taken an instant dislike, and refused her offer of assistance. Plainly reared in London, she had never been allowed the services of a personal maid, and the very thought of the woman's sour, prim offices made the hairs on her scalp prickle. When at last the door had shut behind Eliza's rigid and disapproving back, Patience walked to the window, opened the casement with some difficulty, and leaned out.

So this was her sister's beloved garden – the terraces, the flowers, the arbour, the delightful little stone summerhouse, and beyond, in the foot of the little valley on whose sunlit northern side Wintercombe stood, a great mass of pink and white blossom, indicating the orchard and a good crop for this year's brew of cider and perry. Patience leaned further, breathing deeply. Doing thus in London had invariably brought a choking lungful of dubious odours: horse-dung, filth, dust, river mud and coal smoke. Now, there was only the subtle sweet smell of warm grass, fresh air and the fragrance of flowers.

A very old man, bent almost double, was doing something in one of the knots, just below her. He glanced up, saw her watching, and his weathered face cracked into a smile. 'Good day to ee, maid.'

'Good day,' said Patience, smiling in return. 'What a lovely evening.'

'Aye, 'tis that,' said the ancient. He looked over at the sun, setting rosily on Patience's right. 'But 'twill be main caddlesome the morrow, I reckon.' He bent again over his task, leaving Patience, somewhat bewildered, standing at the window. She wondered if he was being discourteous or was merely of informal and taciturn habit, and generously gave him the benefit of the doubt.

Still smiling, she turned back into the room, wondering which of her small store of gowns to wear. The blue, that fitted her to perfection, but was not so fashionable this year? The grey, so depressingly respectable? Or the rose-coloured wool, unquestionably her best, that Grace had disliked so much? It did become her very well, but the neck was daringly low – would Silence be shocked?

Patience realised, with some surprise, that she actually cared about what her eldest sister might think of her. Silence had always been more tolerant than Grace or Joseph, but a garment such as this, fashionable and undeniably frivolous, might well be beyond the limits of acceptance. And yet . . .

She put on the rose gown and covered the neck modestly with a plain collar. A glance at her reflection in the little mirror hanging above the table convinced her of its suitability. She ran a brush through her thick brown hair, humming the tune of a scurrilous ballad popular in the London streets this year, and deftly knotted it up at the back, securing the heavy twisted mass with a couple of pins, and leaving the rest to fall in flattering ringlets on either side of her face. Then, with a final, satisfied glance at her reflection, she walked without knocking into Joseph's adjoining chamber.

He was mopping his face with a wet cloth, his head bent over the basin. He had removed his doublet, and Patience noticed that he was fast putting on weight, despite the unwonted exertions of the ride from London. She said briskly, 'Aren't you ready yet?'

Joseph lifted his undistinguished face from the cloth and glowered at her. As always, Patience presented a cool, neat, fresh appearance, very different from the grubby child she once had been. At times like this, when he was acutely conscious of neither looking nor feeling his best, her immaculate attire only served to annoy him. Moreover, she was wearing that shocking gown. He opened his mouth to object to it, but his sister, who knew him too thoroughly, forestalled him. 'Well, if you're not ready, I'll go down and wait for you in the hall. Do hurry up, Joseph, there's a dear.' And she swept out in an aura of confidence and rosewater, leaving her brother yet again bereft of speech at her impertinence.

The stairs, she remembered, were just to her right. Filled with a mixture of exuberance at her new surroundings, and exasperation with her brother's slowness, Patience picked up her rose-coloured skirts and whirled round to their head. As usual, she failed to look where she was going, and in consequence collided solidly with someone coming up.

He smelt awful, of cows and dung and worse: for a moment, she thought he must be one of the farmworkers and wondered what he was doing in the house. She said, catching her breath, 'Do watch where you're going!'

'I could say the same of you,' said the young man, with a cheerful smile. His voice held only a trace of the Somerset burr, and that, and his assurance, told Patience of her error. 'I trust you're not hurt, Aunt?'

The thought that she could be styled 'Aunt' by a boy only three years her junior, made Patience at once amused and indignant. She said roundly, 'Please don't call me that – it's ridiculous.'

'No more so than "*Im*patience",' he said, grinning, teasing her with a familiarity that was somehow very annoying. 'Thank Heaven your father didn't have the chance to name any more of you. Sobriety, perhaps? Or Chastity?' Then, seeing her expression, he grinned again and offered her his hand. 'I'm sorry. I'm Nat, as you must have guessed. And you are Patience?'

'Yes,' she said, more curtly than she had intended. Silence was very fond of her stepson, her affection and respect had shone from every mention of him in her letters, and Patience knew that he had been a tower of strength during the terrible years of the war, when hardly more than a child. But somehow, her apologies stuck unspoken on her tongue. She took the proffered fingers with reluctance – they were encrusted with filth and what looked, appallingly, very much like dried blood – and only just resisted the temptation to wipe her hand clean on the wall.

'Don't worry – I've not been murdering anyone, just helping the bailiff with a difficult calving,' said her sister's stepson, with a very disarming smile. 'I'll clean it off before I appear at the supper table, I promise. See you there – do you know where to go? Into the hall, doorway at the end on the right, and up the stairs, that will bring you to Silence's chamber. Everyone else will be there – where's Uncle Woods?'

[42]

'He was a little weary after the journey,' said Patience. 'He is still making ready.'

'And you couldn't wait?' said Nat. 'Just as well none of you *were* called Chastity or Sobriety, isn't it? See you in a little while, dear Impatience.'

She descended the stairs with some indignation, annoyed with him for teasing her, annoyed with herself for letting him do it. The hall was dim, cool and empty, but she could discern, quite clearly, the sound of virginals being played, with a fluency she had never heard in that unmusical house in Paternoster Row. She knew that she ought to wait for Joseph and prove that infuriatingly self-assured boy wrong in his assessment of her character, but she could not resist the temptation to make a grand and sweeping entrance alone, armoured in her London sophistication and her London fashion.

She had forgotten about the spying masks, high above her on the walls. When she arrived at the top of another set of dangerously twisting stairs, the door was already standing open, with an undersized maid, sadly red-haired and freckled, welcoming her within, and her sister and all her family waiting expectantly for her. She had no time to appreciate the old-fashioned but pleasant proportions of this spacious chamber, for William and Deb were clustering about her, drawing her forward to meet two very different girls standing by the empty hearth, introducing her to Rachael and to Tabby.

Rachael, she knew, was Nat's twin, and there was a superficial resemblance in the black hair, the thin pale face and blue eyes. But there was nothing of his teasing friendliness in her expression, only a look of deep and wary hostility that upset Patience considerably. This girl looked as if she strongly resented her presence, and for two pins would say so outright. Patience, who was not to know that her lovely gown, her pretty face and air of overwhelming self-confidence had aroused Rachael's jealousy in the first few seconds of her entrance, wondered what she had done to deserve such a reaction.

The other girl was Tabby, the eldest of Silence's own children, who was almost fifteen. She was a little like her mother, with an air of serene grace and a cloud of astonishing hair, very curly and obviously completely ungovernable, escaping from the inadequate confines of its simple arrangement with an exuberance quite unmatched by the small, lovely face beneath. She smiled shyly, but there was genuine welcome in her eyes, and Patience warmed to her at once.

Deb, who obviously enjoyed taking charge of people, grasped her aunt's arm in proprietorial fashion, and then introduced her to Lily, the little white greyhound, who fawned and wagged her tail and showed her teeth in a grin of welcome that reduced, a trifle, Patience's indifference to dogs, and to the mottled grey and white cat, Misty. 'She's Pye's daughter,' Deb explained. 'Pye was Mother's old cat, but she died last year, and now we just have Misty. Isn't she beautiful?'

Misty, who was used to Deb, refused to be woken from her comfortable sleep on the windowseat, and kept her nose tightly tucked behind her tail. Deb seemed disappointed that there was no one else to whom her aunt could be introduced. Silence, laughing, told her to desist, and added to Patience, 'Where's poor Joseph?'

'He wasn't quite ready when I came down,' said her sister, refusing to feel guilt for abandoning him so ruthlessly. 'He won't be long.'

'Mally's watching for him through the mask in her closet,' William told her. 'Mally is Mother's maid – well, more of a friend, really. That's how we knew you were coming up here.'

'And when Uncle Joseph comes,' added Deb with feeling, 'then we can have supper.'

Poor Joseph arrived a few minutes later, looking harassed and indignant, after being rescued by Mally from lonely bewilderment in the hall, and was likewise subjected to the overbearing attentions of Deb and William. Then Nat appeared, transformed almost out of recognition by soap and water and a change of clothing. His half-sister tried to introduce him to Patience and was firmly dissuaded. 'You're too late, Deb – your aunt and I have already met, somewhat precipitately, on the stairs.' And he added conspiratorially to Patience, 'You'll have to watch young Deb – she'll be dragging you round the whole village if you're not careful.'

'No, I won't!' the child cried indignantly, and was quelled by her mother's reminder that supper would shortly be appearing, and if she wanted it she had best quieten herself. This had a magical effect on Deb's exuberance, and the meal, which was simple and delicious, passed in relative peace.

Patience, whose own childhood had been dreary and restricted by repressive paternal authority, was charmed by her nieces and nephew. On this informal family occasion, they were lively but not rude or bad-mannered, although she had already marked Deb's tendency to become too demanding and loud. William was a delightful child, open and friendly, and Tabby, although much more reserved, gradually revealed more of herself as the evening progressed. It transpired that she had been the player of virginals, and went shyly pink with pleasure when Patience praised her skills. Nat teased her about her devotion to music, and they began a friendly exchange of banter. In the middle of it all, Silence sat, smiling serenely, the still centre of her family, content to let her children be themselves. Patience, glancing at Joseph, mute and gloomy at the other end of the table, sensed his bewildered disapproval. The only boy of the family, he had let the mantle of his father fall on him too heavily. How long had it been since he had simply enjoyed himself and his children, as Silence was now doing?

Candles were lit and the two younger children despatched protesting to their beds, trying to hide their yawns. Despite the warmth of the afternoon, the clear night was chilly, and Mally made up the fire and brought hot spicy wine. Patience, sitting by the new flames, cradling her warm cup, saw Rachael, who had been very silent during supper, looking at her intently. As soon as their eyes met, the younger girl glanced away, but her hostility was plain, and Patience felt renewed annoyance. She could not understand what she had done to cause such resentment.

Joseph, who had also been uncharacteristically reticent, now began a rather tactless inquisition of his elder sister. He had not realised the gravity of Sir George's illness – was he truly dying? And why were the children allowed such unseemly freedom when their father lay so sick?

Patience saw Rachael wince and turn her head away; Tabby looked unhappy and embarrassed; only Nat, gazing abstractedly at the fireplace, seemed completely at ease. Silence, her serene face hiding the sudden stab of irritation within, set herself to explain. 'If I didn't allow them such freedom, as you put it, they'd be cooped up in the house, disturbing their father and resenting him. Of course they're concerned for him, we all are, even Kate, who's really too young to understand what's happening. They know he's very ill, and I think Deb at least suspects the truth, but there will be sorrow enough in a little while. Why make them unhappy now, when there is as yet no need for it?'

Joseph, ill at ease, muttered something about respect and duty in a voice that mumbled away into nothing. Silence, glancing at her sister, saw an expression of mild contempt on her face, and sighed. It was true, Joseph was a weak man, fussy and conventional, with opinions that, although strongly held, bent like a sapling at the first blast of a contrary opinion. His wife Grace seemed to be a much more stalwart character, and Silence wondered suddenly if it had been her idea to despatch the troublesome Patience to Winter-combe.

'In any case,' said Rachael, fiercely and too loudly into the embarrassed pause, 'Father isn't going to die, so you've no need to concern yourself, Uncle. Of course it's better that the younger ones are let out of the house — how else could he get all the sleep he needs?' She glared round at Tabby, and added with venom, 'And you ought to stop playing the virginals. You know he doesn't like it, and he can hear you, and it disturbs him — he said so only this morning.'

Tabby, so quiet and shy, stared at her half-sister in astonishment, and then said furiously, 'I don't believe he said any such thing! Why didn't he tell me himself, this evening? And anyway, how can he hear me, with all the width of the hall between us? And nothing, *nothing*, will make me stop, ever, so you'll have to put up with it.'

'That's quite enough, from both of you,' Silence said, with a severity that startled Patience. 'If you can't sit here without arguing, and in front of our guests too, you can both go elsewhere.'

Rachael shot her a vicious glance and said meaningfully, 'Very well. I'll go see how Father is.' She rose and marched out haughtily.

'I am sorry, Mother,' said Tabby, her wide hazel eyes gazing at Silence. 'But I couldn't help it — she's always so nasty about my playing, and I *do* wish she wouldn't be.'

'She's unhappy,' said Nat unexpectedly. 'You know what Rachael's like — she's desperately worried about Father, and takes it out on the rest of us. Don't mind our petty feuds and squabbles, dear Imp — every family has them, after all, and underneath all the quarrels and backbiting we St. Barbes are solidly united, aren't we, Silence?'

His stepmother smiled. 'Well, if you say so, Nat, then it must be true.'

For a while longer, they made rather uncomfortable small talk.

At this time in the evening, Tabby usually played, but by unspoken agreement did not offer. Rachael's unkind comments had struck her deep, and she did not want her uncle to think that his sister's children were all beyond her control. At length, however, Joseph rose wearily, and Tabby offered to light him to his bed, with a courtesy that did much to mend his opinion of her. Nat also retired, saying that he must go to see how the cow and her new calf did before he slept, and the two sisters were left sitting on each side of the sinking fire.

It was the first time they had been alone together for sixteen years and Silence was conscious, as never before, of the gulf between them, far greater than the eleven years which separated them in age. She herself had survived the hazards of war and siege, as well as marriage and childbirth, and she was passing skilled at managing household and family, however different it might seem to outsiders. Patience, the sheltered youngest child, had never had to face such difficulties, and yet she sat there, walled terrifyingly about with beauty, sophistication and self-confidence, a creature who might have stepped from another land instead of from their own shared childhood. Silence, looking at the smooth, exquisite face, like and yet utterly unlike her own, could foresee, with apprehension, hearts being broken all over North Somerset, and for the first time felt real sympathy with Joseph.

She said lightly, 'I hope you aren't planning to hurry back to London, after your unfortunate introduction to Wintercombe?'

'Hurry back?' Patience's large brown eyes opened very wide with astonished amusement. 'Joseph would have to truss me up like a boiling fowl and sling me over his horse to get me back to Paternoster Row. No, you're mistaken – I didn't want to come here at first, I admit, but now I *am* here, I hate the thought of going back to London – it's so – so enclosed there, so stuffy and restricted and the air reeks – oh, no, Sister, like it or not, I'm staying.'

'Good,' said Silence, with a firm and genuine pleasure that surprised her. 'I'm glad, I'd hate to think we were keeping you prisoner . . . ' She paused, wondering how best to put the confused mixture of warnings, reassurances and information she wished to convey into words. She said at last, 'How did you find the children?'

'Sitting on a gate,' said Patience, mischievously misunderstanding her. She caught her sister's eye and giggled. 'They're . . .

they're not what I'm used to, but I do like them, very much. William especially.'

'Everyone likes William, because he likes everyone. That's one of life's secrets that he was born knowing, and which poor Rachael has never discovered.' Silence leaned forward to poke some life into the fading fire and added quietly, 'You must have sensed her resentment. Nat was right, he always is, they were born in the same hour, and he knows her better than anyone. She is utterly miserable, and when Rachael is unhappy, she makes life unhappy for all around her. She is very close to her father, and when he dies she will be devastated.'

For a moment, her matter-of-fact tone deceived Patience: then she seized suddenly on the vital word. '*When* he dies?'

'Oh, yes,' said Silence wearily, staring at the fire, her hands methodically stroking the cat Misty, snug in her lap. 'I have known, and the doctors have known, for about a month now, that this time it is mortal. He caught some ague or fever when he was in the army, and each winter since then it has returned a little worse, and a little worse, until when he fell ill this January, he didn't get any better. The terrible thing is that it is taking so *long*, and he is in such pain, and the younger children know in their hearts that this is the end. Even Kate has realised, I think – she is so loving towards him these days. One reason why I am glad you are here is that I shall need a friend very much in the weeks to come. Does that worry you? I am sorry if it does.'

'Of course not,' said Patience, truthfully. She added, 'I shall be glad of a friend too. Someone I can talk *to* – I couldn't talk to Grace at all, she used to talk *at* me.'

'I can well imagine it,' said Silence, who knew Joseph's redoubtable wife from his letters, almost as well as if she had actually met her. She added, not without some misgivings, 'I haven't told anyone at all of the real reason that you've been brought here, and I'm sure you'll agree that's the best course. No one will think it's anything other than a family visit, especially at such a sad time. And if you do ever want to talk about it – well, I am here, and I have had a lot of practice in listening to other people's troubles.'

'Thank you,' said Patience, resolving fervently never to discuss her late excursion into treason with Silence or anyone else. She had no wish to incur her sister's pity, or, worse, her laughter and contempt for something which she could not possibly understand. She produced a yawn, not entirely feigned, which she covered prettily with a pale, slender hand. 'Oh, I am so weary, suddenly! Would you mind very much if I retired to bed, Sister?'

'Of course not,' said Silence, smiling. She wished her a very good night and despatched the red-haired Mally to light her to her chamber.

In all of Wintercombe, perhaps only the children slept entirely restfully that night. Their father, racked with each painful breath, tossed and turned despite the poppy-seed drink intended to promote peaceful slumber. Joseph, afflicted with sores and bruises, failed to find any comfortable position, even within the soft depths of his feather bed. Patience, in the next chamber, lay awake listening to the eerie shrieks of the owls as they hunted over the fields around the house, and thinking of John Jackel and his plots, and the heady excitement of treason. They had failed, though through no fault of their own, and that, she decided, was the only reason for shame. Given the chance, she would willingly enter into such conspiracy again. The unknown young man in Scotland was, after all, unequivocally the rightful and proper King of England, usurped by a dubious gaggle of jumped-up army officers and religious fanatics. Why should she not do everything in her power to restore him to his appointed place, if the opportunity should ever come her way?

It was just as well that her sister had no knowledge of Patience's thoughts. Silence lay wakeful, wanting to sleep, yet unable to restrain her busy mind. The events of the past few days, her sister's arrival, her husband's illness, and above all the grief and turmoil and change that would attend his death, haunted her mind. Guiltily, she tried not to think ahead too far, to the aftermath, to the liberty that would suddenly be hers after a lifetime of submission. She knew already, from those years during the war when she had been temporarily relieved of George's inhibiting presence, that she longed for it with excessive intensity. She must be wicked indeed to pray so desperately for her freedom.

And yet, as she slid at last into an uneasy sleep, she could not be ashamed of her disgraceful feelings.

❦ CHAPTER THREE ❧

'A necessary end'
(Julius Caesar)

On the Monday, the nineteenth day of May, Joseph, his legs and fundament well anointed with his sister's salves against the journey, set off home for London. He was not, on the whole, sorry to be leaving. Although hardly a sensitive man, he found the atmosphere at Wintercombe, compounded of imminent death and suppressed emotion, disturbing enough to make him distinctly uncomfortable. And he would be more than glad to leave behind Patience, so shockingly flippant and worldly. Ahead of him lay the soothing certainties of Paternoster Row and Grace, who always seemed to know best, and their two quiet, obedient little boys. He bade farewell to Silence with genuine sympathy for her unhappy situation, and left Wintercombe in a mood of profound thankfulness.

Silence, for her part, was not altogether sorry to see him go. He had never understood her, nor her unhappy relationship with her husband: he would undoubtedly be horrified, should he ever discover the truth of her feelings for George. In the necessarily tumultuous circumstances of death, she knew that the serene mask, which she had used all these years to conceal her emotions from all but those closest to her, would be torn asunder.

Patience would probably see it, but she did not mind too much about that. She knew already that she liked the adult her little sister had become, despite the girl's undoubted faults. She had worn that rose-coloured gown to church, despite, or perhaps because of, Joseph's scandalised disapproval, and had sat in the St. Barbe pew with the eyes of almost every grown male in the place, save for the vicar, riveted on her as if she were some exotic and dangerous beast. With amusement, Silence saw that her sister revelled in the attention her looks brought her. Master Apprice, two years wed and a man of considerable consequence in the village, had all but fallen over as he bowed to her; Tom Flower had earned black looks from his new bride as he ogled her shamelessly from his pew on the opposite side of the nave; and even Parson Willis, denouncing worldly vanities and the perils thereof from the pulpit, turned his hourglass with a bang and glared at Patience as if she had been placed in the church specifically to provide an example for his text.

After the service was over, Silence had introduced her sister to her friends and acquaintances amongst the better sort, Slopers, Baylies, Apprices and Flowers, and to her relief Patience, with a smile and an apparently genuine friendliness, had set herself to charm them, male and female alike. It seemed to work: the women, initially suspicious or even downright hostile towards Lady St. Barbe's shocking London sister, found themselves warming to her in spite of themselves. Patience had learned her wiles at an early age, the only one of the family who had had any discernible softening effect on her stern father, and had sharpened them subsequently on the hapless Joseph. She rode back to Wintercombe with a sunny, satisfied smile, well aware that she would be the subject of fascinated gossip by hearth or in taproom for some time to come.

The children, too, were infatuated. Deb, of course, would fasten like a leech upon any novelty and milk it dry: her mother hoped that Patience could withstand her demands. William, with his own unselfconscious charm, was enthralled by his aunt's stories of her wicked childhood, his brown eyes wide with delighted horror at her daring. He asked Silence, once, whether such tales were true. With her rueful grin, she assured him that they all were, and not in the least exaggerated either. William's allegiance was henceforward assured.

Kate, self-willed, capricious little Kate, was alike entranced by her aunt's personality, so completely different from anyone else in this quiet rural backwater. Patience, with her laughter, her stories, her air of light-hearted gaiety, her ability to invent delightful games and diversions, attracted her like a magnet. Silence was glad, aware that the arrival of their wonderful aunt would do much to distract the younger children from the impending death of their father.

Tabby stayed in her shell, shy but serious, making up her own mind. On the surface, she seemed to have very little in common with the glamorous Patience, but Silence knew that her eldest child could make surprising friendships, and her loyalty, once given, was fierce and unshakeable.

Nat, for some reason, seemed to have begun on the wrong foot with his stepaunt, as he teasingly insisted on calling her. He was, as ever, open and affable as he was with everyone, from his father's wealthy friends to the humblest labourer's child. But his exchanges with Patience had a barbed quality that Silence discerned immediately, and with sadness. She loved Nat dearly, and he had always, even in childhood, been the rock on which she leant. She hoped unhappily that the two would eventually become friends, and that Patience, so assured and delightful in her dealings with the younger children, would learn to take Nat's teasing less seriously.

But that niggling doubt was as nothing, compared to the worry of Rachael. Silence could understand exactly how her stepdaughter must feel. This interloper, with her cheerful levity, her apparent lack of concern for Sir George's plight, must threaten all that Rachael held dear. Not so long ago, the girl had been close to the other children, William and Deb in particular. Now, spending much of her time with her sick father, doing the duty which she plainly felt should also be shared by the rest of the family, she must watch her rightful place being usurped by this foreigner. To make matters worse, Patience was pretty, confident and startlingly attractive. Rachael, acutely conscious of the fact that she possessed none of these attributes, sulked, and was barely polite to her stepmother's sister whenever they happened to meet.

Joseph had had all the levity beaten out of him in childhood, and could not sympathise with anyone, even his own sister, who had not. He left on the Monday and, by Wednesday, it was clear that Sir George was sinking fast. Silence, guiltily aware that up until now she had somewhat neglected her wifely duty, set herself to make his passing as comfortable as possible. Patience had taken it on herself, unasked, to keep the children amused, happy, and out of earshot, during their hours of recreation, and her sister, grateful for the lightening of her burden, spent much of her time tending George, and welcoming the steady stream of his friends and acquaintances who had come to bid farewell to one of the most stalwart defenders of the Presbyterian faith in North Somerset. Even though he would die in his bed, three years after leaving the army, they all knew that he had given his life, as well as his eldest son, for the Cause, as surely as if a malignant Royalist bullet had struck him down. Silence offered them refreshments and spoke with them quietly as they offered her their comfort, all couched in remarkably similar terms, so that after three days of it she wished never again to hear the words 'Heaven', or 'Grace', or 'the Lord's

Elect'. And none of those worthy men, riding back to Mells or Frome or Bath or Freshford or Shepton Mallet, imagined that behind the calm, serious face of the Lady of Wintercombe there boiled a fury of resentment and dislike.

The elder John Harington was still in London, at Lincoln's Inn, but his son Jack rode over from Kelston to see the man whose daughter he was now contracted to marry.

Rachael saw him enter the courtyard from her stepmother's chamber. They had received advance warning of his arrival, and she had been expecting him all morning, sitting in the oriel window paying scant attention to the cushion cover she was supposed to be embroidering. Yet when the handsome rich bay horse stepped under the gatehouse arch and into the sunlight, she did not at first recognise its rider. Then he dismounted, gave his instructions to Jeremy Walker, the youngest stable-lad, and turned towards the house.

Rachael's thin white face flooded with sudden colour and a sweat broke out on her palms. Her hands shook and she jabbed the needle into her thumb. A bead of bright blood leapt up in its place and was smeared across the work before she had time to control herself. Jack was here – he had come to see her at last!

She stared hungrily down at the foreshortened figure approaching the porch. He wore a sober suit of dark grey, with a single lighter plume in his black beaver hat, very proper attire for a man attending a neighbour's sickbed, if not so appropriate to a suitor. Rachael found it impossible to imagine herself sharing her days with this young man, with whom she had barely exchanged ten minutes' conversation in her entire life, but her father had arranged the betrothal, and he, so beloved, undoubtedly knew what was best for his eldest and favourite daughter.

She glanced round at her maid. Jude Hinton was a placid, even-tempered girl who had been more than five years at Wintercombe, serving Rachael and enduring her tantrums and sulks with the phlegmatic, rather bovine nature for which Silence, knowing her stepdaughter too well, had chosen her. Frequently, her lack of response to her mistress's jibes and insults infuriated Rachael still further, but Jude, who wanted to marry a Norton boy and was assiduously saving her wages to that end, put up with it all uncomplainingly.

She was sewing up a piece of ripped lace on an apron, and looked up with an air of mild enquiry. 'Master Harington be here then, Mistress Rachael?'

'Of course he is,' Rachael snapped. She sprang explosively to her feet and ran to the door of the little closet where Mally Merrifield slept. The listening mask within, its eye-holes disguised behind the face of a king with ass's ears, provided a very limited view of the hall below, but she would be able to hear everything.

'Good day, Master Harington.' The voice of Ambrose Carpenter, the young butler, was clearly audible. 'May I take your cloak, sir? Do you wish to see Sir George?'

'Yes, indeed I do – if he is sufficiently able to receive a visitor at such a time.'

Try as she would, Rachael could see nothing of her betrothed. He was probably standing by the fire, well out of her line of sight. She remembered his voice, measured, slow and solemn, but however hard she tried, she could not recall the details of his face, nor even the colour of his eyes.

'I will go tell him of your arrival, sir,' said Carpenter, with the courtesy which made him such an excellent butler. A man of ambition, he had expunged almost all trace of the thick village burr from his voice, and was well aware that he might soon be approached by one or other of Sir George's acquaintances to take charge of a greater household than Wintercombe. None of the servants liked him: his pretensions had soon antagonised them, and his ruthless efficiency had completed the process.

Rachael heard his diminishing footsteps and peered with renewed urgency through the two stone eyes. There was still no view of Jack. Why had he not mentioned that he had come to see her as well? She could have engaged him in pleasant conversation until her father was ready to receive him.

But, of course, she still could. Her heart suddenly thumping, she withdrew her head from the mask, hoping that the young man below would be unaware of its significance, and went back into the main chamber. Silence was probably in the kitchens, where there were problems with the chimneys. Jude sat in the oriel still, methodically stitching. She looked up, and Rachael said curtly, 'You can stay there – I'm going down to greet Master Harington.'

Jude, who knew of the betrothal in company with the rest of Wintercombe, smiled knowingly and bent her head to her work. Rachael smoothed her skirts, patted her plain linen cap into place, and walked decorously down the stairs.

She had been right: he was standing by the hearth, which was warm and glowing. Even late in May, it could be cold in the high, stone-flagged hall. She came briskly through the curtains, checked, and said, with what she considered to be a commendable semblance of surprise, 'Oh! Master Harington, I did not know you were here.'

Memory had lied. The tall, rather plump young man who bowed courteously before her was not especially attractive: his mouth was too small, and his face too heavy, for true good looks. But Rachael, rising from her deep curtsey, marked only his smile and the imposing figure, and blushed with maidenly modesty.

'Greetings, Mistress Rachael,' he said, and she saw with surprise that his own face was a little red. It had not occurred to her that he too might feel constrained and embarrassed at this unexpected meeting. 'I trust you are well? And how is your father?'

'We think he is a little better today,' said Rachael. Her mouth was dry, and she had to lock her fingers together to stop them nervously twisting the folds of her blue gown. Thank Heaven, it was quite new, and Jude had brushed the hem only this morning, and her collar and cuffs and apron and cap were fresh and clean. Mindful suddenly of her duties, she added after an awkward pause, 'Would you care for wine, sir, or refreshments? Or – or we will dine in a little while, will you stay?'

Jack Harington liked good food, and the reputation of Darby, the Wintercombe cook, was famed all through this part of Somerset. 'I am very sensible of the kindness you offer me, Mistress, and would greatly appreciate the opportunity to stay for dinner. My dear mother is not expecting me to return until later this afternoon.'

At Wintercombe, the younger St. Barbes were used to plain speaking, and only Sir George, when in health, used such an elaborate turn of phrase. The style sat oddly on Jack, who seemed too young for such pomposity. Rachael, trying to emulate him, found her tongue stuttering over the stilted words. 'Thank you, sir. I will inform the cook that you have arrived, and that you desire to d-dine with us this day.'

There was a handbell on the mantel above the hearth, that Silence used on such occasions. Rachael, trying to look as if she did this a dozen times a day, picked it up and rang it, a little too fervently. Wintercombe was a rambling house, but not particularly large, and well-stocked with servants. Someone would be within earshot.

The youngest maid, Hannah Grindland, a rabbity-faced girl with her skin heavily disfigured by the smallpox, appeared, curtsied, and listened while Rachael gave her instructions with spurious efficiency. Although Silence had trained her stepdaughter in all the housewifely arts, directing servants had never come naturally to her, nor had she managed to pass on her hard-won skills to her pupil. As Hannah disappeared in the direction of the kitchen, it occurred to Rachael to wonder if Silence would be offended at this usurpation of her authority. Certainly, in her place, Rachael would have been, but the girl had to admit that in such matters her stepmother was a great deal more tolerant, not to say lax, than she herself.

She turned again to Jack Harington, who had been studying the cheerful morning crackle of the flames, and wondered in panic what she could say to him. She had no knowledge of his interests, beyond the fact that he was extremely godly. His father was known throughout Somerset as a man of learning and culture, but no report spoke of Jack being proficient in Latin, Greek, Hebrew or Arabic. Rachael, who was in any case completely ignorant of all those languages, fell back upon the conventional small talk of chance acquaintances. 'Did you have a pleasant journey here, Master Harington?'

He seized upon the topic with patent relief, and treated her to a discourse of the parlous state of the road between Midford and Hinton. There was a pothole so large it filled almost all the highway, and he had feared for his horse's legs: only the good offices of the Lord had carried him safely past such a shockingly dangerous hazard.

Creeping treacherously into Rachael's mind came the likely words of her twin brother, had he chanced to overhear this utterance. 'More fool him, to trust to Heaven rather than to his horse!'

Uneasily aware that Nat, although he had said nothing at all to her, probably had a somewhat lower opinion of her betrothed than she did, Rachael commiserated with him, and hoped, her face coyly downcast, that he would not be discouraged from visiting Wintercombe again.

If she had thought to provoke him to some display of suitor-like behaviour, she was doomed to disappointment. Master Harington said merely that he hoped too that he would have occasion to ride this way in the near future, though not alas in circumstances any happier, thus leaving Rachael in no doubt that he meant the occasion of her father's funeral. Since she was still trying to convince herself that this was but a passing sickness, serious but not mortal, she found tears filling her eyes. Embarrassed and angry with herself, she turned her head aside and surreptitiously wiped them away with her hand, like the child she had taken such pains to suppress.

A door banged behind the screens and young voices erupted loudly, but were almost immediately hushed. Rachael jerked angrily round and saw Kate, her cap askew, her hair flying, dance in through the curtains. As soon as she noticed the stranger, the little girl stopped, her mouth a roundel of astonishment, and said in her bright voice, 'Who's this, Rachael?' Then, belatedly courteous, she dipped a swift curtsey and stood quite still, her hands decorously folded but her small pointed face sparkling with mischief.

Rachael longed to shout at her, to send her packing, but what would Jack think of her if she did? Struggling to keep the fury out of her voice, she said with a smile that did not deceive Kate in the least, 'Master Harington – this is my youngest sister, Katherine.'

Jack looked completely nonplussed. The child, with the directness that Rachael had dreaded, surveyed him with interest, and said, on a note of discovery, 'You're the one that Rachael's going to marry!'

'I think that's quite enough from you, young lady,' said Patience, coming through the screens to complete Rachael's discomfiture. She wore her everyday blue gown, but its quiet air of fashion – not for nothing was she a draper's daughter – the immaculate collar and cuffs and her tumbled, gleaming brown curls, all contributed to a picture at once modest and attractive. She turned to Jack with a charming smile and a swift curtsey. 'I am so sorry, Master Harington. Kate can be shockingly impertinent.'

Jack was gazing at her like a lost sailor at a beacon. Bitterly, Rachael acknowledged that beside her stepmother's sister she was nothing, a skinny, gawky little girl trying on adult attitudes that did not fit her. Patience was only three years older, but, it seemed, a century more mature. She had already stolen the children from her: was she trying to steal Jack, too?

Patience realised, belatedly, that it might be very unwise to flirt with Master Harington. She was sorely tempted: he looked such a boring, godly person, that it would be most amusing to lead him on and shock his prim Puritan principles to the core. But there was Rachael, staring at her like a basilisk, to consider, and Patience, who was well aware of the younger girl's resentment and had by now guessed the probable reason for it, did not really want to make an enemy of her. It would upset Silence, and she had no desire to add to her sister's considerable burden. She said briskly, 'I am Lady St. Barbe's sister, come from London for a visit. Pray excuse me, sir – the children must be attended.' And in a faint, delicate fragrance of roses and orris root, she took Kate's small brown paw firmly in her grasp and whisked her unceremoniously from the hall.

It was fortunate that Carpenter returned at that moment, thus saving both Rachael and her betrothed the necessity of finding something further to say to each other. 'Sir George is ready to see you now, Master Harington. And he directed me to ask you to attend on him also, Mistress Rachael.'

They were ushered into the chamber together. Jack Harington, who had last seen his future father-in-law at his sister Moll's wedding in January, was shocked by the change in him. This grey, wizened, gasping old man, propped up on pillows, looked to be at death's door. Jack mentally compared him with his own father, the same age but still hale and hearty, and knew that the end could not be more than a few days away. It was a pity, for his father had wished to see his old friend once more, but even if the summons went out to London today, he could not reach Wintercombe in time.

Formally, he expressed his sympathy, and his father's, and uttered the pious hope that the dying man in front of him would soon recover his former vigour.

'Nonsense,' Sir George whispered. 'Dying – know it well.' His head turned, painfully, towards Rachael, who was standing miserably beside Jack. 'Glad – see you with him – chance of talk.'

Over the past few days, as her father's breath had become ever more limited, Rachael had grown accustomed to the brevity of his words, and understood what he meant to convey. 'Yes, Father. We have talked – a little. Master Harington is to stay for dinner.'

'Good,' said Sir George. He began to cough, splutteringly. Stone, his manservant, who had shared the nursing duties with Silence, held a kerchief to his lips, and supplied him with a cup of honey and betony water to ease him.

Jack, stalwartly healthy himself, began to feel distinctly

depressed by the overwhelming atmosphere of sickness within the chamber, the dread imminence of death. Silently, he began to pray, both for the man in the bed and for his own continued freedom from accident, ailment and disease. So intent was he upon this task, that Rachael had to call him back to reality with an urgent whisper. 'Master Harington!'

He became aware that Sir George was beckoning them closer to the bed. Rachael, who had only just stopped herself in time from digging her betrothed in the ribs, moved forward, and Jack, hiding his instinctive repulsion, joined her.

'Daughter – hand,' Sir George wheezed, his skeletal fingers twitching on the coverlet. Rachael, her face flushed with distress, leaned over and took it in hers. Her father shook his head impatiently. 'No – his!'

Suddenly shy, flushing deeper, Rachael turned to the tall young man standing beside her, wearing an expression of complete bewilderment on his face. She hid, successfully, the surge of irritated impatience, and said softly, 'My father wishes us to join hands, Master Harington.'

After a pause, he raised his fingers to touch hers. His palm felt sweaty and hot. She had expected some frisson of emotion at the contact, but there was nothing. She told herself that this situation was hardly conducive to romantic feeling, but there was, nevertheless, a lingering trace of disappointment. Resolutely, she turned back to Sir George, Jack's hand tentative in hers. 'Yes, Father?'

'Betrothed . . . good,' said the sick man painfully. 'Both agree?'

Rachael's fervent nod coincided with Jack's more formal, 'Yes, indeed, I thank you, Sir George.'

'Good. My blessing . . . on you both. Wedding . . . not too soon, not seemly . . . mourning . . . New Year . . . '

Rachael opened her mouth to say that the wait was far too long, and closed it again. Her father was right, as always. If, *if* he was going to die, then a delay of at least six months before the marriage festivities was only right and proper. And she thought, glancing shyly at the stranger who held her hand, it would give her the chance to become better acquainted with the man to whom, so astonishingly, she would be wed.

'Son . . . old friend . . . what we both wished . . . pay my respects . . . to your father,' Sir George whispered, and his mouth stretched to a ghastly semblance of a smile. It turned to a prolonged fit of coughing, and this time it was Rachael, as she had done so often before, who held the soothing water to his mouth, and wiped his brow. At last her father, a little eased, lay back on the pillows and gulped air with hoarse, rasping breaths. Then she stared unhappily down at the bed, unwilling to weep in front of Jack. It was her helplessness that distressed her the most. If love and will could save him, she would give all she had, but nothing that her stepmother's nursing or the physicians' nostrums could do seemed to have the power to arrest this terrible and relentless decline.

'Are there no doctors in attendance?' Jack asked her. His own father, who suffered minor maladies with the exaggerated attention of one who was never seriously ill, always availed himself of their services. Bath, after all, was full of them, from respected and competent physicians, graduates of Leyden or Padua with charges to match, to quacks and charlatans scraping a meagre living from those too poor, ignorant or foolish to demand any better.

'Of course,' Rachael said, hearing the note of surprise in his voice.

Sir George, who had also heard, opened his eyes and added, 'No good . . . all quacks . . . send 'em packing.'

'You can't say that, Father,' Rachael cried, and even Jack noticed the anguish in her words. 'They might be some help!'

'No help . . . the Lord's will . . . ' said Sir George. Before Rachael could protest, he went on, 'Now . . . all pray.'

And his daughter, on her knees beside the bed, fighting her tears and her grief, bent her head and silently demanded the impossible, with all the fervour and ferocity of which she was capable.

*

Silence, informed that her stepdaughter's betrothed had arrived and was staying for dinner, was conscious of mixed feelings. Jack Harington was a worthy enough boy, she was sure: it was just that she did not think him at all suitable as a husband for the intense and moody Rachael. She did not relish the prospect of making polite conversation with him, of hiding her true feelings once more behind the hypocriticial mask. On the other hand, perhaps in less formal company, a quiet family dinner surrounded by children, he might reveal qualities hitherto unsuspected.

But, as ever, nothing seemed to turn out quite as she had imagined. Kate began it. She came up to Master Harington as they gathered in the hall before the meal, curtseyed with her usual flyaway grace, and said, with apparently genuine remorse, 'Aunt Patience says I am to apologise to you, sir, for being so rude before.'

Jack, completely unused to children, stared at her in astonishment, and muttered something. Kate, smiling prettily, then compounded her earlier felony. 'Are you *really* going to marry Rachael?' she asked, in tones of complete disbelief.

Embarrassment and outrage warred on Jack's rather heavy, stolid face. Silence saw Rachael's horrified expression and felt she should come to the rescue. 'Kate! One more *word* out of you, and you'll be sent back to Doraty in disgrace. Only children who behave themselves are allowed to dine with our guests.'

Kate, wilful and forward as she was, nevertheless heard the note of absolute authority and dropped her gaze to the floor. 'Yes, Mama,' she said, so subdued that Silence was tempted to laugh.

Despite all her efforts to make dinner a relaxed occasion, the atmosphere in the dining parlour soon became stilted and awkward. Rachael, obviously nervous and too keen to make a good impression on her betrothed, chattered inanely until, obviously, a prod from her irreverent twin brought her to a flushed, resentful and self-conscious halt.

William and Deb, normally so outgoing and cheerful, did nothing to fill the gap. They had decided between them that, if this rather ponderous-looking young man were really to be admitted to the bosom of the St. Barbe family, they must set a good example and try to cancel out the harm that Kate's childish prattle had already done to their reputation. Silence, looking with amusement at their unwontedly virtuous faces, the perfect offspring, seen but not heard, wondered what on earth Jack Harington must think of her ill-assorted brood.

He was, in fact, too intent on his platter to pay much attention to his betrothed or to her family. He had dined at Wintercombe before, but not for some time, and the tenderness of the sweet spring lamb and the fresh carp, each perfectly complemented by sauces of spearmint and fennel, delighted his hungry belly. However, when his appetite was almost satisfied, and when the second course, comprising a chicken fricassee, buttered eggs, a currant and raisin tart and new cheese, had been placed on the table, he found Sir George's heir, seated opposite, engaging him in pleasant conversation. Earnestly, Jack discoursed of local affairs, of his father's failed hopes of setting up a classis of the Presbyterian worship in North Somerset, and the preacher in Bath who had spoken for two hours on redemption through grace, and had never once repeated himself.

Silence, listening, smiled inwardly. Two more different young men could hardly be imagined, despite the similarity in their ages and upbringing. Nat, the younger by a couple of years, had always possessed an old head on young shoulders, with the wisdom and cynical humour of his grandfather, dead these seven years. Jack, his future mother-in-law realised, would never allow any question of levity, any joke however mild, to lighten his earnest, plodding progress through life. He did not appear to have discerned that Nat, at this moment seemingly as pious and godly and pompous as himself, was making gentle game of him. However, it was alas obvious that Deb and William, bright-eyed and prick-eared at the nether end of the table, had realised it.

So had Patience. Up until now, mindful of Rachael, so jealous and insecure, she had sat decorously on Nat's left hand, applying herself to her food and to the children on her other side. But as the conversation between Nat and Jack grew interesting, she found herself listening to it, while trying to attend to Kate and Tabby as well. A spark of mischief flowered in her mind. For once, Nat's teasing, clever brain was not employed at her expense: and just so had she privately mocked the earnest divines present at those treasonous gatherings at the house of Minister Love. She waited for a suitable pause in the talk, which had turned to affairs of state, and then said, with every appearance of seemly modesty, 'That all our enemies are confounded, and at peace with us, must mean that our actions are pleasing to God — as it says in Proverbs, chapter sixteen, verse seven. Do you not think so, Master Harington?'

Since this was an oft-voiced opinion of his father, Jack had no choice but to agree. Patience bestowed upon him one of her most dazzling smiles, and added, 'Of all things, civil war must be the most displeasing to the Lord. We must bless God for his mercy, that he has favoured our cause and thereby brought peace to this suffering and discordant land.'

Silence, listening astonished, did not dare look at any of her children. As Patience, lately discovered plotting for the King of Scots, waxed lyrical upon the benefits of the peacemakers, God's children, she stared intently into space, furiously repressing the bubbles of laughter springing up inside her. She was thankful that no one else at Wintercombe knew of her sister's dubious past: she could imagine only too clearly how Nat, in particular, would delicately, subtly, turn her argument on its head and tear it to shreds.

But Patience's excesses must be curbed, and quickly, or Rachael would surely explode. The meal was all but ended: she rose to her feet, and suggested that wine be taken in the winter parlour, which looked out on to the garden. Then, ushering her family and Jack from the room, she caught her sister's arm to detain her, and hissed, 'Please – remember Rachael!'

It was hard to forget her: all through that mischievous conversation, the girl's hot blue eyes had been burning with hatred. Patience, suddenly and genuinely contrite, gave her sister a remorseful smile, the mirror-image of Silence's own. 'I know. I'm sorry – I couldn't resist it. Shall I take the children into the garden?'

Silence assented, with heartfelt relief. It would not look very well if Jack Harington's betrothed were incited to attack her supposed rival in his presence.

Fortunately, there was no further incident, and Rachael relaxed so far as to exchange a few words with her suitor in a manner that was almost natural. But Silence, who had found Jack's conversational style somewhat lacking, was not sorry to see him leave an hour or so after dinner. To have Patience, from pure mischief, deliberately set out to ensnare Rachael's future husband, was a complication she had never dreamed might arise. Surely, surely, even her Imp could see the harm she would do thereby?

But she had no chance to speak with her further, for that afternoon George took a sudden turn for the worse. The doctor was again summoned from Bath, despite her husband's feeble protests, and stayed all night. By the morning, he had sunk into unconsciousness, and the end, the physician told her gravely, could not now be more than an hour or so away.

The children were brought, unnaturally subdued, to bid farewell to their father. Silence wondered what their true feelings might be as they gazed down at the comatose, gasping man lying in the bed in which their grandmother, also, had died. Would William, with his cheerful, untidy mind, and complete absence of any sense of sin, grieve at the passing of the parent who had done his utmost, in vain, to beat, coerce and cajole him into a proper respect and obedience? True, Deb was weeping, but tears and contrition came very easily to her, and she, by nature loud,

[63]

demanding and self-centred, had never accorded well with her father either. But William's dark eyes were dry, his expression serious, as he stood by the bed.

Tabby, her beloved, shy, secretive Tabby, was also solemn, but there were no tears on her face either. The early, gazelle-like promise of beauty, the small pointed face, the clouds of honey-gold hair, had come now to flower: soon she would be fifteen, as unaware of her loveliness as a lily of the field. She had never chosen the path of confrontation with Sir George, save only in her music: she was as fanatical and obstinate in its defence, as were others for their religion. Father and daughter had inhabited completely separate worlds, and there had never been any understanding whatsoever between them. Because she was, first and foremost, her mother's partisan, and had a hidden streak of fierce and ruthless justice, Silence knew, with sudden insight, that Tabby would be remorselessly glad that her parents would no longer have the power to fuel each other's unhappiness.

That concealed vein of ferocity in her supposedly sweet, gentle eldest daughter was something which had once deeply disturbed Silence, but which she had reluctantly been forced to accept. It was a trait she shared with her half-sister Rachael: but the elder girl, until recently, had never made any secret of her tempestuous nature. She had taken up her position on a chair by the bed, as close to her father as she could, and Silence knew that it would be pointless to persuade her to move until all was over. Already, her heart quailed at the explosion of grief and fury that would erupt from Rachael at her father's death.

Not so Nat. There had never been much love lost between her stepson and Sir George, who had early discarded him as a feeble weakling, unlikely to survive long, and of no particular account. But, against all prediction, Nat had lived, and grown to manhood, not vigorous, but no longer so delicate, while the beloved eldest son, Sam, his father's pride and joy, had been cruelly slain in the service of Parliament. Nat was now his heir, but to George perhaps even William, harum-scarum, undisciplined but delightful, was preferable in his heart to the young man whose independence of mind and lack of filial obedience and respect, had made in recent years an enemy of his own father.

No, Nat would shed no tears, and nor, yet, had Rachael. But Kate, little dancing Kate, her youngest, the quicksilver minnow, took one look at the almost lifeless figure of her father, and burst into floods of frightened, inconsolable tears. She tore herself free from Patience's restraining hand, and flung herself on the bed in a paroxysm of grief, howling over and over again, 'No, Papa, don't go, don't go!'

Not even that onslaught revived her father, who lay unmoving, only the difficult, intermittent fall and rise of his chest revealing that he still lived. Silence, her eyes suddenly wet for her child's anguish, tried to pull her gently from the bed. In the end, she, Nat and Patience had to drag her away by main force from the dying man. It took some time to persuade her into Doraty's firm but sympathetic care: and when Silence turned back into the chamber, there was utter quiet.

Stone, his expression grave, was bending with the doctor over Sir George, whose chest was still, whose harsh and painful breathing no longer filled the room, and then turned to her with a face contorted with distress. 'Oh, my lady — he be gone, he be safe at last with the Lord.'

So ended her marriage, long and bleak and empty: now would begin the days of her widowhood.

❦ CHAPTER FOUR ❧

'A will most incorrect'
(Hamlet)

She sat in her favourite niche in the lowest terrace wall, watching the horses grazing in the orchard. The sun had long since disappeared behind clouds, and the smell of rain, that the old gardener, Diggory, had taught her to recognise, lay heavy on the air. Her flowers would be glad of it: she herself, lost in her thoughts, would scarcely have noticed if a thunderstorm had broken over her head.

She was a widow. She wore black, the black she had worn in mourning for her mother, her father, her little son George who had died of a fever, and for her stepson Sam. She had worn it with grief for her beloved father-in-law, Sir Samuel, and more reluctantly for his bitter and venomous wife, who had done her best to make Silence's life a misery, and who had died abusing her. So much black, so many dead: and now, after a lifetime of servitude and duty, to father and to husband, she was free.

She had feared, once, the probable strength of her feelings at the hour of her liberty. She had been terrified of the joy her release would bring, even though it was purchased at the price of her husband's life. She had armoured herself in guilt and in the efficient performance of her wifely duties, nursing and soothing and consoling, suppressing her true emotions, lest they betray her. She had expected to feel happiness or, more acceptably, relief that George's sufferings were ended, and that he was now reunited with his beloved mother and eldest son in Heaven.

But she felt nothing: nothing at all.

Her old mare, Strawberry, had a foal at foot, a lanky mottled colt who would one day be the roan colour of his dam. Nat's outgrown Cobweb, dappled like a shadow under the apple trees, had dropped a dark grey filly a few days previously, and the two babies slept in infant abandon, a smudge of soft colour in the grass, while their mothers stood nose to tail beside them, dozing peacefully, unaware of the momentous event that had overtaken Wintercombe. And the lady of the house, who should have been speaking to the vicar, to Master Apprice, to the sexton and the servants and her children, who should be penning notice of the death and the funeral to the gentry of Somerset and Wiltshire, sat instead in her favourite place in the garden, and gazed with vacant eyes at the horses in the orchard.

Her little dog, Lily, whined softly and pushed her cold wet nose into her mistress's lax hand. Silence, roused at last out of her bleak reverie, bent and stroked the long white muzzle. 'Oh, Lily,' she said softly, speaking her thought to the dog as she sometimes did, 'why cannot I *feel* something, do something? But all I want is to hide here all day.'

'You'll get rained on if you do,' said her stepson's voice from immediately above her head, so appositely that Silence wondered if she had been unconsciously aware of his presence. She turned and looked up, to see Nat, his black hair hanging, leaning over the balustrade. He gave her a gargoyle smile, and said, 'Sorry if I startled you, but I couldn't resist it. Do you mind if I inflict my company on you for a while?'

'Not at all,' said Silence, and indeed she would be glad, she realised, of a dose of Nat's astringent intelligence. She made room for him in the niche, and he came lightly down the steps to sit beside her. He was fourteen years younger than she was, and in all the crises of her life since marrying into the St. Barbe family, he had been her prop, her anchor, and the keeper of her sanity. She depended on Nat's sense, his ability to cut to the heart of any argument, to see all sides of a dilemma without prejudice or emotion or the blinkers of Puritan morality.

He said, without preamble, 'I've seen Parson Willis, and we've agreed that he will be buried on Monday. I've sent word to Mells, and Kelston, and Freshford, and Bath – those are the most important, I'll inform the others later. Most of the gentry will turn out, I should think – and I mean to make sure that none will complain of any lack of filial respect.'

His voice held a bitterness that Silence had never heard before. She realised afresh how deep and savage and unhealed must be the wound of his father's contempt for him, that he had borne for all of his life. She said, with a rush of compassion, 'There is only one who would ever have done that, and he is gone.'

'And you and I are both free,' said Nat. 'There is no need of hypocrisy between us two, is there? No pious phrases of regret, save that he was not a better husband, or father. And yet, by most people's lights, he did not fail in his duty.'

'Rachael would certainly think that he had not,' said Silence. Her stepdaughter, her grief supplanted and overshadowed by Kate's noisy explosion of sorrow, had vanished to her chamber as soon as the physician had pronounced Sir George to be dead, and had locked the door. No amount of persuasion by Silence, or Nat, had been able to effect an entry, or even a response: and she wondered now, uneasily, about the girl's state of mind. Rachael's emotions, when overwhelming, were usually loudly and publicly displayed. This concealment of her undoubted anguish was somehow much more disturbing.

'And for Rachael, it was true,' Nat said reflectively. 'She is still locked in her chamber, by the way, but she told me to stop bothering her, in no uncertain terms, when I last knocked, and Jude has taken up something for her to eat. She'd have to be in extremis indeed, to forgo her dinner.' He glanced at the still, slender profile of his stepmother, gazing at the glorious pink and white of the orchard, spectacularly vivid even on this dull afternoon. 'Am I talking too much?'

'No,' said Silence. She turned her head, transferring that wide, clear stare to Nat's face. For a long moment, their eyes met, and then, with difficulty, she produced a feeble smile. 'Oh, Nat – why don't I *feel* anything? Anything at *all*? I should be crying, or laughing even, and instead I feel . . . numb.'

'Tie a limb too tight, for too long, and it feels nothing once it's freed,' said her stepson. 'Don't worry, in time you will . . . and I doubt you'll be weeping.'

'I doubt it too,' Silence said. 'But I can't even feel guilty – I've been married more than fifteen years, and yet my husband's death means nothing to me.'

'Oh, yes, it does,' said Nat. Suddenly intent, his blue eyes sharp on hers, he put his hands on her shoulders and gave her a little shake. 'It means your freedom, my dear Silence – your *freedom* – and mine! There will be no more worries, no more criticism, no more guilt. You can direct the servants as you please, I don't care so long as I have a meal on the table at roughly the right time, and don't have to wade through heaps of dirt and rubbish to reach my chamber. I am very easy to please, as you know – and so are you. Father has been unwell for so long, his death will make little difference to the running of the house – you have all the summer before you, to relax, and grow, and enjoy your garden.'

'Perhaps,' Silence said. She paused for a moment, and then

added, 'I have played a part and worn a mask for so long, save with you and a very few others, that I do not know how I can put it aside so readily. And yet I don't seem to be able to play the sorrowing widow very well, either.'

'You don't have to,' Nat said. 'People will assume it – indeed, they already have. Master Willis, and the sexton, and Eliza, all think you are here because you wished to be alone with your grief, and I've done nothing to dispel that impression.'

'Thank you,' Silence said. It seemed woefully inadequate as an expression of her gratitude to Nat: the size of the debt she owed him, both now and in the past, was too great for any words. She added, 'I suppose we had best go in before it rains.'

'It'll hold off a while yet,' Nat told her, with a countryman's confidence. He stared at the unpromising sky for a moment, and then said quietly, 'Freedom has another aspect, does it not, besides liberty from your husband. It also means that you are free to seek another.'

Silence, jolted out of her mood of dreary numbness, stared at him in bewildered astonishment. 'Another? Oh, Nat, he's hardly cold – you can't be serious!'

'Never more so,' said her stepson, leaning back against the dressed stone of the niche. 'Pity Father ever came back from the wars, really, wasn't it? But you are free now.'

Returned from the wars, to a wife who had secretly cuckolded him, and kept it hidden from all save her maid and the twins. Returned to father, as he thought, a daughter who was in fact the child of a Cavalier captain. Returned, to a wife whose changed character bewildered and antagonised him, and to a son and heir he despised.

She knew what Nat was suggesting, and the old agony, suddenly, was struggling to the surface. She had spent the last six years trying to forget the man who had taught her true happiness, who had loved and valued her as her husband never had, who had ridden out of her life that September day, leaving George once more in possession of his home and his wife. Though the original agony of grief had long since dulled to sad acceptance, she had never succeeded in casting him utterly from her heart. His books, Lily, who had been his gift to her, his memory, so clear, sweet and sharp and anguished, and above all the mischievous little girl who was his daughter, all brought him back so vividly to her mind, often at unexpected or inopportune moments. Nat had known, even approved, of their brief and passionate affair. But he did not know of that last terrible night, with the Roundheads encamped beyond the gate, when Silence, suspecting her pregnancy, terrified of the shame and horror it would bring to her as a proved adulteress, had begged Nick Hellier to take her away with him. And he had told her that he could not: for he was already married.

He had told her of his wife, and his own children, and she had known, her heart breaking, that she could not, for his sake and theirs, reveal that she was carrying his baby. She had only been saved from scandal and ostracism by the fact that, unbeknown to her, the Commander of the Parliament forces surrounding Wintercombe was her husband. Still grief-stricken at her lover's departure, she had closed the shutters over her anguish, and welcomed George back into her bed. And he had never, ever suspected that his wife had deceived him, and that his beloved, spoilt, mischievous little Kate was not in fact his child.

And now, six years too late, as Nat had said, she was free.

'Free for what?' she said, unable to keep the sadness, the bitterness out of her voice. 'I don't know where he is, or even if he is still alive. Oh, Nat, the very thought of it is impossible – how can I ever allow myself to hope?'

'You could try to find him,' said Nat. 'Or are you so enrutted in your cosy little world, no hurt, no pain, no love, that you dare not even look out?'

The harshness, the unfairness of his words, stung her out of her lethargy, as perhaps he had intended. She cried passionately, 'I can't, Nat, I can't – he has a wife already!'

In the utter quiet, cows lowed in the distance, and the roan mare Strawberry whickered softly to her foal. The look on Nat's face made her wonder why she had ever thought him hard or ruthless. His strong sinewy hand, brown and calloused from helping on the farm, came down gently over hers. 'I'm sorry,' he said at last. 'I had no idea.'

'He only told me on the last night,' Silence said. She realised that in a moment or two she would begin to weep – and not for her husband, that was the irony, but for her long-gone lover, and the mistaken choices of her life, which had not in fact been choices at all. 'And so I knew I could not tell him – that I was going to have his child.' She glanced at Nat, for they had never spoken of this before: indeed, had not spoken of Nick for six years, until now, when the danger had gone. He must have guessed Kate's true parentage, though, for it was obvious, to one as perceptive as Nat, who had known Nick, and the truth.

He saw her glance at him, and smiled. 'Oh, yes, I knew all along about Kate. I think Rachael knows, too, although she hasn't said anything to me. Have you noticed, how she has never been as fond of Kate as she is of Deb or William?'

Silence had, though she had tried to ignore it, and the implications. She nodded, thinking of the child with her father's chestnut eyes, weeping wildly for the death of another man. And then, suddenly, all the pent-up torment and anguish of the years she had spent trying to cast her brief happiness into oblivion burst to the surface, and she turned her head into Nat's steady, unemotional shoulder, and wept for all that she had lost, and the longed-for freedom that was no use to her.

But tears would not cure her grief, nor fill the emptiness of her days. For what point was there in having her chains unlocked, only to find herself in a larger prison? She could not search for Nick, for another woman had prior claim to him, and so did his legitimate children. She could only tend her house, her family and her garden, that in all her hours of sorrow had been her greatest solace. George was dead, but her life would not be so greatly changed. She was thirty-five years old, in excellent health, and could expect many more years of life, rearing her children, watching them grow, and marry, and give her grandchildren. And at this desolate moment, such a cosy domestic prospect no longer held any appeal for her.

At least she was no longer in thrall to George, and she had lived without Nick for so long, she could continue to do so in the future. Make, do, mend, she said to herself fiercely, repeating the words of her fishwife grandmother, whose pragmatic, sensible nature she had inherited. A few deep breaths, and she was returned to a semblance of calm. She sat up, wiping the last of the tears from her eyes, and said, 'I'm sorry. Do I look very bedraggled?'

'As a grieving widow should,' said Nat, smiling. 'And no one will ever suspect that it is not your husband you have been mourning. Are you very tired of all the lies and deception?'

'Unutterably,' said Silence, with weary sadness. 'But the complications attendant on any revelation of the truth are such that I think I shall lie for evermore. Oh, Nat, I don't think I can thank you enough for all you have done — and above all for *understanding*. How many men would approve of their stepmother cuckolding their father?'

'Not many, I suspect,' said Nat drily. 'And perhaps, for the sake of the general morality of the Commonwealth, it's as well that there aren't. I, my dear Silence, am the exception rather than the rule. Aren't you lucky in your stepson? I can't imagine Jack Harington, for instance, being so generous.'

'Nor can I,' Silence said. She added, 'What is your honest opinion of him?'

'Of Jack? Oh, a worthy enough fellow, though not half the man his father is. He's far too puffed up with his own importance.'

'So is his father. The old King is supposed to have said that you could see his pride shining through the hole in his stocking. But I agree – Jack is worthy, earnest and godly. The question is – is he suitable for Rachael?'

'Of course he's not,' said Nat, with a briskness that surprised her. 'Oh, come, you know that as well as I do. But she's set on it, because it was Father's fondest wish to marry his eldest daughter to his old friend's eldest son. If you have no knowledge of Rachael's character, it looks an excellent match, but she'll be completely miserable, and too proud to admit it, and in consequence she'll vent her spleen on all around her – you know Rachael as well as I do. Whatever her faults, I can't let her blight her future, and allow her to go into that marriage with all Father's blinkers fixed firmly in place.'

'You'll have to,' Silence said. As he stared at her in surprise, she added, 'I had not meant to tell you this yet. I'm not even supposed to know, but Master Harley told me. George changed his will before he died. Amongst other things, all the girls are to have a thousand pounds each for their dowry – but if Rachael refuses to marry Jack, all her portion is forfeit, and shared amongst the others.'

This time, the pause threatened to stretch out for ever. Then Nat, usually so cool and detached, said softly and viciously, 'The bastard! Does he think to bend us all to his will, even though he's dead? What in God's name was Harley doing, to let that past?'

'That isn't all,' said Silence with bitterness, and told him what else his father had ordained.

Nat swore, with a fluency and vehemence she had never suspected he possessed. As she stared at him, rather shocked, wondering bemusedly where he had learned such words – at Oxford, she supposed – he leapt to his feet, and turned to face her. 'A good father? A good husband? Is it good, to compel you to rely on my charity or live miles away in a place you loathe? Good, to force my sister into a marriage that will surely bring her nothing but opulent misery? I'm surprised he didn't find a husband for you, while he was about it.'

'Master Harley prompted him to consider that I might remarry,' Silence told him. 'I don't think it had entered his head.'

'No — his self-esteem couldn't encompass the thought that you might want someone else,' said Nat. He ran a hand through his hair and grinned at her wryly, his anger abruptly evaporated. 'I wish, you know, I wish that in the last moment of his life I had been able to tell him the truth about you — just for the pleasure of seeing his horrified amazement.'

He was hard, she realised, but his father had made him thus, and his sense of justice was as sharp as any man's, if perhaps somewhat more unconventional. She said sadly, 'What good would it have done? I wanted to make him understand, before he died, how much I . . . I disliked him, how much I had suffered from him down the years — how cruel he had been, without ever intending it, or knowing it. I was so sorely tempted — and yet I could not, because that too would have been cruel.' She looked up at Nat, who had that ruthlessness she entirely lacked, and added, 'I do not really regret it. Even that will . . . he was only trying to do his best for Wintercombe, and you all.'

'Really?' said Nat, eyebrows raised. 'Then at best he was guilty of unbelievable insensitivity. He knew how much you love this house, how much you dislike the one at Chard — and yet you are to have no right of residence in your own home, unless I die! And the family lawyer feeling he must intervene on your behalf rather than see you forced to live on my charity — it's as well for him that he has passed beyond the reach of my tongue, or he'd soon know what I think of him.'

'And William, compelled to make his own way in the world — he still wants to be a soldier, and there are no fortunes to be made in that trade,' Silence said. 'And if I'm honest, I don't in the least want to have the burden of Chard laid on me again, absolutely unsupported. *And* it's all but a ruin. If you will have me here, Nat, I will endeavour to be your housekeeper, until you find a wife.'

He laughed, and held his hand out to her. 'You don't need to ask it. And what would I want with a wife? I'll leave that for a day or two, I think. It's starting to rain — come in, or you'll be soaked.'

She allowed him to help her to her feet — 'As if I were in truth an old widow' — and took his arm as they ascended the steps. She no longer felt numb: beneath their friendly banter, her emotions were scraped raw and bleeding with wounds she had thought were long since healed. But at least she was alive; she cared; and her freedom, that an hour before had meant nothing to her, now beckoned with cautious enticement.

She took a deep breath of the rain-soaked air, savouring the wet earth and the damp fragrance of her flowers, and smiled sideways at Nat, with love and gratitude. He smiled back, in perfect accord as they had always been, and the heir to Wintercombe escorted his stepmother, a widow now for five brief hours, into the house.

*

Half of the Somerset gentry, it seemed, wished to pay their last respects to Sir George St. Barbe. Silence, the desolate widow, made sure that the guests would be sufficiently well fed, and plied them with the customary burnt wine and spiced ale. It had rained for days, and the roads, according to Nat, were a quagmire. They had not prevented nearly three hundred friends, acquaintances and old comrades from attending the funeral.

Among them were Jack Harington, who received mourning rings for himself and his father, under one of the more unexceptionable terms of Sir George's will, and Master Jonathan Harley.

By now, Silence had become accustomed to the lawyer's presence. The brilliant green of his eyes no longer disturbed her, nor the smooth urbane courtesy, common to all professional men whose livelihood depended on being agreeable to their clients. She found his manner pleasant enough, and the hint of more human feelings — sympathy for her, indignation about her late husband's provisions — made her inclined to like him. When those less close to the St. Barbes had made their way home, or to Bath for a night's lodging, Harley was amongst those who lingered, talking to Nat, then to Jack Harington, and finally seeking her out as she was directing Carpenter to broach another cask of wine in the buttery. 'Good afternoon, my lady.'

'Good afternoon,' Silence said. Carpenter, efficient and obsequious, melted out of sight behind the hall screens, and she suffered a sudden mischievous temptation to ask him something shockingly inappropriate. Would the words, 'Did you enjoy my husband's funeral?' shatter that unctuous mask? Patience might have succumbed, but Patience, whose behaviour could always be perfectly conventional when it really mattered, was plain and decorous in black, and talking to the Vicar, well away from Jack Harington.

'I have not had the opportunity,' he said gently, 'to tell you how very sorry I am, my lady, about your late husband's death.'

At least, she thought, giving him the sad, hypocritical reply, he does not spout pious phrases, tell me he is with the Lord or elected into Heaven. Master Harley, like everyone else, went to church and listened to sermons, but he had never given her the impression of being a truly godly man. She realised suddenly that she knew very little about him, save that he was unwed, a little older than herself, and had inherited his father's practice in and around Bath on old Master Harley's death three or four years ago. Up until then, he had lived in London, at one of the Inns of Court. He had the reputation of being a good man of law, perhaps too sharp for the liking of those who were not his clients. But he had done his best to persuade George to alter that unjust will, and it was not his fault that he had only partly succeeded. She knew, none better, how mulishly stubborn her late and unlamented husband had been.

'I have been speaking with Sir Nathaniel,' he said. Silence realised, with some shock, that Nat was now a baronet, the third St. Barbe to hold the title. The dignity did not suit him, she decided: it was much too pompous.

Harley was continuing. 'It seems from what he said to me, that he has now some knowledge of his late father's will.'

'He has,' Silence said, raising her wide eyes to meet his. 'I told him, after my husband's death. I thought it best that he was informed of the general provision, though of course you must acquaint him with the particular.'

'As indeed I will — he has already asked me to ride over tomorrow.'

'Then you must stay for dinner,' Silence said. He smiled at her, and she found herself smiling back. 'Thank you, my lady. I shall look forward to it with great anticipation. Darby's cooking is always something to savour.'

*

The day of the funeral had exhausted her, and she should have fallen asleep as soon as her head touched the pillow, but this night slumber eluded her. Misty curled under the bedclothes in the

[75]

warmth, and Lily, uttering tiny whimpers and twitching as she chased rabbits in her dreams, lay stretched at her foot. But their mistress turned restlessly, thinking of her stepdaughter. Tomorrow, Master Harley would come to discuss the will with Nat. Surely, two such clever brains could find some way of ensuring that Rachael was not forced into a marriage she might come to regret even before the banns were cried. The estate was wealthy: perhaps Nat could dispose of some land, or a few of the properties in Bristol, to provide her with another dowry, so that she could attract a husband more suited to her.

With this comforting thought, she drifted at last into sleep, and found all her certainties dissolved on the morrow.

Master Harley arrived in the middle of the morning, and antagonised Eliza, who was supervising the sweeping of the hall, by dripping rainwater all over the rolled-up rush matting. One of the maids, Meg Coker, took his soaked cloak and hat, and another ran for hot ale. Then the lady of Wintercombe was there, calm and smiling in a sensible gown of warm black wool, commiserating with him over the weather, and offering a change of clothing, which he declined. There were no St. Barbe males of his long, lean build – they did not seem inclined to height – and he had no desire to appear ridiculous in garments too short. His own attire, though likewise plain and sober, was always immaculate, and the thick broadcloth cloak had kept much of the damp from his dark blue suit. He accepted the steaming ale with appreciative thanks, and noted that his hostess, although outwardly her usual serene self, had shadows beneath her eyes that betokened lack of sleep. Today, in the thin grey light of a rainy morning, she looked neither young, nor pretty.

Unlike her sister, who followed on her heels, all dark curls and smiles. She also wore black, though the drab colour served to emphasise her looks rather than to obscure them. 'Good morning, Master Harley,' said Patience, with a flutter of eyelashes and a flourishing curtsey, and he realised abruptly that this forward young woman was attempting to flirt with him.

Well, he had no interest whatsoever in her, despite her undoubted physical attractions. He responded coolly, refusing to be tempted, and Lady St. Barbe said, 'We have an hour or so to discuss our business, Master Harley. My stepson will be here shortly – he has been talking over farm matters with the bailiff. What are you going to do, Patience?'

Harley realised that she was well aware of her younger sister's wiles, and Patience knew it too. She glanced at Silence, smiled once more, dazzlingly, at the lawyer, and said demurely, 'I have promised to sit with Tabby while she plays. I'll see you at dinner, then, Master Harley.' And with a defiant levity in her step, her head high, she whisked out of the hall.

Silence found herself meeting Harley's eyes, a smile on her face. His expression was amused and understanding, but he said merely, 'Shall we to business, my lady?'

Nat, joining them a little later in the study, thought that the lawyer had made himself quite at home. He was sitting in one of the leather chairs by the fire, his tankard of ale still warm in his hands, and chatting amicably to Silence, while Lily and Misty, enjoying the heat from the cheerfully glowing embers, had snuggled up together at his feet. Nat, surveying the scene, realised that in this matter he and his late father were, almost uniquely, of similar opinion. There was something about Harley, some elusive quality in the man that he could not describe or evaluate, but which he did not like. Nevertheless, he greeted the lawyer with his usual friendly directness. 'Hallo, Master Harley. I hope your journey has not been too mudridden?'

'A little uncomfortable, sir, I must confess. But the good offices of Lady St. Barbe have quite restored me.'

Slimy unctuous toady, thought Nat immediately, though he knew he was being unfair. He drew up a chair and sat between them, making a fuss of Lily, who always greeted him with wagging enthusiasm. In this informal setting, he was well aware that both he and Silence were at an advantage compared with the lawyer, who by the very nature of his business would be accustomed to the defensive bulwark of a desk or a table.

If Master Harley felt himself ill at ease, however, he gave no indication of it. He finished his ale, set the pewter tankard down in the hearth amongst the warm scattered ashes, and said, 'And now, I take it, to our business, Sir Nathaniel?'

'Of course,' said Nat. He leant back against the cushions of the chair, one hand still idly playing with Lily's ears, and went on, 'Just how are you able to justify drawing up a will such as my father left?'

Harley's green eyes stared at him in surprise. 'It is not my place, Sir Nathaniel, to set aside the last wishes of a dying man. I must confess, I find some of his provisions as puzzling as do you — and

Lady St. Barbe, of course. Even though all my training and experience spoke against it, I did try to persuade him to a more . . . a more considerate will. But on some matters he was adamant, and so I had of course to accede to his wishes.'

'Of course,' said Nat. The irony in his tone was not lost on his stepmother, who knew him so well: whether the lawyer had also noticed it was not apparent on his lean, unemotional face. He went on, bluntly, 'Tell me, Master Harley, in plain words and few. Is it possible, in any degree, to set some of the more objectionable provisions of this will aside?'

'I doubt it,' said the older man, and proceeded to explain exactly why not, in words neither plain nor few. Silence, after the first few sentences, found her mind wandering, and forced herself to concentrate.

'If my sister Rachael should not wish to marry Jack Harington after all,' Nat said when he had finished, 'would it be possible for me to provide her with a dowry from, say, the proceeds of the sale of part of my inheritance?'

Master Harley frowned. 'There is nothing set down in the will to prevent you from doing that, Sir Nathaniel. Whether it would be a wise move, to thus diminish and encumber your estate, is another matter.'

'But,' Nat pointed out gently, 'it will be my decision, will it not, Master Harley? And it may not be necessary, after all. What happens if Master Harington changes his mind, and no longer wishes to marry my sister? Which, of course, none of us desires – but all possibilities have to be considered.'

'There is nothing in the will which mentions such an eventuality,' said the lawyer, after a pause for thought. 'In fact the wording, as I recall, is very clear. Only if your sister refuses the match is her portion forfeit. Your late father does not seem to have considered the other possibility at all.'

'I see,' said Nat, and the small smile that twitched the corner of his mouth made Silence glance at him sharply, well aware that it meant mischief. She herself would have liked nothing better than to take Jack Harington, or better still his father, on one side and persuade him, by any means to hand, that Rachael was not the best wife for him. But such a tactic was hardly fair, and certainly not to her stepdaughter, who at present desired the match so desperately. Silence, not for the first time, and undoubtedly not for the last, thought with bitter dislike of Sir George who, for reasons that seemed to him entirely excellent, was manipulating his family from the grave.

'In truth,' Harley was saying, 'it would be best if you were to read the will yourself, Sir Nathaniel. I have it here — your father gave it into my hands for safe keeping.'

The disputed document was not long, two pages only in the lawyer's clear, unequivocal hand. Nat scanned it once, rapidly, and then a second time in more detail, while Silence, consumed with curiosity, had to curb her natural but unladylike desire to peer past his shoulder. Then he passed it to her abruptly. 'You read it too, Mother — you are one of the beneficiaries, after all.'

He had not called her 'Mother' for years: in recognition of their friendship, and the fact that he had reached adulthood, he used her Christian name now. But, perhaps thinking that Master Harley would not understand, he had reverted to the conventional form of address. She took the thick parchment in her hand, trying not to touch the ink, and perused it with care.

She was not at all versed in legal matters, and it had always been a matter of puzzlement and dismay to her, the power that lawyers wielded in the land. How could these pieces of stiff cured skin have all the force of any Act of Parliament? More force, since even Parliament was now but a feeble Rump, subservient to its masters in the Council of State.

She glanced at the minor bequests: mourning rings; dispensations for the funeral; small amounts of money left to loyal servants, here and at the other house in Chard. There was a cottage and pasture at Lyde Green, the huddle of houses past the Mill, for his manservant, Stone, to occupy for his lifetime, and gifts of clothes and coin to the poor of Philip's Norton. The dowries of his four daughters, Rachael, Tabitha, Deborah and Katherine, were to be provided out of the revenues from his lands in Somerset, properties and shipping interests in Bristol, and the mines, one for lead and one for coal, in Mendip. And there it was, clear and forthright and unambiguous. 'If my daughter Rachael does not wish to marry John, eldest son of John Harington Esquire of Kelston, as she has been contracted, then her portion is to be forfeit, and the moneys divided equally between her sisters, the said Tabitha, Deborah and Katherine.'

Nothing, as Master Harley had already stated, to say what would happen if Jack were the one to change his mind. She read on, the old useless anger knotted deep within her, to the part which ordained that she must inherit the house and land at Chard, in defiance of her dislike for the place, and gave her no right of residence at her beloved Wintercombe. And, most insulting of all, Nat, not herself, was appointed guardian of the children.

'Is there no disputing all this?' she asked, raising her eyes to Jonathan Harley. He shrugged. 'Like all wills, it must be proved at the court in London, and letters of administration granted to Sir Nathaniel. If there is dispute, between the beneficiaries of a will, then the court will decide the outcome. But in this case, I fear, it can be proved that Sir George was of sound mind when the document was drawn up, and very firm and decided in his purpose. It will be very difficult to persuade the court to set his wishes aside.'

And of course, Nat thought cynically, to do so would cost the St. Barbes a great deal of money, and line the attorney's own pockets most handsomely. But for Rachael's sake, and for William, for whom no adequate inheritance had been provided, he must find out all he could concerning his chances of success.

He discussed it with his stepmother later, after the lawyer had dined, to his evident satisfaction, and departed replete in new sunshine. 'If the conditions of a will are unreasonable, then it has a good chance of being declared null.'

'But it's not exactly unheard of, for a man to decree that his daughter marry a specific person, and no other,' Silence pointed out gently. They were walking on the bowling green, a sadly neglected square of rough grass, unused as such for several years, and a favourite hunting ground of her cat Misty. She prodded a humped, glistening molehill with her foot. 'Perhaps Diggory can organise a team of hale and hearty young fellows to come and scythe all this down to its former glory, and then we can invite all the eligible young gentlemen and women of these parts to a bowls match.'

Nat's comment on this stratagem was a derisive snort. He added drily, 'I'll lay you odds of ten to one that the only person at Wintercombe to benefit thereby will be Patience. And there is something else which is not my father's fault, but which has been exercising my mind. I'm not yet twenty-two, and I've seen virtually nothing of the world. He packed me off to Oxford purely to get me out of his way — it was none of his intention that I should enjoy myself there, but luckily I did, and I don't regret going in the least. Since I returned, I've been little more than his unpaid deputy, and received small thanks for it. I would like one day to marry, and be able to converse with my bride on matters a little more exalted than the lambing or the price of wheat. I had hoped, perhaps, to be able to spend some time abroad, in Italy or France, and enlarge my education. You could manage Wintercombe without me, I know. And yet, how can I go, and leave all this tangle, and desert poor Rachael?'

Silence was blowing absently at a dandelion clock, thereby irresponsibly scattering the plumed seeds all over the garden, borne on the breeze. The sun was shining now, for a miracle, but grey clouds to the west, towards Frome, promised more rain. She smiled at him, her face clear and calm, more serene by far than it had been before her husband's death. Already, after the days of rain, her garden was smoothing out the lines between her brows, bringing a spring to her step and a touch of happiness, subtle but unmistakable, at the corners of her mouth. She said quietly, 'You love this place as much as I do – and it is your right, as much part of your inheritance as your title. How can you think of leaving it, even for a year?'

'It would not be for long,' said Nat. 'But you do understand, my dear Silence? I cannot spend all my life here, or I shall dwindle into a country farmer, interested in nothing beyond my nose. And before I can consider any travel abroad, I must find out what chance we have of freeing Rachael from that iniquitous will.'

'Even if you beggar your inheritance to do it?'

Nat grinned at her, his mood changing as abruptly as his twin's did. 'Oh, no. Credit me with just a little sense, my dear Silence. And perhaps a miracle will happen, and the perfect young man – handsome, lovable, tolerant, generous and above all *placid* – will present himself out of the blue, and all Rachael's problems will vanish in a puff of smoke.'

'And I pray she'll be happier than I was,' Silence said, knowing that Rachael, no quiet Puritan mouse despite all her efforts, would not easily attract such a paragon. Therein, surely, lay much of her desperate desire to marry Jack, the only husband so far offered to her.

'So do I,' said Nat. 'Which is why I want time to find the right man. And why I mean to instruct Master Harley to seek out some way of contesting that pernicious document. Don't worry, please – I'm well aware that Master Harley has been rubbing his hands in gleeful anticipation of a nice, long, costly, lucrative law-suit, and I have no intention of beggaring myself, and enriching him, in pursuit of a lost cause. But I need good, honest information as to my likely chances of success. There are other lawyers in the world besides Harley, and I intend to consult several others before I commit myself.'

Silence nodded, relieved. She had known that Nat — cautious, cunning, careful and cynical beyond his years — would not foolishly hazard his wealth for a will-o'-the-wisp chance. But she wished, with all her heart she wished, that George had never laid this problem upon the son and heir he had so much disliked, and despised,

❧ CHAPTER FIVE ❧

'His mouth full of news'
(*As You Like It*)

Patience, free of London, free of Joseph and above all free of his domineering wife Grace, was enjoying her liberty. It was a shame that her arrival at Wintercombe seemed to have engendered such resentment in Rachael, but she had managed to resist entirely, for at least two weeks, the temptation to flirt with Jack Harington, now a frequent visitor. In truth, she could not imagine anyone being roused to a passion of jealousy over such a boring young man, and mischief alone had prompted her to attract his attention in the first place. However, for her sister's sake, if not for Rachael's, she had desisted. Judging from the mystified glances that Jack occasionally sent in her direction, he might have thought that she had been secretly substituted for some other woman, decorous, demure, and yet still fascinating. For once, Patience was glad that her dowry would probably be much too small to interest him, compared with Rachael's thousand pounds.

It was also a pity that Sir George should have chosen this time to die, and thereby plunge the household into mourning. True, she had never expected Wintercombe to be a hive of social activity, but the presence of the twins had led her to hope for it. The only visitors seemed to be Master Harington and his father, recently returned from Lincoln's Inn, and the lean but strangely attractive lawyer. He, however, had shown himself to be emphatically uninterested in Patience, however charmingly she might smile, and she, never one to cast her charms upon stony soil, decided very soon that Master Harley was not worth her pursuit.

Besides, she had noticed, with surprise and not a little amusement, that he seemed to be attracted instead to her sister.

Silence, of course, appeared to be completely unaware of it. How could she, married for nearly sixteen years to a man much older, have any experience of the complicated and subtle game of courtship? Patience, veteran of three abortive betrothals and several relationships with young men (including John Jackel) which had not reached such formalities, had seen it at once. There was, admittedly, very little on which to base her opinion, and instinct and intuition had played a considerable part in her judgement, but she was certain that she was right. Still, she had no intention of mentioning it to Silence — not yet, at any rate.

So, bereft of eligible male company, Patience set herself to enjoy the friendship of her nieces and nephew. She found them all delightful, even Deborah, once the child had got over her urge to impress. Tabby seemed very shy, but by praising her musical skills, and showing an interest in her playing, her aunt found that she could breach the reserve. Kate and William, sunny and friendly by nature, were easy to enthral, and in their company Patience, somewhat to her surprise, was able to discard the veneer of London sophistication, and to enter again into the childhood which, because of her father's harsh authority, she had never enjoyed for herself.

Under William's unprejudiced, expert eye she made great progress on horseback. Nat had allotted her one of the family's riding horses, a rather fat and elderly dark bay gelding inaptly called Spark. Led by the younger children, she explored Philip's Norton and the villages round about, and then, the highlight so far of her sojourn at Wintercombe, rode with the whole family to Bath for a day's jaunt.

She had thought she might suffer from boredom, so deep in the country. One look at Bath, packed with shops, inns, lodging-houses and the Quality, come to take the healing waters, decided her. This place might be small, no more than a market town, but in matters of fashion and sophistication it could almost rival London. Patience, casting an experienced eye over the wares in the mercers' and drapers' shops, decided on a new gown or two, once a sufficient period of mourning for Sir George had elapsed. Joseph had given her a reasonable sum of money for her keep, and Nat, very generously, had supplemented it with a handsome allowance. She might even be able to afford some of that very pretty amber silk — or the sapphire blue — or even, most expensive and daring of all, the rich blood red that she knew instinctively would become her so well.

Whether she could persuade Silence's tailor, who was doubtless some easily shocked Puritan, to make it up in the off-the-shoulder style that all the fashionable ladies in Bath seemed to be wearing, she did not know, but she certainly intended to try.

It was not easy, curbing the exuberance of the children in these crowded streets. Patience had doubted the wisdom of letting Kate come, but the little girl, who had turned five a week after her father's death, had begged and pleaded for the chance to spend her birthday shilling. Patience had already noticed how the child was . . . not exactly spoilt, but definitely indulged by her mother and by Deb and William, who tolerated behaviour from their little sister that they would not have countenanced in each other. Nat, too, seemed especially fond of her, as was Tabby, and with one on either side of her, each firmly holding a small brown paw, Kate would have little chance to get into mischief. She kept up an unceasing chatter, from the moment they left their horses at the White Hart in Stall Street, all through their winding and haphazard progress past shops, booths and stalls, avoiding refuse heaps and the unpleasant and fly-ridden debris outside the butchers' shops. The maid, Mally, carried two large plaited straw baskets, which quickly became filled with the necessities on Silence's list: needles, linen thread; embroidery silks; lace; four yards of fine holland for cuffs, collars, kerchiefs and falling bands; a quantity of ribbon in assorted colours, sleek and shiny; pins and cords, all from the draper's shop.

'Are you going to spend your shilling here?' Patience asked Kate, who was peering on tip-toe into a basket of bundled ribbon on the shop counter, while her mother, a draper's daughter, watched the unfolding of the holland cloth with an eagle eye for impurities in the weave.

'No,' said the little girl, with her usual air of decision. Patience had noticed that she always knew her desires exactly, and spared no effort to obtain them. 'I don't know what I want yet, but I will when I see it.'

The apothecary's shop was next, dark and mysterious and aromatic, with bunches of nameless objects hanging from the ceiling, and a stout youngish man, smiling and knowledgeable, to discuss her needs with my lady St. Barbe, whom he evidently knew well. Patience, who like both her sisters enjoyed excellent health, lost interest and went to stand in the doorway, gazing idly at the processing crowds outside. William and Deb, full of self-importance, had been despatched to the tailor to collect the boy's new summer suit, ordered some weeks previously, and Rachael, fidgety and nervous because they had been invited to dine at the Haringtons' Bath house, just by the Abbey, was examining the bunches of dried herbs and jars of dubious potions on the shelves with a spurious air of housewifely interest. Beside her Tabby, her lips moving soundlessly, read the labels, so evocative of exotic and far-flung places: oil of mace and quicksilver; fenugreek and aniseed; frankincense and galingal and caraway; orris and ambergris.

'Well, what do you think of our fair city?' said Nat at Patience's ear. 'How does it compare with London?'

His teasing tone no longer seemed to arouse her antagonism: instead, she had discovered the satisfaction of answering like with like. 'Oh, a very little,' said Patience, opening her brown eyes very wide. 'But there are more ladies and gentlemen of fashion here – I think they must all have moved to Bath for their health.'

'They all look in the best of health to me.'

'Perhaps that's a result of living in Bath,' she said. There were several handsome young men passing, in fine garments much belaced and beribboned, who were assuredly not of the godly persuasion. They saw Patience studying them, and made several appreciative comments. The object of their attentions, Nat noticed, neither blushed nor simpered, but looked as if she made a habit of this. He was thankful that his stepmother was still inside the shop.

A young man came after, in the plain travel-stained russets of the countryman, though obviously a prosperous one. Like the group in front of him, he glanced at Patience, and then stopped, so abruptly that a woman almost cannoned into him. Patience smiled despite herself, pleased at her effect, and then realised, returning abruptly to earth, that he was not looking at her at all. She turned her head, and saw that Nat, his blue eyes narrowed, was also staring at the other man. Then he left her side, moving suddenly into the crowded street, and she heard him say, evidently with surprise and pleasure, 'I know you – you're Tom Wickham, aren't you?'

Patience watched as the stranger, a similar expression of delight on his face, was escorted back to the relative tranquillity of the shop doorway. He was tall, possessed of a goodnatured face, rather weathered and scattered with freckles, pleasant without aspiring to good looks. 'Nat!' he said, evidently amazed. 'Nat St. Barbe! This is splendid – I had thought to ride over to Winter-combe, but I was not sure . . . ' He paused, obviously a little uncertain, and looking at Patience.

Nat grinned, at his most cheerfully mischievous. 'Oh, this is my

Aunt Imp. Patience, may I present Master Thomas Wickham, whom I have not seen for . . . nearly six years, it must be. And in rather less happy circumstances, eh, Tom?'

'Indeed,' said Wickham.

Patience, determined to make her mark, said briskly, 'I will place on record, sir, here and now, my objections to being called "Aunt". Not only am I no blood kin to Nat, but I do not consider myself sufficiently in my dotage to be styled thus.'

'What about the Imp?' enquired Nat, grinning wider. Patience, her own mouth stretching into an answering smile, shrugged. 'As for that, I have grown used to it. You can call me what you will, so long as "Aunt" is not included.'

'Excellent – I'll take you up on it,' Nat said, his eyes glinting. 'Tom – Mistress Woods here is my stepmother's sister, who has come to stay with us from London, and she is, I hope, enjoying her first taste of Bath. And what brings you here? I had thought you might have feared recognition.'

'The war ended six years ago,' the other man pointed out. 'I have paid my fines and dues long since, and am now as good a citizen of the Commonwealth as any other. Certainly, several people have looked at me rather hard, on this occasion as previously, but I have no fear of denunciation in the street.'

Patience was becoming increasingly puzzled. This young man, who could be little older than herself, seemed once to have been a Royalist soldier. But how was Nat even acquainted with him, let alone upon friendly terms?

Nat must have sensed her bewilderment, for he gave her a swift explanation. 'Tom was part of the garrison at Wintercombe for nearly a year, and we have not seen him since.'

'I did not think it would be . . . appropriate to return,' said Wickham. 'You, and Lady St. Barbe, I know would always welcome me, and any other members of the garrison – but there are some who might not understand our friendship.'

'That is not so now,' Nat said. Wickham took his meaning at once. 'Yes, I have heard of the sad death of your father, as has most of Somerset. I must admit that I had thought of returning home tomorrow by way of Wintercombe, for old times' sake.'

'Then do,' said Nat. 'Why not save the price of a lodging? Call on us this evening, when you've finished your business here, stay the night, as long as you can spare – and we can all talk over old times together.'

'That I'll do gladly,' said Wickham, smiling with such huge delight that Patience could not help but be infected by it. 'Pray present my regards, and my best wishes, to Lady St. Barbe – is she here in Bath?'

'Yes, but busy shopping,' said Nat. He winked at Patience, plainly not wishing her to mention that Silence was, in fact, not fifteen feet behind them, and so deep in conversation with the apothecary that she had not realised what was happening outside the door.

Kate had noticed, however. She emerged, small and brown in her black mourning, her hair escaping from her rather crooked white cap, and gazed up at the new face with bright chestnut eyes, before dropping into a perfect curtsey.

Tom Wickham stared at her as if, thought Patience, he had seen a ghost. Nat gave him a swift shrewd glance, and then said casually, 'This minx is my little sister Kate, who has just celebrated her fifth birthday. What *are* you going to spend your shilling on, Binnick?'

'I don't know,' said Kate. 'The man had a dried up crockydile, but he said he wanted more than a shilling for it.' She did not sound very disappointed: Patience knew that if she had set her heart on it, her protests would have echoed all round Bath. She grinned up at Wickham, with that huge three-cornered smile that people found so very difficult to resist. 'Are you a friend of Nat's? I don't know you.'

'Yes . . . yes, I am,' said Tom. He seemed almost dazed, and pulled himself together with a visible effort. 'I used to be his friend, oh, long ago before you were born, but we lost touch – and now I am invited to Wintercombe this evening, so I will see you again. Your servant, Mistress Woods, Mistress Kate – forgive me, Nat, but I have much business to complete here before I can leave. Pray excuse me.'

And with sudden, almost embarrassed haste, he sketched a swift bow and strode off down the street, pushing between the crowded people as if he had just encountered old enemies, not friends.

Patience was about to comment on his peculiar behaviour, when she noticed Nat's face. He was looking neither bewildered nor offended: instead, his expression was thoughtful. Kate, her eyes following Wickham's retreating figure until he disappeared amongst the crowds in Cheap Street, said happily, 'I do like that man, he's nice. I'm glad he's coming to see us. Does Mama know him too?'

'Does Mama know what?' Silence appeared in the doorway with the rest of her children behind her, and Mally, clutching baskets whose burdens had been significantly increased. 'Who were you talking to, Nat?'

'Oh, just an old friend,' Nat said, winking at Patience again, with the eye that his stepmother could not see. 'He said he'd drop by sometime to visit me – you do not mind, I hope?'

'Oh, no, of course not,' said Silence, and then cried sharply, 'Kate! Kate, come back!'

For her youngest daughter, completely without warning, had dived out into the street. A flurry amongst the crowd revealed her passage: she appeared to be making for the Guildhall, a fine, stately, modern building dominating the High Street. Shouting her name, Nat plunged after her, and Patience, not to be outdone, followed hot in his wake, using heels, elbows and ruthless determination in a manner which she had early learned in the streets of London.

The Council chambers of the Guildhall were situated on the upper storeys: below, the market stalls spilled out from under the arched columns, full of country people selling produce live, dead, grown and manufactured. Patience arrived breathless at the nearest corner, and almost fell into a display of neat butter crocks and round soft new cheeses. She saw her smallest niece standing a few feet away, proffering her precious shilling to a man in charge of a veritable Tower of Babel, comprised of caged singing birds.

'Kate,' Nat was saying, briskly scolding, 'what are you thinking of, to run away like that? You can't possibly want one of these.'

'I do,' said Kate. Her warm brown eyes, huge and imploring, turned up to her brother's face. 'I remembered he had a linnet, but he hasn't got any linnets today, and please, oh please, may I have that one?'

'That one', to Patience's amusement, was undoubtedly the most exotic and expensive item for sale in the entire market, if not in Bath. It sat chained to a perch in the freedom of the air, hunched and malevolent, and scratched its wicked-looking, curved beak with a scaly blue talon that contrasted oddly with its sharp green plumage.

Nat began to laugh. 'The popinjay? Oh, Kate, you can't be serious. That will cost a great deal more than a shilling.'

'Aye, for certain, sir,' said the bird-seller, with a hopeful glint in his eye. 'All the way from the forests of Hy Brazil she d'come, little maid, and cost I dear in the getting. Far-vaught and dear-abought, she be, and not a penny less than five pound in gold will I take for her, sir. Tis robbery plain and simple, even at that price.'

The bird shuffled round on its perch, revealing a large patch of plucked, pink flesh. Kate gave a little gasp of sympathy, but Nat said decisively, 'I'm not having any beast with mange in my house.'

By this time Silence, with Tabby, Rachael and Mally, had arrived. She took in the scene with one brief glance, and added her opinion to her stepson's. 'No, Kate – no. You have no more than a shilling, and that's far too little. Besides, the bird is clearly sick, and what will you do if it dies?'

The bird-seller, plainly growing desperate, hastened to assure her that it was not unwell, that it had merely pulled its own feathers out of itself from boredom, and that what was needed to restore it was the company of a lissom little maid to enliven its days.

'No,' said Silence again. 'No, Kate, I am sorry, but it isn't possible. Look, there's a robin in that cage – why don't you have that instead?'

But Kate, her heart fixed on the popinjay, would not even consider it. Nor, somewhat to everyone's surprise, did she disgrace the St. Barbes with a display of infant fury, shrieking and stamping her feet, such as was becoming increasingly common at Wintercombe. She just stared longingly and fixedly at the emerald parrot, disconsolate on its perch, while the bird-seller attempted, with growing urgency, to persuade the adults to change their minds. By degrees, the price came down, the bird's virtues were extolled, its perfect imitation of human speech, its docility, its ideal qualities as a child's pet.

'Buggered if I'll do that!' said the parrot suddenly, fixing Nat with an evil eye. 'A health to the King!'

'That settles it,' said Silence, with finality. 'A profane and Royalist papingo – we'd never live it down. And we must be late – Lady Harington is expecting us at eleven, and we have to find William and Deb. Kate, take my hand, and Rachael's – oh, I'm sorry, Binnick, but it's impossible, and much too expensive. I pay some of the servants only a little more, and for a whole year's work. We'll find something else to spend your shilling on.'

Kate, spoilt and wayward Kate, did not wail her disappointment, but Patience was touched to see that tears were pouring down her face. Her head hanging, utterly woebegone, she stumbled away between her mother and her sister, Mally following after, laden with baskets. Patience, surprised at her feeling of sympathy – for her own childhood had been one of harsh and dreary obedience, in contrast to the affectionate and loving indulgence which surrounded Kate – was preparing to follow them, when she became aware of conspiracy.

'I've got five shillings,' Tabby was saying urgently to Nat. 'How much have you got?'

'Quite a lot – six crowns, and several shillings,' said her half-brother. 'More fool us, but she's heart-broken – and I can't wait to see Jack Harington's face when the bird says its piece.'

Patience, staring at him in amazement, saw an expression of lively mischief on his face, and Tabby, so quiet and shy and retiring, was sparkling in answer. She realised that there were moods and dimensions to this family that she had, up until now, entirely failed to discern. But certainly, the idea of a swearing and Royalist popinjay in residence at supposedly Puritan, godly Wintercombe was a very attractive one, full of enticing possibilities. Entering into the spirit of the conspiracy, she fished in the soft leather purse at her waist. 'Here. All this must surely be enough.'

The bird-seller's hopes were beginning to revive. 'Four pounds to ee, kind sir, and give that little maid of yourn a treat.'

'That's strange,' said Nat witheringly. 'You'd reduced the price to two, just now – and this is all you'll get, because it's all we have. Take it or leave it.' He held out his hand, his six crowns and a little pile of shillings balanced on it, pale and shining in the morning sun.

The bird-seller knew when to grasp at a rare opportunity. He took the coins greedily, checked each one with his teeth, and nodded. 'Very well, sir, she be yourn. And you can have the perch, and that sack of grain, all thrown in. And I d'hope the little maid d'like her gift, sir.'

'Oh, she will,' said Nat. 'And if it dies within the month, I'll come back and hang it round your neck as a warning to any other customers you might have been fortunate enough to ensnare. And you can deliver it tomorrow, to me, Sir Nathaniel St. Barbe, at Wintercombe in Philip's Norton, and I'll have another crown for you then. Understand?'

'Aye, sir, don't ee fear, I'll be there with she,' said the bird-seller, pocketing the coins and beaming from one side of his face to the other. 'Thank ee, sir — thank ee.'

'And whether that was a mistake or no,' said Nat to Patience and Tabby, as they hurried to catch up with the rest of their party, 'only time will tell. But what with the popinjay, and Tom Wickham, this day and the next are going to be full of surprises.'

*

Silence, sitting in the winter parlour that evening, the door and windows open on the warm fragrant garden, thick and bright with June roses, had no conception of the plots which her devious stepson was hatching behind her back. Nor did Patience, demurely trimming a new collar with some lace she had bought in Bath, attempt to enlighten her. Through the other door, which was open, Nat was bringing the estate accounts up to date. They could hear the quiet, methodical scratch of his quill, mingled with the birdsong in the garden, the distant calls and shouts of Deb, William and Kate as they played some game in the orchard, and the nearer but more fragile sounds of Tabby at her evening practice on the virginals in her mother's chamber. Nat, for some reason, had asked that supper be served a little later than usual, and Silence was beginning to feel quite hungry. She glanced at the clock on the mantelpiece. Perhaps half an hour before eight, and the faintest, savoury tang from the direction of the kitchens was beginning to whet her appetite.

She tried to concentrate on her gardening book. Every year, she made notes of what seeds she had sown, and where, and how they had fared. All the stresses and upheavals of May had interrupted her usually meticulous and accurate records. Now, a month and more after sowing, it was hard to remember what she and Diggory, the gardener, had done.

To add to her difficulties, she could not fix her mind on the task. It kept returning, like a dog on a treadmill, to the dinner at the Haringtons' Bath house. It could indeed have been much, much worse: the children, even Kate, had behaved with quiet decorum, and Patience had seemed as meek and mild as a mouse. But Rachael, who had been nervous and bad-tempered all morning, had retreated into her apparently sullen shell, and spoke only in monosyllables. Silence knew full well that it was the overbearing presence of Lady Dyoness Harington that had inhibited her step-daughter. True, Rachael was not yet at the stage of easy conversation with her betrothed, but at least they could now make polite small talk. Her future mother-in-law, however, was the daughter of an earl, and had a haughtily grand manner to match, despite her genuine attempts to put Silence and her family at their ease. There were two other Harington children present, Will, who was twenty, and Phoebe, a year younger than Tabby, a thin serious girl who had nothing to say unless addressed directly. Silence, who was extremely sensitive to moods and atmospheres, had wondered, as the awkward occasion progressed with tedium to its end, whether Lady Dyoness had in fact approved this arrangement for her elder son. Certainly, she was courtesy itself, but her demeanour told a different story, and poor Rachael was obviously thoroughly intimidated. And if Lady Dyoness had been doubtful before, then how much more reluctant must she be now, to support her husband's choice of this sulky, graceless young woman for her beloved Jack.

It was such a tangle, Silence thought, sighing. Whatever happened, whether the marriage took place or not, Rachael would be hurt. She still did not know the details of her father's will, for Nat and her stepmother had agreed that it would be best if she were kept in ignorance of it. Quite apart from its effect on Rachael's desire to marry Jack Harington, Silence knew that she should not be told of Sir George's efforts to coerce her into that marriage. Let the girl retain her loving memories of her father, untainted by the true nature of his regard. For George, as Silence had discovered to her cost, love was always dependent on obedience. He had died without realising that his wife and his children could not be forced into affection, and that love is in no wise conditional.

Someone knocked on the study door. She heard Nat's instruction to enter, and the painstakingly clear and cultured voice of Carpenter, the butler. 'A gentleman to see you, sir – he says he is expected.'

'Ah, yes,' said Nat.

Silence, listening with unabashed curiosity, heard him go to the door and out towards the hall. She glanced at her sister, and surprised a look of gleeful anticipation on her face. 'Patience,' she said suspiciously, 'do you know anything about this?'

In a way she vividly remembered from their childhood, her sister's expression smoothed instantly to a demure, bland mask. 'It is something that Nat has arranged, I think,' she said innocently, and bent her head industriously over her sewing.

Silence looked at her, unable to suppress a smile. She said affectionately, 'You can't fool me. What have you and Nat been hatching between you?'

'Nothing,' said her sister, blinking with guiltless surprise. As Silence continued to stare at her, she burst into sudden giggles, irrepressible as ever. 'It was Nat's idea not to tell you – it's that old friend he met in Bath.'

'But which old friend?' Silence asked in bewilderment. At that moment, Nat walked through the door, ushering in a tall young man in country russets, with the dusty bloom of travel on his breeches. As Silence laid down her book and got to her feet, he doffed his plain brown felt hat and bowed.

Patience, glancing curiously at her sister, saw that she had gone suddenly white. Then the colour washed abruptly back into her face, and she said, obviously scarce able to believe her eyes, 'It's – it's Lieutenant Wickham, isn't it?'

'Indeed it is, my lady,' said their visitor, smiling more broadly. 'But no lieutenant now – I have long since exchanged my sword for a ploughshare. I hope I have not startled you – I did not realise that Nat had omitted to tell you that he had met me this morning in Bath.'

'I'm sorry,' said Nat, not in the least apologetic. 'But I thought it a good opportunity to surprise you.'

'Or to put me in danger of an apoplexy? More fool you,' said Silence. She had, with something of an effort, regained a little of her usual composure. 'Poor Master Wickham – used as a pawn for your mischief. So Nat met you in Bath, and invited you over for supper? I hope he also remembered to ask you to stay the night.'

'Of course I did,' said her stepson, grinning. 'I was relying on your sense of hospitality and duty.'

'What nonsense – Master Wickham will always be welcome in this house, and I distinctly recall telling him so, six years ago.'

'I insist,' said the former soldier, with the pleasant smile she now remembered so well. 'Please, my lady, call me Tom. All my friends do likewise.'

'Why not, indeed – you are unquestionably a friend,' Silence said. She glanced at Patience, who stood, butter unmelted in her mouth, by the empty summer hearth. 'My sister Patience Woods – may I present Master Tom Wickham, who was once part of the King's garrison in this house, and so should have been our enemy, and was not.'

'We have already met,' said Wickham.

Silence smiled at her wayward sister. 'I thought you might have done. Well, Tom, you must be hungry after your ride — you'll be delighted to learn that Darby is still with us, and cooking better than ever, and supper will shortly be set on the table. Patience, can you call the children in from the garden? And find Rachael, she is probably reading in her chamber. After eating, we must talk over old times together, and Tom can tell us what he has been doing since we saw him last.'

Patience, rounding up her nephew and nieces from the orchard, where they had contrived the usual tally of torn clothes, grass stains and grazed hands, wondered afresh why Tom Wickham had remained on such friendly terms with the family whose house he had once invaded. She remembered, vaguely, the stories of what had happened at Wintercombe during that terrible year: privation, terror and murder had all played their part, according to the hints dropped by Joseph, and the distinctly brief accounts in her sister's letters. Silence had been fortunate to survive such an experience, and it was a miracle that she had done so with her sanity, as well as her family and household, more or less intact. How, then, did the former Lieutenant Wickham come to be a friend, a visitor welcomed with surprise and delight?

She would have to find out. She doubted that Silence would tell her, even if asked directly, for her sister was not usually forthcoming on matters which obviously affected her so deeply. Perhaps she was in love with the lieutenant, Patience thought idly, towing a reluctant Kate up the terrace steps. But surely not — he must be ten years younger than she is, he'd have been a mere boy then, and not especially handsome either — he's just an ordinary farmer now. For a moment, she felt a twinge of envy for her sister, whose otherwise humdrum life had, for a space, held the excitement, danger and adventure which she herself, in her wilder moments, had craved, and which had led her into intrigue against the Commonwealth.

The children, cleaned and tidied, appeared punctually in the dining parlour, with its dark wainscot panelling and the fine carved wooden fireplace. They stood in a neat group beneath the stiff, old fashioned portraits of their grandparents, Sir Samuel and Dame Ursula St. Barbe, and smiled in friendly fashion at the tall stranger. William had only the vaguest memory of the soldiers, and none at all of Wickham: after all, he had been just three years old when they left. Deb had some recollection, imperfect and imprecise, but she beamed at him and assured him, with confidence, that she remembered him very well. Tabby, who had been nine, could say it in truth: she told him so, shyly, and added in a voice so quiet he could barely hear it, 'You were a friend of Captain Hellier, weren't you? Do you know where he is now?'

Patience, alert and observant, wondered why both Nat and Wickham glanced at Silence, but her sister's face, calm and unemotional as usual, revealed nothing. Then Tom said, 'At the moment, no, I do not exactly. But I have had several letters from him over the years, and so far as I know, he is well. He taught you the virginals, did he not? I remember him speaking highly of your talent. Do you still play?'

'Yes, I do,' said Tabby, and added, with a sudden and brilliant smile that reminded Patience vividly of Kate, 'I would love to play for you later, Master Wickham, if you would like it.'

'Nothing would please me more,' he said, and received a still more dazzling smile in response.

Silence, presiding over the supper table as her family and their guest worked their way with enthusiasm through pigeon pie, an onion tart and a sallet of fresh peas, endives and sundry herbs, thought that Nat's little surprise could not have been more welcome. On reflection, she might have liked some warning, some indication that a friend from the past was about to return to their lives, but she had managed to conceal most of her amazement – and her initial, bitter disappointment that it was only Wickham. She remembered him well: a nice boy, the same age as Sam had been, reluctant to acquiesce in the brutality of his commanding officer, and a friend to the man who had been her lover.

Tabby had asked him about Nick, and she wondered if her face had betrayed her. Certainly, if they had been able to hear the thundering of her heart, they would all have discovered her feelings, that she had tried these six years to suppress. Nat knew of her affair, and so did Rachael. She had often wondered if Tabby, quiet and observant, had guessed it too. She glanced at Wickham, seated on her right hand, and saw his eyes resting on Kate, who was chattering happily at the end of the table. He had known Nick well, he had been his friend. Had he also known of his Captain's love for the Puritan lady of the house?

From the way he was looking at Kate, it certainly seemed that he might be speculating. The child resembled her sister Tabby more than anyone else at the table, but she was also Nick's daughter, marked as his by her warm, chestnut-brown eyes. Silence felt suddenly uncomfortable. How long would it be before her secret became common knowledge?

Stop thinking like a wife, she told herself with annoyance. You are a widow now, and no one has dominion over you. Nor do you care anything for the opinion of those who are not your friends. No one can touch you — scandal cannot affect you.

But still, she thought of Rachael, silently and urgently eating her pie on Nat's left, and knew with sadness that scandal was nothing, compared to the effect her affair had had on her stepdaughter, and upon the girl's feelings for Kate.

If Wickham knew, or guessed, he would be sympathetic: she was sure of that. He had news of him, or so he had told Tabby. Soon, she might hear in more detail of what her one-time lover had been doing in the six years since he had left Wintercombe. She was a widow, but she still had no right to him. His wife and children had prior claim to his love and his care. She would never seek him out, nor attempt to remind him of the overwhelming love and passion they had once shared, nor tell him of the existence of his daughter. She had learned strength, in the years without him, for her own sake and her children's. She did not wish, now, to re-open old wounds that were better healed. But she wanted, with all her heart, to hear of him, and to know that he was well.

Despite their protests, the younger children were sent off to bed, and Silence gave instructions that Nat's old chamber — he had moved into the one occupied by his father until his death — be prepared for their guest. Then she led the way to her own room, where Mally waited with fruit and wine and sweet comfits set out on the table, and the windows flung wide to the soft summer evening.

Tabby, unprompted, sat down at the virginals. She had long since dispensed with music books for much of her playing, preferring either to learn a piece by heart, or to improvise a fresh pattern of sound around a well-known melody. Her gift was very considerable, as Nick Hellier had recognised years ago, and she practised for the joy of it, all music being her obsession. She had never learned to play another instrument, however, for her father had not appreciated her ability, and had considered lessons with a music teacher to be a complete waste of time and money. But Hellier had given her a solid basis on which to perfect her skill, and the music books he had left for her, in addition to those which had belonged to her grandfather or the few she had bought herself, had extended her range and provided an extensive repertoire that had nourished her for years.

She began, softly, with a slow and melancholy Italian fantasia, easier to perform than most from that country. Rachael did not like her to play, for she had tuned her feelings to match her father's, and had derided Tabby's musical skills as soon as Sir George had made it clear that he did. She ignored the glares of the older girl, and played with sad intensity, feeling her sorrow pour from her fingers into sound. Over the years, she had almost forgotten Nick Hellier. She could not now recall his face, only the sound of his voice, and the scarlet cloak he had worn, and above all his delight in music, and his pleasure at his ability to transfer some of that skill and joy to the eager child she once had been. And he loved Mother, thought Tabby, glancing at Silence, and she loved him, and now they are parted for ever — and somehow, somehow, I must find him and tell him that Father is dead, or she will be unhappy for the rest of her life. Now Master Wickham is here, he can tell me where Captain Hellier is, and I can write to him.

In blissful ignorance of her eldest daughter's plans, Silence sat in her favourite chair by the south window, and listened to Tom Wickham's account of the years since leaving Wintercombe. After their surrender, the pitiful remnants of his regiment had scatttered, and he had gone with Hellier and the other officers to Oxford, whither most of those still devoted to the King's cause had made their way. He had then received a letter from his father, who owned a large manor farm near Glastonbury. His older brother had died suddenly, of a fever, and Tom was now the sole heir. His father had appealed to him to make his peace with Parliament, pay the fines imposed upon him, and come home.

Not unwillingly, he had obeyed. The money demanded of him to compound was large, and some land had to be sold to pay for it. There were several years of comparative hardship, as he and his ageing father struggled to mend the damage caused by the war, and to make the land once more profitable. Sadly, old John Wickham had died just as success became assured, and now his son, with the help of his mother and several trusted servants, had achieved a degree of comfort and security. He had often been to Bath in the past with his father, who liked to take the waters several times a year for his rheumatism, but had decided not to visit Wintercombe, suspecting that Sir George would not make him welcome. /

'I don't think he would have,' said Nat. 'My father preferred to consort with those of like mind, and I doubt very much that he'd have proffered any hospitality to someone who, in his view, had made overfree use of it in the past!' He gestured at the wide, pleasant, airy chamber, and the sunlit garden. 'Well, Tom, you see Wintercombe restored, and at peace — what do you think?'

'It's changed indeed,' said Tom, with some enthusiasm. 'As are you all — save for you, my lady, you have not altered in the least.'

'Not at all,' Nat said, grinning. 'For we have all grown much older, and I'll swear she's getting younger.'

'What nonsense,' Silence told him. 'Your flattery is outrageous, Nat, even for you. What do you want?'

'Nothing,' he said, his eyes wide and innocent. She laughed, and turned to Tom. 'I'm afraid we are all sadly lax here, and I hope you do not mind.' Her manner was pleasant and friendly: only someone who knew her very well could have detected the agony of tension within that gracious exterior. Like a blushing girl, shy and terrified by the pangs of first love, she longed to hear his name, and yet feared to, in case her tongue, or her face, would betray the strength of her feelings. Why she was so afraid, when all those present knew, or must surely have guessed, of her past affair with Nick Hellier, she could not imagine. She was only aware of the knot of apprehension within her breast, the sticky sweat on her palms and the racing of her heart.

Nat knew. Nat could always detect her moods and emotions. He glanced at her, and smiled so quickly that most people would have missed it, before turning back to Tom Wickham. 'You said earlier that you had been in contact with Captain Hellier. What has he been doing?'

Silence listened avidly, with the image in her mind, sharp and hard and clear as a diamond, of a man slightly built, brown-haired and chestnut-eyed, reckless and smiling, who had so astonishingly fallen in love with her, a dowdy Puritan housewife. She had prepared herself to hear of his wife and his children, but Tom made no mention of them, and she realised as he spoke that they must play as little part in Nick's life now, as she herself did.

'He stayed in Oxford, I know that, after I returned to Somerset,' Wickham was telling Nat. 'I don't exactly know what he did after that — I heard nothing from him for a couple of years. Then I had a letter saying that he was in the Low Countries, and had been fighting in the German wars. He gave me no address, and there was no more until late last year, when he wrote to me from Scotland.'

'Scotland?' It was Rachael's voice, loud and squeaky with surprise. Tom glanced at her, and she blushed at once, turning her face away. A long, long time ago, as a green girl hardly more than a child, she had felt the first sharp pains of calf-love for Nick Hellier: only to discover, in the most painful manner, that he had instead embarked on an affair with her stepmother. She felt bitterly ashamed, now, of her foolishness, of her lovesick mooning over a man who had been nearly twice her age: but still, five or six years later, her memory of him was surprisingly vivid.

'Yes, Scotland,' said Wickham. 'He was most uninformative, but I can only assume that he is with the King of Scots.'

There was complete quiet within the chamber. Silence felt that the sudden wild thumping of her heart must be audible to everyone. The eldest son of the late, executed King Charles had gathered a following and gone to Scotland, the land of his Stuart forebears, where the Presbyterians had welcomed him and, in exchange for certain concessions regarding the enforced practice of their worship in England, had crowned him King of Scots. The Council of State, unable to ignore this looming threat on their borders, had despatched General Cromwell and the army north, to deal with it. This they had done with their usual ruthless efficiency. Report had spoken of several battles and skirmishes, in which the Scots had been soundly defeated. It had been common knowledge for months, however, that the young King planned to invade England, to take his rightful place on the empty throne. And it was for conspiracy to this end that the plotters in London had been taken up.

A conspiracy, of course, in which Patience had been involved. Silence looked at her sister. She sat in the windowseat, her legs tucked up beneath her like a contented cat, and on her face was a thoughtful expression which, to Silence, boded no good. Oh, no, she thought despairingly. Please, Imp, amid all my other problems and worries, do not begin your treasonous plotting again!

'And he is well?' Nat was saying, intuitively sensing which questions his stepmother would most like to ask. Wickham shrugged. 'He was when he wrote – but that was in December, and there have lately been several minor skirmishes. You know as well as I do of the varied fortunes of war, and it is six months since he wrote.'

I would know, Silence thought, feeling her nails dig tight into her palms. I would *know* if he was dead – I am sure of it, as sure as I am of the sun rising. And she prayed, the words burning in her mind, for his safety, and for his happiness: even if she were never to see him again, he would be for ever dear to her.

Wickham had no more information to impart, and the talk drifted to other matters. But much later, when all had gone off to their beds, she sat curled in the windowseat where her sister had been, gazing out of the open window into the dark garden, alive with the subdued squeaks and rustles of its night life, and thought of Nick. Sometimes it all seemed to be a dream, so impossible was it now to believe that she had once loved, and been loved in return. She had entered willingly into adultery, the greatest of sins that a wife could commit. She had only to look at Kate, to know that, yes, once she had been mad, and risked her children, her position, her home, for a man not her husband; and that, given the chance, she would do so again, and gladly, for she had learned from him the nature of happiness, and the true import of love.

But the opportunity would never come again. A realist at heart, she could not hope for any more such joys, but she had her memories, and Kate, and that small, warm, comforting glow about her heart, for once she had been beloved, and no power of Heaven, or Earth, could take that glory away from her.

'Oh, Nick,' she whispered to the owl-haunted air. 'Wherever you may be – keep safe, and happy, and prosperous, and I shall remember you with love, for the rest of my days.'

CHAPTER SIX

'A rare parrot-teacher'

(Much Ado About Nothing)

'There is a Personage at the door, my lady,' said Carpenter, his voice, indeed his whole bearing, redolent of disgusted disapproval. 'He claims to be here by order of Sir Nathaniel, to deliver a Bird. Shall I turn him away?'

Silence stared at him in amazement, her mind wrenched rudely away from the peaceful contemplation of the contents of her still-room. 'A *bird*? You mean, some poultry?'

'No, my lady. It is not a creature with which I am familiar, but I believe it to be some sort of popinjay.'

Mally, picking earwigs out of a basket of rose petals, let out a squawk of astonishment, and then clapped a hand over her mouth. Silence stared at the butler, willing the laughter rising up within her to subside: she did not wish to lower her dignity in front of this haughty and pompous young man. 'A popinjay? Is it a brilliant green, with some feathers missing?'

'It is indeed, my lady, and a most disreputable-looking bird. Shall I turn the man away?'

'No – no, I'll see him, since Sir Nathaniel has had to go over to Hassage this morning, after those missing heifers. Tell him that I will be with him shortly.'

When Carpenter had gone, still radiating disapproval, she untied her apron and threw it, with some exasperation, on to a chair. 'I might have known it – Tom Wickham wasn't the only surprise Nat hatched for me yesterday.'

'He've bought that there popinjay for Mistress Kate?' said Mally, briskly squashing an earwig between her thumb and the table. 'Well, tisn't my place to say so, m'lady, but your little maid will turn out despeard forweend if all on us do spoil her so.'

'Undoubtedly she will – she shows signs of it already,' Silence said. 'But since Sir George died, she has been so subdued – and she didn't throw a tantrum yesterday when I said she couldn't have the wretched bird, she just wept and wept – she cried herself to sleep last night, thinking of it, because Deb had reminded her of it again.

And now it seems Nat has been conspiring to undo all my good intentions, and I really haven't the heart to send it away.'

'Then more fool you, m'lady,' said Mally, who, by virtue of nine years in Silence's service and friendship, was often extremely forthright in private. 'A popinjay! What in the name of Heaven are we to do with one of they?'

'Keep it,' said Silence, with resignation. 'And she'll probably be bored with it inside a week, or it'll die and she'll be inconsolable, if I know Kate. And to cap it all, the bird talks — well, you heard it, Mally. What on earth will Parson Willis think of a popinjay that swears like a trooper and toasts the King?'

'He'll think you should have wrung its neck, most like,' said her maid drily. 'And I can't say as how I'd blame he.'

The bird-seller stood in the hall, distinctly ill at ease under Carpenter's hostile eye. It had been raining earlier that morning, and he presented a most bedraggled and disreputable appearance. In contrast, the parrot, obviously enjoying its new surroundings, sat on its perch and looked about it with bright, interested eyes. As soon as Silence entered from the screens, the bird uttered a wild, soul-wrenching shriek, and flapped its wings urgently. Several emerald feathers descended to the floor, and one of the maids appeared from the other side of the hall, wide-eyed and startled, one hand to her breast. 'Oh, that fair gallersed I! Whatever be that bugabo, m'lady?'

'It's no fiend, Meg — it's a popinjay that Sir Nathaniel has bought,' Silence told her.

'A health to His Majesty! A health to His Majesty!' squawked the parrot, its head on one side. 'A pox on all Puritans!'

Silence dared not look at Carpenter, nor at the maid Meg, who came of a very respectable and godly family. She fixed the bird-dealer with a stern eye, and said firmly, 'Well, I see you have brought the bird. Sir Nathaniel is not here at present, and I know nothing of this creature. What must be done to keep it in good sort?'

'Her d'like water to drink, m'lady, and good grain to eat, and nuts and apples if ee do have them, and her will do well enough,' said the poor man, visibly cringing with embarrassment.

'And if I do not like what it says? Can it be taught to unlearn it?'

'I don't rightly know, m'lady. I ain't never had nothing like she afore — I had her from a gentleman who was going into foreign parts.'

'And cheaply too, I don't doubt,' said Silence drily. 'You refer to the bird as 'she' — how can you tell that it is female?'

'Her laid an egg once, m'lady, or so that gentleman said.'

'I see. Well, Sir Nathaniel has bought her, and so I must accept her. Carpenter, take this man to the kitchen, and make sure he is given some refreshment before he leaves.'

'But, m'lady, Sir Nathaniel — he said as how there'd be a crown for me when I delivered she!'

'Then my butler will see that you are given one,' said Silence. 'Thank you, Carpenter.'

As the two men left the hall, she failed to avoid Mally's eye. Mistress and maid stared at each other for a moment, and then burst into laughter, while Meg, clutching her broom, looked from one to the other in bewilderment.

'Health to His Majesty!' the parrot said cheerfully. It ran up and down the length of its perch, rattling its chain, and uttered another ear-cracking whistle.

Mally, tears streaming down her freckled face, collapsed into a chair. 'Oh, m'lady, m'lady — whatever will Parson say?'

'You said he'd tell us to wring its neck,' Silence reminded her. 'Well, I could easily wring Nat's neck. We shall have to keep it away from Master Harington when he comes to call, for I doubt he'll want to marry into a family with a parrot, particularly not a Royalist parrot.'

'So it won't be staying in the hall,' said Mally, eyeing the bird, who had just left abundant evidence of its presence on the rush matting below the perch.

'No — I think my chamber is the best place. Although what Misty will think of it, I cannot imagine.'

'Maybe her will solve all your problems, m'lady,' said Mally darkly. 'She d'like to catch birds, after all.'

'Give us a kiss!' the parrot shrieked, and followed it with a howl of maniacal laughter that raised the hairs on Silence's neck, and drove poor Meg in terror from the hall.

A little later, the erring bird was duly installed on its perch in the upstairs chamber, busily cracking grain in its wicked-looking beak. Mally had spread an old cloth beneath, to catch the debris, and offered it, somewhat dubiously, a bowl of water. The reactions of the cat and dog were more extreme. Misty, every separate hair on her body stark with fright, leapt up the bed-curtains and took refuge on the canopy, from which safe vantage-point her head could be seen, peering over the edge with eyes as round as an owl's. Lily, intrigued and excited, jumped around the perch uttering enthusiastic yaps, earning a torrent of abuse from the parrot which stretched even Mally's eyes. At last, however, some calm prevailed. Lily was ordered to her usual place by the hearth, and Misty coaxed down from her refuge with a piece of sweet biscuit, a titbit she loved.

'I think your point is answered, Mally,' Silence said, when it had become apparent, after repeated attempts at introduction, that Misty was not willingly going to venture within ten feet of this new and terrifying creature. 'I don't think our popinjay is in any danger at all. If anything, it's the other way about.'

There was a tentative tap on the door, and Nat put his head hesitantly around it, an expression of such comical guilt and apprehension on his face that Silence could not help laughing. 'Am I still welcome here? I see you are in possession of the beast.'

'Nat, you are incorrigible – and Kate will be hopelessly spoilt. What are we to *do* with this infernal bird?'

'Keep it, I suppose – I don't reckon it would make very good eating,' said her stepson, shutting the door behind him. 'I'm sorry, but I couldn't resist it – the thought of Jack Harington's face made it a necessity.'

'Jack Harington isn't going to see it, not if I can help it.'

'No? But I thought that would have suited your purpose admirably,' said Nat, grinning. 'Still, I'm sure we can contrive something. Have you been subjected to all of its repertoire yet?'

'We've heard quite enough, thank you,' said Silence firmly. 'Even Mally was shocked, and I thought that Carpenter would give his notice there and then. Nat, you *know* what Kate's like, not to mention William and Deb – how could you even think of introducing a profane parrot into the household?'

'Easily,' said Nat. He put out an exploratory finger, and the popinjay, quick as thought, gave it a sharp nip with that evil beak.

As he recoiled, Silence snorted. 'That serves you right indeed. Not only will it teach the children to swear and blaspheme, but it'll take large pieces out of them as it does so.'

'I'll have it in my chamber if you like,' said her stepson, retreating to a safe distance. Silence shook her head. 'Oh, no – why should you have all the amusement to yourself? But if it disturbs my peace, it goes.'

'I agree,' said Nat. He was, she saw, quite unrepentant: besides, he was well aware of that reckless, hidden side of her character, that delighted in the unusual, and even the shocking. 'Does Kate know that it is here yet?'

'No. She and the other children are with Patience in the winter parlour. She is apparently attempting to teach them French.'

'*French*? Your sister can speak *French*?'

'Well, yes, she can,' Silence told him, a little sheepishly. 'I know it doesn't figure very highly on the list of approved Puritan accomplishments, but somehow she must have persuaded Joseph to pay for lessons. She suggested imparting her knowledge to the children, and I agreed.'

'William can barely write in English, let alone a foreign language,' said Nat. 'What a surprising person your pretty Impatience is. I wouldn't have thought that she would have the, uh, patience to apply herself to the study of French.'

'She probably hasn't. If I know her, the French master was young and handsome and gave her smiles and curls a good report. And, yes, I did notice your pun, and, no, I did not think it worthy of comment — too many people have derived too much amusement from our names, over the years.' Silence sat down on the windowseat, and stared up at the slender, black-clad figure of her stepson. 'Do you approve of her?'

'Patience, or the parrot? Oh, Patience amuses me — such a wondrous mixture of innocence and sophistication. She even contributed some coin towards the purchase of the parrot. And, by the way, it was Tabby's idea to buy it, so it is her blame entirely — and she can have the naming of it. I know what I'd call it, though.'

'And what is that?' Silence asked. Nat grinned, knowing that he was about to shock her. 'If I had my way, I'd call it Ursula.'

'Nat! You can't give your grandmother's name to a *parrot*!'

'Why not? They have so much in common — both venomous, abusive, malicious and terrifying old birds.'

'You can't,' said Silence, trying unsuccessfully not to laugh. 'You really can't. I can probably, if I'm extremely lucky, and even more extremely careful, explain away a parrot, even one with Royalist views and a profane vocabulary. I cannot face the servants knowing that it has been christened in memory of my mother-in-law.'

'Who has been dead for six years, and therefore can't very well object. No, I do take your point,' said Nat, sitting down at the table by her windowseat. 'And Tabby can always be trusted to find a suitable name. Also, it occurs to me that the problem of spoiling Kate can be avoided if we treat the parrot as a gift to you, not to her. It won't make her any less delighted, and at the same time she has not entirely had her own way.'

Silence smiled wryly. 'A good idea. I know she is too much indulged, and I do try not to — but I find it very difficult.'

'I understand,' said Nat. His eyes met hers, very blue and direct. 'Did it please you, to have such unexpected news of Nick?'

'Oh, Nat,' said Silence. To her embarrassment, her eyes filled with sudden unwanted tears. She turned her face away and wiped them fiercely with her cuff, like one of her children. 'Oh, Nat, of *course* it did — you can't imagine what it means to me, to hear that he is alive and well, even if he is with the King of Scots. And although we'll never meet again, all I want is for him to be happy.' She decided that her face was now sufficiently calm to return to his scrutiny, and met his gaze with something of her usual self-possession. 'And that *is* all I want. I may be free, but he is not. I have no claims on him, and no right to him. By now he has probably forgotten me entirely. And for Kate's sake, it should remain thus. She was so fond of your father — how would it damage her, to discover that she was not his daughter at all, but another man's bastard foisted on him without his knowledge?'

'I agree, that when put like that it sounds despicable,' said Nat. 'But it is your decision, Silence, and I respect it. Like you, I love Kate dearly, despite all her naughty tricks, and I would not see her hurt. But you will have to accustom yourself to other reminders of Nick — I told Tom Wickham that he should make a longer visit, when work on his farm permits, and he will undoubtedly take me up on it. Do you mind?'

'Of course not — he's a very pleasant young man.' Silence paused, a sudden idea springing into her mind, and then added wickedly, 'He might be just the sort of steady, hard-working husband that Patience needs.'

Nat gave a shout of laughter. 'Patience? *Patience*? Oh, poor Tom — if only he knew! You can't want to shackle him to your mischievous little sister — it's grossly unfair.'

'To Tom, or to Patience?'

'To them both. She'd be bored inside a week, and gallivanting with half of Glastonbury the next. Don't even think of it, my dear Silence — your Patience wants someone much more exotic than a plain Somerset farmer.'

'I know she does,' said his stepmother. 'I was only teasing – and don't you dare mention it to her!'

'My lips will be sealed,' Nat promised. 'Nor will I breathe a word to Tom, when next he comes.'

*

June turned to July, and the roses in Silence's garden gave way to poppies and lavender. There was some wind, more sun, and a great deal of rain, which at least saved Diggory, the ancient gardener, and his assistants the labour of watering the terraces and knots. Much hay was spoilt by a sudden downpour, and had to be left longer to dry in the fields. In Nat's opinion, they would be fortunate indeed if most of the crop did not turn musty. A large estate such as Wintercombe could absorb these unexpected losses: the smaller farmers, eking out a living on an acre or two of close or meadow in the fields around Philip's Norton, would not be so fortunate.

The household had adjusted to the death of its head with surprising swiftness. Of course, he had been ill for months, and Nat had managed the farm in all but name for much longer, but Silence still felt guilty at the easy way in which her husband's demise had been assimilated into the passing events of the year. Something that should have been devastating and momentous had actually had as little effect, in the long term, as a pebble thrown into still waters.

Except of course, for the will he had left.

Master Harley, as Nat had instructed, had made enquiries, and had even visited London for a short time to consult with his colleagues at Lincoln's Inn. At least once a week, his tall lean figure could be seen, riding up the track from the Wellow Lane on his handsome brown mare and, after a month or so, Silence had to admit that she rather welcomed his visits.

She was not lonely: it was nothing to do with that at all. Nat had been very much preoccupied with the farm and all his new responsibilities, and Patience had not yet become the companion for whom she had longed. For her sister could never know, and would assuredly never understand, about certain episodes in Silence's past, at present occupying her mind. They could chatter amicably together about their shared childhood, about the children and life in London and in the country, but for Silence there was always that secret barrier, the threshold she dared not let Patience cross. In truth, she had absolutely no idea of how her sister might react, if told of her adultery, and about the truth of Kate's parent-age. Nor, if she were honest with herself, did she feel that she yet knew Patience well enough to trust her with such a momentous secret.

She knew that she was still thinking like a wife, and a Puritan one at that. She knew also that Patience, the devious plotter, was probably perfectly capable of concealing the truth. But somehow, she could not bring herself to tell, to risk the arched brows, the knowing glance, the whispered entreaties to reveal more, that she feared. She was very fond of her sister, but that immaculate sophistication, allied, as Nat had pointed out, with a certain mis-chievous innocence, was surprisingly awesome.

She could not, of course, confide in Master Harley either, but then she had never been tempted to. He would spend an hour or so closeted with Nat, and then, as smooth and smiling as velvet, would climb the stairs to her sunny chamber, to take wine and cakes before his return to Bath. He always brought some titbit of news: the latest doings of the Mayor and Council, an interesting scandal, the weekly sermon, and details of events from the greater world outside this small corner of Somerset.

She had wondered about his reaction to the newest denizen of her chamber. Emerald, as Tabby had dubbed the parrot, had been preening herself when Harley was announced, two days after the bird's arrival. On the entrance of a stranger, she had let out one of her apoplexy-inducing shrieks, and had then surveyed the lawyer with interest before announcing fervently, 'Buggered if I will.'

This, if anything, would be a test of Jonathan Harley's character, and Silence had waited to see how he would react. Approvingly, she noted that he did not blench, nor wince at the profanity. He returned the parrot's scrutiny, and then said, 'I did not know that you were in possession of such a bird, my lady.'

'I was not, until two days ago. My stepson bought her as a gift for me, and because Kate had set her heart on her. The blacksmith in Norton is making a palatial cage.'

'A health to the King! A health to the King, you scurvy knave!'

'And is he also making a gag?' Harley queried.

Silence heard the note of dry mockery with appreciation, and smiled. 'That will probably be the next order. Master Harington has not yet encountered her, and may not like such a, uh, wide vocabulary.'

'I'm certain he will not,' said the lawyer. 'But I trust that Mistress Kate was pleased with her gift.'

'Beyond words,' said Silence, thinking of the child's rapt, wondering eyes, the glory of delight that had transformed her face. What was a little spoiling, when set against such overwhelming joy?

To the accompaniment of whistles, clicks and dark mutterings from Emerald on her perch, they discussed the weather, the price of bread, the paucity of really good preachers, a particularly juicy Bath scandal, and the rumoured imminence of a Scots invasion. If the unusual interest of Lady St. Barbe in affairs north of the Border surprised him, he did not show it. Instead, urbane and courteous, he told her what he knew, promised to do his best to discover more, and took his leave.

Over the next few weeks, Silence found herself looking forward to his visits with considerable anticipation. Sometimes he had no tidings for her at all, and she must take great care to hide the sharp pangs of disappointment which she felt. On other occasions the news was bad. There was a battle somewhere in Scotland, at a place with an outlandish name, during the last week of July. Harley spoke casually of terrible loss of Scottish life, and left her shaken, forced to conceal her anxiety, desperate to know whether Nick was safe, and no way at all of discovering more.

She sat, her heart sick within her, fighting for reason. Why feel like some silly lovelorn girl, for a man who had probably forgotten both her face and her name, who was six years in her past, whom she would never see again? And yet she could not help it, she yearned for him still: all the long labour to repress and disguise and deny her true feelings had gone for nothing at the moment when Tom Wickham had spoken of Nick. Now the pain was back with all its old agonising force, and she no longer had any defences against it.

She hardly listened as Master Harley, apparently in blissful ignorance of her anxiety, went on to inform her that Minister Love, the architect of the conspiracy in which Patience had been involved, had recently been tried and sentenced to death, along with one of his accomplices, but had won a brief reprieve. That worry seemed so remote now: her sister Impatience, smiling and delightful and enchanting the children, might have been another creature entirely from the stubborn, treacherous, ungovernable plotter who had so terrified poor Joseph. Now, all her fears were for Nick.

She dreamed that night, at first of pleasure, of a splendour that she had not experienced for six years, warm and beloved by a man whose eyes were autumn-coloured, like Kate's. And then the slender, lithe body in her bed changed before her horrified gaze to a torn and bleeding carcass that was dead, and yet not dead, for it grasped her hand and drew her towards it for a ghastly, blood-dabbled kiss . . .

She woke crying in terror, though not loudly enough to rouse Mally, asleep in her closet. Was Nick dead? Was that the meaning of this dreadful nightmare? Or was it God's way of telling her to desist from her sinful, wicked and lustful thoughts towards a man already married?

She was afraid to sleep, lest she dream again. She lay wakeful for the rest of the night, trying to force her rebellious heart into some acceptance of reality. As dawn came, she thought that she had at last succeeded, and she prayed, with silent and desperate fervour, to be delivered from this agony of the spirit. And, drifting into a brief slumber before Mally came to wake her, she believed that the illusion of peace that had eventually enfolded her was the reply.

It was not unremitting pain, of course. In a house such as Wintercombe, busy and crowded, there was a great deal for its lady to do, especially in these bounteous months of high summer. Preserving, distilling and bottling the fruits of her garden occupied much of her time, and her mind. The shelves of her still-room groaned under the new weight of cordials, salves and healing waters, while the stores had been augmented with all manner of bottled fruits and conserves, to be opened in December or January to give the flavour of summer to winter tarts and pies.

There were the perennial problems in the servants' hall. Young Jeff Hinton, brother to Rachael's maid and in her employ for scarcely six weeks, had been beaten by the cook for idleness, and even his normally placid sister Jude was distressed. One of the dairymaids, Jane Stone, was being courted by a Hinton lad, and Eliza suspected that the boy had, as she primly put it, 'Taken advantage of her'. And Eliza herself, plain, godly and repressed, had then announced to her dismayed mistress that she wished to be married after Michaelmas, and would be leaving Wintercombe after fourteen years' employ.

'Good riddance,' said Patience flippantly, when told. 'I can't imagine how you've endured that long Friday face all this time.'

'But I doubt we can manage without her,' Silence said despairingly, thinking of how Eliza, despite all her faults, had kept the house clean, tidy and warm, and a succession of young and more or less flighty serving maids in order, and was now abandoning them to till her own furrow. 'Wherever shall I find one as good?'

'Ask around,' said Patience. 'Discover another family with a housekeeper to match her, find out how much she is paid, and then offer her more. It's quite simple, really.'

'And if I do, I'll be shunned by all the gentry for ever more, for poaching their best servants — I already pay Joan Coxe far more than I should, but good dairymaids are almost impossible to find.' Silence squinted at the needle which she was trying to thread. She was at that moment absorbed with the problem of the gaping void which Eliza's departure would leave in the servants' hall, and so was taken completely by surprise at her sister's next question.

'Why are you suddenly so interested in the King of Scots?'

Silence dropped the needle. It rolled off her lap and on to the floor, and her urgent need to pick it up, before one of the animals could tread on it, gave her time to school her face and compose her answer. Nothing, however, could disguise the hot fiery blush that had swept over her as Patience spoke. She could only pray that her sister had not noticed it.

The errant sliver of metal safely in her grasp, she sat back on her chair and said calmly, 'If he is planning to invade England, then of course I am interested. As I imagine you must be, since you went to the lengths of inviting him to do it.'

She had not meant to sound so sharp, but she had successfully deflected her sister's curiosity. Patience gave her the sort of defiant, mutinous stare that must have been all too familiar to Joseph and Grace, and said, 'That was months ago.'

'Perhaps, but if he does invade, then I should pray that your secret remains hidden. Master Harley told me that Minister Love has been tried in London, and condemned to death.'

Patience became suddenly very still, and pale. Silence felt guilty: she would never have mentioned it, had it not been for the need to direct her sister's inquisitive mind away from her own concerns. Yet, was it fair to keep the girl in ignorance of the fate of her fellow conspirators, or indeed in ignorance of the inevitable consequences of such foolhardy behaviour?

She added gently, 'He has been reprieved, so Master Harley said, at least for a little while. But if the King of Scots does invade, I do not think they will be inclined to mercy.'

Patience, her careless, merry Imp, had a haunted look, her beautiful eyes wide and dark in her white face. She said, her voice almost normal, 'Was – did Master Harley talk of anyone else?'

'There was another man condemned and reprieved with him, I think, but I cannot now remember his name.'

'It wasn't . . . was it Jackel? John Jackel?'

Joseph had spoken of the man, in the disgusted tones of one whose trust and regard has been drastically misplaced. Silence shook her head. 'No, definitely not. Gibson, or Gibbons, I think it was.'

All the taut tension drained away from her sister's stiff, upright figure. 'Oh, thank God,' she said, her relief transparent. 'Thank God for that.'

'He may be in prison,' Silence reminded her, wondering whether Patience had at last committed her wayward heart to this mysterious conspirator. It did not seem very likely, despite her obvious concern for him. Would a girl deep in love flirt quite so blatantly with almost every eligible young man she met? Even sensible, plain Tom Wickham had not escaped, unsuitable though he might be.

'He hid himself,' said Patience. She had recovered her poise: she glanced at her sister from under her thick dark lashes, and said playfully, 'I know what you're thinking, and you can rest assured that it's not true. I know Joseph was thinking of him as a husband for me, but that was before he knew about the plot. I liked John, but I only went to all those meetings with him because I was so bored. I wouldn't dream of *marrying* him!' She pulled a comically ugly face to indicate the strength of her feelings, and made Silence smile. 'That's better,' she added. 'Why do you hardly ever laugh? Are you nursing some Secret Sorrow?'

This was uncomfortably close to the truth. 'But I do laugh!' Silence protested hastily.

Patience shook her head. 'Oh, no, you don't. And it isn't because Sir George is dead, because I know you didn't love him at all.'

'How can you possibly be sure of that?' Silence asked, at once startled and curious.

'It's very obvious. I can't blame you. I only ever met him a few times, and again when he was dying, but I can't imagine anyone loving him. He was a boring insensitive arrogant old prig.'

Her contemptuous assessment of the man who had shared

sixteen years of her sister's life should have been deeply shocking. But it was also largely true, and Silence, in this matter at least, was weary of dissimulation. So she did not protest, but said warningly, 'I should keep that thought to yourself, if I were you. It wouldn't help your relations with Rachael. She would be furious, and deeply hurt and upset.'

'Don't worry,' said Patience, after a pause in which Silence wondered, uneasily, if she was about to offer a similarly dismissive opinion of her stepdaughter. 'Don't worry about her. I promise not to speak ill of the dead, in her hearing at least. And I've kept my other promise, have I not? I haven't so much as looked at Jack Harington.'

'I know – and I'm grateful. But one thing worries me above all else – for how long will we be able to keep him and Emerald apart?'

Patience glanced at the parrot, now sulking inside her splendid new cage, equipped with perch, drinking bowl and food tray. Despite these luxuries, the bird missed her old perch and her chain, and for days had refused to do anything other than shriek and flap her wings. Even Kate, offering her unripe apples, or illicit strawberries and raspberries, had had little effect on her black mood, until Nat suggested that Emerald might want to stretch her wings every day. Now, each morning, her cage was removed from the clothes closet, where she had spent the night quietly under covers, and hung on a hook in the south window. Then, all the doors and casements were closed, and the bird allowed half an hour of precious freedom. Mally grumbled at the mess and the destruction – Emerald liked to sharpen her beak on items of wood, the costlier the better – but there was no doubt of it, the parrot was the happier for it, and liked best of all to sit on Kate's shoulder and nibble her hair, while the child fed her sweetmeats and titbits.

Up until now, there had always been warning of Jack Harington's visits, but there was a good chance that he would stay for a night or two fairly soon. Emerald would not take kindly to being shut in the closet all day with a blanket over her cage. Patience said doubtfully, 'Perhaps we can put her in the nursery for a time. Kate would love it, and so would William and Deb.'

'And Doraty would leave. We'll just have to hope for the best,' said Silence, with her rueful smile. 'Perhaps Emerald will feel constrained to moderate her vocabulary in the presence of such godliness.'

'Buggered if I will,' said the parrot, so aptly that the sisters exploded into laughter.

They were not the only members of the family to be concerned. Rachael, having had no part in the purchase of Emerald, thoroughly disapproved of the bird. It was dirty, obviously diseased, had cost a shocking amount of money, and was a monster of profanity. She could not imagine what had come over Nat, and in her usual forthright fashion had told him so, shortly after the popinjay's arrival.

To her fury, he had laughed. 'Oh, Rachael, don't be such a kill-joy! Whatever harm can there be in a parrot?'

'It blasphemes,' said Rachael, whose own vocabulary, when she lost her temper, could be even more extensive. 'The children will learn from it.'

'It says nothing they can't already hear in the barton or the stables.'

'"God save the King"?'

'Well, that I admit hasn't been said at Wintercombe for many a long day. But the justices can hardly hang a parrot for treasonous utterances, can they? And I can always claim to have bought it in ignorance.'

Rachael gave a derisory snort. 'You should never have bought it. *Why* did you buy it?'

'I bought it for Kate,' said Nat, tactfully omitting to add that the thought of shocking his twin's betrothed had also weighed heavily in the scales.

'Kate's just a spoilt brat,' said Rachael, with contempt.

Suddenly, all her brother's cheerful insouciance dropped away. For once completely serious, he laid a hand on her thin, taut shoulder, and turned her towards him. They were sitting on an old wooden seat on the sunny side of the shaggy bowls lawn. The afternoon light fell sharply on Rachael's pale, pinched face, revealing with cruel clarity how it would look in her bitter old age. Nat, his own expression softened with a love he rarely showed openly to the stormy, tormented girl who was the darker side of his own coin, said gently, 'She isn't, and you know it. Does it still rankle, after all this time?'

Rachael, who knew exactly what he meant, chose to profess bewilderment. She said sullenly, 'I can't imagine what you're talking about.'

'You can.' Nat glanced around. There was no one within

earshot to listen to the home truths he was about to deliver. He went on, quietly. 'Kate is Nick Hellier's child. We both know that, do we not?'

Rachael's expression, fierce, reluctantly acknowledging, was his answer. Choosing his words carefully, as he had learned long ago to do when speaking to his turbulent sister, he said, 'But that is not her fault. She cannot help what she is — indeed, she does not *know* what she is. She thinks that she is Father's daughter. She loved him as dearly as you did, and he loved her. I know it isn't easy — I know that, for Father's sake, you resent her.' He omitted, deliberately, to mention the obvious jealousy that the mutual love between Sir George and the little girl had awakened in Rachael's unhappy heart. 'And I realise also that you still somehow feel that sin should be punished, although you know the inevitable consequences that will follow.'

She could not deny it: she was not without intelligence. Long ago, she had realised that such a scandal was, for her father's sake if for no other reason, best left buried. She had also, even if she tried to deny it, some small understanding of her stepmother's feelings in the matter, of how loneliness and neglect had helped to lead her astray. Any impulse she might have felt, to reveal the whole sorry tale after Sir George's death, had been smothered at birth for her own selfish reasons. For surely, Jack Harington would repudiate a bride from such a tainted family?

She flushed, and turned her head away. Once, enduring the torments of adolescence, she had thought that growing up would spell an end to all doubts and confusion and uncertainty. But now she was twenty-one, nearly twenty-two, and still she did not seem to have fixed views upon anything. Her stepmother had been dreadfully wicked, and yet she had not betrayed her. She loved her father, yet she had not told him that his youngest child was not his. And although she wanted most desperately, urgently to marry Jack Harington, she could not suppress the little worm of doubt that whispered in her head. 'Do you *really* want to marry him, and live at Kelston under his mother's eye, and spend half your life in prayer and charity?'

Fiercely denying that voice, she said savagely, 'Of course wickedness should be punished. The Lord will do that, I am sure of it.' But she was not: and certainly Silence did not seem to be suffering very much from heaven's disfavour.

'Then you do see, don't you, that to take out your very natural feelings of resentment on Kate is a little unfair?'

With anyone else, Rachael would have defiantly brazened it out. With Nat, her twin, who knew her better than anyone else, she could not pretend. She dropped her gaze, and after a while muttered, 'Yes, I suppose so.'

'She *is* spoilt,' said Nat. 'But not beyond redemption. And open dislike will not help her. You love the other children, you've always been their friend, you're so good with them – but never Kate. Let her in, Rachael – please.'

'I can't!' Rachael shouted, suddenly and overwhelmingly angry. 'I can't – not now *she's* here!'

Nat knew whom she meant. Since the day Patience had arrived at Wintercombe, Rachael had felt threatened by her, in almost every aspect of her life. Her betrothed, her appearance, her place in the household, her special relationship with William and Deb, all seemed to be under attack. Her resentment had festered in secret for months until now, under Nat's gentle, probing pressure, the bitterness was lanced, and boiled to the surface. Her brother held her as her loathing, her fear and her rage at her stepmother's sister, and above all her deep, desperate and unspoken grief at her father's death, ruthlessly repressed for too long, all burst forth in a torrent of tears.

She wept into Nat's shoulder until the black cloth was sodden and darkened. He had not known her give way to such a storm of anguish for many years, and knew that it could only do her good. Perhaps now, his sister, who had attempted to distort and hide her real self in order to please her father, could at last relax a little, and attempt some happiness.

But of course, he remembered, she could not, for fear of losing Jack Harington.

He cursed his father bitterly, under his breath. When at last the sobbing had stopped, and she was mopping her face with a kerchief, he said quietly, 'Tell me the truth, Rachael. Do you really want to marry Jack?'

She took the kerchief away from her eyes and glared at him. Like this, her face raw, red and swollen with weeping, she still seemed a child. He wondered sadly if she had learned anything over the past few years, save that which would best please her father. Silence, only half joking, had once told him that he had been born old. Rachael, at the beck and call of every passing mood and stray emotion, might never have left adolescence.

'Of course I do,' she said belligerently. 'You know I do.'

Nat did not know anything of the sort. He had long wondered if, in this as in so many other things, her desire to fulfil her father's hopes and wishes had overcome more natural feelings.

'You don't have to, if you don't want to,' he pointed out. 'No one will think any the worse of you if you change your mind. It'll be too late for that, once you've entered the church.'

'I'm *not* going to change my mind!' Rachael shouted, with a fervour that made him instantly suspicious. '*You* may not want me to, but *I* do, and I will.'

'Very well,' said Nat, who did not in the least want the whole of Wintercombe to overhear their quarrel. 'I accept that it is your desire, and your decision.' He was tempted to tell her that her father had not in fact given her any such choice, but remembered his stepmother's thoughts on the subject. Silence had enough to worry her already, and so did Rachael.

But there was one matter which he must try to resolve. He said, 'I know you don't like Patience very much, and I can understand why, even though I don't in the least share your feelings — '

'Do you *like* her?' Rachael cried, her voice sharp, hostile and disbelieving.

'Why not?' said Nat, trying to hide his sudden annoyance. 'She is Silence's sister, after all, and a very pleasant young woman.'

'You're just fooled by a pretty face and a wandering eye,' Rachael said venomously. 'All men are. She's just a conniving deceitful little bitch who's no better than she ought to be, and if no one else will tell you the truth, then I will!'

There was a short, furious pause. Rachael saw, with a mixture of alarm and satisfaction, that she had roused her cheerful, cynical twin to real anger. He said, his voice very level and quiet, 'That is an opinion which is insulting, untrue, unfair and unworthy of you. She has her faults, I grant you, but you have no right whatsoever to cast doubt on her morals. And if I hear even a whisper about her that can be traced to your insinuations, I shall make you regret the day you were born. Do you understand? And jealousy is no excuse.'

Her face livid with rage, Rachael leapt to her feet and dealt him a huge, ringing slap that left the print of her fingers scarlet across his cheekbone. Then she whirled round and ran at full pelt for the safety of Wintercombe, away from the twin, close as her own soul, who had in the end failed to be a friend in all adversity.

CHAPTER SEVEN

'So pestered with a popinjay'
(Henry IV, Part I)

Many of Silence's chickens came winging inevitably back to roost on a hot day in the second week in August.

For the past month or so, Wintercombe had not been a particularly happy place. It was obvious that Rachael and Nat were not on speaking terms. For such a thing to last a day or two was not rare, but when four weeks had gone by without any sign of a reconciliation, Silence began to be worried. Nat had said nothing whatsoever to his stepmother, which was in itself unusual, since they tended to confide in each other. Rachael kept much to her chamber, read her Bible a great deal, and ostentatiously ignored her twin. Nat occupied his time with his inheritance, made himself pleasant both to Patience and to Jack Harington, and weathered his sister's glowers with apparent unconcern.

The younger children were disturbed at this turn of events. There had been some late-night, whispered discussion between Tabby and Deb, and they had come to the conclusion that Jack was the bone of contention. For, as Tabby pointed out, Rachael was silly enough to like him, and Nat had too much sense.

It might have given even Rachael pause, had she realised how much her half-sisters, and brother, had come to dislike her betrothed. Privately, Tabby had early summed him up as a self-righteous and pedantic bore, and nothing she had seen of him since had changed her opinion. Despite their early attempts to impress, Deb, William and Kate had independently come to the same conclusion, and the meeting with the rest of the Harington family had not changed their minds. They knew their half-sister well enough, however, to accept that she would never be persuaded into altering her opinion. It was Jack who must be discouraged.

Tabby had, like Nat, to whom she was very close, immediately seen the possibilities of the parrot. She had wanted to buy it for Kate's sake, and the little girl's enchantment was reward in itself. But if, somehow, seemingly by accident, Jack and Emerald could be brought together, and the bird persuaded to give full rein to her repertoire of abuse, the godly young man would undoubtedly be shocked, outraged and horrified that his betrothed's family should allow such a creature under their roof, let alone as a pampered pet.

It would probably make Silence very angry, but Tabby, who had always had an intuitive understanding of her mother's true feelings, knew that she must secretly share her children's antipathy to Jack. She wanted to be fair to Rachael, of course, so she would not say anything against the match. But if by some means, fair or foul, the betrothal could be dissolved, with as little hurt to Rachael as possible, Tabby was sure that Silence at heart would be glad.

Another way of achieving her end, of course, would be to find Rachael someone that both she, and her family, liked better. Together, the four children had discussed the young gentlemen of their acquaintance, Horners, Ashes and others, with serious consideration from the older three and pert comments from Kate. All were too old, too young, too solemn, too wild, too unlikeable, or, if none of these things, invariably already married or spoken for.

Tabby had an idea, which dropped unsought into her head one night as she was in the pleasant stage of drowsy limbo between wakefulness and sleep. She pondered it, half-dreaming, and found little flaw in it. Even in the clear light of morning, it did seem to be a most appropriate solution.

She would not, for the moment, confide in the others. Deb and William were children still, while she was now fifteen, and almost adult. Besides, the essential reserve of her nature had always inclined her to secrecy about the things that mattered most to her. So one morning, under the guise of practising her handwriting, sitting at the table in her mother's chamber, she took paper and quill and ink and embarked upon a letter of some importance.

Dear Master Wickham,
I write on behalf of my brother, who has not the time to spare at present, being so busy with the farm.

He desires you to know how much he delighted in your late visit to our house, and he is most anxious, as are we all, that you come to us again, as soon as may be. If you do not long delay your journey, you will be able to stay a little space before the harvest. My lady mother presents her affectionate regards to you, as does my sister Rachael. As for myself, I would be pleased to have news of our mutual friend, if you have received any since last we spoke.

Pray be assured that you will always be welcome at Wintercombe, with or without due notice to
Your friend and servant,

Tabitha St. Barbe

It did not quite convey her intent with the subtlety that she had
wished, but surely he would take the hint. Careful not to attract
attention, she sanded it, sealed it when no one was looking, and
addressed it to Master Thomas Wickham, of Longleaze Farm,
Glastonbury, Somerset, to be left for collection at the White Horse
in Glastonbury. It was the work of just a few moments, on the
family's next trip to Bath, to take one of the White Hart's servants
aside, give him one of her stored shillings and instructions to
ensure that postboy or carrier would take it on to its destination.
The servant, eyeing the quietly-spoken and very pretty girl,
smiled indulgently, thinking that the letter went to her secret
sweetheart, and Tabby, guessing exactly what was in his mind,
did not enlighten him. She returned to Wintercombe, certain that
she had done the right thing, and settled down to wait for the reply
or, better still, Tom Wickham himself to arrive on the doorstep.

This he duly did, a fortnight after receiving Tabby's letter. It had
surprised him somewhat, but he welcomed the warmth and
friendliness that seemed to radiate from the page. His land could
do without him for a little while: his bailiff was competent and
trustworthy, and so long as he returned in time for the harvest, he
would not be missed for several days.

Besides, his brief stay at Wintercombe had given him a
reminder, long overdue, that there was a world outside his own
limited acres, and people with whom he had once been friends, and
whose company he wished to enjoy again. His mother, still
young-looking and cheerful, was thinking of marrying again, and
his three older sisters were long since wed themselves. He had to
admit that the lonely evenings in the parlour were long and dreary.
Hard work and aching muscles, even a well-filled coin chest, were
no substitutes for pleasant surroundings and interesting talk.

So he said goodbye to his mother, who was undoubtedly
looking forward to entertaining her suitor without her son's somewhat inhibiting presence, and gave detailed instructions to his
bailiff. Then, on a lovely August morning, the hedgerows dizzy
with butterflies and the larks joyful overhead, he saddled Hodge,
his chestnut nag and a steed very different from the cavalry mounts

he had once ridden, and set out towards Philip's Norton. He travelled all morning in blistering sunshine, through Shepton Mallet and Frome, and arrived at Wintercombe in the middle of the afternoon, somewhat later than he had intended, and hungry, dusty and thirsty.

*

Silence had had a particularly exhausting day. Not only had Jack Harington appeared that morning, an hour earlier than expected, but he had brought his father with him, unannounced.

Chaos had narrowly been averted. After all, Wintercombe was used to such crises, and had weathered many similar, or much worse, in the past. Mally had whisked Emerald into the clothes closet, much to the parrot's disgust, and flung the cloth over her cage with a lack of ceremony that silenced even the bird's vituperative tongue. The children were bundled upstairs to change into their best clothes, and Rachael spent half an hour making Jude Hinton's life a misery before she was satisfied with her appearance.

John Harington, Esquire, of Kelston, was a tall man much leaner than his son, with an aristocratic face and a small, old-fashioned beard, relentlessly trimmed. Like his wife, he had an air of hauteur which did not enhance his efforts to be pleasant to the widow and family of his old friend. Moreover, as one of the executors named in Sir George's will — the other being Master Jonathan Harley — he had necessary business to conduct with the heir of the estate.

So Silence had played hostess to his son while Nat and the two lawyers were closeted close in the study, which must have been unbearably hot and stuffy on such a warm, sunny day. The children, packed like barrelled herrings inside their stiff prickly satins and silks, perspired freely and grew quietly mutinous, despite the efforts of Patience, who herself looked very cool and fresh in her new gown of muted mulberry taffeta, the wide collar and cuffs and apron all snowy white.

Beside her, Rachael felt, as usual, acutely at a disadvantage. Still clad in black, both by convention and by choice, she knew that she must seem a gawky, sallow girl. The colour did little for the extreme pallor of her complexion, and emphasised the hollows and angles in her face and figure. Miserably aware of Jack's covert glances in the direction of her stepmother's sister, she retreated

[122]

into her shell, lacking the confidence with which she might have been able, a little, to shine.

Silence was glad when at last Nat, Harley and Harington appeared, looking somewhat grave of face, and they could go down to the dining parlour for dinner. There had been suspicious muffled sounds from the closet, where Emerald was protesting her incarceration in darkness, and it had required all her skills in polite conversation to distract Jack's attention. As she spoke of harvest, of Parson Willis's sermons, and of the dispute over which parish was responsible for maintaining one of the bridges on the Bath road, she could see the young man's eyes sliding to the closet door, as if he had heard something. She wondered if he thought it might be rats, and did not know whether to be relieved or dismayed at the possibility, although the presence of Misty, curled mottled and comfortable on the south windowseat in the sun, would hardly imply the presence of vermin.

The elder Harington was heavy with news, which he imparted to the company over dinner, and the reason for the long faces became at once apparent. It was no legal tangle, but a much more serious threat to their peace which had disturbed them. The King of Scots had invaded.

Silence sat quite still at the head of the table, her face serene. Only the width and darkness of her eyes betrayed her feelings, as Harington described how the Scots army had marched over the Border several days ago, and was believed to be heading for Lancashire. The Lord General's army in Scotland was, of course, hot in pursuit, and other Commonwealth forces in the north-western part of the country could be expected to fall on the invaders. But Harington, obviously perturbed, seemed to think that if the Scots were not halted and destroyed, they would attempt to seize the towns and cities on the western side of the country, which in the days of war had tended towards Royalist sympathies: Shrewsbury, Worcester and Bristol.

Silence saw Nat looking at her, and sent him a smile of reassurance. She was no child, to be buoyed up with lies and false hopes. Moreover, this invasion was, to any right-minded person, extremely unwelcome. It was one matter to bring the young Charles Stuart back to the throne on a wave of popular acclaim. It was quite another, when that support was lacking, to attempt to force him on to the country with the help of a foreign army.

John Harington was a Presbyterian, though no Royalist, and

some who espoused that religion had, in London, conspired with the Scots. It was evident, however, that he disapproved whole-heartedly of the invasion, and was quite prepared to do everything in his power as a justice to thwart any Royalist conspiracy in Somerset. Already, the call had gone out from the Council of State to the Militia Commissioners in all counties, urging them to make ready in haste to meet this threat to the fragile peace and stability of the young Commonwealth. Known Royalists were to be appre-hended, their houses searched, arms and horses confiscated as a precaution against any insurrection in support of the invasion.

A brisk discussion followed as to whether the invaders would act as assumed and make for the West, or instead aim straight for London, which was being hurriedly put into a state of defence. Silence listened, while her traitor's heart, unnoticed beneath the stiffening of her narrow bodice, beat like a drum the rhythm of danger. Once, war had brought her misery and horror, but it had also delivered Nick into her life, to change it, and her, for ever. As the plans for meeting this invasion were related in vivid detail by Jack, who had once, briefly, been a captain in the New Model Army, she wondered bleakly if history would repeat itself, and the tide of battle wash up to Wintercombe's shores once more.

It did not seem very likely. She knew, from the talk she had heard in the village over the past few weeks, that there were none prepared to take arms in support of Charles Stuart, none indeed who even spoke favourably of him. In Philip's Norton, as over most of the West Country, memories of soldiers, both Royalist and Parliamentarian, disrupting their peaceful lives with their appropriations and brutality and free quarters, were still unpleasantly vivid. Even the militia, paid for by yet another 'assessment', was universally disliked. Men and women in Somer-set cared nothing for Parliament nor King of Scots, Presbyterian nor Independent, it seemed, so long as they could be left alone to rebuild their war-shattered prosperity in peace. And surely, the vast majority of people, rich and poor, throughout the country, must share their feelings.

The general opinion around her table seemed to be that General Cromwell, and Major-Generals Lambert and Harrison, would put an end to Scots pretensions once and for all, before they had penetrated more than a hundred miles into English territory. They were probably right. She thought unhappily of Nick, perhaps a member of that army, perhaps already dead. Of course, she reminded herself sternly, there was no proof beyond Tom Wickham's information, more than half a year stale, that he was with the Scots at all. By now, he could be anywhere, though she could not believe that he would desert the royal cause until all hope was gone. She remembered the Nick she had known, reckless, inventive, deprecating his courage and loyalty, yet in desperate straits as brave and honourable as any man could be. Was he a part of the invasion? And would he share its surely inevitable downfall?

She would probably never know. The invasion, according to the men around her, seemed certain to expire almost before it had begun. By now, he could be a fugitive, or a prisoner, or a corpse, and even Tom Wickham, who had so unexpectedly brought her news of him, might never be able to discover his fate.

She willed her mind away from such morbid speculation and glanced at her children, seated decorous and quiet at the foot of the table. Tabby was apparently daydreaming, while Kate and Deb applied themselves with dedicated efficiency to the clearance of their platters. William, for once not intent on his food, was covertly listening to the military talk, his eyes glowing with the love of soldiers and battle that had been fostered by Wintercombe's garrison when he had been scarcely more than a baby, and something of a mascot to the troopers.

William, whose warm, wild, undisciplined soul was quite unsuited to the sober future, as parson or lawyer, that his father had wished for him. Afresh, she wondered whether Nat had come to any decision yet regarding her husband's will. He could hardly ask John Harington about the question of Rachael's dowry, since it concerned the other man so closely. But the presence of Master Harley might well prompt him to ask whether some provisions could be set aside, and the elder Harington, a respected and highly experienced lawyer himself, would doubtless give him sound advice.

So many problems: the will, and Nat, and Patience, and the profane parrot, and Rachael, and the impossibility of finding an adequate replacement for Eliza, and above all the nagging fear, sometimes a dull background ache, sometimes a pain much sharper, for Nick. She felt suddenly weighted down by her burdens, and the old longing, to run away, to hide from her myriad responsibilities, crept over her again. All she had ever wanted was to live in peace and tend her children and her garden.

Why was such a simple ambition apparently doomed to be thwarted, yet again?

Lady St. Barbe straightened her shoulders and ruthlessly eschewed self-pity. Make, do, mend was her creed, and she would obey it as she always did. She regarded her guests, blissfully unaware of her inner conflicts, who were contentedly picking over the bowls of raspberries and late strawberries, tiny and sweet, that had comprised most of the second course, and suggested that they all retire to her chamber for sweet wine and comfits, there to continue their talk.

The children, by earlier agreement, were released from any further duties, and hurried with barely-concealed enthusiasm to their own quarters, there to change into their everyday clothes, before escaping to the freedom of the countryside on their ponies.

For once, Tabby was not sorry to be counted with the younger three. She found the Haringtons, and Master Harley, to be tedious in the extreme, and the responsibility of keeping Deb, William and Kate out of mischief for the afternoon was nothing, compared with the relief from adult company. Besides, they had, during the course of the meal, given her all the information she could desire concerning the Scots invasion. Perhaps Tom Wickham, if he replied to her letter, would be able to tell her more. She had liked Tom very much, judging him, correctly, to be a helpful and good-natured young man, and had already enlisted him in her mind as an ally.

She was so preoccupied that it was not until they were half-way down the track leading to the Wellow Lane, that she noticed Kate's bright eyes and huge grin, her air of suppressed glee. It was a mood with which Tabby was entirely familiar. She leaned over to her smallest sister, sitting pillion behind Deb on the fat, old, brown pony Dumbledore, who had taught them all to ride, and said suspiciously, 'Kate – what have you done?'

The only answer was an explosion of smothered giggles. William pulled up his chestnut, a sturdy little gelding called Firebrand, and looked round. 'I think it's something to do with Emerald.'

Kate put both hands across her mouth and nose. Her chestnut eyes looked over them, dancing with mirth, and her narrow little shoulders shook. An awful suspicion crossed Tabby's mind. She recalled that her sister had been, by some way, the last down the stairs from their mother's chamber before dinner. Trying very hard not to succumb to the child's infectious merriment, she repeated her question more forcefully. '*Kate*! What have you *done*?'

Kate looked at her, with that vast, mischievous grin, and let loose a peal of uninhibited laughter. 'I took the cover off Emerald's cage. Are you cross?'

Deb giggled, and William gave a loud cheer. Tabby could no longer suppress her laughter. She had a vivid memory of Nat saying, 'I can't wait to see Jack Harington's face when the bird says its piece.'

'I'm not cross,' she said, grinning. 'But whatever is poor Mother going to do?'

*

In the comparative calm and cool of Silence's chamber, the bottles of sweet wine, the cakes, sugared nuts and candied flowers and fruits, a miniature banquet, had been set out on one of the tables. In these more informal surroundings, already familiar, Jack Harington was able to relax, to take his betrothed to one side and to discuss with her, most earnestly, her views on the rearing of children in full and pious knowledge of the Lord. Rachael, filled with the entrancing thought of babies who would be her own, and not subject to seduction by such as Patience, gave the answers that were expected of her, and even managed to look quite animated. Her future father-in-law stood ramrod straight before the empty hearth, where a jug of dried lavender and rosemary sweetened the chamber, and made lawyer's talk with Nat and Jonathan Harley. Silence and her sister dispensed refreshments as required, and joined in the conversation when it seemed to be expected of them.

There was a brief lull, filled by a sudden ghastly shriek from the direction of the closet at the southern end of the chamber. Jack Harington, belying the martial air which he had been at pains to display over dinner, turned pale with shock, and even his father was startled. 'Lady St. Barbe, whatever was that dreadful noise?'

Silence, horrified, had glanced instantly at her stepson. Nat did not look amazed, or apprehensive, or even guilty. There was the merest wry twitch of a smile at the corner of his mouth, and the suspicion of a shrug. Knowing that she could rely on his support, whatever might happen, she turned to her guests. Master Harley, she noticed, was looking at her with something like sympathy. She laced her hands together and said mildly, 'I do beg your pardon, sir – I am sorry if that sound alarmed you. It is only a bird that the children are fond of. The cover must have slipped off its cage.'

Another furious call blasted from the closet: Emerald was growing bored. Mally, tiny and efficient, came to her rescue. 'M'lady, shall I put the cover back on?'

'Please do, Mally,' said Silence, with relief. Perhaps, even now, some decorum could be preserved. Her hopes were shattered as the maid opened the closet door, and the parrot welcomed the arrival of human company with a cheerful cry. 'Hallo, sweetheart — give us a kiss!'

There was a startled pause, once more shattered by Emerald. 'A pox on all Puritans! God save the King!'

John Harington looked as if he could hardly believe his ears. His son had blenched in horror and astonishment and, beside him, Rachael's face was scarlet with mortified fury. Silence felt suddenly sorry for her. She turned to her appalled guests with a bright, brave, desperate smile. 'Pray forgive me — it is no nest of Cavaliers, I promise you, but only a talking bird.'

'A talking bird?' Harington walked disbelievingly to the closet door. Mally was hurriedly fumbling for the cover, which had somehow fallen behind a huge clothes press, several feet from the cage. As she straightened with the material at last in her grasp, the bird glared at John Harington, transfixed in the doorway, and announced, 'Buggered if I will!'

Silence saw the look of frozen horror on his face and felt a terrible impulse to laugh sweep over her. Mally flung the cover over the cage, cutting off Emerald's malevolence in mid-squawk, and Harington, outraged, swung back to face his hostess. 'Surely, madam, you do not consider that profane and blasphemous creature to be a fit companion for your children!'

'She doesn't,' said Nat calmly. 'I am afraid I am to blame, sir, for the parrot's presence here. I bought it from a man in Bath as a present for my little sister Kate, but unfortunately I did not discover the true nature of its vocabulary until some time had elapsed — and by then, of course, the bird-seller had long since made himself scarce. We are at present trying to find a home for it, with very little success, I regret to say.'

'Were I in your place, sir,' said the older man, his expression forbidding, 'I would wring the creature's neck forthwith.'

'That, alas, would greatly upset my younger sisters,' said Nat, an expression of pious regret upon his face that was, Silence knew, totally spurious. 'They have conceived a misguided affection for the bird. Most unfortunate, as you can imagine, but there is very little I can do about it.' He smiled, with the charm that was one of his most attractive attributes. Silence, looking at him with affectionate appreciation, thought that it was just as well that he had inherited his grandfather's characteristic ability to make himself pleasant to everyone, high and low, of whatever religious persuasion, and thus to pour oil on uneasy waters.

John Harington, mollified, allowed himself to be drawn away from the closet, and Mally, her thin orange brows set in a line of some severity, shut the door firmly upon the delinquent parrot. There was a barely audible grunt of protest, and then blessed peace.

Silence, however, was not to be granted any respite. Scarcely had the Haringtons accepted a small second glass of wine, than Carpenter knocked briskly on the door and entered, the picture of deferential courtesy. 'If you please, my lady, Master Wickham is below.'

With a feeling that the day had slipped altogether beyond her control, Silence fought down her rising sense of panic and, worse, a lunatic impulse to laugh. Tom was an old friend, that was all, and there was no need for the Haringtons to connect him with the Royalist garrison that had held Wintercombe for the last year of the war. She said calmly, 'Thank you, Carpenter. Please show him up.'

'Master Wickham?' Harington enquired, as Carpenter vanished downstairs. He looked, Silence thought despairingly, as if he was wondering where he had heard the name before.

Nat came to her rescue once more. 'Tom Wickham is an old friend of mine, sir. I hope you do not mind if he joins us — he lives some distance away, and we do not often see him.'

'Ah,' said Harley. 'Did you meet him at Oxford, Sir Nathaniel?'

'No, he didn't,' said Rachael. Her voice was somewhat higher in pitch than usual, and there was a bright spot of colour on each cheek. 'He was — '

'Interested in breeding a new strain of cattle, using one of my bulls,' said Nat, with a significant glance at his twin. Rachael realised, somewhat belatedly, that revealing the origins of Nat's friendship with Tom Wickham would hardly help the progress of her betrothal, and repressed her rage with some difficulty. Why did the wretched man have to choose this afternoon, of all times, to inflict his company on them? It had been bad enough on the last occasion; one look at that pleasant, unassuming face, and she had been transported back six years, a vivid reminder of events that she desperately wanted to forget, and humiliating experiences that she had buried as deeply as possible, at the back of her mind.

But to no avail. What must he think of her? Did he remember the furious, hysterical child who had shot the garrison's commanding officer with his own pistol, and thereby set in motion an inexorable series of events that had very nearly brought all her family, and Wintercombe, to disaster? She knew that he must still see her as that wilful, undisciplined girl, and not the mature person she so urgently wished to be.

But Tom Wickham had not, on his earlier visit, at first connected the well-dressed, rather thin young woman with the girl who had attempted to murder his colonel. It was only after some hours that he had suddenly realised who she must be, and had felt surprised and intrigued, so different was this quiet, almost sullen Rachael from the loud-mouthed hoyden of his memory. So when he stepped into the high, airy room and saw her standing by the window, his first impulse was to smile at her. He was not at all disconcerted by the frosty unwelcoming glare which he received in return. She had always been contrary and subject to moods, and perhaps she had her own reasons for not wishing to appear too friendly towards him.

He had heard of John Harington, as a justice, a member of Parliament, and a man of considerable stature in the country. His son, a big self-important young man, was introduced as Rachael's betrothed, and he understood her antipathy now. Doubtless she feared he would make some blundering reference to that long-ago shooting, or to another embarrassing incident from the past. It was a shame that he could not reassure her. But it was also a pity that her future husband should be apparently so uninspiring: he thought she deserved better. It was her own choice, however, and he would respect it, and keep his opinion to himself.

He did not have much opportunity to further his acquaintance with the happy couple, for Patience, with her dazzling smile and her low, infectious laugh, was at his elbow with wine and a platter of sweetmeats. He would have preferred a more substantial meal, having eaten only bread and cheese for dinner, but at this hour, and arriving without warning, could expect no better.

Patience was enjoying herself. Jack Harington was not for her, however much he might glance in her direction whenever he thought that Rachael, or his father, was not looking. Nor was this tall, fair-haired farmer in her usual line, and she did not find him especially attractive. But he was young, and male, and at least not hideous to behold, and so she opened out her warmth to him like a flower turning its petals to the sun, and engaged him in light-hearted conversation about the tribulations of his journey, ignoring the resigned expression on her sister's face and the mildly disapproving looks of John Harington.

It was an enormous relief when at last the sun crept round towards the west, and Silence's guests announced their intention of leaving, since they wished to return to their homes before dark. Elaborate farewells were said, good wishes for the journey offered, hopes of another visit expressed. Rachael and Jack exchanged chaste kisses in the hall, and with smiles and waves the Haringtons, and Jonathan Harley, rode out of Wintercombe, back towards Bath and Kelston.

Harington, deep in thought, said nothing for the first few miles. He was beginning to regret the plan to marry his son to Rachael St. Barbe. It had all seemed very suitable and fitting, a few months ago, and he had been delighted to agree with Sir George's suggestion. Now, however, he was not so sure. His wife had her doubts, and had expressed them to him with her usual brusque clarity. But Dyoness adored her eldest son, and Harington suspected that the best natured, most wealthy, most beautiful and accomplished girl in all the Commonwealth would be, in her eyes, totally inadequate as a wife for her beloved Jack.

The more he saw of Rachael, though, the more he doubted the wisdom of this match. That awkward, sullen-looking young woman, with hardly a word to say for herself, would have to change indeed to make a fitting lady for Kelston, when he and Dyoness were gone. Although she was obviously strictly reared, and imbued with all the correct godly attitudes, he wished he could say the same for the rest of her family. Her brother had responded with a marked lack of enthusiasm to his suggestion that he take an active part in promoting Presbyterian worship, and the younger children were allowed altogether too much freedom. That parrot! No right-thinking person would ever have permitted it to cross the threshold, and he himself would have had its neck wrung, however much the spoilt little sister might weep and wail.

But he had promised his old friend, papers had been signed, and he would not go back on his word. Jack seemed quite content, and the girl appeared fond of him, and that, he supposed, was what mattered most. Rachael was very young for her age, and had led a sheltered life. She was, Harington decided, probably of a shy and retiring disposition: his own dear little Phoebe was much the same.

Still . . . there was something about the younger St. Barbes and their mother, which made him uneasy. Lady St. Barbe was an excellent housewife, and no fault had ever been found with her, though he was aware that Sir George had not paid much attention to her wishes and opinions in any matter. She was very much her husband's junior, after all. Although she had always seemed the perfect wife, there was some quality in her face and manner, especially in her eyes, that had led him to the conclusion that her true feelings were completely opposite to what appeared on the surface. Her forward hussy of a sister also prejudiced his opinion.

Frowning, Harington twitched his horse's reins and urged the animal up beside Jack. 'Did you enjoy your visit?' he enquired.

Mildly surprised, the boy looked round. 'Yes, I did, Father,' he said.

'And you are quite happy with all the arrangements that have been made on your behalf?'

The rather bland, plump face, very like his mother's but without her forcefulness, looked even more startled. 'Of course, Father. Rachael is a good and godly girl, and I could not wish for a better wife.'

And with that, Harington supposed he must be content for the moment.

*

If her betrothed was satisfied, Rachael St. Barbe was not.

Tom Wickham had set the seal on her mood. As if the profane and Royalist parrot were not enough, they must also play host to an old Cavalier. The very idea horrified her. Whatever would Jack think if he found out?

He had been decidedly shocked by Emerald, and she had almost – almost, but not quite – sprung to Nat's defence. The habits of a lifetime died hard, and the twins had once been very loyal to each other. But, Rachael reminded herself sternly, she was nearly a Harington now, and her allegiance must be given to her new family. So she spoke disapprovingly of the bird's purchase, and was relieved to see Jack's frown disappear.

Despite her agony of apprehension, Wickham gave no hint, by word or deed, of his unsavoury past. That did not diminish her feelings of anger and resentment towards him, which lingered long after the Haringtons had gone. They were still simmering balefully within her when she walked down through the garden to collect the children from the orchard before supper, and came upon him leaning over a balustrade.

Her first reaction was to be rude. 'What are you doing here?'

There was no hint of offence in his brief smile and doffed hat. 'Hallo, Mistress Rachael. I was admiring your stepmother's garden. I see the sundial has been mended, and so well that you would hardly guess how badly it was damaged.'

A grenado explosion had shattered it, six years before. Rachael said shortly, 'I have no interest in the past, Master Wickham.'

'I can understand that,' he said, meaning only to be sympathetic. Rachael stared at him, her blue eyes starkly hostile. 'I doubt very much that you can. Why did you come here today?'

Tom was beginning to realise the depth and extent of her enmity. He said carefully, 'I believed that I was welcome here – and certainly the other members of your family have done nothing to alter that impression.'

'Well, you're not welcome to me,' said Rachael viciously. A voice, remarkably similar to Nat's, whispered within that she was being childishly, unforgivably offensive. She ignored it, intent only on making herself so unpleasant that Tom Wickham, and all he represented, would never darken the threshold of Wintercombe again.

But he had never been quick to hurt, or to anger. He remembered the similar moods of his turbulent eldest sister Mary, and how marriage and babies had calmed and soothed the fury she had once felt against the whole world. Moll had not known what she wanted from life until it was thrust upon her, and he guessed that this girl was very much the same. It was a pity that her affianced husband seemed to be such a tediously worthy young man, who would most probably fail to comprehend his bride's wilder moods, but that could not be helped. And after all, she had chosen him.

'I am sorry about that,' he said, with genuine regret. 'I had hoped that we could be friends.'

'Well, I'm afraid you must hope in vain,' Rachael snapped, her fury increasing at his lack of reaction. What must she say to him, in order to send him packing? 'Why don't you go away and leave us in peace? I can't think why you bothered to come back.'

'He came because I invited him here.'

Rachael had not noticed the approach of her half-sister. Tabby's movements were always quiet and graceful, never obtrusive, and her progress up the steps from the orchard had been almost without sound. Wickham, who possessed an incongruously vivid and sensitive imagination beneath his very ordinary exterior, was reminded of a young deer by her air of alert watchfulness, and the wide hazel eyes. At their last meeting, she had hardly spoken to him at all, in contrast to the straightforward friendliness of the boy who had once been the soldiers' pet, and the rather strident behaviour of her younger sister. He had put it down to shyness, the natural female modesty of a young girl just leaving childhood. Now, he saw that he had been quite mistaken.

'You *invited* him?' Rachael's voice climbed the scale of indignation. 'You meddling great gawcum, why on earth did you do that?'

Tabby stood in front of her half-sister, wrapped in a cloak of calm serenity that was very reminiscent of her mother. Even in her ordinary gown, a rusty dusty mourning black that had seen better days, and which did nothing to enhance her looks, she was lovely, and gave promise of greater beauty yet to come. She seemed quite unruffled by Rachael's abuse, and it required no great feat of the imagination to guess that she had often suffered it before. She said, with a mildness that would probably only infuriate Rachael further, 'I wanted to. Is there anything wrong?'

Rachael stared at her, nonplussed. She realised suddenly that she could not challenge Tabby further, without revealing the reasons why she did not want Wickham at Wintercombe. And those reasons seemed all at once so hideously confused, so embarrassing and childish and impossible, that her heart quailed at the thought of bringing them half-formed into the open, for the interested scrutiny of Tom Wickham and her sister.

She wanted to scream, to shout, to stamp her foot and utter obscenities as she had done not so very long ago. But that was the action of a child, and a selfish and unpleasant one at that. She had accused Kate of being a spoilt brat: suddenly, humiliatingly, she saw herself as Wickham must, a child too wayward and wilful to grow up, in painful contrast to Tabby, six years younger and apparently more mature by far.

[134]

A great flood of scarlet washed across her face, as the weight of her misery descended across her shoulders like the burden of the world's woes. To her horror, her eyes filled with tears, and she could feel her lip trembling. 'Nothing,' she said, suddenly desperate to leave this impossible situation, into which her own fury and resentment had led her. 'Nothing's wrong at all. I – I must go fetch the children.' She turned and ran blindly down the steps towards the orchard, stumbling and almost falling in her haste to escape.

Tabby's face was thoughtful and sympathetic. She glanced up at Wickham, and said quietly, 'I'm sorry. Poor Rachael, it must be very difficult, not knowing what you want.'

As Tom stared at her in surprise, she added, 'She doesn't really mean to be so rude, you know. If she could only stop to think . . . but then we're none of us perfect, are we?'

It was such a mature statement to come from the lips of someone little more than a child, that Tom was startled. Unaware that she had quoted one of Nat's favourite phrases, he shook his head, bemused and smiling.

'I hope you don't mind that I invited you,' Tabby continued gravely. She had turned to gaze over the crowded fruit trees in the orchard, where Rachael's voice, sharp and angry, could be heard telling Kate not to answer back, or she would probably be sent to bed without her supper.

Tom smiled. 'No, of course I don't, Mistress Tabitha.'

'Oh, please don't call me that – everyone calls me Tabby.' She turned and grinned at him, a sudden vivid flash of friendly mischief. 'I'm afraid the letter I sent you was a little bit of a lie – but only a very, very small one. Nat didn't ask me *directly* to invite you. I thought that he would like it, though, so I did.'

'And I'm very glad of it,' said Tom. 'Was Nat pleased, do you think?'

'You saw that he was,' Tabby told him. Tom, remembering the spontaneous delighted smile that had leapt to her brother's face when he entered Silence's chamber, knew that she was right.

Deb's voice came loud and clear from the orchard, arguing with her half-sister. Tom said slowly, 'I hope I have not upset Mistress Rachael too much. I did not know . . . I had no idea that she harboured such resentment towards me. I don't even really know why.'

'I expect you remind her of things she'd much rather forget,'

Tabby said candidly. She swung round to face him, her expression serious. 'Please – please don't take it too much to heart. She's so unhappy at present – she loved Father very much, and she still hasn't really recovered from his death.' Something in the quality of her voice disclosed that she herself had already done so. 'And then there's Jack Harington . . . Father arranged the betrothal before he died, it was his dearest wish that Rachael should marry him – Jack's father is one of his oldest friends, you see. And I think Rachael feels that – that she *has* to marry him, for Father's sake, even if in her heart of hearts she doesn't really want to.' She grinned again. 'It's almost as if Father left him to her in his will.'

The apt absurdity made him smile in response. He said, 'And you think she doesn't really want to?'

'I don't *know* – if she doesn't, she'd never ever say so. She tells you she's happy, but I don't believe she is,' Tabby said thoughtfully. 'When Rachael's bad-tempered, it always means she's miserable. And she wouldn't *be* miserable if she was madly in love with Jack Harington, would she?'

'I doubt it,' said Tom. He was beginning to feel very sorry for Rachael, and oddly grateful to Tabby, who in the space of five minutes had given him more information about her family than he could have assimilated in a week's stay at Wintercombe. 'Your poor sister. Can't she change her mind?'

'You don't know Rachael,' said Tabby. 'I think the moon would fall on her head before she'd admit she'd been wrong. But we're all trying to persuade her, nevertheless.' She glanced towards the orchard, where the sounds of dispute were growing hotter, and then said abruptly, 'Did you know . . . the King of Scots has invaded at last? Master Harington told us at dinner.'

It was hardly unexpected, for rumour had run riot over the past few months, but, even so, it startled him. 'No,' he said. 'No, I hadn't heard – when?'

'Several days ago, I think. Do you – do you think that Captain Hellier might be with the Scottish army?'

Her small, pointed face was anxious. He wanted to reassure her, but did not know what she most desired to hear. Besides, his dawning respect for this odd, direct, thoughtful child precluded any kindly lies. So he shook his head. 'I don't know, Tabby – I honestly don't know. I've heard nothing from him since that letter more than six months ago. And – and a great deal has happened since then.'

[136]

'I wish there was some way we could find out,' said the girl wistfully. 'He was such a good friend to us all – how I would love to see him again!'

'I don't think that is really possible,' Tom pointed out. 'It would be different if the whole land were to rise in the King's support, but there isn't much hope of it, I'm afraid. People are sick of war and uncertainty, of killing and destruction and hardship. They don't really care who is on the throne, or off it, so long as they are left to work the land and live their lives in peace.'

'Instead of being in the power of men like Colonel Ridgeley,' said Tabby, and shivered. 'I *hated* him. If Rachael hadn't shot him, I think I would have done it.'

Tom was shocked to see the fierce, implacable expression that suddenly and utterly transformed her delicate, gentle face. He said, appalled, 'But – but you were only a child!'

'I was eight or nine,' said Tabby. 'And if I'd had a pistol, I'd have done it. He was disgusting, horrible, evil – do you know, they say in the village that no grass will grow on his grave? And his ghost is supposed to walk the churchyard on nights with no moon, all covered in blood, and laughing?'

It was children's nonsense, of course, but all the same a thrill of superstitious fear trickled down his backbone. He stared at this outwardly fragile and graceful girl. Who would have thought that such a gently-bred child could harbour such bitter loathing?

But the war had taught her, young though she was: had taught her how to fear, and how to hate. How many other children, up and down the land, had their minds distorted by cruelty and suffering, by witnessing, or even enduring, appalling scenes of brutality and rape? It was a dreadful thought, and he was glad, suddenly and overwhelmingly glad, that he had chosen peace, and returned quietly to his lands. Though he might have forsaken honour, if not glory, at least he could live in harmony with his conscience.

Tabby was studying him. She said, echoing his thoughts with eerie precision, 'Why aren't you going to join the King of Scots?'

Startled, he stared at her. 'Because I dislike – no, I hate war. And this invasion is pointless and futile. It would be different if we were all suffering under this rule of Commonwealth, but on the whole we're not. Oh, there are taxes to pay, and everyone grumbles about that. But we know now what the cost of rebellion is – and it's a price that no man in his senses will ever wish to pay again. The only way that a change in government can come now is by the will of all the people. No longer can an outsider attempt to impose it by force – especially if he tries to do it with a foreign army.'

'But he is King still,' said Tabby slowly. 'And I expect, if you asked most people, they would say that he ought to be on the throne – it's his right, after all.'

'But if you asked most people, they would probably also say that it was not worth another war, with all the suffering and bloodshed and misery, to put him there,' Tom pointed out gently. 'And I for one have had my fill of fighting. A simple farmer I have become, and a simple farmer I intend to stay.' He glanced at her. 'Unlike Nick – Captain Hellier. But he was always a restless soul – I don't think he would readily settle down to the farming life. Though I must say, I did not think that he would lend his support to this invasion, either.'

'Perhaps he hasn't got anything else to do with the rest of his life,' said Tabby sadly. She looked up at him, with the shy sweet smile that was so misleading. 'I hope he is happy, anyway. Thank you for talking to me, Master Wickham. And please – don't say anything to anyone else about that letter, will you? Please.'

He gave his promise readily, and watched her walk back up to the house, those gloriously abundant honey-gold curls bouncing on her slender shoulders. She was a likeable child, and intelligent too. One day, that ethereal beauty would grace some wealthy man's household, and he thought wistfully of his own empty home, the busy loneliness waiting for him at the end of this brief visit.

Tabby took the steps to the top terrace at a run, her eyes glowing. He had never guessed, she was sure: he had made the same mistake that most strangers did, thinking of her as just a child. Only her half-brother Nat knew just how devious she could be. Tabby had from infancy made other people her study, and she knew her own family best of all, seeing their virtues and defects with a clear, yet sympathetic eye. She had gained the information she wanted without connecting Nick Hellier and her mother at all. She had gently planted in Tom Wickham's mind, without seeming to do so, the idea that, whatever she might profess, Rachael did not in fact really want to marry Jack Harington, and that the betrothal was therefore not so certain as it appeared.

Smiling with the success of her plotting, she stopped by the door that led into the screens passage, savouring the scents of the thyme and marjoram and camomile that grew between the cracks in the flagstones, to be aromatically bruised by passing feet. There still remained the problem of Nick Hellier's whereabouts, and she could hardly send off a letter addressed to the army of invasion. But Tom Wickham would be the first to receive any news, and whatever he heard, he would tell her.

As she set her hand to the latch, a shout from the garden made her turn. Wickham was running up the steps, his yellow-brown hair flopping across his face. 'Tabby! I have thought of something that might help you – if you do want to find out about Captain Hellier.'

'Oh, I do,' she said, with a child's eagerness. 'What is it? Do you know where he is?'

'No, no, I don't – but I know where his *brother* is.'

Tabby stared at him. 'His brother? Has he got a brother?' Somehow, she could not imagine Nick Hellier encumbered with relatives, like lesser mortals.

'He has a brother who lives in Worcester – I don't know his name, but I'm fairly sure he's an apothecary.' Tom beamed at her, pleased. 'I've only just remembered it – he spoke of his brother very seldom, and it hadn't occurred to me until now. If anyone knows where he is, it'll be his brother. Does that help you?'

She gave him a smile of unalloyed delight. 'Oh, yes, Tom – oh, yes, of course it does! Thank you so much!' And she planted a swift grateful kiss on his cheek before dashing inside, leaving him to shake his head with amusement.

Tabby spent all that evening composing a letter, discarding several sheets that were blotched and misspelt before arriving at the final version. In her round, neat, childish hand, it begged Master Hellier's pardon for putting him to inconvenience, informed him that she was a past friend of his brother's, and wished, for old times' sake, to correspond with him. She hoped that Master Hellier could give her some idea where a letter might reach his brother, and thanked him for his trouble, remaining his servant, Mistress Tabitha St. Barbe.

On her next trip to Bath, she gave it into the hands of the sympathetic servant at the White Hart in Stall Street, who must have wondered that this young, innocent-looking girl apparently possessed two sweethearts, in different parts of the country. She rode home, well pleased with her efforts on her unsuspecting mother's behalf. She had done her very best to find Nick Hellier. Now, she must wait, and rely on good fortune, and the good nature of strangers, to bring the news she wanted to Wintercombe.

The small scrap of paper, insignificant and yet momentous, made its slow, erratic way towards Master Hellier, apothecary, of the City of Worcester. At the same time, much further distant, the heterogeneous army of the King of Scots, many thousand strong, progressed in similar fashion southwards, towards the faithfully Royalist cities in the lands on the borders of Wales.

PART
❦ II ❦

THE SOLDIER OF FORTUNE

(August–September, 1651)

❧ CHAPTER EIGHT ❧

'Royal hope'
(*Macbeth*)

For five years, since the defeated Royalist garrison had marched out of its gates past the besieging Parliament troops of Colonel Rainsborough, the City of Worcester had enjoyed comparative peace. The brief uprising of 1648 had passed it by, and despite the usual grumbles – taxes, free quarter, iniquitous fines imposed on those who had only done their duty by supporting their anointed King – the citizens had been able to regain something of their previous prosperity. Worcester lay at the crossing of many important roads, to Wales, the North, the Southwest, and London, and possessed the only bridge over the Severn for some miles. In consequence, the innkeepers and merchants had always done well, and the late unhappy wars had provided a comparatively minor interruption in their assiduous gathering of wealth.

Master James Hellier, apothecary, had done very well for himself. He was one of the Forty-Eight, the Capital Citizens on the City Council, and a freeman, and he had high hopes of being elected alderman, or even mayor, one day. A small and slightly paunchy man in his forties, already going grey, he applied tireless energy to his business, to the garden where he grew all kinds of beneficial plants, and to city affairs. If his wife Jane, who was a stout, quietly capable woman a few years his junior, felt herself neglected by her bustling husband, she was too loyal to say so. Instead, she contented herself with the household and the children. Six had been born to them, and although three lay in the churchyard of St. Swithin's, dead severally of fever, croup and the measles, John, Sarah and Robert seemed happy, lively, healthy brats.

Master Hellier, though, was not entirely satisfied with his lot. A larger house, finer clothes, greater status, were what he wanted, and in furtherance of these ambitions he spent much time and money making himself congenial to the most influential of the city fathers. And of course his young family must reflect his sense of his own importance: his wife must always appear in public immaculately clad, the children likewise, and perfectly behaved.

Once, it had suited his purpose admirably, that his harum-scarum younger brother, after several most unsatisfactory episodes, had risen to be a captain in the Royalist army. He had acquired the habit of referring to him casually in conversation – 'My brother, Captain Hellier' – in tones that implied that Nick would be a general before long. But when the King's men were defeated, and the Worcester garrison surrendered, Master Hellier hastily expunged all mention of his brother from his talk. Times had changed, and it was no longer politic, nor even safe, to boast of Royalist connections.

He had heard from his brother occasionally, since the end of the war. The fool had chosen to go into exile rather than make his peace with the victors, but Master Hellier could accept that. He and his brother had both been apprenticed to apothecaries, James in Worcester, where he had married his master's only daughter and inherited the shop and the business, and Nick in Bristol. His young brother, disgracefully, had run away before his time was finished, to sell his sword in the German wars. He was a soldier, and there was no employment left to him in England, thank God. James felt no twinge of fraternal feeling or regret. He was relieved to have such a potentially explosive problem safely out of his hands and overseas. The few letters, battered and sometimes almost illegible, which arrived at his shop did not change his mind, though his wife seemed to welcome them, and the children, particularly John, who was the only one with any memory of his uncle, always greeted word of him with enthusiasm.

So when Tabby's letter was brought to him, after a week's rather haphazard journey from Bath, his first feelings were of annoyance and bewilderment. This young lady – it was unmistakably a child's hand, painstaking and clear – had no right to disturb his privacy. What did she think he could tell her? Was he his brother's keeper? And, with the King of Scots and his army loose in the land, and reliably reported to be heading for the Welsh Borders, was this the time to remind him of his Royalist connections?

But he did not succumb to his initial impulse, which had been to throw it on the fire. Whatever link this Mistress Tabitha St. Barbe had with his scapegrace younger brother – and it was unlikely to be respectable, child or no – there might be some advantage to be gained by a courteous reply. St. Barbe was a name of note in the Southwest, a large family with many branches and interests. Quite how a rising apothecary could be of service to them, he could not clearly see, but no man of ambition could afford to let even the slightest opportunity of advancement slip by without grasping it.

He wrote to Mistress St. Barbe, assuring her of his best endeavours, and informing her that, although he did not at present know his brother's whereabouts, he would do his best to discover them. Meanwhile, if she cared to send a letter for Captain Hellier to his address, he would send it on as soon as he had ascertained his brother's direction, and he was always her servant, Master James Hellier.

He gave it into the care of the Post on Tuesday, the twelfth day of August. And ten days later, the King of Scots and his army entered the City of Worcester in state.

The crowds turned out to cheer him: every one of the city's inhabitants, it seemed, and a goodly proportion of the surrounding villages, packed the streets and hung out of the windows and even, dangerously, from the rooftops, waving and shouting. The Parliament garrison, some five hundred men, had chosen the better part of valour and had fled to Gloucester as the Scots army approached, hastened on their way by shots and stones from the citizens, many of whom were staunchly Royalist, and proud of Worcester's previous loyalty to the crown.

James Hellier, with the clear eyes of the self-interested, saw that the King and his men were doomed. Common sense, a quality which he possessed in abundance, told him that this depressed, exhausted army, far from home and already diminished by desertion and disease, would be easy prey for the sharp military skills of General Cromwell and his immaculate, highly-trained and enthusiastic troops. But like everyone else, he closed the shop in good time, collected his wife and children, and joined the crowds about the Foregate, in the northern part of the city wall, to watch the King make his formal entry into Worcester.

The Mayor, Master Lysons, who was tall and stout and, to Master Hellier, over-full of his own importance, bore the City Sword before the King. The apothecary gazed with envious eyes at Worcester's chief citizen, arrayed in crimson satin, his three chins newly shaved and his linen spotless. The effect, he noted with some satisfaction, was a little spoilt by the Mayor's horse, which was a handsome, high-spirited, black belonging to one of the aldermen, and somewhat too light-boned for its rider's weighty pomp. Little Robert, in the front rank of the crowd, pressed against his mother's skirts, said in his high, carrying voice, 'Mama, why is that horse all covered in soap?' Heads turned, and Master Hellier hastily hushed his younger son with a glower that hid his secret amusement.

The King rode next, acknowledging the cheers and rose petals and late flowers with a gracious smile. He did not in the least resemble his small, pallid, martyred father, whose portrait had hung in the council chamber, until the late sad events had made its hasty removal a matter of policy. The twenty-one-year-old monarch was a very tall, dark young man, with a swarthy complexion that would have better suited a farm labourer. He could not have been described as handsome by the most besotted maiden, but there were smiles and blushes and blown kisses from every young girl in the crowd, and King Charles showed that he was well aware of it.

Behind him came a body of men on fine horses, their harness polished and gleaming, although Master Hellier's sharp eyes spotted many patches, threadbare areas and signs of wear on leather and cloth. These, he supposed, must be the King's Lifeguard: and even as the thought crossed his mind, he noticed a familiar face amongst them.

He had not seen his younger brother for nine years, not since the war broke out, but Nick Hellier had the type of face, and physique, which was not much subject to change. Like his brother, he was not tall, and was slightly built, although the years of soldiering had given him an air of lean, wiry energy which the thick buff coat could not disguise. James was conscious, suddenly, of an incongruous stab of envy. Long ago, he too had cherished childish dreams of knight errantry, of travelling to distant lands in search of fame and fortune. However, in his headlong rush to acquire wealth and status, he had never had the opportunity, and never, until now, felt the lack.

He wondered sourly how his brother, with his comparatively humble birth and scant monetary resources, could have risen so far. James, who had an inflated opinion of his own abilities, found it hard to credit that his brother's native talents might have something to do with his present exalted position.

He made no attempt to catch Nick's eye, but his wife Jane supplied the deficiency. She had always had rather a soft spot for her brother-in-law, and so far forgot her dignity as to wave her kerchief. Amongst the crowd of women and men doing the same, her gesture might have been lost, but something made Nick's eyes slide to his left. Briefly, his gauntleted hand was raised in acknowledgement, and then he had passed by, and the broad space of The Cross was filled with the massed ranks of the aldermen, and the Twenty-Four, the most important councillors.

They were followed by the Scots, a hangdog unshaven disreputable-looking crew, a strange sight in their outlandish blue bonnets and coats of dull hodden grey. Even more extraordinary were the shock-headed, bearded men in short plaid skirts, showing their hairy legs. His daughter Sarah hid her face behind her hands as they tramped past, for she had never seen such an alarming sight before. Then came the Scots cavalry, mounted on scrubby ponies, very different from the tall horses of the Lifeguard. Many carried long lances, which looked decidedly unwieldy, and as dangerous to their friends as to their enemies. Seeing the dour, miserable faces, the shambling weariness of the Foot, James Hellier wondered afresh at the folly of this invasion. It was one thing for the citizens to line the streets and cheer their King, but, he suspected, quite another to muster the courage of their convictions and take up arms in his support.

Already the people around them were dispersing, eager to be in the front row at the Guildhall for the next part of the ceremony. Jane was holding Robert and Sarah, and she and the eldest, John, were looking at him expectantly. With a sigh, James Hellier nodded. 'Yes, very well. If we go round by Powicke Lane and up Cooken Street, we'll avoid the crush.'

Everyone else, however, had had similar ideas, and, greatly to the children's disappointment, there was little to be seen over the bobbing heads of most of Worcester. All of them, including Robert, who was four, were too big to be carried on their father's shoulders, even if he had felt inclined, and their view was blocked by a particularly tall and sturdy gentleman in a high-crowned sugarloaf hat. Sarah cried, and Robert wailed in echo that he wanted to see the King.

For James, it was the final straw. Annoyed with the Scots army for disturbing their peace to evil purpose, with his brother's handsome grey horse and exciting life, with his wife's shining eyes and above all with the Mayor, who had decreed that only the Twenty-Four, and not the Forty-Eight, of whom James was one, should take part in the procession, the apothecary gathered up his whining family and marched them briskly back to their shop in New Street, deaf to their complaints.

He had feared that his brother would visit. His neighbour, Master Guise, a tailor, had Parliament sympathies and was always poking and prying into others' affairs. When the inevitable happened, and the government called the foolishly loyal citizens of Worcester to account, he did not wish the name of Master James Hellier, apothecary, to be connected too closely with the King's army.

But, to his relief, and the disappointment of Jane and the children, the day passed and Nick Hellier, with his buff coat and gleaming sword, failed to darken the door of his brother's house. Instead, four Scots officers were quartered in his nice, clean, sweet home, despite his urgent protests, and Jane made herself unnecessarily busy organising beds and supper and even, to her husband's annoyance, fresh hose and shoes for their unwanted and uninvited guests, while the children hovered, round-eyed, and young Thomas, the apprentice, had to be chased back to his work, weeding the physick garden, no less than five times.

He went to the service in the cathedral the next day, and stood amongst the packed soldiers and citizens to hear the preacher, Master Crosby, tactlessly affirm that the King was supreme in all his dominions, over everyone, including the Church. The Presbyterian Scots listened to this arrogant English preacher expounding philosophies quite incompatible with their beliefs and the Covenant that the King himself had signed, and took considerable offence. The preacher had to be admonished and the rift seemed to be healed, but Master Hellier, trudging home in the rain, wondered how that disparate army, bigoted Scots and Royalist English, could ever be kept welded together for long enough to face their enemy.

But welded they were, albeit precariously. Each depended on the other, and the Scots were far from home. Any thoughts they might have had about further marches were quickly dispelled. This place was loyal, welcoming, capable of defence, and well watered and supplied. Here they would stay, bring in eager recruits from Wales and the western counties and regain their strength, before facing the attack that must inevitably be launched against them.

Every house in the city had its share of quartered soldiers and, from the reports of his neighbours, James Hellier came to the conclusion that his own four were unusually clean and courteous examples of the breed, for all he could barely understand one word of their uncouth speech. There were guns, flimsy leather field pieces, on the bastions around the walls, and outside the Sidbury Gate a derelict earthwork, left over from the war, was reclaimed from sheep and undergrowth, and the soldiers set to work on rebuilding it. Orders were sent out to the constables of the surrounding villages instructing them to send men to help with the fortifications, but only a handful of foolhardy yokels appeared.

The King took up residence just round the corner from the Helliers, in a very commodious house next to St. Martin's Gate, and there was much coming and going at all hours, keeping the children awake and excited. His general officers were scattered all around the wealthier houses, especially near the cathedral, where there was an enclave of wild young English officers, headed by the Duke of Buckingham, roosting in the Deanery, and working their way with enthusiasm through large quantities of claret and sack provided by the city fathers. The most important Scots had taken over Master Wyld's house, the Commandery, just outside the Sidbury Gate. Young John, who went to the King's School just by the cathedral, reported with huge delight that he and the other boys had christened the Commandery the Crow's Nest, from the flock of black-gowned Presbyterian ministers who infested the place.

Without much conviction, his father chided him for his insolence, and watched his eleven-year-old son prance into the house, still gleeful at the stupid jest. Here, in his little half-acre strip that ran up to the crumbling bulk of the eastern portion of the city wall, he had tried to create a physick garden, such as could be found in Oxford, or London, or Bath. He had enjoyed mixed fortunes. Some plants had flourished, but others, inevitably the most rare and valuable, had unaccountably withered and died, or failed to thrive in any quantity. Moreover, at this season, with autumn approaching, the whole plot looked distinctly untidy and ragged, some plants already harvested or cut back ready for their new growth in the spring, others yet to come to fruition. The apprentice had been lax with his weeding: tutting under his breath, James bent and pulled a tendril of bindweed from around the nearest stalk of golden rod, an excellent remedy against bleeding wounds.

'Father!' John's high voice, pitched sharper still with excitement, echoed down the garden.

Wincing, the apothecary straightened and surveyed his son's precipitate return without enthusiasm. 'How many times have I told you, boy, not to screech like a night-owl in the garden? The neighbours do not want to hear such a caterwauling.'

'But Father,' said John, with only a moderate lessening in volume. 'He's here – Uncle Nick is here!'

Instinctively, James glanced around the garden, and those on either side, separated from his plot by wall and hedge and fence. Was that a flicker of movement in one of Master Guise's windows? Cursing his son's and his brother's indiscretion, he brushed John aside and hurried up the path. His embarrassing visitor must be kept out of sight within the house.

Too late. Before he had taken three strides, the figure of his brother had appeared, making his way between the hedges of lavender and rosemary near to the house, bordering the patch where Jane grew herbs and sallets for the kitchen. He was clad in his yellow buff coat, and carried his plumed hat in his hand.

With some trepidation, and more resentment, James Hellier halted, and watched Nick approach. A quick glance to his left revealed that the windows of the Guise house were innocent and empty. He hoped, without much conviction, that the brief movement had been no more than a figment of his imagination.

The man who stood before him now, brown and unsmiling, seemed superficially to be the same boy who had run away from his apprenticeship to be a soldier, more than fifteen years ago. Unlike some other men, including his brother, age had not added to Nick Hellier's girth, nor removed any of his brown, thick hair. It had graved a few more lines, of laughter and recklessness, around his mouth and eyes, and given his face a rather hard, careless, dangerous expression. James realised, with a profound sense of shock, that if this man had been a stranger, he would have been afraid of him.

But it was only his brother, seven years younger, whom he had watched grow from a baby, and he knew, reluctantly, that despite his misgivings, blood was after all thicker than water. They had shared a childhood, and such things could not be denied. His face cracked in a stiff, rather unwilling smile. 'Well – welcome home, brother.'

Nick studied him with the warm, chestnut eyes that he remembered all too well, and which had become disconcertingly shrewd. 'Welcome? Are you sure?'

'Of course I am,' said James, with the bluff open good humour that had won him some friends — though not yet enough — on the council. 'We have been waiting on tenterhooks for you to visit us, for two days now.'

'I plead pressing duties,' said Nick. He grinned at John, who was gazing up at him with round worshipful eyes, and looked suddenly ten years younger. 'Keeping Scots hands from English throats, and vice versa, is a task that takes up an inordinate amount of time, believe me. This garden is very fine — much better than the one your Grandfather Hellier had, John, which was little better than a midden and a rubbish heap. But there were trees at the end, just by the wall, very useful if we wanted to escape our duties for a while.'

'You may have done,' said James, not wishing to be included in his brother's memories of disobedience and misdeeds. 'But I can't recall joining you.'

John's thin, lightly freckled face had a yearning, wistful look, as if he, too, wished for a means of escape. Nick gave him a glance that his brother interpreted, correctly, as sympathetic, and continued. 'I see you are growing some of the new sunflowers. Have you found a specific use for them, or are they purely for show?'

The plants in question, giants of whom their owner was inordinately fond, grew against one wall, their vast golden faces turned to the evening sun. James, unwilling to confess that any inhabitant of his prized garden was not there for a useful purpose, said stiffly, 'The buds and seeds are said to be pleasant eating.'

'But meanwhile they look very handsome, and you're doubtless the envy of all your neighbours,' said Nick, grinning. 'So, what news? You look well, brother James — Jane's cooking obviously agrees with you.'

John giggled. His father glared at him thunderously. 'Go inside, young man, and take your insolence with you.'

'Yes, father,' said the boy meekly, and turned back towards the house. His obedience was only for show, however: he began to whistle, defiantly, a tune which Nick, to his amusement, recognised as 'When The King Enjoys His Own Again'.

'Mannerless brat,' said James, glowering, as his son disappeared within doors. 'Yes, I am well, and my dear Jane, and the children. We have had four more since you went away to war, but alas three died, and little Robert is the youngest.' He glanced curiously at his brother. 'And you? In all your wanderings, have you never thought to take a wife?'

'I might have done, had the opportunity offered,' said Nick, staring past him at the faded red stones of the city wall. 'But it did not, and I am glad of it now, for the sort of life I've led is hardly fitting for any woman of sensibility. It's a precarious business, eking out a living on plunder and a soldier's pay. Once or twice I thought I might have to sell my sword in earnest – but, as you see, it still hangs by my side.'

'And how did you come to take service with the King of Scots?' James asked, curiosity overcoming his natural caution. He was also eager to divert the conversation in case his brother should ask him for money.

'It's a long story,' Nick said. 'So long, if I had all night I'd hardly finish it before dawn. Suffice it to say that the wars in Germany seem to have ended, for the moment at least, and there is precious little employment there for a mercenary such as myself. I had some coin saved, enough to allow me the luxury of following my inclination instead of my purse, and so I offered my small services to the King. He accepted, and so you see me before you. It was touch and go,' he added with that disarming, lazy smile that had saved him from more childhood beatings than James, unendowed with similar charm, cared to remember. 'I nearly deserted the Cause in Scotland. Those meddling, bigoted, fanatical preachers were more than I could stomach – almost more than the King could stomach either, for all he knows he won't get his kingdom back without them. You heard of the slaughter at Dunbar almost a year ago? Well, the ministers were to blame for that, they told General Leslie to abandon his position and attack – but, before he could move against the English army, Cromwell seized the advantage and turned the tables.' He smiled grimly. 'At least some good came out of it – the Kirk is no longer supreme, common sense has triumphed over fanaticism, and a good Presbyterian conscience no longer means high rank in the army, even if you hardly know one end of a pistol from the other. They are even allowed to employ reprobate old Cavaliers like me now.'

'It doesn't seem to have done your draggle-tail troops much good,' said James bluntly. 'Cromwell will find them easy meat, and then where will you be?'

'Dead, I expect,' said Nick Hellier, and his smile sent a prickle of appalled horror down his brother's spine: he looked, for an instant, almost as if he welcomed it.

Banishing such morbidly foolish fancies from his mind, he showed Nick the garden, with justifiable pride, and found him surprisingly knowledgeable and interested. He remembered the bewildered letter of the Bristol apothecary to whom his brother had been apprenticed, describing the boy's sudden flight. 'I had not thought he would do such a thing, for he seemed entirely happy and at ease, and already showed no small mastery of his trade.'

He had run away from that trade, at the age of eighteen, with a pocket full of stolen coin, to hazard his life in the German wars and later, after a brief visit to the city of his birth to see his brother, in the English. Again, James felt that twitch of unjustifiable envy, and was angry with himself. Why could he not be content?

But the restlessness of spirit that had driven Nick through half the countries of Europe, also touched his brother, though in a different and more subtle way. For he, too, was never satisfied with his lot, always hungering for new, or more, or better.

They were deep in conversation about the merits of feverfew and its sovereign powers against giddiness in the head, the megrims and melancholy, when Jane came quietly down the gravelled path to tell them that supper was ready. James, who had dreaded his brother's visit, and was still surprised that he actually liked the man, looked with a more benevolent eye on her blushes. She was plain, stout and many times a mother, and her undoubted virtues as a housewife would not attract a man of the world such as Nick.

It was at the supper table, enjoying Jane's mutton broth and lamprey pie and cheesecake, that he remembered the letter from young Mistress St. Barbe. John and Sarah, however, were present and, if his brother had been seducing some well-born child, he did not care for them to hear about it. At least the four Scots officers were not there, being out on their duties.

He waited until Jane had taken the children off to bed, leaving the two brothers with their tobacco and a very good bottle of rich red malmsey, thick and sweet. Then he said casually, 'I had a letter concerning you, not a fortnight ago.'

'Concerning me?' Nick, who had been lighting his pipe from a spill with indifferent success, abandoned his task and stared at his brother. 'One of the Council of State's spies, perhaps? I can't imagine anyone else having an interest in me.'

'I doubt it,' said James. He had imbibed rather a lot of claret, as well as the malmsey, and the unaccustomed quantity had made him less circumspect than usual. 'Unless the Council makes a habit of employing children to do their dirty work for them.' He chuckled lecherously. 'Definitely a child, though, from the hand. Are your women getting younger, brother Nick?'

'Not to my knowledge. What was the name?'

'St. Barbe, she signed herself – Mistress Tabitha St. Barbe.'

Nick, raising his wine-glass to his lips, was suddenly very still. James saw his eyes become wide and dark, as if from some distant, yet well-remembered pain. Slowly, carefully, he set the wine back on the table without tasting it, and stared at his brother. His voice, deepened with some emotion, sounded unfamiliar. 'St. Barbe? Are you sure? What did it say?'

'I'll find it – I have it safe in my deed-box,' said James. There was something in Nick's face that gave him urgency: he blundered to his feet, trying to ignore the sudden wave of dizziness that assaulted his head, and stumbled out of the parlour to his shop, where he kept the stout wooden box, double-locked, in which all his letters and papers were housed.

Nick Hellier found that his mouth was dry, and his heart hammering. He took a gulp of the wine, then another to the dregs, and refilled his glass. Memory had caught him by the throat, at once bitter and extraordinarily sweet. Tabitha, the shy, lovely child, with a fawn's grace and a gift for music which he had discovered and helped to flower. She would be fourteen or fifteen now, and perhaps her promised beauty had also blossomed.

And her mother . . .

For six years Silence St. Barbe had lain in his heart, never to be forgotten. At first, aching with grief and loss, he had sought oblivion in the time-honoured way, drowning his sorrows and finding solace in the bottom of a wine-glass. But he had seen too often the perils of continued indulgence in drink, and had no intention of degenerating into a hopeless sot, all his better qualities submerged in a sea of sack and claret. Once the first sharp agony was past, he had made a determined and successful effort to cast off his dependence on the bottle, and launched himself into action. When the moribund Royalist cause no longer offered any satisfactory drug for the senses and the memory, he had sold his horse and almost all his possessions save those he most treasured, and taken ship for the Low Countries. The dying years of the German wars had afforded him some profit, a little from pay and rather more from plunder. Once, in England, he had loathed the war and its terrible effects on the unhappy population. The sights he saw in Germany, whole landscapes laid waste, made him realise afresh how fortunate England had been.

And now here he was, in company with the Scots army and a few hundred exiled Englishmen, part of an invading force that seemed to be reviled and loathed by almost all his countrymen. He smiled wryly into the bottom of the wine-glass, delicately spiral where the blower had twisted the slender stem. Where had disappeared his conscience, his scruples, his sensitivity? The young King deserved his right, but not at the price of war, of hatred, of further bloodshed and tragedy to mar this prosperous land, and rip open scars that had only just healed over.

No, he was here, part of this unloved and unlovely army, for the most maudlin and trivial of reasons. He had cast aside all remaining scruples to become a professional soldier because he could not face the alternative. He could not bear to settle down quietly in some peaceful town, marry a wealthy widow, and turn again to the only other trade he knew, that of apothecary. And he did not want a wealthy widow, or indeed any woman: he wanted Silence, still, after six years.

He could recall every line of her features so exactly, even now: her level brows, the clear calm expression that disguised such a tumult of feeling, the large tranquil eyes, like water, neither brown nor green but something of both. And because she was married, even though she disliked her pompous elderly husband, she was forever denied him.

He had been a fool to come back to England, he realised, to put himself at risk from long-repressed memories. In Germany, France, the New World even, amongst alien faces and strange tongues and unfamiliar landscapes, he was safe. But even in Worcester, so different from Bath or Philip's Norton, there were women who could remind him of his lost love, in their smile or their dress or the turn of their head.

A loud crash came from the shop, and some cursing. Nick poured himself another glass of malmsey, and grinned despite himself. Brother James had no head for wine, that was certain: he had probably imagined the letter, and would return empty-handed.

But no: he stood in the doorway, flushed with triumph and malmsey, flourishing a battered sheet of paper in his hand. 'Here it is — a letter from your lady love!'

'Hardly,' said Nick, resisting the stab of annoyance that urged him to lose his temper. 'Mistress St. Barbe can't be more than fifteen, and it's six years since last I saw her. How in God's name did she find your direction?'

James shrugged. 'Can't think. Someone must have told her, if you didn't. Here it is, anyway.'

The few clear, straight lines were disappointingly unrevealing. There was no mention of the rest of her family, no indication of how she had come by James Hellier's address, only a direct and courteous request for information. And even in that he thought he saw the spirit of the Tabby he had known. For a moment, longing swept over him, a yearning so intense that he closed his eyes, and saw again the terraced gardens of Wintercombe, the flowers and bees and the cherry arbour, the laughing children, and Silence in her plain mulberry gown, leaning over the balustrade, turning to him with a smile of welcome . . .

James was saying something, and with an effort he brought himself back to the prosaic dark reality of the little parlour. 'Yes?'

'I said,' his brother repeated, somewhat aggrieved, 'I said that I'd replied to her — oh, ten days ago or more — can't quite remember. Said she could send you a letter and I'd send it on if I could find you. Someone must have told her you were with the King of Scots, I reckon.' He belched comfortably. 'Another friend of yours, perhaps?'

'Perhaps,' said Nick, ignoring his brother's overt curiosity. 'Let me know if it arrives, will you? Though I doubt the Post will want to come within ten miles of Worcester at present.' He tucked the letter into his sleeve. 'Say goodnight to Jane for me, will you, and thank her for the delicious supper. I have to go — there's a muster at Pitchcroft meadow tomorrow, and I'm supposed to be one of those in charge.' He smiled crookedly. 'That's always supposing, of course, that anyone turns up. Enthusiasm for the Royal Cause doesn't seem to be running at a high level hereabouts.'

'You couldn't find a more loyal city than Worcester!' James protested, forgetting his own doubts and equivocations.

Nick's smile became chillier. 'Loyal, perhaps, I grant you. Eager to fight, no. I suppose they can't be blamed, but still. The King is desperate for English recruits, and Welsh ones, and I fear that tomorrow he'll be sorely disappointed.'

*

The larks of the morning, with dew upon their breasts, sang over Pitchcroft meadow in the warm sunshine, and Nick, seated on the sturdy, tough, dapple grey mare he had bought in Scotland, stifled a yawn and tried to prevent his mind from wandering. Behind him, the low voices of his men, and the chink of their own and their horses' harness, prompted him to stay awake. He glanced round at the empty field, and then at the sun. Probably past ten, and still no answer to the muster.

Tom Blagge, one of his brother officers, caught his eye significantly, and Nick shrugged. He did not particularly like Blagge, who was full of bombast and had several dubious episodes in his past. His loyalty to the King, however, could not be doubted, and he had been in exile since the end of the war. Blagge had been a Colonel of Horse and of Foot, with the governorship of Wallingford, an important garrison, and stood high in the young King's favour. So did the Duke of Buckingham, who had spent most of the march south sulking because Charles would not make him lieutenant-general in place of the popular, but Scottish, Middleton. He was sulking still, his bored, exquisite features turned away from the other men, the petulant set of his shoulders reminiscent of a child disappointed when an expected gift fails to arrive. Nick sighed. What with the youthful Duke's moods, and General Leslie's air of extreme misery, and Lord Wilmot's drunken carouses at the Deanery, it seemed as if the whole of the Royalist Command was disintegrating around them. And whatever the vices, or virtues, of General Cromwell, it was tolerably certain that he would not while away the days in a fog of wine fumes.

At least the King was not susceptible to such temptations, although a pretty girl would always catch his eye. Nick had met him years ago, when he was still a boy and Prince of Wales, and had liked his enthusiasm and lack of pretension. The boy had become a man, but those qualities had not disappeared with maturity. Charles was now playing soldiers in earnest, and he showed some ability at the deadly game, and more skill in diplomacy. Nick knew that only his tact and soothing words had prevented open fighting between certain sections of his ill-assorted army, and the fact that so many Scots, of different backgrounds and beliefs, had joined him, was also due to his influence. His cheerful, encouraging words had done wonders along the fortifications, urging the men on as they laboured, and he had not baulked at joining them, throwing off his rich doublet and hat to take a turn at spade or shovel himself.

What a pity, someone had said, that his father had not been like this. Nick, who respected his young sovereign's common sense and quick wits, and enjoyed his dry sense of humour, thought that if the first King Charles had indeed been less stiff-necked, more inclined to compromise, more in touch with his people, then civil war might never have come to England. The young man, who was at present urging the soldiers building the earthwork outside the Sidbury Gate to greater efforts, deserved a triumphant return to his rightful place, not this raggle-taggle army and inevitable disappointment, if not worse.

Someone was approaching. He looked up and saw, coming from the north, a small body of horse, no more than thirty or forty strong, and most indifferently mounted: indifferently equipped, too, he realised as they drew closer. Still, at least someone had obeyed the summons, and he hoped most earnestly that these first would not be the last.

They were not. Hardly had he ascertained the name of their leader – 'Colonel' was too exalted a title for the commander of such a paltry body of men – than another group appeared from the city, having presumably come over the bridge from the west. All had to be noted, the names of the officers, the number of men, the details of their arms and horses. Almost all were cavalry, but Sir William Hart brought in a motley collection of foot soldiers, half of them completely unarmed, the rest equipped with pikes of assorted lengths and various degrees of rust, and muskets that looked as if they had spent the years since the war hidden in someone's thatch. Fortunately, the Horse were somewhat better prepared, everyone having a sword and most at least one pistol, if not a brace. But it was not enough: not nearly enough.

The King came down himself to greet the arrivals, with his charming smile and warm words of welcome. But the afternoon dragged on, and the trickle of support had altogether ceased. Nick reckoned that hardly more than a thousand men had attended the muster, very different from the flood of recruits that the optimistic Charles had expected. The disappointment was evidently most bitter, but he hid it as best he could, and talked hopefully to Buckingham and Leslie, who had joined them, of the enthusiastic supporters who were surely even now gathering in the distant blue hills of Wales.

The last body of men were under the command of Lord Talbot, son to the Earl of Shrewsbury, who had earlier brought in several troops of Horse. There were only sixty of these, but Talbot, with aristocratic arrogance, insisted on being addressed as 'Colonel'. For once, both Nick and Tom Blagge were united in their irritation. The sight of his deputy, an amiable young gentleman all aflow with ribbons and lace, did not increase Nick's confidence. Asked for his name, he drawled languidly, 'Lieutenant-Colonel Mervyn Touchet, my dear fellow.'

Nick found an ill-placed smile twitching the corner of his mouth. He controlled his wayward sense of humour and wrote down the name, while the elegant gallant in front of him played idly with the fringes of his riding-glove. The rather long face, the dark hair and eyes seemed oddly familiar, and suddenly he placed the resemblance. Set them side by side, and it would not seem so apparent, but this tall dark aristocrat looked a little like the King, though more handsome by far.

The thought amused Nick, even more than the officer's name had done. He waved the man on, ignoring the affronted expression that crossed Touchet's exquisitely groomed features, and turned his attention to his captain. Both he and Blagge, who though a gentleman born had at least the virtue of plain speech and dress, were thoroughly weary of these beautiful young aristcrats playing at war. Besides, as he remarked to Blagge later, when they were returning to their quarters in a house hard by the cathedral, who could take seriously anyone with the unlikely name of Mervyn Touchet?

'He's brother to the Earl of Castlehaven, and wed to Talbot's sister,' Tom Blagge said. 'Papist, he is – wears a cross under his coat, and carries a rosary. How those black crows in the Commandery will like that, I don't know. Talbot's a Papist too, and his father Shrewsbury – a whole nest of 'em.'

'As long as they can fire a pistol and fight the enemy, I don't greatly care,' Nick said. It had been a weary and dispiriting day, and his usual good humour had deserted him. 'We need every man we can lay our hands on, whether Papist, Presbyterian, Jew or Mahommedan.'

'And pray God the Welsh come down from their hills,' Blagge said grimly.

But the Welsh did not, and through the last week of August, hot and dusty, the King and his army waited at Worcester for the support that never materialised. The soldiers were too busy, throwing up earthworks, breaking bridges and improving defences, to notice the lack, but the officers were well aware that they were in a frighteningly vulnerable position. General Leslie had the aspect of a man expecting to be hanged next week, and was no longer on speaking terms with Middleton, his second-in-command. In the Deanery, Buckingham consumed vast quantities of wine with old sots like Wilmot, and spent hours bemoaning the unfairness of the King, who refused to promote him to the position that was his by right. The more energetic English officers – Massey, Blagge, Carliss – followed their King's example, and did their best to encourage and hearten the dispirited soldiers. At least they were well fed, well clothed, sheltered and healthy. They had only to give that Roundhead Cromwell the long-overdue beating he deserved, and all England would be at their mercy.

It was a delusion, and Nick knew it. But he knew also that miracles could happen in war. Cromwell had been even more dispirited, and heavily outnumbered, before the fight at Dunbar. Leslie's mistake had given him the opportunity to snatch a God-given victory. This time, opportunism, luck and good generalship might turn the tables.

On the evening after the Pitchcroft muster, he went again to his brother's house in New Street. Cromwell was fast approaching from the north – he had last been reported at Stratford, and it was said that the militia of many eastern and southern counties had been called out. There would be battle, or siege, and Nick knew that, even if James did not leave Worcester, he should send his wife and children out of the city.

James agreed, but Jane proved surprisingly stubborn. 'I am sorry, Nick, but I am not deserting my home, or my husband. I do think that the children should be sent away, though. A cousin of mine lives in Malvern, they've been there before, and it will be like a holiday for them. But I am not moving.'

He could not help remembering another stalwart lady, who had refused to flee despite a danger even more desperate. But Jane, plump and small and dark-haired, was nothing at all like Silence. He promised to arrange for a pass that would allow the children, escorted by their mother's maid and Thomas, the apprentice, to leave Worcester, and went back to his quarters with the first grey tendrils of despair twining their chilly way into his heart. They were doomed, unless a miracle happened, but for honour's sake, and for the young King, they would fight, and die. The irony of it was that now, with that last mercy for a restless spirit and an empty life almost within his grasp, he had more reason to keep himself alive than at any time in the last six years. For slipped within his doublet, as yet unopened, but containing all his hopes, was a letter to him from Tabitha St. Barbe.

It was not until very much later that night, when the other officers who shared his quarters had rolled into their beds, or settled down for a session of cards or drinking, that he had the opportunity to discover what she had written. He had ensured privacy for himself: usually, he could school his face to reveal nothing, but against the pain, or joy, that might lie in her words, he would have no defences. He had wondered, ever since James had shown him her first letter, why she wished to contact him once more. She could surely have no more than vague memories of him, and he doubted whether a child so young could have been aware of the relationship between him and her mother. But she was not a child now, and perhaps she had discovered something about that strange, terrible, wonderful year, when enemy soldiers had garrisoned her home, and one of them had become more than friendly with the lady of the house . . .

Or perhaps there was other news. He had steeled himself for the worst, for he had seen death arrive in many guises, and knew that it could come unexpectedly, even to a healthy woman of . . . thirty-five, he supposed she was now, a year older than himself. And would she have changed, if she still lived? Would she have grown fat and placid, like Jane?

Something in him did not want to find out: wanted only to remember her as his lover, passionate and gentle, her delight in him shining in her face. But Tabby had written to him, and something of importance must have happened to make her go to these lengths to seek him out. Presumably the other members of the family had not considered making any effort to contact him.

Well, he would never find out if he did not open it. He sat down at the little table in his chamber, drew the letter from his doublet and carefully eased his thumb under the seal.

There was just less than a page, in her neat, rather childish hand: with a strange mixture of apprehension and joy, he read:

Dear Captain Hellier,
I do not know if this will ever find you, but your brother most kindly did promise to send it on to you, should he discover your direction, and so I have taken the liberty of writing to you in the hopes that you will one day receive it. Pray thank him for his courtesy, should you do so.

Nick found himself smiling at the adult phraseology that seemed so earnest and accorded so little with the dreamy, musical, secret child he remembered. His eyes slid down to the next paragraph.

It was Master Wickham, who was your lieutenant, who told me how you might be reached. He has visited Wintercombe several times, and is a good friend to us, my brother Nat in particular. He has given us news of you, but news is a poor substitute for your self, and we would dearly love to see you once again, if your circumstances allow it. We all have fond memories of you, especially my lady mother, who has been a little cast down by my poor father's death −

His heart lurched, and he stared at the clear round hand. No, he was not mistaken: it was written there in solid black and white, no figment of his wishful imagination. 'My poor father's death, this May last'.

He was dead, then, the red-faced insensitive Roundhead colonel, whom he had cuckolded six years previously. Dead, leaving his wife a widow, free − after a decent interval, of course − to marry again.

Nick put his head in his hands, fighting for control. That all his hopes, long held, long derided by his common sense, should have come to flower now, when he faced such danger − what bitter irony that he should have discovered it at this moment. And in a week, or two, or three, unless the miracle was vouchsafed, he would be dead, or a prisoner, or a hunted fugitive, and Silence and all her serene strength and hidden beauty would be lost to him for ever.

Better, almost, not to have known, he thought, shivering with the intensity of the emotion that gripped him. Better to go to his grave, or into exile, with the memory still fresh of a love that had seemed perfect, yet as impossible and star-crossed as any match between Montague and Capulet. For it is not utter despair that destroys: it is the sliver of hope, as slender and silver as the new moon, that tears the heart asunder.

He looked down at the letter again, seeing the knuckles of his hands clenched white with tension. Deliberately, slowly, he calmed himself, breathing slowly to relax his muscles, until he was able to concentrate on Tabby's remaining words.

You would find Wintercombe just as you remember it, save that there are now no soldiers. Darby still rules in the kitchen, but Eliza is to be married soon. My mother's sister Patience resides here now, and is our great friend. We still have Lily, but poor Pye sickened and died last year, to our great grief. Her daughter Misty flourishes, and she has bred ten kittens this year. And we have a popinjay now, which I have called Emerald, and is Kate's dear friend, and talks most profanely, to Nat's great delight. He is trying to teach it to whistle a tune, but it sits most obstinate and will not obey. The garden has grown yet more beautiful, and all of this family wish that you were here to see it, none more so than your friend and servant,

Tabitha St. Barbe

He wondered who Kate was: perhaps a maid, or a companion to Silence? There had been no one of that name at Wintercombe six years ago. He smiled at the inconsequential flood of news, and even more at the afterthought squeezed in below her firm signature.

It may please you to learn that I play daily upon the virginals, and have never forgotten your teachings, which have afforded me so much delight.

At least, he thought, folding the letter with care, I have left some good behind in the world. He sat for a long while, silent, by the candle, staring into the past, returning again in his mind to the house that held all that he had ever truly desired in life, and which for six years had been denied to him.

One day, if he lived, if the King came into his own again, if he could, he would go back to Wintercombe, and find his heart once more.

❧ CHAPTER NINE ❧

'A foregone conclusion'
(*Othello*)

General Cromwell, in command of forces nearly thirty thousand strong, was supremely confident. The Scots had mustered only half that number, and were reliably reported to be ill-armed and low in morale. His own men were well trained and disciplined, excellently equipped, and filled with enthusiasm for their cause. There was universal loathing for the Scots, and the countryside had significantly failed to rise in their King's support. They had been forced to take refuge in Worcester, which had misguidedly welcomed them. He could afford to let them fester there, apprehensive and isolated, whilst he prepared the rope that would encircle them and draw them into the noose, ready for the kill.

Edward Massey, a Presbyterian who had done signal service for the Parliament during the war, but who had since changed his allegiance, had been sent to garrison the way over the Severn at Upton, some miles south of Worcester. Their destruction of the bridge had been thorough, but not thorough enough. Major-General Lambert, sent by Cromwell to investigate with a small party of men, found that someone had left a plank across the gap between the arches, so that the townspeople could get over. At dawn, eighteen picked soldiers crept across and barricaded themselves in the church, while the rest of Lambert's men forded the river, made shallow by the long hot rainless August, and attacked the Scottish troops. Massey, agonisingly wounded in the hand, could not rally his men. They were driven out of Upton and fled back to Worcester, leaving the triumphant Lambert in command of the vital crossing.

Cromwell was delighted and rode over to Upton that afternoon to thank his troops in person. Now, they could approach Worcester from two sides. The knot was about to be slipped.

In the city, the news was received with shock and dismay. Tidings had already come in of the defeat of the Earl of Derby, whose small band of recruits had been smashed at Wigan. Derby was reported to be wounded and in hiding, and many valuable men were dead or taken prisoner. A bare paltry handful had trickled in from Wales, a travesty of the mighty flood of enthusiastic support that had been confidently expected not so long ago. And now, the experienced soldiers in the King's army knew well that they were trapped. They must stand and fight, or try to break out against vastly superior odds. Nick was not the only one to acknowledge in his heart that their cause was hopeless.

But the young King did not lose faith, and his cheerfulness was an example to them all. Even when the enemy placed a battery on Red Hill, to the south, and began a steady bombardment of Fort Royal, the earthwork outside the Sidbury Gate, he could be seen striding about the fortifications, his black hair flying and the silver lace gleaming on his doublet, encouraging the gunners in Fort Royal to greater efforts. The sixteen antiquated leather field pieces, which had been brought from Scotland, replied as fervently as if their supplies of powder and shot were unlimited. The standard of gunnery, however, was not very high, and a great deal of precious ammunition was wasted.

A raid was planned to deal with the Parliament battery on Red Hill. Although it was meant to be a secret, and surprise was essential to its success, someone talked too freely. The Scots attackers, ghostly white in their shirts, crept up through the bushes and hedges, only to find the enemy soldiers awake, and murderously expectant. Several men were killed, including an experienced and competent major, and the intrepid raiders, cursing their ill fortune and the unknown spy, fled back to Worcester in disarray.

The following morning, soldiers came to the house in New Street that lay next door to Master James Hellier, apothecary. His wife Jane, peering in alarm from her chamber window at the commotion, saw Master Guise the tailor, white-faced and struggling, being unceremoniously hauled away by a group of stalwart Scotsmen in hodden grey, while his screaming wife clutched at the soldiers and begged them to let her husband go, he had done nothing, where were they taking him?

The tailor's poking and prying had gone beyond mere nosiness. Somehow, he had got wind of the Scots attack and had warned the Parliament men. He had been seen leaving Friar's Gate by a curious and Royalist acquaintance, and someone else had spotted him slinking unobtrusively up the lane that led to the enemy positions at Perry Hill. Furious, smarting from the failure of their stratagem, the Scots High Command showed no mercy. Before the day was out, Master Guise's twisted corpse was swinging on a gibbet, and his wailing wife was being comforted by Jane Hellier, more from duty than out of any liking or sympathy for the woman. Guise had been a fool who should have known better than to play the spy and, worse, to be caught. His wife was well known to be a greedy shrew, ever with an eye to the main chance, who had doubtless encouraged her husband in his folly. Jane mixed possets, looked after her children, and turned a cold stare on Mistress Guise whenever her lamentations turned to cursing the wicked ungodly Scots who had so foully murdered her husband.

And still the bombardment went on, more annoying than dangerous to the city itself, for the emplacement on Red Hill was out of effective range of all but the southernmost quarter, around Sidbury Gate and the cathedral. But the heat and the constant dull thud of the guns, that might have been thunder but was infinitely more menacing, sapped the energy and morale of the citizens. It had seemed fine enough, only ten days ago, to welcome their rightful sovereign back to their city, and to hear him proclaimed King of England, Scotland, France and Ireland by their own mayor. They had even, gladly, lavished supplies and quarter on these dour, alien soldiers, and small children had gawped at them in wonderment, while young girls blushed and giggled and simpered at any handsome man in a buff coat, to the scandal of their parents and the ministers. They had believed that supporters would flock to the young King's standard, although, of course, they themselves were mostly too busy, had too much to lose, too much at stake, to arm themselves. Others, better qualified and experienced, could do their fighting on their behalf.

And now General Cromwell, with a huge army, aided by militia forces from all over the country, was camped within a mile of the gate, and suddenly, brutally, reality had intruded. The more prudent, who had relatives in the country, sent wives, children and valuables to safety. Some gathered in stocks of food, believing that a prolonged siege was most likely. James Hellier, knowing that his wares and his skills would shortly, unless a miracle happened, be desperately needed, spent much time making wound salves and restorative cordials, while his wife replenished the stocks of bandages and plasters, and worried about whether the children were behaving themselves at Cousin Jones's house in Malvern. Nick, drilling the paltry bands of new recruits on Pitchcroft, or supervising the labours on Fort Royal amid falling shot and incessant noise and heat, knew that, one way or the other, this nightmare of dread would soon be ended.

General Cromwell had made his plans. He had no intention of wasting time and men on a siege. The Scots were firmly ensconced in their snug, defensible city, and must be drawn out to give battle. His main force, under Fleetwood, would attack the enemy who were stationed to the south-west of the city, around the village of Powicke on the River Teme, near to the place where it joined the Severn. In the meantime, the bombardment from Red Hill would be increased as a distraction while Fleetwood dealt with the Scots, before the rest of the Parliament army joined in the attack to secure the victory.

It was a measure of the General's confidence that he could consider splitting his force in two. But if the malignant Scots, the men of blood, were to be ejected from Worcester with the least possible expenditure of time and men, such a strategy was essential. Bridges of boats were needed to cross the Teme and the Severn in such strength, and the little town of Upton became a collecting point for all the craft that Fleetwood's soldiers could lay their hands on, moored rocking together in the strong Severn current. While their indignant owners complained in vain, children and adults stared curiously and wondered why all these vessels, from trows and barges to rafts and rowing boats, had been gathered here.

On Wednesday, the third of September, a year to the day after his glorious victory over the Scots at Dunbar, and therefore a date of good omen, Cromwell planned to attack.

*

The King and his officers, English and Scots, had known for some time that something was afoot. Scouts, threading their way with difficulty and danger through the Parliament lines encircling the city, reported much activity at Upton, and to the south and east of the city. There might still be time, some of the more faint-hearted thought, for the Scots to break out of the trap and flee homewards. But only a day or so previously, the Earl of Derby, wounded in the fight at Wigan a week before, had managed to reach Worcester with a few followers. He reported that there were enemy horsemen all over Lancashire ready to intercept any fugitives. He himself had only narrowly avoided capture, and owed his liberty to the devoted assistance of a Papist family, who had hidden him, dressed his wounds, and sent him on his way to rejoin the King. Nick, seeing the pale, drawn face as he imparted the tale of his escape to the Scots and English staff in the Commandery, wondered if the Earl regretted exchanging his safe refuge for this threatened, beleaguered city.

He himself wished only for an end to it. Like all of them, his nerves were flayed by the waiting, the heat, the flies and dust and stink in the overcrowded streets, the bombardment that did no real damage save to morale, the certainty of imminent attack and the likelihood of defeat. General Leslie was in the depths of despair: he had already spoken of his belief that they were all doomed, and that his men would not fight. It was becoming apparent that many Scots thought the same. If it had not been for the youthful enthusiasm of the King, holding his disparate and dispirited army together like glue binding a worn-out pot, many more would long since have deserted, whatever the odds against their safe return home across hundreds of miles of hostile country.

A curious mood of fatalism had descended upon Nick in these last few days. Since reading Tabby's letter, with the chance it offered of hope, after all these years bereft of it, his keen awareness of the ironies and absurdities of life had led him to a deep premonition of doom. He was not superstitious: he despised men who ruled their lives by the stars or the casual movements of significant animals, or even the pronouncements of the pulpit. But in the thirty-four years of his erratic, shifting, rootless and pointless existence, he had never had such a dream fulfilled. He had learned to exist for the moment, living from day to day, never looking too far ahead or behind him, for if he did, he might well find that such a bleak prospect would be too much to bear. He had not thought that anyone, save himself, would care if he lived or died. Even his brother James had grown too far distant, too enmeshed in his own narrow little concerns, to regard Nick as anything more than a temporary hiccup in the steady upward climb of his fortunes. Jane might shed a tear or two, but not for long: her heart was given over almost exclusively to her children. And he had thought, hoped, that Silence, in her lovely old house, her family all around her, would find that the wounds of love healed quickly.

But it seemed that they had not — or why else had Tabby written to him?

He could not, for the sake of his sanity, allow himself to dwell on what might have been. He had duties and responsibilities, and the instillation of something resembling military competence into those new Worcestershire recruits was his present task. He put aside his instinctive mistrust of Lord Talbot, and his wayward impulse to laugh at the exquisite person of Mervyn Touchet — he was a professional soldier, after all — and set about informing these raw young farmers how to handle a horse, draw a sword and fire a pistol at approximately the same time, without falling off or dropping anything.

Fortunately, there were some who knew what they were about. Lord Talbot had seen some service in the Royalist army in the dying days of the war, and Touchet, his brother-in-law and lieutenant-colonel, proved to have had experience in Ireland. Colonel Carliss, a Staffordshire man who had raised a couple of troops of horse, appeared resourceful and capable, a man after Nick's own heart, not afraid to bend the rules or abandon convention to achieve results. Between them, they managed to force a little life-saving knowledge into the skulls of young men who had been children when the last war was fought, and who wanted now to snatch at a late chance of glory.

At least, Nick thought, surveying them as they wheeled and trotted raggedly around Pitchcroft in the evening sunshine, their horses still fidgety at the distant gunfire from Red Hill and the nearer flash of drawn swords, they were now a little less of a danger to themselves than they were to the enemy. And in spite of the dour, watching ring of Scottish faces, their enthusiasm for the Cause shone from their eyes and voices and their heartening willingness to learn. Given another two or three weeks, he thought, soothing his restless mare, who was probably coming into her season, and he might have made real soldiers of them.

But they did not have two or three more days, let alone weeks. The next morning Cromwell launched his attack.

*

Like many of those preceding it, the dawn air of Wednesday, the third of September, was crisp and fresh, giving promise of yet another fine day to come. The orchards around Worcester lay flushed and fruitful, the trees laden with apples and pears. Harvest had been gathered in, somewhat earlier than usual on account of the fine weather, not to mention the Scots. No one wanted the most promising yield for some years to be ruined by a pack of soldiers doing battle across ripe golden fields. Cattle, fat and sleek from summer grazing, and sheep just beginning to look woolly again after shearing, had been turned into the stubble. The hedgerows were graced with unripe blackberries and dull-coloured hips and haws, promising an autumn bounty for man and bird and animal. Old people had already studied the signs and the aches in their bones, and prophesied a hard winter.

But on this warm sunny morning, cold and snow and frost seemed very far away. Although logic dictated that Cromwell must surely attack at any time, the day had begun as usual. Nick, with the other officers who shared his quarters, had broken his fast with bread and cheese, cold bacon and herring and small beer in the little dark house by the cathedral, and all over the city their men were doing the same, in varying degrees of comfort. There were a few outposts in the villages to the south and west of the city, and one of these was due for a rather rude awakening.

The boats that Cromwell had ordered to be collected at Upton, six or seven miles to the south of Worcester, had been sent on their way at dawn, rowed by hardy volunteers and river men, while Fleetwood's section of the army kept pace on the bank. It took all morning, with only the larks, otters, herons and a few of the more foolhardy local people, to look on. After nearly ten years of intermittent warfare in England, soldiers were no longer a novelty, but a menace to be avoided and feared.

There was only an outpost, some two or three hundred Scots, at Powicke itself. Despite being vastly outnumbered, they resisted Fleetwood's men with vigour, and a hot battle for the churchyard ensued. Meanwhile, one of their number set spurs to his horse, forded the river and galloped back to Worcester to warn the King and his command that the dreaded attack seemed to be under way.

They were already aware of it. The cathedral tower afforded a magnificent view over the surrounding countryside, and the low line of hills on the far side of the River Teme, around Powicke, could clearly be seen. In the hot, windless air, the men on watch at the top of the tower could hear the distant sharp crackling of musket fire, and see puffs of smoke, although the distance and the intervening trees obscured the details of the conflict, even when studied through a perspective glass.

On the tower leads, King Charles and his staff hastily conferred, listened to the report of the man from Powicke, and decided on their strategy. It was plain that Cromwell had launched most of his men on this southern attack. The Scots were outnumbered overall, but if the man from Powicke spoke the truth, and the reports of other scouts were reliable, then the enemy gun battery at Red Hill was now guarded by a comparatively small brigade of horse and militia.

It was an opportunity too tempting to miss. Charles had always admired and envied his bold and dashing cousin, Prince Rupert. He resolved to do as Rupert might have done, in similar circumstances, and to stake all on a daring venture that, if it succeeded, might well turn the battle in his favour, against all the odds.

The Scots Major-Generals, Montgomerie and Pitscottie, were sent, with some four or five thousand men, to defend Powicke Bridge and the south-western flank of the city against the Parliamentarian onslaught, while the Scots lancers, under General Leslie, took up the reserve position on Pitchcroft, ready to assist where they were most needed. The rest of the Royalist army, a mixture of Scots and English horse and foot, would be sent against the guns on Red Hill when the best opportunity offered.

Nick Hellier, officially a Captain of the King's Lifeguard, found himself somehow at the head of the Worcestershire recruits. Massey, still in much pain from his shattered hand, had apparently suggested it. Lord Talbot, arrogantly at the head of his sixty horse, looked decidedly aggrieved, and Nick, the tradesman's son, smiled inwardly at the irony of it. But Massey was essentially practical, and had never let a man's birth stand in the way of his ability. By any yardstick, Captain Hellier had more experience in the field than these aristocratic colonels of a handful of horse, sitting resentfully behind him with their noses thoroughly put out of joint. He hoped that, in the exhilaration of the charge, they would follow his lead and obey his orders.

The heat blazed down on his bare head: he would not put on his helmet until the order came to advance. They were assembled in the College Green, below the cathedral, out of reach, though not earshot, of the bombardment from Red Hill. In the intermittent gaps in the gunfire, they could hear the more distant sounds of battle to the south. The Scots around Powicke, encouraged and heartened by the flying visit of their King, urging them to fight to the end and hold the line at all costs, defended the watermeadows along the River Teme against almost the entire might of Cromwell's army. Men and horses here were restless and on edge, knowing that before the day was done they would have seen battle, some for the first time, and perhaps died in it. Those who had never fought before could be marked by their air of tense watchfulness, sitting taut in the saddle awaiting instant action. The more experienced men had dismounted to allow their horses to rest and relax, while they conversed quietly or snatched a quick meal from supplies prudently carried in saddlebag or snapsack.

Nick had carefully tried to empty his mind: it was the only way to dissipate the dreadful apprehension that always gripped him before action. In the thick of battle it was different, there was no time for fear or thought, every instinct glued to the twists and turns of the fight. Then the mood of reckless exhilaration would overtake him, when his mind seemed to break free of its shackles, and direct his hand and eye as if they belonged to someone else. And afterwards, the reaction, the shivering relief that could only be dissolved in wine, women and song.

If there was an afterwards. He had been lucky: all the years of soldiering had given him an impressive array of scars, noticeably on his back, but no wound had yet threatened his life, nor even been especially serious. But today the conviction had deepened within him that he would not survive this imminent conflict. Once, in the days of bleak despair after leaving Silence, he might have welcomed it. Now, though, he was aware more keenly than ever before of the beauty of this late summer day, the sweetness of the birdsong in the trees on the green, the sharp nutty flavour of the cheese crumbling in his mouth. And above all there was that hope, wild, improbable yet unutterably joyous, that one day, some day, the miracle might happen and he might see the lady of Wintercombe once more. Yet he still could not rid himself of the belief that this door, opened so recently, would today be brutally and finally slammed in his face.

'Hot work, eh, Hellier?'

It was Mervyn Touchet's languid drawl in his ear. Any distraction, even this, from his disobedient thoughts would be welcome. He glanced at his horse, who was dozing peacefully in the sunshine, her smoky tail swishing the flies away, and then turned to Lord Talbot's lieutenant-colonel with a smile that was not entirely due to the amusement that Touchet always seemed to inspire in him. 'It is indeed,' he said. 'More for those poor devils down at Powicke than for us at the moment, I fancy.'

'Doubtless it will be our turn at some point this afternoon,' said Touchet, as casually as if he were discussing a day's hunting. He was beautifully dressed, in a pristine yellow buff coat, its sleeves decorated with bands of scarlet, his neckcloth knotted in the latest dashing style and so snowily white that Nick had to avert his eyes from the dazzle. He wondered disparagingly how long Touchet thought such glorious cleanliness would last in the thick of battle, at risk from sweat, powder smoke, dirt and blood, not to mention more lethal hazards. His own clothing was plain, but serviceable: the buff coat that had protected him through several seasons of campaigning in all weathers, just a shirt beneath, a plain cloth about his neck, narrow lace only on his cuffs. But his sword was razor sharp, and cleaned so that he could see his face plainly in the sleek shiny metal, and his wheel-lock pistols, in their holsters on either side of the mare's saddle, were in perfect order, ready to load and span when the time came.

'They tell me you are a native of this place,' said Touchet, as condescendingly as if Worcester were a collection of squalid hovels, instead of a proud and prosperous cathedral city.

Nick had learned long ago to ignore such slights, real or imagined: he had other ways of doing battle. 'I am,' he said courteously. 'Indeed, my brother and his family still live here.'

'Really? Oh, yes – the apothecary, is it not?' Touchet's narrow, dark eyes scanned him up and down, as if mentally vesting him in humble tradesman's garb, and providing him with mortar and pestle. 'But you have not been here for many years, I understand.'

'I have not,' Nick agreed. The sun had passed mid-day, the flies were buzzing, and surely the far sounds of battle to the south had grown more intense? He no longer possessed the energy to think of a witty or cutting riposte: the heat and the waiting seemed to have sapped his strength. And he had already decided not to furnish this arrogant man with the details of his life, even in the expurgated version. He added, 'You yourself have seen some service in Ireland, I understand.'

To his surprise, the handsome face abruptly darkened. 'Yes,' said Touchet curtly. 'And that, sir, is why I have hazarded my life and my estates in the struggle against the Arch-Fiend.'

Nick, after a startled pause, realised that Cromwell was thus described. It seemed a surprisingly powerful epithet, until he remembered that Touchet was apparently a Papist, and that the Lord General had a somewhat bloodstained reputation after the massacres in Ireland. That, of course, explained the preponderance of Catholics in the English section of this heterogeneous army. They were probably frightened that Cromwell, having disposed of their friends in Ireland, would next turn his malevolent attention to the English recusants.

He's even more likely to do so now, Nick thought, since most of them seem to be in arms against him. He muttered some words of condolence, but he had been reared to mistrust Papists, and later tolerance had not entirely erased that feeling. It was not so very long, after all, since they had conspired to blow up King James and all his Parliament.

'I lost good friends at Drogheda,' said Touchet. 'Men, and women, priests and children were slaughtered there. I have longed ever since for the chance to wreak some revenge. Are you of our Catholic faith, Hellier?'

'I am not,' said Nick, whose trust in any deity had long since grown faint and erratic. 'But I have no desire to meddle, or to condemn those whose opinions and beliefs differ from my own.' He added, prompted by some aberrant imp of mischief, 'Unlike a certain proportion of our force.'

Touchet appeared to have no levity where matters of religion were concerned. His frown deepened. 'This army will not prosper while such fanatic heretics remain in its ranks.'

'It would look a little thin without them,' Nick pointed out drily. A stir and bustle behind them caught his attention, and he turned, ignoring Touchet's rather affronted stare. The King, accompanied by his staff and the Scots Command, had arrived.

He had already galloped down to Powicke Bridge to exhort the Scots troops there to resist attack with all their might and, from the sounds of conflict that had lingered on the edge of hearing all morning, he had succeeded. But in spite of the heat and his exertions, Charles, King of Great Britain, France and Ireland, looked enviously fresh and enthusiastic. Nick would not, in his position, have bothered to put on the heavy black armour that attracted the heat so thoroughly, nor would he have chosen the splendid chestnut stallion that instantly marked him out as a target for enemy bullets. However, he was young, only twenty-one, and Nick suspected that this was still very much a game to him. Standing on top of the cathedral tower to direct the movements of men and horses like chess pieces was well enough, and so were fine rousing speeches to his troops. Once in the grim reality and confusion of battle, with real blood, real fear, real death all about him, and it would all be very different.

Nevertheless, despite his cynicism, Nick had to admit that the boy showed true promise. In a while, the young King told them, with the frank and open smile that had won hearts all over Worcester, they would be sent in to the attack. He was depending on them to swing the tide of battle. So far, the brave Scots were holding Powicke Bridge, against overwhelming odds. They were giving their lives to win back his kingdom, to defeat Cromwell and his usurping regicide masters. 'And since the Scots can fight so bravely,' said Charles, his dark eyes glowing with eagerness, 'then I'll trust you English to match them. There's no honour in shirking our duty, and no glory either – we can defeat them, we can drive their fanatic army into the Severn, and I know, my friends, that you'll all be in the forefront of the battle!'

In cold blood, it was not a particularly inspiring speech, but they cheered him till the sound echoed round the cathedral tower, mixed with the more pessimistic thud of the Parliament's guns on Red Hill. And Nick, disregarding his doubts, and the secret stone of despair around his heart, roared with the rest.

Down by the Teme, the fight raged on, the Scots resisting the enemy advance with all their strength and dour persistence, against odds of three or four to one. Gradually, bitterly, at push of pike, they were driven back from hedgerow to hedgerow. But the outcome still hung in the balance: a lucky chance, a bold stroke, could send it either way.

Then the long-awaited order came to the troops drawn up on the College Green, in the Cathedral Close, in the grounds of the Commandery and within the half-finished earthen ramparts on Fort Royal. The enemy battery on Red Hill, comparatively unprotected and vulnerable, was their target. The leather field guns on Fort Royal, and the older, more conventional pieces left over from the war in Worcester, would provide covering fire, and the King himself would lead them.

At last, after standing idle for most of the day while their fellows fought and died without their support, they could attack.

The mass of men, horse and foot, musketeer and pikeman, Scots Presbyterian and English Royalist or Catholic, poured out of the Sidbury Gate under the dispassionate eye of the afternoon sun, already sliding westwards: in three hours, it would be setting. There was a brief halt in the space between the city walls and Fort Royal, to group, to assimilate several Scots regiments that were already positioned there, and to receive their final orders.

Then the trumpets sounded for the advance, the drums rolled

and, with the King at their head, his Lifeguard packed behind him, the long column of men and horse filed out from the protective bastions of Fort Royal, and marched steadily up towards the Roundhead positions on the hill, less than a mile away. The Duke of Hamilton, at the head of most of the Scots, was to attempt to capture the guns at Perry Wood, to the north, while the King, with his Lifeguard and the English contingent, almost all cavalry, would engage the main enemy battery at Red Hill.

Nick had been at the battle of Langport, in the dying days of the war, and had seen the Roundhead Horse charge up just such a road as this, the hedges lined with musketeers, towards the Royalists at the top of the hill. Then, the impressive discipline of the New Model Army had eventually won the day, overcoming the superior position of the King's men. Now, the boot was on the other foot, and he and his comrades must run the gauntlet of that hidden fire, while all the while the field guns, in front and behind, kept up an ear-splitting, deadly duet.

But the Roundhead musketeers, despite their discipline, could not achieve impossible rates of fire. It took almost a minute to reload, and in the meantime they were vulnerable. The Royalists, shouting their watchwords, galloped up the lane in a packed, irresistible mass, almost unscathed. His apprehension vanished, Nick urged the grey mare onwards with the rest, heedless of bullets or the furious resistance of the Parliamentarians guarding the guns. In the heat and smoke and confusion, he had forgotten his forebodings, forgotten fear, forgotten everything except the dreadful exultation of battle, the ceaseless rise and fall of his sword arm as he hacked and fought his way towards the guns, intent only upon reaching them.

It was a long and bloody fight. The militiamen guarding the enemy position, many of them raw young men from Cheshire and Essex seeing real battle for the first time, neither wavered nor ran, but defended their ground with bitter tenacity. But slowly, inexorably, the superior numbers and weight of the King's men began to tell. The Roundheads fell back, and with a huge triumphant shout, the Royalists surged forward to take possession of the disputed guns.

Nick, gasping, reined in his mare. Under his helmet, his hair was soaked and dripping with sweat, and the saltiness of it stung his eyes, while the metal chafed skin and restricted his vision. He glanced round, seeing the exultant faces of the men he had led in

that last frantic charge, and on impulse unbuckled the uncomfortable headgear and took it off. The relief, as the cooling breeze struck
his face unimpeded, was enormously welcome. They had the
guns, though at considerable cost. All around him, in the grass and
ditches and hedgerows, the dead and wounded of both sides
marked the bloody line of attack. And at last, the air was silent.

But they had no gun crews, he realised, save the small number
of Scots manning the pieces at Fort Royal. At least someone
seemed to have ridden down to tell them the good news, for they
too had stopped firing. For a brief, strange moment, there was
almost no sound on the broad, tree-scattered slopes of Red Hill,
nor from the thicker foliage of Perry Wood, where Hamilton
seemed to have had similar success. Just to his left, in a ragged
hawthorn bush, a robin began to sing as if nothing had happened,
and a small brown butterfly danced past, weaving erratically
between the groups of breathless, blood-spattered, exultant
soldiers.

This respite, though, could not last. Already he could see the
enemy regrouping at the top of the hill. They themselves had
virtually no ammunition left, and he had seen musketeers using the
butts of their weapons in that last desperate struggle. Now, if ever,
was the time for General Leslie, in command of the reserve of
Scots cavalry, to come to their support and press home the
advantage.

But there was no time. Cromwell, warned of the threat to his
remaining forces, had sent reinforcements back to Red Hill, while
the bulk of his men put the Scots to flight along the Teme. The
cavalry arrived first, joined their fellows on the top of Red Hill,
and launched their counter-attack.

This time, they had the advantage of numbers. No reserves had
come up from Worcester, no supplies of powder and shot to
replenish empty muskets and pistols. Nick's wheel-locks were
useless. He just had time to pull his helmet back on his head before
the Roundhead cavalry poured over the long brow of the hill and
smashed down into the King's forces around the guns below them.
And then they were fighting for their lives.

Their brief moment of triumph had been a cruel illusion, he
realised, as he parried a vicious thrust. They had never had a
chance of victory, with or without the support of Leslie's reserve.
Nevertheless, in the thick of the fighting, above the crash of shots
and the whine of musket-balls and the screaming of the dying, he

heard a vain, despairing voice shrieking, 'Where are the Scots? Where are the bloody Scots?'

He slashed his opponent across the chest, and saw him fall backwards, only to be replaced by another Roundhead, young, earnest, his lips moving in prayer as he pushed his horse forward, his sword darting and weaving in a deadly dancing pattern. Nick fought him doggedly, ignoring the heat, the weariness, the clogging sweat, the fact that, little by little, he and all the men around him were being forced back, away from the guns they had captured only a short while before, down the hill towards Fort Royal and Worcester.

The foot broke first. They had fought bravely, but against this relentless attack of the New Model Horse, they had no defence. They threw down their useless empty muskets and ran back through the rough pasture and thorny hedges, ignoring the frantic attempts of their officers to persuade them to stand and die. Nick, despatching the Roundhead with an improvised and desperate thrust that struck fatally home, to his own surprise and even more to his opponent's, found himself almost cut off, as the men on either side began to wheel their horses round and make good their escape. He realised that to do anything different would be to throw away his liberty, or even his life, to no good purpose. Besides, two more troopers were bearing down on him, swords at the ready, bawling the enemy watchword: 'Lord of Hosts!'

Nick had never been one to waste time on unnecessary debate. He dragged the grey mare's head round, and spurred her down the hill in company with the rest. There was still Fort Royal, still the walled city to defend. And the young King, whose enthusiastic encouragement had heartened all his army this day, was already marshalling the fugitives at the ramparts, rallying them and exhorting them to turn and fight.

As well urge the sand to withstand the sea. The militiamen, intoxicated by the scent of victory, poured down Red Hill, followed by the regular troops, both horse and foot. From Perry Hill came the Scots, streaming back in panic and disarray, and Nick saw the fainting figure of their leader, the Duke of Hamilton, carried with them, blood pouring from a great wound in his thigh. There was no time to organise a counter-attack, no powder or shot to fill his pistols, a moment only to draw breath before the trumpet sounded and they must spur their horses again for the ragged charge that was all they could manage. The King rode with them, ignoring the clearly audible protests of his staff officers, the Duke of Buckingham the loudest. Nick found himself riding knee to knee with Mervyn Touchet, who was mounted on a frothing wild-eyed black, which had already acquired a well-deserved reputation for viciousness amongst the English Horse. Touchet glanced at him, and Nick was surprised to see a swift, almost boyish grin on his face, comradely and direct and quite unlike his usual languid self. Then they had struck the Roundhead Horse, and there was no time for anything except the urgent business of fighting and survival.

For an instant, the Roundhead line wavered, then stood firm. While the Horse struggled, the Essex militia had run on, flinging themselves up the earthen ramparts of Fort Royal to bury their swords in the Scots defenders. As Nick fought for his life, side by side with Touchet, a great scream of triumph echoed from the bastions and the Royal Standard, proud red and gold, toppled slowly and ignominiously out of sight.

And still Cromwell's men came on, shouting the battle cry that all the Royalists had come to know too well during the past few hours: 'Lord of Hosts!'

Once more, the Horse had to give way before the attack. As the Essex militia continued their work of godly slaughter within Fort Royal amongst Scots whose courage had not expired, even if their supplies of powder and shot were now exhausted, their mounted fellows turned in obedience to the frantic commands of the trumpet, back to the Sidbury Gate, from which they had issued three hours earlier with such hope.

The sun had almost dropped below the distant hills, staining the light red, red as the blood which dabbled the grass and earth around the gate. Within the walls of Worcester lay temporary safety, and the panic-stricken Scots, fleeing from the vengeful swords of the New Model Army, were desperate to get inside. But the way was blocked by a powder wagon, the oxen drawing it lying dead in the traces, and already the first Roundheads were upon them.

The confusion was indescribable, a tangle of rearing, terrified horses, screaming men trampled underfoot, and the dreadful stink of blood and sweat and fear. Any attempt to rally and fight on would be useless. Yet still some tried paying for their bravery, or foolishness, with their lives, giving the young King the vital few moments he needed to dismount from his exhausted horse and reach the refuge of the city, though he had to crawl under the powder wagon to gain it. Blagge was there, and Levison, the Commander of the Lifeguard, the recognition of defeat writ as plain in their faces as Nick knew it must be on his. The King must at all costs be protected from death, or capture, which would probably amount to the same thing. Somehow, they must hold Cromwell's soldiers at bay so that Charles could make good his escape.

Eventually, Nick managed to squeeze his sweating, nervous horse past the wagon and under the gate. All around him, Scots and English footsoldiers were struggling to reach the safety of the city, illusory though it might prove to be. Just inside the gate, Charles was hastily unbuckling his armour, helped by one of the troopers of the Lifeguard. His normally swarthy face was scarlet with exertion and grief, the black hair stuck wet and flat to his head. Nick, glancing at the body of cavalry that had somehow, like himself, fought their way inside the gate, saw Buckingham, Blagge, Wilmot, Colonel Carliss, Levison, and about seventy or eighty other officers and troopers, Scots and English. Of the Scots reserve under Leslie's command, there had been neither sign nor sound.

Soldiers ran past, bloodstained and terrified. The King shouted at them to stand, to resist, to fight to the death, but they ignored him, intent now only on their own preservation. Buckingham, persuasive and reasonable, was urging him to flee, now, there was no hope left and no point in staying to be captured. Nick was close enough to hear the King's response. 'Where is Leslie? Order him to attack!'

'Your Majesty!' An officer in Massey's regiment had arrived at a run from the direction of the High Street, his face scarlet with shame and exertion. 'Message from General Leslie – will cover your retreat – urges you to leave the city at once, sir – and they're in the streets on the Severn side, sir, they've broken through Middleton's men, you must leave at once or you'll be taken for sure!'

'I'd rather you shot me!' Charles cried. Someone had led up a fresh horse, and he swung himself up on to its back, the dark armour discarded to leave him clad in the buff coat and red sash which he had worn ever since leaving Scotland, the ribbon of his George about his neck. 'I'd rather be shot than left alive to face the consequences – don't talk of retreat!'

Already even that chance was fading. The sounds of conflict outside the gate were growing stronger as the remaining Scots, trapped and fighting hand to hand, died in the red evening light. Those who had struggled into the city did not pause, but ran on up the narrow streets, to hide or to end their lives on Roundhead swords. It was the end, and Charles knew it. Buckingham grabbed his horse's bridle, and turned the snorting, fearful animal about. 'The Martin Gate, sir – all the others are blocked!'

The King took one last look about him, at the exhausted men, the deepening dusk, the confusion and the fugitives. 'Goodbye, friends,' he said. 'I thank you – and God go with you.' And then, with his staff and some of his Lifeguard around him, he urged his horse up Friar's Street towards the north and his only possible chance of escape.

It had not occurred to Nick to go with him. He was a member of the Lifeguard, true, but at this moment it seemed to him that the King's interests would be best served by covering his escape. The Earl of Cleveland, a veteran of the war, was shouting something, and Nick saw Colonel Carliss, Touchet and several others, mostly English, rallying to his side, while more, with expressions of panic on their faces, were already wheeling their horses round to follow their sovereign. 'Fight them!' Cleveland yelled. 'Hold them off – we must prevent the King's capture – cover his retreat!'

It took on the quality of Hell, the City of Worcester that night, as darkness descended on the last remnants of battle. The terrified citizens, Royalist or otherwise, cowered in their houses and wished that they had fled while the chance still offered. Cromwell's men, pouring in through the Sidbury Gate to the south, and over the Severn Bridge to the west, hunted the Scots fugitives through the dim twisting streets, killing them even when they turned and cried for quarter. But despite the utter destruction of the Royal army, there were still some who resisted, who fought on until the bitter end. Cleveland's little band of horse desperately charged again and again, whenever they came upon a group of the enemy, driving them away from St. Martin's Gate, through which they hoped that the King had made good his escape. Men and horses died, shot or hacked to death or trampled as they stumbled and fell on the cobbled streets, made slippery with Scottish blood that ran in little streams and rivulets down the channel in the centre of the High Street by the Guildhall, where a little remnant of English had made a last hopeless stand.

Cleveland's force had come upon a pack of Roundheads near the Cornmarket, just by the King's lodging. Nick hoped that by now Charles had long since gone. He was so exhausted that he could barely move his sword arm, and his grey mare was stumbling with weariness, her hide now streaked with blood from a gash across her shoulder. But she was willing still, in spite of her Scots breeding, and he turned her with the rest, men and horses all as spent as he was, and urged her to one last charge.

The Roundheads did not lack for ammunition. He saw the flashes of their pistols in the deepening gloom, and then abruptly his horse pitched forward, and he was hurled down on to the stones of the Cornmarket. Without taking thought, he rolled as he hit the cobbles, intent only on saving himself from the mare's flailing iron-shod hooves, and somehow struggled to his feet. All around him, men were fighting, shouting, a sword flashed above him and he dodged, weaponless, for his own had been knocked from his hand as he fell. More shots, another horse screamed in agony and crashed to the ground. Every bone in his body ached, and his breath rasped in his throat as he looked for a way out of the mêlée. A Roundhead trooper was charging at him, sword upraised. He flinched aside as the blade slashed down at him, feeling the wind of it along his face, stumbled in the gutter running down the middle of the street, and fell sideways. He felt the movement, the hooves smashing down on the stones as the horse leapt over him. Winded, exhausted, he lay still, his face just clear of the stinking rubbish in the channel, gasping for breath.

The fight seemed to be moving away, the clatter of hooves and the clash of swords no longer just above him. His mind was working quite clearly. He was only a few yards from his brother's door. If the street cleared, could he risk going to beg James for help? Or would he bring disaster on them, as well as on himself? Mistress Guise, next door, would undoubtedly betray him if she suspected anything. But, without James's assistance, he doubted very much whether he would escape from Worcester at all. And there was also the very real chance that, even on foot and unarmed, he would be cut down in the dark and confusion.

The fighting had indeed moved away, though he could still hear shouting, and, suddenly, the distant squeal of a horse in pain or fear. Very cautiously, he raised his head. There was no moon tonight, and the street was dark, shadowed and threatening, with no lights showing anywhere. He could see, humped still and dead just in front of him, the bulk of his horse. Slowly, inch by inch, he slithered snakelike towards it.

A hand came out to touch him. He froze, rigid, waiting for the *coup de grâce*, from sword or pistol. But a voice hissed in his ear. 'Is that you, Hellier?'

It was, unmistakably, the aristocratic tones of Lieutenant-Colonel Mervyn Touchet.

❦ CHAPTER TEN ❦

'Under a bush, like a beggar'
(*As You Like It*)

'You can't stay here.' James Hellier stared at the two men standing in his kitchen, exhausted, stained with dirt and sweat and blood and refuse, but still undoubtedly military. 'It's too dangerous. They could break into this house at any minute – listen to them!'

The sounds of shouting and battle rose from the street outside. Jane plunged into the small dim room, her arms full of clothes, her round face pale with alarm. 'Here – take these and put them on – quickly!'

Nick had already pulled off the filthy buff coat that unequivocally proclaimed him a soldier. The grey breeches were unremarkable, and would not cause comment, but the heavy boots must also be discarded. He took the patched, rather threadbare green doublet that Jane held out to him. It was much too big, and of a very old-fashioned cut, with a waistline that had been outmoded for twenty years. 'It was my father's,' said his sister-in-law, her Worcester accent made more noticeable by stress. 'I was going to cut it up for floorcloths, but it'll make you a good disguise.'

Nick, shrugging it on in haste, realised that Touchet was still standing in the low, smoke-stained room, so tall his head almost reached the rafters, and making no effort to divest himself of his outer clothing. He said sharply, 'I should take your coat off, at the least, or you'll be spitted as soon as we set foot outside.'

'My dear fellow, do you seriously expect me to wear a garment such as that?' said his brother officer, in his most outraged drawl. 'It's hardly the habit of a gentleman.'

'It will be the better disguise, in that case,' said Nick, unable to keep the annoyance out of his voice. Of all the men in the entire thirteen thousand or so of the King's forces, Touchet was the last he would have chosen to be his companion in such a desperate situation. But chance, or plain bad luck, had thrown them together, their horses both killed under them. They were faced with the choice of surrender, or the almost impossible task of escaping from a city packed with marauding, victorious and bloodthirsty Roundhead soldiers.

Unless they climbed the wall at the bottom of James's physick garden, for by now all the gates would be impassable. Nick, having survived thus far, with the faint hope of freedom dangling before him, had no intention of letting Touchet's high-bred sensibilities ruin his chances.

'Please, *hurry!*' Jane said, almost crying in her urgency. 'Please, sir, put it on, or you'll be captured for sure, and we'll all be plundered or worse – *please!*'

Her distress, Nick noted sourly, moved the chivalrous officer more than his own voice of reason. 'Very well, Mistress Hellier,' said Touchet reluctantly, and began with infuriating slowness to unbutton his buff coat. There was more shouting from the street, and a great cry of pain and terror, ending in a bubbling moan. The hated Scots were being killed out of hand.

The sound at last spurred Touchet into some sense of urgency. The buff coat, with its flamboyant scarlet bands on the sleeves, joined Nick's in a heap on the stone floor, and with his lip curled in disgust, handling it with the very ends of his fingers, he took the second doublet, an ancient affair in russet, with a prominent patch on one elbow and sweat stains under each arm. With an expression so dismayed that, under other circumstances, Nick might have been tempted to laugh, he shuddered himself into it. Although the green was far too large for Nick (Jane's father had evidently been of somewhat portly build), on Touchet the russet doublet was strained across his shoulders, the shortness of the sleeves exposing a considerable quantity of exquisitely sewn shirt. Swiftly resourceful, Jane scooped up a handful of soot and ash from the smoking hearth, and smeared it liberally over the astonished man's expensive linen. 'Go on, sir, make yourself dirty, then your face won't give you away.'

'Good God, woman, what are you doing?' Touchet stared in horror as she then snatched up a kitchen knife from the table.

Jane said briskly, 'You can't go out with your hair like that. Let me cut it for you, sir, please.'

'With that knife?' Touchet cried, aghast.

Nick finally lost his patience. 'If you want my company on this venture, I should let Mistress Hellier do what she wants. You won't get a hundred yards with lovelocks like that.'

With grim satisfaction, he saw the wind taken from Touchet's sails. In an astonished, sulky silence, Jane was permitted to hack away the scented black curls, while James, frantic to get the two men away from his house, performed the same office for his brother. There only remained the question of footwear. Jane had brought two pairs of shoes, roughly made in country fashion, with old mud still caked on them. These presented no problem to Nick, whose feet slipped easily into the smaller ones, but Touchet, a much bigger man, found that the others would not fit him, despite all his efforts. Jane, still exhibiting much greater presence of mind than her husband, quickly used the knife to slit the ends of each, and with his stockinged toes poking through the gaps, Touchet could at last stand up, his disguise complete.

And completely ridiculous, like a caricature of a country yokel. Nick doubted that he himself looked any better, but at least he was aware that his liberty, and possibly even his life, depended on the convincing nature of his attire. At present, Touchet seemed to regard it all as an unnecessary and repellent inconvenience. He said to his brother, 'We must go. Thank you, James, and Jane – we owe you our freedom, at the least.'

James, who had not wanted to let them in, who had only opened the door because he was afraid that the two fugitives on the step would attract unwelcome attention, who was terrified in case soldiers came beating the door down, looked embarrassed and muttered something. Jane, more practical, was thrusting a bag into his hand. 'Here, Nick, take this – you'll need something to sustain you, there's bread and cheese. Goodbye – and God go with you!'

He had time to tell them to hide the buff coats and boots and swordbelts – anywhere, down the well, under the floor, buried in the garden, so long as soldiers could not find them – and then he and Touchet were outside in the garden, hurrying down the path that he had walked so recently in daylight, to the city wall and freedom.

Scots patrols had marched along here, earlier in the day, but now the long black line of it, sharp against the stars, was empty. Noises, screams, the sounds of destruction came from behind them, further down New Street, and Nick, glancing back, saw that something was in flames. He prayed silently that his brother and his wife would be safe. By the rules of war, a captured city was sacked, and thus had Cromwell justified his massacres in Ireland that had so enraged Touchet. But surely, in England, he would be more gentle?

Nick could not know. The only certainty was that James and Jane would surely suffer grave punishment if they were discovered to have helped two fugitive Royalist officers. He glanced at Touchet, who was staring up at the dark-shrouded wall, and said very quietly, 'It's stone. There are footholds, but we'll have to help each other up. There's a ditch on the other side, probably full of rubbish and nettles. I suggest we get as far away from the city as we can, and find somewhere to hide for the rest of the night. Then we can decide where we're going.'

Touchet said nothing, as if bemused by the whole situation. Nick wondered, with weary anger, if he resented a man who was his inferior in rank and birth giving him orders. But if the other man had assumed the lead, they would still be dithering in Jane's kitchen. With a muffled exclamation of impatience, he bent his back, bracing aching legs and arms, making the first step for Touchet's ascent of the wall.

Mercifully, it was an easy climb. Touchet reached the ramparts, and turned, stretching a hand down for his companion. Nick, fit and agile from years of soldiering, did not need it. Just as he swung himself on to the top, a great hammering and shouting broke out in the house at the other end of the garden. At the same time, he saw out of the corner of his eye a small bobbing group of lights, approaching along the wall from the direction of St. Martin's Gate.

It was time to be gone. He prayed that the drop would not be too steep or too dangerous, and that Touchet would follow him immediately, instead of lingering, a betraying shape against the sky for anyone looking out of the house to notice. He swung himself between the battlements, held on for a few wrenching moments by his fingers, and then dropped.

There were nettles, and broken pots, and something cold and foul and sticky. He rolled into the bushes, and struggled to his feet. Touchet followed him, with a muffled curse: at least he seemed to have understood the need for quiet. They crouched together in the kindly enveloping dark, beneath a hawthorn whose prickles had already ripped through Nick's hands, and waited until the small band of Roundhead soldiers had gone by, searching for fugitives, and evidently elated by their victory. Then, slowly and painfully, they extracted themselves from the ditch, and began to move along the hedgerows and orchards that lay outside the walls of Worcester.

'Good morning, my lady. I thought somehow that I would find you here.'

Silence, walking in the cool under the cherry arbour, long since come to fruit, shaded her eyes against the sunny dazzle at the end. She knew who it was: that voice, as smooth and dark and courteous as fine wine, could only belong to Master Jonathan Harley. This was his fourth visit this week, and she had begun, a little, to be irritated by his constant appearances at Wintercombe. Had the man no other clients to attend?

His smile was warm and charming, and he offered her his arm as she drew near. Ashamed of her churlish feelings, she took it with a smile, narrowing her eyes against the brightness of the sun. Her garden was not looking its best — virtually nothing had been in flower for a month now — and the long period of heat and drought had withered some of her choicest plants, despite Diggory's daily watering. But the apple harvest would be excellent, as good as the crop of grain gathered in over the past week, and although this sunshine brought her skin out in lines and freckles, she could not help but welcome the contented, sleepy warmth of it that encouraged all her cheerfulness and made her glad to be alive.

'What news, Master Harley?' she enquired. He had only last week asked her, with that incongruously warm smile, to call him Jonathan. Not without feelings of guilt, she had declined. The man had done them excellent service, and even Nat seemed to have modified his opinion of him. But she could not, still, bring herself to be on more intimate terms with him. Very few people had ever called her Silence: it was a privilege granted, without exception, only to those she most loved.

While Jonathan Harley was a good friend, a charming companion and a reliable servant, she had no intention of letting him approach any closer. Besides, she could not forget that other man, so very different from the smooth-tongued lawyer, who had asked her to call him Nick, as all his friends did. Seeking only friendship, she had done so, only to find that rather more than friendship was offered.

It was not possible that Master Harley sought anything more. She was a widow, thirty-five years old, almost in her dotage, and doubtless screwing up her eyes in the sun like this added at least ten years to her age. And none knew better than Master Harley that she was hardly a tempting prospect on the marriage market. No looks, only the Chard property, which she loathed, to enrich her, and four young children in need of her care and nurture. Besides, she did not want a second husband. The petty tyrannies and restricted freedom of another marriage did not in the least attract her.

'News, my lady?' She noticed suddenly that there was a spring in Master Harley's step, a smile of satisfaction in his voice. 'Splendid news — which is why I have ridden out here today to tell you.'

Her heart had begun to pound, slowly and ominously. She stopped, withdrawing her arm from his, and stared up at him. Against the sun, she could see only the shape of his head and shoulders, the sun turning his fair hair to a silver halo, and the sudden gleam of his smile. She managed, with all the skill perfected over years of hypocrisy, to make her expression one of polite enquiry. 'Oh, Master Harley? What is it? It must be exceedingly important.'

'It is indeed,' he said. 'General Cromwell has caught the Scots at Worcester, and utterly defeated them, with great slaughter.'

Even her dissembling could not keep the blood in her face. She stood very still, using all her strength to hold herself calm. 'When — when did that happen?'

'Wednesday last — three days ago. The news came to Bath yesterday evening, and the Mayor ordered all the bells to be rung, and thanksgiving prayers in the churches tomorrow for our delivery from the Scots. Do you feel well, my lady? You look very pale.'

'Do I? Strange, when it is so hot,' said Silence, as lightly as she could. But his intent scrutiny was uncomfortable: surely, he must see how this news had affected her.

She walked past him to the balustrade, looking out over the orchard. The apples hung like scarlet lamps on the trees, sun-flushed and ripening above the shimmering grass. A few white clouds, as blurred and insubstantial as wisps of wool, drifted in the blue distance.

Three days. He might have been dead for three days, and she had not known: might never know. Don't be ridiculous, she said to herself fiercely. He probably wasn't even there — and even if he was, he must have had a good chance of survival — Nick would not be careless of his life.

But once, he had been. She turned, sick at heart, and said

[189]

quietly, 'We must all thank God for this victory. What of the Scots? Is the King captured?'

'Apparently not,' Harley told her. He was still looking intently at her, as if he suspected something – and yet what, thought Silence sadly, was there to suspect? 'But he is, they say, of somewhat swarthy appearance, and his corpse may have gone unnoticed amongst the common soldiers. The word is that they have taken so many prisoners that they hardly know what to do with them all – Scottish dukes, earls and lords by the score, colours and generals and colonels and lieutenant-colonels and majors – oh, yes, I think the Scottish menace is ended for ever, and once they have the King, if he has not been killed, there'll be no more foolishness from the English Royalists either.'

'What do you think they will do with him?'

'With Charles Stuart? He undoubtedly deserves to be hanged for bringing in the Scots. Certainly they will make an example of him, and of the other important men they have captured. They would be extremely stupid not to do so, for otherwise they'll invite rebellion for ever more.'

There was something about Master Harley's certainty that made Silence, essentially a Puritan, a supporter of the Commonwealth and steadfast for peace, want immediately to contradict him. She resisted the temptation to do so: instead, she said calmly, 'He is hardly more than a boy, and very much in the grip of people who should know better. I, for one, would be sad, and sorry, to see him come to grief. I met him once, when he was a boy – a most pleasant child, a little younger than Nat.'

'You met him?' Harley was jolted out of his usual urbanity. 'I did not know that you had – when did it happen?'

It had been a mistake to mention it, Silence had known since the words left her mouth. With no choice but to soldier on, she said, 'Oh, long ago – when we had the garrison here during the war, and he was brought over to inspect the fortifications. I liked him, child though he was – and very different from his father, I think.'

'None of that alters the fact that he richly deserves punishment,' said Harley, as angry as she had ever heard him. Her look of surprise must have reached him, for he added more quietly, 'Forgive me, my lady, but this matter is something which greatly concerns me. There is no chance for peace and prosperity in this country if armies continually march across it, and I have as little patience with rebels as do the Council of State.'

'So do I,' said Silence. 'But I pray you will excuse me my womanish soft heart, Master Harley.'

He must have heard the irony, rich in her voice, but he only glanced at her rather sharply. Then he said thoughtfully, 'I have some business I wish to discuss with Sir Nathaniel. Where may I find him?'

'He went down to the mill an hour or so ago,' Silence told him. 'He should be back soon – why not take some refreshments, while you are waiting?'

Harley accepted, as she had known that he would, and they walked together back to the cool of the house. There were fat bunches of grapes hanging from the vine that covered most of this side of Wintercombe, promising a feast in a few weeks' time. Only rarely did they enjoy such a harvest, but one autumn, six years ago, Diggory and his assistant had gathered a good hundredweight of grapes, and she had made wine from them. The result had been rather thin, yet light and refreshing. It looked as though this year would be just as good, and Silence wondered suddenly if this bounty presaged some change in her life, that once had seemed to be linked to the fruitfulness, or lack of it, in the vine.

Superstitious nonsense, she told herself sternly, and walked into the dim, blessed coolness of the stone-flagged hall.

Much later, when Harley had returned to Bath, his business with Nat completed, she told her stepson the news about the Scots.

'It's no surprise,' was his comment. 'Hundreds of miles from home, probably demoralised, badly equipped, tired, outnumbered – and the countryside didn't exactly rise in their support, did they? Rather the reverse, in fact – the Somerset Militia at least were most enthusiastic.' He glanced at Silence, who was sitting on the windowseat, her cat Misty on her lap. The sinking sunlight lit her face from the side, emphasising its turns and contours and lines, transforming her mouse-brown hair to a flaring and incongruous red. She wore black still, for it would have been shocking not to do so, but in no other respect did she resemble the grieving widow. Nat added quietly, 'You are thinking of Nick, aren't you?'

'Of course I am,' she said, almost angrily. 'And I have told myself a hundred times how foolish it is, like a lovesick ninny – but it's no good, Nat, I can't forget him – I shall never ever forget him, as long as I live.'

Nat did not answer for a while, but continued to stroke Lily, who rested her long pale nose on his knee. Then he said, 'I have never loved anyone like that. I am not sure, even, if I am capable of it — whether there is a flaw in me, or whether all men are the same, and love is a gift granted only to women.'

'But Nick loved me,' said Silence, and the face she turned towards him had lost all its sorrow, and had acquired the glory of remembered delight. 'And knowing that, how can I ever complain of my lot?'

*

'I am sorry, Hellier, very sorry, but I can go no further. You must leave me here.'

Nick looked at Mervyn Touchet with active dislike. Muddy, dripping with sweat and river water, a hank of green weed unnoticed in his shorn and ragged hair, he was not an object of great beauty, and Nick suspected that he himself looked even worse. At least no one, save the deeply hostile, would ever take these two desperately unprepossessing vagrants for escaped Cavaliers. They had already had dogs set on them twice, and a couple of ragamuffin brats had thrown stones at them. But it was as beggars that they had been persecuted, and Nick, reverting to the thick Worcestershire burr he remembered from his childhood, had probably deflected all suspicion. He had managed to persuade Touchet, with some difficulty, to keep his mouth shut.

They were now in urgent need of food and shelter. They had failed to find any isolated barn in which to lie in hiding, and had spent the first night after the battle huddled in a copse. The sound of a large body of cavalry had woken them before dawn, and the whole area around Worcester seemed to be infested with enemy soldiers. In hushed whispers, they had discussed their plan of escape. Touchet, whose family had lands in Wiltshire, favoured a move in that direction, or, better still, to Ireland. At any rate, taking ship from some port seemed to offer the best chance of freedom, and with this Nick was in agreement. The question was, which port?

London was large enough to hide them both without trouble, but London was over a hundred miles away, and they could not reach it without help. There remained Bristol, where Nick had been briefly apprenticed in his youth. He knew it well, but doubted that he would be recognised after so long. There, surely, they could find a ship that would take them away from England.

Bristol it was. Reaching it, however, had proved to be far more difficult than either of them had at first thought. Nick had suggested that they avoid the main roads, which would surely be teeming with soldiers, and follow instead the route of the River Severn. It was fairly direct, unmistakable, and perhaps they might be able to hide on one of the boats which plied up and down between Worcester, Gloucester and Bristol. They might even, if they managed to clean themselves up a little, pay for a passage. Touchet had a quantity of gold sewn into a belt under his shirt, but Nick was in possession of only a few coins – all he owned in the world, he had thought ruefully, counting the scant pounds and shillings. But he was alive, and unhurt, and that, after the dread premonition of death which had loomed over him on the day of the battle, was worth far more to him than any gold or silver.

For two days they had struggled along the river. It had taken them all of Thursday to reach it, avoiding patrols and regiments by hiding in ditches or hedges or woods. As a result, by sunset Nick doubted whether Touchet's own mother would have recognised him. His clothing torn, his beautiful well-kept hands soiled and scratched and his black hair hanging in lank rats' tails around his dirty face, he looked very different from the elegant aristocrat of Nick's first acquaintance. His voice, however, with its modish, languid drawl, would inevitably betray him. Fortunately, after one incident in which he had upbraided an old woman who refused them apples from her garden, and seen the look of astonishment on her face at his incongruously well-born accent, he seemed to have realised the necessity of letting Nick speak for them both when other people were within earshot. Alone, however, he kept up an unceasing round of complaint about his attire, his shoes, the mosquitoes, the dreadful nature of the terrain they were covering, and above all the lack of food. His reluctant companion, trained to endure, walked on grimly, his hands clenched tight, battling the urge to bury his fist in that aristocratic face.

But even Nick must acknowledge, after two days tramping without any form of sustenance save what they could beg or steal, and precious little of it, that they needed help. He was exhausted, his legs, unused to long walking, ached furiously, and he could think of nothing but platefuls of food and cool ale. The hot sun, that had burned all day in an almost cloudless sky, had set his head swimming, and hunger compounded it. He did not dare sit down, in spite of the overwhelming urge to sink like Touchet into the cool long grass by the river's side, and lean his back against that friendly willow. If he did, he doubted very much whether he would be able to get up again. He walked back to his companion and stood in front of him, frowning. 'I have no intention of leaving you here. Get up, and we'll ask for help at the next house we come to.'

'And what if they prove to be a nest of fanatics?' said Touchet, who had an objection to every suggestion that Nick made.

He was too weary to argue about it. 'To be honest, I don't really care. But if we can find a kindly house, throw ourselves on their mercy . . . then we have a good chance of reaching Bristol.'

'And if we don't – '

'Then we'll be captured, I expect,' said Nick. 'But isn't even that better than what we're enduring at the moment? At least the Roundheads do feed their prisoners, so I understand. And,' he added, clinching it, 'I'm sure we have enough coin to hire a couple of horses.'

Touchet must have discerned the anger in his voice. The younger man stared at him for a moment, his dark eyes narrowed with dislike. Then, with ostentatious difficulty, he stumbled to his feet, ignoring Nick's outstretched helping hand, and turned away from the broad, flowing river, towards the low-lying lonely fields and meadows, where a distant hump of trees and roofs betrayed the presence of a village. In an inimical silence, Nick followed him.

The first house they came to was a mill, some distance from the village, set astride a small tributary of the Severn. The wheel was turning, and the noise of rushing water obscured their approach. Nick would have chosen caution, but Touchet, ignoring his advice, limped painfully up the track in plain view, a sight to make any respectable miller rush out to drive the trespasser away.

Which, of course, he did, with three noisy leaping dogs and two small children for support. Nick, some paces behind, heard the man shouting, and saw Touchet stop, brought to a halt by the barking, furious animals. For an instant he stood there, swaying, and then, quite abruptly, crumpled into a sprawling heap in the middle of the track.

A master-stroke, thought Nick, admiringly. If genuine, he at least gains my sympathy. If not, he not only earns my respect for his stratagem, but their concern as well.

The collapse did look uncommonly convincing: one of the dogs was worrying his hair. Nick hobbled forward to face the miller.

He said above the din, 'We mean you no harm, sir. Can you call your dogs off?'

The miller was a short, stocky man, young, but already balding. He reminded Nick a little of his brother, but with a belligerent, truculent air that James Hellier entirely lacked. He shouted something, and the two children, a boy and a girl, grabbed the dogs by their collars and hauled them away with loud scoldings. Nick knelt down by Touchet, and set a finger to his wrist. The pulse within beat with reassuring strength.

'Are you Scots?' said the miller, his voice rich with suspicion. Nick, glancing up, saw that he had a stout wooden stave grasped threateningly in one hand. He struggled to his feet, with some effort, and said quietly, 'No, sir, we are not.'

The small grey eyes stared at him with hostility. 'But you're Cavaliers, just the same,' he said. 'Go on – we don't want you here. Get out, before you bring trouble on us all.'

'I would,' said Nick, letting the Worcestershire tones creep into his voice. 'But I cannot leave until my friend here has recovered himself sufficiently to walk away. As you can see, he would be somewhat difficult for me to carry in that condition.'

'What is it, Harry? Who are they?' A woman came running down the track from the mill, the children behind her, and another girl, plainly clad in grey, who was probably a servant. 'Are they beggars?'

She was young, and pretty. Nick gave her the benefit of his most charming smile. 'No, Mistress, we are not, though we must beg of your charity. My friend here is sick, and can walk no more at present. If you could but bring us a little water, or even some bread if you can spare it, I will attempt to revive him, and we will be on our way without troubling you further.'

'You'll do no such thing,' said the miller's wife, with a fierce glare at her husband which deflated the man's resistance like a pricked bladder. 'Harry, you go get Robin from the kitchen, and carry him in – Bet, have the truckle bed made up in the parlour, and some broth for them both. And hurry now!'

There was no doubt, Nick thought, watching bemused as she shooed them back to the mill with brisk hands, who wore the breeches in this household. She turned to him, dusting her palms together. 'Are you Scots, or English?'

'English, both of us,' he said. 'And I am from Worcester, Mistress, so am not a stranger to these parts.'

'You live in the city?' she said, looking him up and down. 'You certainly do not seem to be a soldier, sir.'

'I am not,' Nick told her. He had decided on this particular lie some moments ago, without reference to Touchet. 'I am an apothecary from Worcester, and my sympathies are with the King. As you can imagine, I was forced to flee after the battle – my house plundered and burned, and the soldiers most anxious to find me. I fell in with my friend here, and we resolved to travel to Bristol together – he has a house there, where we will be safe. But the way was harder than we thought, because of our need to travel the byways. And we are now sorely in need of assistance, Mistress. Would you, in charity, be prepared to give it to us?'

'Of course,' she said, her smile fairly dazzling him. He had evidently lost none of his charm. 'Don't mind Harry – my husband – his bark's always much worse than his bite, like the dogs. He'll not betray you, not if I have anything to say in the matter.'

The mill was a low, dark building that gently echoed and creaked with the grinding of the wheel at its further end. The miller and a sturdy boy who seemed to be his apprentice carried the comatose Touchet into the parlour, where the serving-maid, Bet, had already made up a truckle-bed. With capable hands, she propped several pillows behind him, and her mistress bathed his muddy face with scented water.

The attention revived him, with a groan and some disjointed mutterings. The dark eyes opened, slid wildly from side to side, and focused on the lovely blonde woman hovering above him, a cloth in her hand. 'An angel!' Touchet cried, so entirely in character that Nick, in his exhaustion, could hardly keep from laughing. 'I must be in Heaven!'

'No, sir,' said the miller's wife, prosaically. 'You're at Bow Mill, near Tewkesbury. Now lie still, sir, and sup some of this good broth – you look sorely in need of it to me.'

Nick watched with a sardonic eye, as his travelling-companion was spoon-fed like a baby with the fragrant stew. Standing in the shadows by the door, he seemed invisible to them both, and wondered if he was intended to fetch his food himself. It was all very well for Touchet's dark good looks to inspire such an act of mercy, but if he overstepped the mark, he did not think that the miller was the sort to be tolerant.

'Here, sir.' The maid, Bet, had not forgotten him: she was

thrusting a pewter bowl, hot and brimming, into his hands. 'Eat this, it'll properly hearten you up.'

He was almost too hungry to swallow, but spooned the steaming broth into his mouth, nearly scalding himself. The contents disappeared too fast, and Bet, with a smile, took the bowl away and brought it back full to overflowing. He ate more slowly, savouring the taste and the warmth in his belly, and at last laid his spoon down, replete.

'You can stay here tonight,' said the miller, with gruff reluctance. Evidently he did not relish the prospect of two fugitives under his roof. 'No longer, mind you – I can't take the risk. But I don't reckon they'll think to search here – we're too far from the road, see. Just for tonight, and then be on your way.'

'That is very kind of you,' said Nick, without sarcasm. When death was the penalty for aiding rebels, he could not blame the man for his caution.

His wife, however, was not so circumspect. She rose from Touchet's bedside and fixed the miller with a steely blue stare. 'They'll leave when they're ready, Harry, and not before. Can't you see they're half dead from hunger and weariness? Do you want their deaths on your conscience? For shame on you, and you a good godly Christian man!'

The miller slunk off like a beaten hound at the end of this tirade, and did not repeat the mistake of speaking his true thoughts in front of his formidable wife.

That night, Nick lay in the feather-lapped comfort of a bed under the eaves of the old mill, listening to the ceaseless yet comforting noise of the stream, and the soft settlings and rustlings of an ancient house at rest. His dreadful clothes, muddy and stinking, had been removed for burning, and Mistress Powell, the miller's wife, had provided him with a clean and prickly nightshirt belonging to her husband. Tomorrow promised food, rest, comfort, and some relief from Touchet's never-ending complaints. For the moment, all energy spent, he could think no further ahead.

Outside, an owl shrieked, and the water rushed endlessly through the dark like a lullaby. Nick turned his head gratefully into the softness of the pillow, and slept.

Touchet, never one to miss an opportunity, took full advantage of Mistress Nan Powell's kind heart. Washed, his hacked hair clean and trimmed and combed, he looked almost presentable, and his dark eyes gleamed at her approach. The miller's wife seemed to take his outrageous flattery and wheedling with a bucket of salt, but Nick suspected that she was more affected than she cared to admit. He did not begrudge Touchet his success with women: he himself was not unaccomplished in the field, but this pretty sparkling young female, at once brisk and tender, was not really to his taste, not with the miller's resentful eye looking on. He could hardly have any scruples concerning cuckoldry, not with his past, but he preferred not to do it in the presence of the lady's husband.

Clean, well fed and taking his ease, he was able to give some thought to the immediate future. How were they to reach Bristol safely? He did not wish to presume on the Powell family's kindness for longer than was absolutely necessary, despite Touchet's shameless exploitation of the situation. But he doubted they would get very much further without advice and help.

He broached the matter to Mistress Nan in the kitchen after supper, the day following their arrival. Bet was scouring pewter, and Robin and the miller out mending some item of equipment. Touchet, still on his truckle bed in the parlour, was asleep, as were the children.

'You can stay as long as you want,' said Nan, mixing some potion with a wooden spoon. The unmistakably pungent aroma of feverfew filled the kitchen, and he thought suddenly of Silence, at work in her still-room at Wintercombe. The memory, sweet and bitter at once, caught him by the throat so that he could not speak, such was the longing that had flooded through him. As he stared at this very different woman, mute and anguished, she added, 'They'll never think to search here, don't worry. We haven't seen a soldier for months, and if we do, we can spy them from a long way off, so there's plenty of time to hide you. It's quite safe.'

'I wasn't thinking about us,' Nick said. 'I was thinking of what would happen to you, and your family, if we were discovered here. Mistress Powell, it is not a risk I am prepared to take.'

She glanced at him with sharp blue eyes. 'And your friend? He's not plain Master Thomson, is he?'

Nick smiled wryly. 'It's best if you don't know who we really are. Best, also, if we leave here as soon as he is fit to travel.'

'On foot?' said Mistress Powell, with a scorn that demonstrated that Touchet's flattery had not perhaps had quite the effect he desired. 'You wouldn't get five miles, either of you. You need a horse.'

'Two horses, in fact,' Nick pointed out, straight-faced. 'Two horses, to carry a man and his apothecary to visit his sick sister in Bristol, or some such tale. We have coin, Mistress Powell, we are not dependent on your charity, only on your help.'

'And as that's free, you can have it, and welcome,' said Nan Powell. 'Are you truly an apothecary?'

'I was apprenticed as such, yes.'

'Then what else should I put in this cordial for headaches and megrims? There is feverfew, and honey, and rosewater – is that sufficient?'

'For that particular remedy, yes,' Nick told her. 'But oil of lilies is also good – or rue steeped in vinegar, and used to anoint the head twice a day. Why – has my friend the headache?'

'No, but my husband has.' Nan decanted the mixture carefully into a muslin bag laid over another bowl, to strain it. 'Caused by you and your friend, of course.' Her face suddenly crinkled with mischief. 'He's a tall dark man – and so is the King of Scots, they say. And fond of a female face.'

'Rest assured, Mistress Powell, you are not entertaining the King of Scots unawares under your roof.'

'I didn't think we were,' said the miller's wife, with regret. 'But then I never did have much luck in life. You want a couple of horses, Master Harrison, or whatever you call yourself? Well, we'll do our best to find some for you.' She grinned suddenly. 'Not but that I'll be sorry to see you go – this is not the liveliest of places.'

A fact for which Nick, at least, was profoundly grateful.

The servant, Robin, was sent into Tewkesbury to gather news, and to buy two horses, serviceable but unremarkable animals. He came back full of rumour and speculation, gleaned from various taproom conversations. The King was dead, was captured, had been seen disguised as a Roundhead soldier, a beggar, a lady of quality, a washerwoman; there was a party of Cavaliers in the neighbourhood, preying on honest travellers; more Scots had invaded to avenge the defeat and slaughter of their comrades. None of these wild tales had the ring of truth, and Nick hoped that King Charles was safely in hiding. He was more concerned with what Robin had to say about any soldiers in the vicinity, but the boy was somewhat lacking in intelligence, and could say little beyond the fact that he had seen some troopers in the town. He did, however, have the horses, and he led them proudly forward for Nick's and Touchet's inspection.

'No,' said the Lieutenant-Colonel, shuddering in disgust. 'I cannot *possibly* bestride one of those spavined jades – it is quite out of the question, Hellier, and you must tell him to take them back to the slaughterhouse, or wherever he found them.'

One of the despised animals was an old, fat mare, doubtless past her foal-bearing years, with a sunken back the breadth and shape of a table, and a dulled, weary eye. The other, by contrast, was young, a tall, bright, snappy, bay gelding with a white blaze that covered most of its face. It was also cow-hocked, ewe-necked, goose-rumped and displayed almost every fault of conformation that could possibly mar a horse. In addition, its mean and rolling eye proclaimed other, less obvious vices. For once, Nick had some sympathy with Touchet. He could not relish a ride on either beast, whatever the need for disguise. However, he did not intend to reveal as much to his companion. 'They're all we have, and we must make the best of them. We can hardly ride about on anything much better, if we want to avoid unwelcome interest.'

Touchet's only reply was a snort of contempt. His days of rest had restored his spirit, and even in his borrowed clothing, a plain suit of mulberry, he looked every inch the haughty aristocrat. Disdainfully, he strolled forward to the bay, which at least had showed some spirit, and put out a hand. The coarse head snaked wickedly out with the speed of an adder, and he leapt back, swearing, a large rip in his cuff showing where the animal's teeth had attempted to remove his hand. 'I repeat, Hellier, I have no intention of riding either of these brutes.'

'Hellier? But I thought your name was Harrison,' said young Robin, with guileless interest.

Nick mentally consigned the indiscreet Touchet to perdition. 'Ride these, or walk,' he said, ignoring the boy's curiosity.

Touchet stared at him, as if about to protest. Then, he swung on his heel and strode away, stamping childishly on the cobbled stones of the mill's courtyard. Nick knew that, with or without him, preferably the latter, he must leave tomorrow. Already there had been several visitors to the mill, mostly local farmers bringing grain to be ground or buying flour. Touchet had not bothered to conceal himself, and had in consequence drawn several interested glances. It would be foolhardy to linger here.

The Powells refused payment for all but the horses and their tack, which surprised and touched Nick, though Touchet grumbled mightily at having to hand over good money for such sorry jades. Nan filled their saddlebags with bread and cheese and some thick collops of cold bacon and, as the sun rose amid puffy apricot clouds, they rode away from Bow Mill, with a relieved Harry Powell waving them an enthusiastic farewell.

The first few miles proved uneventful. Touchet had insisted on having the bay, which was at least up to his weight, despite its vicious nature, and Nick was left with the old chestnut mare, who could not be persuaded out of a leisurely amble. Before they had joined the road to Tewkesbury, Touchet had been nearly thrown three times, and the animal had also attempted to crush his rider against a tree. Nick, watching his companion's struggles with an unsympathetic eye, wondered how long it would be before self-preservation defeated pride, and Touchet decided to exchange his flighty mount for the placid mare.

Whatever his faults, the man was an accomplished horseman. Firm application of his heels, and a switch cut from the hedge, produced some result, and by the time they rode into Tewkes-bury, the bay, though foam-flecked and resentful, had at least been persuaded to show some obedience to his rider's commands.

It was a market day, and the town was crowded. The two men, urging their nags through the press, attracted little notice, and the way south to Gloucester lay before them, sunlit and dusty: but not empty.

Nick saw the small body of cavalry approaching, and his heart sank. It was too much to hope, a scant fifteen miles from Worces-ter, that there would not be patrols. Two men in ordinary clothes, one plainly of good birth, even mounted on such poor horses, would be bound to attract their notice.

'Turn aside,' said Touchet, gesturing with his switch down a lane that led towards the marshes lining the Severn. 'They'll think nothing of it — turn aside!'

'They'll be certain to think it suspicious,' said Nick. 'Brazen it out, that's the best way — and for Christ's sake, remember who we're meant to be!'

Touchet glanced at him contemptuously, and jabbed his heels into the bay. The gelding, who had not expected such treatment, leapt with a squeal and reared up, fighting the bit. The patrol, some dozen troopers, were treated to the amusing spectacle of man versus horse, which the bay, after a titanic struggle involving much use of hands, heels and stick, not to mention profanity, eventually won. He bucked unexpectedly, and Touchet, who up until now had kept his seat only with some difficulty, fell ungracefully off into the ditch.

Nick could not help it: he laughed. As Touchet's bedraggled head, crowned with burrs and bindweed and smeared with mud, rose furiously into view, he was reminded irresistibly of an episode in *Macbeth*. The soldiers pulled up their horses, and sniggered.

'Are you in some trouble, sir?' said their leader, a fresh-faced young captain. He was having difficulty with his expression, which would keep breaking out into a smile, despite all his efforts.

'No, thank you,' said Touchet, in tones of aristocratic hauteur. He rose, like Venus from the waves, girded with mud and foliage, and retrieved his battered and filthy hat. The bay, relieved of the burden on its back, grazed with fervour a few feet away, swishing its tail angrily. Nick slid down from the mare and moved carefully towards it, his hand outstretched. The horse, well aware of his intent, sidled crabwise out of reach.

'Would you like us to help you catch it, sir?' said the Captain, looking at Touchet: Nick had evidently been dismissed as a mere servant.

'If you would be so kind, Captain,' he said, waving an expressive hand that made the bay twitch nervously. Nick, despite the wild impulse to laugh, could not help but admire his aplomb. The young officer issued orders to his men, who formed their horses in a ring around the errant gelding. With every appearance of docility, the contrary animal permitted himself to be caught by his erstwhile rider, and even to be mounted with no more than laid-back ears and a flick of the tail.

'Thank you kindly, sir,' Touchet said, from his rather insecure perch. 'Tell me, what news have you? Is that rogue the King of Scots taken yet?'

Nick did not dare look in his direction. As a good servant should, he stared straight ahead between his horse's ears, and tried not even to think about what would happen if Touchet aroused the soldiers' suspicions.

'Not that we have heard, sir,' said the Captain. 'But we are ever vigilant. Have you come far?'

'From Tewkesbury only,' said Touchet. 'I doubt we have seen anything that might interest you – nothing unusual, and certainly no fugitive Scots.'

'They have all gone north, I hear,' said the officer, with a note of regret: he had obviously given up all hope of making any capture himself. 'Well, we must ride on. I bid you good day, sir. Are you heading for Gloucester? Well, if you should meet with any other patrol, mention of my name should ensure your passage in case of difficulty. I am Captain Bartlett. I wish you a good journey, sir, and Godspeed.'

'And to you, Captain, and my thanks.' Touchet smiled, and bowed courteously from the waist – a risky action, Nick thought, in view of the gelding's unpredictable nature. Then the Roundhead patrol had spurred on towards Tewkesbury in a choking cloud of dust, leaving the fugitive Cavaliers to their relief.

'How far is Gloucester?' Touchet demanded, mopping his brow.

'No more than a dozen miles,' Nick told him. 'We'll be there by dinner time, if there are no more mishaps.'

His companion glared at him, opened his mouth as if to utter something rude, and then thought better of it. 'Good,' he said curtly. 'We shall stay the night there, at least. I intend to buy some clothes – and a horse – that are more fitting for a gentleman.' He turned his unruly nag's head around, and set him off at a brisk canter towards the south.

Unfortunately, it was where Nick wished to go too: and besides, the other man had all the money. It seemed, like it or not, that for the moment he and Touchet must travel together. With deep misgivings, he urged the mare into a shambling and reluctant trot, to follow in his companion's dusty wake.

CHAPTER ELEVEN

'Liberty into bondage'
(*As You Like It*)

Patience Woods had heard of the defeat at Worcester with dismay. Her distress was compounded by the fact that, as only Silence knew of the real reason for her exile from London, she could not openly mourn the death of her hopes. But at least the King seemed to have escaped, for the moment, although the list of captives and slain was a long and depressing one. If he should chance to come by Wintercombe, thought Patience fiercely, I would not fail him — I would give him food and help and shelter. However, since all report, and sense, indicated that the King was fleeing north to Scotland, this did not exactly seem to be a likely proposition.

She fretted, itching for action, and yet knowing that it was impossible. Life at Wintercombe, that had once seemed so pleasant and lazy, now dragged most tediously. The weather had been too hot to ride out in comfort, and Patience had too much care for her pale and exquisite complexion to linger long out of doors. She spent much time before the mirror, examining herself for freckles, and came in for a great deal of teasing from Nat, who caught her peering at the imperfect reflection in a window pane of the winter parlour. At first irritated, she found herself enjoying these barbed exchanges, giving as good as she got, with wits honed on the London streets. It became an entertaining game, and went some way towards relieving the long slow autumnal days.

At last the weather broke, in a cracking thunderstorm that rattled the windows and flooded the lower part of the orchard, and the following day dawned cool and fresh and inviting, the sun's skin-threatening glare hidden behind a prim veil of wispy cloud. That afternoon, Patience succumbed to temptation and the eager importuning of her nieces and nephew, and ordered her horse to be saddled.

She was guiltily aware that she had not paid the children so much attention of late, save for Tabby, whose French lessons she had continued. They certainly provided ample proof of the harmful effects of too much sun and fresh air, being all as brown as hazelnuts, the tanned skins of William, Deb and Tabby a startling contrast to their pale hair. Kate, chestnut-coloured all over, looked like a small and mischievous monkey.

'We've got something to show you,' said Deb, self-important as ever, and William added, 'We've been making it all summer. We were going to ask you to help us, but you haven't been riding recently. Now it's finished, you can come and look.'

'What is it?' Patience asked curiously, and Kate hugged herself, grinning. 'Wait until you see it!'

So, an hour after dinner, they rode out of Wintercombe and down the hill. Tabby, on her little chestnut, Dowsabel, led the way, riding properly side-saddle, her back slim and straight and elegant, balanced easily on her lively mount. Patience followed her, somewhat less secure, and conscious of an uncharacteristic twist of envy. Once, years ago, she had been young, innocent and eager, just like her niece. Now, this fresh and lovely child made her feel a haggard old spinster. She was twenty-four, and not yet wed – and without much prospect of it, either.

She put such self-pitying thoughts from her mind, and listened to Deb's stream of chatter as she pointed out the watermeadows, the slopes of Hassage Hill and Baggridge to their left, and the invisible line of the Bath road on the ridge to the right. For a change, they had turned away from the village, and were riding along the narrowing valley that led towards Wellow, the next settlement to the north-west. The sun was still behind cloud, but Patience was taking no chances: she had bought a wide-brimmed, black felt hat in London, and wore it pushed firmly down, shading her face from the harmful light. Deb, bare-headed and riding astride fat Dumbledore with Kate pillion behind her, had no such scruples.

Tabby was thinking about Nick Hellier. Her mother had told her of the battle that had ended the pretensions of the young King of Scots, and Tabby's quick perception had seen past the calm words to the distress that lay beneath. There were so many uncertainties, so much she did not, and could not, know. But if Nick Hellier had been with the Scots army, if he was at Worcester Fight, if he had survived, was he a prisoner, or a fugitive? And had he received her letter?

The fortunate coincidence which had brought him back to the city of his birth, might also bring him back to Wintercombe. Realistically, she could not expect it, but it would be a crying shame, thought Tabby, if all her plotting and scheming were in vain.

'Tabby!' William's ear-splitting yell brought her rudely back to the present. 'Where are you going? It's up here, remember!'

She jerked Dowsabel to a halt, and realised that, lost in her daydream, she had ridden past the track. She turned the chestnut mare round, and joined the others.

Patience peered dubiously upwards. Here, the valley had narrowed until the shoulders of the enclosing hills rose up steeply from either side of the Norton Brook, leaving barely enough room for the lane. There were trees now growing thickly about them, and a path led off to the left, into the stream and out of it, to vanish up the slope of Baggridge. 'There?' she said.

'You might have to get off and walk,' said William, eyeing her judiciously. 'The trees come in very close for a bit, and you might hit your head on a branch. It'd be a shame to spoil those ostrich plumes.'

'We're not so tall as you, you see,' Deb explained. 'Except for Tabby, of course, and she hasn't got any plumes.'

'We'll tie the horses here,' William said. 'We won't be long. Then we can ride over to Wellow and ford the Wellow Brook – it's sure to be deep after all that rain yesterday, but it was almost dry last week, so Eliza said. And then we can come back by Charterhouse Hinton.'

Patience stared at the dank, and somehow menacing little path. Whatever could they have to show her up there? But as she kicked her leg reluctantly free from the pommel, the sun emerged triumphantly from the shrouding clouds, and Kate giggled. 'Hurry up, or you'll get freckles!'

Laughing, Patience allowed herself to be drawn into the dim shade of the wood, Deb officiously taking one hand and Kate the other. It was wet after the night's rain, and the earth smelt damp and grateful. Beneath the trees, mostly oak and ash, with coppiced stools of hazel, there was a fair amount of undergrowth, nettles, brambles and grass, and she gathered up the thick ample folds of her skirts and draped them over her arm. William had remained behind to secure the horses: he came running up behind them, through the thick damp grass. 'Are you all right, Aunt Imp?'

'Don't call me "Aunt",' she reminded him. 'It makes me feel so old.'

'But you are old,' said Kate, and diluted the unfortunate effect of this with a stream of giggles.

'That's not at all a nice thing to say,' Tabby told her, as sternly as Patience had ever heard her. 'Now, say you're sorry.'

'I'm sorry,' Kate said pertly, not at all abashed. Patience, despite being considered so ancient — although of course she was to Kate's five-year-old mind — could not be angry with her. After all, her own sharpness of tongue had often led her into trouble as a child, and later.

'Here. Here it is,' said William proudly, coming to a halt just in front of her. 'This is what we've been making.'

They had reached a small clearing created by a long-fallen tree, surprisingly sunlit and pleasant, with butterflies dancing in the warm rays of the sun. The path twisted on up the hill and vanished once more between the trees. Try as she might, Patience could see nothing that could possibly have been made: there was only the grass, a few late flowers, the rotting, fungus-covered trunk across the clearing, and a large bramble bush a little distance from them.

It occurred to her that this might be a joke at her expense, save that neither their manner nor their characters suggested it. Then she realised that there had been no other such bramble bushes on the brief walk up from the lane, and that on closer inspection this one appeared not to have grown, but to have been woven.

'Our hiding place,' said William. 'Have you seen it yet?'

'Is it the bush?' Patience asked, with more uncertainty than she in fact felt, and was rewarded by delighted grins.

'Yes, it is,' said Kate. 'We spent *ages* making it! And we all had to wear gloves, and it was William's idea, and he and Deb and Tabby gathered the brambles because they've all got leather gauntlets and I haven't yet, but I did the floor. Come on, come inside and see!'

Deb took away a few branches, and revealed a dark hole, distinctly uninviting. Patience removed her hat with the precious plumes, dyed a defiant Scottish blue, and approached with some apprehension. A damp skirt seemed to be the least of her worries, and she did not relish the prospect of having to repair any rips caused by the fierce thorns infesting every briar.

She ducked under the trailing brambles, and found herself in a round shelter, some three or four feet in height, and long enough to lie down. The floor, she realised as she put her hand on it, was carpeted in soft moss, and felt surprisingly dry. There was a heap of sweet-smelling hay at one end, into which Kate dived and rolled with squeals of glee, and a couple of rough seats formed from logs of wood nailed together.

'I made those — they're quite safe to sit on,' said William, with some pride. He added formally, 'I pray you, Mistress Woods, will you rest and take your ease? Lights, please!'

'The tinder's wet,' said Deb, furiously scratching away with flint and steel over a box which she had removed from some recess. 'I can't set it alight.'

'Let me try,' said Tabby. Her calmer approach paid off, and soon a small soft spark illuminated her face as she blew gently on it. Deb lit a candlestub, and set it within a battered lanthorn at the centre of the mossy floor. Patience hoped that it would not be knocked over: she did not like to think about what might happen, should this flimsy structure be set on fire.

'Well, what do you think of it?' said William, waving a hand around. The walls were lined with thick hanks of grass and branches and bark, all woven together to make a surprisingly warm and cosy shelter. Certainly, very little of last night's rain seemed to have penetrated.

'It's very well made,' said Patience, with sincerity. 'An excellent hiding-place — but what is it for?'

'We can hide in it when we're naughty!' said Kate, her tangled brown head arising abruptly from her nest of hay. 'Mama would *never* find us here!'

'Probably not, but I would,' said William. 'And you're the only one of us who's ever really naughty, so you're the only one who's likely to need it — imp!'

'I'm not Imp — Aunt Patience is Imp!'

'If we found any escaped Scots, we could hide them here,' said Tabby quietly. Patience stared at her in astonishment, and saw a swift red flush run up under her fine skin, turned golden by the candlelight. But her eyes were huge and dark and utterly serious. 'I hadn't thought of it before,' she added. 'We could, though, couldn't we?'

'If there are any,' William said. 'But Mama said they'd all go back to Scotland, so they're not likely to come here, are they?'

'Not really,' said Patience, successfully managing not to laugh. They were so earnest, and so innocent, and so utterly unrealistic. As if a fugitive Scots officer, or English for that matter, would wish to make use of such a primitive and comfortless shelter! And the chances of any such finding their way to this unfrequented little valley in the depths of Somerset were undoubtedly rather remote.

Tabby, who in her heart had some reason to hope it would prove otherwise, did not enlighten her.

*

The fair City of Gloucester boasted many pleasant inns, well appointed, comfortable and furnished with everything that a traveller could desire. Mervyn Touchet, who had some small acquaintance with the place, made unerringly for the most expensive. Nick, cast inexorably in the role of servant, and unwilling to jeopardise their safety by protesting, rode silently behind, wondering with foreboding how long it would be before someone's suspicions were aroused. Touchet, even in ordinary garb, was not exactly inconspicuous, and his superficial resemblance to the King had already been remarked by Nan Powell. He hoped that there was no one in Gloucester eager to gain the favour of the Council of State.

The ostler at the Swan took Touchet's coin with a cheerful smile, and led away the two weary nags as if they were fiery, aristocratic steeds. He did not seem to notice their owner's incongruously bedraggled appearance, and Nick began to wonder if he had overestimated the problem. Certainly Touchet, behaving like a lord, was not acting in a furtive or suspicious manner. Who would believe that a fugitive would willingly make himself so conspicuous?

The landlord showed them to a chamber which, he claimed, was the best his hostelry could offer, and certainly the big feather bed, with its heavy damask curtains, looked extremely comfortable. There was, he added with a cursory glance at Nick, a truckle bed for Master Thomson's servant. Touchet, in a few moments of questioning, ascertained the direction of the best tailor in the city, explained that he was in need of a horse, and was given the names of several people of the landlord's acquaintance who might be able to supply one. Then, with Nick silent and self-contained behind him, he sallied majestically forth in search of a suit of clothes more fitting to his station.

The tailor, unfortunately, was a sharp-eyed little man with an ominously plain style of dress, though the half-finished garments being sewn by his apprentices were far from Puritan. He surveyed Touchet, tall, elegant and lamentably clad, with a gaze bordering on the suspicious, and listened in thoughtful silence to his instructions. A suit of clothes, of the latest fashion, to be made of any fine cloth that the tailor might have at his disposal, and to be ready by tomorrow evening at the latest.

'That will be difficult,' said the tailor, stroking his chin. 'As you can see, we have much to do at present, sir. May I ask why you are in so much haste? Another day, and there would be no problem.'

'I suffered a mishap while on my journey,' said Touchet, waving a languid hand. 'My baggage was quite ruined, and I was forced to borrow another's clothes. However, we must reach Bristol as soon as possible, to see my sister, and I do not wish to arrive so poorly clad.'

'It will of course be necessary to charge extra for such rushed work,' said the tailor. 'However, I think it can be done . . . and we have a bolt of blue woollen cloth, very fine, ideal for riding-clothes . . . if you would care to examine it, sir, step this way, and my journeyman will take your measurements afterwards.'

They emerged at last from the dim little shop, Touchet wondering aloud how anyone could sew a straight seam under such conditions, and began the search for a horse. The second name on the landlord's list proved most helpful, and offered to send round two geldings to the inn that evening, so that the gentleman could inspect them both, and take his choice.

'And you can have the bay,' said Touchet to Nick, as one conferring a signal favour. 'He's a good enough ride, now that I've tamed him.'

This assessment proved to be a trifle premature. On their return to the Swan, they were accosted by the furious ostler, limping heavily. It transpired that the bay had kicked him as he went to fill its manger, and his ire could only be appeased by a liberal tip. Touchet, none too pleased, stamped up to their chamber, calling for strong beer, a bottle of wine, and his supper.

It was brought by a plump young serving-maid, her corsetry artfully arranged to reveal just enough to whet the appetite. Nick had already decided that adopting the stance of detached observer was the only way to preserve his sanity, and Touchet's good looks, if not his life. He watched her lean forward as she placed the tray on the table, and smiled inwardly. By the expression on his companion's face, she was not wasting her efforts. She fluttered her eyelashes at him, bobbed a curtsey, and asked meaningfully if there was anything else the gentleman required.

'There might be, if you come back in a little while,' said Touchet, giving her a look full of lingering lechery. The girl giggled, and retreated in a fluster of maidenly blushes.

'She's no more a virgin than I am,' Nick said, as the door shut behind her. 'Do you think the landlord's hospitality extends to the debauching of his serving-maids?'

'Certain of it,' said Touchet, through a mouthful of roast chicken. Nick, watching, thought it a pity that his table manners were not appropriate to his aristocratic demeanour. 'Known for it, this place — 's why I chose it.' He took a greedy draught of wine, and glanced at Nick, quietly consuming a pastry that purported to be venison. 'Why don't you go down to the taproom, eh, and find a willing girl for yourself?'

'I might,' said Nick, wondering how Touchet had managed to survive so long without someone murdering him. True, the man's money was paying for this handsome chamber and generous supper, and probably for the girl as well, but he had no wish to be beholden to someone whom he held in such dislike. Yet their ways must lie together, for the next few days at least, and he found himself hoping fervently that there would be a ship bound for Ireland lying in Bristol harbour, and another to take him to France or the Low Countries.

A coy knock announced the return of the maid, before the two men had finished the fruit tart and cheese. She carried another bottle of wine, and a glass. As she placed them on the table, Touchet grabbed her round the waist and pulled her on to his lap, amidst a stream of giggles. 'Ooh, sir,' said the girl, making only a token attempt at resistance. 'What are you doing, sir?'

'Only trying to kiss you, my pretty,' said Touchet, expertly capturing her hands. 'Now, have you half an hour to spare?'

'Ooh, I don't know, sir . . . well, perhaps,' said the maid, as his hands briskly unlaced her bodice. 'I don't do this with just anyone, you understand, sir — ooh! — but you're such a fine-looking gentleman.' She giggled again. 'One of the other girls said as how you looked just like the King of Scots — they say he's tall and dark and handsome, too.'

Nick, who had made up his mind to go downstairs, froze in his chair. Touchet laughed softly, his hands roving as boldly as the girl's. 'Well, I wouldn't deny it, would I? And you never know what you might be able to boast of one day, eh?' And his mouth came down on hers, effectively halting all further conversation.

Seething with suppressed fury, Nick left them to it, and stamped down to the taproom. It would, he decided, be very pleasant to get drunk, and forget all about the irritation, the annoyance and the lunatic indiscretion of Lieutenant-Colonel Mervyn Touchet, but he would very likely need all his wits about him this night. He sat morosely with a tankard in a dark corner, taking small sips of the Swan's particularly fine brew, and hoped that Touchet would flail himself into a seizure upstairs.

There was small hope of that, of course. In rather more than an hour, the maid appeared, flushed and dishevelled, still giggling, to take up her more regular duties. Aware that part of the reason for his black mood had been envy, pure and simple, Nick ignored her. He was not going to demean himself by taking Touchet's leavings.

Afterwards, however, he wished that he had.

They were still asleep, on the following morning, when someone knocked thunderously on the door of their chamber. Nick, with the speed of the professional soldier, was awake instantly, and on his feet reaching for his sword before he realised, belatedly, that he no longer possessed one. Then, as Touchet stirred sleepily within the curtained fastness of his four-poster, someone bawled, 'Open up — open up in there, in the name of the Commonwealth!'

For a brief, wild instant, Nick considered the alternatives. Escape through the window was a possibilty, but involved a twelve-foot drop and the likelihood of broken limbs. They had no weapons, and armed resistance would in any case be futile. No, their only chance was to brazen it out.

He thrust his head between the red damask curtains, and met Touchet's sleepy, bewildered gaze. 'For God's sake, remember our story,' he hissed, and added, 'Use that captain's name, if you have to.'

The hammering redoubled in force. With deceptive calm, Nick walked to the door, unbolted it, and lifted the latch.

There was a Roundhead officer outside, large and threatening in his buff coat, with a pistol in his hand. He stared at the slight, brown-haired man standing in his nightshirt in the doorway, an expression of courteous bewilderment on his face. 'Yes, sir? What can I do for you?'

He was thrust aside as the officer pushed into the chamber, with several troopers following, swords drawn. One of them flung the bed-curtains back to reveal the outraged stare of a gentleman rudely and unjustly aroused from guiltless slumber. 'What is the meaning of this?' Touchet demanded, with considerable fury. 'What are you doing, sir? Get out at once, and leave honest men in peace!'

Nick, his arms firmly held by two of the troopers, could only admire his companion's acting ability. One false move, and their freedom, perhaps eventually their lives, would be at an end, and yet the man showed no sign of alarm, only the perfectly understandable rage of the innocent.

'Not until you have answered our questions,' said the officer, waving his pistol: it was a firelock of the latest design, Nick noticed, and something which he would dearly love to possess for himself. 'There's a serving-maid in this inn says you claim to be Charles Stuart, King of Scots. Are you?'

To the officer's evident annoyance, Touchet burst out laughing. 'Charles Stuart? That's rich indeed! King of Scots! What a silly little baggage!'

'Then you never admitted to her that you were Charles Stuart?'

'How could I?' said Touchet in bewilderment. 'Since I so evidently am not?'

The officer gazed at him, nonplussed. He said at last, curtly, 'Will you stand up, sir?'

Touchet gave him a haughty stare. Finally, after sufficient time had elapsed to make his attitude clear, he climbed with dignity from the bed and stood beside it, clad like Nick only in his nightshirt. Fortunately, Nan Russell had trimmed his hair, as she had done for Nick, into a neater and more conventional style. It still fell far short of a gentleman's lovelocks, however, and contrasted a little strangely with Touchet's aristocratic mien. Moreover, his height was immediately distinctive.

'A tall, black-haired man, some two yards high,' said the officer. 'Is that not a fair description of yourself, sir?'

'I beg your pardon, sir,' said Nick quietly. 'May I be allowed to point out a matter of relevance?'

The Roundhead swung round, and stared at him as if he were a small and insignificant insect. 'Yes?' he said with hostility.

'I have never set eyes on this Charles Stuart, sir,' said Nick, trying to give a convincing impression of a humble servant, his Worcestershire burr pronounced. 'But I have heard it said that he's a dark-skinned, swarthy man – and only twenty-one. Which, as you can see, sir, my master assuredly is not.'

The officer frowned at him, and then turned back to Touchet. 'You now claim not to be Charles Stuart. Have you any proof of this? Who are you? What is your business here?'

'My name is James Thomson, of Calne in Wiltshire, and this is my servant. We are on our way to Bristol, to visit my sister.'

'But Gloucester is surely some distance out of your way,' said the officer, his voice heavy with suspicion. 'What are you doing here?'

'I was visiting lands near Tewkesbury in which I have an interest,' said Touchet curtly. 'Is that sufficient explanation, or must I give you all the most trivial details of my journey as well? I must protest, sir — this is an ungodly hour to be woken so rudely. Really, I cannot imagine what your superior officers can be thinking of, to sit idly by whilst honest men are hauled from their beds and questioned on the flimsiest of pretexts. If you are satisfied, be on your way, and leave us in peace.'

'If you are not Charles Stuart, you may well be Scots,' said the officer suspiciously. 'Search their baggage!'

This did not take very long. The Roundhead stared at the crumpled, unprepossessing heap of clothing in the middle of the floor. 'Is that all?'

'A misfortune befell my bag, as the landlord of this establishment will confirm,' said Touchet. 'It was lost in a stream when my horse fell and lamed itself, and so I was forced to make use of a most sorry jade, and borrow a suit of clothing to replace what was spoilt. Now, to add insult to injury, I am put to the inquisition by you, sir. Without doubt, I shall complain most bitterly to your commanding officer — especially since one of your fellows was so kind as to assist me after my mishap, and could not have been more helpful.'

'One of my fellows?' The officer glared at him. 'Who, pray?'

'One Captain Bartlett. He told me that mention of his name would be sure to smooth any difficulty which we might encounter on our journey. He certainly did not take us for rogues or Scots, and I fail to see why you are so suspicious, sir.'

The other man stared at him for a long, tense moment. Nick, still held in the troopers' grasp, became aware of an annoying tickle at the end of his nose. Touchet, the picture of righteous indignation, stared back. Being clad only in a nightshirt did not seem to make him feel at a disadvantage. Then the officer swung round to the men holding Nick. 'Let him go. My apologies for having disturbed your rest, sir. Good day.'

Nick shut the door behind them, and bolted it. With a feeling of enormous and disbelieving relief, he listened as the sound of booted feet heavily descended the stairs, and died thankfully away into the distance.

Touchet roared with laughter. 'Your face! Did you think we were done for? Well, it takes more than some addle-pated lieutenant to outwit Mervyn Touchet!'

'If it hadn't been for your conceit, we'd have been left in peace,' said Nick, his voice low and furious. This wave of suffocating anger had taken him by surprise, and he knew that he should not give way to it, but the pent-up rage and frustration of the past ten days had all come boiling to a head, and would not be suppressed. 'Dear God, anyone would think you *wanted* to be captured! You may think yourself a fine gentleman, sir, and your brother may be an earl and your wife the daughter of another, and you may have inherited blue blood and manners and money, but your wits seem to have been left out of the bargain!'

Touchet gaped at him, utterly astonished. Nick, knowing that he had gone too far, decided to burn his boats with a vengeance. 'For the sake of my own freedom, I'd be better off without your company — at least I can take comfort from the fact that if I'm caught, it'll be my own fault, and not by reason of your stupidity! And if you want me to travel with you, you'd best mend your ways and start thinking like a fugitive, or you'll be in jail before the week's out, and I for one have no intention of keeping you company there! And,' he added, deciding to make this point unequivocally clear, 'I am prepared to play the part of your servant in public, but I'll be damned if you treat me like one in private. Understand? You accompany me on my terms, or not at all.'

Touchet seemed at a loss for words. Finally, he said stiffly, 'Were you a gentleman, sir, and armed, I would call you out for what you have said.'

'Well, you're lucky I am not, because ten to one I'd spit you where you stand,' said Nick, exasperated. 'Dear God, man, come down off your high horse and *think*! A gentleman and his servant, travelling quietly together, are not exactly an infrequent sight. Our best chance of escape lies that way. If you are not prepared to demean yourself by adopting a disguise, then at least you'll have to behave with some circumspection, or you'll run both our heads into a noose.'

Touchet turned away to stare out of the window. Down in the street, the troopers were mounting their horses, while the curious peered out of windows and doors. A long silence followed, in which Nick wondered if he had better take the bay gelding, and make his way to Bristol alone. Touchet was so plainly eaten up with pride and the niceties of gentlemanly conduct, that he could not be persuaded to see reason, and Nick decided that he was not altogether sorry, even if his companion was unfortunately in possession of all the money.

But he had underestimated the man. The aristocratic, languid voice, for once almost devoid of affectation, seeemed to have accepted his argument. 'Very well. If you wish it, we will continue together.'

No word of apology, no promise to act with more caution in future, but at least he seemed to be ready to behave more appropriately to their circumstances. Words were easy, however, and Nick wondered how he would react in reality?

It might seem the height of foolishness to linger at the Swan, and yet, as Nick pointed out later, to leave immediately after the soldiers' interrogation would invite suspicion. Moreover, Touchet's new clothes would not be ready until the evening. 'And if I am to play the part of a gentleman,' he said unanswerably, 'then I must appear convincing. Which I most assuredly do not, in these sorry garments.'

That was true. Nick grunted something, reluctant to start another argument. They might loathe each other, but for the moment at least they must stick together, or surely come to grief.

Nick spent all that day wondering whether the Roundhead officer who had nearly arrested them that morning would try to contact Captain Bartlett. If he did, his suspicions might be lulled – or he might realise that the story Touchet had given him did not quite tally with the truth. The longer they stayed in Gloucester, the greater the risk of discovery.

He went to the tailor to collect Touchet's new clothes, the other man having declared himself unwilling to venture forth clad, in his words, like some wandering vagabond. The tailor was greatly harassed, there being another gentleman's servant in the shop to complain of poor fitting, so he had little time to spare for close scrutiny. Nick took the parcel, neatly wrapped, and bore it back to the Swan with some relief. Now they could be gone at first light.

Touchet did not like the suit. It was not the colour he had expected, the doublet was too short, he did not want to look like a damned Frenchman. It was, however, an excellent fit, and Nick told him so. He was no longer prepared to mince his words. He had given Touchet the choice, and the other man had opted to stay in his company. If he did not relish plain speaking, it was too bad. Certainly in the fine wool, with the fresh linen of his new shirt modishly displayed, and a pair of sturdy riding-boots, he did look much more the gentleman.

The horse he had bought was a spindly chestnut, with a fiery eye and a mouth like iron. It seemed to be sound, but Nick doubted it would stay thus for long. The mare was left as part payment for their accommodation, and on the morning of Saturday, the thirteenth of September, ten days after the battle, they left Gloucester at sunrise, and set off towards Bristol, nearly forty miles to the south, in an inimical silence.

*

Rachael, watching at the window of her stepmother's chamber, beheld her betrothed riding in under the gate. With a sudden stab of panic, she realised that her first emotion on seeing him had not been joy, but annoyance.

No, she thought fiercely. Jack will be my husband in a few months' time – I will love and honour and obey him, and be a good and dutiful wife in all things. Of course I'm not cross that he's come just now – but I was planning to visit Nell Apprice, and I haven't seen her for days, and I was rather looking forward to it . . . it's not Jack's fault, how could he know?

But she could not help greeting him with a little less than her usual smile. Jack, who had ridden over out of politeness and duty, not to mention a certain fondness for Darby's cooking, found himself annoyed in his turn. Really, when he had come all this way, along very mediocre roads – his father should have a word with the local justices about that pothole at Hinton – he had a right to expect more from his future bride than a cool greeting and a peck on the cheek.

He could not, for courtesy's sake, voice his displeasure openly. Instead, like his father, he retreated into a stiff and chilly formality which, in its turn, irritated and alienated Rachael still more. By dinner time, they so clearly had nothing to say to each other that Silence, presiding over a fragrant and steaming table, eyed her simmering stepdaughter and wondered if, at last, Rachael was having second thoughts.

She knew better than to broach it to her: the girl would instantly run the contrary way, whatever her real opinion. Besides, if her dowry were to be saved, it was not Rachael, but Jack, whose mind must change.

It seemed, according to Harley, that there was no chance of altering George's will. She was highly suspicious of legal processes, which seemed to have more to do with lining lawyers' pockets than with honest justice, but supposed that he must be right. If there was an opportunity to embark on a costly lawsuit, he surely would have taken it. And in all the business of running the household, she had little leisure to sit down with Nat and ask him pertinent questions.

Nat did not give the appearance of one unduly worried. He had ignored the sullen figure of his twin, and the less morose one of her betrothed, who was applying himself with dedication to a piece of succulent beef, and was conducting a cheerful conversation with Patience and the children. The subject of freckles, she noticed, was still very much to the fore, and soon Tabby was turning to her and asking, with mischief, whether she had any good remedies for these.

'I am told that fresh hare's blood, smoothed over the face, is excellent,' Silence said gravely. As her sister's pretty nose wrinkled in disgust, she added, 'Of course, it has to be killed at the full moon. If you ask Diggory nicely, I'm sure he can find you one. It won't work unless you skin it yourself, of course, and – '

'Ugh,' said Patience. 'I'd rather have the freckles.'

'Nell Apprice always uses watercress juice,' said Nat. He glanced at his twin, who had studiously ignored him all through the meal, as indeed she had done for some weeks past. 'Or so Rachael tells me.'

'I have nothing to do with such frivolities,' said Rachael forbiddingly to her plate. Her face was a cold pale mask, but inside her misery and fury boiled like a cauldron. Oh, to escape from here, from her family who knew altogether too much about her, to make a fresh start with Jack! And yet she knew, with rage and dread, that after a few more such dinners, when her twin seemed to forget that they had a guest in their midst, Jack would have been made privy to all her most embarrassing foibles and secrets, and she would have nothing left to hide.

'The Lord gave each of us our face, fair or foul, and it is in my opinion an impertinence to enhance or disguise His work,' said Jack, looking earnestly around the table. Rachael, horrified, saw Nat's mouth quirk upwards in mockery. Surely he would not be so ill-mannered as to laugh?

Patience, who had a fine array of bottles, lotions and perfumes jostling on the table in her chamber, shook her head so that her glossy, scented dark ringlets bounced alluringly on her shoulders. 'Oh no, Master Harington, do you really think so? Surely the Lord will not be displeased if His work is made still more lovely. My sister's garden is full of flowers which you will not find growing wild, they have been nourished and enhanced by man's efforts, and yet their beauty must surely be a compliment to their Creator?'

Which, her sister noticed with secret amusement, effectively silenced Jack Harington.

Nat was looking very thoughtful, usually a bad sign. As the maids, with Carpenter presiding, cleared away the first course, he beckoned young Hannah Grindland over and whispered some instruction to her. With some misgivings, Silence watched her leave the room, to return a few moments later with pen, ink and paper.

'What are those for?' Kate asked, curiosity as usual getting the better of her manners. Nat grinned at her. 'Mind your own business, Binnick. You'll learn soon enough.'

There were oysters, buttered eggs and a rabbit fricassee, as well as fruit, plums and new rosy pippins, and cheese. Nat ignored it all, frowning, chewing his quill and ostentatiously hiding his paper from prying eyes. Patience, sitting opposite, felt her excitement bubbling over into laughter. It had something to do with her, she felt sure: he kept glancing in her direction, with mischief as plain in his face as it usually was in Kate's. 'What is it?' she asked eagerly, unable to contain herself any longer. 'What are you doing, Nat?'

'Mind *your* own business,' he said, laughing at her. Once, a very long time ago, it might have irritated her. Now, used to his light-hearted teasing, she laughed in response, and made a swift grab across the table. He was too quick for her, and whisked it out of reach. 'Ah, have patience, Patience!'

'Children, behave!' said Silence, not very sternly. Poor Jack was looking increasingly bewildered, and Rachael's expression seemed to be graven in stone. Kate, by now thoroughly over-excited, was squealing with merriment. If that parrot hasn't discouraged Jack's

intentions, her mother thought ruefully, then this fair approxi-
mation of a bear-garden certainly will.

'I have finished,' said Nat portentously, and put a flourish at the
bottom of the page. 'What I have here is for Mistress Im-patience,
and she may reveal its contents to this undisciplined mob, or not,
as she pleases. Here you are, madam — an ode!'

'In praise of my radiant eyes, of course,' said Patience, smiling.

He rose, bowed, and handed the folded piece of paper across the
table to her, while the children watched with bright-eyed curiosity. 'No — to your radiant freckles!'

She unfolded it, and stared at the writing, a little hasty and
smudged. A verse, extempore — and, knowing Nat, none too
flattering. She would not read it aloud, just yet.

My lady Imp her skin must hide,
So fine and white it be:
The summer sun she can't abide,
His rays she dare not see.
But why hare's blood must wash her face,
That's yet as fair as silver lace,
Is a mystery to me!

It was not at all as she had expected. Absurdly, she realised that she
was blushing. She looked up and met his gaze, mocking, teasing,
and yet entirely serious, and her blush deepened. This is ridiculous, she thought. He's my nephew, he's three years younger than
me — and he looks at me like that! The impertinence of it!

But of course, he was no blood relation to her at all. And male
flattery, even somewhat disguised, had been a rare commodity of
late. A small warm glow of satisfaction settled in her breast, and
she gave him her most dazzling smile in return.

'Read it, please!' Deb was urging her, one hand tugging her
sleeve. 'Please, Patience, please read it to us!'

She glanced at Nat again.

He was leaning back in his chair, highly amused, the blue
eyes crinkled with laughter. 'Well, at least I haven't called you
ugly.'

'I should hope not,' said Patience sternly, with a creditable
attempt to return to her usual casual, light-hearted manner. As she
declaimed the lines of doggerel, she caught sight of Jack Harington's disapproving face, and realised that she had just put herself
beyond his pale.

But it hardly mattered, for now she had a new, more exciting and more promising game to play.

*

'This 'ere be Dursley, sir,' said the ancient labourer, leaning on the gate. 'Be ee a'staying the night, sir? A power of soldiers in the town, you won't find a room for love nor money.' He cackled maliciously, and Touchet and Nick exchanged glances.

It was exactly what they had not wished to hear. They had seen several bands of troopers on their journey from Gloucester, some riding south with great fury, others north. Each encounter had been more alarming than the last, until at the sight of what appeared to be a full regiment bearing down on them at a hand gallop, in a narrow hedge-lined part of the road. Touchet's nerve had almost broken, and his horse's certainly had. The chestnut had reared, squealed, attempted to join the herd thundering past, and had generally proved so difficult that it had taken his rider a considerable time to quieten him. To Nick's secret satisfaction, his own excitable bay had been much easier to control. Then, before they had gone on a mile, Touchet's horse went dead lame, and proved to have cast a shoe. Fortunately, there was a smithy nearby, and all might have been well, had not the blacksmith commented idly that he had just had half a dozen soldiers ask him if he had seen any fugitive Scots.

'And have you?' asked Nick. He was holding the chestnut's leg, and felt considerably relieved that his companion, who had in gentlemanly fashion left such mundane matters to his supposed servant, was standing outside, examining the attributes of a farm girl swilling buckets at the village well. 'I thought they'd all gone off back home – those that haven't been killed, or captured.'

'And hanged, I hope,' the smith had said, spitting unerringly on to the glowing metal of the new shoe. 'And strange gentlemen too,' he said. 'You're from these parts, I can hear it, but what of him?' A jerk of his head indicated the fine new suit and handsome dark head of Master Mervyn Touchet, alias Thomson. 'Ain't never seen *him* before.'

'It's not surprising – he's from Wiltshire,' said Nick. It was astonishingly easy, in the thick red dim light of the smithy, hot as Vulcan's forge, or Hell, to seem as casual as true innocence. 'We're on our way to Bristol, but we won't reach there today. Where's the best place hereabouts to stay for the night?'

The smith's eyes had glinted in his sooty, sweat-streaked face. 'Dursley, most people stop. It's about five or six miles from here. But you want to be careful, you and your master — there ain't no outwitting a Dursley man, proper sharp they are, so you watch your master don't get charged more than he should be.'

The combination of that information, and now the news that the town was full of soldiers, was enough to induce a feeling of anxiety in any fugitive Cavalier. But Touchet tossed the ancient labourer a groat, with a lordly gesture, and rode into Dursley as if he owned the place. Nick followed, trying not to obey his instincts, which screamed at him to become as inconspicuous as possible.

As the old man had predicted, the best inn was full, given over to the officers of the regiment quartered there, and the landlord, though apologetic, professed himself quite unable to help. Nick resisted the temptation to ask if there was any room in the stable, and made his way to the next establishment, while Touchet sat his high-strung chestnut, fortunately exhausted by its exertions during the day, and ogled any pretty girl who happened to pass.

He had better fortune at the third hostelry, where they were offered a small chamber under the eaves. There was one slight disadvantage: it was otherwise packed with soldiers.

There was no alternative but to brazen it out. Aware that Touchet's height, looks and manner had already attracted several curious glances, Nick prayed that his companion had acquired some discretion after the events in Gloucester, and led the way into the inn's courtyard.

The chamber was small and cramped, with only one half-tester bed, and no hearth. Touchet glared round in disgust, saw Nick's face, and wisely said nothing. The window gave on to the main street, near the market place. There were sounds of disturbance and excitement outside, and Nick opened the casement, with some difficulty, and leaned out.

A proclamation was being read, it seemed, and people were crowding round to listen. Nick could hear only snatches above the general street noise, but they were sufficient to give him a good idea of its contents.

'Treacherous and hostile manner with an army . . . said Charles Stuart is escaped . . . malicious and dangerous traitor to the peace of this Commonwealth . . . make diligent search and enquiry for the said Charles Stuart, and his abettors and adherents . . . safe custody before the Parliament . . . as Justice shall require . . .

whosoever shall apprehend . . . Charles Stuart . . . a reward for such services, the sum of one thousand pounds.'

One thousand pounds. An unimaginable sum to the vast masses of the poor: enough to set up a man, and his family, in comfort for the rest of his life. It was not cold, but Nick shivered. He turned abruptly and shut the window.

'What's happening?' Touchet enquired. He had taken his boots off, and was lounging at his ease on the bed, smoking the pipe he had bought in Gloucester, along with a less than fragrant wad of smoky Gloucestershire tobacco.

It was a habit of which Nick, who enjoyed a pipe himself, was fast becoming intolerant. He controlled his irritation, and said quietly, 'They're reading a proclamation from the Council of State. The people are urged to apprehend Charles Stuart and all his followers. And the price on the King's head is one thousand pounds.'

Touchet stared at him in horror. 'A thousand pounds? Mother of God, they must be desperate! And with that bait, what man could resist such temptation?'

'Let us hope, then, that there are still some honest poor men in England,' said Nick grimly. 'But at least we can take comfort from one thing – they'd hardly offer such a fortune if they'd already caught him.'

'Perhaps,' said Touchet. He brooded for a while, the noxious fumes rising in a cloud from his pipe and wafting in a throat-catching haze around the patched, beamed ceiling. 'Was there mention of a reward for the capture of the King's followers?'

'None that I could hear, no. But I doubt any who betrayed us would meet with the Council of State's disfavour, somehow.'

A knock on the door put an abrupt end to the conversation. It was the landlord, a long thin gloomy man, quite unlike the stout jolly sort popularly supposed to be typical of the breed. He surveyed his two non-military guests morosely, and asked whether they would be travelling on the morrow as it was a Sunday.

'What has that to do with it?' demanded Touchet, before Nick could stop him. 'We must be in Bristol as soon as may be.'

A change, slight but significant, came over the innkeeper's long face. His eyes sharpened, and he said, 'You are bound for Bristol, sir? To take ship there, perhaps?'

Belatedly, Touchet seemed to realise the value of caution. 'No, of course not,' he snapped. 'I go to visit my sister, who is sick.

Naturally, I wish to be with her as soon as possible. Her husband sent me a letter saying her life was in danger, and I do not wish to arrive too late.'

'Indeed, sir, I am sorry to hear it,' said the landlord. Nick, unregarded by the window, saw his narrow, assessing gaze, and realised suddenly that they were under suspicion. Yet how could he, in his guise as a servant, presume to answer for the man who posed as his master?

'In which part of Bristol does your sister live? Forgive my curiosity, sir,' said the innkeeper, not in the least apologetic. 'But we have much concern here to watch out for strangers who may be adherents of Charles Stuart.'

'I know that – my servant here heard the proclamation a few moments ago,' said Touchet, somewhat curtly. 'And what business is it of yours, if my sister lives in Bristol or London or High Germany?'

'If I may presume, Master Thomson,' Nick said quickly. Something had to be done to avert the disaster that was surely about to befall them, and once more due to Touchet's intransigence. 'It may indeed be none of his business, but it will smooth matters somewhat if he knows. Mistress Adams lives in St. Thomas Street, sir, and her husband is a merchant of some importance.'

It was the name and address of his old master, the apothecary, to whom he had long ago been so unsuccessfully apprenticed. He prayed that the landlord had no more than a slight acquaintance with Bristol. If he knew the city well, they were surely undone.

It seemed he did not. 'My apologies, sir,' he said, with an astounding change from the suspicious to the more usual obsequiousness. 'Pray forgive me for having disturbed you.' And with a bow that almost banged his head on the floor, he removed himself from the chamber.

Touchet, of course, was exultant. Almost before the door had closed, he had let out a crow of glee. 'Soon put him to flight, eh? Damned nosy old Roundhead – "Are you travelling on a Sunday, sir?"' His voice was a cruelly accurate imitation of the rather nasal tones of the innkeeper. 'I ask you, Hellier, do I look like some canting Puritan who won't even scratch his arse on the Sabbath?'

'No,' said Nick. 'But I expect that's why he was suspicious.' Although Touchet seemed to think that all danger was past, he himself was not so sure. How long had the landlord lingered before knocking on the door? Had he heard anything incriminating? Above all, had his suspicions really been allayed by Nick's description of the address of Touchet's fictitious sister?

The answer came with a brisk hammering on the door, a few minutes later. Nick, expecting their supper, which they had ordered earlier, went to answer it, and found himself looking, not at a serving-maid, but at the long and unwavering barrel of a horse-pistol. 'Good evening, sir,' said the soldier pleasantly. 'Kindly sit down – and you sir. You are both under arrest.'

Sick at heart, Nick pulled up one of the chairs to the table by the window. Touchet remained lounging on the bed, still non-chalantly puffing his pipe. 'Under arrest?' he said, in tones that indicated what he thought of such a ridiculous statement. 'What nonsense is this?'

'No nonsense, sir,' said the officer, still as courteous as if making a social call. 'The landlord of this inn has certain suspicions, which he at once communicated to me. Accordingly, I am confining you both to this chamber, until our enquiries can be carried out.' He glanced at Nick. 'Who are you?'

'My name is Nick Harrison, sir, servant to Master Thomson here.'

'And how long have you been in his service?'

'Two years and more now, sir,' said Nick, letting the Worces-tershire tones colour his voice.

'You certainly seem to know his business better than he does himself, by all accounts,' said the officer drily. He seemed a pleasant man, and under other circumstances Nick might have liked him. Now, however, he represented the rock upon which their hopes of freedom had foundered, a conscientious and diligent officer. 'Why did you not wish to give the landlord your desti-nation, sir?' he added, turning to Touchet.

Cool as a cowcumber, he stared back. 'Do I have to give every last detail of my business to some ferrety little innkeeper?' he said, with aristocratic indignation. 'It seems I must, or risk arrest.'

'You would do well not to arouse suspicions in these dangerous times,' the officer told him. 'Especially since your very appearance may lead to speculation.' His gaze lingered on the black hair, the long sprawled length of the man on the bed, his fine linen and the gently fuming pipe. 'And you claim to be visiting your sister in Bristol? Have you any papers which will prove your story, or indicate that you are who you say you are?'

Touchet spread his hands. 'Alas, sir, I have not. As my servant here will confirm, I had an unfortunate mishap near Tewkesbury, and all my baggage and effects were lost in a river. I have had a most unfortunate journey, and this ludicrous situation is the final straw.'

'My apologies, sir,' said the officer. 'But if you are indeed innocent, you will have nothing to fear, merely a little inconvenience. It will not take long to ascertain the truth of your story. In the meantime, you will not, I am sure, find it too irksome to be confined in this chamber for a few hours. Your supper will be brought to you soon, and I wish you a good night, sir.'

The door was shut behind him by a burly trooper, evidently under orders to stand guard outside, and the key turned in the lock with a sound of utter finality.

They were prisoners.

CHAPTER TWELVE

'Hairbreadth 'scapes'
(Othello)

'There's no escape,' said Touchet. 'No way out. This is the end.'

Nick resisted the temptation to apportion any blame for this situation. Matters were desperate enough, without exacerbating the bad feeling between the two men. He glanced around the narrow, unpromising little chamber, and said, 'I wouldn't give up hope – not yet.'

Touchet glared at him. 'You think you're the clever one, do you? Well, I'd like to see you extract us from this pretty pickle!'

They had spoken in whispers, ever mindful of the trooper on guard outside the door. Supper had been brought to them, as promised, but neither man had been able to muster much appetite, and they left much of the food to congeal on the plates. Now, it was growing dark, and there was little to be seen in the chamber, beyond the shadowy shapes of the furnishings and the sharp grey-blue outline of the window. Nick got up and walked over to it. He had wondered if it would be possible to climb out of it, but one look convinced him of the suicidal nature of such a bid for freedom. It was a dormer window, with a sharply sloping tiled roof immediately below it, and a length of guttering that did not look as if it would bear the weight of a drizzle's worth of water, never mind two escaping Cavaliers. Below, there was a drop of some fifteen feet to the stones of Dursley's main street.

But still, there ought to be a way. Nick had never been a prisoner before, and he found the prospect of it somewhat infuriating, even more so since they were within a day's ride of their destination. It would be so tempting to give way to his rage and frustration, and add to the list of his crimes by strangling Touchet.

That would certainly end any chance of freedom. He grinned to himself, glad that he still possessed the vestiges of a sense of humour, even in a situation as dire as this. But they must escape, or face long imprisonment, perhaps even death if they were chosen to be an example. Touchet, a Catholic, would be particularly at risk.

The window was impossible, and the door was guarded. He glanced upwards, trying to assess the ceiling. It was steeply pitched, and plastered. He could not see any easy way out by demolishing it, and such activity would certainly bring them to the attention of the guard.

Perhaps not tonight, then: but surely there might be a chance to escape on the journey to London, or wherever they were to be taken. And, of course, there was always the possibility, albeit very small and fragile, that enquiries would not damn them.

He was an optimist: even in the darkest hour, the tightest corner, his mind continued to work, seeking a way out. He would not give up, for he was a born survivor. He made his way back to the bed and lay down on it, trying to gather his thoughts. Touchet, despite the uncomfortable lumps and hollows on the mattress beneath them, had apparently fallen asleep.

Nick could not. As the darkness outside deepened, and the town of Dursley settled down peacefully for the night, he ran various plans through his head, rejecting them all. Somehow, they must extract themselves from this chamber before dawn, and almost inevitable discovery. Preferably, they must be able to take the horses: he could not imagine Touchet getting very far without them. Yet to carry on towards Bristol, mounted, under their old aliases, would be to invite trouble.

He could not fix his mind on the problem for very long: he was weary after the day's ride, and the events of that evening had not helped matters. As the bustle and noise of the inn below him died away into sleep, his thoughts drifted hazily on the borders of slumber . . .

He came awake suddenly, the answer as bright and clear as sunlight in his mind. Every vestige of exhaustion had vanished. He slid from the bed, taking care not to rouse the sleeping Touchet, and walked softly to the window. The moon was in its second quarter, but obscured by clouds: as he watched, careful that no one outside should notice him, it began to rain.

He stayed there for a long time, looking down on to the silent, deserted street, while the rain beat harder against the window, and bounced down the tiles to the flooded gutter. Then, noiselessly, he went back to the bed, and set about waking Touchet.

Perhaps an hour later, an observer, if there had been one about on such a wet and unpleasant night, might have seen the dormer window open, very quietly, its hinges greased with the congealed fat from the mutton chops uneaten at supper. For a long moment, nothing else happened: then, as cautiously as if it too were at risk, a dark snake slithered over the sill, and was lowered down the stone face of the inn. It passed a window, but the occupants had been asleep for hours, and would in any case have noticed nothing amid the steady drumming of the rain. It was too short, by some six or seven feet, but that did not matter. Nick, peering over the sill as far as he dared, could not see the end, but knew that the drop would be safe, so long as neither of them slipped on the wet stones beneath.

So far, so good. He had no idea of the hour, but calculated that it must be one or two o'clock in the morning. The lateness, and the rain, had emptied the street long ago. There was a chance of freedom, and anything was better than staying here, to await their fate with spineless apathy.

He had had some difficulty in persuading Touchet of the merits of his plan. Woken after considerable effort from deep sleep, his companion had not been in the most friendly or receptive of moods, and had poured scorn on Nick's whispered suggestion. 'You're mad, man! We'll break our necks, or our legs at the least. Now leave me to sleep in peace.'

'Very well,' Nick had said, in a voice tight with fury. 'I shall go without you – I'll probably have more hope of success if I do.'

He had begun to tie the blankets together before Touchet, reluctantly, had come to help him. There were four on the bed, rough but strongly and tightly woven. They were difficult to knot, but their dark colour would be much less noticeable. If . . . if . . . their luck held, it might be dawn before anyone discovered that they were missing.

It would be impossible to take the horses, which were stabled behind the inn, and certainly well guarded. It would be more arduous, but safer and less conspicuous, to travel on foot. Touchet, who had only just stepped back into his true, aristocratic self, at first flatly refused to put on again the mean garb which he had been given at the Powells' mill, but after Nick had pointed out that his blue suit would be ruined by climbing down the blanket rope in the rain, and that he could hardly play the gentleman without a horse, he gave way with ill grace.

They had so little baggage that it would not be difficult to take it with them, slung in a bag over Nick's shoulder. He hoped that their captors would assume that Touchet would be wearing the blue. A tall Cavalier afoot, in fine clothes, was a very different kettle of fish from a slouching labourer in his mud-stained and shrunken old mulberry doublet.

There remained only the rope. Nick had tied it to the bedpost, and prayed that it was secure. He had persuaded Touchet that he himself must go first, being the lighter of the two, to test its weight. He had no intention of being marooned in the chamber, his escape aborted and his guilt proved, should Touchet's heavy bulk cause the makeshift rope to break, and lead to inevitable discovery.

He had tested the knots before sending the blankets over the sill. There was no time to waste: every moment they lingered now would add to the risk of capture. He swung himself over the sill, uttered a brief prayer to a deity who had doubtless washed His hands of him many years ago, and trusted his weight to its strength.

It held. His hands, strong from years of gripping reins and sword and pistol, clung to the thick rough fabric. He inched his way down to the gutter, and took a deep breath. Now, or never: his last chance. With infinite care, he negotiated the soft leaden gutter and slid slowly, hand over hand, down the rope.

It was as well that he had moved cautiously, for he found himself passing a window. It was shuttered against the rainy night, but if he had been swinging out of control it would have been impossible to stop himself crashing against it. His arms were beginning to ache. He had counted the knots, and knew that he was nearing the rope's end. He glanced down. The rain beat on the cobbles, which seemed too far away, but this was it, there was nothing more below his hands. He hung still for a moment, preparing himself for the drop, and then let go.

The force of his landing jarred his legs and hips. He fell, rolled over and struggled to his feet, ready for flight. But no one shouted, there were no cries of discovery. He peered up through the driving rain, splashing on his face and eyelids and obscuring his vision, and waved to Touchet.

Here, if anywhere, would come the flaw in his plan. He was agile, light, and quick-witted. Touchet, especially in this resentful mood, his self-assumed superiority removed, was none of these things. All too clearly, Nick could imagine the rope breaking, Touchet letting go, or crashing with disastrous effects against the window. He watched, hardly daring to breathe, as his companion began his laborious descent to freedom.

But, as before, he had underestimated the man. In less time than he remembered taking himself, Touchet had dropped from the end of the blanket rope, and was standing beside him on the wet stones, a smile unexpectedly gleaming on his face.

'Well?' said Nick. 'What are we waiting for?' He turned and walked up the street.

For a moment, Touchet stared after him, and then, trying not to make too much noise on the rain-soaked cobbles, he followed at a run. 'Where are you going?' he hissed urgently, as soon as he caught up. 'You're going back the way we came!'

'It's the one road they won't think of searching,' Nick pointed out. He paused by a garden wall, peering at his companion through the rain. 'Keep to the side of the street, and as quiet as possible – once we're clear of the town, we'll strike south, and go over the hills to take the other route.'

He could not see Touchet's face in the murk, but he doubted very much that it registered pleasurable anticipation. He grinned to himself. He did not exactly relish the prospect of a long tramp in torrential rain and thick mud either, but they had no other choice.

A dog barked at a farm on the edge of Dursley, but there was no human reaction. Very soon afterwards, they had climbed over a gate and were heading up across the steep fields towards Bristol, some twenty miles distant.

*

The tavern, in an alleyway just off Bristol Key, was small, hot, smoky, crowded and unbelievably noisy. Sailors, whores, dock labourers and other lowly denizens of the city drank, talked, shouted and swore at each other, and somehow amid the crush and the din did business. As Nick had suspected, everyone was too intent on their own affairs to pay any attention to the two shabbily-dressed men who sat quietly in a corner, swallowing ale (it had not been Touchet's choice, but to call for fine wine in such a place was to invite trouble), and keeping unobtrusive watch on the comings and goings in the taproom.

He had decided on this place, rather than a more salubrious establishment, because it better suited their appearance. Even so, his companion would always attract a second glance, especially a female one. They had already fended off several whores, to Touchet's regret, although, as Nick had forcefully pointed out, any such frequenting this disreputable place would undoubtedly be pox-ridden, haggard, and ancient. And here, amongst the sailors with their wind-leathered faces, the traditional striped breeches and stockinged caps, they must assuredly have word of a ship bound for France or Ireland, whose master would turn a blind eye to two dubious passengers if offered sufficient gold.

Nick took a deep draught of ale. He had not set foot in Bristol since before the war's end, but he had spent several unhappy years here as an apprentice, and there was always the chance that someone might recognise him – though he doubted that anyone from Master Adams' respectable house ever ventured into this den of whores and thieves. Merchant Bristol, fat and prosperous from the trade in sugar and tobacco, drew its rich skirts fastidiously away from such places, and liked to pretend that they did not exist.

But the boy Nick had found his way here, wide-eyed and all afire with talk of strange places and distant lands. He had stolen his master's money to buy a sword that he could hire, a passage on one of those crowded ships to freedom, and a lifetime of impecunious irresponsibility which he had never questioned, until he met a woman called Silence . . .

He would not see her again. He knew that now, and it was vain hope to pretend otherwise. He was doomed to spend the rest of his life in exile, eking out a precarious hand-to-mouth existence like all the other old Cavaliers, sinking slowly into a morass of poverty, drink, debt and regret. The prospect appalled him, and yet he had little choice. He possessed no money, no land, no trade but the sword. He knew, because his self-respect demanded it, that he would strive to collect enough coin to buy a passage to the New World or the Indies, to try to begin his life again. He had nothing left but his mind and his will, but many had risen to the heights with no more.

If he had not been a fugitive, he might have sought employment in the Roundhead army. The idea caused him some amusement – he, Nick Hellier the roistering Cavalier, comrade in arms to those psalm-singing, self-righteous Puritans! But he was not so near despair as that. If he had been younger, his heart less bound to a long-dead and hopeless love, he would have looked forward with keen anticipation to a new beginning in a new land.

Sternly, he put such pessimistic speculation from his mind, and glanced at Touchet, who was in the act of draining his tankard. The last two days, spent trudging up hill and down dale through rain and sun and wind to Bristol, had not made him like his companion any better. Touchet was too conscious of his aristocratic station, too ready to complain about things which could not be altered, and above all too condescending, for that. But at least their brief imprisonment at Dursley seemed to have thrust some sense into his skull. He spoke only when it was essential, forced a faint country burr into his voice, and adopted a menial slouch and an attitude of humility that almost made Nick laugh aloud. But it had worked: on the two days of their tramp, buying food and shelter from farm or inn, no one had ever looked at them with suspicion. Now that they were safely absorbed into the bustling anonymous mass of sea-faring Bristol, Nick felt it might be possible to relax a little.

He had already spoken to the pot boy, claiming to be a servant enquiring after a passage to France for his master. He had concocted a simple but plausible tale of a flight from angry creditors, and the boy seemed to have swallowed it, though Nick had no high opinion of his intelligence.

And here he was, pushing his way through the throng with a brimming jug, and followed by a most disreputable-looking man with a scarred face and one eye. 'This 'ere be Tom Gifford – he d'reckon he can help ee,' said the lad, banging down the jug on the table and holding out his hand.

Nick, who had possession of all their more humble coin – Touchet still wore the precious belt around his waist, with almost fifty pounds in gold sewn inside – dropped a couple of pence into it. 'And another jug and a tankard for Master Gifford,' he said.

There was a stool under the table: the one-eyed man pulled it out and sat down, looking from Nick to Touchet and back. 'I hear you wants to get to France in a hurry,' he said, in tones more reminiscent of London than Bristol. 'Why's that, then?'

Nick repeated his story, and Gifford listened with an impassive face that gave no indication of whether or not he believed it. He jerked his head at Touchet, who had remained silent up until now. 'This your master?'

'No – he is staying quietly at the Red Lion,' said Nick. 'This is Jem Thomson, my fellow servant.'

Gifford's shrewd gaze roamed over Touchet's shabby appearance, the shrunken, mud-stained mulberry doublet, the shorn hair and grimy face. His expression plainly stated what he thought of any gentleman who would contenance such a pair of down-at-heel rogues in his service, but he restricted himself to a curt nod.

The boy reappeared with another jug and a tankard. Gifford, who seemed to be a man of remarkably few words, filled and drained it before he spoke again, while Nick and Touchet swallowed their own ale, and tried not to look as if too much hung on what the one-eyed man might say.

'I knows of a ship.' Gifford swallowed the last of his beer with a noisy gulp. He smelled strongly of sweat, filth and drink, and Touchet's nostrils had visibly quivered at his approach. 'The *Anne* of Bristol, sailing for Dunkirk with the morning tide on Friday. Captain might take you, he's done work of that sort before. Cost your master a pretty penny to get the three of you across, depends how desperate he is, eh?'

'How much?' Nick asked, his heart sinking. Today was Monday: how were they to survive undiscovered in the city for four days, until the *Anne* was ready to sail?

'Dunno, but I'll find out,' said Gifford, grinning. He did not exactly seem to be the most trustworthy sort, and Nick had no intention of relying on him too heavily. He arranged to meet again at the same time, same place tomorrow, and watched the one-eyed man weave his way out of the packed tavern.

'Is it true?' Touchet asked quietly. 'Can we trust him?'

'I don't think I'd ever trust anyone completely again,' said Nick grimly. 'But we have a day to find out if there is any such ship — and perhaps do business with her master ourselves. Gifford will doubtless take his cut of the passage money — or betray us to the authorities.'

Touchet glanced about the tavern in some alarm, as if soldiers were about to burst through the door to arrest them. He said in a hissing whisper, 'Do you think that's likely?'

'No — but as I said, you can never trust anyone,' said Nick. He drained his tankard. 'Well, I can't speak for you, but I've had enough of this place for the present. It's only two hours or so to curfew. Shall we go find a bed for the night?'

Bed proved to be a flea-ridden pallet in an attic chamber shared with three other men, all of whom snored. After an almost sleepless night tossing, scratching and trying to block out extraneous noises, Nick was in no mood to listen to Touchet's complaints. As he chewed his way sleepily through the coarse gritty bread and hard cheese that formed their breakfast, however, he was jerked rudely back to wakefulness by his companion's latest outburst. 'And I'll tell you plain — that's the last night I spend in this guise!'

There were few people in the inn's common room, but his forceful tones, even lowered almost to a whisper, brought several interested glances. Nick put his bread down on the table and stared at him. 'Is your freedom not worth another three nights of scratching, then?'

Touchet, unrepentant, glared back. 'I've had quite sufficient after one, thank you, Hellier. Why we should live like paupers when I've enough to feed, clothe and house us both for a year, never mind until Friday, I fail to see.'

'Because it's our best chance of survival,' said Nick wearily. 'Every time we've played pauper, we've attracted no attention. People are suspicious of strange gentlemen, but no one looking at us now would suspect that we were anything other than servants – as long as you can refrain from bemoaning your lot.'

Touchet's expression radiated venom. 'By God, I'll be glad to be rid of you, Hellier. Why in the name of Mary Mother I put up with your company so long . . .'

'I know the answer to that,' said Nick, brutally honest. 'Because without me, you wouldn't have lasted an hour, and you know it. And I'd be grateful if you didn't address me by my real name – I'm Harrison, remember? Now, are we going in search of the *Anne*, or are we going to sit here arguing all day?'

In a cloud of mutual animosity, they left the mean little inn in Marsh Street, where they had spent the night, and made their way back to the waterfront.

It was one of the wonders of the land, the Key at Bristol, like a street of water with houses on either side, and packed with ships, a forest of masts and spars. From here they voyaged across the oceans to the West Indies and the New World, Virginia and Barbados and the Bermudas, to the Levant and the Spice Islands, and, closer to home, the ports of Europe and the Mediterranean Sea. To find the *Anne* amongst such a fleet seemed almost impossible, but at least they had all day in which to try.

The first men they asked professed complete ignorance: the next directed them to a vessel right at the other end of the Key, which proved to be the *Anne* of Bridgwater. It was as they were making equally fruitless enquiries of a sailor on the next ship, that Nick realised that there were soldiers further down the waterfront.

Behave as though you are innocent, he thought, and they won't even notice you in this crowd. He glanced at Touchet, whose height made him so conspicuous, and saw him eyeing the soldiers

[235]

nervously, plainly the possessor of a guilty conscience. He thanked the sailor whom he had been vainly questioning, and made his way down the gang-plank to join his companion on the quayside. Amid the bustle of loading and unloading, swarms of men intent only on their own business, it was obviously wise not to stand about aimlessly. He dug Touchet in the ribs, and said in his ear, 'Act as normal – pretend they're of no account.'

'Do you take me for a complete fool?' the other man said, with the clarity of anger. A woman who had been lounging by a pile of barrels, talking to a group of sailors, turned and gave them a long and assessing stare. For a moment, Nick feared the worst, and then realised that it must be professional interest: with her painted face and revealing gown, she was evidently just another whore. She said something to the sailors that brought guffaws of laughter, and then sauntered over.

From a distance she had seemed young, and quite attractive. Close to, the ravages of her trade were plain beneath the paint, and her eyes were bright and hard. 'Looking for someone, sirs?' she said, her voice strongly flavoured with Somerset. 'Perhaps I can help ee.'

'I doubt it,' said Nick drily, but Touchet, his eyes lingering on her neckline, was already speaking. 'You must know most things here. Do you know a ship called the *Anne* of Bristol?'

The woman glanced at him, her eyes glinting at his height and his evident interest. Nick could not understand why Touchet, so fastidious in other matters, should be so utterly indiscriminating when it came to women. This one, though she had once been boldly handsome, looked as if she would sell her own mother for the price of a drink.

'Why do ee want to know that, sir?' she asked, taking Touchet's arm in a proprietorial gesture.

'I wish to do business with her Captain,' he told her, while Nick wondered that he did not flinch away from her touch. 'But perhaps I might do business with you too, eh?'

He had, Nick realised, spoken with his habitual aristocratic drawl. The whore did not appear to notice. She giggled, an incongruously girlish sound, and then, leaning up on tiptoe, whispered something in Touchet's ear. He laughed lecherously: evidently she had suggested some obscenity. Nick felt his hackles rising. The soldiers were not far away now, and they seemed to be searching the quayside and asking questions. But, he reminded himself, he and Touchet now looked very different from their appearance at Dursley. What could be more ordinary, than a casual conversation with a whore? They would not expect any fugitive to behave in such an open and careless manner.

The woman had also noticed the soldiers. She glanced at Nick, and he saw her gaze sharpen suddenly, as if in recognition. Then she turned her attention back to Touchet, pulling his dark head down for a practised kiss.

How he could bear to touch those scarlet lips, Nick could not imagine: the very idea revolted him. He preferred his women clean, and wholesome, and to climb into his bed for love or lust or liking, but not for money. He turned away to find a trooper at his elbow, and it took all his training not to react with a start of guilty surprise.

'We're looking for Cavaliers,' said the soldier, his voice betraying his London origins. 'Have you seen anyone suspicious, asking questions, trying to buy a passage out of the country – anything of that sort?'

Nick shrugged, and shook his head. 'No – sorry, I've seen nothing.'

'And him?' The soldier indicated Touchet, comprehensively entwined with the whore, but there was no response. He grinned at Nick, and moved on.

Touchet disentangled himself a little, and winked. 'Jealous, my friend? Well, let's all go back to the Dove and buy a drink or two – and maybe more, eh?'

The woman laughed. She was still handsome, despite her rotting teeth: her hair was so dark as to be almost black, and her blue eyes had perhaps once sparkled with innocent merriment. Now, in her slatternly faded red dress, all too obviously designed to incite lechery, and with the paint thick across her face, she had only a poor shadow left of the youthful beauty she had once possessed. Nick thought of spending the morning in that foetid tavern, drinking ale he did not want and watching Touchet and this raddled harlot pawing each other, and found that the prospect disgusted him. I must be getting old, he thought. But such pastimes had never really appealed to him, even in his wild youth.

'I'll leave you two alone for a while,' he said, with patently false jocularity. 'You look as if you want to become better acquainted, after all. I'll continue to look for the *Anne*.'

'Oh, very well, Hellier,' said Touchet, waving the hand that was not clasping the whore's waist. 'Do as you please — I've other fish to fry!'

'Hellier?' The woman had stiffened, and her eyes shot to Nick's face. 'Hellier? I thought I knowd you!'

He stared at her for a horrified second, wondering where he had seen her before, and how he had earned the sudden blazing hatred on her face. The memory came back to him at the same instant as she said viciously, 'Yes, you do know me, don't ee — Leah Walker, I be, and I've a score or two to settle with ee, Captain Nick Hellier!' And she turned suddenly and shouted at the soldier, now some yards distant. 'Here — here be one of your Cavaliers — come and take him!'

Touchet, his face suddenly white, aghast, tore himself free from her clutching hands and ran back down the Key. Without waiting to see how the soldiers had reacted to Leah's denunciation, Nick sprinted after him.

There were more soldiers in front of them. Already the hue and cry was starting up, and shouts of 'Stop! Stop them!' echoed along the waterfront. Nick dodged two drawn swords, flung an empty barrel into the path of his pursuers, and caught sight of Touchet's dark head, just vanishing up an alleyway. With a muttered curse, he punched a sailor blocking his way and flung himself in pursuit. Somehow, they must get out of the city, or capture was certain.

Touchet, for all his superior height and muscle, was not so fit and agile. He was forcing his way past people by dint of sheer weight, while Nick, swift and wiry, was able to dodge or evade those quick-witted enough to realise that the running men were in flight from justice. And just as he was drawing level with his companion, a new cry rose from behind. 'It's the King! I'm sure it's the King! It's Charles Stuart! After him!'

'Oh, Christ,' Nick muttered, wishing that he had never laid eyes on Mervyn Touchet. The entire population of the Key, drawn as if by a magnet to the prospect of a thousand pounds' reward, was pouring in pursuit. They must lose them, somehow, in the maze of streets and alleys in the packed, dark, narrow city, and then attempt to leave by one of the gates, as if nothing had happened. Once the Bristol authorities, impelled by avarice and public duty, heard that Charles Stuart might be within their walls, they would search the place so thoroughly that not even a mouse would be able to evade them.

'Down here!' he said, grasping Touchet's arm. For an instant the

[238]

other man resisted, and then, as the howl of pursuit grew louder, turned and ran with him down a narrow street. People stared curiously at them, and an old lady burdened with many bags and baskets was rudely shoved aside. Nick, who had several times as a boy been chased through these streets by irate shopkeepers, or as part of some 'prentice game, knew exactly where to go. They dodged between two tall houses, down a dark stinking alley where surely no sun ever shone, across a wider street and another narrow way, and emerged panting into the broad, crowded space before the Bristol Bridge.

Here was much bustle and activity. One of the sleds used for transport within the city was passing, laden with barrels and drawn by two straining horses in tandem. Nick was suddenly aware, as the sled crashed noisily past over the cobbles, that for the moment they must have lost the pursuit.

'Across the Bridge,' he said softly to Touchet, whose face was scarlet and dripping with exertion. No one was looking at them and, with luck, they would not be noticed. They walked past the church of St. Nicholas, and between the tall jostling houses that lined the Bridge, much like London's, but much shorter. Here, there was no sense of crossing water, since there was no gap between the houses. Nick looked back as they drew near the end. The press of people was considerable, but he could see, suddenly erupting above the heads bobbing behind him, the unmistakable shape of a mounted trooper.

He quickened his pace, and Touchet, after one glance behind, did likewise. Shouting broke out at the other end of the bridge. They dodged another sled, found themselves face to face with a huge merchant in purple velvet, avoided him with some difficulty and hurried on. In front of them, the way parted, and Nick led his companion down the right-hand street. They had attracted no further attention: their shabby attire blended in amongst the crowds, and certainly no one seemed to be connecting them with the fugitive Cavaliers being sought at the city end of the bridge.

'They can't know that we've come down here yet,' Nick said softly as they walked down Temple Street. In this suburb of Redcliffe, the crowds were much thinner, and they could walk more quickly. By the same token, however, they would be more visible. The sun was out, and it was a warm day. Nick glanced at Touchet, and said, 'Take your doublet off.'

'Eh?'

'Take it off. There are plenty in shirtsleeves here, and they'll be looking for a man in a mulberry doublet – for Christ's sake, take it off!'

For a moment, he thought Touchet would hit him. Then, still walking, he fumbled with the buttons, shrugged the doublet off and slung it over his shoulder. No one gave him a second glance, and yet his pride had evidently received a severe battering. Out of the side of his mouth, he said furiously, 'You do not do likewise, I notice.'

'Oh, but I will,' said Nick. A ridiculously inappropriate feeling of light-heartedness – or foolishness – had come over him. On this lovely September morning, amid the narrow stinking streets of Bristol, he knew that for once his luck was with him.

There was, as usual, a great press of people about the narrow Temple Gate. Someone had brought up an overburdened cart, laden with baulks of timber, and was engaged in a furious argument with the gateward, as to whether it would pass through the gap. Nick glanced behind, and saw in the distance, at the other end of the long straight length of Temple Street, soldiers gathering.

Many of the bystanders had joined in the discussion, with some heat, shouts and waving fists. Nick saw Touchet staring at the crowded gateway, and set his face firmly to the front. The guards did not even notice the two ordinary, shirtsleeved men squeezing past the disputed cart. And now they were free of Bristol, walking away down the road between gardens and orchards, as swiftly as they dared.

There were no sounds of hue and cry, and Nick began to wonder if they had escaped. It seemed almost too good, too easy to be true, but the city lay well behind them now, and still there was no pursuit.

The River Avon wound its leisurely way through the fields to their left. Touchet said suddenly, 'Who was that woman?'

Nick stopped. There was a rider coming towards them, a plainly-dressed man obviously a farmer, on a sturdy feather-heeled cob. Touchet eyed it enviously as it trotted briskly past the two men, and continued. 'If I'd realised you might be recognised in Bristol, I'd never have agreed to go there! Who was she? And how did she know you?'

Nick was tempted to point out that all might have been well if his companion had remembered to address him by his false name. He resisted it, with some difficulty. 'She was a maidservant in the house where I was garrisoned during the last year of the war,' he said. 'And an unpleasant young woman she was, too – her present situation is richly deserved, I can tell you.'

'Garrisoned – hereabouts?' said Touchet. 'Then you know this country?'

'Tolerably well,' said Nick. He had already decided not to reveal just how well he had known Bristol, and the consequent risk he had run of being recognised. But he had never imagined that Leah Walker, whom he had completely forgotten until she made herself known, would denounce him. That had been a most unfortunate mischance, and there was no hope now of a return to Bristol to find the *Anne*, since every citizen would be eager to capture the supposed King of Scots and claim the reward. And Leah, plying her trade on the quayside, made it quite impossible.

'Then I'll tell you this, Hellier,' said Touchet, fixing him with a hostile stare. 'I refuse utterly to spend any more nights in such a fleapit as the last, nor under a hedgerow or in a barn. Nor do I wish to tramp the countryside like a vagabond, disguise or no – especially when I have more than enough coin to travel in some style. I propose we make for London, we'll be safe enough there – unless the city whores have some acquaintance with you too?'

'No,' said Nick shortly. He added, 'Do you then contemplate walking to London?'

'Walking?' Touchet's laugh was loud and contemptuous. 'Over my dead body, sir. You know this country – you must be aware of some friendly house that would offer us shelter and assistance.'

Nick had thought of it already, and rejected it. The household of a Roundhead colonel, though lately deceased, could hardly be described as 'friendly'. And yet, they were so close, hardly a dozen miles away, less if they travelled across country. He thought of Silence, suddenly and miraculously within reach, when he had only yesterday acknowledged her to be lost for ever. Would she be changed? Had she carried him within her heart all these years, as he had held her in his? Would Wintercombe still be as lovely, golden and peaceful, balm to the restless, fugitive soul? What had the children become, sunny William, stout Deb, grave and sensitive Tabby, the fierce tormented Rachael, and Nat wise and old beyond his years? With a shock, he realised that the twins would be twenty-one, and adult: so fast had time sped.

There was the danger, of course, to Silence and her family if they were discovered to be harbouring Royalist fugitives. But surely, such an eminently Puritan household would not fall under suspicion? He remembered that Tabby's letter had spoken of a visit from Tom Wickham. What did it matter if he himself was recognised, if no one knew that he was a fugitive from Worcester? The servants who remembered him would assume that he was paying a courtesy visit, just as Tom had obviously done.

Touchet, of course, would have to be explained away, and since the animosity between them crackled the air, Nick realised that to introduce him as a friend would strain the credulity of the more perceptive. That, however, was a minor problem, and so were the difficulties attendant on their walking up to the door clad like beggars. He would think of something: and the vision of Silence, and Wintercombe, his Grail suddenly became reality again, set his blood singing.

'Well?' said Touchet impatiently. 'Is there such a place?'

'There is,' said Nick. 'It's to the south of Bath, quietly situated, and I know for certain that we'll be welcome, whatever our circumstances. But it's a day's tramp, probably – can you manage that?'

Touchet must have heard the note of derision in his voice. He drew himself up to his considerable height, and glared at Nick. 'Of course I can,' he said. 'Which way is it?'

'Along the highway for about six miles, until we reach a village called Newton, as I remember, and then we can turn aside and go over the hills,' said Nick. 'Perhaps twelve miles in all, by the most direct route. And with luck, we'll reach it by nightfall.'

Twelve miles, under a hot sun and along muddy tracks, would not be an easy stroll, but he did not care. At last, after six long years of heartache and exile, he was going back to the only place where he had ever felt at peace, to the only woman he had ever loved: and in his sudden flood of joy, a thousand miles would not have seemed too great an obstacle, if he could be assured of seeing Wintercombe, and Silence, again.

CHAPTER THIRTEEN

'Travellers must be content'

(*As You Like It*)

The sun smiled on them as they walked eastwards towards Bath, and there was no sign of any pursuit. Probably the troopers were still fervently searching Bristol for the supposed Charles Stuart and his Cavalier companion. As the long muddy miles reeled out under their trudging feet, Nick found his stride growing lighter and lighter. It was as if he were coming home, after long absence. And if home is where the heart is, he thought, smiling, then Wintercombe has been so, long since.

Behind them, they were pursued only by the clouds, which had been building up, black and heavy in the west, all morning. They bought bread and cheese in the little village of Newton, just as the first rain began to fall. The goodwife who sold it to them looked suspiciously at them both, but in particular at Touchet. Nick chatted with her, letting slip the tale that they were sailors, temporarily ashore, going to visit relatives near Bath, and she seemed to accept his story without further question. They ate the food under a thick hedgerow, sheltered from the gathering wind, and washed it down with a flagon of beer. Then they turned away from the road, and took a narrow, tree-lined lane that led south, along the side of a valley.

It fast became apparent that this latter part of the journey would be a little more difficult than the first. The rain had settled down to a morose, steady drizzle, soaking their garments with peculiar effectiveness. The lane was thick with mud, and although it was comparatively level, their progress was slow, tiring and treacherous. Then the way turned west, in quite the wrong direction, and they had to strike upwards, across the fields, a steep and exhausting climb. There was an unfortunate encounter with a herd of playful and curious bullocks, and another with a belligerent farmer, who chased them off his pasture with shouts and threats. It was only after a heated argument that Nick managed to persuade Touchet not to go back and, as he had put it, 'Teach the scurvy rogue a lesson he won't forget.'

At last they struggled down into a small village, perched on the side of another valley, that Nick well remembered. He hoped that no one would recognise him as the implacable and hated Cavalier captain who had come here all too often, foraging with his troops, more than six years ago. But such was the disreputable nature of his appearance, bedraggled, muddy and wet, that he doubted even his own brother would know him now.

From here, he knew the way. It was only a few miles further, but Touchet, whose shoes had split and were leaking mud and water, squelching at every stride, demanded the exact details. He obviously thought that they were lost, and that Nick was leading him on some insane wild goose chase. After two or three laboured and miserable miles along deeply muddy tracks, he said so, forcefully.

'I told you,' said Nick. Like Touchet, he was soaked, tired, and heartily sick of tramping up hill and down dale with no apparent end in sight, but he knew that there were only a few miles left, and the thought of seeing Silence again, perhaps this very day, had kept his spirits buoyant. 'I know exactly where we are – I used to bring foraging parties all over this country. We've just crossed the highway that leads from Bath to Wells, and the village down there in the valley is, if I'm not mistaken, Combe Hay. And this lane here is the one we want to take.'

Touchet stared despairingly at the track thus indicated. It led down to a fast-flowing stream, forded it, and climbed straight up the opposite hillside. 'For God's sake, how much further?' he demanded.

Nick sighed. 'To the top of the hill, down into a village called Wellow, across the river, and Wintercombe is perhaps two miles further. We'll reach it easily before dark.'

The rain had stopped so gradually neither of them had noticed when it ceased. Touchet looked dubiously at the sky, which was clearing rapidly. The position of the sun could now be seen, and it was obviously lower in the sky than he would like. He muttered something ungracious, and stamped laboriously off down the lane that led to Wellow. Nick followed him, with a rueful smile.

They attracted some notice in Wellow. A crowd of small children followed them through the village, with much abuse concerning beggars, and several thrown stones. By this time, both men were too exhausted to do anything other than hunch their shoulders and plod onwards. Nick's legs ached, and his back where it had been struck by what felt like a small boulder. He was hungry, thirsty and unutterably weary, and yet their destination, the fulfilment of all his hopes, lay only a mile or so distant, and banished all feelings of pain and discomfort. Yet he knew, despite his yearning, that they could hardly knock on Wintercombe's door in this condition – it would invite suspicion. Somehow, they must find a way to make contact with one of the St. Barbe family.

The lane grew dark and gloomy, lined with thick trees. Through gaps in the branches, Nick could see the westering sunlight, shining golden on the leaves and grass further up the hill, on his left. There was a stream running on the other side: he remembered its clear cold waters, and realised how thirsty the steady bright rippling sound had made him.

'Want a drink?' he said to Touchet, and without waiting for a reply, he left the lane and knelt by the brook, at a place where the sheer banks, like miniature cliffs, gave way to a shelving sandy shore. The icy water was blissfully refreshing on his filthy skin, and he rubbed his hands all over his face, feeling the rasp of unshaven stubble, and grinned. Doubtless he looked like the worst kind of villain, if Touchet's appearance was any guide to his own. His companion, kneeling beside him taking great noisy gulps from his cupped hands, was no longer recognisable as the exquisite earl's son. He looked, instead, like the sort of beggar most safely stoned out of town, or confined in the stocks.

Nick heard nothing at all above the noise of the water, until some sense warned him that he was being watched. He leapt to his feet with the speed of a soldier, or one possessed of a guilty conscience, and beheld a very small child, staring up at him with the calm, bright-eyed curiosity of a tame bird.

'Are you Scots?' said the child, her gaze travelling over his appalling garments with an air of wondering disgust that brought a smile suddenly to his face. He had not been in the company of children for so long, and he had forgotten how astonishingly honest they could be.

'Or are you beggars?' she added. 'I haven't got any money, so you can't take it off me.' She was, he reckoned, perhaps four or five years old, and rather grubbily clad in a brown dress, with an apron that was probably her mother's despair. She was too young for him to know her, and he could not imagine who she might be. With that small sharp face, her dark hair and chestnut brown eyes and light build, she bore no resemblance whatsoever to his memory of the fair-haired, rosy-cheeked and sturdy St. Barbes.

'I wouldn't dream of taking your money,' he said. There was, nevertheless, something familiar about her face, or her look, something that lurked tantalisingly on the edge of his memory. He added quietly, 'No, we are not beggars – nor are we Scots, and we will not hurt you. What is your name?'

A huge three-cornered smile of pure mischief flashed across her face, and she danced backwards, well out of his reach. Beggars or not, she was obviously taking no chances. 'Shan't tell you!' she cried, giggling. 'You'll have to guess.'

Unfortunately, her game was doomed to early disappointment. A group of rather older children, leading ponies, had appeared, making their way down a path which wound between the crowding trees. 'Kate!' one of them called, in furious tones. '*Kate!* Come *here!*'

'Do you know them?' Touchet asked, still kneeling by the stream.

Nick, without taking his eyes off the children, nodded with quiet delight. 'Yes,' he said. 'Yes, I do.'

The child Kate glanced round at the others, her expression mutinous. She took a token step backwards and stood firm, her gaze once more fixed upon Nick. And suddenly, everything came together in his mind, and his heart turned over.

She was perhaps five years old, and undoubtedly a St. Barbe, for these approaching were the rest of the brood. Brown, and small, and quick, with a streak of merry mischief, and eyes that had seemed familiar because they looked back at him from mirrors . . .

No, he thought, staring at her. *No*, it can't be – it's not possible. And yet he knew that it was not only possible, but quite likely, that the brief month when he and Silence had been lovers, had borne fruit, in the shape of this sparklingly naughty little girl.

'Why are you looking at me as if you know me?' said Kate, with a recurrence of that delightful giggle. 'I don't know *you!*'

'I know your brother and sisters,' said Nick. And as Kate's chestnut eyes widened in amazement, he walked forward to greet them.

Even after six years, despite the fact that many children alter out of all recognition during such a time, they had not essentially changed. That stalwart small boy, hair as shiny as a gold coin even in this heavy gloom under the trees, was assuredly William, and was what that bright lovable infant had become. The plump strapping girl beside him, scowling her suspicion, must be Deb. Behind them, older, taller, almost adult, with her hair as he remembered it so vividly, a great tangled honey-coloured mass around her face, was Tabby.

She was staring at the two tatterdemalions by the stream with an expression of wonderment, as if her dearest dream had come true, and yet he did not think that she had recognised him. Then he realised that in fact she was looking at Touchet. He had risen to his feet, and his height and bearing, even in his filthy ragged clothes, were conspicuously aristocratic. With a fluid grace that caught suddenly at Nick's memory, Tabby sank into a deep and flowing curtsey.

'Why are you doing that?' Deb demanded stridently: advancing maturity had evidently failed to moderate her forceful character.

William shot her a look of indignation. 'They're Cavaliers,' he said, as if that explained everything. 'They must be.'

'Or Scots – or beggars,' said Deb suspiciously, but none of the other children paid her any attention.

Tabby rose from her obeisance and walked forward to the two men. All that early promise of beauty had come to flower, the fine-featured face, the cloudy glorious hair, the huge hazel-green eyes that were so like her mother's. But the expression in those eyes was direct and honest and trusting, and her slim graceful body was still a child's. She said to Touchet, 'Are you Scots? Or Cavaliers? Please don't be afraid, we are your friends, and we want to help you.'

To his disgust, Nick saw naked interest on Touchet's face. To look at an innocent child like that, as if she were a whore ripe for the plucking, utterly repelled him, and he longed to smash that lascivious expression into oblivion with his fists. But she had always been sensitive beyond her years, and a very slight frown began to mar the space between her fine, slightly arched brows. He said quickly, 'Tabby?'

She whipped round to face him. He saw incredulity in her eyes, and then a sudden and overwhelming joy. 'Is it – it is – Captain Hellier!'

'The same,' he said, smiling.

A younger child might have hugged him. This one, who had always been rather shy, merely took a deep breath, her eyes shining, but her delight was plain, and touched him deeply. She said, 'Did you receive my letter?'

Touchet was staring at them, obviously mystified. Nick had no intention of enlightening him, for the present. He devoted his full attention to the girl. 'Yes, I did. And thank you, Tabby. You must have made great efforts to find me.'

'Oh – Tom Wickham told me where your brother lived, so it was easy,' she said, and turned to the younger children, who seemed almost as bewildered as Touchet. 'Look – it's Captain Hellier!'

William's eyes grew very round, and rounder still as Nick said cheerfully, 'Hallo, Caligula!' Then the boy grinned, rather sheepishly, and bowed.

Deb, never one to mince her words, stood still by her pony, staring at him, and then said, 'How do you know he's Captain Hellier? He could be *anyone* under all that muck and skummer!'

For reasons which none of the others could understand, Tabby and Nick were touched into laughter. Kate, unused to being ignored for so long, tugged at her eldest sister's sleeve and said imperiously, 'Why are you laughing? Who are they? Who *are* they? Are they Scots?'

'Hush, Binnick,' said Tabby, capturing the small bony brown paw. 'I'm laughing because this is Captain Hellier, who was our friend before you were born, and I'm glad to see him, and I expect he's glad to see us too. And this – ' She glanced at Touchet again, with that same look of awed speculation. 'This is a friend of Captain Hellier's. And they're in danger, and we must hide them.'

'In danger? Who from? Who's chasing them?' Kate demanded.

Nick looked at her again, more assessingly, wondering if his earlier intuition had been correct. Was this talkative, quicksilver child really his daughter? She belonged to Silence, but was she also his? There was no doubt as to the eyes, his own warm light brown, quite unlike the darker colour of William's and Deb's, or Tabby's hazel. He saw the older girl staring at him, and her face suddenly flushed pink.

She smiled briefly, and then looked round at the others. 'We shouldn't stand here, should we, right by the road. Let's go back up to our shelter, and we can talk about what we're going to do.'

He had to acknowledge the sense of that, and did so. She gave him a quick, friendly grin, and said, 'Follow us. We'll lead the ponies. Have you got any horses?'

'No,' said Touchet, in tones that indicated the depths of his dissatisfaction with this lamentable state of affairs. 'We have walked all the way from Bristol today, and we need food and shelter, Mistress . . . '

'St. Barbe,' Tabby told him. 'We live at Wintercombe, which is a mile or so down the lane, nearly at Philip's Norton. You've walked from *Bristol*? Today? But it's been raining for hours – '

'And that, dear Tabitha, is why you didn't recognise me,' said Nick. They had forded the stream, which had added considerably to Touchet's discomfort: his split and flapping shoes squelched water and mud at every step. By now, it was almost dark under the trees, and they followed the line of the path, climbing upwards through the undergrowth. The children walked briskly, sure-footed in the slippery clay, while the two men toiled in their wake. Nick did not realise that they had stopped until he bumped into the warm shaggy bulk of one of the ponies, which sidestepped and nearly trod on Touchet's foot.

'Here we are,' said Tabby. 'We do have a light – can you find it, William? Deb, tie the ponies up, and make sure Dowsabel can't get loose again – that's why we're here so late, you see, it took ages to catch her.'

'She unties the knots!' her younger sister complained indignantly. She led the three ponies aside, still grumbling to herself, and Nick saw a dark hump a little distance from the path, evidently the shelter. 'Come on – come inside,' said Tabby, indicating the darker doorway with an outstretched hand, and welcomed them within as if it had been a palace.

Touchet, bent double, entered with an expression of extreme trepidation on his face. Nick followed, hiding his own smile. This might be better than a flea-ridden pallet in a communal inn chamber, better than a damp lodging under a hedgerow, but it was undeniably not the warmed feather bed for which his companion had yearned.

The soft floor – moss? heather? hay? – was surprisingly dry and comfortable. Nick sat in almost impenetrable darkness, and listened to William trying to light the tinder, with muttered curses that he might have learned as an infant from the soldiers, and realised how tired he was. Walking over the hills, intent only on reaching his destination, the dream of Silence always before him to spur him on, sore feet and aching muscles and the onset of utter exhaustion had been easy to overcome. Now, half-lying, half-sitting in the soft, cramped, womblike shelter, he wondered if he would ever be able to get up again.

William's soft hiss of triumph heralded the production of the light. Nick was glad to see that the candle was placed securely within a lanthorn, probably filched from the Wintercombe stables. He looked around him, much impressed. Considering that it had been built by four children, and of gentle birth, it was surprisingly well constructed, warm and dry and draught-proof. Deb and Kate crawled in, and pushed a door made of woven branches into the entrance hole. They squeezed together in the remainder of the space, which was not exactly large, and stared expectantly at their adult visitors.

Nick almost smiled at the absurdity of it. Here they were, two fugitives who faced certain imprisonment and possible death, being entertained by four young children in a makeshift hut half-way up a remote Somerset valley. And the children were treating this as earnestly and seriously as if it were some great adventure, quite innocent of the possible consequences to themselves, and their guests, if they were discovered.

He said quietly, 'It is very kind of you to offer us shelter here. We were almost captured in Bristol this morning, but I doubt very much if they have even realised that we have left the city. Most people on our travels have taken us for vagrants, or beggars — we don't exactly look like escaped Cavaliers, do we? It's quite possible that no one, except yourselves, knows we have come this way.' He paused, well aware that he must warn them of the risks they ran, but unwilling to frighten them unduly. Yet, he and Touchet were forced to take advantage of the help they offered, for the sake of their liberty.

'I know what you're going to say,' Tabby told him, before he could go on. 'You're going to tell us that we can get into trouble for hiding you. Well, we know that, and it doesn't matter. We decided, as soon as we heard about the battle, that we must help any Scots or Cavaliers who came this way — even though we didn't think there would be very many.'

'And have there been?' asked Nick, straight-faced. She shot a glance at him, and grinned flashingly, like Kate. There was a definite resemblance between the two sisters, enough, certainly, to allay any suspicion about the younger child's parentage.

'Of course there haven't,' she said. 'All the Scots went north. No one even knows where the King is.'

Her eyes went involuntarily to Touchet, and Nick realised, a little belatedly, that she was in some danger of making the same mistake as the good citizens of Bristol. He said hastily, 'This is Lieutenant-Colonel Mervyn Touchet, of Lord Talbot's regiment, and my travelling companion since Worcester Fight.'

He wondered why Tabby's eyes gleamed suddenly — surely she was not acquainted with French, or with the language of sword-play? But she seemed somewhat unconvinced. Touchet, his dark eyes shining with appreciation, bowed as flamboyantly as he could, given that he was sitting in a shelter some four feet high, and said, 'I am charmed to meet you, Mistress St. Barbe. Now, if you will lead us to your house — '

'But you can't come to Wintercombe — not yet, anyway,' said Tabby. 'Jack Harington is staying the night — he caught a chill in the rain this morning, and Mother said he could rest until he's recovered, and that's why we all came out here, to get away from him.'

'He's so boring!' Deb added. 'I can't think why Rachael ever said she'd marry him.'

'And he was a captain in the army, and very hot for Parliament,' Tabby finished. 'I'm sorry, but we can't possibly try and smuggle you into Wintercombe while he's there.'

'We could try tomorrow,' said William thoughtfully. 'If we planned it thoroughly, I'm sure we could get you inside without being seen.'

'We could hide you in the roof!' Deb cried. 'Where we went to escape from Black Jack Ridgeley — do you remember, Captain Hellier?'

'I remember your escape,' he said. 'But I've never been up there.' He noticed that Touchet was looking more and more disgruntled — there would be small chance of a feather bed in such a garret.

'It won't be very comfortable,' said William. 'But nobody ever goes up there, so you'll be quite safe.'

'Much safer than here, in fact,' Tabby pointed out. 'And it would be a lot easier to bring you food. We can't take a great deal out here, it would look too suspicious. And then when the hue and cry has died down, we can lend you clothes and horses and you can go — wherever you're going.'

'And Patience could help,' Deb added.

For a moment, Nick thought that she was referring to the

personal quality most necessary for enduring incarceration, whether voluntary or not. But Tabby said at once, 'Yes, of course she could – that's a good idea!'

'Patience?' said Nick, gently querying. 'Do I know her?'

'She's our Aunt Imp!' Kate said, giggling with delight. 'Im-Patience, Nat calls her.'

'She's Mother's youngest sister,' Tabby explained. 'She came to stay with us a few months ago, just before Father died – to cheer Mother up, I expect. But she's very nice, she's our friend too, she's teaching me French and we often ride out together – she knows about the shelter, and I'm sure she'd help us.'

Nick wished that he could share her optimism. He had only the vaguest knowledge of Silence's family in London, but remembered that there had been a brother, and several sisters with equally outlandish Puritan names. Surely this Patience must be fully adult, and in consequence would be exceedingly unlikely to assist her nieces and nephew in such a hare-brained scheme. He said slowly, 'Can she be trusted?'

'Of course she can!' Deb cried, with some indignation.

Tabby said, more thoughtfully, 'Yes, I'm certain she can. She told me a week or so ago, when we first heard that the Scots had been defeated, that she thought they should have won. I know she'd do everything she could to help us. She's clever – she's got that sort of mind.' She glanced at Nick, and added slowly, 'I don't think anyone else ought to know. Certainly not Rachael – she's in such a strange mood at the moment.'

'She might tell Jack Harington,' said William.

'No, she wouldn't!' said Deb stoutly: she had always been her half-sister's supporter.

'She'd think it was her duty,' said Tabby. 'I think it's safest not to tell her, at least for the moment. And keep it from Nat, too. After all, he's the one who'll be in trouble if we're found out. It's best if he doesn't know anything about it.'

Nick found it passing strange, to sit here in this stuffy little hut, listening to the children who had once played such a part in his life, discussing other members of the family with the air of seasoned plotters. A glance at Touchet showed him to be still completely bewildered.

'And Mother?' said William. Nick looked up involuntarily, and met Tabby's gaze, resting on him thoughtfully. She smiled, and he realised that she must know something of his affair with Silence.

The other children had surely been much too young to be aware of it, and certainly had no idea now that he was any more than an old friend. But Tabby, watchful and observant beyond her years, must have sensed something in the air, long ago, and might even have guessed Kate's true parentage.

He wondered suddenly how many other people knew of this. He prayed that they would be discreet, for he had no wish for the woman he had once loved so much to be subjected to Touchet's assessing, lecherous stare.

Oh, Silence . . . 'Not yet,' he said, in belated answer to William's question. 'It wouldn't be fair. She'd feel she had to help us, for the sake of old obligations. Later, perhaps . . . but for now, I think only the four of you, and Patience, if you do feel sure that you can trust her, should be party to the plot. And don't tell anyone — anyone at all, not even your closest and dearest friends.'

'You must swear, all of you,' William said earnestly. 'Swear not to tell *anyone* — on the Holy Bible.'

'We haven't got a Bible here,' Deb pointed out.

'Well, we'll just have to *imagine* one, then. Go on, Kate, put your hand out and swear — say after me, "I swear on this Holy Book . . ."'

The child's voice, high and unwontedly serious, followed his. One after the other, the four children affirmed their solemn oath to keep this secret, and Nick felt another pang of guilt. This was so patently a game to them, a glorious adventure into which they had entered with wholehearted enthusiasm. He and Touchet were shamelessly exploiting their willingness to help, but at least, if they were discovered, the children would hardly be punished. They were so young, and of otherwise exemplary birth and character, that a stern warning about their misguided and foolish behaviour would be the worst they could expect. Adults, however, would have no such defence. And, despite his misgivings, he knew that he and his companion were in urgent need of assistance, and there was no hope of obtaining it anywhere else. They would have to do their best to ensure that the children did not suffer for it, should they be caught.

'We must go,' Tabby said, when the oath-taking had finished. 'The last thing we want is for people to come looking for us, and we're late already. Will you be all right, here in the woods? It's quite safe, no one ever comes here except us. And tomorrow we'll bring you some fresh clothes, and we'll find a way to get you into

Wintercombe without anyone seeing. I'm sorry we can't do that tonight, but it's nearly dark already, and with Jack there it'd be much too dangerous. You do understand, don't you?'

'Of course,' Nick said. 'It's the most sensible plan.' He was almost falling asleep where he sat, and doubted that Touchet was in any better case.

His companion still wore that petulant expression, which seemed to fill his face whenever he disliked a situation, but could do nothing to alter it. He said now, with elaborate courtesy, 'Tell me, Mistress St. Barbe . . . do you have any food with you? We have had almost nothing to eat all day, and we are sorely hungry.'

'Oh, I'm sorry, I forgot!' Tabby's face showed lively consternation. 'How could I – but we haven't very much, have we – and there's no chance of going back to get more. You brought something, William – what you have got?'

'Only a bag of apples,' said her brother, and scrambled out of the shelter. He returned a moment later, rather sheepish, with a large bag that proved to contain three fat rosy pippins, and several well-chewed cores. 'Sorry,' he said, almost comically crestfallen. 'I seem to have eaten most of them – I'm keeping the cores for Strawberry and Cobweb and their foals.'

Deb's apron pocket yielded a couple of squashed-looking plums, split, over-ripe and sticky, and Kate produced a hunk of cheese, covered in bits of fluff and rather gnawed-looking around the edges. Ignoring Touchet's look of horrified disdain, Nick accepted these offerings with gratitude, and brushed aside Tabby's apologies. 'It doesn't matter – it's hardly your fault that you didn't come prepared to feed a brace of hungry Cavaliers!'

'There might be some blackberries ripe, further up the hill,' said William helpfully. 'And you could always make a snare and catch a rabbit and cook it – there's plenty of dry wood behind you, and we'll leave the flints and tinder.'

Nick tried to imagine Touchet catching, flaying, gutting and cooking his own rabbit, failed comprehensively, and lapsed into laughter. Tabby grinned at him, and Kate joined in, with her infectious giggle.

'Can't you catch a rabbit, sir?' said William, who must have noticed the appalled expression on Touchet's face. 'I caught my first one when I was seven,' he added, in the incredulous tones of a country-bred child.

'Perhaps Master Touchet hasn't had the same opportunities as you did,' Tabby pointed out kindly. 'Come on, we must leave — we aren't usually back so late, and we don't want to make anyone suspicious.'

Reluctantly, the younger children crawled out into the gloom, and Nick watched them go, feeling curiously bereft. They represented a vision of fresh, warm normality, of peace and rest and laughter, in sharp contrast to his present life, full of stress and war and danger. He realised that he could so very easily come to rely once more on the solace that they, and of course their mother, could give him. Realistically, he knew that he must continue to fend for himself. To depend too much on other people, particularly on a brood of young children, was most foolhardy, and could even be dangerous in his present circumstances.

But he wished, how he wished, and for reasons quite different and less practical than Touchet's, that he could go back with them tonight to Wintercombe, and see Silence once more, see her serene face and the sudden smile of delight that could give her beauty, put his arms around her and draw her close, sheltering within her calm and her passion as once she had sheltered in him, and share her quiet strength and gentleness and humorous wisdom. Yet it could never again be the same as it had once been. Six years had elapsed since he had seen her last, and he knew that as he had changed, so must she. And he could not bear it, if the dream and the memory that he had kept all this time in his heart should prove in the end to be a cruel and bitter illusion.

Tabby paused by the door, her face lit golden and soft in the candle's glow, almost supernaturally lovely, as if she were some ethereal spirit of the forest. She said softly, 'I'm sorry about the food. We'll bring some tomorrow, as soon as we can.' She glanced at Touchet, then at Nick, and her eyes gleamed suddenly. 'Thank you, Captain Hellier — thank you so much, for coming back.'

*

Patience sat at her table by the window of her chamber, preparing for the night. She had anointed herself with lotions to soften the skin and whiten the complexion, waters to dissolve freckles and stave off wrinkles, and now she was brushing her hair. Sometimes Silence lent her maid Mally to perform this task, especially when Patience wanted a more elaborate coiffure than the usual simple knot at the back of her head, or when washing or curling was required. Tonight, however, she had contented herself with brushing hair as soft and shining and lustrous as Cathay silk.

The room smelled sweetly of rosewater and camomile and orris root. Patience laid down the tortoiseshell brush, and gazed at her reflection in the mirror. Smooth, pale, immaculately lovely, her face stared back. She wrinkled her nose at it, and put out her tongue. Unabashed, the reflection mimicked her perfectly.

This is ridiculous, she thought, getting up to stare out of the window at the moonlit garden. Absolutely ridiculous. He is three years younger than I am, for heaven's sake, he's not handsome or imposing or gallant – he's nothing like the men I knew in London, he helps with the calving and comes home with blood on his hands and dung on his doublet. But he's the wittiest person I ever met, and I do like a man who's good company.

She smiled at the memory of Nat at supper, mocking Jack Harington so gently that the victim was unaware of it – although Rachael, from her thunderous expression, certainly realised. Patience had joined in, as subtle as Nat, and the smile he had sent her was friendly, admiring, and in perfect accord. It certainly added spice to her life at Wintercombe to flirt with her sister's stepson, but Patience was beginning to recognise, somewhat belatedly, the consequences if she allowed herself to stray out of her depth.

Nonsense, she told herself, remembering that she was the veteran of half a dozen more serious affairs, skilled in the charming, empty game of courtship, even though no man had ever done more than kiss her. You, of all people, know what you are doing. And at least he responds, in that light-hearted manner – more than anyone else in this rustic little place has done so far!

A knock on the door interrupted her thoughts. She got up and went to open it, wondering who it might be, her mind running fantastically on midnight assignations.

Tabby stood there, a night-rail wrapped round her chemise, barefoot and with her hair tangled on her shoulders. Patience noticed again her air of suppressed but overwhelming excitement. She said, rather hesitantly, 'Can I talk to you for a little?'

Patience pulled the door wide, surprised but rather flattered. Tabby was notoriously reluctant to reveal her inmost thoughts. 'Of course,' she said. 'Come in.'

She did not know what she expected: some tale of first love, perhaps, or advice sought on a childishly trivial matter, but the girl sat down on the bed, straight-backed and serious and glowing, and said softly, 'Can you keep a secret?'

'Of course I can,' said Patience, startled.

'This one will have to be kept,' Tabby told her. 'Oh, Patience, do you remember the hut we built in the woods above the Wellow Lane?'

Puzzled, her aunt nodded.

'Well – I think the King of Scots is hiding in it!'

Whatever she had suspected, it was not this. Patience stared at her, utterly dumbfounded. 'The *King*?'

'Shush!' said Tabby urgently, a finger to her lips. 'No one else must know – *no one*! Jack Harington's only just down the passage – think what he'd do if he found out!'

'But the King of Scots . . . ' Patience said, still incredulous. 'The King, here . . . it can't be!'

'I think it is,' Tabby assured her. 'He's young, and very tall, and dark, and he's obviously of high birth, you can see it plain, even in the rags he's wearing. Who else could it be?'

'Does he *say* he's the King?'

'No,' Tabby admitted. 'But he says he's called Mervyn Touchet.' She grinned. 'And that *can't* be his real name, can it? He *must* have made it up.' She made imaginary swordplay movements with her arm, finishing with a ferocious thrust. '*Touché!* Nobody could really be called that.'

'I don't know,' said Patience. It seemed much too good to be true, but the younger girl's excitement was infectious. 'Perhaps he's French.'

'I'd swear he's as English as you or me. And the best of it is, he's not alone – Captain Hellier is with him!'

Patience listened to her account of the meeting with the two men, and began to think that this mysterious Touchet might indeed be the fugitive Charles Stuart. Captain Hellier, who had once commanded the Wintercombe garrison, she dismissed as unimportant, merely the means of presenting her with the perfect opportunity to serve the King far more effectively than she had been able to in London. She said, when Tabby had finished, 'Did this Captain Hellier behave as if Touchet was the King?'

'Well, no, I suppose he didn't,' her niece said slowly. 'But it's not the sort of thing you'd reveal to just anybody, is it? Especially in front of a little prattler like Kate. I expect he thought it was best if they kept up the disguise. And they are *very* well disguised – I didn't recognise Captain Hellier at all, until he said my name.' She grinned. 'They looked just like beggars — and smell like it, too. I said we'd find some fresh clothes for them.'

'And where are we going to hide them?'

'In the roofspace, above the hall. A stair goes up from the closet in Mother's chamber, and another from the closet in Nat's. There's a huge loft up there, you could hide a regiment in it and nobody would know.'

'They'd know if we kept walking through with food,' Patience pointed out.

Tabby grinned. 'Not necessarily. How often is Nat in his chamber? And he doesn't have a manservant to sleep in that closet. It's easy, you'll see.' She hugged her knees, and Patience suddenly felt aeons older, and wiser. 'I promise you, no one will ever, ever find out.'

*

'That little maid was a beauty,' said Touchet, with reminiscent appreciation. 'A peach of a girl — a wood-nymph, a veritable dryad!'

'She is fifteen years old, and still a child,' Nick said, through lips stiff with anger and disgust. 'And if you treat her as anything other than a wholly innocent young maiden, I shall take the greatest pleasure in pushing your teeth down your throat.'

Touchet looked round at him, affronted. 'My dear fellow, I would not dream of doing anything at all improper to such a delightful creature — but a man may surely express his admiration for such perfect, untouched, flower-like loveliness?'

'Not in my hearing,' said Nick. The comfort of the soft moss had proved illusive, and he had woken sore in every joint, with a raging headache and a stiff neck to add to his aching legs and empty belly. 'I have a certain care for her. I taught her to play the virginals, when I was here during the war.'

'The virginals?' Touchet stared at him. 'I did not know you could play.'

'Not many people do — the opportunity to display my skill has been a trifle limited of late,' said Nick drily. He rubbed his aching neck, and gazed at the dappled morning sunlight in the clearing that surrounded their shelter. Some devil of mischief made him add, 'I'm pretty sharp-set. A nice fresh roasted rabbit should put me to rights.'

Touchet glowered at him. They had been awake ever since the dawn birdsong made further sleep impossible, and both men were hungry, bad-tempered and on edge. Nick felt he would have given a fortune, if he had it, for a thorough wash, even a bath, and a suit of fresh clothes, and another for a good hearty breakfast. He thought of crusty new bread, still warm from the morning's baking, sharp fresh cheese, collops of bacon, even hot frumenty, which he had never particularly liked, and found his mouth watering in vain anticipation.

'It's my belief those children won't come,' said Touchet, after a while. He peered down through the trees. 'Should never have trusted it to them — they'll be bound to prattle.'

'I don't think so,' said Nick, curbing his annoyance. 'You can't expect them too soon — they'll have lessons and duties to do before they can slip away without arousing suspicion. And I'd trust the eldest one, Tabitha, with my life.'

'Tabitha? Damned Puritan-sounding name for such a pretty girl!'

'Their father was a Roundhead colonel,' said Nick, and had the satisfaction of seeing his companion's jaw drop.

'A nest of infant Roundheads? Good God, man, as soon walk into a cockatrice's den! What are you thinking of?'

'Food, beer, and a bath,' said Nick concisely. 'I told you — they are friendly. You must have seen that for yourself. Oh, I grant you, we began as enemies — but by the time my garrison surrendered, the family were all on the best of terms with us. My lieutenant seems to have visited them since — and as for the Roundhead colonel, he's been dead for months.'

'So what of the rest of these St. Barbes — their mother, and the others they mentioned?'

'Lady St. Barbe would undoubtedly help us, but it might not be wise to involve her unless absolutely necessary. We will probably only need to stay for a few nights, until the hue and cry has died down. I do not want to bring any more trouble to Wintercombe — they suffered enough during the war. As for the others — Nat, who must be the heir, was very level-headed and old for his years, and certainly not a Roundhead. His sister Rachael was always more difficult. If she is betrothed to this man Harington, she could prove to be a problem.'

'I don't like it,' Touchet said. 'The thought of relying on a pack of children, and this Patience female — sounds most unlikely to me, she'll probably betray us on the spot, or chatter about it to that Harington man.'

'You'll have to like it,' Nick pointed out, with unanswerable logic. 'Where else can we go for help?'

This at any rate had the benefit of silencing Touchet, for at least half an hour.

The sun had climbed past its zenith before they heard faint, distant voices. Then, as they tensed, ready to dive into the hut, someone began to whistle a bouncing, jaunty tune. The sound was pure and true, and Nick relaxed so far as to grin at his companion. 'It's all right,' he said. 'That must be Tabby. She's whistling "Packington's Pound", which is one of the pieces I taught her.'

Touchet looked at him doubtfully, and then got to his feet. The voices were coming nearer, and then Kate came dancing up the path and into the clearing, her brown hair flying, her face glowing with excitement. She ran to within a few feet of the men, stopped, giggled, and swept them a flowing curtsey. 'Hello,' she said demurely, rising and clasping her hands together. 'Did you sleep well?'

'Tolerably well, Mistress Kate,' said Nick gravely. The more he saw of this wayward, delightful child, the more certain was he that she was his daughter. But were his thoughts a reflection of the truth, or a distortion produced by his own sentimental wishful thinking?

Only Silence could tell him, and yet he must be kept secret from her.

'Kate, how many times have I told you, you mustn't go running ahead like that!' said Deb, puffing perspiring into view with the fat old brown pony behind her. 'You don't know what you might meet.'

'I do — I met them!' Kate grinned impartially up at Nick and Touchet, her warm brown eyes glowing. 'We've brought lots of food for you, and clothes, and Tabby even managed to borrow Nat's razor, so you won't look like beggars any more. And Aunt Imp has come with us, and she's going to help you too.'

This, approaching with Tabby and William, must be Patience. To Nick's surprise, she bore little resemblance to her sister, being dark and pretty where Silence was quietly plain, and her careful curls and becoming russet-coloured riding-habit spoke of an interest in her appearance that Silence entirely lacked. She was flushed and breathless from the ride and the climb in warm sunshine, but this did not in the least detract from the very attractive picture she presented. Predictably, Touchet watched her with considerable interest, as she walked over to the shelter and, like Kate, dropped an impeccable curtsey. Then, she stood, gazing with covert awe at Touchet's height, and Nick knew exactly what she was thinking. Somehow, he must contrive a way to take Tabby aside and tell her, in no uncertain terms, that his companion was not the King of Scots.

'This is Aunt Imp,' said Kate, unnecessarily.

Tabby performed the more formal introductions, and then the saddlebags were unloaded. Nick saw his fantasies unpacked and laid out on the grass in a sunny spot a few yards from the shelter. There was fresh bread, its delicious aroma alrady scenting the air, cheese and cold bacon and, most welcome of all, a couple of leather bottles that proved to be filled with cool, frothy beer.

Their hunger was too great for any attention to manners. Nick and Touchet fell ravenously on the food, while Kate sat and watched them with bright-eyed interest, and the older children and Patience tied up the ponies and laid two more bulging saddle-bags on the ground beside the two men.

At last, they had eaten and drunk their fill, and there were few crumbs left for the birds. Nick was amused by the intent watchful-ness of the four children as they sat in a circle around them. He stretched, replete, and said gravely, 'None over for you, I'm afraid.'

'We've already dined, thank you,' said William, equally solemn, while Kate giggled behind her hand. 'Was that sufficient? We couldn't have brought you any more – as it was, Darby was suspicious.'

'Darby is our cook,' Deb explained. 'But of course you remember him, don't you, Captain Hellier?'

'I remember his food – fit for angels, as I recall.'

'It still is,' said William, with relish. 'We had a wonderful roast capon for dinner, with apple sauce and two sallets and – '

'I'm sure that Captain Hellier and Master Touchet have other things to discuss with us,' Patience said gently. Despite her fine clothes, she sat with the children on the grass, heedless of stains or damp. She caught Nick's eye, and grinned at him. 'I hear you know this crew of old.'

'Except for Kate,' Deb pointed out. 'She wasn't even born when Captain Hellier was here before.'

'Yes, I was!' said the infant, obviously proposing to be contrary.

'No, you weren't, you were born the next spring, and I remember it very well,' said Deb crushingly. 'You screamed so loud that the whole house could hear it.'

'No, I didn't!'

'Yes, you did!'

'Be quiet, both of you,' said Patience sharply. To Nick's surprise, both girls subsided, with mutual glares. Their aunt turned to the two men, her smile friendly and captivating. 'I do apologise for these two. They don't usually display such ill manners.'

'Think nothing of it, Mistress Patience,' Touchet told her gallantly. 'These children have already been of such help to us in our troubles — leading us to this shelter, and bringing us food and clothing. But I do hope that we are not forced to spend another night here.'

'"Oh, I have passed a miserable night",' Nick quoted mischievously. As he had suspected, no one else was acquainted with the works of William Shakespeare, and they looked at him blankly. He added, 'Tabby has some idea of hiding us in the roofspace above the hall.'

'I know,' Patience said. She clasped her hands round her knees, thoughtfully. 'It does seem to be the best place. I went up there with Tabby this morning. It's dark, and dusty, but unless you draw attention to yourselves by moving around a great deal, there's small chance of discovery. We took a couple of mattresses up, and some blankets and quilts, candles and food and books — you'll be quite comfortable.'

'How did you manage that without being seen?'

'Oh, quite easily — we went up the stairs from the closet in Nat's chamber, and took the mattresses and bedding from there as well. He's ridden to Bath today, to see Master Harley — which is a pleasant change from Master Harley coming to see us. He's Nat's lawyer,' she added in brief explanation. 'There's some tangle over the inheritance, apparently.'

'Is he a Puritan too?' Touchet demanded abruptly. Patience looked at him in some surprise, and spread her hands. They were white, Nick noticed, and beautifully smooth and well kept. 'I don't know, sir. He dresses soberly and plainly, but the cloth is always of very good quality. It isn't obvious that he is — not like Jack Harington, whose only topic of conversation seems to be last week's sermon, or the iniquities of the Scots.' She grinned. 'But at least he left this morning, so one of our difficulties has gone. We'll have to smuggle you into the house without being suspected, which might not be easy – but what I propose we do, is this.'

She outlined a stratagem which, in its simplicity and boldness, left Nick acknowledging, reluctantly, that this stylish young woman was also a natural and devious plotter. Which, he thought gloomily, was more than could be said of Lieutenant-Colonel Mervyn Touchet.

❧ CHAPTER FOURTEEN ❧

'Concealment, like a worm'
(*Twelfth Night*)

The four St. Barbe children and Patience had ridden out, as was their habit, immediately after dinner. They returned, flushed and laughing, perhaps two hours later, to a house that, in the middle of a warm afternoon, was quiet and peaceful. Nat had gone to Bath, and Rachael was walking in the garden, where Silence was consulting with the ancient gardener, Diggory, on the best place to plant the new tulip bulbs which she had asked her brother to send her from London. Most of the servants were busy in their quarters where, with luck, they would be clearing up after their own dinner. Patience looked round the empty hall, and smiled with rich satisfaction. So far, all was well.

William had been delegated to lead the ponies round to the stable, and to keep the grooms occupied with some tale of temporary lameness. It was essential not to have anyone's eyes too often on the gravelled courtyard in front of the house. It did not much matter if the two fugitives were seen to enter Wintercombe, but no one must be given the chance to realise that they had not left.

The one stumbling-block might prove to be Carpenter, the officious butler. Patience, however, had given strict instructions to the two men, to be acted on should he open the door.

It sounded a hare-brained scheme, but Nick had heard worse. He knew, moreover, that anything unusual could be made to seem ordinary, if the actors in the drama could carry it off with confidence and aplomb. Certainly, trying to smuggle them into Wintercombe in secret would be very difficult. What could be easier than walking straight up to the front door?

He put on his new clothes. Like all the rest he had borrowed on his journey from Worcester, they were an indifferent fit, being made for a man rather heavier, but the quality was good, and the shoes were almost the right size, for which he was profoundly grateful. Touchet did not grumble, even though the garments provided for him, with apologies from Patience, were slightly too small, and rather more worn than those given to Nick.

'You won't have horses, of course,' Patience had said, admiring them as they stood before her in all their glory. 'But if Carpenter does open the door, he'll think that the grooms have already taken them to the stables, and of course if William plays his part, the grooms won't even notice any visitors.'

They had followed the children from the shelter, down through the trees to the warm sunlit line of the Wellow Lane. Ahead, perhaps a mile away, Nick could see the tower of Philip's Norton church, jutting up out of the trees and the hill that lay between. He had not travelled this road for six years, and it seemed passing strange to be walking along it now, in the wake of Silence's children and Silence's sister, returned without her knowledge to the place that had once meant so much to him.

And did still. He had forgotten how the summer trees hid its gables and chimneys, and the sudden vision of Wintercombe, as they climbed the hill, took his breath away. Somehow, it was smaller than he had remembered, but even more lovely. Abruptly he realised the source of his yearning, the feeling of desperate hunger that had been with him since yesterday.

He wanted nothing better than to stay here, rooted like a tree in the red-brown Somerset soil, with his child and the woman he loved. And after all the years of restless, aimless wandering and soldiering, he desired no other life.

Unfortunately, it was a vision of his future that was distinctly unrealistic.

'Stay here,' Tabby said, coming back to them, slim and young and graceful on her frisky little chestnut. 'If you lurk behind this tree, you can't be seen from the house. In about five minutes, William should be safely in the stables, and the rest of us in the house. If there's anything wrong, we'll send Kate back to warn you. If you don't see her, you can come up and knock on the door. Patience should answer it, but if Carpenter gets there first, you know what to say.' She grinned. 'Good luck!'

The two men watched her retreating figure as she rode back up to the house. Touchet, wisely, uttered no further comments on her appearance. He said, 'Mistress Patience is a surprising young lady.'

'She is indeed — and nothing whatsoever like her sister,' said Nick, wondering how the bleak, unhappy childhood which Silence had described to him, long ago, could ever have produced the sophisticated, merry and devious Patience. 'If the house is indeed as quiet as she thinks it will be, then we have nothing to fear, but I run the risk of being recognised, if we encounter any of the household who knew me before.' He ran a thoughtful finger across his unshaven chin, the stubble now long and bristly enough, he hoped, to be a fairly effective disguise. 'This should help, but I lived in that house for nigh on a year. If any of the rest of the family see me, they'll be in no doubt who I am, and then we'll have even more people party to our secret. The fewer who know, the better.' He glanced at his companion, who looked remarkably different when washed, shaved, and clad in respectable clothes, and added, 'I reckon they all think that you're the King – and I notice you didn't do anything to correct that impression.'

Touchet smiled smugly. He had certainly been most gallant to Mistress Patience, and she, evidently a born flirt, had responded in kind, to Tabby's patent amusement. 'I suppose it's an understand-able error,' he said, with totally spurious modesty.

It was strange: perhaps it was the influence of Wintercombe, but Nick found himself almost warming to the man. Like his name, he was too absurd to be taken seriously. He laughed, and clapped the supposed King familiarly on the shoulder. 'I suppose so. Come on, it must be time to make our move.'

Every yard of the way was beset by memories. Here, the musketeers had hidden behind the hedge, to rake the attacking Roundheads with bullets. Here, he had turned for one last look at Wintercombe, and seen Silence watching from her window, bereft for ever. The house itself, even though he had not set eyes on it for six years, held so much that was dear, that he felt he knew every stone of it. His commanding officer had ordered the low wall bordering the front courtyard to be raised, and it was still at that height, though the new work had weathered in to blend with the old. The watch-tower, once a dovecot, now seemed to have resumed that function, to judge by the number of pigeons sitting on its conical roof.

He led Touchet under the gatehouse, sparing a quick glance at the farmyard, called the barton by the household, where the stables were situated. It was satisfactorily empty. The gravel, neatly raked, crunched under his feet. Ahead lay the main wing of the house, grey-gold, gabled, with two beautiful oriel windows looking down at him. Nothing at all had changed, and yet there was a quiet, a deep sense of peace and tranquillity, that Winter-combe had never worn in the days when almost a hundred soldiers had been garrisoned here.

That time, all too brief, had brought him the greatest happiness of his life. He knew that he could not expect any more. He had first ridden up to this lovely place as an enemy captain, in a position of power and authority. He came now as a hunted fugitive, whose presence must be kept a secret, even from his beloved Silence, and though he longed above all to see her, and speak with her, he must recognise the core of fear around his heart. Wintercombe had not altered, for six years was but a brief moment in its long existence, but would those years have wrought as great a change in the woman he loved, as in her children?

In Worcester, he had wondered idly and sadly if she had grown stout and plain, as his brother's wife had done, and whether her heart had forgotten him. Now he was almost glad that he would not see her, so afraid was he that his dream might prove to be an unbearable illusion.

He pulled himself together, with an effort, and banged the door-knocker twice, briskly. In the gloom of the porch, it was hard to see much of Touchet's face, but he hoped it did not appear too arrogant.

There were footsteps, and the door opened wide. It was, unfortunately, not Patience who stood there, but a neat, plainly-clad young man with a supercilious expression. This must be the butler, Carpenter, who would not recognise Nick. He stared at the two men in the porch, and said forbiddingly, 'Yes?'

Nick hoped that he could remember his instructions. 'We've come to see Mistress Woods, sir,' he said, letting his voice slide into its old Worcestershire habit. 'Concerning a matter of some garments she ordered in Bath, sir. She be expecting us, I d'believe.'

Carpenter's eyes travelled coldly over Nick's rather dusty clohtes, and he wondered if the door was about to be slammed in their faces. Then there was the sound of briskly tapping feet, and Patience herself appeared, smiling. 'Ah, I thought so! Thank you, Carpenter – I've been expecting Master Hill for a day or so. He promised to take some measurements, and one of my old gowns for a pattern. Do come in, Master Hill – and is this your assistant? Oh, yes, I remember you. That will be all, Carpenter.'

'Will the gentlemen require refreshments?' said the butler, evidently accustomed to Patience in full flight. She glanced at the two men, not in the least disconcerted, and nodded. 'Yes – I am sure they would like some beer. If you will bring it up to my chamber, as soon as possible? Thank you.'

Carpenter retreated in the direction of the buttery, where the barrels of beer and cider were stored, and Patience drew Nick and Touchet inside, still talking. 'My niece will assist us — Tabby? Ah, there you are! Here's Master Hill, come to measure me. This way, please, up the stairs.'

Nick, dazed by her swift confident chatter, followed her up the narrow, twisting stone staircase that he remembered so well. He wondered which chamber she occupied, and if it had been wise to order Carpenter to bring the beer up to them. It might have seemed odd had they declined refreshments, after their supposed journey from Bath, but surely the most urgent need was to ensure that they reached their hiding-place as soon as possible?

Patience and Tabby led them into the little suite of rooms at the top of the stairs. Six years ago, Nick's commanding officer, Black Jack Ridgeley, quite possibly the most unpleasant man he had ever encountered, had occupied these pleasant chambers overlooking the gardens, and had made them foul and squalid. There was no trace of his presence now. The little antechamber, with its yellow-curtained bed and tapestry hangings, was neat and sweet-smelling. On the elm clothes-press by the window lay a woman's gown of a rich dark blue material, a length of tape, and a pair of fearsome-looking shears.

'Oh, yes,' said Patience, shutting the door behind her. 'This has all been planned down to the last detail. I thought you'd better have some beer, it might have seemed suspicious if you had not. I wish Carpenter hadn't been so quick to answer the door, but apart from that, it's all gone very well, hasn't it?'

'So far,' said Nick, who did not believe in counting his chickens so long before hatching. 'Where's Rachael? And Lady St. Barbe?'

'In the garden,' Tabby said. 'You can probably see them, if you look out — but be careful!'

He went to the window's edge, screening himself behind the curtain, and stared down. The neat, formal pattern of the terraces was laid out below him, gravelled walks and intricate knots, their patterns designed to be viewed to best advantage from above. He saw Kate and Deb, skipping together down the steps, squealing with excited laughter, the picture of innocence. A stocky boy knelt with basket and trowel, weeding, and beyond him was surely the stiff unyielding figure of Rachael, still giving that impression of spirit and hard-held temper, walking slowly along the cherry arbour.

And there, by the sundial, talking to the ancient gardener whom he remembered from six years ago – surely *he* was not still alive? – was Silence.

She had not, at least, grown stout. She wore black, presumably for her husband, but somehow it did not seem as unrelentingly severe as her stepdaughter's mourning gown. She was smiling, and he saw the swift gestures of her hands as she spoke. The urge to fling open the window, to call to her, to let her know that he had come back, was so overwhelmingly strong that he clamped his hands together.

'We had the sundial mended,' said Tabby softly, at his side. 'I wish I could tell Mother that you are here.'

He glanced at her, and saw an expression of sad compassion on her face. 'Perhaps you can,' he said. 'We'll see how matters progress.' He turned, and moved away from the window. He did not in the least want Touchet to suspect that his feelings for the Roundhead colonel's widow were anything more than mild friendship.

There was a knock on the door. He remembered his supposed role, and took up the tape that Patience thrust urgently into his hands, while Touchet stood to one side, trying to imitate a tailor's assistant with some conviction.

Carpenter, walking in with a tray of beer, did not seem to see anything out of the ordinary. Nick, remembering his own encounters with tailors, went through the motions of measuring the width of Patience's back. Out of the corner of his eye, he saw the butler put the tray down on the clothes-press, and return to the door. 'Thank you,' said Patience, dismissing him. 'That will be all. Master Hill won't be very long, and I will probably show him out.'

'Of course, Mistress Woods,' said Carpenter, bowed, and went out.

The door shut behind him with a sharply final sound. They listened to his footsteps, clattering briskly down the stairs and into the distance. Then Patience, her eyes sparkling in triumph, whirled round and smiled at the two men. 'I told you – he doesn't suspect a thing! Now, we only have to smuggle you up into the roofspace, and you'll be safe.'

'I don't doubt it, Mistress,' said Touchet, smiling warmly back. 'But might we be permitted to drink our beer first?'

Which, thought Nick, as he swallowed the cool frothy liquid

with great pleasure, and tried not to think about the woman in the garden, was probably the first sensible thing he had said since leaving Worcester.

Tabby opened the door with great caution, put her head outside, and listened. She glanced back into the room, and beckoned. Nick, Touchet and Patience hurried to join her. 'It's all clear,' she hissed, and, with a comically conspiratorial air, the three followed her across the passage, to a door almost opposite.

Six years ago, this had been occupied by Silence's mother-in-law, a fearsome old termagant whose sudden demise had caused little grief. Now, it seemed to be Nat's chamber. Although empty, it bore all the signs of his occupation: a small library of books stacked on chairs and tables, piles of papers and writing implements, and a row of interestingly miscellaneous objects ranged along the mantelshelf. Nick remembered the boy Nat, and his passionate curiosity concerning the world around him. It seemed as if that characteristic, at least, had not changed.

Tabby led the way to the unoccupied closet, and pulled back the hangings that disguised one wall. Behind lay a small, narrow door. She lifted the latch and opened it, to reveal a flight of tiny, steep stone steps twisting upwards in the thickness of the wall. Nick, who had never been in the roofspace, but knew roughly what to expect, said, 'Is there any light?'

'I have it,' Patience told him, and lifted up a small lanthorn, the twin of the one in the shelter, and already lit. 'Shall I lead?'

The stairs were very steep, and difficult, but at least not worn. He glanced back and saw Touchet, an expression of deepest doubt on his face, preparing to follow. Above him Patience, her skirts bunched in one hand and the lanthorn held high in the other, was climbing slowly and carefully.

It seemed a long time before the steps ceased abruptly, and there was a sudden, looming space before them. Patience stood at the top, the lanthorn casting a rich yellow glow about her. Behind Nick, Touchet arrived at the top, brushing his doublet free of dust and cobwebs, and stared in open dismay at their hiding-place.

The space between the shallow-pitched ceiling of the hall below, and the steep-sloping rafters of the roof above, seemed vast in the light of that one flame. Nick, peering forward, could just make out the dark arch at the other end, forty feet away, that led down to Silence's chamber, by a stairway identical to the one which they had just ascended.

'Good God,' said Touchet, appalled, at his elbow. 'Are we to spend days cooped up here, like rats in the dark?'

Patience turned and stared at him, a look of rather indignant surprise on her pretty face. 'I am sorry if it is not to your liking, sir,' she said. 'But it is the best we can do.'

'Perhaps you'd prefer to return to the shelter,' said Nick, unable to disguise the anger in his voice. Touchet seemed incapable of expressing any sort of gratitude, and yet these children, and Patience, had risked a great deal, and gone to considerable trouble, to make them secure and comfortable. As his annoyance got the better of him, he added in a whisper, 'If it were not for their kindness, we'd be camped under a hedgerow still.'

For a moment, the other man was silent. Patience said, with a rather false brightness, 'We have mattresses and blankets here — and we can bring up some more food later, if all is clear, and books if you want them, and more candles — whatever you require. And it isn't cold.'

It certainly was not, being somewhat stuffy under the stone-tiled roof. Nick walked down from the step, and sat on the nearest mattress. Planks and boards had been pushed together to make a small platform, balanced across the joists of the ceiling below. By the feel of it, he was sitting on feathers, and a sudden longing for sleep came over him. Touchet sat down beside him, evidently surprised by the comfort of the bedding.

'I'll light the other lanthorn,' said Tabby, kneeling down to do it. With the extra illumination, the roofspace seemed somehow even more huge and threatening, as the two flames threw their shadows looming across the floor and walls.

'Don't tread on the space between the joists,' Patience warned. 'It's only plaster, and you'd be likely to go through the ceiling.'

'And then people would be bound to notice us,' said Nick drily. He looked up at the two girls, and added quietly, 'Our thanks for all you have done for us. You have taken great risks, and for no possible reward.'

'Reward?' Tabby's voice was rich with scorn. 'Rubbish, Captain Hellier! Our only possible reward is to see you safe.' She smiled down at him. 'Which I hope you soon will be. Meanwhile, I trust you will be as happy as possible up here. Only remember, the hall is below, and people may be able to hear you, if you talk too loud.'

'Small fear of that, Mistress St. Barbe,' said Touchet, stifling a yawn. 'These beds of yours are damned comfortable. I think we'll take a little nap.' He winked at her cheerfully, and stretched out his long length. Nick was not a little amused to see that his feet overhung the end of the mattress by some inches.

'I think we ought to go, in case we're missed,' said Patience. 'If you want to sleep, you could blow out the lanthorn – although it might be difficult to light it again. We'll bring some food for you later.'

'Goodbye,' said Tabby, and a sudden mischievous smile, the image of Kate's, flashed across her elfin face. 'And pleasant dreams!'

Nick lay listening to their retreating footsteps, and then the quiet closing of the door at the foot of the stairs. Touchet, his hat over his eyes, seemed to be already dozing, despite the apparent discomfort of his position. At least, Nick knew from past experience that he did not snore.

He regarded his companion with exasperation. There was no doubt, the younger man was possessed of a multitude of faults, not least his insistence upon the comforts to which he, an earl's son, was accustomed, and considered his right. But although he was arrogant, impetuous, wrong-headed and generally extremely annoying, at least he was not actually ill-natured. Nick had met many much more unpleasant people on his travels, and not least of them, Lieutenant-Colonel John Ridgeley, who had once commanded the garrison at Wintercombe, until his timely death.

Sleep seemed elusive. He found his thoughts dwelling, unwelcome, upon Ridgeley, his cruelty and excesses, and then, as if in antidote, upon Silence. The woman he had glimpsed in the garden, whom he had never thought to see again, had not apparently altered: he had been transported back six years by that brief sight of her slender figure, the black dress concealing the body he remembered like his own, even after all this time.

A wave of desire swept over him, almost suffocating him. He rolled over in the deep softness of the mattress, and buried his head in his hands. It was such a desperate coil, he could see no solution. Here he was, hidden without her knowledge in the house of a woman who had once been his illicit, secret lover, and assisted now by her sister and her children. He knew how easy it would be, to get up and step carefully across those joists to the stair that led down to the closet off her chamber, perhaps still occupied by her maid Mally. His imagination walked down those steep stone steps, slipped through the tiny closet, and entered the bright airy space of the room beyond, the windows flung wide to the garden, and the afternoon sun streaming in. He would sit, as so often before, on the cushioned windowseat and play with Lily, the little white greyhound that he had given her, long ago, and wait for her footfall on the stair. And then the door would open, and she would enter, the same Silence, cool and calm and smiling, her sweet serenity masking the secret, reckless, passionate woman within. And her face would light up with joy, at the sight of him, and she would open her arms . . .

He clenched his fists in frustration. It was too dangerous, and he would not put her at risk. Better, safer, for her sake and his peace of mind, if she knew nothing at all about the two uninvited guests hidden above her head. Patience seemed to know what she was doing, had entered this plot with open eyes, and the children were too young to be punished.

But he did not think he could bear it, to be cooped up here for days on end, no dark and no daylight, knowing that only a few feet away Silence lived and moved and laughed and slept, quite unaware of his presence. He wondered if there was some way in which he could appear openly, as himself. Touchet, so dangerously distinctive in appearance, was another matter, but surely, if Tom Wickham had been received here as a welcome guest, it would raise no eyebrows to see him also pay a visit to the house which he had once garrisoned?

He would have to ask Tabby — Tabby, whose letters had drawn him here, he now realised, for they had brought Silence and Wintercombe back to the forefront of his mind, and had given him hope. She had told him that her father was dead, and he was certain now that she was well aware of the implications of that information. She knew about his love for her mother, she had guessed the truth of Kate's parentage, and she wanted to bring them together again.

But what she did not know was that once he had lied to Silence, and had, for reasons that had seemed entirely admirable at the time, told her that he was married already. Thus, he had dissuaded her from deserting her home, her husband, and her children to follow him, knowing that if she did so, their new-found love could not survive poverty and exile.

Now, it was different. Now, she was a widow, and there was no obstacle to their marriage, and, he realised, marriage was what he wanted. He did not care if they could not live at Wintercombe, did not care that he had nothing to offer her, save his heart and his soul. The Silence he had loved would not have baulked at such obstacles.

But was she still his?

There was only one way to find out, and that seemed to be denied him. Somehow, he vowed, lying sleepless in the dim light while Touchet slumbered blissfully beside him, somehow, he would reach her, and discover whether she had changed.

*

'And what have you all been doing, today?'

The St. Barbe family were gathered round the big table in the dining parlour, while the stiff painted faces of Sir Samuel and Dame Ursula, the children's grandparents, stared woodenly down from either side of the fireplace in seeming disapproval. As always, Silence sat at one end, Nat at the other, with the rest distributed on either side. The atmosphere tonight, relaxed and full of laughter, was in complete contrast to yesterday's supper, which had been inhibited by Jack Harington's worthy and snuffling presence: even a severe summer cold had not prevented him from doing full justice to Darby's cooking. However, Silence, always receptive to her children's moods, had already marked the air of suppressed excitement, especially in Kate, whose giggles were unusually frequent, even for her, and who mischievously ignored the glowering looks of her elders.

'Nothing,' said Deb, with an air of injured innocence that did not ring true to her mother at all.

Patience added casually, 'Oh, we all rode out towards Wellow after dinner, and Kate and Deb had a race back.'

Kate's eyes opened very wide with shocked surprise. 'No, I didn't! Mama said not to!'

'Oh, yes, you did,' said Deb, who had divined her aunt's purpose. She followed it up with a swift kick to the shins under the table, and William, who was sitting on Kate's other side, leaned over and hissed something into her ear.

His little sister had, obviously, been about to wail her displeasure, but Silence was interested to see the effect that William's words, whatever they were, had on Kate's behaviour. She flushed very red, her eyes dropped, and then she turned to her mother and said, with a most uncharacteristic humility, 'I am very sorry, Mama. I know you said we shouldn't race our ponies, but I forgot.'

'Well, don't forget again, either of you,' said Silence, with some attempt at severity. 'It is dangerous, both to yourselves and your poor ponies — what would happen if you fell? You'd hurt yourself badly, and the pony too. Do you promise me you won't, Kate?'

Kate hung her head, and her whispered, 'Yes, Mama,' could barely be heard.

'And you, Deb?'

'I promise, Mother,' said Deb, with her usual ringing confidence.

'Good,' Silence told them. 'And please remember it.'

The meal resumed, and Patience decided on the words she would use to them later. This was not a game: this was real, far more real than the conspiracy in which she had been involved in London. The man in the roofspace might, or might not, be the King: he certainly looked, and spoke, as if he was, although some of his utterances had been distinctly lacking in royal dignity. Yet the other man, Hellier, whom Tabby held in such high regard, did not exactly treat his companion with proper deference. She would *like* the man introduced as Touchet to be Charles Stuart, but, if she considered the matter honestly, she could not really believe that he was.

However, King or no, they were still fugitives, with a price on their heads, and the penalty for aiding them would be severe, if they were caught. She had no fear for the children, but she was beginning to realise the foolishness of involving one so young as Kate, who was too little to understand the absolute necessity of secrecy.

She smiled to herself suddenly, as she remembered that she had not drawn her nieces and nephew into her plot. In fact, they had involved her in theirs.

'Penny for them,' said Nat. Patience's eyes flew open, and beheld him gazing at her with quizzical amusement. 'You look as if you are pondering some particularly thorny problem,' he added. 'Can't you decide which sort of lotion to put on your hands tonight?'

Despite her anxieties, Patience could not suppress a delighted giggle. No other man of her acquaintance had ever talked to her in this teasing, oblique manner, with such a lack of deference, and in her usual contrary fashion, she relished it. 'Actually,' she said solemnly, 'I was trying to decide whether the camomile water or the cornflower and honeysuckle would be best.'

A snort of contempt from Rachael, opposite, indicated her opinion of such fripperies. A lively discussion ensued, to which Silence listened with her usual quiet amusement, watching Nat and her sister crossing verbal swords like fencers. She was glad that they now seemed to accord so well: when Patience had first arrived, she had feared for the fragile peace of her family, as her wayward little sister seemed to set everyone by the ears, with her frivolous, sophisticated London ways. But at least she now appeared to be on excellent terms with Nat, and although Rachael's early hostility had not dissolved into friendship, she must be grateful that the danger of open conflict now seemed to be over.

She studied her stepdaughter with sympathetic eyes. The girl would never be pretty, for her nature as well as her face ensured that. She was not ill-looking, she had a slender figure and good features. If only she could learn to relax, to laugh and smile as Patience did.

But Patience was utterly different, she reminded herself. She might as well compare dog and cat. Rachael, locked into her father's mould, still missing him sorely, compelled by pride and duty to welcome the unprepossessing Jack Harington as her suitor, was unequivocally her own worst enemy, a prisoner of her own conscience. Silence, looking at her little sister with clear, affectionate eyes, wondered whether Patience even knew the meaning of the word.

A movement, glimpsed out of the corner of her eye, attracted her attention. Deb had, most unusually, left a good half of her helping of pigeon pie on the side of her plate. Now, after a quick furtive glance around, she scooped it up in her hands and thrust it into her lap and thence, presumably, into her apron pocket. As her mother continued to watch her, while still appearing to listen to Patience's banter with Nat, she helped herself to another slice, and proceeded to consume it with enthusiasm.

Vaguely puzzled, Silence wondered what Deb could want with a piece of pigeon pie. Surely her middle daughter, though notoriously fond of her food, did not feel so hungry at night that she had to steal at supper, for consumption later on? She found her mind dwelling on remedies for worms, and smiled to herself. Deb, in bounding and ruddy-cheeked good health, did not look like a child afflicted by such debilitating parasites.

Something made her look next at William. Much more open

than Deb, he usually had some difficulty in concealing any wrong-doing, and his movements now, as he slid four thick slices of mutton from his plate to his lap, positively drew her attention. Silence found herself consumed with curiosity. Something was happening, under her nose, some childish conspiracy from which she, and presumably the elder three, were excluded. Kate's excited mood had already betrayed that something was afoot, and Deb's and William's behaviour confirmed it.

Was Tabby involved? She had not seen her eldest child conceal-ing food, but that meant little. Her platter was clean, and she was nibbling an apple while, obviously, enjoying the talk of Nat and Patience. Tabby, who inhabited a dreamy world of her own for much of the time, was surely not part of any plot. At the precise moment at which this comforting thought crossed her mind, she saw the girl exchange a plainly conspiratorial glance with William, sitting opposite her.

Whatever it was, Silence decided, it was unlikely to be very serious. Kate was the only one of her offspring who had the recklessness and imagination to do something spectacularly foolish, and she was as yet too young. Rachael, once, had been capable of terrible things, but her carapace of religion and duty seemed now to have forced such impulses out of her character.

It's probably something to do with their secret place in the woods, she decided, and dismissed it from her thoughts.

After supper, the younger children had perhaps an hour before their bedtime, which was supposed to be devoted to quiet rec-reation in the house or in the garden. It was a fine evening, and she had presumed that they were all playing bowls on the green, which Nat had ordered to be scythed close, for the first time for many years. Patience, whose knowledge of the game was yet another of her surprising accomplishments, had been teaching the St. Barbes for some days, and even Rachael had seemed to enjoy it.

But as Silence walked down the corridor beyond the kitchen, intending to check on the quantities of various essential items in the store-rooms, she was astonished to see Deb emerge cautiously from the dairy, which lay at the end. She gave a start of guilty surprise when she realised that her mother had seen her, and stood by the door, her hands clasped in front of her apron, her dark eyes wide with spurious innocence.

'Deb, whatever are you doing here? I thought you were in the garden.'

'I felt hungry, and I wanted some cheese to nibble,' said her daughter. 'I'm sorry, Mother. I won't do it again, I promise.'

She had always been too ready with explanations and apologies, and Silence delivered her customary admonition, which she feared, as was also customary, would have its usual lack of effect. Deb, looking suitably chastened, walked away up the corridor, her head bowed submissively. It was only as she turned the corner by the kitchen that Silence realised that her hands, placed so demurely in front of her, had seemed to conceal a very large and heavy bulge in her apron.

Puzzled, she put her head round the dairy door. The cheeses, both hard and soft, were drying on their shelves, and the dishes and pots lay in neat rows, clean and scoured and scalded, ready to receive the morning's milk. Everything seemed in order. If Deb had taken any cheese, it was surely a very little piece.

Or a whole cheese. Shocked at the implications, she went into the room and counted the fruits of the dairymaids' daily labours. There were smaller cheeses, called truckles, wrapped in cloth, at one end of the lower shelf. She thought that one had gone: she was not sure, but she could ask Joan Coxe, who was in charge here, tomorrow.

A whole cheese. Whatever could Deb want with one? Silence pondered the problem as she checked her stores with the swift competence of long practice, and failed to arrive at any convincing answer. Stocking up their hideout in the woods seemed to be the most likely explanation, but an entire truckle, weighing upwards of five or six pounds, seemed excessive even for her children's hearty appetites. It was hardly probable that the girl was planning to run away, as Rachael at the same age had so often threatened to do. Deb was a child who liked her comforts, and always preferred the more devious methods of getting her way, rather than direct action. Moreover, both William and Tabby seemed to be in the plot as well, and she could not envisage them absconding either.

She wondered if there was some poor child, or family, which they had conceived it their duty to feed. It did not seem likely that Deb, whose concerns were still stalwartly self-centred, would enter upon such a project of her own accord, but William had always been a very generous child, and Tabby had the imagination and sensitivity to conceive such an idea. If that was the case, their covert action was entirely commendable. But why the secrecy?

No nearer to an answer, Silence went outside to the bowls lawn.

She found a lively game in progress, with much laughter and discussion, not to say distortion, of the rules. After an amusing attempt to play herself, she collected Kate, under protest, and escorted her off to bed, leaving the rest to enjoy one more game in the last of the evening's light.

She might, she knew, have gleaned some information by skilful questioning of her youngest child, but such a tactic seemed unfair, not only to Kate but to the three older ones. Besides, although stealing food in quantity was a serious matter, she could not help but remember her own dreary and repressed childhood. That had been made bearable only by the secret world which she had shared with her sisters and, to a much lesser extent, her brother and her mother. She herself was no ogre, and had always taken care to ensure that her son and her daughters enjoyed the happy, relaxed childhood she had never known, but there was surely still a need for that enticing secret life, into which no adult could enter.

She told Kate a story while Doraty, the nurse, gathered up clothes and put out fresh ones for the morrow, and then bade her smallest child goodnight. The chestnut-brown eyes, so hauntingly reminiscent of someone else, gazed sleepily up from the pillow, still with that infuriating yet beloved spark of mischief. 'Mama,' said Kate. 'Mama, I've got a secret, Mama, and you don't know what it is!'

'A secret?' Silence came back to the bed, smiling. 'What secret is that?'

''Twouldn't be a secret if I told you — and I promised!' said Kate. She hugged herself with delight. 'So it's *my* secret, and not yours, Mama.'

'Is it a nice secret?' Silence asked softly.

The little girl nodded drowsily. 'Yes, it's a *very* nice secret. I wish you could know it too.'

'Well, if it's a nice secret, I don't mind you keeping it to yourself,' Silence said. 'If it's nothing naughty or wicked or unpleasant — you enjoy it, and tell me one day, perhaps, when it's all over?'

''Course I will,' Kate said, and yawned. 'G'night, Mama.' And she snuggled down into the warmth of the bed, and closed her eyes.

Her mother stood looking down at her for a long while, as she drifted into sleep. If she had ever wished to forget Nick Hellier, this child was a daily, delightful reminder: spoiled, wilful, charming, and utterly beloved. In the soft candlelight, bathing her smooth young skin in a golden glow, the long lashes laid angelically on peach-bloom cheeks, a naughty thought might never have entered her head.

'She d'look as if butter wouldn't melt in her mouth, bobbant little minx,' said Doraty fondly.

Silence smiled. 'And it probably wouldn't. William and Deb will be up soon — they wanted one last game of bowls before dark.' She paused, wondering whether to ask the nurse if she had seen or heard anything untoward, but decided against it. Kate's nice secret, whatever it was, should be left to find its own way to the surface.

As she left the nursery, she heard the soft click of a latch. It seemed to come from Nat's chamber. Remembering that she had not yet asked him how his business with Master Harley had gone, she knocked briefly on his door, and went in.

It was not Nat who stood just beyond the bed, wide-eyed and startled as a fawn. It was Tabby.

Surprised, Silence stared at her. 'What are you doing in here? I thought you were all playing bowls.'

'Yes, we were — but Nat asked me to fetch something,' said Tabby.

It might have been a convincing explanation, if Nat had been in the habit of ordering his sisters to run errands for him. Tabby, praying that her mother would not notice the tray of purloined food and beer that she had hastily pushed under the bed, knew that it was a poor excuse, but could think of none better. Yet part of her wanted their secret to be discovered, wanted her mother to know that the man she loved, and thought beyond her reach, was hiding only a few feet above her head.

I can't, Tabby thought unhappily: we agreed not to tell her. She hated to deceive Silence, to whom she had always been very close. Nevertheless, her honesty told her, she herself had initiated that deception, when she had written to James Hellier, in Worcester.

'What's going on, Tabby?' Her mother's voice was quiet and resigned. '*Something* is — I've seen Deb and William hiding food, and Kate said she had a nice secret. What's happening? Can you tell me?'

Tabby swallowed painfully, her heart banging against her ribs. She was beginning to realise that it was not a game. If — *if* — the man above them, the ridiculous Mervyn Touchet, was in fact the

King, then the penalties for harbouring him were very severe. She thought that they would do nothing to her, or the younger ones, if they were discovered. It would certainly be unpleasant, but they would suffer no serious or lasting punishment. If it could be proved, however, that Silence, or even Nat, were involved, then fines, disgrace, imprisonment must surely follow.

No, Tabby thought, with a new and desperate maturity. No, this is not a game, but only the children can play it. She said softly, 'I'm sorry, Mother, but I don't really know. It's something to do with the shelter in the woods, I think, but I'm not sure. I don't think there's any harm in it, though.'

For a long moment, their eyes, such a similar hazel, stared at each other. Then, Silence smiled. 'Good. I don't mind if there's no harm in it, but tell Deb that stealing a whole cheese is perhaps a *little* excessive.'

Tabby's grin, bright and vivid with relief, flashed at her. 'I'll certainly tell her. It's only a silly game, after all. Thank you, Mother.'

Silence gave her another long, careful look. Then she said, 'That's all right, then. Remind William and Deb, when you go down again, that it's time for their bed, will you? And then, perhaps, the rest of you can come up to my chamber, and you can play. You haven't practised today.'

'Nor I have,' said Tabby, surprised. There had been other matters occupying her mind, and her beloved virginals had, for once, been neglected. Perhaps, if she played loudly enough, Captain Hellier would hear her. She grinned happily. 'Yes, that would be lovely. I'll play something from that new book of dances that I bought in Bath.' She knew that she had not managed to allay her mother's suspicions, nor her curiosity, but for the moment she had got away with it.

'I'll see you in half an hour or so,' said Silence, smiling, and went out.

Tabby waited until her footsteps died away, and then pulled the tray out from under the bed. She brushed off the fluff, blew the dust away, and hurried into the closet to open the concealed door. At any minute, Nat might appear, and he, unlike his stepmother, was not to be fobbed off with transparently false excuses.

The man called Touchet was sleeping like a baby, peacefully lapped in blankets and the feather mattresses that she and Patience had hauled with such difficulty up those narrow little stairs. Nick

Hellier, however, was awake, lying on his back with his hands behind his head, watching the top of the stairs. He smiled at Tabby as she appeared, and sat up.

Very carefully, she set the tray down noiselessly on the platform, glanced at the sleeping Touchet, and whispered, 'Can I talk to you? About Mother?'

His eyes, that she had noticed from the first were like Kate's, opened very wide. He nodded, and very cautiously got to his feet, Touchet did not stir as he stepped carefully over him, and joined Tabby by the top of the stairs. He saw, with a pang, that she was now almost as tall as he was. Yet this willowy, lovely, resourceful girl was still the child he had known, and loved.

She sat down on the step, her back to Touchet, and he joined her. Below them, there was no sound, although he had heard voices, off and on, all through the afternoon. She said softly, 'Mother suspects something. She's just found me in Nat's chamber. I tried to give her a good explanation, but I don't think she believed me. At least she didn't see the tray, I managed to hide it. But she knows that Deb and William have been stealing food.' She grinned. 'So have I, but I took good care she didn't see me.'

'Thank you, Tabby,' he said. 'I don't know where we'd be without you – half-starved under a hedgerow, probably. Dear girl, what you have done may be praiseworthy – but is it wise?'

'They wouldn't do anything to me, or to the little ones,' she said stoutly. 'That's why we don't want to tell Mother, or Nat, isn't it? But I *want* to tell her, Captain Hellier – it would make her so *happy* if she knew you were here.'

There was a long pause. He stared at her intently, as if trying to ascertain the truth. Finally, he said softly, 'Would it? Would it really? Are you sure?'

'Of course it would,' said Tabby, astonished that he could ever doubt it. 'She's never said anything to me, but I – I *notice* things. I think I knew, even when I was little, that you loved her, and she loved you. And then there is Kate. She is yours, she must be, her birthday's in May.'

His heart leapt at her words. So his yearning hopes had not been purely the product of wishful thinking, and he had to smile at her practical analysis of a subject that most people would consider highly improper for a gently-bred young girl to know, let alone to discuss. She had been close to Nat, he remembered, and some of the boy's refreshing lack of hypocrisy and self-righteousness seemed to have rubbed off on his half-sister.

'That isn't necessarily so,' he reminded her. 'But at present it isn't so important. Are you sure that your mother will be glad to see me – even under these circumstances?'

'I *know* she will be,' said Tabby emphatically. 'When Master Wickham came here – when he spoke of you – I saw her face. She hasn't changed, Captain Hellier, even after all this time. She still loves you.'

Nick closed his eyes, afraid to let her see the overwhelming relief that must lie raw in his face. He did not doubt that she spoke the truth, as she saw it. She was intelligent, observant and sensitive. But would Silence welcome him as a dangerous and inconvenient fugitive, even if she did still love him? He did not want her joy to turn to anxiety, desperation, grief or anger. And yet the urge to see her once more was threatening to dissolve his usual common sense.

'It would make it much easier to bring you food, if she knew,' said Tabby slowly, evidently thinking aloud. 'And I think she would *want* to know. After all, it isn't as if she's not used to danger.'

'But this is different,' said Nick. His head was arguing against his heart, so far with indifferent success, for the power of emotions suppressed and denied for six years was coming to overwhelm all rational thought. 'If we are discovered . . .'

'We won't be,' said Tabby. 'Who'd suspect Colonel St. Barbe's family of harbouring two Cavaliers? Or even . . .'

Involuntarily, she turned to glance at Touchet, still enjoying the sleep of the just, and Nick seized his chance. He said softly, 'I'm sorry to disappoint you all, Tabby, but Mervyn Touchet, improbable though it might seem, is in fact only Mervyn Touchet.'

She produced a grin that was sharply reminiscent of Silence. 'It was silly of me to think that he was anyone else, really, wasn't it?'

'Not necessarily,' said Nick drily. 'You weren't the only one to make that particular mistake, unfortunately. In Bristol . . .'

The pause threatened to drag out for ever. Tabby, not liking the expression on his face, said hesitantly, 'What happened in Bristol?'

'I was recognised,' said Nick. His heart had begun to hammer out, slowly and strongly, the rhythm of approaching nemesis. 'I was recognised by someone who could link me with Wintercombe. It was later that they started to shout out that Touchet was the King . . . but the damage was done already.'

'Who? Who recognised you?' Tabby's voice had dropped to a hiss of urgency.

He said slowly, 'Leah Walker.'

'*Leah*? What was she doing in Bristol?' Tabby's eyes caught his, and she blushed suddenly. 'I do know. It's still talked about, in the village. I don't think her father and brother have ever forgotten or forgiven you – even though it wasn't your fault.' She frowned. 'I never did like her, even before she went with that . . . that dreadful man Ridgeley. She was always saying things that seemed amusing, and were actually quite cruel. And she had no morals at all.'

'Neither had the other maid . . . what was her name? Red-haired girl, was going to have my drunken lieutenant's bastard.' Briefly, he had forgotten that he was speaking to a sheltered, fifteen-year-old virgin.

The shy and sheltered child grinned, with no discernible embarrassment now. 'Bessie Lyteman. She had a little girl whom she called Mary. And last June she had *another* bastard, a boy this time. But I like her, she's still cheerful and jolly, even if Eliza does call her the village harlot. Lack of morals doesn't always mean that you have an unpleasant *character*, does it?'

'I hope not,' said Nick gravely.

Tabby caught his eye, and had to stifle a giggle. Then she added, abruptly serious, 'Do you think that Leah will tell the soldiers in Bristol that you might have come here?'

'I don't know. It doesn't seem very likely, to someone with no knowledge of the truth, that I would come here again, does it? On the face of it, we should be enemies. But they must have asked her how she knew me, and they might look here, if only because they have no other trail to follow.' He fell silent, thinking of the logical consequences. Soldiers hammering once more on the studded oaken door of Wintercombe, demanding to search it, frightening the children, upsetting and bewildering their mother. Did he really want Silence to endure that nightmare again?

But there was nothing he could do to prevent it. Even if he and Touchet left the house tonight, the soldiers might come tomorrow, or this week, or the next. It would depend on what Leah had told them, and how likely they thought the chance that the King was hidden at Wintercombe, and how desperate they were to catch him. He did not want Silence to discover, too late, that he had been hidden here, and yet made no effort to speak to her. That, he realised, would hurt her very deeply.

And if she knew that he was at Wintercombe, as Tabby had pointed out, their concealment became very much easier.

He came to the decision which he had wanted to make, and felt in his heart that he was right. Unless she had changed very much — and Tabby had said that she had not — she would be overjoyed to see him. And the Silence he had known would have dismissed the danger to herself, thinking only of her children's safety, and his own.

'She would rather know,' he said softly. 'You are right. It isn't fair to embroil her in this without her knowledge. We should go, as soon as possible — we must not be found here, for all your sakes. But I must see her, tonight. Is Mally still her maid?'

'She is,' said Tabby. 'She wouldn't give you away, ever. But in any case, you don't need to worry about her, because she isn't here. Her grandmother is ill, and Mother said that she could go and nurse her. She's been away for two or three days now, so Mother will be alone, after we've gone to bed.' She gave him a conspiratorial smile. 'Shall I tell her? Or do you want to surprise her?'

'I'll tell her,' said Nick. He felt suddenly ridiculously light-hearted. Tomorrow, the soldiers might come: tomorrow, they would have to leave Wintercombe, or risk discovery. The thought of resuming the dangers and difficulties of his travels should lie heavy on his mind, and yet he could dismiss it all utterly, so sudden and glorious was the knowledge that he would see her tonight.

Tomorrow was another day, another time, another place. This night, he would see Silence, and all the years of emptiness and longing had coalesced into a desire that burned him to his soul. Even if the worst happened, he had been granted this one dispensation, this one chance to snatch at happiness. And this time, he would not turn it aside. He might have no future beyond tonight, but tonight was all that he wanted.

PART
III

THE GALLANT CHILD

(September, 1651 – June, 1652)

CHAPTER FIFTEEN

'Night and silence'
(*A Midsummer Night's Dream*)

Wintercombe had settled into its night-time quiet, the children's voices stilled into slumber, the virginals at peace. Silence paused by the keyboard, and pressed with an exploratory finger. A small sharp sound, bearing no resemblance whatsoever to the glorious flood of music that Tabby could unleash from this same instrument, was her only reward. Silence smiled sadly. She had no such ability, she could not even sing in tune. Her daughter's gift for such things was unexpected, and yet not really surprising. These virginals had belonged to Tabby's grandfather, Sir Samuel St. Barbe, and it must be his love for all kinds of music that she had inherited.

A cold breeze whispered in through the open window, and she moved to close it. September was more than half over, and the air smelt of autumn. It was a season she loved, all smoke and colour and sudden frost, with the store-cupboards full, the harvest gathered and the house provisioned and snug, ready for the winter. A time to reflect, to take stock of the past year, and to look ahead to the next.

But this year had not given: it had taken away. She was a widow now, had been so for four months, and, she realised guiltily, not for one day of that time, not one hour or one minute, had she missed her husband, or mourned for him. Neither, she suspected, had her children, with the exception of Rachael. Instead, they had blossomed after his death.

She found that she could now think of George without anger. Her chief emotion was pity, for a man who had been so singularly unable to command affection from those closest to him. His friends, in Somerset and Wiltshire and in the army, had held him in the highest regard, but his family seemed the happier for his passing. Like her own father, he had demanded their love and respect with an imperious tyranny that had obliterated any such feelings.

Now he was dead, and she was free: but it was an empty freedom. She had her children, she had Wintercombe, but somehow her life lacked flavour, like meat without salt and sea-soning: flat, pleasant, but very bland. She wanted the moon, and she knew it, and could even smile at her presumption.

But that did not diminish her desire, did not stop the despair she felt sometimes, late at night, when her bed seemed so wide and empty and somehow threatening, and even the generous, uncon-ditional affection of Lily and Misty was not sufficient. Like Kate and the parrot, she wanted something which she could not have. And unlike Kate, she had no kind benefactor to speak the magic spell and give her her heart's desire. She could only draw up all her strength, take comfort in the past, and endure this eternal pain until one day, as it surely must, it faded away.

A breath of chill air coiled round her face, and lifted the hairs on her neck. She shivered suddenly, and drew the curtains. Foolish to leave the window open for so long, but she loved to listen to the night-time noises, the owls in the orchard, the wind sighing soft round the house. Eliza had lit the fire before retiring, but she had no one to help her undress, to talk to her of the day's events, and to keep her thoughts at bay with her companionship. She had let Mally go to nurse her grandmother willingly, knowing how much it meant to her maid, who had already lost her father, grandfather and stepmother, but she missed her cheerful presence. Mally could always put her darker feelings in perspective.

Lily whined softly, and then growled very low, deep in her throat. Silence turned, puzzled. 'What is it, Lily? Ssh, don't be silly, there's no one there.'

But there was.

Her heart seemed to stop. Someone was standing in the doorway to Mally's closet, clearly outlined against the very dim light behind him. There was a single three-branched candlestick lit, on the table by the east windows, and she could see only that the figure was male, and lightly built.

Once, she would have known him anywhere. Once, she would have followed him to the ends of the earth, and had been rejected with love, for their love's sake. Now, so unbelievable was this apparition, this revenant, that she closed her eyes, afraid to open them again lest he prove an illusion, brought to spurious life by her hopeless longing.

Lily growled again, but more questioningly, and she could hear the little dog sniffing the air, trying to identify this mysterious intruder. And, no illusion, he said softly, 'Silence?'

She opened her eyes. He had come forward, into the light. Lily was watching him warily from a distance, obviously beset by remote memories. Silence stared at him, unable to believe what she saw, that the man she had once loved so much had at last returned to her, as if she were a sorceress able to conjure up his presence from desire.

He looked older, harder than the laughing, reckless, loving Nick whom she remembered so vividly. The heavy growth of beard could not disguise the lines around his mouth, nor the shadows of strain and exhaustion under his eyes. Then he seemed suddenly uncertain, as if he did not know what her reaction would be, as if he feared it . . .

'Nick?' she whispered, incredulous, feeling the joy beginning to run free in her, spilling over in a glorious unstoppable flood. 'Is it – is it really you?'

'It's not likely to be anyone else, I hope,' he said, with the dry understated humour that she had always loved in him. She found, to her surprise, tears beginning to fill her eyes, and at the same time laughter welled up from within. She did not remember moving, and yet she was suddenly in his arms, sobbing, while his hands stroked her hair, wiped away the tears and turned her face towards him for his kiss.

Then there was no more need of words. Long hunger, long denial had made them both desperate with yearning. She had thought, once, that she could well remember the passion they had so briefly shared. Yet that memory was but a pale wraith beside the suffocating, overwhelming, devastating reality. They clung together as if drowning, shaken to the heart by the force that consumed them both alike. Without making any conscious decision, she found that they had moved to the bed. And any last spark of conscience, or guilt, or Puritan morality, vanished into the incandescent glory of desire.

It did not take long. With frantic urgency, their hands explored each other, renewing old feelings, old memories, and their bodies fitted together as if sprung from one molten mould. The heat and the tension soared to almost impossible heights, to an explosion of sensation that came to them simultaneously, and left her weak, shaking, sobbing with breathless laughter and tears.

They had not, she realised, even managed to take their clothes off.

'Crying?' said Nick. He leaned on one elbow, and traced the

[291]

path of a tear. 'Why are you crying? Surely I haven't lost my touch?'

It was, she realised, as if they had never been parted: as if those six long and empty years had never intervened. Perhaps if they had talked, instead of embracing, it would have been different, less easy, more constrained. But in the aftermath of such lovemaking, there could only be joy, and the truth.

'You haven't,' she said. 'Oh, no, my dearest love, you surely have not. But . . . oh, I'm just so *glad*, so very very *glad* . . . I thought you were gone for ever, I thought you might be dead.'

'I don't think I am,' he told her gravely. 'Though I won't deny, I've come quite near to it once or twice of late.' He paused, his eyes searching her face: Kate's eyes, but older, wiser, yet no less mischievous. 'You are singularly lacking in questions, my herald of joy. Aren't you even going to ask me what I'm doing here?'

'You haven't exactly given me much opportunity to ask you,' Silence pointed out. She pushed the tears away with an impatient hand, thinking that she ought to be regretting her impetuous action, which might well produce a result that could not be so readily explained away as Kate.

Kate. She must tell him. There were so many things, suddenly, that she wanted to ask. She said slowly, 'Well, what *are* you doing here?'

'You won't like my answer,' he told her. 'I'm sorry, my love – I've put you in danger by coming here. But at the time, there didn't seem to be any alternative.'

'In danger? Are you being hunted?' She sat up, found her bodice sliding down to her waist, saw his expression and began to laugh. 'Oh, Nick, Nick – at this moment, I don't care if the hounds of Hell are on your trail, I don't *care* – just to see you, to touch you –' She pulled up her bodice, and Nick promptly reversed her action. They wrestled playfully for a moment, breathless and laughing, before he managed to remove the disputed garment altogether. Then, he pulled her close and kissed her. She laid her head on his shoulder, feeling the warmth of reality beneath the rough linen of his shirt, the firm steady beat of his heart, the arms encircling her. An hour ago, less, she had been thinking of him with hopeless longing, knowing he was forever denied her. And now, beyond all belief, beyond all hope, she lay here in his arms, and her yearning was for the moment assuaged.

'I am here by invitation,' he said, so quietly that for a moment she wondered if she had misheard him. As his words struck home, she tried to sit up, and was pulled back with gentle ruthlessness. 'Invitation?' she said, in astonishment. 'Whose?'

'Tabby's,' he said.

Completely bewildered, she stared at him. 'Tabby? *Tabby* invited you here? *How*?'

'I'll tell you, but it's a very long story. Are you sleepy?' She shook her head, and he smiled, the long lazy grin that she remembered so well. 'Shame on you – you ought to be, after what we've just done. And you may not want to laugh,' said Nick, suddenly and extremely serious, his eyes searching her face. 'I should not have come here, for you, and Wintercombe, may be in danger.'

He told her of the battle at Worcester, and about Tabby's letter, which had informed him of Sir George's death. She listened with disbelief and indignation to the tale of his misadventures with Mervyn Touchet, at present sleeping in the roofspace above her hall, and with alarm to his encounter in Bristol with Leah Walker. Six years ago, she had dismissed the girl from her service for fornication with the dreadful Colonel Ridgeley, and she could understand Nick's fear that, because of Leah, Wintercombe might now be searched. But she could still hardly believe that such malice might still fester, so long after Leah's enforced departure.

'She certainly has no love for me,' said Nick ruefully. 'Nor would you readily recognise her – she has succumbed to the usual hazards of her trade. If I stood in no danger from her spite, I might even be tempted to feel sorry for her.'

'I don't – she has brought it upon herself,' said Silence, hearing the ghost of her stern and implacable father speaking. She added, unwilling to think of Leah and her treachery, 'What happened after you left Bristol – in something of a hurry, I should imagine?'

'No, at a decorous walk, or we'd have aroused even more suspicion. Touchet is very tall, and distinctive in appearance – no wonder they thought that he was the King. So did Tabby, to start with. It took her a little while to recognise me – I had to prompt her before she realised who I was.'

'I'm not surprised, with that growth of beard – it makes you look quite different.' Silence trailed her finger over the harsh bristles, feeling the sharp lines of the bones beneath. She added, 'How did you meet Tabby, then? Were you making for Wintercombe?'

'Yes, we were. Touchet wanted to sleep in comfort instead of under a hedge, and it was plain we wouldn't get very far – no food, filthy clothes, on foot, wet through – we looked like beggars,' Nick said, with a faint and reminiscent grin. 'I'm sorry, sweet Silence – we should never have come here.'

'Don't say that!' Her voice was suddenly fierce, and anything but sweet. 'I told you, I don't *care*! You don't know how it has been, without you – how wonderful it is, to see you and touch you and speak with you again.'

'Oh, but I do,' said Nick softly, and the remembered pain in his eyes told her that he spoke the truth. 'My herald of joy, I do. And in the end, when the chance offered, I found that I could not bear to keep away. Even if I have to leave tomorrow – and I may – we have still had this night.' He hesitated, and then added, 'Even after what Tabby told me – and she knows about us, she wanted me to come here, so if any blame is to be apportioned, then she must share in it – even after that, I wasn't sure. I thought that you might have wanted to forget the past.'

'Never,' she said, shaking her head. 'Never, never, never. It gave me the strength to – to survive, afterwards. But *Tabby* . . . I never dreamt she'd try to find you.'

'She was lucky,' Nick told her. 'If her letter had reached my brother just a little later, I would already have fled Worcester – and doubtless be sleeping at this very moment under some hedge, or in a barn, in the belief that Wintercombe, and you, were forever denied me.' He stretched luxuriously. 'I am very grateful to your Tabby.'

'So am I,' said Silence. 'But you still haven't said how you came to be here – how you managed to enter the house without anyone knowing.'

He told her, and she listened in astonishment to the tale of her children's conspiracy, the shelter in the woods, and, with rising disbelief, the involvement of Patience.

'Your little sister,' said Nick, amusement colouring his deep voice, 'is quite a surprise. She's not very like you, is she?'

'She lacks common sense,' said Silence, unable to suppress a smile. 'And suffers from at least one of the deadly sins.'

'Which one? Vanity?'

'How did you guess? She has set all of Philip's Norton by the ears, and flirts shamelessly with every man she encounters. Did she flutter her eyelashes at you?'

'No. She was too busy looking at Touchet. I think, like every-one else, she hoped that he might be the King. I've told Tabby that he isn't – he is very aristocratic and exquisite, to the point of imbecility at times, and an earl's son, so it's an understandable mistake.' He grinned. 'And because of his complete disdain for the proper precautions, it's a miracle we ever reached here safely. The militia of three counties must be hunting for us.'

'And will doubtless be knocking on the door tomorrow,' said Silence. 'But even if Leah does prompt them to seek you here, surely no one with any local knowledge will believe we could be hiding you. They'd think we'd denounce any Cavaliers as soon as they came to the door. The idea that you could take refuge at Wintercombe would seem unthinkable. I'm sure you're in no danger – and that's not just wishful thinking, that's my own common sense speaking.'

'Then you are willing to hide us?'

'Of course I am – *more* than willing, glad, eager – it's danger-ous, I know, but I have faced worse, and survived. After Ridgeley, the might of the New Model Army doesn't seem very menacing.' She smiled into his eyes. 'And the two of us can surely curb any recklessness and lunacy to which my dear little sister and your companion may be tempted. Now, for the final time, will you please tell me how you were smuggled in?'

She listened with reluctant admiration, as he described how Patience had boldly and openly brought two escaped Cavaliers into this ostensibly Roundhead house. She had already guessed that they must be hidden in the roof, for it was the obvious, indeed the only place at Wintercombe in which to conceal hunted men. But a thorough search was bound to find them. If the worst happened, and soldiers did come looking for the man believed to be the King of Scots, the only hope was, somehow, to allay their suspicions. If knowledge of the fugitives was limited to herself and her family, the task would be much easier.

'Nat should know,' she said, when he had finished, with a lyrical description of Touchet, wrapped in warm blankets, catching up on several nights of lost sleep. 'He has the most devious brain of us all – if there is any danger, he could disarm suspicion so much more effectively. And you need have no fear – he won't mind, he'll welcome you gladly. He has always spoken of you with affection and respect, and he'll be so pleased to see you again. But Rachael . . . '

[295]

'The children said that she was to be married to a man called Jack . . . Harrison?'

'Harington. A truer Presbyterian never breathed – *and* he used to be a captain in the army. Poor Rachael is so confused – she hasn't changed, not *really*, though she has done her best to be a dutiful daughter to her father. When he died, she seized on the marriage because she knew it fulfilled his dearest wish. But sometimes I wonder if, in her heart of hearts, she really wants to marry Jack. He is a worthy boy, but very serious, even dull, and rather self-righteous, and although it's a very good match – his father's one of the foremost gentry hereabouts – I think she has doubts.'

'And what do you think?'

'I think she wouldn't be happy for a week,' said Silence bluntly. 'But there is nothing I can do – I'm sure you can remember what Rachael is like.'

'I certainly can,' said Nick, with an all too vivid picture of the adolescent Rachael, fierce, uncompromising and awkward, filling his mind. If she had indeed not changed, and was betrothed to this rampant Presbyterian into the bargain, then it was imperative that she knew nothing about the men concealed in the attics.

He said as much, and Silence nodded in agreement. 'I think it's wise. I know she once had a fondness for you, calf-love I suppose, but she is so volatile, you would never be able to predict her reactions. She has been at loggerheads with Nat, hardly deigning to notice him – I suppose he must have spoken his mind about Jack. I could see her altering her allegiance, from St. Barbe to Harington, little by little, day by day – and the episode of the parrot was the final straw.'

'The parrot? Tabby did say something about one, in her letter.'

'Kate's parrot, at present sleeping in its cage over there. Nat and Patience and Tabby bought it for her, from a man in Bath Market, and it swears like a Cavalier and denounces all Puritans.'

'I don't believe it,' said Nick, entertained. 'What do all your godly neighbours think of it?'

'Well, the Haringtons were not impressed. We have to keep the cage covered whenever Jack visits, in case it tells him to bugger off again.'

She stopped, for Nick had rolled over and buried his face in his hands, shaking with helpless laughter. His voice came, rather muffled. 'My God – I do wish I'd seen it. A sight for sore eyes, I should think.'

'It was.' She hesitated, and then put a hand on his shoulder. 'Nick – I must tell you something.'

The seriousness in her tone alerted him. He turned and sat up, his hair tangled round his face, staring at her, still flushed with laughter. 'Tell away, sweet Silence.'

She swallowed, and said, her voice low, 'It's about Kate.' Astonishing how difficult this was, to speak the truth. What would be his reaction to the news that he had a bastard daughter, and one, moreover, whom many might think disgracefully wayward and naughty?

She need not have worried. He smiled suddenly, in pure delight. 'Don't look so anxious. Are you trying to tell me that she is mine?'

Silence nodded, not trusting herself to speak. A lump had appeared in her throat from nowhere, and her nose was beginning to run.

'I guessed when I first saw her,' he said. 'The eyes give it away, don't they? But I thought it might be my own hopes deceiving me, until Tabby told me outright, a few hours ago. There's not much that escapes that daughter of yours. My love, Kate is adorable, a child of whom any man could be proud . . . why, oh why, are you crying?'

Silence had been struggling furiously against the tide of emotion that threatened to engulf her. Why now, she told herself fiercely, why weaken now when the moon is within your grasp?

Because it never had been: because, she knew in her heart, all this was an illusion, tempting and glorious, promising a future that could never exist. She mastered herself, and sat up, forcing calmness into her face and her voice. Her answer, when it came, was very quiet and level. 'She is your child – but she thinks her father was my husband, as did he, and they loved each other dearly. And whatever happens in the future, she will never know she is yours – you can never take your rightful place in her heart.'

'Why not?'

She shook her head impatiently. 'You know very well why not. Your wife . . '

'My *wife*? Oh, Christ,' he said savagely. 'Oh, Christ, I had forgotten all about that.'

'Forgotten you had a wife?' She stared at him in disbelief, her hazel eyes very wide, and from somewhere forced a smile. 'Oh, Nick, that is somewhat careless of you.'

'It's nothing to laugh about . . . my love, I have a confession to make. I don't know if you will be glad, or angry, to hear it – I can only ask your forgiveness. I lied to you.'

'You lied?' Deep inside, a small sudden spark of hope had sprung to life. She tried to ignore it, and added quietly, 'What did you lie about?'

'About my wife.' He took a deep breath, his gaze steady on her face. 'I have never had one.'

Incredulous, astonished, she stared at him. 'But you told me – '

'I know. It was a lie, all of it. I described my brother's wife Jane, and his children. I thought – forgive me, my love, but I thought it would make it easier for us to part.'

'Why – why did you want it to be easy?' She found that she was shaking with an emotion which she recognised as anger. 'Why did you lie, Nick, why, *why*? All this time, I thought there was no hope – even when George died, I knew there was none – and now you tell me you lied, you've never been married – *why*?'

'You wanted to leave your husband and children, and come away with me,' he told her. 'And I knew it wouldn't work – you would be miserable, in poverty and exile, missing your children, missing Wintercombe – and I did not think I could bear it, if you ever came to regret your decision, and perhaps even to resent me. And there would have been no going back, ever.'

In her heart, she knew that he was right, but it did not lessen the hurt, or the renewed impact of all the unnecessary years of pain and loss. She said, 'I suspected that I was with child. That was why I asked you to take me with you – because I knew I would lose Wintercombe and the children anyway, because of my adultery.'

'Oh, Silence,' he said, and pulled her into his arms, feeling her body trembling beneath his hands. 'Oh, my love, if I had known – if only I had known.'

'And I didn't tell you,' she said, her voice muffled in his shoulder. 'I didn't tell you, because I thought it would make it worse for you.' The absurdity of it struck her suddenly, and she struggled upright, a wan smile lurking behind the tears. 'But it all came right in the end – because it was George who was waiting outside the gate, to take his house back, and I was able to make him think the baby was his. He was so pleased . . . he never thought, it was so easy, he never dreamt it could be another man's – he never thought me anything other than a virtuous wife, right to the end. Master Harley had to persuade him to make provision for me in his will if I should marry again, the idea obviously hadn't entered his

[298]

head – and even though Kate was a girl, he doted on her . . . ' She smiled rather shakily. 'Poor George . . . I duped him so thoroughly, without a qualm, for the children's sake as much as my own . . . and he never knew.'

'Much, much better that he did not – think of the grief that it would have caused him, the children, everyone, not least yourself, if he had found out.' Nick set his hands on her shoulders and stared into her eyes. 'You cannot surely feel guilty about that.'

'You're right, I don't. And I am being very foolish – we are talking about what happened six years ago, and we can hardly alter it – no use a-crying after the milk be spilled, as Doraty would say. The future is what should concern us.'

'The immediate future? Or do you wish me to take a slightly longer view?' Nick's hands tightened on her shoulders. 'My sweet Silence, my perfectest herald of joy – the fact that I do not at present have a wife, does not imply that I do not want one. I want you.'

Her mouth had gone dry, and her voice sounded strange. 'What did you say?'

'You heard me,' he said, grinning. 'If ever I should come safe through this present coil, and find myself able to show myself at Wintercombe without fear of arrest . . . Silence, all I have ever wanted is you – I want to marry you.'

The moon was in her grasp after all. Hardly able to believe it, she stared at him. 'Do you? Do you really?'

'Of course I do,' he said, with some impatience. 'Dear fool, of course I do – I have spent the last six years aimlessly and fruitlessly wandering this earth, and I have met nothing and no one to compare with you – all I want is to marry you, and settle down with you and the children, and perhaps breed one or two more if we are not too late – I'll warn you now, I have no money, we won't be rich, but I'm not ashamed to live off your jointure – pride has never been one of my sins. Will you? Will you cast caution to the winds again, and make an honest man of me?'

She kept him waiting, teasing gently, though her answer was plain in her eyes. At last, when it was obvious he could bear the suspense no longer, she smiled, and drew his face close for her kiss. 'How could you doubt me?' she said softly. 'With all my heart, I love you. And if we could, I would marry you tomorrow.'

'I would agree wholeheartedly with that. Let us hope that my aristocratic friend in the roofspace has learned some sense and discretion over the past weeks,' said Nick, unable to keep his delight from his face, despite the seriousness of his thought. 'If he has, the two of us will make our way to London, lie low for a while, and then I will come back openly. If Tom Wickham has been here without questions being asked, then I can too. I am not important enough to be a danger, to be locked up with all the other lords and generals they took off to the Tower.' He smiled at her. 'Perhaps we will be allowed to have our hearts' desire after all. It depends upon Leah Walker, perhaps – and on Touchet.'

'Let us pray that he has learned his lesson,' Silence said, feeling a swift surge of anger against the man who might hold their fate, their happiness in his hand, and yet seemed so careless of what he did. 'For I don't think I could ever forgive anyone who destroyed our future now, not when it is so nearly within our grasp.'

*

Much, much later, when the little clock on her table showed an impossible hour, when they had made love again, for longer, more leisurely and tender and yet no less passionate or spectacular in the conclusion, he left her lying sleepily in the wide bed with its heavy green curtains, and crept back up the narrow secret stairs to his hiding-place in the loft. She listened to his departing footsteps, and stretched as lazily and luxuriously as a cat, drowsy and sated with love.

It did not seem possible, that he had come back to her: still less likely, that he would be free, and desire her to marry him. That was something so glorious, so wonderful, that it seemed to be part of a dream. Yet this superbly glowing, fulfilled feeling was real, and the hollow that his head had made in the pillow, and the warmth his body had left, close by her beneath the blankets.

She closed her eyes, shivering with happiness. She had not cared, six years ago, that he was a penniless soldier of fortune: she did not care now. She smiled wryly at the fact that George and Master Harley had ensured, for quite different reasons, that she had enough money to support them both in a little comfort, and perhaps the children as well. Her mind wandered forward, hovering on the edge of sleep. They could live at Wintercombe – or, if Nat ever married, they might move to Chard, where she could remake the garden, and transform the dark, gloomy old house with love and laughter.

If. It was unlucky to count chickens, she reminded herself

sternly. She must not look too far ahead, must not take their happiness for granted, when there was so much risk, so many chances that it could all go tragically wrong. Bad luck, malice, betrayal, stupidity, foolhardiness, could wreck everything still. She had learned long ago not to hope for too much, for life had never treated her very kindly. It would be entirely in keeping for her to believe now that her wildest dreams were about to come true, only to have her happiness snatched brutally away at the last minute.

But she could not keep from smiling, as she drifted at last into sleep.

*

'Nat? Can I speak with you for a moment?'

Her stepson looked up from the papers on his desk in the study. It was a dark and gloomy morning, with rain falling heavily in contrast to the fine evening of the previous day, and he had pushed the table over to the window to take advantage of the light. He smiled, in a rather preoccupied way. 'Yes, of course – so long as it won't take all day.'

'It won't,' said Silence, coming to stand beside him. He was adding the previous day's purchases in Bath to the accounts, and she watched as his swift clear hand set the next item down. 'Lump sugar, 20 pounds and a half, one pound six shillings.' Wondering how she could broach her subject, she said drily, 'No wonder Deb always seems to have the toothache, she eats so much sugar.'

'I thought it turned teeth black – I didn't know it made them ache as well.' Nat put his quill back into the inkwell, sat back and surveyed his stepmother with amused affection. 'But you didn't come here to discuss Deb's eating habits, I feel sure – gross though they are. What do you want to talk about? And why are you looking as if there's a candle lit inside you?'

She had not realised that the wonder of last night still showed so clearly. She realised that she was blushing. She said very quietly, 'Something has happened, and I was only told about it last night. I thought you ought to know too – there may be danger involved.'

'Danger?' Nat's blue eyes gleamed suddenly. 'Don't tell me – we now have a regiment of Cavaliers hiding in the stables.'

Silence swallowed the impulse to laugh. She said, 'Very nearly. Two, in the roofspace.'

It was suddenly extremely quiet. Nat stared up at her. 'Say that again.'

'There are two Cavaliers hiding in the roofspace above the hall. They've been there since yesterday.'

'That's what I thought you said. How did they get there?'

'Patience and Tabby and the children smuggled them in.'

For a moment longer he stared at her, while she wondered in panic whether, even after all their years of friendship, she had misjudged his reaction. Then, suddenly, he broke into genuine laughter. 'Patience? And Tabby? No, no, you're gulling me, you must be. *Patience*? She thinks of nothing beyond her own skin.'

'On the contrary, she's a seasoned plotter,' said Silence, and told him why her sister had been removed from London.

Nat listened with interest, his mouth quirking in amusement. 'Well, well – I would never have suspected it. So I suppose when these two Cavaliers presented themselves, she thought it only right and proper to assist them? And what in God's name were they doing at Wintercombe in the first place? We're a long way from Worcester, not to mention Scotland.'

She could not remember hearing Nat take the name of the Lord in vain before. She could only stare at him, rather shocked, while he studied her betrayingly fiery face in return, and then smiled. It was a warm, friendly and entirely affectionate expression. He said, very softly, 'And is one of those Cavaliers by any chance Captain Nicholas Hellier?'

She had never been able to deceive him, even when he was a small child. Smiling ruefully, she nodded. 'How did you guess?'

'It wasn't difficult. I could see something different in your face, as soon as you came downstairs this morning, and that in itself set me wondering . . . and combine that with two Cavaliers, at Wintercombe, and I was able to put two and two together. I'm very glad for you,' Nat said, leaning back in his chair. 'But what are we going to do with them?'

'I was hoping that you would be able to help us,' Silence told him. She explained about Leah Walker in Bristol, and about Touchet's apparent resemblance to the King. 'Nick said there would be danger, but I'm not so sure. Even if Leah told the soldiers where she had known him before, they would hardly think it likely that he would come back here, where he was the enemy.' She smiled. 'Only a few people know that the reality was very different.'

'Including Leah?' Nat gazed at her thoughtfully. 'I can't remember what happened to her — I know you dismissed her, but I can't recall when it was.'

'I sent her packing, the day that Ridgeley was killed. She couldn't possibly know about me and Nick — I didn't myself, then. In fact, I don't think she even realised that he'd played a part in Ridgeley's death. She *can't* be a danger, Nat, she *can't*.'

'I tend to agree with you,' said her stepson. 'But if you can always prepare for the worst, it won't happen. Since they can hardly expect us to shelter them indefinitely, they must have plans. Where do they want to go?'

'London, or so Nick said. I know it sounds risky, but they would be safer there than anywhere else, unless in France or the Low Countries. And when the hunt is over, when the country is quiet again . . . ' She paused, her eyes on Nat's face, wondering if this would sound absurd and unbelievable to his practical, cynical mind. 'He wants to come back openly, and marry me.'

'And about time too,' said Nat, grinning. While she was still absorbing the implications of his reaction, he added, 'But I thought — didn't you say he already had a wife?'

'It was . . . a misunderstanding,' said Silence, unwilling to explain, even to Nat, Nick's reasons for misleading her. It all looked so ridiculous in the clear light of day, and her present happiness. Besides, she did not want to admit how nearly, six years ago, she had come to deserting Wintercombe and her children.

He looked at her rather sharply, but said mildly, 'A rather considerable misunderstanding . . . are you sure he hasn't got a wife tucked away somewhere?'

'Quite sure,' said Silence firmly. 'Nat . . . do you disapprove?'

He gave a shout of laughter, and leapt to his feet. With astonishment, she found herself being comprehensively embraced. 'Do I disapprove?' he demanded, looking at her with that quizzical expression which Mally would doubtless describe as 'old-fashioned'. 'Oh, my dear Silence, I thought you knew me better than that! I am delighted — after all this time, it's like a miracle — but,' said Nat, descending abruptly from his congratulatory mood, 'there is a great deal of water to flow under that bridge, before it can be crossed. If they are to reach London safely, they must have clothes, baggage, money, horses — all of which we can supply. You will have to feed them while they're here, and make sure none of the servants finds out. And make sure, too, that Kate doesn't prattle.'

'She already has done,' said Silence. 'Fortunately, so far as I know, just to me. But I will have a long and serious talk with all the children — and Patience. I think the younger ones treat it as a game — and it's rather more than that.' She smiled. 'And certainly, they should be more discreet about purloining food.'

'Ah, you noticed that. As much vanished into Deb's apron pocket last night at supper, as went in her mouth. I wouldn't like the task of washing out that apron — or William's pockets, either.'

'I'll have to find a more reliable way of feeding our uninvited guests,' Silence said. She paused, and then added slowly, 'Nat . . . is this as foolhardy and dangerous as it seems to me now, in the clear cold light of day? Or am I seeing obstacles and risks where none exist?'

'Perhaps,' he said thoughtfully. 'But if we are sensible, and discreet, and plan our strategy carefully, there need not be any great danger involved. The fact that this household would prob-ably be regarded by most people as being above suspicion must help us. But the quicker we make everything clear to the children, and Patience, the better . . . where are they all now?'

'In my chamber, doing their lessons. Rachael is in her chamber, sulking — she wanted to visit Nell Apprice this morning, but the weather intervened.'

'Then I hope she stays there, for the present. I don't think Rachael need know of this at all,' Nat said, and in his voice, stripped of its usual dry light cynicism, there was a note of sadness, and regret. 'She is my twin, we were born in the same hour, and yet now I don't seem to know her at all . . . it's as if she was a stranger with Rachael's face. I've tried, but I can't reach her any more. And . . . it hurts me to say it, but if she should ever find out about Nick and this other man, I think she might do something we would all regret — and herself most of all, in the end.'

The word 'betrayal' hung in the air, unsaid, and yet as plain as if he had uttered it. Silence shivered suddenly. Six years previously Rachael had shot and wounded the terrible Ridgeley, with his own pistol. The girl who had once attempted murder would be quite capable, if her motive were strong enough, of giving away the hiding-place of two Cavaliers. And no doubt, as had happened after her attack on Ridgeley, she would regret what she had done, most bitterly.

No, Rachael must never know the secret. Silence thought with grief of her stepdaughter, seemingly condemned to be forever the outsider, the misfit, lonely and friendless. And yet, how much of her present unhappiness was her own fault?

'If *only* we could persuade her not to marry Jack,' she said despairingly. 'She'll be miserable as Mistress Harington, I know she will – and yet there is nothing we can do.'

'It doesn't matter about the dowry,' said Nat. 'Lands can be sold, if necessary, to provide her with another. Harley does not seem to think that there can be any objection, and my inheritance is sufficiently wealthy to bear the burden. But short of force, and that would do more damage than letting the betrothal continue, there doesn't seem to be anything that will discourage either side. If even the parrot didn't work – and I won't deny, I had some hopes of it – then we are powerless.' He smiled wryly. 'Let us pray that, like so many other things, she does not regret her marriage when it is too late. Well, since all the other conspirators seem to be gathered conveniently in one place, shall we go talk to them?'

Since Silence's chamber occupied the whole of the upper, eastern part of the house, and was reached only by its own stair, there was little chance of a family discussion being overheard. She climbed the stone steps with Nat, listening with amusement to sounds which indicated that quiet study was not taking place on the other side of the door. A bright dance tune came sparkling from the virginals, and there was much laughter and tramping of feet, interspersed with Lily's high-pitched yelps of excitement.

Silence, smoothing her face into as severe an expression as she could muster, flung open the door. The music stopped abruptly, and she stared at the frozen tableau before her, hoping that she would not spoil the effect by laughing. Tabby, of course, sat at the keyboard, and Patience was clutching the hand of a scarlet-cheeked, rather sheepish William. Kate, with her brilliant, three-cornered smile, clasped her dancing-partner, Deb. A chair had been overturned, the window-cushions were all on the floor, and a large chunk of Mendip coal had fallen unnoticed out of the hearth, and was smouldering balefully on the rush matting in front of the fire.

Lily, the only one lacking a guilty conscience, came bouncing up, wagging her thin curled tail in welcome. Nat brushed past her and kicked the offending coal briskly back into the flames. Silence said sternly, 'I would not describe this as a little quiet study.'

'I was teaching them a dance,' Patience explained, quite unabashed. She looked delightfully pretty, her face flushed, her dark eyes bright with merriment and her hair in some disorder. 'Don't worry, it's quite decorous really.'

'It didn't sound very decorous,' said her sister, finally losing her battle with the amusement bubbling within her. 'And how did you learn to dance? I hardly think it was one of Joseph's preferred accomplishments for a modest and godly young woman.'

'My friend Ruth taught me – her stepfather engaged a dancing master for her,' said Patience blithely, though a note of defiance had crept into her voice. 'He thought it was admirable exercise for young ladies, and gentlemen, making the body active and strong and graceful.'

'You don't need to justify yourself to me, my dear Impatience,' said Nat, grinning. 'Unlike your brother, I wouldn't care if you danced naked in the churchyard on a Sabbath.'

'Nat!' said Silence. Her amusement was not helping her attempts to sound stern and shocked, and the scandalised, delighted giggles of the children were making matters worse. Only Tabby was sitting still and quiet, her expression alert and thoughtful as she stared at her half-brother.

'In September? Too cold for me – and wet,' said Patience, rising to Nat's bait with bright-eyed enthusiasm. 'But I understand the ladies of ancient Greece and Rome wore very little, though in hotter climes than this.'

'Really?' said Nat, though he must have been aware of it. 'I had considered visiting Italy – perhaps you would like to accompany me. After proper thought and due preparation, of course.'

Silence, aware suddenly that there were undercurrents to this conversation which muddied still further the turbulent waters of her household, said firmly, 'Nat – can I remind you of our reason for coming up here?'

'Of course,' her stepson said, entirely unrepentant. He glanced round at the laughing, flushed faces of his half-brother and sisters, and added, in a very different tone, 'Come and sit by the fire, all of you. Your mother and I wish to talk to you, on a matter of very great importance.'

Nat was so rarely entirely serious that the children sobered at once. They exchanged glances, and Silence, watching them, saw their happy mood drain away abruptly into anxious guilt. Even Deb seemed suddenly solemn, without the expression of bare-faced innocence which she habitually adopted when accused of wrong-doing. William walked over to the hearth and sat down on a stool, all his exuberance vanished, and Kate's brown eyes had grown vast with fright. Only Patience, older but not necessarily wiser, retained her insouciant air. She glided over to her chair in a waft of tantalising scent, and sat down with careful grace, arranging her sapphire blue skirts about her, as if sitting for her portrait.

Nat remained standing, looking down at them. Five pairs of eyes, of varying shades of brown, stared apprehensively up. He said quietly, 'I understand that we have uninvited guests in the roofspace.'

'They're not uninvited,' Tabby said at once. 'I asked them to come here.' She added, her face stricken, 'How did you guess?'

'I didn't. Your mother told me. Captain Hellier thought it only fair that she should know what was happening, so he informed her last night.'

Tabby said nothing, but she glanced at Silence, and a small, delighted smile hovered at the corners of her mouth.

'I know all the details of your conspiracy,' Nat went on, his voice very serious. 'And you have no need to look at me quite so anxiously – have no fear, I am not angry. In your position, at your age, I might have done the same. But the fact remains, that by concealing these men in the house, even if one of them is an old and dear friend, you have put all of us in danger.'

It was so quiet that Silence could hear the soft muted patter of the rain against the windows, a blackbird defiantly setting his song against the dying of the summer, and the sounds of her maids cleaning the hall below, with brisk clattering of brooms and mops.

'Are you going to tell Jack?' said Deb, her plump hand to her mouth, her voice very different from its usual stridency. 'Oh, Nat, please don't.'

'Of course I won't,' he said reassuringly. As the children relaxed, their tension escaping in sudden gasps of relief, he added, 'Nor will I tell anyone else. And, just as important, *vitally* so – *neither will you.*'

'But we haven't,' William objected, into the hush. His face was rather red, and Silence suspected that tears were not very far away. 'We haven't told *anyone*! We swore a solemn oath.' He glared round at his three sisters. 'You *all* did – you *promised* not to tell!'

'You may not have told, in so many words,' said Nat. 'But it wasn't exactly difficult for your mother – or me, for that matter – to guess that something was afoot. You and Deb were stealing food, and Kate was bursting to tell somebody that she had a secret.'

'Oh, *Kate*!' Deb cried in disgust, obviously hoping to distract attention away from her own lapses. Her small sister rounded on her at once, her face pale and fierce. 'I didn't tell — I didn't, I *didn't*! I just told Mama I had a nice secret.'

'It doesn't matter now,' Nat said. Without raising his voice, or changing his tone very noticeably, he could quell their strife, and bring their attention back to the matter in hand. It was a useful knack, and Silence wondered where he had learned it. Only much later did she remember that Nick Hellier, Captain of the Wintercombe garrison, had also possessed that trick of unobtrusive command. 'But it matters very much, from now on. This is not a game — understand me, it is *not* a game. It is in deadly earnest. If Jack Harington, or his father, or even one of the servants, finds out that there are two escaped Cavaliers hidden in the loft . . . the consequences will not be pleasant at all.'

One of the maids below had begun to sing as she worked. The faint strains of 'The Lark in the Morning', slightly off-key, filled the pause. Patience was studying her immaculate pale oval fingernails, her face as smooth and practised a mask as her sister's. The children gazed up at Nat, their mouths open, all their attention fastened on his words.

'Do you remember the soldiers?'

They nodded, even Kate, who had not been born.

'Captain Hellier was our friend, but some were not so nice. They were rough, rude and frightening, and when they searched the house, they didn't treat it gently.'

'They smashed Grandfather's writing desk,' said Tabby. 'And they broke the panelling in the winter parlour, and threw things through the windows. I remember it very well.'

'Perhaps, if Wintercombe is searched again, they might be kinder. But,' said Nat, very softly, 'they might not. And if they should find Captain Hellier . . . '

'Will they kill him?' Deb asked, her eyes filled with tears that, for once, were utterly sincere.

'They won't — not immediately, anyway,' Nat told her. 'But they will certainly take him away, and put him in prison for a long time. They'll probably take me away, too, for harbouring him. And even if they don't, I shall doubtless have to pay a very large fine.' He smiled at the children, his reassurance contradicting the terrifying implications of his words. 'I don't think anything like that would happen to you. They wouldn't put children in prison.

But it would be much talked about, and you might well be reprimanded — and much more severely than I would do.'

'I'm not afraid of that,' said William stoutly. 'I'm not afraid of anything anyone could do to me!'

'But you shouldn't be afraid for yourself,' said Nat, still very quiet. 'You should be thinking of Captain Hellier. If any — *any* of you — are careless — if you steal food, or creep furtively round like conspirators, or tell people that you have an important secret, but won't reveal what it is — then it is Captain Hellier, and Master Touchet, who will suffer. They will go to prison, not you.'

'And you might,' said Deb, her nose and eyes moist.

'And I might — though I might manage to wriggle out of it,' said Nat. 'But you understand now how important it is? You must not tell *anyone* — anyone outside this chamber. We are the only ones who know, and that is vital. I know you think that it is very exciting to be helping two Cavaliers, but you must try to behave as if nothing untoward has happened. No more stealing food — your mother can arrange something that won't arouse suspicion. I will find horses for them, and clothes, and in a day or two they can ride away and no one will ever know that they've been here. If, that is, you can all keep the secret. Can you?'

They nodded. Kate's lips were clamped together, as if she feared that all the details of the plot would pop out by themselves if she opened her mouth. Silence, who had wondered whether Nat's approach had been the right one, saw that they had taken his words utterly to heart, and was reassured. She did not like to see her children needlessly frightened, but she suspected that a more gentle touch might not have had the same effect. There was no doubt, now, that all of them, even Kate, were well aware of the appalling consequences, if the two men were discovered.

'What about Rachael?' said Deb suddenly. 'Can't we tell her either?'

'Of course we can't, you gawcum — she'd tell Jack Harington,' William said scornfully.

'No, she wouldn't!' Deb cried. She had always been closer to her half-sister than any of the other children, and was still very fond of her, despite the distance that their father's death, and the betrothal to Jack, had recently created between them.

'I don't think that it would be very wise to tell Rachael just yet,' Silence pointed out, tactfully. Deb eventually agreed, though with a reluctance that boded somewhat ill for her future obedience. Her mother, eyeing her dubiously, resolved to take her on one side later, and impress on her once more the utmost importance of keeping her eldest sister in ignorance of the secret.

Nat was speaking again, the lightness back in his voice. 'Good – I'm glad you all understand how much depends on your good sense. And perhaps one day, when the hue and cry has died down, Captain Hellier can come back and visit us, just as Master Wickham has done, and we can all be friends without this secrecy. Now, I understand that you have some studying to do, so I think you'd best apply yourselves. I shall go up and introduce myself to your guests – and I think it wisest that none of you visit them unless your mother or I know about it. Understood? I know Mally isn't here at present, and if she was I'm sure she'd help, but some of the other servants might not be so sympathetic.'

'We won't go up,' they said earnestly, although Tabby looked rather disappointed. Nat smiled, and watched as they dispersed, quiet and unwontedly thoughtful, to their places around the table.

Only Patience was left, sitting by the fire, her dark eyes staring into the flames, apparently dreaming. But Silence had seen the bone-white knuckles of her hands, the set of her chin, and waited with apprehensive interest for the explosion.

It did not come. Nat said, his voice deceptively pleasant, 'Perhaps I could have a word with you, sometime today, my dear Impatience?'

'Of course,' she said, turning her face towards him, blank and expressionless. 'I will seek you out later, when you have spoken to Captain Hellier. Now, if you will excuse me?'

Her graceful progress from the chamber was just a little too determined, the closing of the door a trifle too loud, to deceive either of them. Nat gazed after her, and then shrugged. 'I've upset her – how, I don't know.'

'Don't you?' Silence said. She glanced quickly at the children, who were all writing with unusually industrious concentration, and went on softly, 'I can't imagine why you included her with the children – since you so evidently appreciate that she's a grown woman.'

Nat, startled, gave her an uninhibited grin. 'My dear Silence, I don't know what you mean!'

To which his stepmother's only answer was a derisive snort that could have been one of his own.

❧ CHAPTER SIXTEEN ❧

'Young fry of treachery'
(*Macbeth*)

Master Jonathan Harley was well pleased with his life. He was still young, he was healthy and pleasant to look upon, he had a flourishing legal practice in a thoroughly congenial city and, with fees and favours, he was well on the way to becoming a wealthy man. In the eyes of the world, he lacked two things only. He should have a wife, to found his dynasty, and breed a son to follow in his father's footsteps, as he himself had done: and he must also acquire sufficient land, and a house, to reflect his growing prosperity. Now, through chance and his own ability to seize and enhance an opportunity, he had both within his grasp.

Over the past few months, he felt that he had come to know Silence, Lady St. Barbe, fairly well. She was gentle, modest and godly, her character apparently all that a wife should be. Yet he was aware also of the spirit that lay hidden beneath that calm unassuming exterior, and found that knowledge tantalisingly exciting. Her boring, elderly husband had evidently been unable to satisfy her. Harley, with memories of his numerous London conquests, and his discreet succession of wealthy and amorous mistresses in Bath, secure and comfortable at the back of his mind, knew that he could improve on the old man's technique. Admittedly, she was no longer very young, but there would be sufficient time to beget the children who would carry on his name and his line, and with four living St. Barbe offspring to her credit, he could be sure that she was a good, and fertile, mother.

He rode through the streets of Philip's Norton, smiling at the irony of it. Sir George, oblivious to this jewel in his bed and at his board, had not even considered any provision for her in his will. She had her jointure, as agreed in the original marriage contract, but it was barely enough to keep her from want. He had not even allowed the possibility that, still comparatively young and not ill-looking, she might wish to marry again. Master Harley, who had this chance very much in mind, had gently pointed out that such a devoted wife might deserve, even need, a competence of her own. The children were provided for, and even the despised eldest son would receive his inheritance intact. Surely Lady St. Barbe might be allowed a measure of independence, that would save her from the indignity of reliance upon her stepson's charity?

It had taken a great deal of persuasion, but Master Harley was a shrewd judge of character, and Sir George, his mind stripped to its bare bones by pain and approaching death, had in the end capitulated. He had decreed that the manor at Chard, with its surrounding lands and two other smaller manors close by, were to be left to Silence, absolutely.

Harley had tried to hide his initial disappointment. He had never seen this house, but knew that it had been left in a ruinous condition by war. It was now let to tenants, who had at least made the place habitable, if not luxurious. He did not know, and Sir George did not tell him, that Silence had detested Chard, where she had spent the first seven years of her marriage, and that inheriting it, far from being welcome, would seem to her like a burdensome millstone around her neck.

The more Harley thought about it, however, the more attractive the idea became. He could rebuild the house in the most modern style, befitting his eminence in his profession. It was a long way from Wintercombe, and from her children, and he had no intention of letting Sir George's brats, a surprisingly froward and ill-disciplined crew, disturb the first few months of wedded bliss. Later, perhaps, when he had safely got her with child, her other offspring would be allowed to visit. The further away she was from that disconcertingly shrewd stepson, the better. Nor did it matter that Chard was fifty miles from his business in Bath. He had never anticipated that marriage would put an end to his enjoyment of other women, and a wife in Chard for high days and holidays, with a stream of complaisant mistresses for his long absences in Bath, would suit him very nicely.

So, he had made his plans. He had sent an agent, very discreetly of course, to inspect her possessions, and had drawn up his own marriage contract in readiness. This would not be a pact between two callow young people, persuaded into an alliance by their parents, as had happened to the eldest St. Barbe girl. This was a marriage between adults, free from any interference. He looked forward to the consummation of all his desires with the satisfied pleasure of the successful strategist. Now, there remained only one small part of the plan to be set into place, the keystone of the arch.

The lady herself could not, he knew, be in ignorance of his intentions. Not long ago, he had asked to be on Christian-name terms with her. She had refused such intimacy, but in a manner which had led him to believe that she would not be unreceptive to his advances. She surely could not be very surprised when he declared himself to her.

It was a shame, he thought, as his horse walked up the long track, sticky with the heavy wet soil, that she would not inherit Wintercombe. The house was old, but still beautiful, and it could easily be altered and enlarged to suit his pretensions. The Chard manor, by comparison, was small and mean, but he meant to see it rival the older house before he was done. Besides, there was always the chance that Sir Nathaniel, who had been such an unhealthy child, would shortly sicken and die, leaving his stepmother as guardian of William, and Wintercombe, until the boy came of age.

He saw his horse taken away to the stables, and the bowing butler welcomed him within, not without some surprise, for Harley had given no warning of his coming. He had timed his visit to a nicety, for it must want only half an hour or so to dinner, and the fragrance of roasting lamb set his mouth watering. He gave Carpenter his cloak and hat, and asked to see Lady St. Barbe.

Carpenter, his polished eyebrows lifting a trifle, said that he did not know where she was to be found, but was somewhere within the house. If Master Harley cared to wait, he would go in search of her.

The lawyer wandered idly about the hall, and toasted himself before the cheerfully blazing fire, glancing upwards now and then at the ceiling, so wastefully high above him. If the house were his, he would insert a floor to make chambers above, parlours or even a library below. There was no doubt about it, the place might seem fine enough from the outside, but within was lamentably old-fashioned and inconvenient.

The lady was a long time in coming. He studied the tapestries, gazed at the portraits of Sir George and his wife hung above him, as stiff and wooden as funeral effigies, and wondered what could be keeping her. It was hardly the weather for gardening, after all.

She arrived abruptly, almost at a run, her face flushed and the hem of her plain black gown laced with dust and cobwebs. She smiled breathlessly. 'I am so sorry to have kept you waiting, Master Harley. I have been helping the maids, and Carpenter could not find me.'

He bowed politely. 'I am sorry to have put you to inconvenience, my lady — and I must apologise for arriving unannounced on your doorstep. It is most remiss of me.'

'Nonsense,' said Silence, briskly. She dusted down her skirts with hands that were themselves a little grubby, and added, 'Carpenter told me that you wished to speak with me. Are you sure that it is not Nat whom you require? He is somewhere about, and will doubtless appear for dinner. Will you stay for it?'

'I thank you, yes, my lady,' he said, wondering why there was that wary, almost alarmed expression in her eyes. If the reason for it was that she had guessed his intention, then he must tread very carefully indeed. 'But it is indeed you whom I wish to see. May we speak privately, for a little while?'

She stared at him in surprise, and then nodded. 'Yes, of course. The children are at their lessons in my chamber, but there is a fire in the winter parlour, and we shall not be disturbed. Would you like a glass of wine?'

He accepted, and she led the way through the screens into the passage behind, past the stairs that climbed up to the main upper part of the house, and through a door on the left that led into the study, where he had often discussed business with Sir George, and latterly his son. There were account books and papers strewn over the table by the window, and a door ajar at the other end of the room.

He had never been in the winter parlour before. It was a pleasant room, with windows looking south and east over the garden, comfortable chairs strewn with cushions, and another crackling hot fire. He sat down, accepted the wine which was brought to him by a plump young maidservant, and watched as Silence sank into a chair on the other side of the hearth, her own glass in her hand. She sipped at it, and made all the usual polite enquiries about his journey, and the weather, and he thought with anticipation how pleasant it would be, to have this woman as his wife.

At a suitable pause in the conversation, he said quietly, 'My dear lady — I have come here because there is something of great importance, which I wish to ask you.'

She looked up at him, startled, her eyes very wide in the gloomy light of a rainy September morning. 'Of course, Master Harley. What is it?'

He had prepared all the conventional speeches in his mind, on his way to Wintercombe, and rejected them. Each one had sounded false, unconvincing, and insincere. He said simply, 'My lady – Silence, if you will – pray forgive me for my presumption. Over the past few months of my acquaintance with you, I have come to hold you in very high regard. I regret that I can no longer keep my feelings in this matter a secret . . . and so, it would do me so much honour, and fulfil my dearest wish, if you would consent to become my wife.'

She stared at him, utterly thunderstruck. At first, when he had spoken of a private talk, she had suffered a moment of panic. Had he discovered something about Nick and Touchet? But a moment's reflection reassured her, for there was no possible chance that he could know anything about the fugitives in the roofspace. Thereafter, she had supposed that it concerned Rachael's betrothal, some matter that would be more appropriate to discuss with her, rather than with Nat.

But this – this was completely unexpected. She had been aware of his sympathy, of course, and that he held her in some esteem, though she could not imagine why. And, true, he had been a remarkably frequent visitor over the past few months. But to ask if she would marry him . . . it was incredible.

And still more so, that she should have received two proposals of marriage, from two so very different men, within the space of twenty-four hours.

So absurd did this seem, suddenly, to a woman who had never thought herself to be anything other than a very ordinary, plain and dowdy housewife, that she wanted to laugh out loud. But to do so would be unforgivably offensive. Master Harley, with his sleek pale hair and those strange green eyes like her cat's, was looking at her very intently, and his proposal had not been made in jest, but in real earnest. She must appear to consider it carefully, with the respect it deserved, even if her answer could be given instantly, and in the negative.

Hastily, she marshalled her thoughts, hoping that her astonishment had not shown too plainly on her face. A modest and maidenly blush was an inappropriate reaction in the circumstances, but a degree of flattered surprise would not come amiss. She liked him, though she knew Nat thought him a cold fish, and perhaps if Nick Hellier had not returned so abruptly into her life, changing all her hopes and expectations with the assurance of his love, she might even have given serious thought to this offer. Harley was an attractive man, with excellent prospects, and in the eyes of the world she could do a great deal worse. Certainly, he might, on the surface, appear to be a much better choice than a humbly-born soldier of fortune, at present in hiding from justice.

But Nick, for all his faults, was warm, honest, loving. This man, she knew in her heart, would never love anyone but himself.

She said quietly, 'You do me honour, Master Harley. This is most unexpected – I had no knowledge of your feelings – pray forgive me if I seem a little confused.'

'I beg you, please call me Jonathan,' he said. 'Whatever your answer, I pray you will grant me that favour, at the least.'

'Of course,' Silence told him, knowing that he deserved no less. 'But . . . Jonathan . . . forgive me, at present I find it difficult to think clearly . . . I do not think that I can accept.'

She had expected disappointment, and that emotion was certainly there, for an instant, in the handsome, usually bland face. What she had not thought to see was the unmistakable flash of real anger in his eyes.

'I am very sorry,' she said, suddenly afraid – but why? He had never been anything other than pleasant and courteous. Whatever she did, she must not give him any indication of her true reason for refusal. What would he do, if she were to blurt out the honest answer: I cannot marry you, because my secret Cavalier lover has a prior claim on my affections.

She must not laugh, either. She mastered her wayward emotions, that had threatened to betray her all morning, and added, 'Please – please, Jonathan, do not take my refusal amiss. I too hold you in high regard, as you know. But . . . your offer comes so soon after my husband's death . . . I do feel that I need more time to accustom myself to widowhood, before contemplating another marriage.' She managed to summon up a smile. 'After all, even if I had accepted you, it would not be seemly for the wedding to take place for some time yet.'

He looked at her, with an expression on his face that she could not read, and found strangely perturbing. He said slowly, 'Then – am I to understand that this is not a final refusal? That at some time in the future, you might be prepared to accept me? There is no other, who has a hold on your heart?'

It was extraordinary: she would never have thought that this smooth lawyer could give such a powerful impression of danger. Belatedly, she realised that he must on no account be angered, any more than was necessary, for he would make a most uncomfortable enemy.

'None,' she said hastily, praying that those disturbingly observant eyes would not notice the lie. 'I can give you no promises, Jonathan – but yes, perhaps, in six months or so, when this time of change and grief is over, you may ask me again, and receive a different answer. I am sorry, so sorry that I can give you no more encouragement than this – will you forgive me, and remain my good friend? We shall see each other often, I expect, and we can take the opportunity to become better acquainted.'

The bland mask was back on his face again, and Silence, who so often employed a similar disguise for her feelings, was aware of a sudden sense of kinship with him. 'Perhaps that would be the wisest course, my dear Silence,' he said, with a smile that did not involve his eyes. 'My humble apologies for troubling you. It may be, that I did not fully consider the implications of my proposal, nor your widowed state. I hope that I have not offended or distressed you?'

'Of course you have not,' she said, wishing that, just for once, they could descend from these hollow courtesies and be honest with each other, and speak from their minds and hearts, with humour and wit and affection, as she did with her children, and with Nick. 'I trust that you will be staying for dinner? We have a lamb roasting, and it promises to be uncommonly sweet and tender.'

'Perhaps, after all, I will not,' he said, rather curtly. She realised with alarm that the hurt she had done him, whether to his pride or to a gentler emotion, had run deeper than she had thought.

He took his leave of her in a somewhat constrained fashion, and rode back to Bath with anger surging inside him, almost too vast and urgent to be contained. How dare – how *dare* she, a widow who would be virtually penniless but for his efforts, refuse him? The force of his feeling surprised him, and the bitter resentment remained, even after galloping his horse hard for several hazardous miles. True, she had not closed the door completely, but he had sensed, in her evasive replies, that she had not given the true reasons for her refusal. Did she – this quiet Puritan mouse – have a secret lover or admirer, whom she preferred even to himself?

If she has, vowed Jonathan Harley, with a savage jealousy that took him by surprise, then I will use every means at my disposal to ensure that I am the victor.

[317]

Silence found that she did not want to tell anyone, even Nick or Nat, about that strange and unsettling encounter. Her stepson would laugh at the lawyer's pretensions, and at her own fears, and somehow both were too real, and too disturbing, to be subjected to his mockery.

And Nick . . . she had to confess to herself that she had no idea of his likely reaction to the news that he had a rival. The Nick she had known long ago had been light-hearted enough, sufficiently sure of himself, to eschew base emotions such as jealousy, or possessive rage. But the man who had made love with her last night had changed, had grown in some ways more vulnerable, in other ways less so. If her lover possessed unattractive feet of clay, she did not at present wish to find out.

She had been in the roofspace when Harley had arrived, and the butler's searching, with the loud assistance of Eliza, had fortunately alerted her before her whereabouts had been discovered. She had emerged from Nat's chamber, breathless and dusty, with the excuse that she had been searching for lost papers. The incident had given her food for thought. How long could this continue without detection by one of her servants, none of whom had been chosen for stupidity or lack of initiative?

There was no doubt of it, she needed Mally's help. Her maid would be delighted to see Nick again, although she might have a few well-chosen words, expressed in her usual pithy Somerset idiom, to say about the danger and foolhardiness of such a conspiracy. But Mally was also unswervingly loyal, was devious and discreet. Unlike Carpenter, always seeking to better himself, or even the sternly moral Eliza, she would hold her tongue.

All the same, Mally was nursing her sick grandmother, and Silence, knowing her maid's affection for the old woman, had not the heart to ask her to return just yet. She was well aware that Mally, however pressing her own concerns, would consent with her usual cheerful obedience, and she could not help thinking that the Widow Merrifield's need was greater than her own.

It had been very difficult to talk to Nick, with Touchet there, as if nothing lay between them but friendship. She had asked for details of their escape, since she must behave as though this were the first time she had seen him for six years, and her face must betray no trace of the love and desire she felt whenever she looked at him. When she thought about the previous night, which was often, it was as if her bones were dissolving to water within her, and the whole glorious, miraculous fact of his return assailed her afresh. They had been given a second chance, against all hope, and she prayed, more desperately than she had ever done in her life, that they would be granted leave to take it.

Nat had explained to the two men that he would procure horses for them, food and clothing, and send them safely on their journey. The big dark man, Touchet, had thanked him with elaborate courtesy. Nat, refreshingly down-to-earth, had dismissed it with a dry smile. 'The sooner you leave Wintercombe, the better for all of us. We have too many people here, who might not be sympathetic towards you. And if I give you horses, you'll go away that much faster!'

Touchet, Silence noticed, had not known how to take Nat at all, and had appeared thoroughly uncomfortable. She could see how he had been mistaken for the King. 'A tall black man, above two yards high,' was an excellent description of them both, though she suspected that Touchet was considerably more handsome than the swarthy, lively boy who had once visited Wintercombe, more than six years ago. Handsome is as handsome does, she thought, studying the arrogant, rather petulant face. If half of Nick's tale is true, the man's got the sense of a headless chicken, and the manners of a churl.

It did not give her any great confidence for Nick's immediate future, that he was shackled to the company of this well-born idiot. But the two had evidently suffered much together, and she suspected Nick was well aware that his companion would not long evade capture without him.

Nat planned to go out this afternoon, to purchase two horses from a farmer in Combe Hay who made a profitable living from dealing in animals of quality. There was a small paddock by the Wellow Lane, where the animals could be pastured overnight. Very early the next morning, if all went well, Touchet and Nick would leave Wintercombe, collect the horses, and be away towards London before the household had broken its fast. And so soon would her lover be gone.

But not without hope this time. This time, she had something to cling to, something to lighten her life. As yet, the thought that, one day, she might actually become plain Mistress Hellier, and settle down in domestic bliss with a man whom she loved, but hardly knew, was at once so wonderful, and so terrifying, that her mind shied away from it. Better to enjoy this brief time together to the full, almost as if it were once again their last, and to take each succeeding day as it came.

*

In contrast to the dull, rainy morning, the afternoon turned comparatively fine. The clouds rolled away, the sun shone and, although there was a brisk wind, the wet garden steamed pleasantly in the sudden heat. Nat rode off to Combe Hay, Silence busied herself with household duties, and the children, released from their studies, played along the terraces.

Rachael had spent the morning in perusal of her Bible. Once, she would have scanned the pages briefly, eager to be out with her brothers and sisters, enjoying their company and the fresh air. Now, she had become almost a recluse, taking a perverse pleasure in her separateness, her isolation from the cheerful and carefree life of the rest of her family. She did not think of herself as a St. Barbe any more. In a few short months, she would be a Harington, a married woman, and in preparation for her new life, she was putting away childish things.

She had thrown herself into pursuits befitting a competent housewife, the arts of healing and physick, the secrets of the kitchen and still-room and dairy. Because Jack was so godly, she must equal his knowledge of Holy Writ, his enthusiastic support of sermons, and his hours of earnest prayer and meditation. Unfortunately, Parson Willis at Philip's Norton was an ineffectual preacher, a middle-aged weathercock of a man who would bend whichever way the winds of his parish, and his government, might blow him. Jack was always talking of the public sermons given in Bath, and she had sometimes wondered if he thought her lacking in godliness. It was not her fault that Nat had no interest in sermons, and avoided those in Bath as he would a house with the plague. Nor was she responsible for Parson Willis's earnest and convoluted expositions of the more obscure books of the Old Testament, which sent three parts of his parishioners to sleep, and failed entirely to gain her attention.

So, she filled the windowsill of her chamber with theological works, and books of sermons by eminent divines. But sometimes, as she pored over the difficult texts, trying to force her brain into some measure of intelligent understanding, that quiet, hateful, cynical voice would ask her why she was doing this, when it gave her no enjoyment, no profit and, above all, no sense whatsoever that such intensive study was moving her any nearer to that elusive state of Grace which Jack seemed to have assumed so easily. Because I wish to marry Jack, and impress him, and gain his approval and respect, she might have replied: to which the voice invariably retorted, do you *really* want to marry this tedious prig?

It was a question which she always pushed away, and battened down with the stern words of duty, obligation, and pride. Yet the conflict and the confusion in her mind could not be so easily repressed, and her warring emotions forced her into a mood of lonely and bad-tempered misery. These past few months had not been happy ones for Rachael St. Barbe, nor had she made life any easier for those around her.

The sunshine, sparkling brightly on the damp garden and left-over raindrops, now beckoned temptingly. The children, who had once been so dear and so close to her, had run outside as soon as dinner had ended. She thought, with a sudden stab of unhappy regret, of those distant days when she had been their friend and mentor. Patience, her rival in so much, had taken her place, but today her aunt had gone with Silence to her chamber, doubtless for a cosy chat over sewing or embroidery.

There were times when Rachael hated the whole world, wanted to pick it up, shake it and harry it into obedience to her fierce desires. This was one of them. She stood in the garden room, listening to her stepmother and Patience climbing the stairs to Silence's chamber, and to the distant happy sounds of the children playing. Her own chamber, her Bible and sermons, held no allure. Drawn unwillingly, as if by an invisible thread, she walked into the garden.

The warmth and sunshine struck her like a blow. She stiffened her back and strolled slowly and decorously along the terrace towards the summerhouse, where once, in happier times, she had played with her twin and their elder brother, Sam, who had been so tragically killed during the war. Beside it, steps led down to the lower level, the shady arbour of cherry trees, and the balustrade that overlooked the orchard, now heavy with apples, glowing red in the sun.

The children were nowhere to be seen, but as she approached the summerhouse, she heard Deb's voice, loud and clear as a trumpet. 'But I can't understand *why* we're not allowed to see them any more!'

Rachael, aware that her shoes crunched on the gravel, stopped at once. Tabby's answer came more quietly. 'Because the fewer people who come and go, the better. What would happen if Rachael found out?'

'She won't,' Deb insisted. 'I'd be *very* careful, really I would!'

'As careful as you were when Mother noticed you taking food?' That was William, unusually scathing.

Deb's reply, somewhat deflated, was inaudible. Rachael strained her ears, but could discern no more. Besides, the gardener's assistant, Jem, was weeding the knots further along the terrace, and had glanced at her already. She turned and, as quietly as she could on the noisy path, made her way back towards the house, her mind burning with curiosity. Who was Deb so anxious to see? What must she herself be prevented from discovering? She had sensed some unusual excitement in the children's mood this morning, but had taken little notice. Now, their shared glances, the whispering, the air of conspiracy, all came back to her with sudden significance. What was their secret, from which she was so unfairly excluded?

Ignoring the undeniable fact that she, over the past few months, had taken good care to exclude herself from the company of her younger brother and sisters, Rachael decided that she must find out. She knew William and Deb well enough to realise that they would be most unlikely to reveal what they knew, unless by means of the kind of forceful persuasion that even Rachael hesitated to use. Nor could she approach Patience, their friend but her enemy, and more than a match for her in guile and sophistication. And Tabby could be so secretive that she would make an oyster seem a blabbermouth.

There was only one possible source of the information she desired. Rachael retreated to the upper part of the garden, where formal knots, edged with clipped lavender and box and hyssop, surrounded an oval pond choked with water-lilies. There were several stone or wooden seats around the perimeter. She sat down on the one nearest to the summerhouse, twisted round to peer through the swelling stone pillars of the balustrade that separated her from the terraces, and waited.

It did not take long for the conspirators to emerge from their hiding-place. Tabby came first, tall and unforgivably pretty, even in her plainest, oldest clothes. Then William, saying something over his shoulder to Deb, who followed them sulkily, red-faced, and scuffing stones with her feet. And, last and smallest, Rachael's quarry.

Kate skipped past the others along the path beside the knots, her brown hair bouncing on her shoulders, singing some tuneless rhyme. Rachael watched her round the last one and come back, hopping this time, obviously intent upon reaching the summerhouse with the use of just one leg. She negotiated William and Deb with some difficulty and much laughter, put the other foot on the ground by accident, and continued her self-appointed task while the remaining three strolled back towards the house.

Rachael seized her opportunity. She stood up and walked purposefully down the steps. Kate saw the sudden movement, and her concentration wavered. With a squawk of alarm, she tripped on her skirts, and fell over on to the gravel.

'Are you all right?' asked her stepsister, with assumed concern. She had never really liked Kate, seeing in her from babyhood her difference, her wild and free spirit which represented all that she herself most loved, and feared, and above all her subtle resemblance to the man who must surely be her father. Rachael had known about her stepmother's affair with Nick Hellier, for whom she had suffered the torments of unrequited calf-love: it had been unbearable to watch Kate, child of secret adultery, slipping, like the quicksilver minnow Tabby called her, into the affections of the man who thought he was her father. For his sake, knowing how he had been gulled, Rachael had never allowed herself to dote on Kate as everyone else did. The child was not a St. Barbe, she was an interloper, a changeling, and not worthy of her love.

Sometimes, when she hurt herself, Kate would make the most of the ensuing attention, crying and wailing as her injuries were dressed. On other occasions, she treated the accident as a brief interruption in whatever was absorbing her, and brushed off all offers of help. This appeared to be the case now, for she ignored Rachael's proffered hand and scrambled to her feet, dusting her palms. 'Didn't hurt!' she said stoutly, and hopped a few experimental paces, her interfering skirts hoisted well out of the way.

'Kate,' Rachael said quickly, her curiosity rising to unmanageable proportions. 'Kate, what's happening?'

The child stopped hopping and turned to stare up at her eldest sister. Her mouth tightened suddenly. She had always been secretly afraid of Rachael, with her abrupt swings of mood and her unpredictable flashes of malice. She said sternly, 'I don't know.'

'Yes, you do.' Rachael glanced around. The other children had gone down into the orchard, and they were alone by the summerhouse. The door was open: she grabbed Kate's thin brown paw, and whisked her abruptly within, out of anyone's sight.

'Let go!' Kate cried, her face at once frightened and angry. 'What are you doing? Let me *go*!'

'Not until you've told me what it was you were all discussing in here just now,' said Rachael. She kicked the door shut. The little room, crammed with garden tools, smelt of dust and earth, and thick grey cobwebs obscured the three small windows, rendering it dark and gloomy. Kate's chestnut eyes, vast and distended with fright, stared up at her tormenter. 'I *won't* tell you!' she said fiercely. 'I *promised* not to tell *anybody*!'

'You ought to tell me,' said Rachael. 'I'm your sister, after all.' Some savage impulse made her tighten her grip, and the little girl gave a huge sob of pain and tried to twist free. 'Let go! *Please* let me go! It *hurts*!'

'I'll let you go when you've told me,' Rachael said, her voice hostile and implacable.

Kate began to cry, and tears dribbled down her face as she vainly tried to escape the older girl's grasp. 'Please, oh please let me go, I promised, I *promised* not to tell, and they'll do awful things if I do!'

'But I won't tell anyone else, if you tell me,' Rachael said cunningly. 'I just want to find out — if you tell me what's happening, I won't let them know.' She smiled, unaware of the wolfish expression on her sharp pale face. 'Please tell me, Kate — I feel so left out of it!'

In the silence, she could hear a mouse softly scuttering about behind the sacks and barrows. Kate gulped, the tears shining on her face, her eyes enormous. She said, 'Really? Will you *promise* not to say anything, if I tell you what the secret is?'

'I promise,' said Rachael firmly, fully intending to keep her word.

For a moment longer, Kate stared at her, her lip wobbling. She said, so quietly that Rachael could hardly hear her, 'But I promised too . . . William made us all swear an oath that we wouldn't tell, on the Bible, except we didn't have one.'

'He'll never know that you've told me,' said Rachael persuasively. 'And it's only fair that I should know. Does Patience?'

Kate nodded. 'Yes, she does. And Nat, and Mother too.'

'Then I ought to know as well.' She crouched down, taking up

[324]

Kate's other hand, gripping both wrists with just enough firmness to hurt. 'Please, Kate, please. Tell me, and I'll let you go.'

Rachael in this guise was almost more terrifying than Rachael in a rage. Kate knew that her mood could change in an instant. She glanced down at her arms. One was already turning scarlet under her sister's fingers. If she did not tell, Rachael would just go on hurting her until she did, out of malice. Then she would probably tell William, Deb and Tabby anyway, from spite. Even at five, Kate was well aware that her eldest sister, for some unaccountable reason, did not like her.

'I'll tell you if you promise to keep it a secret,' she said at last, reluctantly.

A huge, gleeful smile erupted on Rachael's avid face. 'I will, I promise. Come on, tell me – what *is* it?'

Kate hesitated, already regretting her decision. At once the grip on her arms tightened unbearably, and she gasped. '*Tell* me,' Rachael hissed urgently. 'You said you would – now tell me!'

Kate swallowed painfully. Whatever she did, she was sure that no good would come of it. But the agony was too great to be endured. She whimpered involuntarily, and then said, 'There are two men hiding in the attic.'

'What?'

'Two men. Cavaliers. In the attic,' said Kate, beginning to cry again. 'Oh, let me go, please, it hurts so much, you said you would if I told you, and I have!'

'Cavaliers?' Rachael, her grip unrelaxed, stared at her in amazement. 'Cavaliers? Hidden in the *attic*? Oh, don't be so ridiculous!'

'But there are, there are,' Kate wept, twisting her body to and fro in her sister's implacable grasp. 'I *saw* them! We found them on the Wellow Lane and Patience hid them in the attic – I *saw* them!'

'But why would Patience want to hide two Cavaliers in the attic?' said Rachael, in disbelief. 'Who are they, anyway?'

'Don't know – I don't remember!' Kate cried in desperation.

'Well, what did they look like, then?'

'I can't remember!'

'You must,' said Rachael, shaking her. 'What did they look like?'

'Like beggars.' Kate sniffed and sobbed. 'They were all dirty and skummery, but Tabby knows one of them.'

Rachael's heart began to thud, suddenly and painfully. She pushed her face closer to the child's. 'She *knows* one of them? Is it Captain Hellier?'

The tears were flooding Kate's eyes now, a veritable river. She nodded, unable to speak.

Rachael's breath came out in a long hiss. She sat back on her heels, still keeping hold of the little girl's arms. 'Thank you for telling me,' she said. 'But remember — I won't tell anyone else, and you won't either, will you? Or William and the others will be *furious*!'

Kate idolised her brother. She shook her head miserably. 'No, I won't.'

'Good,' said Rachael. 'You can go now.' She dropped her hands. The marks they had left encircled Kate's wrists like two scarlet bracelets.

The child did not run away, but stood firm, wiping the tears fiercely from her face. She said urgently, 'You won't tell Jack, will you? Or soldiers will come and take us all off to prison — Nat said so!'

Rachael felt a surge of anger against her brother, her twin, who had ranged himself against her with all the rest. She tried to smile, but to judge from the sudden fear on Kate's face, it was not very convincing. 'Of course I won't. It's a secret, isn't it?'

'Yes,' Kate whispered. She added, with a sudden flash of her previous spirit, 'And don't you forget it either!' She took a step back, then two more: when Rachael made no attempt to detain her, she whirled round, wrenched the door open with a sob of desperation, and fled.

Rachael had learned their secret, but she did not feel very triumphant. On the contrary, she felt rather sick, and suddenly, agonisingly ashamed of herself. She knelt on the dirty floor, and thought of the child's white terrified face, and buried her head in her hands. What had she done? What had she become? She had tortured — yes, that was the word, *tortured* her five-year-old sister, to reveal something that, if true, if spread abroad, would bring ruin upon her whole family.

No, she would not tell Jack, because if he and his father discovered that his betrothed's stepmother and brother were concealing two enemies of the State, then the marriage contract would undoubtedly be torn up forthwith.

But isn't that what you want? whispered that inconvenient voice.

'No!' Rachael cried aloud. She hugged herself, rocking to and fro in an agony of misery and grief. She had alienated all her family for the sake of a husband whom she did not really want, for love of a father who had rarely noticed her. And now the pit she had dug for herself was so deep that she could see no way out of it.

There were two Cavaliers hidden in the roofspace, or so Kate had said – and one of them was Nick Hellier: involuntary subject, six years ago, of her first adolescent longings; her stepmother's lover; cuckolder of her beloved father; and undoubtedly, to anyone who knew of that affair, the father of Kate.

Belatedly, Rachael tried to calm herself, and to think clearly. She could not tell Jack, nor anyone else, what she knew. This was her secret, now, and yet she must reveal to no one at all, not even the others who were involved, that she was aware of the fugitives' presence. If she did, then her treatment of her little sister would certainly be revealed as well, and Rachael shied away with shame and horror from the consequences of that. She had tried to separate herself from her family, but she was only just beginning to realise how important it was to retain their affection and respect.

Rachael struggled to her feet, regretting her actions most bitterly. No one, not even those whom she had once thought loved her, could condone her spiteful treatment of Kate. No one, not even herself. She went to the door and looked out, hoping even now to see the child, to call her back, to apologise, with tears and hugs and remorse, for what she had done.

But there was no sign of her. The terrace was empty, save for Jem, still diligently weeding.

Dejected, miserable and loathing herself, Rachael trailed back to the house, and the safe loneliness of her chamber.

✥ CHAPTER SEVENTEEN ✥

'Wild laughter in the throat of death'
(*Love's Labour's Lost*)

'At *Wintercombe*?' The Governor of Bristol stared in disbelief at Captain Humphreys, standing defensively on the other side of his desk. 'That's the St. Barbe house, is it not? The woman's wits must be addled with the pox. Sir George fought as well as any man for the Cause — and lost his eldest son in it, too. A man more loyal to the Commonwealth never breathed. No — there's no profit in searching there.'

'If I may explain, sir,' said Humphreys, with dogged persistence. He had spent all day, and most of the previous night, searching Bristol high and low for the man who bore such a remarkable resemblance to Charles Stuart, King of Scots, and had met with dismal lack of success. The fellow and his companion, Hellier, might have vanished into thin air. There were, to be true, reports of them being seen passing through the Temple Gate: but there were also people who claimed to have seen them passing through the Castle Gate, the Frome Gate, and even swimming the Avon, 'Seed 'em sure as ee be standing there, sir.'

The harassed Humphreys was well aware that, if it had in fact been Charles Stuart who had slipped through his clutching fingers, his hitherto steady advancement would now come to an untimely end. In desperation, he had interviewed the woman Walker again. She was a repellent specimen, raddled and undoubtedly infected with the pox, but she was absolutely certain that one of the two men had been Nick Hellier, once Commander of the Royalist garrison at Wintercombe in Somerset. 'I knowd him for sure,' she had said positively, fixing the unfortunate captain with a baleful glare as he dabbed a scented kerchief to his quailing nose. 'And he knowd I too.'

'And he was Commander at Wintercombe, you say? While you were a servant there?'

'Aye — and had his colonel murdered, so I heared,' said the whore. 'A despeard rogue, he be.'

'But why,' Humphreys had asked, with increasing bewilderment, 'why in the name of all that's holy would he want to return there now? A hunted man, fleeing to a place where he was known, and hated . . . '

'Ah,' said Leah, and sniggered knowingly. ''Tis where ee be mistaken, Captain.' She gave him a ghastly leer. 'Lady St. Barbe, she were sweet on him.'

There was a startled pause. Humphreys had met Sir George St. Barbe once or twice, in the days of the war, and could not, by any stretch of his rather rampant imagination, conceive of his being cuckolded by a Cavalier captain. Moreover, it seemed that this man Hellier was comparatively young, while the lady, if the same age as her husband, must be well past fifty. He said sharply, 'Nonsense. What you suggest is a gross slander on a respectable family. Now get out.'

The harlot did not move. She said viciously, ''Tis the truth, sir, plain as ee be standing there. If ee d'want that King of Scots, then do ee look for him at Wintercombe. She'll be hiding them, I don't doubt.'

He had had to send two men to force her from his room, for she refused to go until he took her seriously. He wondered at the depth of hatred this unknown Lady St. Barbe had aroused in her erst-while servant, and deduced, with a fair degree of accuracy, that the Walker woman had probably been dismissed for fornication.

He was inclined to ignore her allegations. They were grotes-quely insulting, too ludicrous to be entertained. But brief enquiries established that Sir George St. Barbe had recently died, and that his heir was a young man of twenty-one, apparently in dubious health, who had exhibited a partiality neither for the Common-wealth, nor for the King of Scots. And if, if, the fugitives had escaped through the Temple Gate, if they were the two men someone had seen tramping along the Bath road, then he must leave no stone unturned.

However, it was a difficult task to convince Colonel Scroope. The Governor was an upright man, reluctant to believe such a scandalous story. He listened to Humphreys' concise explanation in silence, tapping his quill against the side of his nose, and then snorted incredulously. 'The woman's a vindictive whore. There can be no credence in such a tale.'

'I agree, sir. But . . . ' Humphreys hesitated. 'She was very certain, sir, she begged me to discover the truth for myself. And when I told her that there would be no reward, even if the search were successful, she said that she wanted none, whether in coin or in kind — revenge and justice were all she required.'

'I see.' Scroope drew the quill thoughtfully along his upper lip. 'And since these men are no longer in Bristol, apparently, they must have gone somewhere . . . ' He gazed into space for a moment, and then came to a sudden decision. 'If that tall man proves to be the King, we must not be accused of shirking our duty. Take half a dozen men and go over to Bath, at first light tomorrow — it's nearly dark now. You will have to apprise Colonel Pyne of the situation. He is very hot in pursuit of all malignants, and he must be better acquainted with the St. Barbe family than are we.' He smiled, satisfied that a knotty problem had been passed on to someone else. 'And while you are on the Bath road, be sure and make the most thorough enquiry for those men. They cannot have disappeared into thin air. And I need hardly remind you, that your diligence in this matter will not go unrewarded. But be discreet — if the Walker female is mistaken, or merely malicious, such a slanderous accusation will doubtless offend Sir George's heir most grievously, and complicate matters still further.'

So, at dawn the next day, Captain Humphreys collected half a dozen of his most reliable troopers, one of whom had actually seen the hunted men on the quayside two mornings ago, and set off, with some trepidation, for Bath. Pyne was, notoriously, an arrogant despot with all Somerset safely in his pocket. Either he would laugh this tale out of court, or he would descend upon Wintercombe with overwhelming force, and cause great offence to the St. Barbes, if they were innocent.

Or, if they were not, grab all the glory for himself.

Humphreys, brooding, had ordered his men to stop and question anyone whom they met on their way. All, without exception, had received these enquiries with blank looks and shaken heads, and his mood grew blacker. This was a wild-goose chase, he had known it from the start, and he did not in the least relish his approaching interview with Colonel Pyne.

'Sir! Captain Humphreys, sir!' Mitchell, the soldier who had encountered the fugitives on the quayside, was shouting urgently. 'There's an old goodwife here, sir, says she's seen them!'

'Has she, indeed!' Humphreys, his depression abruptly cast aside, stared at the aged woman standing beside her door. 'What village is this?'

'Newton, sir, and she says she sold them food, at about this time two days ago!' Mitchell said exultantly. 'No mistaking it, sir – she can describe them exactly. She was suspicious, so she says, because one of them at least seemed to be a gentleman of quality, but they were dressed very meanly, and told her they were sailors.'

Humphreys smiled, his whole body tingling with anticipation. He did not normally act upon intuition, but in this case his hunch had been proved right. 'Give her a coin, and our thanks,' he said. 'And did you ask her which way they went?'

'They turned off of the highway, sir,' said the old woman, hobbling forward, her eyes bright with curiosity. 'Went over the hill towards Englishcombe, they did, just as the rain were a-ginning to drop. I thought they was up to no good!'

'What else lies along that road?' the captain asked, leaning down from his horse. 'Where might they have been going?'

'I don't know, sir – they didn't say. There be a few villages over that way – South Stoke, Combe Hay, Wellow – or they could be making for Frome, or Wells.'

'Begging your pardon, sir,' said one of the other troopers. 'But I know these parts, I was reared in Stoke. You can get to Philip's Norton along these here lanes, sir, and that's where Wintercombe is, in Philip's Norton.'

It was the moment when intuition and hope fused together, and became certainty. He had six men: more than enough, surely, to apprehend two unarmed fugitives, and then all the honour and glory would be his. He thought of the huge reward for the capture of the King of Scots, enough to set him up as a gentleman on his own land, a man of wealth and consequence. Besides, he would receive the thanks of Parliament and of the Council of State, as well as the rewards which would doubtless come flooding in from all parts of the country, in gratitude to the man who, by his initiative and quick action, had seized the greatest menace to the peace and security of the Commonwealth.

He thought also of Colonel Pyne, who would certainly draw all that glittering reward to himself, when it was he, John Humphreys, who really deserved the credit.

It was an opportunity too great to be missed. If he was right, his future would be miraculously transformed. If wrong, there would be no harm done: the unpleasant Pyne would be none the wiser, and the St. Barbes' tranquil and blameless life barely ruffled by the arrival of a mere half-dozen soldiers on a routine search.

Decided, he waved to the soldiers. 'We'll turn aside, men, and follow the trail!'

If he had not been so certain that the two Cavaliers had come this way, they would soon have lost the scent. It took all morning to discover someone in Englishcombe who might have seen the fugitives, and he was an ancient labourer, lacking teeth, with an impenetrably thick dialect. His arthritic wave of a gnarled old hand towards the fields might have meant anything. The trooper from South Stoke translated. 'He d'think he seed them two day agone, sir, tramping crost that close of pasture over there.'

'Ask him what lies beyond the hill,' said Humphreys, his impatience fretting at him. Two days ago! They could have lain just one night at Wintercombe, and then gone on their way, and the glory would be for ever beyond his grasp.

The old peasant did not seem to share his sense of urgency. He deliberated, spat, and regurgitated a string of syllables which to Humphreys, a Gloucestershire man, might have belonged to the language of Cathay.

'He d'say it be the quickest way to Combe Hay,' said the trooper, an answering gleam of excitement in his brown Somerset face. 'By God, sir, I d'believe ee be right after all!'

'Do not take the name of the Lord in vain, Trooper Wright,' said Humphreys automatically. 'Ensure that he is adequately rewarded, and follow me.'

The sun emerged as they rode down the steep, narrow lane into the beautiful valley of Combe Hay, and the captain's belly was gurgling with hunger. He ordered a halt, while he and his men ate the contents of their snapsacks, and their horses rested and snatched some sweet grass, wet with the morning's rain, from the verge. Inevitably, a knot of villagers, evidently with nothing better to do, appeared to watch these military interlopers with wary, hostile curiosity. Soldiers of any breed were no longer welcome in these sheltered, prosperous villages around Bath, after the depredations of the war, and the widespread misuse of free quarter thereafter.

None of the onlookers seemed particularly willing to vouchsafe any information, whether they in fact possessed it or not. Annoyed, Humphreys ordered his men to remount, and the South Stoke man, Wright, led the way along a tree-lined lane, up and over the hill to Wellow.

Here, there was more certain news. A crowd of dirty children, squealing with excitement, showed gratifying signs of recognition when the trooper asked them if they had seen two strangers passing through the village, a day or two ago. In chorus, they described the beggars, their filthy, shifty, damp appearance, the stones thrown at them, and the direction they had taken: down the hill, across the noisy rushing brook, and over the far side of the ridge.

The next village along that way was Philip's Norton.

His quarry at last within reach, Humphreys turned to his men, his eyes gleaming in triumph. 'We have them at last! Follow me!'

It was a shame that he did not think to ask the children, or their elders who were also crowding round, the way to Wintercombe. Nor did Trooper Wright know the country so well as he had pretended. Beyond the ford, the lane split into three. The seven men trotted briskly up the middle one, and before long were thoroughly lost.

Humphreys, almost crying with impotent rage, asked directions of a farmer whose barn they were passing. His cackle of dour laughter did nothing to improve the captain's mood. 'Ooh, dear me, you have come by the wrong road and no mistake! See that there hill over there? Looksee at the house with the trees all about? That there be Wintercombe.'

So near, and yet so far: an impenetrable wooded valley lay between, and it must have been a mile or more distant. With a keen sense of the damage done to his dignity, Captain Humphreys listened to the farmer's directions, and then turned his horse and led his men back the way they had come. He was beginning to wonder if he would ever reach the place, or if it, and his dream of riches, would prove a bright and enticing illusion, to wither away as soon as he touched it.

*

By an ironic twist of fate, it was Rachael who first became aware of the soldiers' arrival at Wintercombe.

Consumed with guilt at her brutal interrogation of Kate, she had fled to her chamber, there to take refuge first in tears, then, with furious concentration, in study of her Bible. But no amount of Old Testament savagery could erase the bitter shame of her own merciless behaviour, her cruelty towards the little sister whom she had never allowed herself to love.

After a fruitless hour, her restlessness drove her outside again.

The house seemed still and silent, though she knew well that it concealed upwards of two dozen people, all quietly busy about their duties and employment. She had some thoughts of going into the village to see Nell Apprice. It was usual for her to ride the half mile or so to her friend's house by the market place, but today she could not wait for the grooms to saddle her horse. She strode out of the door and down the track, her black skirts lifted clear of the morning's mud, and her misery and anger and self-loathing fuelling every forceful step.

She heard horses as she reached the end of the track, where it joined the Wellow Lane. Resolutely ignoring them, she turned right and tramped along the deep, mired lane towards Norton, wishing already that she had spared the time for her horse to be made ready. Nell was sharp-eyed and even sharper of tongue, and she would not hesitate to comment on the mud now splattering her friend's gown, despite all her care.

She glanced back, and froze with astonishment. The horsemen had come briefly into sight, and she saw one gesticulating towards the track that led to Wintercombe, down which she had just walked.

They were soldiers. Almost before her horrified mind had had time to assimilate the fact, they had urged their horses up the lane towards the house, and out of her sight.

There was only one reason, surely, for their appearance at Wintercombe. Somehow, they must know about the presence of the two fugitives hidden in the roofspace.

Rachael stood still, staring back, while her mind worked furiously. Someone must have betrayed them — why else would troopers trouble to visit a respectable and godly household, that most would consider to be above suspicion? And if the secret was known already, then there was no hope of deflecting the doom that already hung poised above them, ready to fall. The troopers would search the house: the two concealed staircases to the loft above the hall would be discovered; and Nick Hellier and his companion captured, to the disgrace and ruin of the St. Barbe family.

She could see the consequences of that, as sure as evening followed day. The Haringtons, horrified, would withdraw from the betrothal, and she would be forced into a life of eternal and shameful spinsterhood. For who would want to marry one of the tainted St. Barbes?

There is only one way, only one chance, said another, slyer

voice in her panic-stricken mind. *If you can go back to Winter-combe now, and tell them where the men are hiding – then none of the disgrace will fall upon you.*

She thought of the odium she would thereby incur from her family, and dismissed it hastily. If her only chance of matrimony was with Jack Harington, and the only way to keep the betrothal was to betray the two Cavaliers, then she must do it, and let the rest go hang. She would not need them, anyway, as Mistress of Kelston.

And at last, she would be revenged upon Patience, whose arrival had ruthlessly cast her own, hesitant blossoming into the shade.

She gathered her skirts, and began to run back towards Wintercombe.

*

'My lady! My lady!' Eliza, the chief maid, came hurrying breath-lessly into her mistress's chamber without so much as a knock. 'My lady – 'tis soldiers, soldiers be here, oh, do ee come quick, my lady!'

It was a long, long time since Silence had last heard such a warning. Then, it had changed her life and her world. And now, though the men outside were supposedly friends, their potential to bring disaster to Wintercombe was no less great.

Patience had flung up her head like a hind, her brown eyes very wide, her face, with the undeniable scattering of freckles across her small straight nose, suddenly pale with shock. Silence, more skilled in dissembling, regarded her maid with an air of mild surprise. 'Soldiers, Eliza? Whatever do they want?'

'I don't know, m'lady, I didn't stop to find out, I come up here so soon as I seed them a-riding along the lane.' Eliza laid a bony hand across her heaving bosom, and made a visible effort to control her uncharacteristic panic. 'I d'beg your pardon, my lady – it fair gallersed me, to see they come a-riding up here again, just like they did afore.'

'I can't think what they can want – no more free quarter, I hope,' said Silence. She got to her feet, sighing with what she hoped was a convincing weariness. 'Well, I suppose I had better speak to them, and find out. You stay here, Patience – their business surely cannot concern you.'

Eliza, already clattering back down the stairs, did not see the significant glance that passed between the two sisters. 'Warn them

— but tell them not to do anything rash,' Silence whispered urgently, and Patience nodded, quick to understand.

She walked down the steps in Eliza's wake, her heart lurching unevenly against her ribs. If all her surmise were correct — if, if — there could be no evidence to connect the two fugitives with Wintercombe. Probably, these soldiers were still under the impression that the King of Scots was loose in Somerset, and felt obliged to cast their net wide, even in such an unlikely place. Or it could even be a purely routine matter, and nothing to do with escaped Cavaliers at all.

In the next few moments, her fate, and Nick's, and all the happiness they might one day enjoy, were to be decided. She had not even the benefit of Nat's support and quick wits, for he was not yet returned from Combe Hay, with the new horses. This was something with which she must deal on her own, and the safety of all her family depended on her ability to convince these troopers of Wintercombe's innocence.

A younger Silence, untempered by war, danger and adversity, might have quailed in panic, and wished herself elsewhere. But she had faced the worst that the appalling Ridgeley could do, and survived it. These men were friendly, and had fought in the same cause as her husband. They could have no evidence or proof, and she had her unimpeachable position, as the widow of a staunch supporter of the Parliament's cause, to bolster her appearance of innocence. Even if they had, unlikely though it seemed, good reason to single out Wintercombe for their attentions, they would surely think it impossible that such a household would knowingly harbour a brace of Cavaliers. All she had to do was to pretend that the two men in the roofspace had never been there.

An ironic thought reminded her that, if Nick had not visited her the previous night, she would in truth have been innocent. She smiled, thinking that, even if she had faced the certainty of disaster, she would still have welcomed the glories of those brief hours with open arms.

But she prayed, with sudden desperation, as if sheer force of will could grant her desire, that the one night of love which she and Nick had enjoyed would not prove to be their last.

There were only six troopers, and a captain at their head. Her confidence rose as she watched them dismount in the courtyard before the house. Surely, a search party would have been rather larger?

She stepped out of the porch. The afternoon sun was drawing down, and the shadows lay long and dark across the gravel. She stood still, her hands clasped before her, neat and tranquil in her black gown, her white-capped head turned slightly to one side in an attitude of polite enquiry, while Eliza hovered behind her, her long horse face puzzled and alarmed.

The captain bowed. He was quite young, with lank fair hair, and a pockmarked face that showed some signs of intelligence, but there was an expression of questing eagerness in his eyes that she found alarming. 'Lady St. Barbe?' he said. 'Captain Humphreys, of the Bristol Militia, at your service, madam. I do humbly beg your pardon, for putting you to this inconvenience.'

He was scanning her face with interest, and she could not imagine why. She did not know that Humphreys was wondering, for the first time, whether the whore Walker's malicious slander could possibly have been true. This trim, decorous woman was much younger than her dead husband, probably even now only just in her thirties. Suddenly, that mischievous tale seemed much more likely.

'I would be grateful if you would tell me your business here, Captain Humphreys. We have not had soldiers at Wintercombe for a long time, and I am curious. If you will come inside, and your men too, you can explain.'

He followed her through the porch, and into a dim screened passage. She led the way into the hall, lit golden by the westering sun, and turned to face him. Her calm serious face was pleasing to the eye, though beginning, in the smile lines about her mouth and eyes, to betray her age. Humphreys felt his doubts rising again. This woman, plain and serene, was no beauty, and assuredly no adulteress, her open expression utterly innocent of any guilt or fear. She said to the hovering maid, 'Eliza? Would you arrange for beer to be brought for Captain Humphreys and his men? They must be thirsty, after their ride from Bath.'

'We have not come from Bath, my lady,' said Humphreys, still studying her. 'We have ridden from Bristol.'

'Bristol?' There was only bewilderment in her large, direct hazel eyes. 'Forgive me, Captain, but I do not understand – why have you come here, all the way from Bristol?'

More and more, Humphreys was realising that he must be mistaken, misled by his own greed and Leah Walker's malice. This godly widow, in her dull mourning black, could have nothing to do with escaped Cavaliers, or with sheltering the King of Scots. He was uncomfortably aware that he must give her some explanation, and that anything approaching the truth would undoubtedly make him look extremely foolish. He said unhappily, 'My apologies, my lady. I fear that I have been sent out on a wild-goose chase. There have been reports that the King of Scots has been seen in these parts.'

'The King of Scots?' She was having some trouble concealing her amusement. 'I thought that he had been slain at Worcester Fight.'

'Alas, no, my lady — or at least, his body has not been discovered. He is somewhere at large, and was seen by one of my own men on the quayside in Bristol, two days ago.'

'Then he has probably taken ship for France,' said Silence. It was as she had thought. This man, faced with the sober reality of herself, and Wintercombe, was beset by doubts. Her spirits, and her confidence, rose still further. 'Why on earth do you think he might be here?'

Humphreys, floundering, refused to meet her eyes. 'A woman of, er, ill repute, suggested that he might have taken refuge here, my lady. And two suspicious beggars were seen in Wellow, two days ago.'

'A woman of ill repute? She must be far gone in her wits, to dream up such a tale. As for the beggars, we see many hereabouts, since the war ended — old soldiers, for the most part.' She turned as the two scullions, wide-eyed small boys, were shepherded through the screens by Eliza, bearing trays with tankards of frothing beer. 'Thank you, Richard and Jeffery. You may go.'

'One moment, if I may, Lady St. Barbe? A child's eyes are often sharper and more curious than his elders' . . . ' As she nodded, Humphreys addressed the two boys. 'I am searching for two men, escaped Cavaliers. Have you seen any suspicious beggars or suchlike, lurking here during the past few days?'

The boys looked at him, surprised, and shook their heads. 'No, sir,' said Richard Combe, a sturdy and sensible child. 'No, norry a one, sir.'

'Nor anything unusual here, in that time?'

'No, sir,' said young Richard, obviously bewildered. 'We've seed naught.'

It was hardly likely, since they spent most of their time in the kitchen under Darby's vigilant eye, chopping food and scouring dishes, that they would have noticed any dubious strangers unless in regimental quantities, but Silence did not intend to enlighten the captain. Evidently satisfied, he thanked the boys, and she dismissed them.

'I am sure, if any such rogues were hiding here, they would have noticed,' she told Humphreys, when they had gone. 'Richard is a bright lad, and very observant. But you are welcome to search the barn and stables, Captain, even the house, if it will set your mind at rest.'

He stared at her thoughtfully. He still shrank from making such a fool of himself, but he could not return to Bristol without even a cursory attempt to discover the King of Scots. He was tolerably certain that they could not be within the house, not without this woman's knowledge, and she was patently innocent. It was possible that they might have concealed themselves in a barn or hayloft, however, without anyone seeing or assisting them. He said, 'I will indeed search the outbuildings, by your kind leave, my lady, but it is plain that they cannot be within these walls. May I instruct my troopers?'

'Of course,' Silence said, waving a gracious hand. 'Go where you please, Captain, so long as your men do no damage. The barn is full of stored grain and hay at present, so I beg you, for the sake of our winter supplies, ask them to be careful.'

'Of course,' said Humphreys courteously. 'When we have finished, my lady, you will not know that we have been searching.'

*

Rachael panted up the track, her mouth dry and her hands stinging and bloodstained where she had slipped and fallen on the wet muddy stones of the little bridge over the Norton Brook. Her skirts were mired nearly to her knees, and her black hair, ruthlessly scraped this morning into a plain white cap, had escaped and was hanging in witch-locks about her face. She did not care what picture she presented. All that concerned her was to divert the sword of fate, now poised to fall on Wintercombe, from her own head.

She drew level with the yew walk, bounded by a low stone wall, and the shell of one of the three towers that betrayed Wintercombe's martial origins. Belatedly cautious, she crept carefully along the wall until she could see what was happening in the courtyard.

With surprise, she noted that it was almost as usual. One of the stable lads was bringing buckets of water and hay for the seven horses, two brown, three bay and two chestnuts, and the last buff-coated back was just disappearing within the porch. It all seemed very calm. Could this just be a routine visit, merely concerned with taxes, or some trivial local problem?

There was only one way to find out. Rachael dared not risk being seen: quite apart from anything else, the lamentable state of her attire did not add to her self-consciously adult dignity. A little bridge lay behind her, crossing the ditch and leading to a wicket gate, new cut in the wall around the yew walk. She could go through the garden and come into the house from the other side, unseen. Then, she would be able to overhear the soldiers' plans.

She threaded her way through the clipped yews, coaxed by Diggory's careful art, over long years, into pyramids, cones and other fantastical shapes, and past the edge of the bowling green, fortunately empty, though bowls lay scattered on the grass, forgotten. Rachael hurried into the next part of the garden, past the pond, praying that no one was looking down from Silence's chamber, and sprang down the steps, nearly falling again. She ran along the gravelled terrace until she reached the door into the garden room, next to the hall.

The door was open. Rachael heard voices, masculine and alien. She stumbled up the three stone steps, gasping, trying not to make a noise, and paused to control her breathing. There was no one about. She crept very quietly into the little closet, screened by a curtain from the main hall, and pulled it a little to one side, so that she could see.

The six troopers, mud-stained and weary, were drinking from their tankards with every appearance of enjoyment. Their captain stood by her stepmother. Rachael's avid gaze could discern no trace of alarm in Silence's habitually calm expression, no hint of unpleasantness in the demeanour of the captain. Perhaps everything was well. Perhaps the men in the roofspace were unsuspected after all. If there was no danger of discovery, then she would not have to forestall disaster by betrayal.

'The woman's name was Walker,' the captain was saying. 'She claimed to have once been in your employ, my lady.'

'Leah? I suppose you must mean Leah,' Silence said. 'Yes, she was, some years ago, but I was forced to dismiss her. She behaved in a disgraceful manner, no better than a harlot, and she was an unpleasant, sly and vindictive girl to boot. So she still wants to make trouble for Wintercombe? Well, that is no surprise. Nor does it astonish me, that she has taken up the trade for which she seemed so well fitted. I hope you did not give too much credence to her tale?'

Captain Humphreys had the grace to look a trifle embarrassed. 'Well, no, my lady – well, any fool can see that it's all a wild tale spun from spite. I shall make every effort, when I return to Bristol, to have her taken up and whipped for a slanderous and arrant whore.'

'I would not wish her punished on my account, Captain,' said Silence. She turned as a door slammed behind the screens, and childish footsteps and voices interrupted them. The heavy curtains billowed, and through them, like two small sturdy whirlwinds, came William and Deb, supporting a sobbing Kate between them, with Tabby, grave-faced, just behind. They saw the troopers and stopped dead, wide-eyed and shocked.

'What is it? What's happened to Kate?' asked Silence, startled. Her youngest daughter's face, normally so lively and sparkling and mischievous, was crimson and streaked with tears, and on her thin arms, brown from the summer sun, the new bruises stood out an angry, purplish red.

'Someone's hurt her, Mama,' said William, his voice loud with indignation. Cruelty and unkindness had always been quite alien to his open, friendly nature. 'We found her hiding in the orchard, crying and crying, but she won't tell us what happened, or who did it.'

Silence glanced at Captain Humphreys, who was staring intently at the child. She said sharply, 'Surely you cannot think that these two men, whoever they are, have something to do with this?'

'What two men?' said Deb, with an air of innocent enquiry that she had practised too often over the years. 'Why are these soldiers here, Mama?'

Now came the test, and Silence braced herself, and prayed. She could lie successfully to this captain, who seemed a pleasant man, and so, probably, could her self-willed and deceitful Deb, and the secretive Tabby. But could William, so honest and straight-forward, manage not to reveal his guilt, even involuntarily? And was Kate, in the grip of hysterical terror, in any state to keep the secret?

'Forgive me, Captain,' she said, with a rueful smile at Humphreys. 'But the need seems urgent . . . I must take up my maternal duties for a moment.' As he nodded, his eyes still on the weeping little girl, she knelt down to embrace her youngest daughter. 'Kate, Kate, hush now . . . whatever is the matter? What have you done to your arms?'

'I can't tell!' Kate sobbed, between gasps. 'I can't tell – I promised – I *promised*!'

'Can't tell what? Oh, Kate, who did this to you, poppet?'

'I *can't*!' Kate wailed, in an agony of despair. The soldiers, staring at her with a mixture of interest and embarrassment, might have been arras on the wall, for all the notice she took of them. 'I promised!'

'Promised who?' Silence's voice was gentle and coaxing. Kate hiccuped and sobbed into her arms. Rachael waited, rigid with tension, for the inevitable, but it did not come.

'Perhaps,' said the captain, the houndish eagerness back on his face, 'perhaps she met with two strangers . . . pray ask her whether she did, my lady.'

'Was it a nasty man who did this?' Silence asked, reluctantly. She was beginning to realise the danger, and she wished now that she had sent the children upstairs immediately, pretending to a strictness which she never usually employed with her offspring. Whatever the truth of Kate's mishap – and unpleasant Cavaliers were unlikely to be involved – the longer the child lingered here in a state of distress, the more probable it was that she would unwittingly reveal that she knew something more damaging about the men that Humphreys was seeking.

'N–no,' said Kate, sniffing. Her mother gave her a kerchief, and watched as she blew her nose, with some thoroughness.

'Are you sure?' Captain Humphreys, the parent of small children himself, squatted down by Kate's side. 'You saw no strangers?'

Kate turned, noticing him for the first time. Her wide, tear-drenched eyes took in the implications of buff coat, sword and sash, and her face crumpled in terror. 'Don't!' she wailed. 'Don't take Nat to prison, don't, don't!'

Suddenly sick at heart, Silence said quickly, soothingly, 'Oh, Kate, don't be silly, poppet – he's not going to take anyone to prison.'

'But I told Rachael!' Kate cried, overwhelmed by a confusion of

[342]

fear and guilt. 'I told Rachael and now Nat'll go to prison, and they will too!'

The sudden quiet could have been cut with a knife. Silence, still kneeling, her arms round Kate, saw the expression on the captain's face change to the sudden sharp certainty of a hound at last catching sight of its long-pursued quarry.

'Who is Rachael?' he asked softly. Silence opened her mouth to answer, and was forestalled by a strident voice from the other side of the hall.

'I'm Rachael – and I can tell you where you can find the men you're seeking.'

Oh, no, Silence thought in dread, all her worst nightmares suddenly made flesh. She rose to her feet and turned to face the child who had defied her, the girl whose moods had been her despair, and the adult whose turbulent and difficult nature had been the cause of so much strife and dissension in her family; and who now, for some obscure reason of her own, wanted to betray them all.

Rachael stood in the centre of the hall, her face white with rage, or fear, her hands clenched at her sides. Her half-brother and sisters stared at her, aghast. Avoiding their gaze, she said loudly, 'There *are* two Cavaliers hidden here, Captain, and I know where they are.'

'You made Kate tell you!' Tabby cried, and the disgust and horror in her voice took even Rachael aback. 'You did that to her, didn't you – well, I hate you!'

'You know where they are?' Humphreys had leaped up, delighted. 'Where are they?'

Her boats burned with a vengeance, Rachael stabbed a finger upwards. 'There – they're in the roofspace!'

William, his heart hammering, took two steps back, until he felt the heavy screen curtain touch his hand. He glanced round, but everyone's attention was riveted upon Rachael. Unnoticed he twitched the curtain aside, and vanished behind it.

The men in the loft must be warned, and, even more important, they must be armed. In the screens passage, various weapons hung on the walls, a legacy of his father's military career. With some difficulty, and not a little noise, he tugged a pair of swords from their scabbards, and ran for the stairs.

No sounds of immediate pursuit followed him, as he plunged upwards. Gasping with fright and effort, he flung himself into

Nat's chamber, and shut the door. He wondered if he should jam the latch, but decided against it. His quick mind, accustomed to thinking strategically by the games in the orchard, had already told him that Hellier and Touchet had a good chance of escape, if they kept their heads, for there were only seven soldiers below.

Clutching the swords, he dived into the closet, pulled aside the curtain that hid the secret stair, and wrenched the door open with a frantic hand. There was no need for secrecy now. 'Captain Hellier!' he shouted, launching himself upwards. 'Captain *Hellier!*'

One of the swords slipped from his grasp and clattered backwards, and he cut his hand trying to grab it. At least it's sharp, he thought wildly, groping in the gloom, and then a candle's uncertain light appeared above him, and Hellier's deep voice, stripped of its usual dry humour, said, 'William? William, what's happened?'

'Rachael told them!' the boy gasped, struggling up the last few steps. 'She made Kate tell her about you, and now she's told the soldiers where you are and they'll be here any minute and I got you these, only I've just dropped one.'

Nick stared at the proffered sword, naked and slightly pitted with rust. So, it might not be disaster after all, despite Rachael's treachery. He said, 'How many of them?'

'Only seven,' said William, suddenly gleeful. 'So if you come down this way, and Master Touchet goes down the other stairs, you'll only have to face four of them at the most.'

There was shouting below. Nick's face lit up with a reckless defiance, which the men under his command here, six years ago, would have recognised very well. Behind him, Touchet appeared, his expression contorted with alarm. 'What is it? What's happening?'

'Discovery,' said Nick tersely, and thrust the hilt of the sword at him. 'Take it. There are only seven of them — you cross the roofspace and go down the other stairs. They'll have to split up to take us — and this way, at least one of us has a good chance of escape.'

'They've left their horses outside in the courtyard,' William said. 'Nat isn't back yet — if you can get out of the front door, you can take one of their own horses!' His eyes gleamed with a wild delight to match Nick's.

Touchet had not moved: he was clasping his sword as if he had never held one before. Nick turned and gave him an exasperated push. 'Don't just stand there, man, go! Do you *want* to spend the next few years in a Roundhead gaol?'

'He doesn't know the way,' said William, suddenly perceptive. 'Come on, Master Touchet, I'll show you!' And with a careless agility which neither man, particularly Touchet, could match, he skipped over the piled mattresses and bedding, and ran lightly along the narrow planks that had been laid over the joists to form a bridge to the other side. 'Follow me!'

Nick waited only long enough to see his companion begin, rather ponderously, to cross the planks. Then, he turned and plunged down the stairs, up which William had just come.

The dropped sword had slithered down to the bottom. He picked it up, feeling its balance, just as he heard the door of Nat's chamber open. With luck, they would not know that William had warned them. Surprise was, for once, on his side rather than theirs.

He paused for a moment, standing crouched awkwardly on those desperately narrow, twisting steps, judging his moment. Then, as the voices came nearer, he flung back the door, and rushed out.

There were four troopers, in the familiar buff coats that had dogged his footsteps all through the weeks since Worcester. None of them had drawn their swords, and in the confined space of the closet, there was little room for them to do so. Their leader managed to get his weapon half-way out of its scabbard before Nick's sword slashed briskly across the hilt. He dropped it, gasping, and Nick, with the power of desperation, shoved him aside, evaded the clutching hands and pushed his way into Nat's chamber.

There were women there. He saw the Friday-faced maid, familiar from long ago, and Silence, her expression grey and stark with shock and horror. Other servants were crowding the doorway, and they parted, screaming, like the waves of the Red Sea as he ran towards them, until there was only one left to block his path, a stiff thin figure in black and white, her blue eyes desperate.

'Rachael!' he shouted. The soldiers were behind him, he heard shouts and the metallic rasp of drawing swords, and the cries of the women. She did not move. Suddenly brutal, he wrenched her to one side, flinging her against the doorpost, and ran for the stairs, with the four troopers at his heels.

He had miscalculated. There were soldiers coming up.

He thrust at the first one as he reached the head of the stairs, and had the satisfaction of seeing his blade strike home. The man fell backwards on to his comrades, blood pouring from his thigh. But the stairway was now blocked, and in this wild, desperate moment, he could remember no other way down.

There was the gallery, with the hall below. But his pursuers were crowding through the door of Nat's chamber. He watched them, waiting, his sword balanced in his hand, poised like a snake to strike.

'Go on, there's only one of them!' their leader shouted, nursing his bruised hand. One of the troopers advanced a little way, his weapon thrust forward hopefully. Nick had never considered himself a brilliant swordsman, his technique was too workmanlike and unrefined, but at least it was efficient. There was a brief, forceful clash of blades, and the trooper's stout broadsword, made for the service of the Commonwealth in the forges of Birmingham, was abruptly torn from his grasp and sent spinning across the floor.

'Where's the other one, sir? This isn't the King of Scots!' said one of the remaining troopers, on a note of surprise.

'You're right, it isn't,' said Nick, his eyes holding theirs. He saw the movement of skirts behind them, but dared not allow his concentration to wander. He needed all his wits now, or he was lost.

A shout rose from below. 'There he be – get him, you wantwit – *after him!*'

Involuntarily, Nick glanced sideways to the hall, where Touchet must be making good his escape. There was a great crash of falling furniture, a shout of glee that could only come from William, and some most ungodly language. He grinned, and turned once more to face his adversaries, his mind busy with the alternatives. He could leap from the gallery, twelve feet and more to the stones below, and risk a broken leg or worse, with no certainty of escape even if he survived unscathed. Or, he could fight his way through these four men who blocked his path to the stairs. At least he had disarmed one of them, possibly two.

They were advancing. Their leader, hurt hand notwithstanding, was holding his sword in purposeful fashion, and had placed himself most bravely in the van. 'Surrender yourself, sir, in the name of the Commonwealth. You are surrounded, and there can be no escape.'

Nick had remembered the other stairs, that lay in the north

wing. If he could reach those, gain the barton, perhaps snatch a horse, then he might win his freedom after all. He would leave Silence and her children to face the reckoning, but at least he would not be a prisoner.

He smiled at the Roundhead officer. 'Surrounded, you say? Well, yes, I suppose I am.'

Below, the shouts and sounds of pursuit had grown fainter, and he thought he could hear hoofbeats, rapidly receding into the distance. If so, then probably Touchet, with the help of the stalwart William, had made good his escape. Nick, still smiling, lowered his sword a little, and saw the Roundheads begin to relax their guard. As a grin of triumph began to spread across the captain's face, Nick selected his target, a vacant-looking young man with a less than firm grip on his sword, and charged.

Silence, watching horror-struck from the doorway of Nat's chamber, knew that he had no chance. One man, against four – it was hopeless. And yet she understood that vivid streak of reck-lessness within her lover. Once, it had led him to court her, and then, to hold Wintercombe against greatly superior forces, heed-less of the consequences to herself. Now, he was surely doomed.

Nick had other ideas. His opponent was just as incompetent as he had hoped, but he was not the only one. Desperately, he slashed and parried, beating them away, trying all the while to force his way through to the stairs. The two remaining troopers were clumsy, easily fought off, but the captain was another matter. He was quick, well-trained, and determined. Twice, his blade came within a whisker of Nick's sword arm, and his eyes, intent and hostile, betrayed only his eagerness to make an end of this business.

The boards were slippery, polished with care under Eliza's gimlet eye. Nick's arm was growing weary, and sweat blurred his vision. So far, he had remained unscathed, largely because the two troopers apparently lacked the will, and the space, to attack him at the same time. But he knew now, with a deep sick certainty, that the end was inevitable. Unless he could make one last effort, and try to win through to the stairs . . .

He parried the captain's low, wicked thrust, and found the hilt twisting in his hands. The blades were engaged together: for a brief moment, he was helpless. He wrenched his sword free, and hurled himself at the gap between the men facing him, towards freedom.

And Captain Humphreys saw his chance, and took it.

Silence cried out as the Roundhead lunged. She saw the point enter Nick's body as the troopers slashed down. Her lover was flung round by the force of the blows, and she saw blood running as his sword spun rattling to the floor. Then he was falling, and the soldiers closed in for the kill.

'No!' she cried, and ran forward, heedless of the danger. 'No — no, Captain Humphreys — please stop, *stop*!' She grabbed a leather-clad shoulder and pulled it savagely round. 'Captain — for pity's sake, I beg you — stop!'

But they had already put up their swords, for resistance was over. She saw Nick's blood dabbled red on their blades, and felt suddenly sick, and faint. She swallowed the bile that rose in her throat, and stared at Humphreys' grim face.

'It were best you move away, my lady,' he said, and gestured to the crowded people behind her, shocked servants and sobbing children. 'And remove these onlookers, if you would.'

She had not dared to look down at Nick. He might be dead, for all she knew, and to see it for certain would destroy all her defences, all the remaining shreds of her composure. She said urgently, 'I have some skill and experience in healing, sir. If you do not let me and my maids tend this man, you are no better than a savage!'

Humphreys had been expecting tears and feminine vapours, and was nonplussed. The man lying sprawled untidily at his feet was certainly badly hurt, if not dead, to judge by the quantity of blood, and past being any danger. Belatedly, he remembered that he was meant to be hunting the fugitive Charles Stuart, and this Cavalier was assuredly not the man he sought.

'Very well,' he said curtly, and turned away, sheathing his sword. Explanations, accusations, recriminations would all follow in their course, but for now he had other tasks. A man came stumbling up the stairs, gasping some tale of failure and escape. He snapped an order at one of the troopers. 'Guard him. I'll be back shortly.'

But Nick, lying loose and broken on the bloodstained floor of the gallery, was no longer in need of guarding.

❦ CHAPTER EIGHTEEN ❦

'A traitor, and must be hanged'
(*Macbeth*)

'Will someone please tell me, what in Heaven's name has happened here?'

Sir Nathaniel St. Barbe, third Baronet, stood in the doorway of his hall, surveying the servants, and most of his family, herded there like sheep, with two burly troopers standing guard over them. His eyes, blue and watchful, flicked from face to face, reading, in the familiar features of his household, varying degrees of shock, astonishment, distress and indignation, that probably mirrored the expression on his own countenance. Not by one note of alarm or guilt did he betray the fact that he had had a very good idea indeed, ever since he had set eyes on the six strange horses tied up outside his front door, of what had befallen Wintercombe in his absence.

'Nat! Oh, Nat!' His half-sister Deb launched herself at him, wailing. 'Oh, Nat – Captain Hellier's dead! They've killed him!'

He braced himself for the shock of the impact as she hurled herself into his arms, howling with genuine grief. Above her tangled, honey-coloured head – as usual, her cap had fallen off – he allowed his face to register appalled surprise. 'Captain *Hellier*? What's he doing here? We haven't seen him in six years!'

'I told en that, Sir Nathaniel,' said Eliza angrily. 'But he didn't take no heed of what I did say.'

'Nor I neither!' several others added.

Nat stared at them again, seeking someone reliable. His eyes met Tabby's, hazel brown, wide with strain and shock, but promising an account more accurate, and calm, than any which Deb was likely to give. He patted the child's shaking shoulders, and said gently, 'It's all right, Deb – Deb, where's your mother?'

'Don't know!' his sister bawled, in between hysterical hiccups. The nurse, Doraty, dependable and kind, came forward and with gentle, firm hands prised the girl's fingers from Nat's doublet and took her aside.

'Is it true?' he asked, and Tabby, white-faced, thin and graceful in her shabby old black gown, spread her hands.

'I don't know if he's dead. Mother's with him now. But, yes, it is Captain Hellier.'

Their eyes met again, and she gave him a faint nod. He could guess her stratagem, and returned a smile of encouragement. Of all the children his stepmother had borne, this deceptively angelic girl was the closest to him, in temperament as well as in age. He knew that the lovely face and cloudy golden brown hair hid a nature in some ways as devious and cunning as his own, and far more unswerving in purpose. Tabby had been the principal plotter, and her ideas had brought them to the brink of disaster. Now, with equal guile and courage, she was going to do her best to limit the damage which she had done.

'What happened, Tabby?' he asked quietly. The servants were silent, listening. Probably, in the confusion, they had little more idea of what had occurred than he did. He thanked whichever deity watched over him, that he had been unable to purchase any horses, from Combe Hay or anywhere else. To arrive here with two good mounts in tow would not have helped any protestations of innocence.

'The soldiers came to take Captain Hellier,' Tabby said. She took a deep breath, holding his eyes with her own, and added, in a desperate gabble quite unlike herself, 'I'm sorry, Nat, I'm sorry, I really am – I should have told you, but we didn't want to involve you – we smuggled him into the roofspace, and hid him there.'

'We? Who?'

'Me, and Deb and William and Kate,' Tabby told him. She had already decided that Patience, at present helping her mother to tend Nick, was best left out of the reckoning. 'No one else knew.'

'And soldiers came looking for him? I saw their horses outside,' said Nat, playing the part which she had tacitly assigned to him. 'Where are the rest of them?'

'One is guarding Captain Hellier,' said Tabby. 'The other three, and their captain, are searching for the other man.'

'What other man, for Heaven's sake?'

His sister's lip trembled, as if she thought him truly angry. 'There – there was another man with Captain Hellier. I think he escaped. He took one of the soldiers' horses.'

'Did he, indeed.' Nat surveyed her, an alien grimness set hard on his face. 'Well, I'd best talk to your mother. Where is she?'

'She — she's in your chamber, I think,' Tabby told him. 'That's where they carried Captain Hellier. We all had to come down here, and we can't go anywhere until the officer comes to question us.' Her face wobbled suddenly, with genuine emotion. 'Oh, Nat — he may die, and it's all my fault. *Please* don't be angry with me!'

He gave her what little comfort he could, as she sobbed into his arms, and whispered to her, 'Be brave. Can you take it all on yourself?'

'Yes, I must,' she hissed back, under cover of her weeping. 'Please, Nat — it *is* my fault. Remember, you and Mother are both innocent!'

He knew that it was their only hope. Present this situation, however unlikely it seemed, as the unfortunate result of a childish prank, a game begun in naivety and innocence, and perhaps Wintercombe would escape the vengeance of Colonel Pyne, the uncrowned King of Somerset, and his henchmen. It all must rest on the slender, fragile-seeming shoulders of the child whose conspiracy had led them to this nightmare.

He glanced around the hall, seeking the rest of his family. William was there, a small stalwart figure sitting on the settle by the fire. His arm was circled protectively around Kate, who had evidently been crying her heart out, for tearstains streaked her face, and her brown eyes were round and numb with horror. Nat sent the two children a warm smile, and was rewarded by an answering grin, rather feeble, from his brother. Kate, lost in misery, did not appear to notice him.

He could not see Rachael. He gently disengaged Tabby's hands, and asked her where his twin was.

An extraordinary expression, fierce and full of loathing, appeared on the girl's elfin face. 'I don't know, and I don't care,' she said venomously. 'She betrayed us.'

'*Rachael*?' Nothing that had so far been revealed had appalled Nat as much as this news. 'Rachael betrayed you? Did she know about your plot, then?'

'She wasn't supposed to know. We decided not to tell her. She found out,' said Tabby. 'And when the soldiers came looking, not really expecting to find anything . . . she *told* them.'

There were mutterings of distress, or disgust, amongst the servants. Nat glanced at them and saw in their shocked faces a measure of his own horror. They were almost all respectable, godly people, who had no love for Scots or Cavaliers, but with

[351]

very few exceptions their loyalty to the St. Barbes was unshake-able, and half of them had been with the family long enough to remember Nick Hellier, when he had been in command of the Royalist garrison here. He was glad that none had been privy to the conspiracy. Their genuine bewilderment and ignorance would further help his cause.

'I'll speak with Rachael later,' he said. 'For now, I must go see Hellier for myself.'

'I d'beg your pardon, sir,' said one of the troopers, blocking his path as he approached the screens. 'But Captain Humphreys said as how nobody wasn't allowed out of this here place till he returned, sir.'

Nat was shorter than the soldier, by a hand's span at least, but his air of arrogant astonishment was singularly intimidating. 'This is my house, and I'll move around it as I please – especially since I have nothing whatsoever to do with this ludicrous caper. Now stand aside, or I'll report your insolence to your colonel.'

The trooper held his ground for a moment longer, and then shamefacedly gave way before the younger man's confident and contemptuous stare. Reluctantly, he stepped aside, and uttered a parting shot as Nat pushed through the screen curtains. 'But you bain't to go outside, sir – Captain Humphreys said most particular!'

Only those who were nearest heard Nat's brief and pungent dismissal of Captain Humphreys, and a subdued mutter of scornful laughter echoed in the hall, much to the trooper's discomfort.

The door to his chamber was shut, but there were sounds of activity within. Nat paused, gathering his thoughts. He did not know how much Silence might have revealed, in the shock and horror of seeing her lover hurt, of the truth about her own complicity in this sorry affair. He hoped that she had managed to be circumspect, even in those ghastly moments when she must have thought Nick dead, or dying – and if he did not survive, his own grief would be almost the equal of hers.

He hoped most desperately that it would not end thus: and he wished now, with a savage regret that was quite foreign to his philosophical, pragmatic nature, that he had not gone to Combe Hay this afternoon, and left them, unknowing, to the mercy of the soldiers, and Rachael's treachery. He did not know what he could have done to avert this disaster, but at least he would have been able to offer his support and help.

Rachael. The hurt her betrayal had caused him was surprisingly bitter. It was as if she had become someone else, and the years of their childhood had vanished away like smoke, forgotten and of no account. He could not imagine what motive had been sufficiently powerful to turn her traitor, nor how she had discovered the secret. But in doing so, she had earned Tabby's fierce loathing, and his own disgusted anger.

He would deal with her later, however painful it might prove to be. Now, his duty, and his compassion, were given to his stepmother. He mustered his strength, and knocked on the door.

Patience opened it, a Patience he hardly recognised, made plain by fear and shock, her hair tangled around her face and her pretty hands stained with blood. There was a red smear of it across her pale forehead, and more dabbled across her apron and cuffs. She stood staring at him as if he were a ghost, her eyes enormous. 'Oh, Nat – Nat, thank God!'

'Can I come in?' he asked. For answer, she held the door wide. 'Yes, oh yes, please do – oh, I'm so glad to see you!'

He entered his familiar chamber, crowded with the things that gave him interest and pleasure. But his attention was fixed only on Silence, bending over a still figure in the bed. A trooper, incongruous in these domestic surroundings, stood solidly by the closet door, his arms folded, gazing with ghoulish fascination at the wounded man. The air smelt foul, a sickly-sweet mix of blood and the pungent aromas of his stepmother's remedies. Nat said softly, 'How is he?'

Silence stood on the other side of the bed, her hands full of bloodstained linen. He saw at once that her strength was almost at an end, the breaking point very close. She said, in a strained, taut voice, 'I don't know – we've almost stopped the bleeding, thank God, but he's lost a lot – oh, Nat, why did he have to fight?'

It was an unanswerable question. He said softly, 'Tabby has told me what happened. Can I help? There must be something I can do.'

'Yes – you can hold that over the wound,' Silence said, indicating a thickly folded pad of linen. 'Patience – go down to the still-room, and make up an ointment, you remember the recipe – wheatflour, white of egg, a little honey and Venice turpentine, that's on the top shelf on the right side of the hearth, and add some bole armeniac for the bleeding, that's in a jar on the mantelshelf. Mix it all together in a bowl, and bring it up here as quickly as you can.'

'Of course,' said her sister, and ran from the chamber. Nat, holding the pad of linen as he had been instructed, stared down at the man who, only this morning, had spoken to him of his plans for the future, and wondered, with bleak and angry sadness, what future was left for Nick Hellier after this.

He lay quite still, unconscious, which, Nat thought grimly, was probably just as well. The neat, clever, lively face, with its unaccustomed and disguising growth of beard, was grey and slack, the skin cold and clammy to his touch. Silence, her face almost as lifeless, took his wrist in her fingers. Nat glanced down at the pad. So far, no blood seemed to have soaked through. He knew better than to give way to hope, though, so small seemed to be the margin now, between Nick's death, and life.

'How bad is it?' he asked softly. Silence, her eyes vast and haunted, laid her lover's hand down on the bed. With compassion, he saw her desperate effort to be objective. She swallowed twice, and said, in that same strained hoarse voice, 'I don't know. If we have stopped the bleeding, if, I think he will have a good chance. It – it doesn't seem to have pierced his lung, I don't think it has, and the other cuts are superficial. But he's lost a lot of blood.'

Nat took her hands in his, trying to lend her some of his own strength. She pushed him away, with a shadow of her usual brisk asperity. 'No – you must keep pressing on that pad!'

He obeyed her, with a mock smile that drew a very faint answer. 'I'm sorry. I shouldn't neglect my duties.'

'No, you should not,' said his stepmother. She gripped her hands together and, visibly, with several long deliberate breaths, calmed herself.

He waited until she had done, and then said softly, 'Tabby has told me what she and the other children have done. I can hardly believe it.'

Silence stared at him, bewildered. Nat glanced at the trooper, but the man's attention had wandered. He put his finger significantly to his lips, and went on. 'It barely seems credible, that somehow they can have smuggled two men into Wintercombe without anyone else's knowledge – do you know how they did it?'

Exhaustion, grief and the vast, terrible fear that had gripped her ever since she saw Nick fall, had made her wits slow, but she understood him now. She shook her head. 'Tabby has said nothing to me yet. I haven't had the chance to talk to her, it all happened so suddenly — have you seen her? Is she all right? And the other children?'

Under Nat's firm pressure, the pad seemed to shift. He glanced at Nick's face, and saw a sudden tension there as awareness, and pain, returned. 'Yes, they are,' he said briefly. 'Captain? Captain Hellier, can you hear me?'

The trooper looked round, his expression avid and expectant. The man in the bed frowned, his mouth gripped tight. Very slowly, his head moved.

Silence closed her eyes, sick with relief. No matter that a return to consciousness was no indication of future recovery. Her greatest fear had been that he would slip away from her for ever, without any chance of farewell. And she knew that the longer he survived, the better would be his chances. Against all sense and caution, a tiny glint of hope began to illuminate her dread-filled heart.

'You're in my chamber,' Nat was saying to the wounded man. 'My stepmother is tending your hurts.' He paused, wondering how to proceed. In normal circumstances Nick, so quick-witted, would understand the necessity of caution but, in this extremity, could he be prevented from uttering some damning remark? Somehow, Nat must try to give him an indication of the tale he must tell, if Wintercombe was to be saved.

'Is it bad?' Nick's voice was little more than a whisper. 'It should be — it hurts like hell.'

'Apparently you'll live,' said Nat drily. 'Tabby has told me everything — how she smuggled you into Wintercombe — what a stupid, foolhardy prank.'

Nick's eyes opened, Kate's eyes, narrowed against the light from the window, although the day was drawing near to evening. He turned his head until Nat's face came into view. 'We didn't want you to know,' he said, and, unseen by the trooper, managed a wink.

Nat relaxed. At least he now had some idea of the story they must all tell. He smiled broadly. 'Don't worry about it. We'll try to sort it all out. You lie still, and rest.'

Patience rushed into the chamber like a whirlwind, carrying a small pewter bowl, from which a throat-catching smell was wafting. 'That captain's back,' she announced, striding up to the bed and thrusting the ointment into her sister's hands. 'I don't think he caught the other man. He's furious.' She was unable to keep the satisfaction out of her voice. 'He's interrogating the servants now, and when he's finished, he wants to question all of us.'

Silence tested the consistency of the mixture, dipping a finger into the glutinous mass and sniffing it. She said firmly, 'He'll have to wait to see me, until my business is done here. Captain Hellier? I am going to spread this over your wound, and then bandage it all up, with my sister's help. It will undoubtedly hurt, but we will try to be as gentle as we can. Then, you can sleep for a while, if you are able.'

'If . . . ' said Nick, and a trace of wry amusement twisted his mouth. 'To your work, my lady . . . patch up this old soldier of fortune, and he'll swear never to fight another day.'

*

Captain Humphreys was, as Patience had said, absolutely furious. He had spent an hour or more at the head of his three troopers, galloping up and down the streets and fields and lanes of Philip's Norton, seeking the supposed King of Scots, but to no avail. He might as well have disappeared into a puff of smoke like a demon, for all the inhabitants had seen of him, and there was a good chance that he had never gone near the village at all. To add insult to injury, the rogue had taken Humphreys' horse, a handsome chestnut that he had paid for out of his own pocket. In justice, one of the Wintercombe riding horses would have to supply his need for the present, and let the grandees argue about it later. He could hardly return to Bristol riding pillion behind one of his own men.

He rode back to the house glowering, lost in thought. There was no help for it, Pyne must be informed, and the local militia turned out to search for the fugitive. He scribbled a brief note, to summon assistance and to acquaint Colonel Pyne, or one of his subordinates, with the situation, and sent one of his men off to Bath with it. Then, grim-faced, he took his seat in the dining parlour, and began the long and frustrating task of discovering exactly how this godly, respectable Puritan household had come to be sheltering two escaped Cavaliers.

He began with the servants, each one more bewildered and affronted than the last. No matter how closely he questioned them, he could draw from them no admission of guilt or complicity. Even the smooth-tongued butler had avowed that if he had known of the situation, he would have lost no time in denouncing the Cavaliers to the authorities in Bath, and had added that surely

Sir Nathaniel or Lady St. Barbe would have done the same, if they had become aware of what was happening under their roof.

Captain Humphreys regarded this loyal servant with some dislike. 'So you think they did not know?'

'I am certain of it, sir,' said Ambrose Carpenter.

'Then in Heaven's name, who did succour them?'

'I cannot say, sir — but I can guess.'

So could Captain Humphreys, impossible though the idea seemed. He sat in the chair at the head of the dining table, chewing his thumbnail in impotent fury, while one of the maidservants, a shy plain child, lit candles and drew shutters against the dark, and replenished the fire. She dipped a nervous curtsey. 'Will that be all, sir?'

'Fetch the St. Barbe children,' he said curtly. 'I wish to see them at once.'

They came in, white-faced and apprehensive. The little girl who had inadvertently alerted him to the presence of the Cavaliers was evidently terrified. He sent her an unconvincingly jovial smile, and she hid behind her sister's skirts. The boy looked frightened, but obstinately unrepentant. He had helped the other fugitive to escape, by casting a wooden bench into the path of the pursuing troopers, causing them to fall over it. By the time they had extricated themselves, their quarry had seized one of the horses — *my* horse, thought Humphreys, with renewed fury — and fled.

The tall, lovely girl who seemed to be the leader of the conspiracy, put her hands on the boy's shoulders, and stared at the captain defiantly. There was no sign of remorse there, either. Humphreys decided to attack. He said sharply, 'Which of you knew about those men?'

'We all did,' said the eldest girl. She indicated the other children. 'Me, and Deb, and William, and Kate.'

'And your brother, Sir Nathaniel? What was his part in all this?'

'He didn't know anything,' said the girl. 'We didn't tell him.'

'I find that hard to believe,' Humphreys said. He leant forward, glaring at her. 'Why did you not?'

'Because he'd tell them to go, of course, if he knew,' said the girl scornfully. 'And they needed to rest. They'd walked all the way from Bristol.'

'So you discovered them, and offered them shelter?'

'Yes,' she said calmly, refusing to be intimidated. 'We found them on the Wellow lane. I knew Captain Hellier, from when he was with the garrison here, during the war. He was our friend then, he saved our lives, probably – I couldn't just tell him to go away, now could I?'

'And were you aware,' said Humphreys, suddenly jabbing his finger at her, 'of the penalties lately laid down for assisting Charles Stuart, pretended King of Scots?'

Tabby stared at him in bewilderment. 'What has the King of Scots to do with this?'

'You claim to be unaware, then, that the man who has escaped our clutches, thanks to the connivance of your wretched brother, is the King of Scots?'

This, to Humphreys' fury, seemed to cause the girl great amusement. 'The King of Scots? Of course he isn't the King of Scots! Whatever gave you that idea?'

'I have been reliably informed that the man bears a strong resemblance to him.'

'Well, I suppose he might,' said Tabby slowly. 'At least, he's tall and dark like the King – I mean, Charles Stuart. But he can't be the King of Scots, he's much too old – nearly thirty, I should think. And he said his name was Mervyn Touchet, and Captain Hellier said so too.' She swallowed suddenly, the first sign of fear that he had seen in her. 'What are you going to do with him? Is he very badly hurt?'

'He is my prisoner, and will suffer the proper penalty in due course,' said Humphreys. 'That is no concern of yours, Mistress St. Barbe.'

'Yes, it is!' Tabby cried, suddenly and fiercely angry. 'I brought him here, it's my fault he was captured, he's our friend – of *course* he's my concern!'

'So – you admit that you committed the grave crime of treason against the Commonwealth, by harbouring two enemies of the State,' said Humphreys. 'And you expect me to believe that a pack of children had no other accomplices? How old are you, girl?'

'I'm fifteen,' said Tabby. She had begun to tremble, but held herself calm and steady in the face of his attack. 'Deb is eleven, William's nine and Kate is five. I know it was treason, but it didn't *seem* as if it was – he was our friend, we couldn't just leave them there when they needed help!'

'And your mother and brother knew nothing of it?' He switched his attention suddenly to William, and the boy started. 'You! Did your mother know you were sheltering these men?'

[358]

William was beginning to learn a little guile. His face as open as a book, his brown eyes wide, he shook his head. 'No, sir, she didn't.'

'Nor your brother?'

'No,' said William positively. 'We all swore an oath – I made all of us four swear not to tell *anyone*.' He glared at Kate. 'But *she* did – she told Rachael.'

'At least there is one honest person amongst you,' said Captain Humphreys bitterly. 'Where is your sister Rachael?'

The children exchanged glances. 'We don't know,' said Tabby. 'I think she's hiding somewhere.' Her face grew defiant once more. 'She's probably ashamed of what she's done.'

The captain banged his hand on the table. The candles jumped and Kate, transformed by the terror and shock of the afternoon's events into a shrinking, nervous shadow of her usual exuberance, began to cry. 'Enough of this nonsense!' Humphreys shouted. 'Before God, your father would be ashamed of you!'

'What right have you to say that?' Tabby retorted, quick as lightning. '*I* am not ashamed of helping an old friend, nor would my father be, and neither are William and Deb. You can put us in prison, if you like, but no one else had anything to do with it at all, and it's not fair to suggest that they did!'

She was almost shouting at him. He stared at her in astonishment. He had thought her a reserved, gently-reared girl who had unaccountably strayed into waters well out of her depth. But now, she was transformed into a termagant, and he had no idea how to deal with her. It had been a long, frustrating and infuriating day, and he had reached the end of his tether. 'Silence!' he bellowed.

She was staring at him, her head held proudly and her eyes bright. She said, in a very much quieter voice, 'Please, sir, will you be more temperate? You are frightening my little sister.'

He spared a glance for the smallest one, who was indeed sobbing bitterly into her brother's chest. She was the same age, roughly, as his own little Sue. For the first time, he wondered how he would feel, if some overbearing stranger were to bully and browbeat his daughter thus. Belatedly, he controlled his impotent fury, and said, trying to moderate his voice, 'I have heard enough for the present. I may wish to speak with you again, Mistress St. Barbe but, for the moment, you may all go.'

'Thank you,' she said coolly, with not a trace of humility.

'Come on, Kate, it's all over – and time you were in bed. Let's go and find Doraty, shall we?'

He watched, chewing his thumbnail, as the four children left the room. It was beginning to seem as if the eldest girl was in fact telling the truth. He found it hard to imagine her as the chief conspirator, but that anger and defiant honesty had been genuine enough, and the boy had corroborated it. He wondered if any of his troopers had heard anything incriminating.

None of them had. Indeed, the man whom he had placed to guard the prisoner was able to state that every word the wounded man had said, and the talk of Sir Nathaniel and his stepmother, indicated their innocence and bewilderment.

'And how is the prisoner?' Humphreys enquired. He would be sorry to see the man die, Cavalier or no, and greatly regretted that it had proved necessary to injure him in order to capture him.

'Sleeping sound, sir, when I came down,' said the man. 'Lady St. Barbe d'think he'll live, sir.'

'Good. Now, bring my lady and Sir Nathaniel to me.'

The trooper saluted, and went out. A delicious smell of food wafted in through the door before he closed it, and Captain Humphreys felt his mouth watering. He had had little enough sustenance all day, but at least he and his men were assured of a dry comfortable bed tonight, and a hot meal to fill their bellies. Colonel Pyne or his minions would arrive, probably tomorrow morning, to take over the search and the prisoner, and he would be free to return to Bristol, somewhat chastened by his experience. Fool, to place too much credence on rumour, to succumb to his own greed!

The door opened, and Sir Nathaniel St. Barbe stood there, ushering in his stepmother. Humphreys sighed. The children had been most adamant that neither adult had been involved, and certainly he could not believe that this plain, ordinary, sensible woman would have done anything so foolhardy. Nor the young baronet, who looked far too clever to be risking his inheritance and his freedom, by concealing escaped Cavaliers in his roofspace.

'What are you going to do with Captain Hellier?' Silence asked, before Nat had shut the door. She walked up to the other end of the table and stood there, her hazel eyes intent. Humphreys found himself surprised that this woman could lack beauty, and yet resemble her lovely daughter so closely. 'Before I answer any of your questions, if I can, you must tell me that.'

Her stepson put a hand on her arm, but she ignored it. Humphreys said honestly, 'I do not know, my lady. I have sent for Colonel Pyne, or his officers, and I intend to give the prisoner into their care. What happens to him thereafter will depend on their good will, or otherwise. I take it that he was part of the Scots army?'

Just in time, Silence remembered the role which she must play. She spread her hands. 'I have no idea, Captain. I knew nothing about him, until this afternoon.'

'Yet you referred to him as Captain Hellier.'

'That was the rank he held when he was in the garrison here, during the last year of the war,' said Nat. 'I don't know what he is now.'

'They are planning to send all the Scots prisoners, and others, who are below field rank, as bondservants to the New World Colonies,' said Humphreys. 'If he is still a captain, that may well be his fate. They will embark from Bristol – the orders have already gone out.'

'They cannot take a sick man!' she said, horrified. 'He can't be moved from here, let alone taken aboard ship!'

'I repeat,' said Humphreys wearily, 'that will be for Colonel Pyne to decide. He will probably think it most unwise to leave the prisoner here, where doubtless your rebellious offspring would seek to set him at liberty.'

A smile twitched Nat's long thin mouth. 'If I know them, they probably would.'

'Exactly.' The captain surveyed them. 'I must ask you this, Sir Nathaniel. Were you aware of the fugitives hiding in your loft?'

'Not until I returned this afternoon,' Nat said, 'to find my house in uprorar, troopers everywhere and my chamber resembling a butcher's stall.' He allowed the smile to lengthen. 'Believe me, Captain, if I had known of this, I would have lost no time in sending them away..All I desire is to enjoy my inheritance in peace, and harbouring enemies of the Commonwealth is hardly conducive to that.'

'So you disclaim all knowledge? Do you then believe that your sister was the chief mover in the plot? She is hardly more than a child.'

'Appearances can be deceptive,' said Nat. 'My sister Tabitha is a young lady of decided character, with her own ideas of right and wrong. I assume that she wished only to help an old friend, with unfortunate consequences.'

'That, indeed, is what she claims. But I find it equally difficult to believe that she and the other children are solely responsible. I have seen the hiding-place — feather beds, food, blankets, all mighty comfortable. Surely they must have had adult help.'

'Does she say so?'

'No, she denies it emphatically, but . . .'

'Tabby is a truthful child,' said Silence, feeling that her daughter must be defended. This tale would doubtless ring round Somerset before the week was out, and although she could acknowledge the need, for all their sakes, for the blame to be placed where there could in all humanity be no punishment, she hated the idea of her beloved eldest child being branded a criminal, or a traitor, or, almost as bad, a naïve and gullible fool. No matter that Tabby herself had chosen, indeed insisted on this course. Honour demanded that she herself take at least some of the blame.

But where Nick, and Wintercombe, and their future were concerned, honour must for once be rejected. She added anxiously, 'What will happen to her? Surely she will not be punished too severely — she's only a child.'

Humphreys smiled reassuringly. 'I do not think that you will have cause to fear, my lady. She has been foolish, perhaps but, as you say, she is very young, and has evidently not yet reached the age of discretion. Punishment such as you fear would be most inappropriate, in these circumstances. But,' he added warningly, 'that does not mean that she will not be brought to full recognition of the wrong she has done.'

'I think she already has been,' said Nat drily.

Silence could tell that Humphreys believed them: the gradual change in his manner, from anger to considerate sympathy, confirmed it. She said softly, 'Thank you, Captain, for your forbearance under such difficulties. I would like to go now, and speak to my daughter. She must be very anxious to learn what fate will befall her.'

'Of course,' Humphreys said courteously. The aroma of cooking increased, and his belly grumbled hopefully.

Nat remained, studying him thoughtfully. He said, 'I am sorry for the trouble to which you have been put, Captain. You have ridden all the way from Bristol, and had very little reward for it. You will join us for supper, I trust? Your men can be fed in the kitchen, and there are beds for them over the stables.'

Humphreys thanked him warmly. Tomorrow, or more likely

the day after, he might be able to laugh about this escapade with his comrades – not mentioning, of course, the ludicrous mistake about the King of Scots. His mood of frustration and anger had ebbed entirely, and he found himself liking this self-contained, very mature young man. The offer of supper was most welcome, and when a maid appeared with wine, a very pleasant claret, his hesitant feeling of contentment increased. One man had escaped him, but he was certainly not Charles Stuart, and he still had a prisoner, obviously a most desperate villain despite Mistress Tabitha's protestations, to show for his pains. Colonel Scroope would surely look kindly upon his initiative, and favour him when the next position became vacant. The girl would not escape unscathed, either, for her brother would doubtless punish her for her reckless and foolish exploit.

'To the prosperity of the Commonwealth, and the downfall of its enemies!' said Nat, raising his glass, and Humphreys echoed him fervently.

*

If the worthy captain thought that all difficulties had been resolved, his confidence was not shared by the rest of the St. Barbes. Kate, packed off to bed, had cried herself to sleep, and Deb had had to be taken into Nick's chamber before she would believe that he in fact lived. William, unusually subdued, had asked his mother if they were to be punished, and Silence had given him a smile of reassurance. 'No, but we may have to pretend that you are until the soldiers have left. It's all right, William, don't look so worried. We're not angry with you – you did splendidly. It's just a pity that Captain Hellier was captured.'

William was sitting bolt upright in bed, his nightshirt crumpled and his face very serious. He said earnestly, 'Will he die, Mama?'

Silence took a deep breath, and found that her eyes were filling with tears. She blinked them hastily away. 'No, I don't think so,' she told him. 'But he will be ill for some time, and I shall have to nurse him. Nat and I did it before, but you won't remember that, you were too young.'

'In the siege?' William's eyes shone suddenly bright. 'Oh, I do! There were lots of things that went bang.'

'You must have heard about it afterwards – we sent you to Wick Farm for safety,' Silence told him. She watched as he wriggled down under the blankets. 'Good night, and sleep well.'

There remained only Tabby. In deference to her age, she had recently been given the chamber in the north wing, overlooking the barton, that had belonged to Nat before his father's death. Silence found her sitting at the table, staring out into the dark. Only one candle had been lit, and the fire was cold.

'I think it'd be best if I didn't come down for supper, if that man is going to be there,' Tabby said, mustering a shadowy grin. 'I almost shouted at him, and he didn't like it.'

'I'm not surprised,' Silence said. She hesitated, suddenly at a loss. For so long, she had felt so close to her eldest, and favourite child, and now this beautiful, graceful young woman seemed to be almost a stranger. It was humbling to realise how great was the debt she, and all of them, owed to Tabby.

'I'm sorry,' said her daughter suddenly. 'I didn't mean to cause all this trouble – I didn't realise.' She swallowed. 'What I told Captain Humphreys – about not wanting to involve you and Nat – it *was* true, really. It still is true – I wish you hadn't known.'

'I don't,' said Silence. 'I'm glad I did. All I'm sorry for, is that Nick didn't escape.'

'I'm sorry too,' Tabby said. She looked up at her mother, and Silence saw that her eyes were filled with tears. 'I didn't think that it would lead to this. I *wish* it hadn't – I *wish* he hadn't been hurt – I thought it'd all be all right, and one day he could come back and marry you, and now it's all gone wrong, and it's all Rachael's fault – she's a traitor, and I hate her!'

Rachael. Silence had forgotten all about her. In the panic and confusion following the discovery, Nick and the urgency of saving him had driven everything else from her mind. She realised that she had not seen her for some time – not, in fact, since Nick's capture. She said, 'Do you know where she is?'

'No, I don't, and I don't care,' said Tabby, and a look of loathing transfigured her face. 'Betraying Captain Hellier was bad enough, but what she did to Kate was *horrible* – and I won't ever be able to forget it, or forgive her.'

There was nothing, Silence realised, that could be said. It was true: and the memory of Kate, guilty and desperate and sobbing, rose again to haunt her. On this occasion, Rachael's behaviour had plunged from the merely annoying and awkward, to the utterly unforgivable.

And yet, she thought, even after all she's done, I feel so sorry for her. What agonies must she be enduring, now?

But she understood why Tabby's views were so strong. Her eldest child had a fierce sense of justice, and Rachael had far overstepped even her generous limits. She said quietly, 'I think she had her reasons for doing what she did, even though they may seem paltry to us. You know Rachael – everything looms so large in her mind.'

'She probably did it to keep Jack Harington,' said Tabby. 'And it would serve her right if he never wanted to speak to her again, let alone marry her.'

'We shall have to wait to find that out,' Silence pointed out. 'But doubtless the tale will reach Kelston soon enough. And we may find that Sir John no longer wishes to be allied with a family that harbours escaped Cavaliers.'

'Good,' was Tabby's forthright comment. 'Do you know, I don't think Rachael really wants to marry Jack at all. She was doing it for Father.' An incongruously wicked grin suddenly appeared on her face. 'I think that when all this is over, we ought to invite Tom Wickham to stay for a little while.'

Silence stared at her incorrigibly scheming daughter in astonishment. 'Tom *Wickham*? You can't possibly mean . . . '

'Well, I know she said she loathed the sight of him,' said Tabby. 'But he seemed quite sympathetic to her, even though she was really offensive to him. I like Tom.'

'Then why are you thinking of encouraging him?' Silence could not help asking.

Tabby looked at her with surprise. 'Because he'd be good for Rachael. He'd understand her.'

'I thought you could never forgive her for what she'd done,' Silence reminded her, in some bewilderment. 'Now you're planning to throw her into the arms of a very pleasant young man who'd be good for her – or so you claim! What about poor Tom's feelings in the matter?'

'I think he'd rise to the challenge,' Tabby said. She looked at her mother, her eyes wide and serious. 'You think I'm joking, don't you – you still think I'm a child. Well, perhaps I am, in years and experience, but I know *people*, I can understand them, somehow. Yes, I do hate Rachael, no, I don't think I will ever forgive or forget what she did to Kate, and to you – but that doesn't mean I don't want to help her. She is my sister, after all, and if we don't do something about her soon, she'll make our lives unbearable.'

Silence could only stare at her, somewhat bemused. After a

pause, she said, 'You're quite right — you are no longer a child. And perhaps you're wiser than all of us — except for Nat, of course.'

'He's much more cunning than I am,' said Tabby. She looked as if she was about to confide something, but hesitated. Then she went on, 'What's going to happen? What will they do with Captain Hellier?'

'I don't know. Captain Humphreys doesn't either, but he says it'll be Colonel Pyne's business, when he arrives. Humphreys has sent for him, and he'll probably be here in the morning.' She gave Tabby an encouraging smile. 'You may have to tell him your tale all over again.'

'I don't mind,' said Tabby. 'They can't do anything very much to me, can they, and still less to Deb and William. I don't mind if they think I'm a stupid child. *I* know I'm not, and so does everyone here, and their opinions count. Colonel Pyne is a corrupt and arrogant despot, everyone knows it, and I don't give a toss for what he thinks. Mother, don't look so unhappy — I *chose* this, this whole business was my fault, I asked Captain Hellier and that other man to come here, and I didn't want you or Nat to know anything about it. Patience was different somehow, I knew it would seem like an adventure to her, and it did. It's only fair I should take the blame, I *want* to — and if by doing so I save you and Nat from fines and disgrace, or worse, then I'm *glad* to do it! What can they do to me? I'm not afraid of shouting men, or a good scolding. I remember what Colonel Ridgeley was like, and after him no one can ever seem as bad.'

'I feel rather the same myself,' Silence confessed. She looked at her daughter's emphatic face, and wondered how she could ever have thought this child vague, or dreamy. That serene and lovely countenance concealed a strength of will that was astonishing. 'Tabby — you deserve all our thanks.'

The girl's mouth twisted ruefully, much as Nat's did. 'No, I don't — not for doing what I think is right. But there's one thing we haven't really talked about, which is the most important thing of all. How are we going to help Nick escape?'

As her mother stared at her, dumbfounded, she added, 'Well, we can hardly leave him to Colonel Pyne's mercies, can we? Can't you put a sleeping-draught in the soldiers' food this evening?'

'Tabby, he is *hurt*,' said Silence, torn between shocked laughter and bitter tears. 'If we try and put him on a horse, he'll fall off it, and likely die from loss of blood – he's quite unable to ride. He is sleeping now, and that's the best thing. I would much rather he was a prisoner, and alive, than dead.' She added urgently, 'Please – *don't* do anything else. We may all survive this, but if you try to spirit him away, Pyne's retribution will fall on us all like a wall. For your sake, and Nat's, and everyone's, and most of all for Nick – please, please leave it be.'

Tabby's eyes, the same hazel-green as her own, but, she saw now for the first time, far fiercer, far more uncompromising, met hers for a long moment, and then dropped. 'Yes,' she said to her hands, clasped on the table. 'You are right – I will leave it be.'

'Good,' said Silence. 'It's – it's not that I don't *want* him free – I do, most desperately. He has asked me to marry him – we had been making plans . . . '

'Wonderful!' Tabby said, leaping up to embrace her. 'Oh, Mother, I'm so pleased – it's the best thing possible – now all he has to do, is to convince Colonel Pyne that he won't fight against the Commonwealth again, and then they'll let him go!'

Which, Silence thought miserably, as she bade her beloved child goodnight, was undoubtedly an extremely optimistic view of the circumstances.

Rachael's chamber lay next to Tabby's. She paused outside it, steeling herself for the unpleasantness of the next few minutes, and then knocked.

There was no reply, and the door remained obstinately shut. She knocked again, and then lifted the latch.

The door swung open, creaking gently. The chamber beyond was impenetrably dark, and she sensed its emptiness. She walked in, holding up her candlestick, watching the long black shadows move round the furniture. Bed, clothes-press, table, chairs, books – but no Rachael.

An indefinable prickling of dread crawled up her scalp. She glanced around once more, and even, feeling foolish, peered under the bed. But there was only the maid's truckle there, pushed out of sight. The fire was unlit, and there were no candles. Rachael had not, it seemed, been here since before darkness fell.

Her maid might know where she was. Silence walked down the corridor that ran for most of the length of the north wing, and looked into the chamber occupied by the serving-maids, Meg and Hannah, and, the dairymaids, Jane and Anne. It was dark and unoccupied, for at this hour they would all be downstairs, cleaning the dairy or helping to make ready for supper. Still disturbed by that feeling of apprehension, Silence closed the door and went down the back stairs to the servants' hall.

Jude Hinton, Rachael's long-suffering maid, was laying the table for their supper. Her plain, placid face creased with puzzled anxiety at Silence's question. 'No, no, m'lady – I ain't seed her since afore the soldiers come. She towd I she were a-going to see Mistress Apprice, and gived I some sewing to do – and I've been a-sewing in here, m'lady, till the soldiers come. Wherever can she be?'

'We must find her,' Silence said. 'Supper can be delayed for the moment, and I'll organise a search.'

Captain Humphreys, impatiently awaiting his longed-for meal in the dining parlour, was not best pleased by the news that it was not, after all, imminent. Nat, his face suddenly serious, excused himself with apologies. 'My sister is missing, sir, and must be found. I will return to you shortly – in the meantime, help yourself to more wine.'

Rachael was not hiding in any of the store-rooms in the north wing, nor in the chambers above. The groom, Tom Goodenough, who had been at Wintercombe for nearly half his life, directed his lads and the garden boys in a brisk and thorough search of the buildings around the barton, with no result. Nat and Silence, with increasing anxiety, hunted all through the eastern part of the house, even looking in the now deserted roofspace. But dust and shadows were all they saw, and when the seekers gathered, as arranged, in the hall, no one had anything to report. Rachael was nowhere within the house.

The last anyone had seen of her was in the confused and frantic moments when Nick Hellier was fighting for his freedom. Eliza told Silence that she thought Rachael had run down the stairs when the captain fell: Carpenter, however, had been in the hall, and had not seen her. It was as if, Silence thought with terrible foreboding, her stepdaughter had vanished from the face of the earth, spirited away by the forces of darkness.

'I think I know where she might be,' said Nat suddenly. He glanced around the servants, and at his stepmother. 'She might have taken refuge in the summerhouse. If she isn't there, then the Lord alone knows where she is. And . . . perhaps it would be best if I went alone. In her probable state of mind, it can do her no good if we all come bursting in on her.' He smiled reassuringly at

Silence, whose face now showed, indelibly, the marks of the strain of this long and terrible day. 'I shan't be long.'

She waited in the garden room, watching the small yellow light from his lantern bobbing down the terraces and away out of her sight. Her view of the summerhouse was blocked by the small angled turret which carried the stairs to her chamber. She slipped outside the door, and stood shivering in the chilly September night, wondering why she should feel so apprehensive. Surely, this was no more than another of Rachael's tantrums?

*

But Rachael, fleeing the house, had known that, this time, she had put herself utterly beyond the pale. She had seen Nick fall, surely dead, and it was all her doing, as certainly as if she had wielded that lethal sword herself. Anguish and remorse had ripped through her, and, like a wounded animal, she had turned and run blindly, seeking respite from this bitter torment.

Almost of their own accord, her urgent feet had taken her to the pretty summerhouse at the end of the terrace, where, only an hour or two before, she had hurt and frightened her five-year-old sister into revealing the deadly secret. She fell, sobbing, down the steep wooden steps to the little-used lower storey, smelling of apples and damp and dust, and curled herself into the furthest corner, behind a group of pots.

But she could not hide from her thoughts, from the stern ruthless voice which shouted her sins to her until she put her hands over her ears, but still could not shut it out. She was a traitor, and wicked, and evil. She had caused a man's death, from spite and for her own selfish ends, she had alienated and disgusted her entire family, and she knew now that, whatever hopes she might have entertained, Jack Harington would no longer want anything to do with her.

And with good reason. In the long silent hours, as light drained slowly from the dim little room, Rachael looked herself fully in the face, for the first time in her life, and shrank from what she saw. And yet the voice went on, shouting in her head, cataloguing the evils she had done in the name of duty and religion, remorselessly describing, in minute detail, the myriad little cruelties, the despicable arrogance, the general abhorrence of her conduct over the past few months.

As the voice reminded her, unhappiness had been no excuse. Other people were unhappy, but did not take their misery out on innocent victims. She did not have to marry that pompous bore: she had only needed to say so, and her brother would have gently but firmly apologised to the Haringtons, and torn up the contract. In short, she was vile. And the future, ostracised, loathed, unwed and shunned, seemed too appalling to be borne.

As dusk had grown, the idea had come to her. She did not have to go on living with this dreadful guilt, this unutterable emptiness. It was a sin, but what was one more, against those which she had already committed? Her family, to whom she had never really felt she belonged, would be free of her. If I were them, thought Rachael, I would dance on my grave.

Her sense of purpose grew. She got stiffly to her feet. It was cold, and dark, but she had been so long in the dim light that her eyes had adjusted to it, and she could see quite well. She knew what she wanted, and where it could be found. A length of hempen rope, round and prickly. A sturdy wooden tub, upturned. And a hook or beam, around which to fix the rope.

She could see none in this lower room, and almost sobbed in frustration. She had turned her face towards death, and any delay now seemed intolerable. Then she remembered that there were hooks in the wall in the upper part, from which garden tools were hung. Moving with the dead implacability of a sleepwalker, she found her way by touch and instinct to the wooden stairs, the rope in one hand and the heavy tub in the other. It made a noise as she hauled it bumping upwards, but she was past caring.

There was more light up here, for there were three windows instead of one, and they were comparatively clean. She found the strongest-looking hook, lifted Diggory's pruning saws down, and slung the rope around it.

She realised then, with sudden panic, that she had no idea how to make the knot. She knew what was required, but the form it should take was a mystery to her. Sobbing, her feverish fingers experimented until they were raw and bleeding, her desperate purpose increasing by the minute. Soon, they would come looking for her, and she did not want to face their accusations, their loathing, their anger and disgust.

At last, after what seemed like hours, she managed an acceptable slip-knot. She pushed the tub close to the wall, and stood upon it, one end of the rope tied round the hook, the other looped around her neck. And now, whether she went to Heaven or to Hell, she was ready for the final act of contrition.

Nat opened the door. The stony cold, the silence, struck him with sudden dread. He held the lantern high, saying softly, 'Rachael?'

He saw his sister, his twin, her distended eyes staring at him. And below, wound like some life-squeezing snake about her neck, the thick, lethal noose of rope.

CHAPTER NINETEEN

'The lie circumstantial, and the lie direct'
(*As You Like It*)

Silence waited on the steps, listening. Nat had gone within the summerhouse, and she could see the lantern light, window-shaped now. It moved and dimmed as, presumably, he set it down. She wondered what he would say to Rachael, if he found her there. The twins, outwardly so different, had nevertheless once been very close, and Nat understood his sister as, perhaps, no one else did. But what could he say, however understanding, however compassionate, to someone who had betrayed all her family, who had behaved so monstrously to Kate?

'Silence?' His voice, disturbingly altered, echoed softly along the quiet dark terraces. 'Silence, I think you should come down here.'

And the dread which had been pressing down on her so hard, became certainty. Her heart lurching, she ran down the steps and along the terrace. The pale gravel between the knots was easy to see, and the moon, nearly full, drifted with callous serenity between the leisurely clouds.

Nat stood in the doorway, his face ghastly in the lantern light. She said, gasping, 'What's happened? Where is she?'

Beyond his still dark figure, she saw Rachael, lying on the cold stone floor, her head pillowed on a pile of sacking, her eyes closed and her face drained of all life and colour. Around her neck, a great scarlet mark stood out, shockingly vivid, against the pallid skin.

'She tried to hang herself,' said Nat, and in his voice, usually so light and cynical, she heard the harsh rags of a desperate, tearing grief, and pity. 'Thank God, she didn't make a proper knot – no, she isn't dead, but she could so easily have been.'

Silence knelt beside her stepdaughter. The thin chest rose and fell, and the breath rasped in her bruised throat. 'She fainted when I cut her down,' said Nat, his voice still almost unrecognisable. 'Oh, the fool, the fool – *why* does she have to be like this?'

'Because she is Rachael,' Silence said bleakly. She felt for the girl's pulse and found it slow, but firm. 'And I suppose she found that she could not live with what she did today.'

'But why? What did she think we'd do to her?' Nat cried. His face was twisted with anguish: Nat, who was so clear-eyed, and detached, and level-headed.

Silence, close to tears herself, shook her head. 'I don't know. Oh, Nat, I don't know. No one understood what went on in her mind. She must have felt such terrible remorse for what she did.'

Nat stood, looking down at his twin, his face shadowed. He said at last, in something approaching his usual voice, 'We must take her inside – and somehow, I don't know how, keep this quiet. She will find the next few days dreadful enough, without everyone whispering that she tried to murder herself.'

'And what if a justice should hear of it? Suicide is a crime, is it not?' said Silence sadly. She brushed the tears from her face. 'Can you carry her, Nat? And wrap something about her neck, as if keeping her from the cold – you can say that you found her collapsed in here, that she's taken a chill – anything, so long as it's convincing, and no one suspects the truth. If we put her to bed and keep her to her chamber for the next few days, until the marks have faded, perhaps no one need ever know.'

'What about her maid?' Nat was untying the knotted rope. He coiled it around his arm, and dropped it over one of the other hooks, replaced the saws and pushed the tub, right way up, into a corner. The summerhouse was once more empty of significance, innocent of any sinister resonance. He knelt by his sister, and with a gesture infinitely and uncharacteristically tender, stroked her lank black hair back from her brow.

'Jude can be trusted not to tattle,' said Silence, after considering the question. 'She will be loyal to Rachael, I should think, though her task hasn't been easy, even at the best of times.'

'And we must ask Mally to come back, if her grandmother is better,' said Nat. 'We've been in sore need of her, the last day or so.'

'And may be yet,' Silence said. She found her lips quivering, the tears spilling over. 'Nat, Nat – I know this is not the time to say it, but I am so frightened for him, so despairing – what are we going to do about Nick?'

'One thing at a time,' he told her. 'My mind has not neglected that particular problem, you know. But at this moment, I think that Rachael needs us more.'

She watched as he removed his doublet, and then gathered up his sister's unresisting body. Once, years ago, Rachael had been the taller by a head, a stalwart, sturdy girl who had looked far older than her frail, undersized twin brother. But Nat had put on height and strength as he shed his childhood ill-health, and had caught her up and passed her. In addition, she had lost a good deal of weight over the past few months. He lifted her with no apparent effort, her black head laid against his shoulder. Silence took up the doublet, and tucked it warmly around her stepdaughter's neck and shoulders, hiding the ropemark completely. Now, they must get her safely to her chamber.

The waiting, anxious servants crowded round as Nat walked slowly, burdened, into the hall. Silence answered their questions briskly and firmly, hoping that they would not sense that there was more to this than might meet their eyes. 'She was in the summerhouse, and she seems to have taken cold.'

'I've lit the fire in her chamber, m'lady,' said Jude Hinton anxiously. 'And I've put a warming pan in her bed, too.'

'Well done,' Silence told her. 'You need not stay with her tonight – she said she wanted no one near her, for the moment. I'll give her a sleeping drink, and she will probably be better in the morning.'

Rachael stirred as her brother laid her down on the soft warmth of her bed. Her blue eyes opened, still horror-struck, and she stared up at him. 'Nat – please – oh, please . . .'

Her voice was almost lost, reduced to a desperate hoarse whisper by her bruised throat. Nat lifted his stricken face to Silence, standing beside him. 'That's – that's what she said before I lifted her down.'

Rachael twisted violently under his steady hands. 'No – please – let me alone!'

'Listen.' Her brother leaned over her. 'Listen to me, Rachael. Do you think that I would? Do you really think that I *want* you to die? That any of us do? It doesn't matter what you've done – you're alive, and that's all that matters.'

'No,' Rachael gasped, tears of bitter anguish flooding her eyes. Silence said softly, 'Oh, please listen – we love you, Rachael, we all do – and we only want to help, *nothing* is worth losing you like that, *nothing!*'

But Rachael, unable to force any more words past her swollen throat, had turned her head away, and closed her eyes.

'I'll give you something to make you sleep,' Silence said, recognising defeat. Best, for the moment, to give that tortured spirit the oblivion she craved, even if only for a little while. She had taken her precious phial of laudanum, expensive and in very short supply, from the still-room while Nat carried Rachael upstairs. Only a few drops would be needed, mixed in a glass of honey and water. The potion was bitter, and she did not know if the girl would swallow it.

But all the resistance seemed suddenly to have drained out of Rachael. She allowed Nat to prop her upright, while Silence tilted the cup to her lips. The liquid drained down her throat, and she lay back on the pillows, pale and unmoving. Together, they watched as her breathing grew deeper and more even, though still with that rasping painful sound, until they were certain that she was asleep. Silence tucked the blankets around her, for there seemed no point in disturbing her rest by attempting to undress her. Tomorrow, perhaps, she would have recovered her wits a little, and they could begin to repair the damage. Until then, she could sleep in this fragile illusion of peace.

But, Silence remembered, as she closed the door softly upon her stepdaughter's empty shell, there were other reckonings and dues to be paid, come tomorrow.

*

Rachael woke suddenly, with a sensation of acute physical discomfort. Her mouth was dry as dust, she had a raging thirst, her throat hurt, and her head ached. It felt, in fact, as if she had drunk too much on the previous night. She had never been in such a condition before, but knew, from the talk of other sufferers, what it must be like.

She was still wearing her clothes. Her bewilderment increased. She sat up abruptly and then, with a gasp of pain, cradled her head in her hands. It felt as if she had red-hot spears lancing through her temples. A voice, soft and concerned, said just by her, 'Rachael — are you all right?'

Recollection, vivid, humiliating, appalling, flooded through her mind. Yesterday, she had tortured her little sister, and forced her to tell her secret, and then she had used her ill-gotten knowledge to betray her family to the soldiers. In doing so, she had caused a man's death, and brought disgrace and ruin and grief upon her beloved brother, and her stepmother. Too late, she had repented. And, unable to face the consequences of her dreadful deed, she had compounded her wickedness by trying to hang herself.

She had even failed in that. She had tied the knot wrongly, the rope had stretched, and she had spent what seemed like hours, balanced on tip-toe, the rope cutting into her neck so that she could barely breathe, unable to free herself, unable to die. However much she had earlier craved death, she had never been so glad to see anyone, when Nat had walked into the summerhouse, the lantern held high in his hand. She must have fainted then, for the last thing she remembered, with the clarity of nightmare, was the look of utter horror growing on his face, as he realised what she had tried to do.

She had a vague recollection, later, of being put to bed, and the presence of Nat and her stepmother. They must have given her something to make her sleep, and it had certainly worked, although her dreams had been frighteningly vivid.

'Rachael?' said that soft, familiar voice again, through the blinding waves of pain inside her head. She opened her eyes unwillingly, blinking against the light.

It was Patience.

Unwisely, she flung herself back down on the bed. The agony inside her skull increased to almost unbearable levels. Whimpering, she pulled a pillow over her head, to shut out the light, and the presence of someone whom she had always regarded as her enemy.

'Rachael, I have something for you to take – Silence said you would wake with a headache.' For the first time, a note of uncertainty, even pleading, entered the older girl's quiet voice. 'Please take it, Rachael – you'll feel so much better.'

Anything would be preferable to this numbing, shrieking pain. Much more cautious this time, Rachael drew the pillow back from her head, and sat up with considerable care.

Patience was perched on the edge of the bed. For once, she was wearing one of her older garments, a plain but becoming blue, unenhanced by her usual frills and furbelows and lace. Her pretty face was devoid of cosmetics, and pale and taut with strain and anxiety. 'It's feverfew water,' she said, taking a pewter cup from the table beside her. 'Silence says it's an excellent remedy for the megrims, and you'll feel better within the hour. And there's honey for your throat, and plenty of water, too – she said you'd feel thirsty.'

Without speaking, Rachael took the cup. She loathed the bitter aromatic taste of feverfew, but knew that it worked. She swallowed it in one gulp, despite the raw pain in her throat, and tried not to shudder. Then she handed the cup back to Patience, who put it down on the table, and picked up one of the ubiquitous little brown-glazed earthenware storage pots. 'Honey?'

Rachael nodded, and Patience passed her the pot and a spoon. The cool thick sweetness was wonderfully soothing. She swallowed mouthful after mouthful, washing it down at the end with several tankards of cool, refreshing water from the well in the kitchen garden. Already, the brutal agony in her head was beginning to recede, and she was able to think about something other than her own physical needs.

She looked at Patience, sitting there so calmly, with not a trace of the pert lively manner that had once annoyed her so much. She dreaded to see sympathy or curiosity in the large brown eyes, but there was nothing discernible, save an air of practical serenity that greatly resembled her sister's. Suddenly, Rachael realised that she must speak to her stepmother – whether to apologise, explain, or to try to make amends, she did not exactly know, but she could hardly confide in Patience. She tried to speak, but it came out as a half-strangled croak. Impatiently, she tried again. 'See – Silence.'

Patience understood. 'I'll fetch her. She's sitting with Captain Hellier at the moment, but she asked me to tell her as soon as you woke.'

Rachael stared at her in disbelief. Words and questions suddenly jostled in her mind, but could not fight their way past the painful blockage in her throat. She put all her fierce will into the most economical sentence she could manage, and still make sense. 'He – he isn't dead?'

'Of course he isn't,' said Patience, with brisk cheerfulness. 'Oh, I'd forgotten, you couldn't have known – he lost quite a lot of blood, but Silence thinks that he will recover. I hope she's right,' she added, thinking of her sister's face, for once unguarded, as she had looked down at the man lying in Nat's bed. It had come as a startling revelation to Patience, and explained a great deal: Tabby's partisan friendship, his return to Wintercombe, and Silence's obvious distress when he was hurt. She knew that she was not imagining it, for she had spent too many years analysing her own affairs of the heart, and those of other people, to mistake it. Her sister, her calm, serious, responsible sister, thirty-five years old, a widow and a mother of four children, was in love with this reckless and disreputable Cavalier. And the liaison could only have begun six years ago, when he had been commander of the garrison here, and thus nominally her enemy.

So George was cuckolded, Patience had thought, with satisfaction. Good. I've never met anyone who deserved it better. And now, she is at last free to marry Nick Hellier – but he is not.

She had devoted her mind, since, to plotting ways of setting him at liberty. All her ideas, of which there had been several, had foundered on the undeniable fact that he was hurt, and weak, and in no condition to flee anywhere, unless he risked his life. She had almost been glad to sit with Rachael, all night, for Silence had felt that her stepdaughter should not be left alone.

Patience had learned with appalled bewilderment, and a certain small thread of contempt, of Rachael's attempt at self-murder. She herself loved life, had always wrung from it whatever it had to offer, and could not imagine any circumstance in which she would wish to put a premature end to it. But that dreadful mark under the other girl's jaw, her evident desperation, had aroused Patience's reluctant pity. At least, Rachael had felt some remorse for her dreadful deeds.

She rose to her feet, smiling down at Rachael's chalk-white face. 'I'll get her. I won't be long.' Somehow, it did not seem as if self-murder would be attempted again, as soon as she turned her back.

Silence was sitting in a remarkably similar position by Nick's bed, sewing. Captain Hellier appeared to be asleep, but his eyes opened as Patience entered the room, and he gave her a faint, friendly smile. She said quietly to her sister, 'Rachael is awake, and wants to see you.'

'Does she? I'll come at once.' Silence put down her sewing, a cushion cover which she was embroidering in stumpwork, and rose to her feet. She said to Nick, 'Do you mind if Patience watches over you for a space? She'll get you anything you need.'

'I doubt it,' said Nick. His voice was faint, but held a note of laughter that was as obvious as a caress. Patience, her mind once more busy with escape plans, took her sister's place at the bedside, and Silence went to see Rachael.

She had said nothing yet to Nick, concerning her stepdaughter's attempted suicide. Sooner or later, she might judge it right to tell him, if Rachael herself agreed to it, but for the moment, she, Nat, Patience, and Jude Hinton, were the only ones who knew how closely real tragedy had come to them last night.

Patience had left Rachael for only a moment or so, but Silence was still a little apprehensive as she knocked on the door. Her imagination, always inconveniently vivid, showed her a flashing succession of horrific pictures: slashed wrists, severed throats, nooses . . .

There was a rasping sound on the other side of the door. She opened it, and went in.

Rachael was sitting up in bed. She was dreadfully pale, and the evil mark below her jaw stood out as vividly as a scarlet collar. She gave her stepmother a twisted travesty of a smile, and whispered something that might have been, 'Sorry.'

Silence thought that the word was, at the least, just a little inadequate in recompense for what she had done. Yet somehow, her attempt to hang herself, so obviously genuine and desperately desired, had cauterised much of the bitterness and resentment that her stepmother might have felt. They would all suffer because of her betrayal, but none more so than Rachael herself.

At least, however, Nick was not dead; Touchet had escaped, though how long such an arrogant idiot, with his inconvenient resemblance to Royalty, would manage to stay at liberty, remained to be seen; and perhaps Tabby would succeed in deflecting the blame, and the punishment, from Nat and from Wintercombe.

This time tomorrow, they would know their fate. It all depended on Colonel Pyne, and what Silence had heard of him was not precisely reassuring.

But, she reminded herself sternly, nothing, and no one, can ever again terrify me as Ridgeley did. He held all our lives in the grip of his hand, and he valued us as little as he might an annoying insect. That man was truly evil. Pyne is a self-important lawyer who has come to power by relentless scheming, and by packing the Committee and the Militia Commissioners with his cronies. He is a little man, a big pike in a small pond, and in no way is he comparable with Ridgeley.

However, her thoughts would not help her, when the time came to face him.

She smiled at Rachael, and sat down on the chair next to the bed. She said, 'You shouldn't try to talk too much. It will probably take several days for your voice to return to normal. Meanwhile, you can stay in this chamber, until there's no sign left of what . . . of what you tried to do. If, of course, that is what you wish.'

[379]

Rachael nodded fervently. She swallowed several times, obviously in some pain, and then whispered, 'Nick – all right?'

'He will be, if we are granted time, and no corruption enters the wound,' Silence said. She uttered a brief wordless prayer, for if that wicked, deep, almost fatal hole in his shoulder should become infected, he would undoubtedly die. At least she had taken great care to ensure that it was clean. In wounds, as in her dairy, great ills could prosper in dirt.

An expression of huge relief passed over Rachael's face. She closed her eyes, and tears slid from under the blue, exhausted lids. Her lips shaped the words, 'Thank God.'

'Did you think he was dead?' Silence put out a hand to touch the girl's arm. That explains it, she thought. That explains why she was so distracted as to attempt to take her own life, for she knows how much I love Nick. Controlling her voice, she added softly, 'I did too, for a while – I did not think we could save him, he'd lost a lot of blood. He should never have tried to fight against such odds.'

But if he had not, she reminded herself, he would not be Nick, and she would not love him so much, for that reckless defiance in the face of such great danger.

'My fault,' said Rachael, with difficulty, the tears still flowing. 'How can you forgive me? My fault.'

Silence stared at her for a long moment, that heart-felt, whispered plea echoing in her mind. At last, she said reassuringly, 'Things might not turn out to be so bad as we think.'

Rachael made a strangled gesture of disgust, and banged the bed with her fist. 'I – I *betrayed* you!' she gasped. 'Doesn't *matter* what happens!' She doubled over, coughing. Silence poured water and handed her a cup, and her stepdaughter gulped it down, scarlet-faced, her eyes streaming.

'Yes,' Silence said, when at last she was calm. 'Yes, you betrayed us. Was it because of Jack?'

Rachael looked at her, evidently astonished by her perspicacity. She nodded, and then shook her head, and her soundless mouth shaped the words. 'Don't want to marry him now.'

'I think it quite possible that he won't want to marry you,' Silence said, with some asperity. Rachael's attempt to kill herself had forced her to realise the depths of the remorse which her stepdaughter must feel, but it still did not, as the girl herself had pointed out, erase the enormity of what she had done. She knew that Patience pitied her, in a rather condescending way, for her sister had the strong animal's unthinking superiority over the weak. Yet pity and sympathy would not help Rachael come to terms with her treachery, and nor would sweeping it under the mat. She had probably already confronted it, in those lonely hours in the summerhouse, and decided that she could not live with what she had done. But Silence, looking carefully at her stepdaughter, thought that she would not try to kill herself again. There was a subtle, bleak strength in the set of Rachael's mouth, which indicated that she had decided to accept life after all, and whatever of good and bad it had to offer her.

'Don't want to see Jack,' said Rachael, in that almost voiceless whisper, and shook her head violently. 'No – never again.'

Some impulse, some instinct that this was the right time, prompted Silence to say, 'In that case, I think that there is something you should know about the betrothal.'

The girl looked up at her, surprise on her face. She went on, knowing that it was too late now to turn back. 'Nat told you, of course, that your father had left you a dower of a thousand pounds, under the terms of his will. But did he tell you about the condition attached?'

'Condition?' Rachael's voice was quite strong on the first syllable, but died away into a whisper and another fit of harsh, painful coughing. She gulped some more water, and then stared at her stepmother. 'What condition?'

'Your father ordered that the dowry was only to be paid if you married Jack. If you rejected him, if you wanted to marry someone else, you would be dowerless.'

In a way, it was cruelty to shatter the girl's illusions thus, but Rachael had been in thrall to her false memories of her father, for too long, and too miserably. With compassion, Silence watched the dawning realisation in her stepdaughter's face, the understanding of what her words implied. She said at last, hoarsely, 'You mean . . . you mean, he wanted to *force* me?'

'He knew that without a dowry, you would be unlikely to marry anyone else. He wanted you to marry Jack, and I don't think . . . I don't think that your wishes meant very much to him. Even after his death.'

Rachael buried her face in her hands. Her shoulders heaved, and great tearing sobs shook her thin body. Silence put her arms around her, feeling again the savage loathing which her husband had once inspired in her. None of this was really Rachael's fault: all this confusion, this terrible mess of love and hate and betrayal, had sprung from a daughter's desperate desire to be loved, and a father's need to have his wishes at last obeyed. And she did not think that she herself was entirely guiltless.

There was a sudden thunderous knocking on the door, and it was flung open before Silence had time to draw breath. Jude Hinton stood there, her normally placid, good-natured face pale with alarm and fear. 'Oh, m'lady, m'lady, Eliza told me to tell ee — Colonel Pyne be here!'

Rachael, lost in her own grief for what had never been, did not seem to notice. Silence sat still, lending her strength to the sobbing girl, gathering her forces for the confrontation to come. She gave the maid a brief, reassuring smile. 'I shall be down presently, Jude. As you can see, Mistress Rachael has more need of me, at present. Meanwhile, I am sure that Sir Nathaniel is more than adequate to deal with the occasion.'

And that, she thought, as Jude closed the door behind her, evidently not looking forward to imparting such a message to the notoriously choleric Pyne, would cool the man's heels for him.

*

Colonel John Pyne was not accustomed to being kept waiting. He was a thick-set, florid man in early middle age, who by dint of skilful manoeuvre, fanatic conviction and implacable determination, had been ruler of Somerset for the past six years. He had filled the County Committee, while it sat, with his cronies and henchmen, most more distinguished for their loyalty or subservience to him rather than for any talent or service which they could offer to county affairs. When the Committee had been disbanded, nearly two years previously, he had ensured, after a struggle with the moderate John Ashe, a friend of Sir George St. Barbe, that the sequestration commissioners appointed in its place were likewise his men, and turned a blind eye to the many abuses which they had perpetrated. And the officers of the Militia, raised to defend Somerset from Royalist rebellion, were to a man his nominees. Pyne was an enthusiastic seeker after malignant conspiracy, and much admired by the Council of State for his diligence in the public service.

It was fortunate that he had been in Bath, not at his home in Curry Mallet, thirty miles away, when the Bristol captain's message had reached him. The Militia had only just returned from their duties on the Worcester campaign. Most had thought it a great shame that they had failed to arrive in time for the battle. Pyne, whose record in military matters was not especially distinguished, or courageous, had kept his relief to himself, and had earned the approval of the regular soldiers by the thoroughness of his search for the hidden valuables of Worcester's Royalist citizens.

In view of the contents of the message, and the garbled words of the Bristol trooper who carried it, he had thought it expedient, although inconvenient, to come to Wintercombe himself. He had been invited to dine with the mayor today, before returning to Curry Mallet, and his wife Amy. But he could not afford to ignore the slightest chance that the renegade Charles Stuart might be at large in Somerset. If it proved to be so, and the rogue slipped through his fingers, he would be a laughing-stock.

So he had gathered a body of his friend Popham's dragoons, for the foot under his own command would be too slow, and had led them off at first light for the manor of Wintercombe, in the parish of Philip's Norton.

Sir George St. Barbe had been Presbyterian and moderate in his inclinations, and had regarded Pyne as a dangerous radical. Pyne, in his turn, had considered the older man, despite his good service to the Cause in the late wars, to be lukewarm at best, shamefully ready and eager to compromise with the old King. He had never met the heir, who kept out of county affairs, had no known opinions one way or the other, and had spent most of the past four or five years at Oxford, completing his education. Rumour spoke of ill-health, and he had not been invited to join Pyne's militia.

The young man who met him in the hall, however, did not seem to be an invalid. He was pale, but not alarmingly so, and his height was no less than average, although he could scarcely be described as stout. He bowed very correctly as Pyne introduced himself, and, far from displaying guilt or fear, spread his hands in amused resignation. 'My apologies, Colonel. It seems that you have been hauled out from Bath on a fool's errand.'

'I'll be the judge of that,' Pyne snapped. 'Where is Captain Humphreys?'

The captain had imbibed a little too much of the excellent Wintercombe wine the previous night, and had in consequence not felt at his best upon waking, rather belatedly, to the sound of hoofbeats outside his window. He came hurrying in from the summer parlour, on the eastern side of the house, where a bed had been made up for him. He was pouch-eyed, unshaven and dishevelled, still buttoning his buff coat in his haste.

Pyne surveyed him with annoyance. 'Explain why you sent for me, Captain — at once, if you please.'

Humphreys' frantic hands completed their task, smoothed his tousled hair and ran in sudden panic over his bristly jaw. Pyne's hostile, pale blue eyes surveyed him contemptuously, and with increasing disbelief, as the story of Wintercombe's secret was unfolded. Nat, listening with a deceptively wooden face, felt amusement bubbling up, and with it, more seriously, an awareness of danger. This man, ridiculous though his posturing might be, wielded real power in Somerset. He could spin some exaggerated tale, haul Nat off to prison, sequester the estate and bleed it dry before any petition, or justice, could take effect. It had already happened to Sir John Stawell, who languished in gaol on some flimsy pretext, while Pyne's cronies enjoyed his lands and his revenues. But Nat had no intention whatsoever of allowing the same fate to befall his family.

'And you expect me to credit this cock-and-bull story? That *children* are concerned? Surely their elders must have taken the major part!'

'I believe Sir Nathaniel here to be entirely innocent in this matter,' said Humphreys doggedly. 'He had no idea that these men were concealed in the loft, until he returned home yesterday, and found that we had discovered them.'

'You, sir! Is that true?' Pyne whirled round and jabbed an accusatory finger at Nat.

His aggressive, bullying manner was well known, and had been the subject of at least one hostile pamphlet. It might intimidate bewildered yeomen or unfortunate widows, but Nat, as a child, had defied Ridgeley. He did not quail or tremble, but continued to look at Pyne with that same air of friendly frankness. 'It is, Colonel. I knew nothing of these men that my young sister had apparently concealed within the house, until yesterday afternoon. And if I had known, I would have sent them very quickly on their way.'

'Aha!' Pyne said. 'So you would not have performed your lawful duty to the Commonwealth, and denounced them? Even though one was the rogue Charles Stuart?'

'It now appears, sir,' said Humphreys, rather nervously, 'that I was mistaken. The man in question was not the King of Scots, but one Mervyn Touchet.'

'Touchet? Brother to the Earl of Castlehaven? A notorious malignant, and a Papist to boot.' Pyne's eyes narrowed. 'But not Charles Stuart? Are you certain?'

'The girl — Mistress St. Barbe — she seems quite positive, sir. I attempted to question the prisoner, and his response was the same.'

'And what search have you made for this other man, this Touchet? How was he able to get away?'

There was an embarrassed pause. Nat took pity on the captain, and kept quiet. After a while, Humphreys said reluctantly, 'He was helped by one of the children, sir.'

'One of the *children*? Are these brats such monsters of iniquity?'

'My brother is nine years old,' said Nat swiftly. 'I do not think it likely that he appreciated the gravity of his deed. He still seems to regard it all as a game.'

Pyne gave an exclamation of disgust. 'I hope he is to have some sense beaten into him?'

'I will see to it myself,' said Nat reassuringly. Pyne's pale eyes, distended and a little bloodshot, stared suspiciously into his. Then, he swung round on the unfortunate Humphreys. 'Did this man escape on foot, or on horseback?'

'On horseback, sir.'

'Then this child supplied him with a mount?'

'No.' Humphreys licked his lips, took a deep desperate breath, and said, 'He made his escape on my horse, sir.'

'On *your* horse?' Pyne gave a bark of humourless laughter. 'With, or without, your knowledge and approval?'

'Without, of course, sir,' said Humphreys, infuriated beyond the bounds of prudence. 'I was elsewhere, capturing the prisoner.'

'Ah, yes, the prisoner. Is he still alive?'

'Yes, sir, and likely to remain so, I understand.'

'Pity.' Pyne regarded him reflectively, and then turned again to Nat. 'So. You claim to be innocent of this. What of the rest of your household? Apart from the children, of course.'

'They too knew nothing, so far as I can judge,' Nat told him. He glanced at Humphreys, who said hastily, 'I can vouch for that. I have questioned every one of the servants, and they denied all knowledge most emphatically. I would swear to their innocence.'

'And Lady St. Barbe?'

'She too, sir — I have spoken with her, and she was in complete ignorance of what her children had done,' said Humphreys. 'And none of my men has overheard any conversation which would imply the contrary.'

'I see.' Pyne stared at him. 'Well, Sir Nathaniel, Captain Humphreys seems very sure that you are not concerned in this distressing conspiracy. I remain to be convinced. I would like, with your leave of course, to question these children. What are their names, and how old are they?'

Nat had expected it, of course, but it was still unwelcome. Tabby, he knew, would not be deflected from her chosen path, but would the younger ones stand up to Pyne's bluster?

Yes, if Tabby could protect them. He said, 'They are my half-sisters Tabitha, who is fifteen, and Deborah, who is eleven, and my half-brother William, who is nine. I think that the youngest child is too overwrought and distressed to be of any use to you, and she is only just five years old – she cannot have properly understood what the others were planning.'

'Five?' Pyne snorted. 'They'll be plotting in the cradle, next. I agree, Sir Nathaniel – she can be of little use. Fetch the others to me, in a room where we may not be disturbed.'

'I would insist,' Nat said, his voice soft but suddenly implacable, 'that their mother is present. They are very young, after all, and much frightened by the events of yesterday. In humanity, Colonel, I must request this favour.'

Pyne had children of his own, and he was no monster of evil. He nodded. 'Yes, of course. But I would like to question her, as well.'

*

Tabby had been expecting the summons, ever since Jude brought the news of Pyne's arrival, but that did not lessen her feeling of sick dread. On her performance in the next half-hour, on her ability to convince this unknown and frighteningly powerful man that she alone was the chief conspirator, the future of her family and of Wintercombe depended. She rose to her feet, and Nat smiled at her. 'Brave girl. You can do it – I know you can.'

His words gave her the confidence she needed. He added, 'He wants to see William and Deb as well. Try to do as much of the talking as you can. It isn't that I don't trust them, but they might inadvertently let something slip that would damage us.' He took her hand and squeezed it encouragingly. 'You don't have to worry about Kate – I've already convinced him that she's too young to be questioned. Your mother will be with you, too, so you need not fear any violence or ill-treatment. The worst he can do, is to shout at you.'

'If that's the worst, I don't mind,' Tabby said bravely, though her belly felt as if it had turned to water, and her heart seemed to have taken refuge in her throat. She gave him a rather feeble grin, and walked from her chamber to face her retribution.

Colonel Pyne had taken up residence in the dining parlour, in the same chair that Humphreys had occupied the previous afternoon. Tabby, pausing at the door, studied him warily. The captain had been furious at first, but he had soon showed himself to be a moderate and reasonable man. Pyne's hard eyes and intimidating manner gave her no such reassurance. She swallowed hard, and walked into the room, William on her left side and Deb on her right, to stand at the end of the table, stiff with apprehension, her hands gripping the children's.

Pyne stared at her, trying to conceal his surprise. This fragile and exquisitely lovely child did not look capable of harbouring two desperate men, nor of plotting against the State. Humphreys had no doubt been misled by a pretty face, and probably not for the first time. Pyne had not formed a particularly high opinion of the captain. He said sharply, 'You — you are Mistress Tabitha St. Barbe?'

The girl stared at him, her eyes dilated with fear. She swallowed and said, her voice surprisingly clear, 'Yes, sir. This is my sister Deb, and my brother William.' She glanced around the dining parlour, seeing the two impassive dragoons standing at Pyne's back, and then added, 'Where is my mother, sir? My brother Nat assured me that she would be present.'

'She will doubtless be here shortly. We cannot afford to wait for her — I haven't got all day to waste,' said Pyne shortly. 'I understand that you are the instigator of this sorry affair?'

'Yes, sir,' said Tabby, low but clear and resolute. 'It was my idea, and I persuaded the other children to help.'

'And the three of you were the only ones involved in the plot?'

As if pulled by the same string, the three heads, two honey-gold and one fair, nodded in unison. Tabby said, 'We didn't want to tell Nat, or my mother. We knew they'd disapprove. We thought it'd be best if no one else knew at all.'

'I made everyone swear an oath to keep it secret,' said the irrepressible William. 'But Kate didn't — she told Rachael.'

'Kate is the youngest child?'

'She's only five,' said Tabby. 'She doesn't understand.'

'And who is Rachael?'

Deb, who had once been her eldest sister's partisan, gazed miserably down at her feet. Tabby said, 'She is our half-sister, sir, Nat's twin. She told the soldiers where to find Captain Hellier and Master Touchet.'

'Master Touchet? You did not, then, think him to be Charles Stuart?'

'Oh, no,' Tabby said. 'He came here once, when there was a Royalist garrison here, and Captain Hellier was in command of it. I remember him – he's the same age as Nat. Master Touchet is much too old to be the King.'

Her certainty reassured him. Pyne leaned back in his chair, surveying the three surprising offspring of Sir George St. Barbe, who was doubtless even now turning in his grave, at the thought of his children's misdeeds. 'Let me clarify this,' he said, his voice hard. 'You knew Captain Hellier from his sojourn here six years ago.'

'Yes, sir,' said Tabby. 'He was always my friend. He taught me to play the virginals. And when we found him and Master Touchet by the Wellow Lane, they were starving, and I had to help them. He was a *friend*, you see,' she added, earnestly. 'I couldn't just leave him there.'

'He is an enemy of the Commonwealth.'

'So I should have passed him by on the other side?' Tabby said, suddenly fierce. 'Well, perhaps *you* would, Colonel Pyne, but I didn't – and even now, I'm *glad* I helped him!'

'Glad, even though he is now a prisoner, and hurt?' said Pyne unpleasantly.

Tabby flushed, and looked away. Common sense told her that she should be subdued and properly repentant, but it was so hard to remember it, with those inimical eyes boring into her brain. She said unhappily, 'No, of course I'm not – but you don't understand! I don't know anything of this Commonwealth you all keep talking about, and neither do William and Deb. When we met Captain Hellier, we didn't think about him being a Cavalier, or an enemy, we just wanted to *help* him, because he'd helped us before.'

'But you must have known that you were doing wrong,' Pyne pointed out. 'Or you would not have agreed to keep your mother and the rest of your family in ignorance.'

'We thought it was right to help him,' said Tabby, stubbornly. '*They* wouldn't have done – that's why we didn't tell them.' She added sadly, 'As soon as Rachael knew, she informed Captain Humphreys.'

'A pity you did not do the same,' Pyne said grimly. 'So, Mistress St. Barbe, you and your brother and sister, alone and with no other help, smuggled these two men, with no one else's knowledge, into the roofspace of this house, provided them with food and other goods for their comfort, and planned to do – what? Send them on their way after a few days?'

'I suppose so,' Tabby admitted. 'But they really needed horses, and we hadn't worked out how to get them without someone becoming suspicious.' She added, with foreboding, 'What will happen to Captain Hellier?'

'I shall decide that in due course,' said Pyne repressively. 'Meanwhile, I must also decide what to do with you, Mistress St. Barbe.'

William's brown eyes were vast with anger and fright. 'You won't do anything to her!' he said belligerently. 'She's my sister, and I won't let you!'

'But he has to do something,' said Tabby. 'He can't just let us escape scot-free – we've committed a treason against the Commonwealth, after all.' She faced Pyne, her chin raised, her eyes bright with unshed tears. 'I wish you would get it over, sir. You obviously think we should be punished, so why not do it? We've done wrong, I admit it – *and* I'd do it again, if I had the opportunity!'

'*And* me,' said William stoutly. Pyne banged his hand against the table, and Deb, who had not uttered a word, began to cry. At once, William hastened to put his arms round her.

The colonel gazed at them in frustration. He had now no doubt whatever that the girl was telling the truth. There was none of the evasiveness or guilt that characterised most people who tried to lie to him. Yes, she had committed a treason, yes, she and the others were deserving of punishment. But his vindictiveness, so thoroughly employed against adult malignants, stopped short of subjecting these misguided children to the kind of treatment routinely meted out to enemies of the State. He could hardly have them flogged, or fined, or imprisoned. Nor could he punish their brother, who was surely innocent. The young baronet had as yet given no indication of what faction he might be prepared to join. He was wealthy, and could be a powerful enemy. Many in London would listen to him, for his father's sake if not for his own. And Pyne's hold over Somerset had already been challenged once, almost successfully. In the years to come, he might need Sir Nathaniel's support.

The door opened without any preliminary, and a plainly-dressed woman came in. She stared at the children in some distress, and then turned angrily to Colonel Pyne. 'I was told that I could be present when they were questioned! Why have you begun without me?'

'I could not delay any longer, my lady,' said Pyne. He had, with the minimum measure of courtesy, risen to his feet. 'I have been as gentle as possible, under the circumstances.'

'Gentle?' Silence, borne on the wings of her rare anger, indicated the weeping Deb, now clinging to her, and soaking her bodice with tears. 'It hardly seems so, sir. Have you finished with them? Are you satisfied of their guilt?'

'They have freely admitted it,' said Pyne. He stared suspiciously at her, as she stroked Deb's tangled hair. 'And you, my lady? Are you guilty too?'

'I told you,' said Tabby passionately. 'My mother didn't know – we didn't tell her!'

'Is that true, Lady St. Barbe?'

'Yes, it is,' said Silence, looking at him directly. He was an unpleasant man, but not, thank God, of Ridgeley's category of evil. She did not like his eyes, as pale and unyielding as pebbles, but she did not think that he would be cruel. 'I knew nothing of it, until my stepdaughter Rachael denounced the men to the soldiers. I can still hardly believe it.'

'And what would you have done, if you had known?'

'I would have sent them away at once,' said Silence firmly, praying that he would not detect her lies.

'So you would not have informed me, or the nearest justice, of the presence under your roof of two enemies of the peace of the Commonwealth?'

'No,' said Silence, her voice flat. 'No, I would not. Captain Hellier, hard as it may be for you to believe or to understand it, once did my family a very great kindness – indeed, he may have saved all our lives, at a time of peril. Is that how you would have me repay him? It may be how you would treat an old friend, sir, but it is not my way.'

'So you admit you are guilty too?'

'No, of course she isn't!' Tabby cried urgently, rushing forward. The two dragoons eyed her warily, their hands on their swords. 'She isn't guilty — how can she be, she didn't *know!*' She stared at Pyne's stony face, and could not read it. Panic threatened to overwhelm her, and anger, that her mother could thus compromise herself. In this state, crying would be easy, and tears might soften this cold man's heart. She sobbed desperately, 'It isn't fair! It isn't *fair!* She didn't *know!* How can you say she's guilty for something she didn't know and didn't do?'

'Tabby, please,' asked Silence, putting out her hand. Her daughter ignored it. 'Punish me, I'm the guilty one, I planned it all, I knew what I was doing, but not the children, not Mother — please, sir, she didn't *know!*'

'Very well, very well,' said Pyne testily, waving an embarrassed hand. 'I accept what you say, Mistress Tabitha.' Weeping women always made him uncomfortable, and to have this ridiculously lovely child so distraught disturbed him much more than he cared to admit. 'Lady St. Barbe, I am satisfied. Your children may go. But I would be grateful, madam, if you would consider most thoroughly your rearing of these misguided infants. They seem to be lacking in several of the qualities essential to good citizenship of the Commonwealth. And I would remind you also, that though I consider it inappropriate to punish their misdemeanours myself, it is your duty, and Sir Nathaniel's also, to supply the lack. If you'll take my advice, madam, a good beating, or more than one, and a very restricted life and diet for the next few weeks, should ensure that they have leisure to contemplate the error of their ways, and learn some sense. Do I make myself clear?'

There was nothing that Silence would have liked better than to shout her defiance at him, to tell him, in no uncertain terms, that she had never beaten any of her children, and did not intend to begin now. But against all the odds, they seemed to have won, and not for anything would she put that victory in jeopardy. She reined in her anger, and said, 'Yes, Colonel Pyne. Rest assured, I shall do exactly as you say.'

'Excellent, madam. I am glad to hear it. And I sincerely hope,' said Pyne, through shut teeth, 'that the St. Barbe family henceforth follows the proper path. If there are any further transgressions, by any one of you, of whatever age, then I shall not again be tempted to leniency. Do you understand me, my lady?'

'Yes, very clearly,' said Silence, gripping Deb tightly.

[391]

'And you – Tabitha? William? Deborah? Do you understand?'

They nodded mutely.

'Good,' said Pyne. 'Now go.'

The children stared at him incredulously. He waved his hand impatiently. 'Go on. Get out of my sight, before I change my mind.'

They fled, their faces indicating that they could hardly believe their good fortune. He saw, with displeasure, that their mother still lingered. There was some disturbance in the courtyard, and he turned to peer through the window behind him. Two strange horses were being led away by a stable lad, so it would appear that Wintercombe had more visitors.

Silence knew that it was foolish to tempt fate, that luck, and Colonel Pyne's patience, could be pushed only so far, but she had to know. She laced her hands in front of her, and said quietly, 'If you please, Colonel, I would be very grateful if you could tell me what you intend to do with Captain Hellier.'

'And what business is that of yours, pray?'

She would not be intimidated: she would not. She said mildly, 'As I have told you, sir, we perhaps owe him our lives. I am naturally concerned, also, that my nursing is not wasted. He could well have died, and may do so yet, if he is not tended with care.'

'And I repeat, it is no business of yours now,' said Pyne. 'He is my prisoner, to be disposed of at my discretion. I am sick and tired, madam, of supporters of this rogue and pretender Charles Stuart, stirring up rebellion and fomenting discontent, and this Commonwealth will never mend nor prosper until such traitors are stamped out. I have no sympathy for any of them, nor for those who claim friendship with them, and you would do well not to forget it, madam.'

It would be dangerous, and risk all that they had won, to press the matter. Sick at heart, she dropped a perfunctory curtsey. 'No, Colonel Pyne – I will not forget it. Good day to you, sir – I must go see my children.'

'Good day, madam,' he said curtly.

She added, knowing that it was necessary, but hating the words she spoke, 'I thank you sir, for your forbearance.'

She was unutterably glad to escape his hostile presence. She stood outside the door, trembling and sweating with anger, and relief. They were not safe yet – and Nick's fate still hung in the balance, according to Pyne's wishes, or perhaps his whim. But unless any further disaster occurred, Wintercombe seemed to have been saved.

There were voices in the hall. She turned towards them, her knees still weak, and pushed through the screen curtains.

Standing before the fire, grave-faced, was Jonathan Harley. And beside him, his expression even more forbidding, was John Harington.

❧ CHAPTER TWENTY ❧

'A goodly apple, rotten at the heart'
(Merchant of Venice)

She dropped a curtsey, and tried to keep her voice from shaking. 'Why, sir, this is a pleasant surprise.'

'Though, alas, under these very unhappy circumstances, Lady St. Barbe,' said Harington heavily. He was too similar to George, too narrow and self-righteous, for her ever to like him, but he was upright and honourable, his honesty and incorruptibility a byword in Somerset, and he was no friend at all to Colonel Pyne, who had never been able to buy him. Harington also had a vast knowledge of the law, was respected and revered, and still had powerful friends. Whatever the sins of her family, she knew that he would support her against Pyne.

'We understand that Colonel Pyne is here,' said Jonathan, and indicated Nat, who stood unsmiling in the centre of the hall. 'Sir Nathaniel has told us about the events of the last few days, and I think that we have a great deal to discuss.'

His presence, the brilliance of his disturbing eyes, still had the power to make her uneasy. Only yesterday, he had proposed marriage to her. She wondered if he would now be so keen to ally his name to hers, mother of a nest of traitors.

Or, for that matter, whether Harington now was.

'Yes, we have,' she said, looking round at the three very different men who faced her. 'But perhaps it had best wait until Colonel Pyne departs, since we will be talking, I should imagine, about private matters.'

The curtains were thrust apart, and Pyne pushed aggressively through them, his boots clumping heavily on the flagstoned floor. His pale gaze sharpened on Harington. 'Good morning, sir. What brings you to Wintercombe?'

'I am sure that you can guess,' said the older man coldly. 'Since my son is at present betrothed to Mistress Rachael, and as an old friend of Sir George, I felt that my presence here would be welcome at this unhappy time. And I have no need to enquire, do I, as to what brings *you* here?'

'I have come to take a prisoner into my custody, and to ascertain the truth of this sorry tangle,' said Pyne curtly. 'The latter, I have done. The first, I intend to do shortly. Where is this Captain Hellier?'

It was Nat who said sharply, 'You cannot take him away now, Colonel! He is sick, and weak from loss of blood. In such a condition, he's hardly likely to escape, and I would ask you, sir, in all humanity, to leave him here, so that we may care for him.'

'No,' said Pyne with finality. His pale, unfeeling eyes swept round the other men's grim faces, and returned to Silence.

She said, trying to keep the desperation from her voice, 'What my stepson tells you, sir, is true. Captain Hellier will probably not survive it, if you force him to ride to Bath.'

'Well, since you are so concerned for his welfare, madam, you can supply me with a litter or a cart, so that he may be transported in comfort,' said Pyne. 'I do not propose to waste time arguing on this matter, and still less do I intend to leave him in this house, where his presence will, no doubt, incite your undisciplined brood to make an attempt to free him. Well, Sir Nathaniel, the choice is yours. Will you have him ride, and die, or will you supply a litter?'

'We do not possess a litter,' said Nat. He glanced at Harington, whose frown had deepened. 'There is a cart, however, which could be used for such a purpose.'

'Are you set upon this course, Pyne?' Harington asked. 'I agree, the man must be taken into custody at some time but, from all I have heard, he does not appear to present any great danger at this moment.'

The colonel stared at him, overtly hostile. 'I must say, sir, I had not thought to hear you pleading a Cavalier's cause.'

'I am not,' said Harington sharply. 'I am merely requesting that you delay moving him for a few days, so that he may recover his strength a little. Is a dead man of use to you, or any credit to your standing?'

Pyne glared at him. 'I fail to see how this is any concern of yours, sir.'

'It concerns me, Pyne, that you seem to have so little consideration for a sick man, whatever his allegiance,' said Harington. In other circumstances, he would not have taken such a stand, but he loathed Pyne and all he stood for, and his shrewd, argumentative lawyer's brain could not resist this confrontation.

Pyne, however, was not to be persuaded. His mouth hard and

uncompromising as a trap, he said contemptuously, 'In matters concerning the safety of this country, and the Commonwealth, sir, such consideration is of very little importance. I am surprised at you for suggesting otherwise – after all, up until now, your loyalty has not been called into question.'

'Nor will it be, by any godly and honest man,' said Harington, breathing hard. 'Well, Pyne? Are you prepared to take the course of sense, and humanity? Or are you, as usual, going to ride roughshod over all decent feeling?'

Silence wondered whether Pyne would actually explode. He seemed to swell larger, and his face darkened to an alarmingly congested shade of red. 'You will regret you ever said that, Harington!' he said venomously. 'May I remind you who holds the power here?'

'The Lord our God wields the ultimate power in this land,' said Harington. 'And though you appear set on your course, you would do well to remember it.'

Pyne stared at him, opened his mouth as if to say something, and then evidently thought better of it. He turned to Nat. 'Sir Nathaniel – kindly ensure that a cart, and driver, are ready and waiting within a quarter-hour. And you, my lady – since you are so concerned for this Cavalier, perhaps you would wish to prepare him for the journey.'

Silence stared at him. The ultimate horror was upon her, and she had no weapons, no defence, no plan, no hope. She could only, as he had told her, give Nick into the custody of this man, and pray that he would survive the journey to Bath, the incarceration, and whatever would come after it, whether release . . . or something else. And she could hardly, as lady of the house, leave Harington and Harley unattended in the hall, still less in the company of Colonel Pyne, or there would surely be murder done.

Suddenly, all the skills she had acquired over the long years at Chard, and then at Wintercombe, seemed to have deserted her. She could only think of Nick, and his need of her, both now and in the future, and that only a few last moments had been granted to her, to say farewell.

Harley was looking at her with sympathy, and something more. She realised that her eyes were full of tears, and turned away from him, brushing a casual hand across her face. Nat, as ever, came to her rescue. 'You do what you must,' he said. 'I'll send Carpenter to deal with the cart.'

His words freed her from panic. She smiled, though it meant no more than a rearrangement of her face, thanked him, and walked past the unfriendly, implacable figure of Colonel Pyne as if he were not there.

She visited the still-room first, pushing the ointments and remedies he might need into a small stout leather bag: willow-bark water, to her own recipe, for fever; ivywort, for cleansing and healing the wound; plasters and bandages, to protect it. Then to the study, where the estate chest was kept. She unlocked it with the keys on her chain, and drew out one of the small heavy bags of coin. It was full of gold and silver, sovereigns, crowns and angels. She weighed it in her hand, and then put it in with the medicines. Wherever he was going, whatever was to happen to him, he would need money for food and comforts, and to grease his gaoler's palm.

After that moment of panic in the hall, when the habits of years had abruptly deserted her, she was calm, and bleak, and tearless. After all, there was nothing she could do, now, to change the situation. Six years ago, she had wept her heart out for him: she would again, but not now, not with Pyne and Harington and Harley scrutinising her every move. If any of them suspected that Nick Hellier was rather more to her than an old friend, who had once done the St. Barbes a favour, then all their carefully-constructed appearance of innocence, all Tabby's assumption of blame, would be set at naught, and they would lose after all.

She had asked Patience to sit with Rachael once more, before she went downstairs to see Pyne. Eliza, reliable but no friend whatsoever to Nick, had been left to watch over him. However, when she entered the chamber, the bag pulling heavily at her arm, it was Tabby perched on the bed, reading aloud, her quiet clear voice describing the rhythm of the poem as surely as that same voice danced and soared in song:

Go, and catch a falling star,
Get with child a mandrake root,
Tell me where all past years are,
Or who cleft the Devil's foot.
Teach me to hear mermaids singing,
Or to keep off envy's stinging . . .

Silence knew that verse: it was in one of the books of poetry that Nick had given her, six years ago. Her voice mingled with her daughter's:

And find
What wind
Serves to advance an honest mind.

She could still smile, a little. Nick was lying propped up on pillows, wearing one of Nat's nightshirts, and looked a good deal better than he had done the previous day, though his face, under the tan and the beard, was still drained of colour. He smiled in return, but it faded with hers.

Tabby had risen to her feet, the poem unfinished, the book clasped in front of her like a shield. She said, her voice suddenly rough with foreboding, 'Has Colonel Pyne decided?'

'Yes.' Silence stared from her daughter to her lover, and then shook her head. 'I'm sorry. I couldn't do anything. Even John Harington tried to persuade him – and you should be honoured, Nick, to have such a staunch and godly Puritan pleading for your cause – but he was adamant. And he has a score or more of dragoons with him.'

'They can't!' Tabby cried, flinging down the book with a most uncharacteristic lack of respect. 'They can't – he's hurt – it isn't *fair*, it isn't *right*!'

'You can't stop them,' said Nick. His voice was stronger, and a wry smile twisted his mouth. 'I suppose I should be flattered, that they think me so dangerous.'

'That has nothing to do with it,' said Silence flatly. 'And a great deal to do with Pyne's spite.' She looked at Tabby's anguished face, and added, 'We can't say too much, or we put everything else in jeopardy. If he suspects how much I care . . . then Tabby's sacrifice will go for nothing.'

'I don't intend to die just yet,' Nick said encouragingly. 'My dear love, they are hardly going to execute me. Whatever the price of my freedom, I will try to pay it.'

'You can't,' said Silence. 'You can't even pay for a loaf of bread . . . I put some coin in this bag, and some remedies – the willow bark is a sovereign cure for fever, and you must try to put a little of the honey ointment on the wound each day . . . What am I saying?' Silence cried suddenly, on a great tearing sob of anguish. 'I may never see you again, and all I can do is blether on like an old goodwife about wrapping up warm and taking your medicine!' And, to her own shame and horror, she burst into tears.

Tabby came running round the bed, to fling her arms about her.

[398]

'Oh, no, Mother, please don't, *please* – we've been talking, he won't be in prison for long, you'll see – we'll get him out, somehow, it'll be all right!'

Once, she had comforted her children when their trivial hurts, or their greater ones, grew unbearable. It must be a sign of encroaching age, that now the situation appeared to be reversed. She struggled for control, knowing how vital it would be, in a few moments, to be outwardly calm and unemotional. She pushed the tears away from her face, took a deep breath and said shakily, 'Don't – don't plot any more, Tabby, *please*. Look at what happened the last time!'

'Would you rather I had not?' said her eldest child, fiercely. 'Would you *really* rather I had not? There you are, then. And Patience plots as easily as she flirts, or breathes.' She turned and gave Nick, helpless in the bed, her flying gallant grin. 'We must dress you. Nat will want his nightshirt back.'

Silence found that it was quite easy to lose her overwhelming sense of loss and despair in the banal tasks necessary for Nick's survival: fresh bandages, fresh dressings; one of Nat's plainest shirts, since his own was of course ruined by blood and sword; breeches and hose and shoes, all belonging to Nat, and a thick broadcloth doublet and cloak, to ward off the prison cold and damp. Through it all, Tabby kept talking, joking with Nick, keeping their spirits up, holding grief at bay with a sensitivity and maturity that surprised even her mother, who had long recognised and respected her qualities. At last Nick was ready, pale but determined, sitting in the chair by the door.

'Say goodbye to him now,' said Tabby, her eyes suddenly bright. 'Then you won't have to do it under Pyne's horrible fishy eye.' She gave her mother that encouraging grin. 'I'll go down and tell them that Nick's ready.'

'I don't know how she can face him again,' said Silence, when she had gone. 'She held her own in that confrontation – she must have been terrified, but she stood her ground, she convinced him that she was the only one to blame.'

'She is a very remarkable person,' said Nick. He held his hand out, and she took it, kneeling by his chair with her head against his thigh. Awkwardly, he moved his left hand, despite the pain in his shoulder, to stroke her hair. 'She must inherit it from her mother.'

Silence could think of no suitable reply to this. She said, speaking from her fear, 'Please, Nick, please – don't put yourself in danger again. No forlorn hopes, no desperate escapes. You can't be important to them . . . '

'For this accurate estimate of my worth, I hereby give thanks!'

'They are awash with prisoners,' said Silence, trying not to laugh. He had always had this gift of arousing her amusement at inconvenient moments, it was one of the qualities that had first attracted her to him. 'Half of Scotland must be in custody. Sooner or later, they will surely let you go. Please – don't let Tabby and Patience put themselves in danger. Tabby has always let her sense of right overcome her caution, and Patience – well, as she said, Patience is a natural plotter. They both are, in fact.' She gave a rather wobbly laugh. 'My grandmother used to say that children always seem to resemble their most unsuitable aunt, or uncle.'

'My Uncle Robert was an incorrigible wencher and drunkard, who drowned in the Severn when I was ten,' said Nick with interest. 'Perhaps I take after him.' The fingers continued their gentle, soothing motion. After a pause, he added, 'You need not fear for me, my gracious Silence. After all, I have a promise to keep, have I not? I said that I would marry you, and whether it is this year, next year or only sometime, I will.'

'So long as it is not never, I don't mind,' said Silence. She could hear distant voices, coming nearer. She added swiftly, 'Take care of yourself, please, Nick. And remember – I love you.'

'How could I forget that? Herald of joy, I love you too,' he said, and gave her a push. 'Get up, now, or all our subterfuge will be wasted.'

Somehow, pale but composed, her tears dried on her kerchief, Silence was able to watch, apparently without emotion, as Nick walked, astonishingly, on his own stubborn feet out of Nat's chamber. He had thanked her formally for her care of him, and she had modestly replied that she would do the same for any man thus afflicted, as if they were no more to each other than a physician and his patient. Then he was gone, and she was left only with that mercifully numbing sense of disbelief. He had been here – and he was here no more.

She sat down on Nat's bed, that was still warm from his body, and wondered, bleakly, why she could not weep. It had been easy earlier, when he was still here. Why, now, was it so difficult to mourn his departure?

In these two brief days, she had moved in bewildering succession from ignorance, to overwhelming joy, to terror and grief and

[400]

the aftermath of disaster. She was exhausted, numbed and battered by circumstance. Suddenly, she wanted to bury herself in the warmth he had left, and put a pillow over her eyes and ears, and hide from the world.

This will not do, she reminded herself sternly. Nick has gone, and so, thank God, has Colonel Pyne, but Harington and Harley are still here, and I think I know why they have come. Rachael has said that she no longer wishes to marry Jack – and perhaps Jack, too, has changed his mind – or his father has. I shall have to warn her that they are here – and at some time today, I shall have to tell that incorrigible sister of mine to refrain from any escape plots.

It seemed suddenly overwhelming. She sat there, fighting despair with the skills which she had learned long ago, under the iron rule of her feared father, to whom emotions had always counted for nothing beside duty, convention and seemliness. She must make the best of what she had, do her duty to the utmost of her ability, and mend what had already been damaged almost beyond repair. Below her, and all around her, Wintercombe was waiting for her.

She got up, because she had to, and went to Rachael's chamber.

Patience was there, and to her surprise her sister was chatting, with apparent friendliness, about, of all things, London fashions. At last, Silence thought, Rachael might be taking some interest in her appearance. Anything was to be preferred to brooding on her own misery and guilt.

'She's decided,' said Patience, speaking to save Rachael's strained voice. 'She's not going to wear black any more. I must say, I think it's time for her to wear colours again. Not very bright ones, of course – that wouldn't be fitting, not yet. But blue, or murrey, or grey, would suit very well.'

'Good,' Silence said, smiling with more warmth at her sister than she had done for some time. 'But I don't think we have enough cloth here, in any colour, for a gown. You'll have to go to Bath for that.'

'Yes,' said Patience. 'There's a good choice there – and you and I of all people, Sister, ought to be judges of fine cloth!' Her eyes bright, she turned to Rachael, who was looking rather bemused. 'If you have it made in the pattern of my rose-coloured gown – with a long boned bodice, and the shoulders cut to here . . . ' She glanced at Silence, and with a giggle amended it. 'Well, perhaps only to *here* – and a trained skirt . . . '

'Which will pick up every mote of dirt and dust, and need brushing every night, and laundry once a month,' said Silence. 'It's a fashion more suited to the halls of palaces than a plain country manor, I fear — but you can have a trained skirt if you wish, Rachael.'

'And if you have an underskirt of a different colour,' said Patience, with animation, 'you can loop the train up behind to show it.' She jumped to her feet, and pulled up the hem of her gown, displaying a quantity of cream lace-trimmed petticoat. 'Like this, see? Then it doesn't drag on the ground.'

Silence felt that it was time to bring this fashion lesson to a temporary halt. She said, 'Rachael — there are two visitors downstairs.'

At once the old look of stubborn misery clamped down over her stepdaughter's face. She said in a hoarse whisper, 'Is — is it Jack?'

'No — it's his father, and Master Harley. They may be here for other reasons entirely, of course — but I think it does concern your betrothal.'

Rachael stared bleakly into space for a moment. Then she took a gulp of water from the cup by the bed, and said in a terse, emphatic croak, 'Tell them — I've changed my mind.'

'Are you sure?' Silence asked her, startled. Rachael made an impatient noise. 'Yes! Don't want any dowry . . . ' She broke off to swallow more water, and added forcefully, 'Not on those terms.'

It was a thousand pounds, and the chance of any suitable husband, that she believed that she was casting away. But Nat had promised Silence that he would find the money somehow, from the rest of his inheritance. Whatever happened, Rachael would not return to the marriage market undowered.

Besides, as Harley had pointed out some time ago, her portion was only forfeit if she rejected Jack. There was no mention in the will of what would happen to the money if he spurned Rachael. Probably George, in his sublime arrogance, had not even contemplated this possibility, just as he had failed to allow, until the omission was pointed out to him, the chance that Silence might one day wish to marry again.

She said, 'I understand. Do you want to see them?'

Rachael made a noise in her throat. 'No!'

'I'll say that you are suffering from a severe cold,' Silence told her. She rose, hoping that everything had been discussed, but

Patience put out a detaining hand. 'Have they taken Captain Hellier?'

'Yes,' said Silence. And then, her courage at last failed her. Without another word, she turned and almost ran from the chamber, the door slamming shut behind her.

With a sob of despair, Rachael flung herself down on the bed. But Patience, her face thoughtful and her mind busy, stared at the oaken panelling, as if its ancient silvery grain could give her the answers which she, and her sister, so desperately needed.

*

'It is not lightly, or on a momentary whim, that I have come to this decision: it is the fruit of many days of doubt and concern.'

She knew already what he was going to say: had known it, ever since she had first seen his heavy face that morning. Silence turned the slender stem of the wine-glass in her hand, eyeing the crimson depths, and tried to look as though this matter concerned her as greatly, as if it was not in fact a heartfelt relief.

'It has nothing to do with yourself, Lady St. Barbe, or with the rest of your excellent family,' Harington continued. 'Nothing would please me more than an alliance between our names — as, indeed, it was my old friend's last, and dearest, wish. But I have come to realise more and more, over these past months, that Mistress Rachael, while in all respects a young lady of admirable character and disposition, is not suited to my son — and nor, in my opinion, is he suited to her.'

And if you knew the real Rachael, Silence thought, you would be confirmed in your thoughts a thousand-fold. She said quietly, 'I must admit, sir, that I too have had my doubts — and so has Rachael herself. I think that perhaps her eagerness to obey her beloved father's wishes blinded her to difficulties in the match which were not immediately obvious. She has led a sheltered life here, and perhaps is not yet ready for the duties and disciplines of marriage.'

Nat was smiling at her: she must be doing well. Jonathan, too, was nodding. Harington said, 'I have discussed this matter with my son, and he is in full agreement. He and I both feel that a girl of greater years, older and a little wiser in the ways of the world, would suit him better. He has mentioned to me one or two names, and we will proceed with great care and diligence. I trust that you and your daughter, madam, will be happy to do the same?'

'After a seemly interval, of course,' said Silence. 'I think, like your son, that Rachael would like to take stock of her situation, and look about her, before she leaps once more towards matrimony.'

'I am glad that you understand our point of view so well,' said Harington, and smiled. It completely transformed his rather gloomy, ascetic face. 'I have brought my copy of the marriage contract with me, and Master Harley here has custody of yours. Are we then all agreed, that this betrothal is at an end?'

'We are,' she said, in unison with Nat, and watched, trying not to betray her pleasure, as Harley tore the stiff squares of parchment across and across, and thrust them, seals and all, into the hot greedy fire. They curled and cracked, smoked and turned black, and she wished that all her problems and fears could so easily be transformed to ashes.

The business over, she found that the two men, trying to disguise their curiosity, were asking Nat to explain in greater detail the presence of Cavaliers under his honest Puritan roof. Silence listened with half her attention to her stepson's entirely convincing display of exasperated bewilderment. It was evident to her that this incident had been the final straw that had persuaded Harington to abandon the betrothal. Yet, overhearing their polite discussion of their ostensible reasons, an ignorant observer might have thought it hinged entirely upon the fact that the two participants had not been suited to each other.

What an understatement that was, Silence thought. A prosy young bore, old before his time, linked with unhappy, mercurial Rachael – they would both have been ripe for the madhouse before a year was gone.

'So, you knew this Captain Hellier before,' said Jonathan suddenly. She started, finding him beside her, smiling and attentive and yet somehow, to her heightened sensibilities, subtly menacing. She glanced around, but Nat had been cornered by Harington, and was listening, with every appearance of solemnity, to his remedy for ungovernable children. 'Sir Nathaniel told me that he had commanded the Royalist garrison here, during the war.'

'For a time, yes, he did,' said Silence, wondering why she had suddenly become so nervous. She had spun this tale so many times, and should be able by now to give a convincing display of unconcern, but her palms were sweaty, and her fingers had begun to shake. She clasped her hands firmly around the stem of the wine-glass. 'There was another man before him, most wicked and unpleasant, who would have done us all great harm, had not Captain Hellier prevented it. The children took to him, Tabby in particular – I suppose that is why she felt she must help him.'

'A pity she did,' Harley observed. 'This story will hardly help your family's standing or reputation in Somerset, will it? And many people will find it hard to believe that a pack of children, however brave and resourceful, could conceal such men successfully, without adult assistance.'

He had guessed. He had not said so, but she could not mistake the expression on his face, or the tone of his voice, insinuating the truth. She fought down her fear. If she did not rise to the bait, he might think his suspicions were after all unfounded. She said calmly, 'Unfortunately for those people, it is the truth. And at least Colonel Pyne is convinced of it.'

'Your daughter is a remarkable child,' said Harley softly. 'But not as remarkable as Pyne believes . . . my dear Silence, must I make myself so plain? I know full well the extent of your complicity in this morning's affair. At present, I am prepared to keep my knowledge to myself, as a gesture of good will towards you and your family – as you know, I have long held you in great admiration and respect. I had hoped that your answer to my proposal of yesterday would have been more . . . accommodating. Perhaps, in view of my magnanimity, you would be prepared to reconsider your decision.'

A sick, cold feeling had descended into the pit of her stomach, but there was also a hard core of anger. She had thought this man a friend. Now, it appeared that she had encouraged a viper.

She glanced at Nat, but he was still talking to Harington, apparently oblivious. Harley followed her eyes, and said softly, 'By all means inform Sir Nathaniel, when I have gone. After all, I would imagine he has been as deeply concerned in this affair as you – and he has, after all, a great deal more to lose, should Colonel Pyne come to hear of the part he played in sheltering two Cavaliers.'

'You are threatening me,' Silence said, in bewilderment. 'You want me to agree to marry you, and if I don't . . . you'll tell Colonel Pyne that we are traitors?'

'Perhaps,' said Harley. He smiled reflectively. 'And he would also be very interested to learn the reason *why* you helped Captain Hellier – not a very edifying tale, is it, to spread around the West

[405]

Country? Do not try to assure me of your innocence, my dear — I have suspected for a long time that you were not the virtuous wife you appeared to be, and your demeanour today convinced me of it.' He smiled, and it was not pleasant. 'So you see, my lady, you have much to lose, do you not? Your reputation, your wealth, your home, possibly even your liberty — for Colonel Pyne will not allow you, or Sir Nathaniel, to go unpunished, should he come to hear of how thoroughly he has been gulled. And all because you will not marry me.'

Play for time, said an urgent voice inside her head. Play for time, and then consult with Nat. She looked down at her feet, seeing Lily crouched beside them like a heraldic hound, couchant and regardant. She said, hearing and hating the note of despair in her voice, 'Surely you do not find me so — so attractive? Jonathan — I had thought you were my friend — and now it seems you are my enemy. Please — why are you threatening me?'

'Because I want you, my dear,' he said, and his hand touched hers. It took all her powers of control not to snatch it away. 'And besides, you should be grateful to me, that I managed to persuade Sir George to leave you so well provided. I would be most distressed to feel that all my efforts were to be wasted for the benefit of some penniless Cavalier adventurer — or, should he meet with his just deserts, for nobody. Don't you think it only right and proper that I should enjoy the fruits of my own endeavours?' He smiled again, his fingers stroking her palm. 'We shall discuss this more fully, at some other, more convenient occasion. In the meantime, pray think upon my offer again. I think you will find that it is, after all, acceptable to you.'

She was shaking as he moved away from her, with fear and a great surging rage that could not, with Harington only a few feet away, be given any expression at all. Somehow, she must behave as if everything was normal, as if the tall, urbane man, smiling so pleasantly at her, had not just threatened to destroy everything she loved, if she did not marry him.

And still, she could barely understand it. Why did he wish to marry her? She was not young, not pretty, not even especially wealthy. The property at Chard was a possession she had never even wanted, a half-ruined house that still held sad and unpleasant memories of the early years of her marriage, when she had struggled to become the godly Puritan wife and mother and housekeeper that George had expected. Why does he want *Chard*?

she thought in bewilderment. I don't understand – he professed friendship, why suddenly place it all in jeopardy? Surely he cannot want an unwilling wife, coerced into marriage?

The answer stole into her head like a thief. Because he is only a lawyer, as yet – he has made no fortune, bought no lands. If he marries me, he will have an estate to call his own, a wife who might, despite her age, well give him children to found his dynasty.

The thought of him in her bed was utterly repulsive. She would sooner have had George, who at least had married her honestly, whatever his faults, and had not taken her by deceit and blackmail.

Oh, dear God, she thought, what am I going to do? For if the truth were revealed, about Nick, about her involvement, and Nat's, even, appallingly, Kate's true parentage, then the scandal would ring through Somerset and beyond, and, as Harley had told her bluntly, she and Nat stood to lose everything.

The prospect revolved round and round in her mind, as if she were on a treadmill. She smiled and talked and even managed to laugh, while all the time in the grip of nightmare. It was worse to pretend that Harley was still a valued friend, to sit opposite him at dinner, and all the while knowing, as she spoke with him or with Harington, that he plotted her downfall, or her enslavement in another marriage that she did not want. Though she saw Nat looking thoughtfully at her, once or twice, he was, as yet, in ignorance of this new, and terrible threat to the St. Barbe family.

It's no use, she thought despairingly. Not even Nat's devious mind can save us now.

*

Tabby sat at the table in her chamber, chewing the end of her quill ragged. The piles of crinkled ash in the hearth bore witness to the difficulty of the task which she had set herself. She must leave him in no doubt that his presence was urgently needed, but she could not say why. Too many unfriendly eyes, these days, might be interested in events at Wintercombe.

At last, inspiration struck. She dipped the pen into the ink and wrote, in her round clear careful hand:

Dear Tom,
It seems a great while since we have seen you, and much has happened here. We have had an unexpected visitor, who

remembers you with great affection. Alas, however, he could not stay with us long, and is now forced by ill-health to sojourn at Bath, to his great distress, and ours. However, if you will favour us once more with your presence, as soon as you are able, I know that it will lighten the days of my sister, and of your affectionate friend,

Tabby.

She read it over with some satisfaction. It was short, and cryptic to a fault, but surely he could guess something of what had occurred. The invitation, the most vital part of the letter, was quite unequivocal.

She cast her eyes over it again. Her name, though occasionally found, was an unusual one. It was the only clue in the letter to link it with Wintercombe. If she signed only her initial, would he guess that it came from her?

He would know her hand, for sure. Besides, she thought suddenly, I can send one of the stable-lads with it, instead of risking the Post. He can set out now, and be there by nightfall if he hurries — it's hardly more than twenty miles. That way, unless a real disaster happens, there's no risk of the letter being seen by anyone else.

She folded it over decisively, heated the wax in the hearth, and sealed it. Then, she knelt by the bed and fumbled under the mattress. Since her fifteenth birthday last June, Nat had given her an allowance of money, to spend as she chose. Tabby, not particularly interested in fashion or fripperies, had laid out a little on music, a book or two, and a few trifles and presents. She had been saving to buy a guitar, but this was infinitely more important. She tipped four silver crowns and thirteen shillings into her hand, put ten of the shillings back in the bag, and then took them out again. What if the horse went lame, and a fresh one had to be hired, or lodgings bought? Her messenger would need all the coin she could spare.

She tied up the bag, pushed it and the letter into her sleeve, and went in search of him.

Jeremy Walker, who had the misfortune to be cousin to the infamous Leah, was the youngest stable-lad, a gangling, pimply youth of eighteen who was still, even after four years in Wintercombe's employ, very eager to please. Like most of the younger male servants, he was infatuated with Tabby, and there had been several bloody noses exchanged as one or other of them claimed that she had shown them especial favour. Tabby, who saw only her usual familiar face when she looked in the mirror, was completely unaware of this secret, hopeless rivalry. She thought Jeremy a rather tongue-tied, blushing, helpful lad who could be relied upon to carry out an important task such as this.

He listened to her instructions, trying to keep the excitement out of his face. This special errand was a sure sign of her regard, and worth any amount of jibing, abuse, and even black eyes from the other boys, when he returned. The journey presented no problem, for he had been to Glastonbury once or twice on St. Barbe business, and the directions she gave him were precise. Her last order, however, was more unusual. 'Jeremy, I don't want anyone to know of this until you return – and I hope that Master Wickham will be able to return with you. Can you saddle a horse and ride out, without telling anyone where you're going?'

'Twon't be no trouble, Mistress Tabitha,' he said, and his eyes dwelt on her longingly, thinking that he would die for her, if she would just give him the chance.

But she gave him only her unselfconsciously enchanting grin, which caused him to blush an even deeper red. 'This should be enough for your expenses. If you need more, I am sure that Master Wickham will supply you.'

In a daze of delight, he saddled one of the best horses in the stable, and told Goodenough, the head groom, that he was going on an errand for Mistress Tabby. Then, he rode out of Wintercombe, singing a long and cheerful ballad celebrating true love.

Tabby, from her window overlooking the barton, watched him go. Despite her mother's pleas, she had no intention of letting Nick languish in some putrid Bath gaol, to the peril of his health, if not his life, while Silence ate her heart out at Wintercombe, bereft of love and hope. She was certain that, somehow, she and Patience could concoct a plan of escape. Tom, sympathetic, intelligent, and above all unknown to Colonel Pyne, would surely help them.

Besides, there was Rachael to consider. Tabby had spoken the truth, when she had told her mother that she could never forgive her half-sister for what she had done. But she had sensed, with her intuitive perception, that Rachael's troubles stemmed from unhappiness. Tom had shown an interest in her. She would do all she could to encourage him but, after that, it would be up to Rachael to make the most of the second chance she had been offered – so long as she was able to recognise that she had been offered it. Tabby, who had suffered from her sister's malice on several occasions in the past, had no great faith in that, but at least she would have done everything possible, and salved her conscience. That Rachael might be grateful for this attempt to transform her personal affairs was a remote chance at best. Ruefully, Tabby realised that resentment and fury were much more likely reactions – but only if her half-sister realised the extent of her meddling. And she was determined to keep that a secret, for the time being at least.

So many secrets, so many tangled strands of conspiracy, sometimes she wondered if she would ever be able to weave them all together into a satisfactory ending. But she must do her uttermost, for the sake of her mother, her sister, and all her family.

❧ CHAPTER TWENTY-ONE ❧

'Safe in his imprisonment'
(*King John*)

'But Nat – what can we *do*?' Silence stared at her stepson, praying that he would offer some miraculous solution to this new and ugly twist in their fortunes. As soon as Harley and Harington had ridden away towards Bath, she had taken the puzzled Nat up to her chamber, shut the door, and in an urgent, increasingly frantic whisper had told him exactly what Jonathan Harley had proposed, and threatened, that morning.

'Let me get this clear,' Nat said. His face was unnaturally serious, and there was an unaccustomed note of anger in his voice. 'This man we thought our friend had the temerity to propose marriage to you – when?'

'When he was here yesterday. I refused, of course,' said Silence. 'And although he took it quite gracefully, on the surface, I had the impression that he was angry, rather than disappointed. I sensed danger then – it disturbed me. And then today, when you were talking to Harington, he took me aside and repeated his proposal. And he said that if I refused him again, he would tell Pyne the truth about our involvement with Nick and Touchet.'

'And he knows, as we do, exactly what that would mean,' said Nat, his voice even. 'A crippling fine at the very least – Pyne is never less than vindictive, he would probably sequestrate the entire estate, and divide it amongst his cronies. So – the St. Barbe family ejected, penniless, forced to beg our bread from charitable friends and neighbours. Add to that, the scandal attached to you – and possibly Kate – and you have a threat which Harley probably thinks is overwhelming.'

'I can't see any way out,' Silence said. For hours, she had been trying not to give in to despair: to her fear for Nick, for Tabby, and for everyone at Wintercombe.

Now, the terrible strains of the past few days were showing plain on her face, and Nat, gazing at her with love and compassion, could see what she would look like when she was old. He said swiftly, 'But I haven't turned my mind to it yet. Harley thinks he's devious enough to have us dancing on the horns of his dilemma. He probably makes the same mistake as most people do, who don't know me.'

'They think you're an inexperienced boy,' Silence said, trying to smile. 'They underestimate you, just as they do Tabby. You were born a hundred years old.'

'But up until now, my powers have hardly been stretched,' said Nat. 'Perhaps outwitting Harley will allow them full rein.' He got to his feet, and walked over to where she sat. Gently, he took her hands. They were not a lady's, for Silence liked to tend her own garden, and work in the still-room, and had little time for the scented oils and other remedies which her sister Patience employed for dry, roughened skin. Touched, he saw that several of her nails had been bitten down to the quick. He said quietly, 'We can call his bluff.'

'Would you want to risk it?' Silence asked. The feel of his hand had restored a little of her confidence, and besides, she had always tended to rely upon Nat, his clear logical mind, free of prejudice and convention, that had cut through so many tangles. If anyone could defeat Harley, it would be him. Yet, born with an old mind or not, he was still only twenty-one. How could he hope to outwit an experienced lawyer nearly twenty years his senior?

Nat gave her a wry smile. 'No, I would not. There is too much at stake. If he is devious, and ruthless, enough to plot this, then he is also ruthless enough to tell Pyne all he knows – or guesses. But I doubt he has any proof.'

'I doubt that Pyne would need any,' said Silence. Her mind was beginning to work again now, freeing itself slowly of that numbing stupid terror. 'He requires very little excuse to bleed a malignant white.'

'Trying to sequestrate Wintercombe, though, might well lead him into very deep waters,' Nat said thoughtfully. 'Most of the gentry loathe him – he runs Somerset on the backs of a gaggle of fanatic yeomen, half of whom can't even write their own names. Oh, the Council of State hold him in high regard, because he is so hot for the Commonwealth – but sooner or later he'll commit an outrage that even they can't ignore. He's not stupid, mind you, despite all that arrogant bluster. He must know that men like Harington and Sir John Horner would never stand tamely aside and watch him fasten his greedy claws into Wintercombe. But even if they persuaded the Council of State to intervene, it would take months, possibly years, before our possessions were restored to us – and in the meantime, the estate would probably have been milked dry. And the loss of your reputation could never be made good.'

'Does that matter?' Silence said, unable to keep the bitterness from her voice. 'It would not exactly be undeserved, after all.'

'It matters to me, that you are treated with respect, and not reviled as a whore,' said Nat, his eyes intent on hers. 'You did what you did for love, and that is the best of all reasons.'

Silence saw something new in his face, an awareness that had never been there before, for all his cynicism. She found it almost impossible to believe – Nat, in love? And with someone so wildly unsuitable, in every sense of the phrase, that she could see little happiness in store for either of them. She almost spoke, and then thought better of it. There was enough heaped on his platter, and hers, already, without adding to it. But she wished, of all people, he had not fixed his affections on her pretty, wayward and devious little sister.

'For love,' she said, and smiled wearily. 'And yet, Nat, I feel that I hardly know him – he is almost a stranger to me, I have so little idea of his childhood, his history – and yet in other ways, in all the things that matter, we are so close that we have no need of words.' She pushed her hand through her hair, and several pins dropped to the floor. 'And when Pyne took him away, in the cart – it was all I could do, not to run down the lane after them. He could be dead by now, he could have bled to death on the journey, and I wouldn't know.'

'Young Jack Goodenough is driving it,' said Nat. 'I told him to take the greatest care, and not to pay very much attention to Pyne's bluster if he was urged to go too fast for Nick's safety. I also told him to find out exactly where Nick was to be held, and if he could do so discreetly, what arrangements were to be made for his care. And no, I know what you're going to say. At present, we cannot risk any attempt to free him. But I don't think that there can be any harm in making sure that he's being kept in some comfort, do you? And if I am the one who visits him, then no breath of scandal or suspicion can be attached to you. It would hardly seem likely to all these foul-minded gossips, after all, that I would be prepared to give help to a man who'd cuckolded my own father.'

'Nat,' Silence said, after a pause. 'Dear Nat, I don't deserve you

'– how many stepsons in your position would even look on Nick with anything other than disgust and loathing?'

'I don't know,' said Nat, with his usual grin. 'I only know that I don't give a toss for other people's ideas of morality – ideas that Christ himself probably wouldn't even recognise as Christian. I don't claim divine grace or approval for what I think – still less, do I seek to impose my views on anyone else. But love, and friendship, and happiness, seem to me to be the most important things, and to do to others as you would want them to do to you, does not strike me as a bad philosophy by which to live your life. And by that rule, I am only returning a past favour.'

'Only?' said Silence, and Nat laughed.

He had not given her any easy answers to her dreadful dilemma. She suspected that no one could do that. She knew for certain, only that she would rather die than give herself to that devious, reptilian man, in whom she had once, so mistakenly, put her trust.

*

'We *must* free him!' Tabby was saying at that precise moment, quite unaware of her mother's appalling predicament, or of the perfidy of Jonathan Harley. 'We can't just leave him to rot in gaol.'

'I agree,' said Patience. She had regained a little of her colour since the morning, although it owed something to artifice, and seemed once more to be her usual lively, vivacious self. 'The question is, though, how do we do it? We know nothing about where he's being held, how well he's guarded – nothing. We can't just walk in, ask for the keys, and let him out.'

'Hardly,' said Tabby, thinking. 'And somehow, we have to do it so that no possible blame can be attached to Wintercombe – so that this time Nat and Mother really are innocent – and us as well.'

'Which means disguise,' said Patience. She peered into her mirror, and flicked a misplaced curl with her finger. Tabby saw her smile, slow and wicked. 'This could be very interesting. I shall enjoy pitting my wits against that repellent man.'

'Colonel Pyne?' Tabby said, startled. 'But you didn't meet him.'

'No – but I *heard* him. I was listening from the gallery,' said Patience, unblushingly. 'I was quite surprised when Harington spoke up in Nick's defence. I'd always thought him a self-righteous bore.'

'He is – though I know he's also extremely honest and incorruptible,' Tabby told her. 'Unlike Colonel Pyne.'

Patience's smile grew a little absent. She said, after a pause, 'How much coin do you have?'

'None, at the moment. I gave it all to Jeremy Walker when I sent him off with Tom Wickham's letter.'

'A shame,' said Patience. 'I have a little, but it may not be nearly enough to bribe the gaoler, and I can hardly ask Nat for more. This time, no one else is going to be party to our conspiracy – except for Tom Wickham, of course. Not Deb, not William, and certainly not Kate or Rachael.' She glanced at her niece's thoughtful face. 'Why exactly have you summoned Tom?'

To her own annoyance, Tabby blushed. She said, a little defensively, 'I – I thought he could help us to free Nick.'

'Nothing else? Nothing,' said Patience, her eyes suddenly dancing, 'to do with Rachael, who is now free of encumbrance?'

Tabby produced a rather shamefaced grin. 'He likes her, I think. And she needs someone to take her mind off Jack, not to mention everything else.'

'A brave attempt,' Patience commented. 'But I warn you, it may not work.' She paused, glancing at the younger girl assessingly. The information, imparted in confidence, could do no harm, and might even lead to some good. She added, 'You do not know this, but I think you should – you must keep it a close secret, though. When Rachael took refuge in the summerhouse yesterday . . . she tried to hang herself.'

There was an appalled silence. Tabby's hazel eyes, wide with horror, stared at her aunt. '*What*?'

'She tried to hang herself. Fortunately, she can't tie a slip knot, and Nat found her in time, and cut her down. That is why she is keeping to her chamber, and why someone is always with her. She can barely speak, and her throat is badly marked.'

Tabby had begun to weep, the tears slithering down her face unchecked. She wiped her nose on her sleeve, and said miserably, 'Oh, poor Rachael – I hadn't realised – oh, how *terrible*.'

'She was fortunate,' said Patience, who did not have much sympathy for Rachael's plight, considering it to be largely self-inflicted. 'Remember, don't tell anyone that you know. It could cause so much trouble, if the truth were known.'

'I hate secrets,' said Tabby, in quite a different voice. 'They seem to bring nothing but misery – I wish we were rid of them, for ever!' She dried her eyes fiercely, and turned to Patience, her slender body tense with resolve. 'And the only way to do it, is to free Nick somehow. Have you any ideas yet, as to what we can do?'

Patience refrained from commenting on the obvious, that any attempt to set her sister's lover at liberty would inevitably result in still more conspiracies and murky secrets. 'Yes,' she said slowly. 'Yes, I do believe I have.'

And with suddenly shining eyes, Tabby listened breathlessly to her whispered plan.

*

'For you, sir. You are Master Wickham, aren't you?'

Tom, weary, mud-splashed and aching in every joint from following the plough, surveyed the scrawny youth in front of him in some surprise. Letters were infrequent at Longleaze, and messages brought by servants even rarer. Someone must want to contact him very urgently. Even as the thought crossed his mind, he knew who it must be.

He took the folded paper, warm from its place inside the boy's doublet. Yes, the clear schoolgirl hand was Tabby's, the superscription unmistakable. Master Thomas Wickham, of Longleaze, near Glastonbury. He pushed a finger under the seal and scanned the brief lines within, a frown on his face, while Jeremy watched him anxiously.

The boy was aware that this summons must have something to do with the recent shocking events at Wintercombe. The servants, in their usual fashion, had not long remained in ignorance of Tabby's astonishing plot, and had their own ideas about the possible complicity of the adults. For his part, Jeremy had decided that it must be as she had so courageously declared to the unpleasant Pyne, that she had acted alone, and his admiration had soared still further. She was young, lovely, innocent, intelligent and brave, and he would do anything for her.

'Do you know what this is about?' asked Tom, in bewilderment. The message could only mean one thing, but the thought was so appalling that he could scarcely believe it. 'Tell me what has happened at Wintercombe.'

With mounting astonishment, he listened to Jeremy's rather garbled account. The soldiers' arrival, Rachael's betrayal, the fight in which Captain Hellier had nearly lost his life, and the saintly selflessness with which Mistress Tabby had taken all the blame on her own shoulders, seemed scarcely credible. But the boy, plainly lost in admiration of her, seemed to be telling the truth, as he saw it. Tom glanced round his barton, the two oxen being unyoked by Will Everett, his most senior worker, his own team waiting patiently, steaming in the cool dusk, for their turn. There was a great deal to do, as there was on any farm at this time of year, but this matter could not wait. The ploughing could be managed without him for a few days. His labourers were well paid and reliable, and Everett more than capable of directing them himself. He looked again at the paper, seeing the suppressed and desperate urgency of Tabby's words. 'Our great distress.' So, indeed, it must be, even if Jeremy had told him everything that had happened. Although he could not see how he could be of any use to the St. Barbes in this calamity, at least he could offer his support and comfort.

And he would be able to discover the truth of Rachael's part in the affair. The boy, with barely disguised contempt, had spoken of treachery. He could not believe it. He knew that she was rebellious, difficult, and unhappy, but he could not think her capable of informing against her own family in cold blood. Only at Wintercombe could he ascertain the truth.

'I'll ride back with you,' he told Jeremy. 'We'll go at first light — meanwhile, there's a bed for you, and a good supper waiting.'

And Jeremy, who had been hoping for Mistress Tabby's sake that her entreaties would be answered, grinned delightedly in reply.

*

The object of all this tangled conspiracy lay on a hard and uncomfortable bed in a narrow stonewalled cell, contemplating his future, or the lack of it, with an equanimity that surprised him.

At least he was still alive, though the journey from Philip's Norton had been exceedingly unpleasant. The cart in which he had been transported was, of course, unsprung, and had evidently last been used for carrying dung to the fields. Bedded on piles of straw and sacking, wrapped in blankets, the precious bag of coin and remedies concealed beneath his doublet like a talisman, he had set himself to endure and survive and, somewhat to his surprise, had done both. He could not remember very much about the latter part of the journey, but had a rather too vivid recollection of being hauled, somewhat roughly, from the cart before a crowd of jeering onlookers, and half dragged, half carried into somewhere dark, and damp, and cold, which was presumably this place. Then, he supposed that he had lost consciousness.

By the light from the tiny narrow window, it was morning. That cold pale glare had nothing of evening gentleness about it. To his vague surprise, the fierce pain in his shoulder had dulled to a nagging, miserable ache. Carefully, he probed the bandages with his other hand. It hurt, but not agonisingly so, and it did not seem to have bled any more. Although he still felt weak and tired and light-headed from lack of blood, his forehead, when he touched it, was cool and dry. No sign of fever yet, at any rate. Despite the chill in the little cell, the blankets, and Nat's thick cloak, had kept him comparatively warm.

He was lying on his back. Slowly, with care and not without several stabs of pain, he managed to struggle into a sitting position. They had laid him on the bed as he was, not even bothering to unbutton his doublet. Careless, he thought, I could have had a pistol hidden there. But at least the coin was safe, and Silence's potions.

He looked around him cautiously. In the distant days when he had been part of the Bath garrison, the city prison had been housed in the tower of St. Mary's, a disused church hard by the North Gate. Incongruously, the nave and chancel of the same church, suitably adapted, contained the Grammar School, and the young sons of the aldermen and gentlemen of Bath and the surrounding district studied Latin and Greek only a few yards away from the felons in the cells.

He listened, but could hear no sound of young voices. Doubtless they were beaten if they spoke out of turn, just as he had been in his schooldays in Worcester. There were, however, distinct noises from the street outside, wheeled traffic, shouts and cries, the general bustle of a busy morning.

He looked at the window. It was unglazed, and might have allowed a small child to squeeze through its narrow confines. There was no hope of escape that way, and besides, at present he did not have the energy to do anything more than conserve his strength.

The rest of the cell was even less promising. It held his bed, another the same, mercifully unoccupied, two stools and a bucket. The small door in the corner presumably led to a turret staircase. The floor and ceiling were made of oak planks, roughly nailed to the joists, and the stone walls were ancient, the mortar flaking and powdery, stained with damp and mould. He shivered suddenly, and pushed himself down beneath the blankets, seeking warmth.

He was asleep when the gaoler opened the door, with a great noise of rattling iron and creaking hinges. He woke with a jerk, and subsided, wincing, as his injured shoulder forced itself painfully to the fore. He turned his head and saw a large and loaded tray advancing towards him.

For some reason, he had imagined his gaoler to be a long thin gloomy man. This rotund, beaming personage, who would barely reach his shoulder, was the exact opposite. 'Aha, so we're awake, are we?' he said, in accents that were not of Bath. 'And about time too. Breakfast, your worship.'

Nick eyed him suspiciously. This man, unlikely as it might seem, had absolute power over him. The provision of food, comforts, medicines and visitors would be entirely at his discretion, and his whim. Offend him, and life would become exceedingly unpleasant. Grease his palm, and blankets, books, fine food and writing materials, even the passing of messages, might well be procured. He had been prepared to bribe, cajole and plead to obtain what he needed. Now, looking at this jovial little man, he wondered if it would be necessary.

Of course it was. He sat up gingerly, and surveyed the repast set out for him. Coarse bread, probably mixed with barley or even rye, and a watery-looking broth that might contain anything. His appetite not exactly encouraged, Nick looked up from the tray. 'This, I take is, is what you give to all your prisoners?'

'Yes, if they haven't the wherewithal to pay the extra,' said the gaoler, with cheerful candour. He held out a chubby pink palm. 'Have you, sir?'

'Perhaps,' said Nick, guardedly. 'But before I pay you anything, I would like to ascertain the conditions under which I am held. Is there anything which I am not allowed — barring my liberty, of course?'

'Colonel Pyne didn't say, sir. Anything within reason, that's the usual rule — so long as the prisoner pays for it, of course,' said the gaoler, hopefully. 'And a fine Cavalier like yourself, sir, should surely be supplied with ready coin.'

He had taken the precaution earlier of hiding the bag, containing the greater part of his money, beneath the mattress. He fumbled under the pillow, where he had concealed the rest, and brought out a silver coin. 'Take that, and bring me a breakfast that's fit to eat —

if you please. A crown should be sufficient to feed me for several days.'

The gaoler gave him a very sharp glance. He snatched the coin from his hand, bit it, and pushed it deep into a pocket. 'That all depends, sir.'

'On what?'

'On how well you want to be fed,' said the little man. 'If you want roast meat and white bread and fine wines – well, at the Katherine Wheel's prices, it'll barely buy you a dinner. But bread, cheese, ale – plain fare but good, yes, it should last you three or four days.'

'Plain fare,' said Nick. 'I am not, alas, awash with coin. But of good quality, nothing stale or rancid, and plenty of it. I doubt that Colonel Pyne would wish me to waste away.'

'I doubt he'd care overmuch,' said the gaoler bluntly. 'He's got other fish to fry. My orders are to keep you here until you are well enough to be sent to Bristol, with the rest of the Scots prisoners. Your comfort was not mentioned, sir. As is customary, the condition of your confinement depends on my reward.'

'Unusual, to find a gaoler with a sense of humour,' Nick said drily. 'But at any rate, there should be no misunderstanding between us. I have stated my requirements, and given you the necessary payment – would you be so good as to carry them out?'

'Of course, sir,' said the man, and bowed with exaggerated courtesy.

In half an hour, a very different tray was brought to him. New bread, still with a faint lingering warmth from the oven, a solid wedge of cheese, and a leather blackjack of beer. He ate it all with enthusiasm, and then retreated once more within the warmth of the blankets, feeling very much better. The gaoler – Pearce, his name was, Harry Pearce – was as venal as all turnkeys, but not malicious. Anything would be available to him, except his liberty, if he was prepared to pay for it.

He had thought of sending a message to Wintercombe, but decided against it. To do so would only incriminate them further, and he could not risk it. He suspected that, in himself, he did not matter very much to Colonel Pyne and his henchmen. He was merely one more Cavalier prisoner, without high rank or important knowledge, and there were thousands such in London, Bristol, Chester and many other places. Pearce had spoken casually of shipment to the New World, to work as bondservants on the plantations, or, more unpleasantly, in the gold mines of the Guinea Coast. Merchants were apparently already bidding for prisoners. Somehow, he must extract himself from his cell, without suspicion falling on anyone at Wintercombe. He would be no use to Silence labouring in a gold mine in Guinea, but neither could he compromise her further. Which meant that, if he did escape, he must not attempt to contact her for a very long time.

His battered mind, weakened and exhausted by the headlong events of the past few days, could find no way out. It would come to him, he was sure: somewhere amid all the tangle lay the answer. But for the moment, all he wanted to do was to sleep, and regain his strength.

*

At Wintercombe, a precarious air of normality had been attained. The servants, shocked and bewildered by the discovery of fugitive Cavaliers under their roof, no longer gathered in odd corners, whispering, but went about their mundane duties with the appearance of calm. Mistress Rachael still kept to her chamber, and one or two of the more forthright had stated that twere no surprise that the northering forweend wench was too shamed to put her nose out of her door. There were very few people who had a good word for Rachael, whatever their feelings about Scots and Cavaliers. Poor Jude, her maid, sadly aware of the real reason for Rachael's concealment but unable to disclose it, did her best to defend her.

The children were exceedingly subdued. William was too good-natured to be unkind to Kate about her revelation of their secret, but Deb, miserable and confused herself, lost no opportunity to make sly references to it, frequently reducing her little sister to tears. Doraty, exasperated, found herself appealing to a higher authority several times a day, and Silence must put aside her own worries and cares to pour oil on the nursery's troubled waters.

It had been so difficult to preserve her calm, which seemed, she thought with amusement, like a crust of pastry covering something quite different: tainted meat, perhaps. But the years of practice had told, and to her servants and her children, she was her usual serene self: as if her lover had not been hauled wounded off to prison in danger of death; as if her daughter were not guilty of crimes against the Commonwealth; her stepdaughter had not tried to hang herself; and as if the family lawyer were not attempting to blackmail her into marriage. It seemed so fantastic, so absurd, that

[421]

if she had heard of it happening to someone else, she would have laughed in disbelief. Yet she was caught up in this nightmare, and it was not in the least amusing. She knew in her darkest heart that only a miracle could save her from becoming Jonathan Harley's wife.

He would soon return, and demand her answer. The only hope to which she could still cling was that Nat might be able to amass sufficient, in cash or in land, to keep him quiet without resorting to marriage. The thought of bargaining with him made her gorge rise, but there was no help for it. He had no proof, but his certain knowledge of their guilt was a powerful weapon against them. He held their fates in his hands, and knew his power too well.

Once, she had wished that her husband would not return from the war. Once, she had felt ashamed of that impulse, and chastised herself bitterly for desiring his death, however remotely.

Now, with an intensity that terrified her, she understood why murder was done. She found herself imagining how it would feel to plunge a well-sharpened knife into that satisfied chest, to beat that handsome, clever face into an unrecognisable pulp. And she knew, with sick dread, that she would be capable of it, for he threatened her happiness and her children and Wintercombe, and his death might perhaps be her only chance of salvation.

She dared not mention these appalling feelings to Nat. She feared that he, devious and selectively amoral, was quite capable of slipping some deadly potion into Harley's wine, and speaking to him with cheerful fellowship as the poison spread through his veins. Then she was ashamed of her mistrust. Nat was not evil. He was too cynical, too light-hearted, too contemptuous of convention, but he was not so wicked as to encompass, with forethought and deliberation, the death of another human being, however reprehensible that person might be.

That night, at the hour when Nick had come to her, only two days ago, she prayed long and urgently for deliverance from evil, from her dreadful thoughts, and for an answer to her appalling predicament. When she rose from her knees, cold and stiff, weary and heartsick, the stillness and emptiness of midnight was her only reply.

But someone must have been listening, for quite early the next morning, only just after the family had broken their fast, there was a knock on her chamber door, and Mally walked in.

She looked anxious, her small freckled face most uncharacteristically pinched and tense. So unexpected, and so utterly welcome, was her return, that Silence could barely refrain from weeping. The two women, so different in appearance and in position, but united by many years of friendship and loyalty, embraced with much warmth, and she saw, touched, that Mally herself was close to tears.

'I've come back to help ee,' said her maid, once ensconced in one of the fireside chairs, with Misty, who had always liked her, curled purring in her lap. 'It d'seem to me, you d'need it despeard bad, m'lady.'

'You don't know the half of it,' Silence told her, spreading her hands. 'But – Mally, what of your grandmother? Surely she is more in need of you than I am?'

'My sister Christian have come over from Frome,' said her maid. 'Her Tom don't mind. Soon as I heard what was a-happening up here, I sent word to her.' The shrewd blue eyes rested speculatively on her mistress. 'So – your young Cavalier came back to ee, did he? And caused a power of pain and grief thereby, from all accounts.'

Her sharp manner did not deceive Silence. She knew that she could rely on Mally's sympathy and support, as surely as she could anticipate the rising of the sun. She said quietly, 'I had better tell you exactly what has happened.'

Mally listened closely to the whole confused and unhappy tale. Silence spared nothing, not even Nick's night-time visit to her chamber, and its inevitable consequences. She suspected that her maid, ever practical, was wondering if those brief hours of ungovernable passion would produce another child. At this particular moment, she herself did not know, and did not wish to. She had other, more pressing matters to resolve.

'That Pync, he always were a bastard,' was Mally's unequivocal comment. 'He be famous for en – he've all the sequestrators in his pocket.' She eyed Silence, speculatively. 'And he bain't no dummel neither. Be ee *certain* he don't know nothing more?'

'I'm sure,' Silence said. 'Would he lose an opportunity to appropriate a rich estate like Wintercombe?' She hesitated, wondering whether to tell Mally about Harley's threats. The maid, robustly practical, would assuredly advise calling his bluff, and it was a suggestion that Silence did not, for the moment, wish to hear. She knew that her courage had for once failed her, that she would not risk it, and this self-knowledge, that she would willingly lay herself open to blackmail, was not a pleasant discovery. What she needed now was time: time for Nick to heal; time to find a way out of their predicament; time, perhaps, for this nightmare to dissolve away into nothing, like morning mist burned away by the sun.

'And Captain Hellicr? Where be he now?' Mally asked.

'In the city gaol in Bath. Jack Goodenough drove the cart, and brought the word back. He survived the journey,' Silence said, her voice suddenly ragged despite all her efforts. 'That was the best that Jack could tell me. And it would be unwise even to try and find out how he is.'

'I don't see why,' said Mally bluntly. 'By your own tale, m'lady, you spoke of past friendship. What's to stop ee bringing comfort to a sick man? Tis only charity, after all, as Scripture tell us to do. If ee don't want to go see him, I'll do it and willing.' She grinned. 'Chances are, turnkey will do aught for a shilling or two, save unlock the door, of course. Then I can bring ee word, m'lady, and give him your comfort too.'

Silence stared at her, wondering what Nat would say to this. She wanted to have no more secrets from him, and she trusted his instincts above anyone's. He, after all, had most to lose, should Pyne's suspicions become aroused.

But by now, Pyne was probably on his way home to Curry Mallet. And Mally was quick-witted and resourceful. She said slowly, 'It might be possible. Oh, Mally — I only want to know how he is, I am so afraid for him, it's not knowing that is the worst, not being able to help. And if you could visit him . . . '

'Who's to know I hail from Wintercombe?' said Mally, and grinned. 'I could be an old sweetheart from his days in the Bath garrison, and that turnkey won't know any different.' She glanced at her mistress meaningfully. 'Do ee want orryone else to know of this, m'lady? Sir Nathaniel, maybe?'

'Yes,' said Silence. 'Nat, in particular.'

She had wondered if her stepson would find any obvious flaws in her plan, that she had somehow overlooked. But after greeting Mally with a warmth which, she suspected, concealed a fair amount of relief, he listened with evident approval as she suggested that Mally visit Nick in prison. 'An excellent idea — why not? I agree, it would be foolish for you or me to see him, but no one can read any sinister motive into an errand of charity to a sick man — not even our dear Pyne. And who could be more discreet, or sensible, or charitable, than Mally Merrifield?'

At which compliment her maid, surprisingly, blushed.

It was arranged that she would ride into Bath immediately after dinner, since the following day was a Sunday. She would be escorted by Jack Goodenough, the head groom's nephew, who was the only stable-lad available, since Jeremy Walker had mysteriously and worryingly disappeared the previous day. This was not very satisfactory, as Jack was now known to the turnkey, but Mally, ever resourceful, would doubtless ensure that he kept out of sight.

And now, all Silence had to do was to wait for news.

*

'Visitor for you,' said Pearce, flinging open the door to the cell with a cheery crash that wrenched Nick from his peaceful slumber. 'Do you want to see her, or not?'

Nick, dazed with sleep and clutching his injured shoulder, which had been painfully jarred as he sat up, stared in some bewilderment at his gaoler. 'Visitor? Who?'

'She'll cost you extra,' said Pearce, ignoring his questions. He marched up to the bed and, in what was now a familiar ritual, held out his hand. 'Shilling extra, to be exact.'

Nick groped beneath his pillow, and found the right coin. He saw Pearce's eyes, small, bright and greedy, follow his movements, and knew that he had done well to hide the bulk of his money elsewhere. Pearce would undoubtedly have no compunction whatsoever in stealing it, given the opportunity.

'Excellent,' said the fat man, pocketing the shilling. He turned and shouted towards the open door. 'In here, my dear — he's ready and waiting for you!'

He had not known whom to expect. He had recognised that his visitor was very unlikely to be Silence herself — Tabby, perhaps, or even Patience. But for a moment he did not recognise the trim, diminutive young woman, in hood and cloak and plain dark grey, her hair hidden. Then she pushed the heavy cloth from her head, revealing the bright gingery curls he remembered, and gave him a blunt, cheerful grin. 'Good afternoon to ee, Captain Hellier.'

'Mally!' he said, in delight. He had not seen her for six years, but his recollection of her was vivid and pleasant. With her connivance, he and Silence had become lovers, and she had kept their secret faithfully. No one could be more loyal to their mistress, or a better servant, and friend. For the first time since Captain

Humphreys' sword had struck him down, he found himself daring to hope.

'Will you leave us for a while?' he said to Pearce, who was still hovering by the bed.

The man grinned widely. 'Yes, sir, I gladly will – for a consideration, of course. Privacy comes extra.'

Nick glared at him. At this rate, even that reassuringly heavy bag of coin would not last a week. He produced a groat, and pushed it into the plump greedy hand. 'I'm surprised you don't charge for pissing in the bucket.'

'Oh, no, sir, of course not,' said Pearce, his small eyes wide with mock affront. He paused, and added pointedly, 'But I'll charge you for the service of emptying it, sir.' And, chuckling at his own dubious wit, he waddled from the cell. Nick and Mally heard the door slam, and his footsteps receding down the stairs.

'It's good to see you, Mally,' he said. 'You haven't changed in the least.'

'You have, though, Captain,' said Silence's maid, with the forthrightness he remembered. She was carrying a rush basket under her cloak: she walked over to the bed and set it down. 'M'lady packed en for ee. Bread, honey, a nice pasty, cold meats and a fat joint of gammon. And a bottle of restorative for the blood – twill taste tarblish foul, Captain, but she told me to tell en to be sure and take it, twill do ee a power of good.'

'I will indeed,' said Nick. The savoury tang of mutton was rising from the basket, and he realised that he was feeling extremely hungry. 'But I'll have some of that pasty first.'

Like all of Darby's baking, it was well seasoned, succulent and delicious. It seemed that, almost before he had taken the first mouthful, he was mopping the last crumbs from the blanket. Mally watched him with her head slightly on one side. With her rather beaky nose, and sharp features, she reminded him of a bird, though she entirely lacked fragility. She said, 'There bain't much wrong with ee, by the look of en.'

'At this rate, there won't be soon,' said Nick. 'I could have eaten two of those pies.' He leaned back, his hands folded in front of him, his eyes resting on her face. 'How are things at Wintercombe?'

He had spoken very quietly, but still she glanced at the door. There was a small grille cut into it, through which Pearce could observe and listen, but she could see no one lurking there. She was determined to take no chances, though, and knelt by the bed, her face close to his. 'Calm, you could say, Captain. I only came back this morning, so I ain't had much chance to see how the wind d'blow, but there bain't no one despeard betwattled nor gallid — nor m'lady neither.'

'And how is she?' said Nick, and his eyes were suddenly bright. 'Is she well?'

'Well, but fretting,' Mally whispered. 'You know m'lady so well as I, Captain — she d'*seem* all fine and happy, but she bain't — I can see en in her eyen. She be pining for ee, but she d'know in her heart there bain't much hope. She've explained it all to me, about Mistress Tabby and all she did to help ee — brave little lass, she be.' She fumbled with the buttons of her bodice, and drew out a tiny folded piece of paper. 'Mistress Tabby gave me en, just afore I left, and told me most especial to give en to ee secret-like. And you're to burn en when you've read en, she said, leave no trace.'

'How can I?' said Nick. He gestured round the little cell. 'Hardly, when there's no hearth.'

'You could always eat en,' said Mally, stifling a grin. 'Twouldn't be no trace then.'

'Excellent advice,' Nick said, and unfolded the paper.

The writing was not in Tabby's round young hand, but a bolder more dashing stroke that must surely belong to Patience. His eyes flicked over the few lines.

Do not worry. We have not forgotten you. T.W. will help. Do not be surprised at *anything*.

The last word was heavily underlined. He stared at it, feeling at once afraid and exasperated. Could this infuriating young woman never give over her plotting? And once more, she had embroiled Tabby in her web. Well, if she thought she had some crackpot scheme to spring him from prison, she could think again. He looked up at Mally's inquisitive face. 'Tell Mistress Tabby — *and* Mistress Patience — that I am quite happy to stay here for a while, and I am not, repeat *not*, in dire need of rescue. And the last thing I want is that those two nincompoops put everyone else in jeopardy because they've hatched some ludicrous plot to spirit me away to . . . wherever they think I'll be safe from pursuit.' A dry smile illuminated his drawn, pale face. 'The New World, probably.'

'So — you want me to tell them to stop,' said Mally. 'Tisn't my place to do ort like that, Captain.'

He saw the gleam in her eye, and knew better than to take her words at face value. Forthright Mally had never been shy of telling people exactly what she thought, whether it was her place to do it or not. He suspected that she was even now rehearsing what she would say to Patience and Tabby. 'Does Silence know what they are planning?' he asked.

'I don't think so,' said Mally thoughtfully. 'Shall I tell her?'

'No – not unless they ignore you,' Nick told her. 'And perhaps not even then. If she doesn't know, then if something goes wrong again, she really will be innocent. But Mally – please, tell them from me, with all the force and persuasion you can muster, not, not, *not* to hatch whatever escape plot they're planning.'

'I'll try,' said Mally. 'But telling Mistress Patience not to do summat once her mind be set on it, be like that old king who told the tide not to come in. Tisn't possible, not till the sea d'run dry.' She added darkly, 'If tweren't for their godly father and mother, I'd wonder if she was truly m'lady's sister.'

'I think she is,' said Nick drily. 'Unfortunately. But I'm relying on you, my dear Mally – do everything you can, *everything*, to stop that pair of crackpots plunging Wintercombe into disaster.'

He knew, and Mally knew, that he was being less than fair to Patience and Tabby. After all, it was not their fault, in the circumstances, that they had been betrayed. And Tabby, at least, was an intelligent girl, who would learn from past mistakes. But the thought of what might happen if something once more went wrong made his blood run chill. At all costs, they must be prevented from taking such a risk.

'Ain't ee disremembered summat?' said Mally, with a grin. She indicated the piece of paper, still held in his hands. 'Bain't ee a-going to eat en?'

With exaggerated care, he tore Patience's message into small pieces, and put them in his mouth, while Mally watched him solemnly. It was no use: he caught her eye, and both of them exploded into helpless laughter.

'Wash en down with some of this here beer,' the maid advised, in between giggles. 'Oh, Captain, if m'lady could only see your face!'

'If only Patience could see it too,' said Nick, taking her advice. She was right: a good draught of beer swilled round his mouth, reduced the paper to a mushy pulp, easily swallowed. His duty done, he said soberly, 'It's no laughing matter really, Mally.

Patience is living in the real world, not in some French romance, and the sooner she realises it, the better. And she's old enough to know better, too. Tabby . . . I think Tabby has some idea that she can move us all around for our own good, as if we were chess-pieces. But people aren't so biddable — and when she discovers it, she'll be hurt.'

'A brave little wench,' said Mally. 'But I d'reckon ee be right, Captain. I promise, I'll try and wallop some sense into they two gawcums.'

And with that, he had for the moment to be content.

🦋 CHAPTER TWENTY-TWO 🦋

'Sisterly remorse'

(*Measure For Measure*)

Tom Wickham, as yet unaware of the role that Patience and Tabby had assigned to him, rode into Wintercombe, with Jeremy Walker at his side, just before supper. His horse had twice cast a shoe, delaying them for several hours, and he was weary, and rather apprehensive. What had really happened here, and did the boy's wild tale actually approach the truth?

Jeremy was also anxious, but for somewhat different reasons. His fears proved justified when the head groom, Tom Goodenough, stamped out of the barton with a face black as thunder. 'So there ee be, you girt loppus — where have ee been, eh? Not on Mistress Tabby's business, that be sure enough!' And he swung his large fist at Jeremy's ear.

The boy ducked, and dodged behind his horse. Tom, still mounted, said hastily, 'It's all right, Goodenough — Mistress Tabby sent him to fetch me.'

The groom turned, his face wrinkled with astonishment. 'You, sir — oh, tarblish sorry, Master Wickham, I didn't recognise ee. Very well, Jeremy, you can take Master Wickham's horse, and yourn, and we'll disremember what I said, eh?'

With a rather shamefaced grin, the boy took the reins of Tom's white-faced bay gelding, while he dismounted. The front door opened with a bang, and Tabitha St. Barbe, her honey-brown hair bursting from under the plain linen cap, ran down the steps, all aglow with delight. 'Oh, Tom, you're here already! Wonderful!'

She turned to Jeremy, and the boy, who had chattered almost without stopping, all the way from Glastonbury, at once became a blushing, tongue-tied hobbledehoy. 'I done what ee said, Mistress Tabby,' he stated, somewhat obviously, and stared fixedly at her shoes. 'And I didn't spend more'n a shilling or two, neither, and here's your bag.'

'Thank you, Jeremy,' Tabby said, her smile full of warmth. 'You've done very well — thank you so much.' She glanced at Goodenough, who was still surveying them with an air of dour puzzlement. 'I'm sorry I sent Jeremy off without telling you — I didn't think about it,' she explained, with an artless innocence which, as she had intended, entirely melted the stubborn old groom's displeasure. 'Please don't blame him, it was my fault, and not his at all.' She smiled dazzlingly at Tom. 'Come inside, it's nearly time for supper, and you must be ravenously hungry.'

But as soon as they entered the porch, dark and dim, with the door to the house closed so that they were out of sight and earshot of anyone lurking in the screens passage, she put out a hand to detain him. 'Wait, Tom — wait! I've got so much to tell you, I can't say it all here, but I asked you here for a reason.'

'What's happened?' he said urgently. 'I think I had the gist from your letter, and what Jeremy said, but it sounded too fantastic to be true — tell me in plain words — what in God's name has happened here?'

'We hid Nick Hellier in the roofspace, but Rachael found out and told the soldiers,' said Tabby bluntly. She had wrestled long with the problem of her half-sister's treachery, but in the end had decided on the truth. He was bound to find out sooner or later, and there was always the chance that he would not be angered or discouraged. She added, to set the record straight, 'I think she had some idea of keeping favour with Jack Harington. But the betrothal is ended anyway, the contract was torn up, and none of us are really sorry — not even Rachael. She regretted what she'd done, though, once Hellier was taken.'

Tom's pleasant brown country face was a study in bewilderment. 'So Nick was *here*? And is now a prisoner — where? In Bath?'

'In the city gaol,' said Tabby. 'He was badly hurt — he tried to fight his way free — and Mother thought he'd die, but he didn't. And her maid Mally went to see him this afternoon, and she said that he was much much better — sitting up, and eating well, and in good spirits.'

She was not going to reveal what else Mally had said to her, in a brief private moment on the stairs from Silence's chamber, but she was more determined than ever, if that were possible, to free Nick from prison. She knew that it must be his concern for her, and Patience, and Silence too, of course, that had led him to such a forceful repudiation of help. There's no need to worry, Tabby had thought, listening with deceptive meekness to Mally's hissing tirade. This time, we shall be careful — this time, we won't be caught.

She still had to convince Tom, of course, and she could hardly discuss it here in the porch, while anyone who might be in the dining parlour was able to overhear her through the little squint in the wall. Time for that later: for now, he could rest from his journey, and perhaps see Rachael, and be welcomed once more to Wintercombe as an old and valued friend. Nick was not, after all, at death's door — Mally had been very cheerful and positive on that score. For a day or so, he could wait, and regain his strength, until every detail of the plan to free him had been worked out.

She gave Tom a friendly, conspirator's grin, and led him on into the house.

*

Rachael sat at her table, looking despondently into the mirror. The face that stared sadly back was all too familiar, chalk pale, the mouth downturned, the stark blue eyes smudged with the indelible shadows of pain and misery. She essayed a smile, and it looked ridiculous, grotesque, a leer on a gargoyle. I shall never be beautiful, she thought unhappily, never, never, never — and it's pointless even to try.

This evening, she had thought that she might appear at supper, for the first time since that dreadful night — her mind shied away from the words 'suicide', or 'hanging' — after Nick's capture. But now that the hour was upon her, her courage had trickled away, leaving only fear — fear of her family's ridicule, their loathing and contempt, feelings which they would not openly express, but which would stare accusingly from their eyes.

She had not given any explanation of her conduct to anyone. She knew that no amount of justification, no weight of reason, could excuse her treachery, nor her treatment of Kate. Yet, somehow, in the anguish of remorse and despair, all her bitterness and rage had been seared to ashes, leaving only this mood of sad apathy. The only person she hated now was herself. She longed, more than anything else she longed to stand in front of her brothers and sisters, her stepmother and Patience, and speak the truth. I am sorry — so desperately sorry. I have made a terrible mistake, and caused much suffering, and grief. I think and I hope that I have learned from it — I will try so hard to behave better — if you will only give me the chance, and accept me and love me for myself.

But her fierce pride, so often her downfall in the past, would not allow her to abase herself thus. Rather than face their scorn and revulsion, she would hide here, covering the raw scar on her neck, the mark of her shame, with a prim high collar, shut in with her misery.

There was a knock on the door. She ignored it, hoping that the person would go away. It was repeated, more forcefully. With the tone of a condemned man facing the inevitable, Rachael called out, 'Come in!'

Patience stood there, all scented elegance in her low-cut rose-coloured gown, a lace-trimmed neckerchief doing the minimum to preserve her modesty. She shut the door behind her, folded her arms, and said, 'You look terrible.'

Once, that remark would have aroused Rachael to vicious rage. Now, she said listlessly, 'I feel terrible too. I'm not coming down to supper.'

'Oh, yes, you are,' said Patience. 'Tom Wickham's here, and he's going to think it very strange if you don't appear.'

'I've got a headache,' Rachael said, passing a hand across her brow. 'I don't want any supper.'

'You'll fade away to nothing if you don't eat,' said Patience. She glided over to the table, pulled up another chair, and sat down. 'You're getting too thin. You'd be pretty if you were a little plumper, smiled a bit, and had some colour in your cheeks.'

Astonished and disbelieving, Rachael stared at her. '*Me*? Pretty? Oh, don't be absurd!'

'I'm not,' said Patience, for once exhibiting the quality for which she had been named. 'I'm telling you the truth. Do you think I don't know what I'm talking about?'

Rachael stared at her stepmother's sister, at the gleaming, immaculate dark curls, the bright eyes with their artfully darkened lashes, her glowing skin and tinted rosebud mouth. She was a triumph of fashionable beauty, and at that moment Rachael would have sold her soul for a little of the forbidden knowledge of self-enhancement. She said slowly, 'No. No, I don't.'

'Well, I'm not lying,' said Patience. 'Your features are good, you have lovely eyes, and your hair would look so much better if you brushed it. That gown does nothing to show off your figure – your corsets need to be laced more tightly, here, then you won't seem to be so thin. Have you got a really beautiful gown – one which you think is becoming?'

Rachael had always been susceptible to such a mixture of interest and flattery, and Patience's brisk manner left, by design, no room for protest or doubt. She said slowly, 'The yellow — but I don't think it's very . . . '

'Where is it? In the clothes-press?' Patience got up and swept over to the big oaken chest in the corner. She flung back the lid so that it cracked against the painted plaster walls, and rummaged inside. 'This one?'

Accepting the inevitable, Rachael said dully, 'Yes.'

Patience smoothed an expert hand down the rather crumpled folds. 'What a lovely colour — that soft buttery yellow is so much more flattering than a harsh marigold shade would be. Come on, I'll help you put it on, I can't wait to see how you look.'

In the grip of an irresistible force, bereft of the power to fight, Rachael rose reluctantly to her feet. Patience laid the yellow gown on the bed, and briskly unlaced the younger girl's bodice. The sad-coloured cloth slid down her body, to lie in a crumpled heap around her. Rachael stepped out of it and stared at Patience, who was shaking out the yellow. With a half-hearted return to her old belligerence, she said listlessly, 'Are you doing this because you feel sorry for me?'

'Feel *sorry* for you? I've never felt sorry for anyone in my life,' said Patience, with almost the exact truth. 'No, I just don't like to see things, or people, wasted, that's all.' She did not mention the brief but exhaustive conversation she had had with Tabby, just before coming to Rachael's chamber. 'Please, put this on before you change your mind.'

Rachael allowed herself to be assisted into the yellow silk. It was comparatively new, and of a colour she had always favoured, but she had only had occasion to wear it once or twice, before her father's death had abolished vivid colours. The bodice was long and boned, dipping to a point in front, and the full skirt almost trailed on the ground. She looked dubiously at the folds of cloth, and said, 'It's too bright. What will people say? You said yourself, just the other day, that I shouldn't be wearing bright colours yet.'

'Nonsense,' said Patience, robustly. 'Oh, that new gown we were planning, yes, I agree. But just for tonight, don't you think it would be . . . well, rather splendid to wear yellow? To thumb your nose at convention? And who's to see it and be shocked by it?'

'Tom Wickham,' said Rachael. 'Why is he here, anyway? I thought he wasn't going to come back.'

'He probably heard about . . .' Patience floundered, her tongue having run away with her. Rachael took her up. 'About Captain Hellier. Yes. I wonder who told him?'

'I wonder,' said Patience innocently. She was fairly certain that Rachael had at last learned her lesson, and besides, she could no longer feel forced to behave as a Harington, rather than a St. Barbe. But still, she had agreed with Tabby, that they, and Tom, should be the only ones involved in the latest conspiracy. They had wondered about Mally, but her forthright attitude had compelled them to abandon that idea with some speed. At least Mally, whatever she thought, would never betray them. However, it was imperative that Rachael be kept in the dark still. Let her begin to think that Tom had come out of concern for her, thought Patience, remembering what Tabby had said. And once she thinks that he has a good opinion of her, then half the battle will be over.

She pulled the laces tight, and surveyed Rachael with a critical eye. The bulky skirts hid much of her awkward thinness, but the stiff bodice flattened what little breast she had. 'Have you got some kerchiefs?' she asked.

'Yes, in the clothes-press, at the front,' said Rachael, puzzled. 'Why?'

'You'll see.' Patience pulled out several, and screwed the fine white linen into two crumpled handfuls. 'Now, if I undo the lacing just a bit — that's it — and push them down here, and here — you don't mind, do you? And pull up the laces, and there — doesn't that look better?'

Rachael, blushing furiously, not knowing whether to be shocked or pleased, stared at her reflection in the little mirror, held up by Patience. The kerchiefs, stuffed ruthlessly down her bodice, had had a most gratifying effect, and an almost buxom young woman stared back. Astonished at the transformation, she said reluctantly, 'Won't — won't people notice?'

'Goose,' said Patience, with unexpected affection. 'They're meant to. Wouldn't you rather they looked at you?'

'Nat will guess. He knows *everything*,' said Rachael gloomily. 'And then he'll tease me, in front of everyone else.'

'I think you're doing him an injustice,' Patience told her, with an uncharacteristic sharpness that, at another time, might have given Rachael food for thought. 'He wouldn't do any such thing.'

'I'm his twin — I should know,' said Rachael. She twitched despairingly at the shoulders of her gown. 'It's no good, I *can't* wear this, it's not decent.'

'Then wear a collar,' said Patience. 'A nice big lace-trimmed neckerchief, fastened round your neck with a pin or a brooch – it'll hide that mark, *and* make you feel a bit more modest. Like mine,' she added, with a giggle.

Rachael gazed dubiously at the wisp of fine gauzy linen that covered, somewhat inadequately, the other girl's neckline. 'A bit larger than yours,' she said, with minimal enthusiasm.

The battle was won, and Patience knew it. Her face split into the wide, dazzling smile which had enchanted so many. 'Of course,' she said, delighted. 'And then we'll do something about your hair.'

*

Silence, once she had overcome her initial surprise, had been delighted to see Tom. He had apologised, with a smile, for burdening Wintercombe once more with his presence, and she had retorted briskly that he was always welcome, no matter what the occasion.

'I thought that, in circumstances such as these, you might be glad of me,' he explained, with the rather shy, diffident smile that she had noticed before.

'How did you hear of what has happened?' Nat asked curiously.

To Silence's interest, the expression on Tom's face became almost sheepish. He said, after a pause that was evidently for thought, 'I, uh, received a letter. From Tabby.'

'From Tabby?' Silence stared at him. 'Oh – was that what Jeremy Walker was doing? Well, Tabby seems to have taken matters into her own hands yet again.'

'Again?' said Tom, and Silence told him, briefly, of how Nick Hellier and his companion had been brought to Wintercombe.

'And you did not know?' Tom asked, when she had finished.

Silence glanced at his pleasant, ordinary face, already weathered beyond its years, and knew that he could be trusted. 'Not at first,' she said. 'But we had to pretend ignorance to Colonel Pyne. It's not a very noble thing to confess, that Nat and I let Tabby shoulder all the blame. But she wanted to – she knew what she was doing, and she knew that Pyne could not punish her, whereas he could most assuredly punish us. Our only justification is, that Wintercombe was at stake.'

'I cannot in the least blame you,' Tom said, smiling. 'But – what is to happen to Nick now?'

'We don't know,' said Nat. 'For the moment, he seems to be comparatively comfortable in Bath gaol, and recovering better than we had dared to hope. There has been so much rumour about the prisoners taken in this sorry affair – they are to be incarcerated for years, or sent to the Guinea Coast, or set free – no one seems to know, and I don't think that the Council of State do either. But we dare not do anything, for the moment, except send him comfort. Mally took him a basket this afternoon.'

Tom, who lacked neither imagination nor intelligence, began to understand why Tabby had sent for him. Unknown in Bath, apparently nothing to do with Wintercombe, he might yet have a role to play in this drama. And if Nick were indeed to be sent to Guinea, to labour in the gold mines there, he was quite prepared to hazard his own security in order to save the man who had once been his friend, from slavery and ultimate, miserable death.

Yes, he would indeed have to speak at length to Tabby. But nothing must be said, either to Nat or to his stepmother. That at least was very clear.

But he could not help smiling at the thought of Mistress Tabitha St. Barbe, so young, so lovely, and so surprisingly devious.

There was another surprise at supper, which had been delayed by half an hour to accommodate his unexpected arrival. Tabby was there, of course, and so was Lady St. Barbe's sister, Patience. But there was another young woman beside her, wearing a delightful gown of a creamy yellow hue that set off the carefully curled black hair, and made her pale skin look even whiter by comparison.

It was Rachael.

The last time he had seen her, she had told him, blisteringly and with astonishing offensiveness, that he was not wanted at Wintercombe. By this, of course, he knew that she had meant that *she* did not want him. She had reminded him sharply of his eldest sister Mary, who had been utterly miserable, and whose unhappiness had caused her to strike out at the first thing to cross her path. He remembered Rachael's fierceness, her uncompromising nature, the passions that had ruled her life, and could not reconcile that tormented spirit with the quiet girl standing hesitantly by the door, unsure of her welcome in her own house. He found the sight curiously touching, and was glad when Silence, indicating where he should sit, placed him next to her. He was interested in this strange, contradictory young woman, so refreshingly different from all those insipid girls to whom his mother was forever urging him to pay court. He would rather have made advances to one of his own heifers.

There was, not unnaturally, a rather strained, subdued atmosphere in the dark panelled room. Nat stared at his twin, his eyebrows lifted, before saying merely, 'Well, you do look splendid tonight, Rachael.'

Instead of smiling gladly, the girl gazed at him apprehensively, as if she feared that he would say something more, as if she could not believe that he would offer her an unalloyed, undisguised compliment. Then, with the air of the condemned going to the gallows, she took her place beside Tom, with Nat on her other side, and Tabby and Patience opposite. The younger children, presumably, had been despatched to bed.

Because he was interested, and moreover an essentially kind person, Tom set himself to draw a smile from Rachael's pale tense face, and to remove the small frown which was apparently a permanent groove between her thin brows. As a matter of course, he avoided any mention of the terible events of the past few days. Instead, he regaled the table with tales of his nephew Robert, Mary's eldest son, a small boy whose talent for outrageous feats of mischief, related in Tom's understated, Somerset-flavoured voice, soon had everyone but Rachael smiling. She had done no more than pick at her food, and the aura of her unhappiness hung oppressively around her, discouraging further efforts.

Tom was not one to be so easily put off. He paid her no direct attention, but he knew that she loved her younger brother and sisters. Perhaps the story of Robert and the bull would have a greater impact.

It certainly made a good tale: the five-year-old boy, utterly fearless, standing his ground before the irate snorting animal, brandishing a pitchfork twice his size, and shouting, 'Charge, then! I'm not afraid of you!'

'And did he charge?' Tabby asked, her eyes wide as she imagined the scene. Tom grinned. 'Yes, he did.'

Beside him, he heard a small intake of breath. Rachael said, with reluctant curiosity, 'What happened?'

'His father pulled him out of the way just in time – pitchfork and all, with only a few inches to spare. Robert was most indignant. "I could have stopped him!" he kept saying – as if a five-year-old could stand firm before a charging bull!'

Silence gave a shiver. 'I'm very glad that none of my offspring have ever been so foolhardy. I can't imagine anything more terrifying for a mother.'

'I climbed on the roof of the Chard house, once, when I was ten,' said Nat reflectively. 'No, I didn't think you knew anything about it — I made very sure that no one did.'

'Except for me, of course,' said Rachael suddenly. 'I watched you.'

'Because you'd dared me to do it,' said Nat, grinning. 'And, knowing you, you probably wouldn't have taken my word for it otherwise.'

'Of course I wouldn't,' Rachael said. She was beginning to relax. The glass of wine, and the light-hearted conversation, and above all the fact that no one had commented adversely on her appearance — indeed, Nat had even complimented her, *Nat*, the incorrigible tease — all had combined to induce the first small flickers of hope. Perhaps, it might be all right, after all. Nothing, nothing, could ever erase her self-loathing for what she had done. But at least the pillory, the sneering remarks or, worst of all, the pity that she had feared, had not happened. If she tried hard enough, she might be able to forget, for just a little, that she had betrayed her family.

The talk turned to other matters. Nat and Patience had once more embarked on their curious banter, half teasing, half something else to which, so far, Rachael had successfully closed her eyes. She found that her platter was clean, and that she had enjoyed what she had eaten.

'Nat was right,' said Tom quietly.

Rachael started, and nearly knocked over her wine-glass. She turned her pale, haunted face towards him, and said nervously, 'Was he? What about?'

Tom hesitated. He was certain that he would only embarrass her, he could see it in her manner, suddenly taut and strained. But he persevered. 'You do look splendid. That colour — it suits you very well.'

The trite, stilted compliment brought a vivid wash of colour up under Rachael's thin skin. She said, with some intensity, 'You don't mean it!'

'I never say anything I don't mean,' said Tom, with perfect truth.

Rachael stared at him as if she disbelieved every word. Then she

said, in a low, miserable whisper, 'I suppose you've heard about
. . . about what happened to Nick?'

'Yes, I have,' Tom said.

'Aren't – aren't you going to say anything?'

'No. It's hardly my business, after all.'

'You must have *some* opinion,' said Rachael desperately.

'Yes, I have,' said Tom equably. 'But for the present, I'll keep it
to myself.'

Rachael glanced around. No one seemed to be paying them any
attention, though she could have sworn that Tabby had been
looking her way just now. She had not intended to behave like
this, she had thought that she wanted to forget all about her
despicable behaviour. But it was not possible, for some devil sat on
her shoulder and urged her to pick over the wound again, to make
quite sure that this unassuming, friendly young man was
thoroughly acquainted with the depths of her iniquity. She said in
despair, 'You must despise me so much.'

'Despise you?' Tom stared at her in genuine surprise. His face
was tanned and lightly freckled, with a couple of bigger moles on
his cheek, and his eyes were a surprisingly light blue under the
thick, straight brown hair. Rachael, hating herself, gazed miserably back. 'Of course I don't despise you,' he went on. 'We all
make mistakes – though, I admit, yours are a trifle more, er,
dramatic than most.' And he grinned.

It was infectious. The muscles around her mouth actually
twitched before she managed to control them. She said, with some
scorn, 'Oh, yes – everyone has been very understanding.'

'Would you rather they'd shouted at you?' Tom dropped his
gaze to his wine-glass, as if seeking inspiration, and then looked
up. 'Do you *want* me to despise you?'

'No – no, I don't,' said Rachael, floundering in waters that were
suddenly too deep for her.

'But you feel that I should, is that it? That you deserve it? Well,
that's ridiculous,' said Tom, with a light-heartedness that did not
in the least disguise his sincerity. 'I do not despise you, nor do I
even dislike you. Mind you, I am, according to my sister Mary, as
placid as an old ox, and very few things goad me into feelings as
extreme as that.' He smiled. 'Strangely, Mary and I are not in the
least alike. She is very quick-tempered, and before she married she
always seemed to be in a rage about something or other, usually
very trivial. And now, she's almost as placid as I am – she's happy,

you see.' He glanced at Rachael's pale face, no longer seeming quite so taut and tense. 'Your brother's tale about climbing on the roof for a dare reminds me of the time when Mary said I wouldn't be able to climb the tallest tree in the wood behind our farm.'

Tabby, watching with covert interest, saw her half-sister relaxing almost imperceptibly, as she conversed — if listening with hesitant interest to whatever Tom was saying could be called conversing. At least she did not appear to have been unforgivably rude, nor had she stormed out, nor had she hit him. It was all going very well, Tabby thought, with a certain satisfaction. Soon, she must put the next stages of her grand design into effect.

*

Rachael was brushing her hair before sleep, when Tabby entered. The yellow gown lay limp and discarded across the clothes-press, and Jude had lit the fire and put a warming-pan into her bed, for the night was clear, and would be chilly. She looked up as her half-sister entered, and said, without much interest, 'Oh, it's you. What do you want?'

The two girls, so different in temperament and interests, had never been very friendly. In her deepest, darkest heart, Rachael was envious of Tabby, of her loveliness and her musical gifts, and above all of the painful fact that everyone seemed to like her. Tabby would never betray anyone: Tabby, soon, would have men flocking to her, as they had never flocked around Rachael. Above all, Tabby seemed to have gained the confidence, the affection and the friendship of Nat, which should more properly belong to Rachael, his twin.

'Just a chat,' said Tabby. She supposed that she ought to be girlishly confiding, but such a pose was beyond her. Patience, who seemed to have as many different faces as the moon, would have slipped with ease into such a role, but Tabby knew that she would only feel awkward and ridiculous. She should have asked her aunt, or even Nat, to come in her place. If Rachael had emerged at all from her mood of black self-pity, then she might well be suspicious. Everyone knew that Tabby was hardly likely to confide anything to anyone, least of all Rachael.

'A chat?' Rachael's brush had found a knot in her hair. Patience had been right, it was much improved. Tomorrow, she might even ask Jude to bring up some hot water and scented soap and lotions, and wash it. She pulled the tangled strands apart with impatient fingers. 'What about?'

'Oh, nothing much,' said Tabby. She sat down on the bed, and Rachael wondered how someone who took so little trouble over her appearance could still look so fetching. She did not realise that a large part of Tabby's attractiveness stemmed from the fact that she was completely unaware of it.

'It's late,' said Rachael, her manner discouraging. She put her brush down, and turned to stare at her half-sister. 'What do you want?'

Tabby was beginning to realise that she should not have come. Rachael had never cared for her, and any attempt to push her in the direction she planned, would inevitably result in the opposite. She was not infallible, and if this lesser plan could fail, how much more vulnerable was the plot to free Nick. She seized at the first straw that passed through her mind. 'Do you think . . . perhaps . . . I could borrow your yellow gown, sometime?'

Rachael stared at her with some astonishment. 'My yellow gown? *You*? But it wouldn't fit!'

'I've grown since last year,' said Tabby. 'I'm as tall as you, now.'

'It wouldn't suit you either,' said Rachael. She saw that her half-sister's gaze had become somewhat fixed. For a moment, she wondered why, and then remembered. The loose nightgown which she had put on over her chemise, was unfastened and falling open. And the mark on her neck, now dark purple, must stand out like a brand.

Rachael saw the appalled expression on Tabby's face. She said harshly, 'Please go.'

The girl's hazel eyes, so like her mother's, filled suddenly with tears. She said in a whisper, 'I'm sorry – I didn't realise . . . '

'Please go,' Rachael said again, her voice suddenly hoarse with misery. 'Go on – please, leave me alone.'

There was nothing that Tabby could say. All her small designs and childish scheming evaporated into the mist, when put beside the reality of what Rachael had suffered, and was still enduring. She got up and fled to the cosy welcoming warmth of her own chamber, and to the bitter and belated realisation that there were some tragedies that no amount of conspiracy, or well-meaning meddling, could avert, or alleviate. Trying to kindle an interest in Tom Wickham, in the immediate aftermath of Rachael's agony, seemed all at once pathetically inappropriate.

She slept badly that night, wrestling with her conscience, and came down, heavy-eyed and pale, to break her fast. It was raining outside, a damp autumn day, and there was no chance of speaking to Tom privately in the garden, as she had originally intended. Rachael was there, wearing her usual black with a deep, lace-edged collar buttoned high above her neck, hiding the betraying rope-mark. Her eyes, bleak with unhappiness, glared at her half-sister, daring her to reveal what she knew. But that was not the sort of secret which Tabby would lightly confide to anyone. She gave Rachael a smile that she hoped would indicate her sympathy, and support, and turned away to address herself to frumenty and salt herring.

Tom Wickham, who had probably slept better than any St. Barbe, looked enviably refreshed and alert. He was a little surprised when Patience, who had placed herself next to him at the table, glanced around and then said, very quietly, 'We have something we wish to discuss with you, Tabby and I. In the summer parlour, on the other side of the hall, when breakfast is done?' And then, before he had had the chance to do more than nod in bemused agreement, she said loudly, 'I hope you slept well, Tom.'

Nat had been looking at them too closely for her liking. Of all her sister's family, his was the sharpest eye, the most acute and incisive intelligence. He was also the one whom, for a variety of reasons, she most feared, should he discover what was afoot. After all, it was his inheritance which she was risking.

But if it all goes according to plan, Patience thought, running through the details in her mind, worked out through the sleepless hours of two nights until she was sure they were perfect, then no one will ever discover that anyone at Wintercombe was involved.

First, however, Tom's help had to be enlisted. His role was vital, and if he refused to take part, Patience did not know what she could do. Tabby had seemed very certain that Nick's old comrade-in-arms would be eager to assist in his escape, but Patience was more doubtful. She liked Tom, but sensed his caution, his solidity and his essential ordinariness. She suspected that he would prove lacking in the spark of reckless imagination necessary for her scheme.

But she was wrong. Hardly had she shut the door of the summer parlour, having first carefully ensured that no one was lingering within earshot, than he said quietly, 'Is this to do with Nick Hellier?'

Tabby and Patience exchanged glances. 'Yes,' said the older girl. 'Yes, it is.' She paused, uncharacteristically weighing up her words in advance, and then added, 'We think we can free him, but we can't do it without your assistance. Will you help us?'

There was a brief silence. The rain slid miserably down the window, from a dull and depressive sky. The ride to church, later in the morning, would not be a comfortable one. Tom Wickham smiled. 'Of course. I'll do anything that you want me to – within reason, of course.'

He had no idea what plan Patience had worked out. The scheme that she outlined to him, interposed with brief enlargements or explanations from Tabby, was bold and simple and might well work. It was also very shocking, and he said so.

Patience gave him her brilliant smile, strongly reminiscent of Kate in mischief. 'All the better – then no one will suspect me. Well? Are you willing to help us? There is some risk, after all.'

'I can accept that,' Tom pointed out. 'I used to be a soldier, remember.' He looked at the two girls, one fair, one dark, all lit up like candles with their enthusiasm, and decided to introduce a note of caution into the proceedings. 'But everything depends on you keeping your head – are you sure that you can carry it off?'

Patience laughed. 'Of course I'm sure,' she said, with a certain brusqueness. 'I wouldn't be asking you to help if I was not, after all. From what Mally says, there's little to fear from the gaoler. And anyway, there is no risk to you whatsoever, should my part miscarry. All you have to do, is to wait.'

'And that,' said Tom, with a certain grimness, 'is what I've been doing for a large part of my life.'

'Tuesday, then?' said Tabby, and the other two nodded.

'Tuesday,' Patience declaimed, softly and exultantly. 'On Tuesday, God willing, we'll set Nick free.'

And they struck hands on it, like market farmers, to seal their pact.

*

After a wet and windy Sunday, the rain stopped that night, and by Monday morning the sun, rather shy and hesitant, peered out from behind light, swift, lacy clouds. The younger children were despatched to their lessons, complaining that they wished to go out, and Tom, feeling in need of fresh air, decided to go for a stroll in the garden before the weather grew once more inclement.

He saw Rachael at once, standing on the lowest terrace, gazing down at the orchard. There was something so mournful, so utterly dejected in the droop of her shoulders, that his heart was wrung. She had betrayed Nick to the soldiers, an act which, despite his heartening words to her, was something he could not understand. It was plain that she was smitten with desperate remorse, and he felt sharply sorry for her. And yet, he was certain that any display of pity would immediately antagonise her. Again, he remembered his sister Mary, in the depths of rage and grief because she could not marry the wastrel upon whom she had set her heart. His sister had eventually been transformed by a happiness which she had not suspected, and had found love with a man she had never even considered. Curiously, he wondered whether Rachael would be the same.

He walked down the steps to where she stood, leaning against the damp balustrade, the wind blowing her black hair into thin tendrils very different from the careful curls of Saturday night. He put his elbows companionably over the stone rail alongside hers, and looked down at the gnarled trees and wet grass below, the apples long since harvested for pressing into cider. 'It's very peaceful here,' he said, after a while.

Rachael could think of no answer sufficiently offensive. Besides, there seemed to be little point in antagonising someone so determined to be pleasant. Like Jude Hinton, it seemed to be impossible to make him angry, or hurt, or to jolt him out of his cheerfulness. She said, after a pause, 'Yes, it is.'

Tom said, choosing his words with great care, 'This is not the first time that we have stood here.'

Rachael turned her head warily to study him, a marked frown distorting her brows, her blue eyes narrowed. 'No,' she said. 'It isn't.'

'You said that you did not want me here, as I recall.' He saw no reaction in the thin pale face, and went on. 'I was sorry for that, then, although I thought I could understand why my presence here might remind you of things you would rather forget. It would be good, now, to discover that perhaps you were disposed to be more friendly?'

The wind blew a black strand of hair across her face, and she brushed it back. Her eyes unhappy, she said flatly, 'Perhaps.'

'Then will you accept my apologies, for any hurt which I may have unwittingly done you, in the past?'

'You haven't done anything,' said Rachael wearily. 'So there's no need for apologies.' She took a deep breath. Somehow, all her rage and desperation seemed to have vanished, and that fierce angry girl who had been so unforgivably rude, for no good cause, seemed a stranger to her now. And she had vowed, in the long dreary hours of night, to try to be different. She said rather raggedly, 'In fact, I should be apologising to *you*. I spoke very offensively to you, and I am very sorry now that I behaved so badly.'

'It doesn't matter,' said Tom. 'I don't think you were very happy, and that excuses a great deal.'

He had said the wrong thing. A brief spark of anger inflamed her face. She said with exhausted bitterness, 'Does it? I don't think so, Master Wickham — I don't think so at all.'

'I suppose you are the best judge of that,' he told her mildly.

Rachael gave a sob of despair, and spread her hands wide. 'Why are you so nice to me? Why does everyone try to be so kind? I have *betrayed* them, I've done terrible things and all they can do, and you, is offer excuses for me. Well, I don't offer any excuses for myself — I have been evil, evil and wicked and proud and self-righteous, and yet no one will even reproach me for it!'

'You sound as if you want to be punished,' said Tom. He was in uncharted seas here, for nothing in his surprisingly varied experience had prepared him for this unexpected and passionate repudiation of forgiveness. But the strange, tormented girl standing here, pouring out her heart to him, was beginning to concern him greatly.

'I do,' Rachael muttered. 'And yet I don't — I'd do *anything* to unmake the damage, to set it all right, to go back in time and do it different — and I can't!' She stared at him, wild-eyed. 'Captain Hellier is in prison, because of me. Nat and Mother nearly were, because of me. And I — I forced Kate to tell me where he was hiding, she's only five and I hurt her, I made her tell, and when I went yesterday to say that I was sorry, she tried to hide from me, she was so frightened of me.' She had begun to weep without realising it, the tears shining on her agonised face. 'I even tried to kill myself, but I couldn't, I couldn't — I failed in that, too.'

Tom, shaken and appalled, stared at her in horror. 'You — you tried to . . . ?'

Savagely, Rachael ripped the high collar from her neck. 'See? I tried to hang myself.' She was trembling violently. 'And I'll wager not even you can stomach that.'

[446]

She pulled the kerchief back to cover the livid mark, and turned away. She had gone three strides before he recovered his wits sufficiently to grab her sleeve. Somehow, he must help her, undo the damage, draw this terrible burden from her. And yet, he had never encountered anyone so resistant to comfort. 'Rachael!' he said, more urgently than he had intended. 'Don't go – listen to me!'

But she shook off his restraining hand, and ran along the gravelled walk towards the summerhouse. Forgetting dignity, prudence, propriety in the face of her desperate need, he sprinted after her. Even hampered by skirts, she was surprisingly fast, and had almost reached the door before he caught up with her, panting. 'Rachael! Rachael, please stop, I want to talk to you!'

Trapped, she leaned her head against the cool yellow stone and burst into tears. Tom had never felt so diminished, or so helpless. He tried the door. It opened inwards, upon a dim smell of apples and damp stone. He took her thin shoulders in his hands, feeling the shuddering grief coursing through his fingers, and guided her within.

For what seemed like hours, she wept into her hands, on and on, beyond all control. He had a kerchief in the sleeve of his doublet, and gave it to her. At least she did not push it away. Unsure of what to do, he sat beside her on the pile of dusty sacks, and waited for the storm to subside.

The sun was shining strongly outside, with the brightness of mid-morning, before she said, in a small voice quite unlike her usual strident tones, 'I'm sorry. I've soaked your kerchief.'

'That doesn't matter,' he told her. 'Wring it out, and it'll soon dry.'

For a moment, she said nothing. Her face was averted, and he could not see her expression. Then she turned towards him and said, 'I've told you everything now. Do you hate me?'

'No, of course not,' said Tom, unable to keep a certain amount of indignation from his voice. He went on, more calmly, 'We all make mistakes, as I think I have already said to you. But they can profit us, if we learn something from them. Have you?'

There was utter silence in the little room. Tom shivered suddenly. Despite the sunlight outside, the stone room was surprisingly cold. Rachael said suddenly, 'I do want to. I always think I'll change, be better – I pray so hard, I *try* so hard – and then something happens, and I forget. And what I did – a few days ago

– is the worst thing I have ever done. I don't *want* to do it again – I don't! And I can't understand why they don't hate me.'

'But you can't want them to hate you.'

'No,' said Rachael, after a while. 'I thought they would – that was why I tried – I tried to . . . ' Her voice dried up. After a painful pause, she went on. 'But I was wrong. I was so frightened – I found I didn't want to die.'

'I'm very glad you did not,' said Tom. The utter sincerity in his voice obviously surprised her, and she smiled wanly. 'I didn't think that I would be – but I am. It's – it's just so *difficult*. And I feel such a *fool*.'

There was a trace of the old Rachael in her voice. He said candidly, 'That's understandable.'

He could not make out her reaction, and thought that he had blundered again. But she said, 'Not many people know what I tried to do. Mother, and Nat, and Patience and Tabby, and my maid – and now you.'

'I won't tell anyone,' he told her softly. 'I give you my word.'

'Thank you,' said Rachael, after a pause. 'Thank you so much, Tom, for listening.' She stood up, rather stiffly. 'It must be near dinner time, they'll be looking for us soon, if they aren't already. We ought to go.' She hesitated, and then said, 'I feel better – I don't know why, but I do. I feel as if things weren't nearly so bad as I thought – as if talking to you has somehow improved matters.'

'I'm very glad,' said Tom. He had risen also, and was looking down at her. On impulse, he held out his hand. 'Are we friends now?'

'Yes,' said Rachael. 'Yes, I think so.' He felt her hand, cold and dry, gripping his with surprising firmness, and she smiled, with real warmth. 'Thank you, Tom.'

Mary had told him once, not without some irony, that he was an excellent listener, and he had known it for a double-edged compliment. Now, he was glad he possessed that quality. Rachael had confided in him, she seemed to have benefited thereby and, for the present, he was more than content.

But tomorrow, he must present his excuses to Silence, and leave Wintercombe. Tomorrow, he would ride, not back to Glastonbury, but to Bath, there to meet, if all went well, the man who had once been his friend and commander. He had listened carefully to Patience's plan, and could not see any glaring flaw in it, though much depended on her acting skills, and upon her presence of mind. And, as she had pointed out, there was no risk whatsoever to himself.

Why, then, did he have the disturbing feeling that somehow, despite all their care, something was bound to go terribly wrong?

❧ CHAPTER TWENTY-THREE ❧

'All patience, and impatience'

(*As You Like It*)

'Tom!' Silence rose from the table where she had been going through the inventories of her linen chests, and smiled, while Lily greeted him with whines and wriggles of her sleek white body. 'Have you really come to say goodbye? It feels as if you have only just arrived.'

'I have been here for nearly three days,' he reminded her. 'I would very much like to stay longer, but my land is in need of my attention at present. When autumn is further advanced, and there is less to do, perhaps I might return?'

'You know you'll always be welcome here,' Silence said. She looked tired, the clear serene lines of her face taut with anxiety, and he was almost tempted to say something to her, to bring encouragement and hope. But no one must be told, Patience had been adamant on that score. Too many had known the last time. For this attempt, only she, Tom and Tabby would be party to the conspiracy.

He said quietly, 'I feel as though I have been singularly useless. I came intending to bring you some comfort, but there is nothing I can do to help.'

'But your friendship is a comfort in itself,' said Silence. 'And at least Nick is not like to die . . . but it is so draining not to know, not to know if he is well or ill, how he is faring in prison, and above all, what will happen to him.' She gave him a tight, brave smile. 'I should not really be talking like this, Tom, but you are no fool, you must have guessed, in fact I think you did all those years ago. Nick and I had been planning to marry, but his capture rather puts that in jeopardy.'

'I am so sorry,' said Tom, feeling afresh the inadequacy of the word, and the ludicrous nature of the escape attempt in which he was embroiled. 'I had guessed, yes, but I did not know for certain . . . that explains why Tabby was so keen to discover all she could of Nick, a few months ago.'

'She is his partisan, and mine,' Silence told him. 'Oh, Tom, I don't know how it will all finish, I daren't look beyond the end of each day as it passes – but you have my heartfelt thanks, for your support and your friendship.'

Now was the moment to broach the other matter, the one which had kept him awake half the night, even in the warm snug little guest chamber in the north wing, lapped about with soft feathers and thick blankets. Almost, his heart failed him, for if the idea of freeing Nick was ridiculous, how much more so was this half-formed, completely unsuitable impulse. But he remembered the agonised, weeping girl who had confided in him the previous day, and also a different Rachael, still pale, but with a lightness in her bearing and a sparkle in her face, playing bowls in the light of afternoon, her burden beginning to slide from her shoulders. He said diffidently, 'My lady – '

'For Heaven's sake, call me Silence – you are surely friend enough,' she said, smiling.

'Silence, then – this is something that has come on me quite unawares – I am very conscious of the fact that it might be inappropriate . . . ' Tom found himself floundering to a halt, breathing hard, while she gazed at him enquiringly. He tried again. 'If it is acceptable to you, and to Nat, and of course to Rachael – '

'Rachael?'

'Yes, Rachael.' He took a deep breath, and finished in a rush. 'My lady – Silence – I would be grateful for your permission to pay my addresses to your stepdaughter.'

The formal phrases sounded hollow and futile in his country voice. It was the first time that he had ever seen Silence completely taken aback. 'Rachael?' she said incredulously. 'You wish to court *Rachael*?'

'Yes,' said Tom. 'And before you tell me, let me say that I already know about·. . . about everything. Including what she tried to do on the night that Nick was captured.'

There was absolute quiet, save for the sound of Lily, scratching her collar with intense concentration, and the malevolent muttering of Emerald in her cage. Silence said, in quite a different voice, almost hostile, 'Very few people know of that, by intent. It is not the sort of information which we would wish noised abroad, for Rachael's sake above all. How did you come to hear of it?'

'She told me herself, yesterday.'

'Merciful Heaven,' said Silence, after a startled pause. 'You must have uncommon patience – or have gained her confidence to a most unusual degree. Rachael – well, she is not normally willing to disclose anything to anybody.' She smiled at him suddenly. 'I wish you luck – you'll need it. But, Tom – nothing would please me more, you are our friend and you obviously have the fortitude of Job, but Rachael has not. I should warn you, although you have probably seen this for yourself – Rachael has been, and indeed still is, desperately confused and unhappy. She thought she should marry Jack Harington, for her father's sake, and yet she could not have been more unsuited to him – and I think she knew it, deep in her heart. She needs someone who will be tolerant of her moods, someone who will love her unreservedly, someone who, above all, will give her happiness. I did not think that there was such a paragon in all Somerset, leave alone amongst our friends. And you must be very sure of what you are doing, for she craves love, that is why she agreed to marry Jack in the first place. If you raise her expectations and then change your mind, I do not think her sanity will survive it.' She looked at him intently. 'Are you sure, Tom? Are you truly? Or are you just acting on a whim, because you feel pity for her?'

He flushed. 'I have asked myself the same question, and, no, I don't think I am. She reminds me very much of my sister Mary, who was once famous for a shrew, and is now so happy – because she has what she always wanted, and did not know it before she married.'

'But Rachael is not Mary,' said Silence. 'She is herself, only, and you must remember it. And for all her fierceness, she is so easily hurt, and so much damage has been done to her already, by people who did not realise she was so vulnerable. Tom, listen – I don't think it would be a good idea, just yet. Oh, nothing would make me more glad than to see her happily married to you – I am not placing any obstacles in your way, once she is calm enough to think for herself. It is *Rachael* who is my chief concern. And I think the best for her, and for you, would be for you to visit Winter-combe regularly over the next few months, and come to know all of us better, and make friends with Rachael. Say nothing as yet, just take an interest in her, and perhaps you will be rewarded. But nothing formal yet, Tom, please – she isn't ready for it. Is that enough for you?'

'Of course it is,' he said, feeling relieved that she had understood the situation so well. 'And perhaps I will be able to clarify my own feelings, too – and perhaps liking and interest on both sides will grow into something more.'

'I very much hope that it will,' Silence said. 'I am so glad – I have been worried to death about Rachael, as well as everything else. And now, perhaps, there might be some hope for her.' She paused, and then added, 'Tom – you will doubtless learn this anyway, but I think you ought to know it now, in case it influences you one way or the other. Rachael will receive a substantial dowry when she marries, under the terms of her father's will.'

'That would cut little ice with me,' Tom said. 'I am not wealthy, but neither am I poor.'

'No, but some may insinuate that you are marrying her for her money, and comment on the disparity between you. Will that concern you?'

Tom laughed, feeling suddenly more light-hearted than he had done for days. 'Silence, what people might say has never worried me overmuch. Thank you . . . ' He stopped, as something more occurred to him. 'But surely Nat is her guardian? What will he say?'

'I think that I can confidently predict,' Silence told him, smiling, 'that Nat will wish you joy with all his heart.'

And Nat did, when he came in a few moments later, with much cheerful banter that effectively concealed, Tom thought, any doubts which he might feel, concerning the suitability of such a match. Rachael was a baronet's daughter, after all, and though his own father had called himself gentleman, he had not in fact been anything of the sort.

He tried to mention something of this, and Nat cut in sharply. 'I care nothing for any of that, Tom, and you should know it. And as for Silence . . . '

He glanced at his stepmother, and she smiled at him affectionately. 'As for me – well, my father was a draper, albeit a very wealthy one, but a draper nevertheless. And my mother's mother sold fish in Billingsgate when she was a child. Now let's hear no more of your supposedly humble origins, please, for I can cap them with ease.'

At last, knowing that he must be gone, he took his leave of them, and of the rest of the family. Patience and Tabby, demure in their plain, everyday garments, gave no indication of the plan which they had agreed, two days ago, and were now about to put into effect. Rachael was there too, thin and unsmiling, and he gave her no special farewell. Silence was right — time was needed here, and caution, and great care. If, in a while, something came of it, then their new understanding would be founded on a bedrock of friendship. He had a farmer's patience: he could wait.

He rode out of Wintercombe under a bright morning sun, down the track to the Wellow Lane, and turned right, towards the village. By now, he was well out of sight of the house, and no one would realise that he had not taken the road to Wells, and Glastonbury. He swung left at the end of North Street, to follow the highway to Bath, and the inn called the White Hart, in Stall Street.

*

As soon as his solid, reliable back had disappeared out of sight, Patience turned and walked back inside the house. The children were dispersing to their lessons or duties, and she paid no attention to them, or to Deb's demand that she teach her some French. 'No, I can't today — I promised I'd go riding with Tabby.'

Deb made a sulky face. Patience smiled. 'But I'll try and give you a lesson tomorrow, I promise. Now go along to your mother's chamber — I'm sure she has plenty for you to do.'

Once in her own chamber, she went to her clothes-press, and drew out her rose-coloured gown. With scant respect for its integrity, she stuffed it into a small cloth bag. Several of the small pretty jars by her mirror followed, some pins, a comb, a pair of shoes, a soft dark hood and a black mask, of the type now so fashionable amongst London ladies, and those who wished to imitate them. Then she dressed in the russet riding-habit, pulled on her calf-leather boots, picked up her cloak, and went downstairs to meet Tabby.

Her niece was talking to the two horses, the old bay gelding and her little chestnut Dowsabel, which they usually rode. She gave Patience a brilliant smile. 'I told Mother we were riding. I'm sure she doesn't suspect anything. Are you ready?'

Patience was tying the bag to her saddle. 'Yes,' she said. 'Shall we go?'

And, following almost in the hoofprints of Tom Wickham, who had passed that way not half an hour earlier, they set off for Bath.

It was unfortunate that they failed to notice Nat, talking to Jesse Russell in the barton. But he saw them riding under the gatehouse, and wondered where they might be going. After the events of the past week, any sighting of the two arch-conspirators together was sufficient to make his scalp prickle. What was in that bag, which he had plainly seen hanging from Patience's saddle? It would hardly be carried on a jaunt round the lanes between Wintercombe and Wellow. His suspicions rising, he finished his business with the bailiff, and went in search of his stepmother.

She was teaching Deb, without much success or indeed any hope of it, the intricacies involved in keeping and checking household accounts. Deb, breathing hard and with her tongue jammed in the corner of her mouth, was attempting to calculate how much four and a half pounds of sugar would cost, at two shillings and sixpence a pound. Beyond her, Kate was practising writing her name, and William, who had been threatened with the Grammar School in Bath in the near future, was studying his Bible. Emerald, vicious green in her cage in the sun, preened herself, and uttered an occasional epithet under her breath.

'Can I speak to you for a moment?' Nat asked, and drew Silence into the little clothes closet. He shut the door, and she stared at him, puzzled.

'What's happened? It's — it's not Harley, is it?' For four days now, she had been waiting in fear for the lawyer's return, when he would demand her answer to his despicable proposition.

Nat hastily shook his head. 'No, no, nothing like that. This may be unimportant, but I don't intend to take any chances. Where have Patience and Tabby gone?'

She looked at him in surprise. 'Out for a ride — Tabby asked me if she could, and I agreed, it's such a lovely morning, and Diggory says it'll rain before sunset. Why?'

'I don't know,' said Nat. 'I'm probably doing them an injustice. But it did occur to me that they might be plotting mischief again. And why would Patience be carrying a bag with her?'

Aghast, Silence said, 'But I *told* Tabby — I begged her not to interfere, for all our sakes. And she promised me that she would not.'

'Perhaps she did,' Nat told her grimly. 'But Tabby, dear girl though she is, seems to be as good a liar, even to you, as the most hardened felon. I think I shall ride out and see where they've gone. I don't like playing the spy, but we can't afford to allow those two harum-scarum noodles to jeopardise everything.'

'But I trusted her,' said Silence bleakly. 'Please, Nat — don't say anything to her unless you're certain that she has done something wrong. I couldn't bear it if . . . if, as well as everything else, she turned against me.'

'Don't worry,' said her stepson. He smiled, and touched her cheek briefly. 'Trust me. You know you can do that.'

She watched him go out, slight, but somehow utterly dependable. She prayed that he was wrong. Surely, after all that she had said, all that had happened, all the promises, her beloved Tabby would not break her word?

But if she had . . .

Silence stood, irresolute, staring at the bent industrious heads of her three younger children. If Tabby and Patience had indeed hatched some plot to free Nick, then it was vital that she discover it. But she could not go to Bath herself, for if she did, she might draw the wrath of Colonel Pyne back upon Wintercombe, to disastrous effect.

There was only one person who would be her eyes and ears, whom she could trust as she would herself, or Nat. And anyway, she had been too long without word of Nick.

Suddenly firm of purpose, she went in search of Mally.

*

At the inn called the White Hart, in Stall Street in Bath, Tom Wickham introduced himself as Master Reynolds, and asked for a private chamber where he could await his servant, who was at present on an errand elsewhere in the city. In the meantime, he ordered a hearty dinner, and settled down, not without some trepidation, to await whatever this sunny, late September afternoon would bring him.

Not very far away, and not much later, Mistress Richards, for so Patience had styled herself, taking her fishwife grandmother's name, and the maidservant accompanying her, took a chamber on the first floor of the Katherine Wheel. It was a substantial inn on the west side of the High Street, not far from the Northgate, where was situated, in the tower of the disused church of St. Mary's, the city prison.

To Tabby's relief, no one appeared to look twice at Patience, unescorted by husband or father or brother, and still less at the quiet, nervous maid in attendance. Despite her apprehension, her fear that something would miscarry, she appreciated the power of a confident manner to allay suspicion and carry its possessor wherever she wished to go.

'You have the hardest part,' said Patience, once they were alone in their chamber, with a modest dinner ordered and no one, for the moment, to listen. 'You have to wait here until I come back. Can you do that without being too bored?'

'I have a book,' said Tabby. 'I brought Mother's copy of Bacon's *Essays*.' She glanced at Patience, who was removing her rose-coloured gown, now sadly crumpled, from the bag. Suddenly very conscious of the fact that she was the younger, by nine years, she said slowly, 'Are you sure it will work?'

'Of course I am,' said Patience, with some astonishment. 'I wouldn't be here if I wasn't — and neither would you.' She gave Tabby her most encouraging smile. 'Can you help me change, once they have brought dinner?'

The food arrived almost immediately, roast mutton, a good fat trout from the Avon, and a dish of buttered eggs. Tabby had thought that she would not be able to eat very much, but found that apprehension had not in the least diminished her appetite. When the clean plates had been removed, by a maidservant probably younger than Tabby, Patience locked the door, made sure that nothing could be seen through the window by anyone in the houses opposite, and, with her niece's help, began her transformation.

*

Nat had had an annoying morning. Russell, the young bailiff, had waylaid him as he walked into the barton to order his horse saddled. The matter was of some importance, and he could not be brusque with Jesse, who was enthusiastic and far more receptive to Nat's new ideas than Tom Clevinger, his dour old predecessor. His grey gelding had been ready and waiting for fully twenty minutes before he was able to make his escape, and ride off towards Norton, hoping, without much conviction, that his earlier prickles of intuitive foreboding had been wrong.

Old Walker, who had been working for the St. Barbes for years, and who had the misfortune to be the father of the infamous Leah, now whoring in Bristol, was laying the hedge where the track met the Wellow Lane. Yes, Sir Nathaniel, Mistress Woods and Mistress Tabby had passed this way, and gone up towards the village. Nat thanked him, and left him to his painstaking work, cutting and laying and weaving. With his suspicions still active, he rode past the mill, and the cottages, Walker's amongst them, around

Lyde Green. He stopped to enquire of a woman carrying water, and learned that she had seen his quarry, not so long ago, riding along the highway towards Bath.

Suspicion became a certainty. With unwonted grimness, Nat gave her a coin, and clapped his heels to the grey's sides.

They were not in sight, and his mount was fat and out of condition from too much summer grass. By the time he reached Midford, quiet in its steep-sided valley, he had to acknowledge that he was unlikely to catch them up before they reached the city. His latest informant had seen two women riding past, but since then she had been up to the field at the top of the hill, to take her husband his dinner while he ploughed, and had stayed chatting with him for some while before returning. Nat handed over another groat, and urged the gelding, by now hot, lathered, and somewhat resentful, to further efforts.

*

A mile or so in his wake, Mally Merrifield rode pillion behind the stable-lad, Jeremy Walker, thoughtful and unusually quiet. She was wondering whether she should not have told Silence about that note which Patience had sent to Nick. The truth of it was, that whatever she did, whether she continued to keep the secret or whether she told her mistress, it could be construed as betrayal. But her ultimate, fiercest loyalty was to Silence, and when Lady St. Barbe had come to her, her face pinched and white with anxiety, as it had been too often since this whole sorry affair began, with some tale about a possible plot, Mally had ruthlessly abandoned any duty of secrecy which she might have owed to Patience, and told her mistress about the note.

'And I didn't think so much of en, m'lady, I didn't take it too serious, I thought as how Mistress Patience were just a-blathering on as usual – I didn't think to peach on her, m'lady, till now.'

'I'm very glad you did,' said Silence thoughtfully. 'Then Nat was right, they *are* plotting something – probably to free Nick from prison. Oh, how *could* they be so stupid! They'll be caught, and then we'll all suffer, and Nick most of all – oh, Mally, whatever can we do?'

'Well, Sir Nathaniel have gone after them,' Mally pointed out. 'If anyone can stop them, he will. Do ee still want I to go see the Captain, m'lady? Or shall I stay here, and keep ee company?'

'I would like you to go to Bath,' said Silence, after a pause spent urgently collecting her thoughts. 'Nat doesn't know for certain that they *have* gone there – he doesn't know about that note. They might give him the slip, or he might have set out too late to catch them. Can you go to the prison, very discreetly – I know I can rely on you in this – and discover what is happening? I want to go so much, I want to *see* him – but I can't, Mally, I dare not contact him openly, or Wintercombe is threatened.'

'It d'seem to I,' Mally said bluntly, 'that it'd be best if the Captain *did* escape, m'lady. Then it'd save ee a power of grief and worry.'

'Of course it would!' Silence cried in sudden anguish. 'Of course I want him to escape – but one of Patience's hare-brained schemes is hardly likely to succeed, is it? And Tabby – to involve Tabby again, it's absolute lunacy – but I feel so helpless, Mally, what can I *do*?'

'Nothing yet, m'lady,' said her maid, wishing that she had m'lady's sister before her at this moment, and Mistress Tabby too, so that she could bang their addled pates together. 'Do ee stay here, and wait for I. Don't ee fret, m'lady, twill all vay in the end, don't ee fear.'

But despite her heartening talk, she had no great faith in the ability of any plan produced by Patience's fertile brain to succeed. She had said nothing of any of this to Jeremy, who was well known to be a blabbermouth, and who was merely escorting her to Bath on an errand for her mistress, as he had done many times before.

I d'hope en all vays in the end, Mally thought grimly, as the miles up hill and down to Bath diminished steadily under the horse's plodding hooves. For my lady do deserve all the happiness she can find, after all she've suffered, and Captain Hellier d'love her truly, as sure as she love him.

*

Nick was dozing when the key banged into the lock with Pearce's usual lack of finesse. An uneasy dream featuring Touchet, dressed as a washerwoman, bearded and masculine and miraculously undetected, had annoyingly disfigured his slumber. It was hardly worth wasting sleep on his erstwhile companion, still less any anxiety. Presumably, a miracle in itself, he was yet at large, since Nick had not been told of his capture. By now, he might well have reached the seething anonymity of London, and safety, and Nick wished him joy of it.

Prison, while inexpressibly tedious, had at least provided him with the opportunity to rest. In the past four days, he had enjoyed enough sleep to last him a week or more, and had paid Pearce enough to give him three substantial meals a day. His wound, which he had managed, not without some pain and difficulty, to treat and dress himself, was healing nicely, a clean crusty scab with no sign of corruption, heat or swelling. He had to acknowledge that this enforced inactivity might well have saved his life. With such a wound, even if he had succeeded in escaping, he would doubtless have succumbed very quickly to fever and loss of blood.

But now, as he approached full recovery, boredom and all his old restlessness had reappeared. Pearce had told him only that he was to be confined until such time as the fate of the thousands of other prisoners of Worcester, languishing in gaols in London and all over the western counties of England, was decided. Once, bereft of Silence, Nick had contemplated sailing for the New World. But the prospect of being shipped there as a bondservant, or of labouring his health away in the Guinea mines, did not entice him. And what would Silence do, if he were sent overseas?

It was an insoluble problem, though he had wrestled with it through the long tedious hours, desperately seeking a chance, the slightest hope, and finding none.

So, when Pearce stood in front of him, his belly huge before him like a woman with child, and with a lascivious leer told him he had a visitor, he thought at first that it was Mally. It was a little surprising, though, that the diminutive, red-haired maid, with her freckles and her beaky, prominent nose, could arouse such wet-lipped lust in his gaoler.

'Who is it?' he asked, his brain still clogged with sleep, and incongruous images of bearded washerwomen.

'Luscious little piece,' said Pearce, almost salivating with the memory. 'That'll cost you a packet, Captain, and no mistake. Can't let you have your pleasure and not pay for it, eh?' He held out his hand in the well-worn gesture. 'Come on, sir – a crown at the least for this one. Just a crown, and I'll leave you alone and undisturbed with her for at least five minutes.'

It could not be Mally, not in a hundred years. He said again, 'Who is she?'

'A friend, she said – from Bristol. Asked me if your whoring days are done. Shall I tell her they are, then, and have her myself?'

The only whore he knew in Bristol was Leah Walker, who as he had last seen her, raddled and diseased, could hardly be described as a 'luscious piece', unless she had undergone some remarkable transformation, or unless Pearce's powers of discrimination were as rudimentary as Touchet's. The thought of her befouling his cell made Nick's skin creep. Besides, she had probably only come here to gloat. It was most emphatically not worth a penny, let alone a crown.

'You can have her yourself if you like,' he said, pushing the hand away. 'If she's the one I think she is, she's an old enemy. You can amuse her, I'm not interested. Tell her that, if you like.'

Pearce, obviously, did not know whether to be angry at the loss of a crown, or pleased at the prospect of dalliance with the whore. Lust at last seemed to conquer greed, for he gave Nick a lecherous, superior grimace, and waddled out of the room, whistling. Feeling somewhat relieved at his narrow escape, Nick pulled the blankets up to his chin and tried not to think of making love with Silence, the pure gold beside which all else seemed to be no more than base metal, flawed and counterfeit.

He had almost succeeded in dozing off when the key again rattled in the lock, and the door was flung open. He sat up with annoyance, and beheld a young woman who must, assuredly, be the whore. She was not Leah, though her hair was almost as dark, and Pearce had not lied, she was a luscious piece, her prominent bosom much enhanced by the extreme low cut of her gown, and very tight lacing. But the thick paint on her face was smudged and her curls dishevelled, and he saw that her eyes were wide with fear, her breasts heaving dangerously. She shut the door and swept up to the bed, and he realised abruptly that she was not frightened, but angry.

'For God's sake, don't you *want* to be rescued?' she said in a furious whisper.

It was Patience.

Thunderstruck, and appalled, he stared at her, his mouth agape. She went on, urgently, 'Come on, we haven't much time – *please*, Nick, before he comes!'

'But Pearce – where's Pearce?'

'I hit him with a stool,' said Patience, with a look of pure venom. 'He was horrible – what a disgusting man – he tried to paw me . . .'

'I'm not surprised, with you dressed like that,' Nick commented drily. He flung the bedclothes back and got to his feet. To keep warm, he had been wearing shirt and breeches, both very much

[461]

stained and creased. Swiftly he pulled on his stockings and shoes, and shrugged his stiff shoulder into the doublet laid on the other bed.

All the while, Patience was talking in the same low, urgent voice. 'Do you know the White Hart, in Stall Street? Go there as fast as you can without attracting notice, and ask for Master Reynolds. That's the name Tom Wickham has taken. You're supposed to be his servant, who's gone on an errand for him, and he'll be expecting you. How you get out of Bath, and where you go, is up to you, but Tom said you could stay at his farm near Glastonbury for a while, until the hue and cry has died down. Are you ready? Go on, *go*, before that awful man wakes up!'

'What about you? For Christ's sake, girl, you can't wander about the streets like that!'

'My cloak and mask and hood are down in that man's room — you'd be surprised at what they hide,' said Patience, virtually pushing him towards the door. 'Please, Nick, no more questions, please, just *go*!'

He snatched the bag of coin, by now sadly diminished, from under the mattress, and followed her out of the door. They ran down the steep twisting stairs. There was no sign of Pearce. Patience dodged into the little room at the bottom of the tower, immediately below his own, and he had a brief glimpse of the gaoler, felled like a tree, lying half under the table, the stool overturned at his side.

'Here — take this!' Patience pushed an old felt hat on his head. It was greasy and shapeless, and evidently belonged to Pearce. 'You might not be recognised so readily — it'd look strange if you weren't wearing one.' A velvet mask now disguised her face, and she was tying on her hood. She pulled it forward so that her painted skin was in shadow. The cloak, buttoned down from a high neck, did indeed hide everything: she looked almost respectable. Her brown eyes sparkled suddenly, and she gave him her dazzling, mischievous grin. 'Go on, Nick — you're free!'

'Thank you,' he said, smiling in return, and on impulse kissed her cheek, all thick with paint.

'And good luck!' she hissed after him, as he went to the door of the tower.

There was no sound from behind him, nor from the other cells above, many of which he knew to be occupied. No one noticed as he walked confidently out of Bath gaol, as if he had every right to do so. The hat pulled low down over his eyes, he strode away through the crowds around the Northgate, hoping that Patience would not linger in the tower. Not only did she risk discovery, but a fate somewhat worse than that. Pearce could hardly be blamed for taking her at face value.

He was free. The sunny air, the familiar stink of Bath, the yellow stone, the cries of the street sellers, at last forced themselves into his dazed mind. It had all happened so quickly – was he even now dreaming, was he, God forbid, trying to make his escape dressed as a washerwoman?

No, he was wearing breeches. Then, someone trod heavily on his foot, and the sharp pain convinced him. This was real, he was alive, he was free. All he had to do, was to find Tom Wickham at the White Hart, and pretend to be his servant.

Slowly, as the joy grew to life in his mind, a smile spread across his face, and a feeling of reckless delight began to spill over. It was so simple, and it had worked, and he hoped that, one day, he would have the opportunity to thank his lover's astonishing sister as she deserved.

He did not notice the tailor's boy, who was at work as usual in the window of his master's shop just by the Northgate. As he had been paid to do, the child had watched the comings and goings at the prison all morning. When the shabbily-dressed man in the old black hat stepped from the door, the boy's eyes had sharpened, and he put down the breeches on which he was working. A quick word to the journeyman in charge, and then he slipped out of the tailor's shop, careful to keep his quarry in view through the jostling crowds.

Nick, too overwhelmed by the glory of freedom, did not think to look behind him.

*

Patience hoped that Pearce would not wake for a good while yet. The narrowness of her escape still appalled her. She had originally intended to gain access to Nick by bribing the gaoler. Once alone with him in the cell, she had planned to give him her all-enveloping cloak and hood and mask, so that he could make good his escape without attracting Pearce's attention. Then, with Tabby's cloak, which she had worn under her own, to conceal her disguise, she would have slipped out of the tower a little later. But Nick had refused to see her, and the lecherous little turnkey had tried to . . . She shivered again at the thought of his greedy hands on her skin. If that stool had not been so conveniently to hand, and if rage and fear had not lent such strength to her arms, she did not like to think what might have happened. But perhaps it had turned out for the best, even so, for with Pearce unconscious downstairs, it would be very much easier to keep his prisoner's escape a secret for quite some time.

She went back upstairs to Nick's cell. She bundled a bolster under the blankets on his bed, to make it look as though he still slept there: it might deceive someone for a while, and time was vital. She locked the door behind her and ran down again, fumbling with the keys. She did not want to make any attempt to tie up Pearce, even if there had been something she could use. Then, she realised that her own stockings would suffice, although her flesh revolted at the thought of touching that flabby body. And what if he woke before she had finished?

But she must take the risk, she must. The longer he remained helpless, the better were Nick's chances of getting clean away. She set her teeth, and pulled off her stockings, not without some regret, for they were comparatively new, and hardly darned at all. It was her own fault, though, for forgetting to bring any rope. Trying not to flinch, she pulled Pearce's fat hands together behind his back, wound one stocking tightly round his wrists, and tied a ferociously intricate knot of her own devising. To her relief, he did not stir. She hoped she had not done him serious injury, though he was still breathing with reassuring strength. There was a large and blood-stained lump on the side of his head, where she had swung the stool at him. A little less urgently, she bound his legs and then stepped back. It would undoubtedly take him a good while to extricate himself, and meanwhile Nick and Tom Wickham would have left Bath, unnoticed and unsuspected.

To make matters absolutely certain, she locked the door of the gaoler's room. She wanted to lock the tower, too, but someone might well notice her doing it. Better just to take the keys with her, and drop them in the Avon on the way home. She pushed the heavy clanking ring deep into the pocket of her gown, and with an expression of intense satisfaction, slid out of the door, closed it behind her, and walked proudly towards the Katherine Wheel, well pleased with the success of her plan.

No one in the inn so much as glanced at her, as she hurried up the dark stairs to the chamber, the cloak, mask and hood still

[464]

disguising the blatant garment beneath. She would be glad to loosen her stays, to scrub her face, and to step back once more into her safe, respectable russet riding-habit, a gentlewoman of unimpeachable modesty.

She knocked on the door, a single and then a double tap, lifted the latch and swept in, pulling off the hood and mask, unbuttoning her cloak. 'It worked!' she said exultantly. 'We did it — he's free!'

She cast the cloak on to a chair, wondering why Tabby was not speaking, why she had not rushed up to greet her. Her niece was sitting by the fire, the book of Bacon's *Essays* open on her lap, her face unnaturally pale — and streaked with tears.

With a sudden dreadful foreboding, Patience turned, in all her overflowing glory, and saw Nat, standing by the window.

CHAPTER TWENTY-FOUR

'The reward of a villain'

(Much Ado About Nothing)

It was well past dinner time when Jeremy Walker and Mally came down the steep way to Bath, and the bridge over the Avon. They had stopped for a snatch of bread and cheese at a wayside inn, hardly sufficient for a mouse to dine, and Mally, who had a healthy appetite, was ravenously hungry. But she had promised Silence that she would find out all she could in Bath, and so her belly would have to wait a while for its sustenance.

They rode over the bridge and up Southgate Street. There were plenty of people about, fine ladies and gentlemen taking the air, country people, beggars, and, as was usual in Bath, the halt, the sick and the lame, making their way to and from the waters. Jeremy guided the horse between them, and up to the Southgate.

As was also usual, in these still troubled times, there were a couple of militiamen on duty. Their presence was no more than a token one, however, and they were chatting amicably to a group of women obviously well known to them. Mally ignored the twitch of guilt between her shoulderblades, and kept her eyes firmly to the front, past Jeremy's rather prominent ears. Of course, the two soldiers paid them no mind whatsoever, and they passed under the stone arch, with its three weathered stone statues, many hundreds of years old, of a king, a prior, and a bishop.

'Here,' said Jeremy suddenly. 'Looksee, Mally, bain't that Master Wickham? Tis his horse for sure, I'd know that girt bay anywheres.'

Mally stared. Surely, Wickham had intended to go home to Glastonbury. He had certainly said nothing about a trip to Bath. But Jeremy was not mistaken: it was indeed Tom Wickham, his plain pleasant face suddenly very wary, sitting in his solid farmer fashion on the bay gelding with its distinctive white face.

And behind him, almost unrecognisable in humble russets and a greasy felt hat, riding an ewe-necked hired horse, was Nick Hellier.

Mally's heart began to pound erratically against her stiff bodice.

At all costs, she must prevent Jeremy giving away the secret. She could not remember if he knew the Captain by sight, but it would be as well to take no chances. Those soldiers were only a few yards behind them, and she had a sudden dreadful vision of Jeremy, blunderingly innocent, saying in his loud Somerset voice, 'Why, if it bain't Captain Hellier – aren't ee supposed to be in the city lock-up?'

'Good day, Mally – good day, Jeremy,' said Wickham, drawing rein. To her profound relief, she realised that Jeremy seemed to be paying Hellier no mind whatsoever. Perhaps, he had in fact never seen him before. She prayed that he would not query the sudden presence of a servant, when Wickham had ridden to Wintercombe without one.

'Good day to ee, Master Wickham,' said Jeremy. The tips of his ears had become rosily red with embarrassment, for the sight of the other man had reminded him once more of Tabby, and the errand on which she had sent him. Behind him, Mally allowed her eyes to meet Nick's. He looked surprisingly well, although freedom had probably had a beneficial effect on his health, and he had shaved off his week's growth of beard. Without it, he looked younger, more respectable, and quite different from the sickly prisoner she had encountered only a few days previously. Seemingly casual, she touched her finger to her lips, as if brushing something away, and saw that he understood.

'Well, I will not detain you if you are on an errand for your lady,' Tom said. 'Pray convey my regards to her, and my thanks for her hospitality, and I hope that I will soon see you all again. Goodbye, Jeremy – goodbye, Mally.'

'Goodbye, Master Wickham,' she said, and watched him urge his horse past them, his shabby 'servant' following after. She took a deep breath, not daring to glance behind her: it would not be safe, to give this apparently casual encounter any more importance than it seemed to warrant. There was no sound from the direction of the gate, however, no cries or alarms. As Jeremy rode on up through the crowds in Stall Street, she closed her eyes with relief. The Captain was free, and apparently unpursued. It was beginning to look as if, against all the odds, Mistress Patience's plotting had succeeded.

'Where are we to go?' Jeremy asked over her shoulder. 'You haven't said yet.'

'Do ee keep on up Stall Street,' Mally told him. In truth, she did not have any destination in mind, since the purpose of her journey was even now, she hoped, crossing the Avon in Master Wickham's wake. But she would have to think of somewhere, if only to allay any suspicions that Jeremy might have. The mercer's, just opposite the White Hart, would do as well as any. There were bound to be pins or silks or needles required, and inspiration would surely strike her, once inside the shop. Fortunately, she had enough coin in her purse to make the necessary purchase. Then, they could return to Wintercombe, and she would be able to give the glad news to her mistress, that Nick Hellier had, miraculously, escaped.

*

Master Jonathan Harley was in his study, examining various documents in connection with a law-suit which one of his clients wished to pursue, when a loud hammering on the street door disturbed his peace. He raised his head from the crabbed Latin handwriting of a deed nearly two centuries old, and listened. He heard the heavy tread of Mistress Barnard, his housekeeper, the opening of the door, and a child's high-pitched voice. Suddenly alert, he pushed the pile of parchment and paper to one side and got up. Mistress Barnard, as fussy and protective of her bachelor employer as a broody hen, would doubtless send the brat packing, unaware of the probable importance of his message. Only one boy was likely to come to his house in Stall Street with such urgency, and that was the tailor's apprentice whom he had paid, without his master's knowledge, to watch the city prison from his shop hard by the old church.

He flung open the door, and called along the narrow hall. 'Alice? If that is the tailor's boy, show him in. He has a message for me.'

The 'prentice was about twelve years old, a sharp-eyed boy with sandy hair, ears almost at right-angles to his head, and a rather sly, furtive expression. He had readily agreed to the gentleman's suggestion that he earn an extra coin or two, and keep his master in ignorance. And, sure enough, not half an hour past he had seen, from his position by the window, the man of Harley's description emerge from the tower door, and set off down the High Street. He was certain that it was the same one: of medium height, brown-haired, lightly built, and somewhat pale and haggard in appearance. And, though the child had seen plenty of people coming and going at the prison, he was sure that this man was not a casual visitor.

'And I followed him,' the 'prentice finished. ''Twas main simple, sir, for he never looked behind him once. I followed him to the White Hart, and I d'know one of the lads in the stable there, and whiles I were a-talking to him, I seed this man a-riding off with another gentleman, what had been a-waiting for him. Dick, he tellt me his name were Reynolds. But when they rode down to the Southgate, sir, this Master Reynolds, he met a woman riding pillion what knowed him, and *she* called him Master Wickham.'

'Wickham!' Harley said. 'Are you sure?'

'Yes, sir, sure as my name's Sam.'

'And the Captain and this Wickham – where did they go?'

'They went out of the Southgate, sir, and down toward the bridge, and I couldn't see no further,' Sam told him. 'Then I thought as how I'd best come and tell ee, sir.' He paused expectantly, and added, with a greedy glint in his eye, 'Have I done what ee asked, sir?'

'You have, and more,' Harley said, unable to suppress the excitement in his voice. If Lady St. Barbe was still unwilling to marry him, this would surely prove the final persuasion he needed. Her lover freed from prison with the connivance of a man who was known to be a friend of her family – Colonel Pyne, for one, would never believe in her innocence after this. She would undoubtedly know it, and, faced with disaster and ruin, must at last bow to the inevitable, and agree to marriage.

He drew a long, triumphant breath. Now, all his planning had come to fruition, and the surge of delight which flooded him surpassed even the joy he felt when winning a particularly intractable case. He must ride to Wintercombe immediately, and present Silence with the ultimate, inescapable choice. She must agree to marry him, or he would tell Colonel Pyne of Wintercombe's complicity in Hellier's escape.

He became aware of Sam's eager expression and outstretched hand. He thrust a couple of shillings into it. 'Well done, lad. Now be off with you, and remember – not a word to anyone about this!'

'Don't worry, sir, I won't tell a soul,' said Sam, his grubby fingers closed tight around the precious coins. 'Thank ee, sir – and if you d'want ort else done for ee, you d'know where to ask.'

'I do indeed, Sam,' said Harley, although, with all his dreams at last within reach, he could not imagine any further need for the boy's services. He watched the child run out, and then glanced at his handsome new clock. Perhaps three hours to sunset: there was plenty of time to ride to Wintercombe, and lay his offer, for the last time, before the lady whom he wished to marry.

That she might hate him for it, that any future they might share would be blighted by his actions, did not occur to him. It was enough that she must marry him, must submit to his wishes. After all, it was not really a companion, nor a helpmeet, nor a lover, that he sought, for the women of Bath would supply those needs. Silence would bring to this forced marriage a pleasing body, which had already been proved fertile, and a manor sufficient to found his dynasty. Her feelings in the matter were not worthy of his notice or consideration.

Jubilant, he told Alice that he was going out on business, and might be back very late for his supper, if at all. Then, his long, usually impassive face inflamed with excitement, he walked the few doors down to the White Hart, where his horse was kept in the stables.

*

'And what have you to say for yourself?'

Patience had never seen Nat so angry, and in fact had not thought him capable of such fury. Only a moment ago, she had joyfully assumed that her plan had succeeded, that all she and Tabby needed to do was to return innocently to Wintercombe, as if from a pleasant afternoon's ride. Instead, by means which she could not guess, Nat had followed them, discovered their chamber at the Katherine Wheel, and had waited, with Tabby, for her return. By the look on the girl's face, and her tears, that wait had not been a pleasant one.

She was acutely, mortifyingly conscious of the fact that her body was decorated and enhanced and displayed for male delectation, and that Nat, for various reasons, was the last person she would have wished to see her thus. Patience turned her back on him, hoping vainly that her scarlet embarrassment was not too obvious, and picked up the cloak which she had gleefully cast aside, only a moment before.

'Yes, I should cover yourself if I were you,' said Nat. She heard his footsteps behind her, and his hand gripped her shoulder with painful force, pulling her round to face him. He was the same height as she was, and his eyes, glittering with rage, were much too close for comfort. 'What in God's name do you mean by this?

[470]

Tramping the streets like a twopenny whore? What if someone recognised you? Or, worse, what if you were propositioned, or raped?'

Patience found her anger rising to match his. 'Well, I wasn't,' she said indignantly. 'And no one would have known in the street – I kept my cloak well buttoned, and the hood and the mask hid my face. No one knew who I was, or saw me dressed like – like . . . '

'Like a whore? I'll say it for you, if you're too mealy-mouthed to manage it. And Tabby had to watch while you made an exhibition of yourself . . . '

'I helped her!' his half-sister cried, jumping up. 'I painted her face – she couldn't do it without a mirror . . . '

'I didn't ask for your account,' said Nat viciously, rounding on her. 'I've had it from you already. So, Mistress Patience – if you were not parading through the streets bare-breasted and painted, what *were* you doing?'

'Helping Nick Hellier to escape,' Patience told him, in a low, furious voice. '*And* I succeeded – he's free, and no hue and cry, no alarm, and no one knew that I was responsible. You can rant all you like, Nat, but I succeeded, he's free now, and there's nothing you can do to alter it.'

In the quiet, Tabby glanced from one to the other, trying not to cry. She could not understand Nat's savagery, not when their plan had worked. The interrogation to which he had already subjected her had left her far more upset and frightened than had Colonel Pyne's. She had always been close to Nat, had thought him her special friend, and the manner in which he had turned on her left her feeling bereft and betrayed. He had not really listened to her frantic explanations, he had accused her of lying, of stupidity and disobedience, and while she knew that those charges were strictly true, surely the reason justified her actions?

Quite plainly, he had not thought so, and now he was not sparing Patience either. But her aunt was made of strong metal, and had honed her argumentative skills on her father and, later, her hapless brother Joseph and his wife, the formidable Grace.

'You have put Wintercombe in hazard,' Nat said, softly venomous. 'You have risked your freedom, and your sister's, and mine, for some ridiculous notion of escape – after you'd been expressly forbidden to take any further action. My God, girl, you've nearly ruined us once already – isn't that enough for you?'

[471]

'It wasn't her fault!' Tabby interrupted. 'It was my idea — I asked her to help!'

'I don't want to hear another *word* from you!' said Nat viciously. She stared for an anguished moment at his face, and then turned abruptly away, trying to suppress her tears. It was very unfair — they had succeeded, their plan had worked, so why was he so angry?

'Anyone would think I'd put a bill on the prison door, advertising the escape of Captain Hellier, with the assistance of the St. Barbes of Wintercombe,' said Patience. 'And the reason I'm dressed as a whore is so that no one would recognise me. Who would imagine that I'm really a respectable woman? If there had been another way, Nat, I would have taken it, but there wasn't — and I am not in the least sorry for what I have done. Wintercombe is *safe*, as safe as we can make it — I doubt they even know yet that he's escaped. Unless,' she added unpleasantly, 'you've made the whole inn aware of it.'

Nat gazed at her defiant face for a long moment. Then he said curtly, 'We'll discuss it later, on the way home. I presume you did not ride all the way from Wintercombe dressed like that?'

'I doubt you could have been more offensive if I had,' said Patience caustically. 'I suppose that you wish me to change my clothes? Then, *with* your permission, *sir*, I will retire to that closet, and Tabby can help me.' Her eyes hard and unfriendly, she surveyed him. 'And perhaps you would consider using those few minutes to ponder the advisability of a return to more civilised behaviour — *if* you know how.'

She swept up her russet riding-habit and walked over to the closet, Tabby close behind. He received one more withering glance, and then the door was slammed shut.

Nat would dearly have loved to throw something at it, but he had long ago left childhood behind. His anger almost suffocating, he turned and strode to the window, his hands gripping the stone sill, while the bright busy bustle of Bath passed to and fro below him, a never-ending pattern. She had acted with unforgivable stupidity and rashness, she had embroiled Tabby once more in her plots, and then she had insolently defied him. And to walk the streets in that indecent attire, to take the part of a whore . . .

He found his mind dwelling on her body, tempting and undeniably attractive, even if laid out for purchase with all the subtlety of a butcher's stall. Then the realisation struck him with devastating force. He cared not a fig for propriety, he was normally tolerant, to a fault, of all the foibles and perversions and peccadilloes of his fellow humans, so long as they did not harm others. But Patience's disguise had repelled him because he wanted her for himself.

He leaned his forehead against the cool glass. He had flirted with her, he had enjoyed her company, her laughter, her light-hearted sophistication. He had appreciated her beauty, he had tacitly acknowledged, as had she, the spark of attraction between them, rapidly fanning to a flame. But it had taken the sight of her in the rose-coloured gown, shocking and blatant, to force the message home. He desired her, as he had never desired any woman before.

In his years at Oxford, the other students had thought him a dry stick, interested only in books, while they spent their time evading the restrictions of their tutors in taverns and bawdy-houses. Nat had never seen much point in such activity, and had observed that it did not seem to increase their happiness. He enjoyed the company of women, but had not encountered one who could arouse in him more than a night's worth of desire.

Until Patience, infuriating, frivolous, pretty and vain, the anti-thesis of all he had thought he wanted in a lover, still less a wife, had ridden rough-shod over all his ideals. She was three years older than he was, and, more seriously, his stepmother's sister. He did not think that there would be any canonical bar to their marriage, but he was not sure . . .

Marriage, he thought incredulously. What in God's name can I be thinking of, to shackle myself to that maddening, empty-headed female? I must be ripe for Bedlam.

But there was no other way to have her, and have her he must, for the thought of making love with her was enough to turn his bones to water. He knew that he did her an injustice, that she was not unintelligent, nor wanton, and that her qualities of spon-taneous laughter and mischievous delight might well supply a certain lack in himself. And there was the very real chance that she would turn those large dark eyes on him, wide with incredulous astonishment, and, laughing, contemptuous, reject him.

He could live with that: he had suffered rejection and contempt too often from his father, to be unaccustomed to it. However, he had a good sense of his own worth, and he knew that she would be considered foolhardy to turn down such an opportunity.

And yet . . . he wanted her for herself, he wanted her to marry him because he was Nat, not because by doing so, she would become Lady St. Barbe and mistress of Wintercombe, like her sister before her.

You are a fool, he told himself ruefully, all his rage suddenly gone. A fool to fall in love with a woman so completely unsuitable in every way, and still more a fool to quarrel with her so thoroughly that the chance of her ever accepting you is doomed before you even ask.

The closet door opened. He looked round, and saw Patience, his beloved Imp, standing in her decorous russet riding-habit, her face scrubbed gleamingly free of paint, her eyes hostile. 'Well?' she said. 'Am I decent?'

'You'll do,' said Nat, a wry smile twitching at the ends of his mouth. 'Patience — my apologies. I was disgracefully rude to you, and I am heartily sorry for it. Will you forgive me?'

The honesty of it disarmed her. Most men whom she had known would rather have died than admit they were in error, still less have apologised with any grace. She looked at him dubiously, wondering whether he was in fact sincere. His long mouth lifted slightly. 'Would you like me to kiss the hem of your gown?' he enquired, rather acidly. 'Or are mere words sufficient?'

'Perhaps,' she said guardedly, unwilling to capitulate so readily. She had always enjoyed personable young men importuning her, though Nat was so very, excitingly different from the rest.

'And I think that I should also tender you my thanks,' he added quietly. 'But I'll save those until it's certain that he has truly escaped, and no whisper of blame is attached to you, or to Wintercombe.' His sudden smile illuminated his rather sharp, spare face. 'Come on, you two incorrigible conspirators — let's go home and tell Silence what has happened.'

*

Mally took her time in the mercer's shop opposite the White Hart, choosing silks with care, while Jeremy held the horse outside. She thought that he might think it strange if she only visited the one shop. It was hardly worth a visit to Bath, after all. Perhaps they should also go to the apothecary's in the High Street. She considered it as she paid for the needles, and the bright, sleek embroidery silks, and decided that it would be unwise. If Captain Hellier's escape had left the prison in uproar, it were best that she and Jeremy return straight home. Anyone seen in the vicinity, and known to come from Wintercombe, would be bound to raise suspicions, no matter how innocent their errand.

She came to the shop door, blinking in the sunlight. It was a most pleasant afternoon, despite gathering clouds in the west, and they would be returning with good news. With a rather smug smile on her face, she walked out into the street to join Jeremy.

A horseman emerged in something of a hurry from the yard of the White Hart, just across the way, and she recognised the St. Barbes' lawyer, Master Harley. She had never particularly liked him, distrusting his smooth manner and sensing, with country intuition, that his real character was quite different from the face he presented to the world. Of course, her mistress was also possessed of what Mally had long ago termed her 'company mask', but in private she was warm, friendly and pleasant. Mally suspected that the real Master Harley was not nearly so attractive as he seemed.

She slid unobtrusively back into the shop, but too late: he had seen her, and anyway, Jeremy's jug ears and gormless features were amply distinctive. An extraordinary expression, compounded of triumph, vindictiveness and unholy joy, crossed his face. He raised his hand and smiled, a menacing gesture, to say the least. Then, he turned his horse and sent it at a brisk trot down towards the Southgate, ruthlessly scattering those of the crowded pedestrians who were foolhardy enough to linger in his path.

A terrible chill of foreboding had settled on Mally's stomach. She had no proof, nothing but coincidence and circumstance to enlighten her, but she knew, surely and sickeningly, that somehow Master Harley had discovered Nick Hellier's escape, and even now would be calling out the hue and cry after him.

She tried to peer above the heads of the people around her, but she was too small, barely five foot, to see more than a distant bobbing glimpse of the lawyer's smart black beaver, plumed with blue, as he made his way towards the Southgate. Perhaps ten or fifteen minutes had passed since she had seen Wickham and Hellier, and she doubted very much whether they were sufficiently far ahead to escape him.

There was nothing she could do. She could hardly leap on to the horse and gallop in pursuit, for that would only draw unwelcome attention to the situation. She could have cried with frustration. So near to safety, and all now seemed to be undone, thanks to Harley.

She could, of course, be wrong, but she did not think so. There had been no mistaking the jubilant self-satisfaction in Harley's face. She could not imagine why he wanted Hellier recaptured, but surely he could not possibly desire the downfall of a family whom he had served, with apparent loyalty, for so long?

She forced herself to think, aware of Jeremy's puzzled gaze. If only Sir Nat were here, she thought, he be a despeard crafty one, he'd cook that hang-gallise lawyer's goose for him, and no mistake!

But of course, she remembered suddenly, he probably was in Bath. He had gone in pursuit of Mistress Patience, believing her to be arranging the Captain's escape, and since Hellier had escaped, it stood to reason that Mistress Patience was somewhere in Bath, and Sir Nat too. At once, she began to scan the busy street, and then, cursing her lack of height, turned to Jeremy. 'Come on, do ee light so quick as ee can – we can't be volating about all day.'

Jeremy looked as if he were about to protest, but thought better of it. Mally's sharp tongue and brisk manner were legendary at Wintercombe, and it was well known that she had their lady's full confidence. Rather sulkily, and with some difficulty, he led the horse between the crowds to the White Hart's mounting block, across the street.

Once elevated to her pillion pad, it was much easier to see. There seemed to be no alarm at the Southgate. Master Harley's purpose, however malicious, apparently did not involve raising the hue and cry in pursuit of the escaped prisoner, but Mally's suspicions were not dispelled. Her hands decorously round Jeremy's scrawny waist, she studied the faces passing by, but without success. She said, thinking hard, 'If ee d'see Sir Nathaniel, do ee tell I right away – I've a message for him, from m'lady.'

'Aye,' said Jeremy, bewilderment plain in his voice. 'But where do I go?'

'Do ee go on up Stall Street,' Mally told him firmly. 'And don't ee forget to keep a sharp look out.'

But Nat's pale, distinctive face did not appear amongst the shifting crowds, nor were there any others whom she knew, and could ask. Mally's practical soul was not given to panic, but she could not stop her mind tracing, with inexorable clarity, the path which Master Harley would take on his way out of the city. By now, he must have reached the bridge over the Avon, and be crossing it. And only a little further on, completely unaware of the danger in which they stood, Master Wickham and Captain Hellier rode up towards the downs, headed for – where? She hoped that they would avoid Wintercombe, and make instead for Wells. Master Wickham lived near Glastonbury, she knew. Surely that would be his destination, surely he would not be so foolish as to return to Philip's Norton, and Wintercombe.

Mally was not given to piety, but she prayed now, with unusual fervour, that Harley would not catch up with his quarry.

'There he be,' said Jeremy, cheerfully unaware of her desperation. The sense of his words barely penetrated her thoughts. He said it again, more forcefully. 'There he be. Sir Nathaniel – over there!'

The miracle had happened. Mally saw him too, on his handsome grey, picking his way unhurriedly down Cheap Street towards its junction with Stall Street, and behind him, in tandem, his half-sister Tabby, and Mistress Patience. Joy and relief burst into Mally's voice, as she waved her hand and shouted. 'Sir Nathaniel!'

Her voice carried urgently across the twenty yards or so between them, and heads turned curiously. Nat had seen her, and he pressed the grey to walk a little faster. To Mally, foaming with impatience, it seemed an age before he came up to them. In the press of people, with Jeremy prick-eared in front of her, she would have to be extremely discreet. Somehow, she must convey the vital importance of her message, without arousing anyone's suspicions. In a crowd such as this, who knew who might be listening with unfriendly intent?

'I've a message for ee, sir,' she said, hoping that her eyes and her voice would communicate what her words could not. 'From my lady. She d'ask ee to return to Wintercombe, so sharp as ee can.' She stared at him intently, willing him to understand. His eyes narrowed, and then he smiled, and nodded. 'Thank you, Mally. Of course I will.'

'And,' she added, 'I've just seed Master Harley, not five minutes agone, a-riding down to the Southgate. Do ee scanter along, you'll catch him for sure.'

This time, there was no mistaking the impact of her information. Nat's brows snapped together in an expression very reminiscent of Rachael. 'Has he indeed? Well, we'd best be after him directly – there's a matter which I wish to discuss with him, urgently. I'll see you later, Mally – and thank you.'

It was out of her hands. She turned, with heartfelt relief, to watch him urge his horse down Stall Street, with the two girls, pale and looking somewhat anxious, following behind. She had done all she could, and it was up to Nat now, to stop Master Harley's mischief and save Captain Hellier from recapture. If anyone could succeed, it was Sir Nat: she had the greatest respect for his cunning and intelligence.

'Where do I go, Mally?' Jeremy asked her plaintively. She pulled her thoughts together with an effort. 'To the 'pothecary's in the High Street,' she told him. 'And then we can go home.'

*

Jonathan Harley rode briskly across the bridge, his horse's hooves rattling out a tattoo on the cobbles. A mood of exultation filled him to the brim, so that it was all he could do, not to shout his triumph to the passers-by, the statues, the trees overhanging the river, the cows in the meads. Everything he had worked for had suddenly come to fruition, and his greatest ambition, to become a landed gentleman, was at last within his grasp.

He tried to urge his horse into a trot up the steep hill rising from the Avon valley. But the animal could not sustain the pace for more than a few strides, and he had to curb his impatience as it slowed to a safer walk. He thought of Silence, her pleasing face and figure, the key to his fortune, and smiled. Once married, he would be able to exert his charm, and his skilful love-making, to woo her. If, unaccountably, he failed, well, he would have his house and his lands and, if fortune smiled as he hoped, his heir.

He came at last to the fork in the road, high above the city, and debated for a moment while his mare rested. Ahead, the way climbed up to Odd Down, and thence to Wells, or to Philip's Norton by an easy route. To the left, there was a narrow steep track, that led to South Stoke, and was also a short cut, for those in a hurry and not too concerned for their mounts' legs, to Wellow and Norton. His brown mare had only recently recovered from lameness, and he was not so impetuous as to risk being benighted on the high, cold, deserted downs with a broken-down horse. He took the Wells road.

It was growing late in the afternoon now, and to his right, above the blue, hazy autumn hills towards Bristol, the sun had sunk into a bank of deep stormy clouds, racing from the west. Up here on Odd Down, the wind blew hard and chill, a reminder of the coming cold of winter. The few trees were planted in the combes that folded the landscape, and hunched against the sheltering downs for protection against the icy blasts of January. It was a bleak, unwelcoming place, inhabited mostly by sheep, and at this hour, and with rain fast approaching, there were few people about.

But ahead of him, on the long straight road that led along the ridge between Combe Hay and Englishcombe, he saw two riders, close together. They must, surely, be Wickham, and Nick Hellier.

Harley hesitated only for a moment. The pleasure of seeing Hellier's face as he realised that his escape was known, and his future endangered, would only be exceeded by Silence's acceptance of marriage. And he would not be long delayed. He set spurs to his tired horse, and the mare lumbered into a canter.

Tom heard the hoofbeats as they approached, and glanced apprehensively round. But there was only one rider, plainly not a soldier, catching them up. He relaxed, and took his hand away from his sword. One man could surely present no danger, and he was, in any case, probably only a traveller anxious to reach Paulton before dark. He drew his horse to the side of the highway to allow the rider to pass unhindered, and Nick, beside him, did the same.

But the other man was slowing down, pulling his horse into a trot, then a walk, and the long lean figure, the distinctive yellow hair, were somehow familiar. With mounting bewilderment, Tom recognised the man he had met once at Wintercombe, who had been introduced as Jonathan Harley, the St. Barbe family's lawyer. This could not be coincidence, he realised suddenly, with a sick feeling of dread. This man had come in pursuit.

'Good day to you – Master Wickham, is it not?' said the lawyer, baring his teeth in a smile that was far from pleasant. 'And, I believe, Captain Nicholas Hellier, late of Bath City Gaol?'

Somehow, God only knew how, it had all gone terribly wrong. But there was only a single man facing them, not a regiment, and Tom had never been one to give in without a fight. Nor, as he knew only too well, had his companion. He glanced at Nick, and saw that his face, still pale with ill-health and the exertions of the ride, was tense and watchful.

He decided to try to brazen it out. 'Captain Hellier? You are sadly mistaken, Master Harley,' he said. 'This is Ned Wingfield, my servant.'

The lawyer shook his head with mock reproof. 'Oh, no, Master Wickham – your lies do you no credit. This is Captain Hellier, I know beyond a doubt. I saw him as he was carried from Winter-combe last Friday, and it is undoubtedly the same man. Perhaps you have been misled, sir?'

'What do you want?' Nick enquired sharply. He had no recollec-tion of seeing this man before, and had no idea how he might have come to be at Wintercombe, but Tom knew him, and his instincts, infallible in such matters, were shouting to him of danger.

'What do I want? Nothing of you, yet,' said Harley, and showed his teeth again. His horse, blowing hard, sidled hopefully towards the grass, and he jerked the reins. Two travellers, heading for Bath, glanced at the three men curiously as they passed, and trotted on out of sight. The rain had almost reached them now, blurring and then obliterating the western hills. The lawyer went on. 'Indeed, I may not want anything of you at all. Just for you to know that I am privy to your secret, that you are not so safe as you thought — that is all I require of you, for the present. And then, you may go on your way to — where, precisely?'

'I am hardly going to tell you that,' said Tom angrily. His hand itched to draw his sword, and slash that smug, triumphant leer off the man's face, but for the moment, he held back. The lawyer also carried a weapon, but it was hardly honourable to strike a man without warning.

'It doesn't matter,' said Harley, with a dismissive gesture. 'It should not be too difficult for me to discover it, if necessary. In any case, neither of you form any part of my plans — save as the means to an end.'

'And what end is that?' Nick asked softly. He could read Tom's mind as clear as daylight, the hovering hand, the pose of watchful readiness. He himself was unarmed — it was hardly proper for a servant, after all — but there were more ways to kill a man than with a yard of steel.

And yet — he still could not understand. Why had this man Harley pursued them, if he was not to arrest them?

The lawyer did not reply directly. He said abruptly, 'I believe that you are Lady St. Barbe's lover, are you not?'

Nick stared at him in furious astonishment. 'What the hell is that to do with you?'

'I like to know who my rivals are,' said Harley, smiling. 'I was on my way to Wintercombe when I saw you, and could not resist the opportunity to tell you something of my plans. It would hardly be kind, to allow you to live any longer with false hopes, now would it? I intend to ask Lady St. Barbe to become my wife — and I confidently expect her to consent.'

Nick controlled his rage with considerable difficulty. 'I doubt that, sir,' he said, between his teeth. 'On the contrary, I have every reason to believe that she wishes to marry *me*.'

'Oh, she may *wish* to marry you — but she will find it impossible. I have a proposition to put to her, which she will certainly be unable to resist. For if she refuses to agree, I will inform Colonel Pyne, whom I am sure you know very well, of her complicity, and Sir Nathaniel's, in your concealment at Wintercombe, and in your subsequent escape from captivity.' He smiled. 'And I am also sure that you can well imagine the likely consequences to the St. Barbe family, and to Wintercombe, if I do.'

Nick saw Tom looking covertly around him, and knew what he was thinking. The rain had begun a little while ago, in huge heavy drops, and would soon become a downpour. The light was fast draining away into an early dusk, and the road was empty. Murder would undoubtedly ensure their freedom — for the moment. He could not imagine that the man in front of him, well-dressed and evidently prosperous, would die without a struggle, nor would his killing be ignored. Doing the deed with a sword would hardly imply that robbers or footpads were responsible. Yet it seemed that only Harley's death would ensure his own safety, and Silence's freedom from another forced marriage. His mind working urgently, he decided to play for time.

'Why do you want to marry her?' he asked.

The lawyer laughed. 'You should know the reason, since you are of the same mind. The lady is possessed of everything that is necessary in a wife, after all — a face neither haggard nor wrinkled nor pocked, a pleasing body, and a handsome fortune. Reason enough, don't you think? And since you have already bedded her, you must know about her more intimate attractions. Is she good sport, between the sheets?'

Nick, goaded beyond sense, dug his heels into his horse's sides. The elderly hireling, hardened to such treatment, flung up his ungainly head, and dug in his toes. Harley laughed again, and drew his sword with a menacing rasp. 'Or perhaps she will look on me more favourably when she knows that there is no hope of any other offer. You're a hunted man, Captain Hellier, and it is my duty to apprehend you — and if you resist, I can hardly be blamed for killing you.'

On the last word, he lunged. Tom, whose horse was more responsive than Nick's, thrust his own sword between them. There was a ringing clash of metal, and Harley disengaged, moving his own mount back. 'Well, it seems that I'll have to kill you too, sir — a pity, but it cannot be helped.'

'Get away!' Tom shouted at Nick, as Harley closed again. Go on, you fool — *ride!*'

Nick had no intention of abandoning his friend to his fate. He could do nothing on this useless horse, he would be faster and more mobile on foot. He jumped down, leaving the animal to graze by the roadside, and ran to grasp Harley's reins. The other man's sword, whistling down, sliced within an inch of his face. Feeling the wind of it, he dodged, and dodged again, trying to keep the horse's head between himself and the weapon. Then Tom, who had once been a cavalry lieutenant, and who had been trained to fight on horseback, came to the rescue, waving his workmanlike broadsword with a military flourish.

As the two armed men clashed in the failing light and lashing rain, Nick cast desperately around him for a weapon, anything, even a rock or a branch, with which to ward off attack. There were few trees, and only a small and haphazard pile of stones at the roadside. With some wild thought of throwing it at Harley, he picked up the largest, and hefted it in his hand.

*

The single aim in Nat's mind, as he pushed his tired horse up the Holloway, with Tabby and Patience toiling some way behind him, was to stop Harley, somehow, from reaching Nick and Tom. It was clear, from what the girls had told him, that the two men could not be far in front of the pursuing lawyer. In his heart, he knew that he was unlikely to reach Harley before he caught up with them, but, even if he did not, he might still be in time to prevent . . . what?

With dread, he spurred his grey into a gallop as soon as they reached more level ground. Tabby and Patience, riding side-saddle on smaller horses, could not match his speed, and besides, Patience, despite her months in the country, was still a far from confident horsewoman. Her hat at a perilous angle, breathless and bouncing in an uncomfortable and highly undignified fashion, she dared go no faster than a gentle canter. Tabby, far more competent, resisted the temptation to leave her behind, and kept her own pretty, lively Dowsabel to the same pace, while Nat, his hair and cloak flying, sped up towards Odd Down in frantic haste, and the clouds swept up black and ominous from the west, like a portent of doom.

He reached the crossroads at the top, and glanced around. To the left, the road led to Midford, Charterhouse Hinton and, eventually, Philip's Norton and Wintercombe. To the right, the way went downhill, towards Newton and Bristol. And ahead, the old straight Roman road, known as the Fosse Way, ran clear for miles, along hill and valley, to Shepton and Wells.

There were figures in the distance, too small, and far, and blurred by the increasing rain, for him to discern any detail. But they seemed to be standing still. His tired, lathered horse was in no condition to be urged to further efforts, but he dug his spurs into its heaving sides, and persuaded it into a gallop.

'There they are!' called Tabby, reaching the crossroads a few minutes after her brother. She glanced back at Patience, flushed, wet and dishevelled, her sturdy old gelding reduced to a gasping walk. 'I'm sure that's them – see, along the Wells Road? Come on!'

Patience had a stabbing stitch in her side, and the driving rain stung her face. Despairing and furious with her inadequacy, she picked up her stick and smacked her horse's rain-darkened rump. He was not enjoying the ride or the weather either, and he laid back his ears and swished his tail in ill-tempered fashion, while Tabby's game and willing little mare galloped obediently on ahead, going further and further away. Almost sobbing with anger and frustration, Patience put all her strength into one vicious slap of the stick. Her mount, at last stung into action, flung up his head, banging her painfully on the nose in the process, and lumbered resentfully into a trot.

Nat could barely make out what was happening ahead of him. There were certainly two men on horseback, and one on foot, with another animal grazing riderless by the roadside. He wiped the water from his face, and peered above his mount's lowered head and flattened ears. He saw arms waving, in an appalling and unmistakable pattern, and the pale swift sweep of a sword. Then the man on foot seemed to throw something at one of the riders, and Nat realised that it was Nick, hatless, his brown hair dark and sleek with rain. Then his horse burst in amongst the fighting men, and he shouted, 'Stop! For God's sake, stop!'

Harley wheeled his brown mare, his face set with an unholy strength of purpose that lifted the hairs on Nat's scalp. 'Stay out of this, boy – out of my way!'

Nat gripped the reins, forcing the grey to stand still. He was unarmed, for he rarely carried a sword save on formal occasions, and in any case had received only the most perfunctory training in its use. He faced the lawyer whom he had once believed to be honest and loyal in his service to the St. Barbes, if never quite a friend. 'Harley – for God's sake, man, put up your sword! This doesn't solve anything – let's talk in a civilised manner, shall we?'

'On the contrary,' said Harley, his smile suddenly and chillingly intent. 'It solves everything. And if I kill you too, I can gain control of Wintercombe as well, until your brother comes of age, and who's to say you have not been slain by these rogues here? No sword, I see – you may not live to regret it.'

Nat had read the movement in his eyes, a fraction before the weapon thrust at him. He wrenched his abused and weary horse to one side, only just in time. And then Tom Wickham was pushing past, urging his mount to the attack. Nat, feeling uncharacteristically useless, tried to get out of his way. He saw Nick, a stone in each hand, running towards Harley, and shying his impromptu missiles with more haste than accuracy. One missed altogether, and the other knocked off the lawyer's hat.

Tabby, approaching at a gallop, saw it all too clearly. Four men, two armed, two defenceless, three mounted, in a confused mêlée. Harley and Tom engaged swords, and she saw Nat trying to bump and jostle the lawyer, and the gleam of wet steel as Harley slashed at him. Then quite suddenly Nat was lying on the ground, his frightened horse shying away wild-eyed, and she gave a great howl of fear and fury.

Her mare was nearly up with them now. She needed a weapon, something, anything, but she had no stick, her lovely Dowsabel had never needed one. The little chestnut swerved to one side to avoid Nat, prone in her path, and Tabby prayed in terror that he was not dead. Someone, Nick, was shouting at her, yelling at her to get back, but she had no intention of running away, not now when all her family's future depended on it. The harsh metallic clash of the swords beat inspiration into her mind. She pulled off her hat, guiding Dowsabel with one hand, while she fumbled with the mass of her ungovernable hair, already running wet and tangled with rain. It was secured at the back with pins, each four inches long, and sharp as a needle. Her frantic fingers found one and wrenched it out, coils of hair falling in its wake. A finger's length of steel was no match for a sword, but she had other plans.

Harley was pressing his advantage against Tom, his arm seemingly tireless, intent on victory as the other man gave ground. She saw Nick bending over Nat, as the two mounted men moved further away. With a sob of grief, she urged Dowsabel up unnoticed beside Harley's much taller brown mare, and with all her strength plunged the pin into the rain-blackened rump.

The brown mare squealed in pain, and reared up. Harley, taken completely by surprise, lost his balance and his stirrups and fell backwards, even as his horse slipped in the wet mud, and crashed down on top of him.

Tabby, gasping, her hair whipped by the wind across her face, brought Dowsabel at last to a shuddering halt, and stared at Harley's horse, thrashing in agony on the ground. She could see nothing of the lawyer but a jerking arm, pinned under the brown mare's frantic bulk.

At last, the horse managed to struggle to her feet, hobbled a few steps, terribly lame, and stopped. She stood, head hanging, the saddle broken and twisted and smeared with wet earth and other, darker stains.

Harley, pressed and ground like a sack of grain into the soft mud of the Fosse Way, lay quite still.

Tabby felt suddenly sick. She turned her head away and saw Tom Wickham, his face a study in amazement, staring at her.

Oh, God, she thought, Nat — what of Nat? Afraid to look behind her, she kicked her legs free of stirrup and pommel, and dismounted. Her knees refused to support her, and she collapsed on to the wet road, sobbing with fear.

Someone touched her, and a voice, dear and familiar, said, 'What are you crying for, Tabby-Cat?'

No one else called her that. She turned her drowned, mud-streaked, bedraggled face, and saw her beloved half-brother, kneeling beside her. 'You didn't think I was hurt, did you?' said Nat, smiling. 'I ducked too sharply, and fell off and winded myself. What in God's name did you do to Harley's horse?'

She was still holding the pin, clenched between her fingers. She lifted her hand to show him. Nat drew a long breath, and released it in a whistle. 'No wonder it reared up.'

'Nat?' It was Tom Wickham, his freckled, pleasant face display-ing a mixture of relief and distress. 'Nat, I think he's dead.'

'Don't move, and don't look,' he told Tabby, and got, rather painfully, to his feet: the fall had jarred his shoulder and back. He followed Tom to the side of the road, where Harley lay as he had when the horse had heaved itself off him. Nick was bending over the lawyer's body. As the other two men approached, he glanced up, and shook his head.

All three of them had seen death too often to mistake it. Jona-than Harley lay sprawled flat in the mud, his eyes fixed in a sightless glare, his face, twisted in its last agony, oblivious to the steady rain beating down on it. 'Crushed,' said Nick succinctly, and rose to his feet. 'He was probably dead before the horse got off him.'

They stood staring down at the lawyer's broken body. Only a few minutes ago, he had menaced all of them. Now, the threat he presented was of a more subtle, yet no less dangerous kind.

'What's happened? Are you all right?' Patience cried above their heads. She had never managed to persuade her unwilling horse into anything faster than a shambling trot, and had been forced to watch helplessly as it carried her, unbearably slowly, towards the four men fighting in the road. She had seen Nat fall, and feared the worst. The flood of relief, when she saw him move, had almost overwhelmed her.

'We're all unharmed,' he told her, coming over to her horse. Her face was pale, distraught, and he gave her a reassuring smile. 'But Harley . . . '

'He's dead, isn't he,' said Patience. She stared for a brief moment at the lawyer's body, and then looked down at Nat. 'I thought that you were, too, for a moment.' And suddenly, to her shame, the tears welled up and spilled down her cheeks, mingling with the rain, and she sat on her uncooperative mount, and sobbed.

Tabby, her own tears vanished, saw her brother walk up to the horse, and hold out his arms. Patience, in an undisciplined flurry of damp skirts, dropped from the saddle, and into his embrace. At once pleased, and a little embarrassed, she turned away from them, and encountered Nick Hellier.

He looked exhausted, his hair soaked and sleeked like a seal's to his head, his eyes shadowed. He said wryly, 'I can't pretend I'm sorry he's dead, but it poses almost as many problems as it solves.'

'It was an accident,' Tabby said. She was trying, unsuccessfully, to pin her hair back into its usual knot, but her fingers were too cold and wet, and she gave up. Nick, looking at her with a rather wary respect, thought that she resembled nothing so much as Medusa, her mass of rain-sodden hair snaking round her pale, lovely, implacable face, her hazel eyes bleak. She went on. 'His horse fell on him, and crushed him. It's always happening — a man from Beckington died that way last spring. There's no one about, no one saw — who's to say any different?'

Nick's respect was changing to admiration, and a certain disquiet. There had always been a fierce, ruthless side to Tabby's nature, but there was something very chilling about her expression now, as she discussed the death of a man, in which she had been the principal agent, as unemotionally as an avenging angel. One day, she must realise that the people around her were not divided purely into evil and good, but were all a greyish and variable mixture of both.

It was getting dark, and the rain fell heavier than ever. Somehow, they must find shelter, or run the risk of catching chills and lung fever to add to everything else. He knew what must be done, but his extreme weariness was rapidly numbing his mind, and sapping his powers of thought. He looked round for Nat, and wondered, with rather remote amusement, whether it was permissible to embrace an aunt, even if no kin to him by blood, with quite so much passion.

As if aware of his thought, Nat and Patience stepped apart. In the dim light, it was hard to make out the expression on the girl's face, but he thought that she looked dazed, and disbelieving. Nat smiled, and said something to her, and then came over to Nick and Tabby. Tom had been busy by Harley's body: as he got up to join them, Nick saw that he had found the lawyer's sword, wiped it carefully clean of mud on his cloak, and replaced it in the scabbard.

An accident, Tabby had said, almost callously, from the depths of her hatred. And Nick began to see that it would be quite possible to conceal the dangerous and unpalatable facts behind this sudden death.

'You two must go on,' said Nat, his face pale and quite serious, though there was a gleam in his eyes that hinted at another mood entirely, behind the solemn exterior. 'You're supposed to be going home — we can't have you party to this, or everything is wasted.' He glanced at Harley. 'We'll put the body over my horse, which isn't an impossible feat for a man and two women, and take him back to Bath. We can say that we came upon him, and the cause of his death is quite obvious — no one will have any reason to think that we are not telling the truth. But you two must go, now, and perhaps you'll reach Paulton in time for supper, and then on to Glastonbury tomorrow. You'll be far away, and safe. Leave the rest to us, and I'll send you word, when the hue and cry has died down.'

Nick and Tom exchanged glances. Neither relished the prospect of leaving Nat and the two girls alone on the downs in company with a dead man and a crippled horse, with nightfall almost upon them and the rain falling. But they could see the sense of it. They had only to ride onwards, and into Nick's freedom, from imprisonment and possible slavery. Harley was dead, the only enemy who knew for certain how deeply all the St. Barbes had been embroiled in this affair. And with him had vanished the threat to Silence, and to Wintercombe.

Nick smiled suddenly, as the full impact of it struck him, for the first time. 'You're right,' he said. 'We must go, and quickly. I don't want to risk lung fever, when I've barely recovered from that wound.'

Tabby and Patience stood huddled together by their horses, trying to shelter a little from the rain. They watched as the three men, with some effort, pulled Harley's body from the sticky grasp of the mud and slung it over Nat's tired grey. The animal, uneasy, stamped and sidled, and Nat secured its ungainly burden with the stirrup leathers. Then there were farewells, brief, urgent, and yet not without hope.

'We'll see you all soon,' said Nick, his eyes on Tabby, smiling. 'And give my dear love to your mother, and tell her that there is no need for her to worry, any more.'

'I know there isn't,' said Silence's daughter. 'But she will, until you're both together again, and safe.'

'It won't be very long, I promise,' Nick told her. 'Goodbye, my dear Tabby — and thank you, for all you have done.'

She watched as he and Tom mounted, and rode off in the rainy dark towards the shelter of Paulton, some five or six miles distant. Despite the appalling weather, Tabby, shivering in her wet cloak, distinctly heard him whistling as they went.

Nat helped her and Patience into their saddles, and took the reins of his grey, with its grim burden, and Harley's limping brown mare. Then, they turned back towards Bath, and the unsavoury task of convincing the justices that the death of Jonathan Harley, man of law, of Bath, had been no more than an unavoidable and tragic accident.

🦋 CHAPTER TWENTY-FIVE 🦋

'Joy delights in joy'
(Sonnets)

Silence had waited all day, and all night, listening to the rain beating remorselessly against the windows, trying to take comfort in the warm furry presence of Misty, snuggled next to her, just as her mother Pye had once done. All day, she had tried to go about the house as usual, supervising all the humdrum tasks, making herself busy, avoiding idle moments when all her fears, and her feelings of helplessness, would threaten to overwhelm her.

As the day drew to its close, and there was still no sign of Tabby and Patience, or Nat, or Mally, she was forced to the bitter knowledge that all was not well. What had happened? Had Nick escaped? Or had something gone dreadfully wrong, and was he, or Nat, even now in prison?

She could not disguise her anxiety from the younger children. She had told them that the older ones had gone to Bath for the day, but her explanation had sounded forced, even to her own ears. William had looked at her doubtfully, but had said nothing. Deb had been bad-tempered and quarrelsome all day, and Kate little better. When she came to kiss Nick's daughter goodnight, with a smile that inadequately concealed her sick fear for him, the little girl had looked up at her from the pillows, her chestnut eyes wide, and asked curiously, 'Mama, where have Nat and Tabby and Patience *really* gone?'

'To Bath — I told you,' said Silence briskly. 'Now go to sleep.'

'But they're not back, and it's dark, *and* it's raining.'

'They won't be long — you'll wake up and see them in the morning,' said Silence, with false hope. 'Now, for the last time, go to sleep, Binnick.'

Shortly after that, she had heard hoofs in the barton, as she was saying goodnight to Deb and William. She flew down the stairs, to find Mally, dripping, white-faced, and unusually subdued.

She had news, but of a very limited kind. Yes, Nick had escaped, she had seen him herself, and Tom Wickham with him, and she supposed that Tabby and Patience must have had some part in it, though she knew no more than that. She described how she had seen Master Harley, almost certainly following in pursuit, and how Nat had gone after him, with Tabby and Patience. She had then gone with Jeremy Walker to the apothecary's shop in the High Street, but had seen no great clamour or alarm round the prison by the Northgate, so it seemed safe to assume that Nick's escape, miraculously, had not then been discovered. So, with a mixture of hope and fear, she had ridden back to Wintercombe with Jeremy, overtaken by rain and dark.

Grateful for her company, even if her story had provided more cause for anxiety than rejoicing, Silence sat up until midnight, trying to read, trying to sew, with her heart hammering, dull with dread, inside her ribs. She had told Mally about Harley's threats, and the full extent of his enmity, and both women knew that he must have followed Nick and Tom with evil intent.

Eventually, almost by main force, Mally persuaded her into bed. But she could not sleep, and lay wakeful, her thoughts treading over and over what her maid had told her, wondering what had happened. Had Harley caught up with Nick and Tom? Had Nat managed to reach them in time? What had happened to Tabby and Patience?

Her lover, her beloved child, her sister, and Nat who was so dear to her . . . so many of those who were most precious to her, in hazard. Sick with apprehension, she rose at first light, having slept not at all, and saw the hollow-eyed, haggard stranger in her mirror with no more than a remote sense of surprise. All morning, she slid through the routines of Wintercombe like a sleepwalker, deflecting the bewildered questions of the children, making excuses to the servants that sounded hopelessly lame, and trying to counter the shrewder suspicions of Rachael, who was by now well aware that something was very wrong, and that she had once more been excluded.

Rachael, pale with strain, the fading mark on her throat well hidden behind a high linen collar, was not easily deterred. She managed to corner her stepmother in the little closet off her chamber, where clothes and linen, and sometimes Emerald, were stored. 'Please tell me, *please* – what is happening? Where are they all?'

'I don't know,' said Silence. She looked at the girl's gaunt figure and pleading face, and was tempted to tell her everything. Surely, Rachael had at last learned her lesson. Surely, the very act of trusting her with a secret of such enormous importance would do much to mend the damage?

She hesitated. Beyond the open door, she could hear the scratching of pens, and the murmurs of William and Deb as they conferred about some aspect of their study. Emerald shook out her feathers, gave a contemplative squawk, and muttered, without much conviction, 'A pox on all Puritans!'

An involuntary smile pulled quite unexpectedly at Rachael's mouth, and Silence came to a sudden decision. She might regret it later, but, somehow, she doubted it. She closed the door, softly, and in a few whispered sentences, told her stepdaughter what had happened on the previous day.

She had done right. Rachael's eyes widened with astonishment, followed immediately by concern. 'But if Nick is free – where are Nat, and Tabby and Patience? What's happened to them?'

And there were no answers in her stepmother's distraught face. Rachael, moved by an unusual compassion, put her arms about her, trying to give comfort.

'M'lady? M'lady!' Mally's voice rose loud in the chamber next door. 'M'lady, they be back – Sir Nat have returned!'

She ran with Rachael and the children to her oriel window, looking down into the rainy courtyard. There was Nat on his grey horse, and Tabby, riding Dowsabel, with Patience just behind. They dismounted wearily, and gave their mounts to Jack Goodenough. As the lad walked the animals towards the barton, the three gathered together for a moment, evidently conferring, before vanishing into the porch.

Despite their damp, bedraggled garments, and their evident exhaustion, there had been something about the reckless angle of her sister's head, in Nat's bearing and the graceful swirl of Tabby's cloak, that told Silence that perhaps, despite her fears, diasaster had not after all befallen them.

She ran down the stairs to greet them. For the moment, the more practical things – dry clean clothes, a hot meal, an hour or so of warmth in front of a roaring fire – were what was needed. Explanations could follow later, when they had rested, and when there was a chance of absolute privacy, away from the curious eyes and flapping ears of the younger children, and the servants. She could be patient, for she knew already, from their reassuring, exultant smiles, that the news would be good.

That afternoon, Nat, on his own, and with a very strange and uncharacteristic blend of elation and seriousness, took her walking in the garden, in the fitful sunshine that had followed the rain of last night and that morning. They strolled together down the steps that led to the lower terrace, and leaned in a companionable quiet over the rough lichened stone of the balustrade. She listened to the peace and stillness that always seemed to belong especially to autumn, lovely and melancholy, one of her favourite times of year, and waited.

In that stillness, she heard, with astonishment, and shocked amusement, of her sister's plan to release Nick from prison, related by Nat with more than his usual dry understatement. Her imagination struggled to envisage Patience in her indecent disguise, and could hardly encompass it. She said, torn between anger and laughter, 'I'm not surprised she went unrecognised.'

'I think that was her intention,' Nat commented. He was gazing thoughtfully at the apple trees in the orchard. After a while, he said slowly, 'I do not know quite how to tell you this, but despite all her preposterous antics, your dear Imp and I have . . . come to an understanding, I believe is the phrase.'

'It isn't unexpected,' Silence said, deliberately echoing his dry tone. 'I can't imagine that you are eager to rush into matrimony, though.'

Nat laughed. 'You're right, I'm not. It is much too soon yet to be sure of anything, save that we are attracted to each other, and besides, I'm not at all certain that we will be able to take it any further. We are no blood kin, and I know that a husband's family are regarded as being separate to the wife's, should they wish to marry, but there may still be some impediment . . . I don't know.' He grinned at her ruefully, her dear friend. 'And courting your Impatience will not exactly be a quiet stroll along the primrose path, I am sure. Do you disapprove?'

'I don't think so,' said Silence, cautiously. 'But I must say, I wouldn't have thought that the two of you were very well suited. Still . . . I may become used to the idea, in time.'

'So may I,' said Nat, grinning wider. 'And I'm under no illusions at all. It may always be difficult, unlike you and Nick, which has ever seemed so . . . so easy, somehow.'

'It was, and is,' said Silence. She took a deep breath, still apprehensive, even though all the omens and portents were good, and said very softly, 'Tell me, Nat, please — what happened next? Where is he now?'

The tale did not take long, but she found it hard to sort out the events in her mind, and harder still to understand how Harley had become involved. Nat could not tell her. 'I have no idea. Perhaps he had some minion watching the gaol – I don't know. But he set off after Nick, not to denounce him, it seems, but to tell him what would happen if he attempted to return to Wintercombe, or to marry you. He may have intended to come here afterwards, and demand your answer, knowing that you could not refuse him.'

'I would have done,' said Silence, shivering suddenly. 'Somehow, I think I would have found the courage – I hope. Perhaps we could have bought him off, though I doubt it. But I have spent too many years of my life shackled to a man whom I neither loved nor respected, and I do think that my second husband should be one of my own choosing, and selected for love and liking, and not out of fear.' She stared bleakly at the hazy sky, beyond the green shoulder of the valley. 'And now Harley is dead, and it seems that we may be safe – although it will be a long, long time before I can be truly happy. How did he die, Nat?'

He had been dreading this, and he knew of no way to make it easier. He thought of Tabby, his beloved and lovely sister, turned by love and hatred and circumstance into a secret plotter, who had slain Harley as surely as if she had plunged that pin into his heart. And yet, with her clear, terrifying sense of justice, she seemed almost untouched by her deed. He remembered also the dreadful things that had befallen Wintercombe, six years ago. Had the damage inflicted on her, and on all the children, by that terrible and violent year, struck much deeper than they had supposed?

He could not tell. He knew only that he feared for Tabby, their beloved avenging angel, for her peace of mind, and for her future.

Briefly, he told Silence what she had done, and, to his surprise, she did not weep. After a long while, she said bleakly, 'I liked Harley, once. I thought that he was my friend, and yet he was no more than a Judas, waiting for the moment to take his advantage. How he must have despised and envied us! And Tabby – what will become of her? When Rachael tried to kill Ridgeley, the shock and guilt of it almost destroyed her wits. But has Tabby *ever* felt guilty?'

'Perhaps one day she will – but I doubt it. And anyway,' said Nat, covering his own disquiet, 'we owe her so much. Remember, Harley was trying to kill us – he announced his intention to me quite clearly. No jury on earth would blame her for what she did.

She acted in defence of us, with the only weapon she had to hand. I don't think she meant to kill him at all — she intended only to disable him or distract him, and give Tom the chance of fighting back. But when she found that he was dead, she was not exactly stricken with grief. And when we managed to get back to Bath at last, after that dreadful journey in the rain and the dark, she *seemed* almost unaffected by it all. Even the weeping and wailing of Harley's housekeeper seemed to make very little impression on her.' He glanced at Silence. 'There have been no awkward questions asked about his death. I said that I had ridden after him in the rain, because I wished to speak with him about a family matter, and that we came upon him soon after his horse fell on him. It is very nearly the truth, after all. He will be buried in the abbey, in three days' time — I made all the arrangements, since the housekeeper was prostrate. He has no kin in Bath, though I believe that there is a sister in Salisbury. And I feel that I must attend the funeral.'

'And Nick?'

'Should by now be safe in Glastonbury, with Tom Wickham. He'll stay there for the time being, until everything is quiet. I made enquiries, very discreetly of course. Apparently the gaoler, the one whom Patience laid out with a stool, didn't recover until his wife came to bring him his supper, and found him locked up in the guard-room. No one seems to have seen anything, and all the gaoler could remember was some garbled tale about a whore from Bristol — so a couple of militia men were sent in that direction this morning.' He smiled at her. 'I don't think, somehow, that they'll find anything. My dear Silence, Nick is free, and safe — and now all you have to do, is to wait a while, until it has all been forgotten.'

'It's not so easy as that,' Silence told him sadly. 'He's still a hunted man — how can he ever come back to Wintercombe?'

Nat looked at her, and shook his head in mock reproof. 'Haven't you remembered? You may have cause to thank Harley after all — and my father. I agree, he can't come back to Wintercombe for a very long time. But are you not now in possession of a certain house at Chard?'

*

The spring of the year 1652 was cold, and wet, and unpromising of finer weather to come. The roads had not dried out, making travel a difficult and tedious business, especially along the river valleys. But this day, the first of June, had relented somewhat. There was enough blue amongst the high white clouds to make a sailor's breeches, one of old Diggory's famous weather saws, and perhaps it would stay fine until the evening.

The house just outside Chard had been in the St. Barbe family for several generations. It was old, and had once been dark, cold, uninviting and inconvenient, lacking entirely the warmth and grace and light of Wintercombe. Silence had spent the first seven years of her marriage there, and had always loathed the place which, for her, held so many unhappy memories. She had not laid eyes on it since the beginning of the war, and had never missed it: indeed, she had been glad when news arrived of its plunder and destruction by fire.

But she could no longer link the crowded hall in front of her, cheerful and sunny and full of life and talk, with the dark dreary memories of a place which no one had seemed to like very much. All through the winter, Nat had organised masons and glaziers, carpenters and joiners, and caused this miraculous transformation. The tenant farmer who had inhabited it had been housed elsewhere, in a dwelling much less grand but far more comfortable, and Nat had made regular journeys, all through the worst of the winter weather, to ensure that his orders were being carried out to his satisfaction. It was, he had told Silence, by way of being his wedding present to her.

It had been hard to believe, in the cold darkness of that winter after Worcester Fight, that there would ever be a happy ending to her story. Militia soldiers had come back to Wintercombe, to hunt for the escaped Cavalier who had once hidden there, but had of course made their rather perfunctory searches in vain. There were no more enquiries, and in December the militia was disbanded. Malignants who had been arrested as a precaution after the Scots invasion were ordered to be released, and Colonel Pyne, busy consolidating his position as ruler of Somerset, had little time to concern himself with the doings of a family so distant from his sphere of influence. As the tedious weeks crept by, with rain and frost and snow, the St. Barbes at last began to realise that they seemed to have escaped the ruin that had so nearly befallen them.

Then Tom Wickham had come to Wintercombe, just before Christmas. He brought Silence a long and loving letter from Nick, and cheerful news of him. She had seen Rachael's pale face become pretty in his presence, and allowed herself to hope, a little, for some happiness for her stepdaughter.

The Chard house was being made ready, and she began to make plans. Tom, a frequent visitor all through the chilly months of spring, brought letters, and took hers back to Nick, idling quietly at his farm near Glastonbury. At the beginning of May, Nat reported that the Chard house was almost ready, and that, in accordance with her wishes, he had instructed the banns to be read by the minister at Chard, for the forthcoming wedding between Silence, Lady St. Barbe, widow, now of that parish, and Master Nicholas Hellier, bachelor, of Worcester. And in preparation for the day, set for the beginning of June, the entire St. Barbe family, and Mally, had left Wintercombe and journeyed south.

Nat had told the rest of the servants that his stepmother and her children were removing to Chard for a while, to live quietly while certain alterations and enlargements were carried out at Wintercombe. He had long thought that the house would benefit from the addition of another wing, to house more bedchambers, and perhaps a library. He asked Silence for her opinion, since she loved the house as much as he did, and was told that, so long as her beloved garden was not obliterated, she would trust to his taste and judgement.

So, they had arrived at Chard three weeks ago, without leaving any suspicions behind them, at Wintercombe. Silence, knowing what was to come, had managed to endure those last few days without fretting, though they seemed to be the longest of her life. After nearly seven years, after so much pain and grief and separation, it did not seem possible that she and Nick could ever be together.

But no one had denounced him, and the banns had been called without anyone pointing out that Master Nicholas Hellier was an escaped Cavalier. Curious acquaintances in Chard had been told only that he was an old friend of the family, and that the wedding was to take place quietly, in view of her recent widowhood. On the last day of May, he rode with Tom Wickham up to the handsome new gates of the Chard house, and back into her life.

And this day, she had married him: had stood beside him in the church, while the minister pronounced them man and wife, for better or worse, richer or poorer, and he had smiled at her with the chestnut eyes that were so like Kate's, and she had known that she was rich indeed, to have the love of this man. Then, they had returned to the place she had once hated, and which now, she knew, would give her memories of her second marriage that would be so much happier than her first. Already, she had plans for the garden which lay, walled and neglected, around the house. Nick would be with her, and her beloved children, and her sister, and together they would become a family.

She looked around her at her guests. Nat and Patience were talking together, their dark heads almost touching, and she could sense the spark between them, that more than half a year of argumentative courtship had not diminished. As Nat had said, it would not be easy, but she knew now that they could not bear to wait much longer. Soon, there would be another wedding, probably at Wintercombe. Whether love would bring as much joy to Nat as it had given to her, she did not know, but could not deny him the same chance of happiness that she had received. And, she thought with amusement, it will take Patience off my hands — and off Joseph's.

Her brother was here, with his cold-eyed wife, Grace. His complaints about his journey from London, and the appalling qualities of his hired horse, had begun even before he walked into the house. But he had met his match in the talkative, balding, paunched man who had cornered him at the other end of the hall, and who was, astonishingly, Nick Hellier's elder brother, ridden down from Worcester for the occasion. Silence had liked his wife, Jane, on sight, and they had already exchanged recipes and remedies. Their eldest child, Nick's nephew John, had disappeared to play in the garden with William. Looking at her own brother, and her husband's, she thought that at least if the two of them were boring each other to death, they were not at liberty to inflict their tedious conversations on anyone else. It was a shame that her other sister, Prudence, could not have come as well, but she was seven months gone with child, and thus unable to travel so far.

The sound of a fiddle being tuned attracted her attention. They had not been able to bring Tabby's precious virginals with them to Chard, but her daughter had declared that she did not mind so much, being quite absorbed at present in learning to play the guitar which Nat had given her as an early birthday present: she would be sixteen in a few days' time. But Nick had managed to borrow a fiddle, and had promised to play a couple of dance tunes, to celebrate his wedding in some style.

The only trouble with that, Silence thought, was that he could not dance with her and play at the same time. But it did not matter: nothing more mattered, save that he was here, and they were married, and there was nothing now that could snatch away her happiness. She watched, smiling, as James Hellier led out his little daughter Sarah, and Nat danced with Patience, resplendent and shocking in a new gown of amethyst silk that completely bared her shoulders, her hair wired into immaculate ringlets. Grace had looked very sourly at the expanse of flesh thus revealed, and Silence felt some sympathy both for her and for her sister. At least, Patience would not have to return to her narrow life in London: a much more delightful future lay in store for her.

She saw Tom Wickham, with a smile, offer Rachael his hands, and her stepdaughter accepted with a gracious incline of her sleek black head. Over the last few months, as she had suggested, Tom had managed to gain the girl's confidence, and then her friendship. Nothing appeared to have been said, yet, about marriage, or even love. But Tom, as she had hoped, had given the wild, tormented, guilty Rachael the greatest gift in his possession, which was happiness. The breathless, laughing girl being whirled around amongst all the other dancers, flushed with delight, seemed to be another creature entirely from that Rachael who had, not so very long ago, tried to take her own life.

The music stopped, and Nick put down his bow, claiming lack of practice. Silence saw him making his way over to her, Kate hanging on to his arm and chattering merrily. She did not know if she would ever tell her youngest child the truth about her father. The little girl seemed to have conceived a great fondness for Nick, though, and for the moment, that would be enough.

He took her hands, and kissed her, and she heard his voice, dark and rough with happiness, soft against her ear. 'Oh, my Silence, perfectest herald of joy – I love you so much.'

She emerged from his embrace, feeling that her own joy and delight must at any moment burst out of her, and wondered how long it would be before they could, with propriety, slip away to the comfortable, sunny bedchamber upstairs, and bolt the door on her beloved family, and enjoy their first night of legitimate, unsinful passion. But it was still many hours till sunset, and they would have to be patient. They had waited so long for this moment, and a little more delay would only serve to whet, and heighten, their desire.

Kate, irrepressible, was giggling at her. Beyond the small brown figure of her youngest child, bright as a jewel in her new dress of kingfisher taffeta, she saw Tom and Rachael, hand in hand, slipping out of the door that led to the garden. Amid her own flowering happiness, she had time to wonder whether another happy ending, against all the odds, was lying in wait for her stepdaughter.

'What a lovely morning,' said Tom Wickham, still keeping hold of Rachael's hand. Suddenly shy, she looked away from him, and saw William and John Hellier, frozen in guilty surprise, half-way up the wall at the other end of the garden. Once, she would have ordered them down, but it seemed inappropriate on a day such as this, when delight and joy seemed to fill the air about them as visibly as the sun and clouds above. She felt so easy with Tom now, an old and trusted friend, that it was almost impossible to remember that once, not very long ago, she had regarded him as an enemy. The touch of his hand made her feel at once nervous and excited, as the thought crept slowly into her mind. This is not just friendship – this must be something more.

She had envied Silence her happiness: she had seen the growing love between Nat, her twin, and Patience, who had once too been her enemy. She had never thought that it would ever happen to her, and had contemplated a life of spinsterhood with sad certainty, oblivious of the man who now stood at her side, tall and fair and reassuringly solid and ordinary, and whose attractions she had failed to perceive – until now.

The garden was rough and overgrown, long neglected. Tom drew her down between an avenue of rose bushes, straggling and hung around with trailing weeds, and out of sight of the two noisy small boys climbing the wall. Rachael thought of the children, who had never really forgiven her for her betrayal. It still made her feel sad and guilty, and those scars might never heal completely. But somehow, out here in the sunshine, with Tom so close beside her, it was not her past which mattered to her now, but her future.

She took a deep breath, smelling damp earth and wet grass and, somewhere, roasting meat. Tom said, 'What are you thinking about?'

Startled, Rachael turned to face him. She could see herself, in her lovely soft yellow dress, her hair carefully arranged by Patience, reflected in his blue eyes. She said shyly, 'I was wishing that I could be as happy as Nick and Silence are, one day.'

'One day?' said Tom, and she realised suddenly that he was as unsure of himself as she was. There was something very endearing about his hesitant smile, as he went on, 'What's wrong with today?

Rachael — we have known each other for some time now . . . can I . . . will you . . . will you?'

She stood there, her sunlit face turned up to his, all the old lines of tension and temper vanished as though they had never been, and read in his face the question which he had not managed to ask. 'Yes, if you like,' she said softly, and smiled with new delight as he drew her face near to his, for their first kiss.

William St. Barbe and John Hellier, perched on top of the old stone wall surrounding the garden, had noticed. They hooted and whistled their approval, but the couple entwined amidst the rose bushes were too involved in each other to pay them any mind.

Such an event was much too important to be kept to themselves: so the two boys, risking twisted ankles and skinned knees, leapt joyfully to the ground and rushed inside, to spread the glad news to the rest of the company.

Here is an extract from **A Falling Star**, *the third book in Pamela Belle's compelling* Wintercombe *series . . .*

It was so much smaller than he remembered.

Strange, that a place that had loomed so large in his life, that had driven him away, that had called him back, should be so insignificant. Low, gabled, built in the grey-gold stone that still thrust like bones through the earth in the surrounding fields, it seemed hardly more than a farmhouse. He had seen the palaces of Europe, he was familiar with great houses in four or five countries, and beside them, Wintercombe was nothing.

And yet . . . it has been the home of the St Barbes for nearly two centuries, and now it was his, possessed by right of inheritance. He had been born here, passed his childhood within and without the rough grey walls, had known a little of happiness, and rather more of its opposite. It had not been able to hold him, and as soon as he could, he had escaped.

Home. Home was here: not Amsterdam, nor Den Haag, nor Aunt Kate's pretty château by the wild Loire. And after nearly fifteen years, he had come home for good.

Or had he? There was no one about, save a couple of men chopping up a wind-blown tree down by the Wellow Lane. He could still change his mind, deny his past and his destiny, and defy his father for the last and most decisive time. He could turn his horse about, and ride back to Bristol, to take ship for his old life, his regiment, and for Johanna and the careless debauchery of the other English exiles, voluntary and involuntary, who crowded the towns and cities of Holland. If he did . . .

If he did, Charles would have Wintercombe by default. And he was damned if he would make a gift of his inheritance to Cousin Charles.

The decision, after all, had already been taken, long since. He smiled rather grimly, and twitched the horse's reins.

Henry Renolds, the most junior stable boy, had doubts, and expressed them nervously. Surely Mistress Louise should not be riding Shadow? If she must venture out on this chilly February afternoon, why not take Nance, her usual mount?

Louise Chevalier stood unmoved in the centre of the stable yard, tapping her whip gently against the thick dove-grey folds of her

French riding habit, and let the boy's thick Somerset dialect trail away into confusion. 'I told you, Henry,' she said calmly. 'I wish to ride Shadow. Go saddle him at once, if you please.'

The boy, faced with vastly superior tactics and weaponry, gave up. 'Aye, mistress,' he muttered, and scuttled into the stables. Louise waited, now and then glancing at the sky, which was high and white today, threatening neither rain nor snow. If only the wretched child would hurry, before someone discovered what she was about.

But no one shouted from the windows looking down over the stable yard, no one came bustling officiously out to ask her what on earth she was doing, going riding alone, and on the most notorious horse in the stables into the bargain. She knew that she should be sitting decorously indoors, stitching, or talking French to her cousin Amy, but today the prospect appalled her even more than usual. She had to break free, or suffocate, and once this wild mood was on her she would brook no opposition.

Shadow appeared, already frothy around the bit and under the girth. He was a big, well-made gelding, young and fast and hot-headed, and emphatically not a lady's ride. Young Henry, who was only fourteen, struggled to hold the horse's head as he danced and fretted, cooped up, like Louise, for too long, and desperate to run. She admired his looks, the dark, almost black hide, the white blaze on the proud head, the curving, well-muscled quarters and white-splashed legs. She loved all horses for their power and grace and beauty, but Shadow was the pick of Wintercombe's stables.

With some difficulty, Henry persuaded Shadow to stand still by the block for the few vital moments necessary for Louise to mount him. She arranged her skirts, made sure that her small, dashing hat, in the latest French fashion, was perched securely on her head, and grinned at the boy, letting the wild bubbling excitement surge out of her at last. 'All right, Henry – let him go!'

Shadow, released at last, found that he was not, after all, in control. His rider had a confident seat and a firm grasp of the reins. Moreover, she carried an efficient-looking whip, and would undoubtedly use it. He subsided with a wicked, rolling eye, and Louise, well aware that the slightest slackening of her hold would reap the whirlwind, steered him briskly out of the stable yard, with a smart tap to remind Shadow who was in charge.

There was another rider ahead, coming up the hill from the Wellow Lane. Curious, Louise narrowed her eyes. The horse, though obviously weary, was a magnificent animal, a big strong-boned dappled grey, its mane and tail a pure and flowing white. She tightened her grip on Shadow's head, having no wish to be deposited ignominiously at the visitor's feet, and urged him into a brisk trot, the quicker to investigate. Personable strangers were rare at Wintercombe.

And this man, she saw as she drew nearer, was rather more than personable. Like the horse, he was uncommonly tall and strongly made, with wide shoulders and a slouching, easy posture that betrayed the habitual horseman. He wore an unadorned dark suit and a hat decorated only with a single plume, and the black hair that drifted untidily in the gentle wind was plainly his own, and no periwig. And Louise, now close enough to have a good view of his face, knew his identity with a sudden jump of her heart.

She had not seen him since . . . Thirteen, she had been, a wild skinny hoyden with a passion for horses and a direct and belligerent manner that had been the despair of her governess, and now, nearly seven years later, made a more sophisticated Louise blush to recall it. He had seemed almost godlike, her splendid cousin, descending on her stepfather's château and turning it upside down with a breathtaking ease that had delighted the rebellious child. And her wayward, mischievous mother had seemed to revel in the disruption of her usually well-ordered household, had laughed off her husband's complaints and the outraged appeals of the senior servants, and entered into an unholy alliance with his disruptive nephew that had scandalised the district. Louise, in some ways more adult than her mother realised, had known that there was nothing improper in Kate's behaviour, however much the neighbouring aristocracy might gossip and whisper. There had been no lingering glances, no touched hands, no secret assignations. Louise had seen such things before, when her stepfather had been her mother's secret lover while his first wife, ailing and jealous, was still alive. No, it had simply been that Kate, still young and lively, had relished the arrival of a kindred spirit whose inventiveness, audacity and brilliance had dazzled almost everyone around him.

He had dazzled Louise too. Her vivid memories still had the power to make her giggle at inopportune moments. The time he had ridden his horse into the dining room . . . the day when the entire household had been smoked out of doors by his unauthorised alchemical experiments in the still room . . . the race, involving riding, swimming and running, that had ruined everyone's clothes and nearly drowned her stepfather's young cousin, although Alex, godlike in this as in all else, had brought him miraculously back from the dead.

That wonderful summer, seven years ago, had coloured her behaviour for months after his departure. She had wanted so desperately to look like him, to have the sapphire-blue eyes and lively, lazy features, the black hair which he wore thick and long, scorning a periwig, an affectation entirely characteristic and the subject of much adverse comment amongst people whom Louise thereafter despised. She was his cousin, his mother's sister's grandchild: why had she failed to inherit his beauty?

All that she saw in her mirror was the same Louise, with her narrow pointed face, rather lifeless in repose, unfashionably olive skinned and dominated by a nose, alas, that already threatened to become aquiline. Her eyes were good, being like her mother's, large, and an unusual shade of chestnut brown. Louise, unaware of the sparkle that transformed her expression when she talked or laughed, had long ago decided that she would never, despite all her longing, look as glorious as her English cousin Alex, for she too greatly resembled her Guernsey father's family.

She could ride like Alex, though, and she had set herself to excel in the saddle, bruising herself severely in the process, breaking her arm and acquiring a reputation for daredevilry throughout the district. When he returned, as he surely would, she could dazzle and impress him with her skill and dash.

But he had not come back. Whispered family gossip spoke of scandal in England, both political and amorous, hasty exile in Holland, a string of mistresses, and service in the army of the Dutch, enemies of France. And Louise, to her horror and indignation, was sent away to school near Blois, protesting until the moment her stepfather pushed her into the coach, to acquire, as her mother pointedly told her, some polish and sophistication. If Alex had visited during her enforced absences, she had never come to hear of it.

And now here he was in the flesh, riding towards his polished and sophisticated little cousin, and she was tolerably certain that, seeing her here in England, hundreds of miles from her mother's family, he could have no idea of her identity.

She reined Shadow in with a flourish just in front of the grey's nose, judging the distance to a nicety, and raised her eyes to Alex St Barbe's face.

Amusement, Louise had expected, perhaps even interest: she might not be pretty, but she was confident of her attractions. What she had not thought to see was his hostile blue stare, nor to hear the hard voice full of malice. 'What the devil do you think you're doing, madam?'

Submission and decorum had never been amongst her long suits. Louise's chin came up dangerously. 'I might ask the same of you, sir. Whom do you wish to visit at Wintercombe?'

Shadow, balked of his extended gallop, was beginning to sidle and fret, chewing at his bit. Specks of froth splattered the ground, and she gave him a warning tap with the whip. The inimical eyes surveyed her and her restless mount. 'Hardly a lady's ride, is he?' said her cousin, in the sort of contemptuous drawl that had always infuriated her when she heard it employed by aristocratic Englishmen.

'Perhaps you think you can manage him better?' she suggested, with a withering glare that indicated her thoughts as to the likely outcome of such a situation.

'I intend to,' said Sir Alexander St Barbe, 'since he is, I assume, my horse.'

Louise gave him the haughty stare down her undoubtedly aquiline nose (it did have some uses, after all) that she had practised before her mirror for the quelling of an impertinent young Vicomte. 'Your horse, sir? How strange – I was under the impression that it belongs to Sir Alexander St Barbe, and you surely cannot presume to an acquaintance with him.'

For a moment their eyes met, mutually antagonistic, and it took every scrap of her bravado not to flinch from the unpleasantness in his gaze. All her expectations, and her disappointment, had crystallised into her swift-rising anger, and she would have given anything now to call those words back, instead of leaving her insult hanging between them like a cleaver.

'I think you know very well who I am,' he said softly. 'As to who *you* are, madam, making free with my property—'

'*Moi?*' said Louise. She had annoyed him, the cousin she had once worshipped, with a few ill-chosen words fuelled by her quick temper, and she did not intend lingering to make matters worse. She gave him a brilliant smile, full of false mischief, and employed the French he must speak almost as well as she did. '*Moi, Monsieur? Vous me connaissez bien – je suis une Guernesiaise!*'

And she gave Shadow his head at last, and sent him flying down the hill towards the Wellow Lane, heedless of the mud that her mount's hooves might scatter all over the man who had once, in another and more innocent lifetime, been her childhood hero.